A SEA OF
SKULLS

ARTS OF DARK AND LIGHT

BOOK TWO

A SEA OF SKULLS

VOX DAY

CASTALIA HOUSE

A Sea of Skulls
Vox Day

Published by Castalia House, Switzerland.

Cover Design: Kirk DouPonce

ISBN: 978-3-03944-034-4

This is a work of fiction. Names, characters, places, and incidents are products of the author's imagination or are used in a fictitious manner. Any similarity to actual people, organizations, and/or events is purely coincidental.

To the Selenoth fans

Your long wait is finally at an end.

You can stop calling me Vox RR Day now.

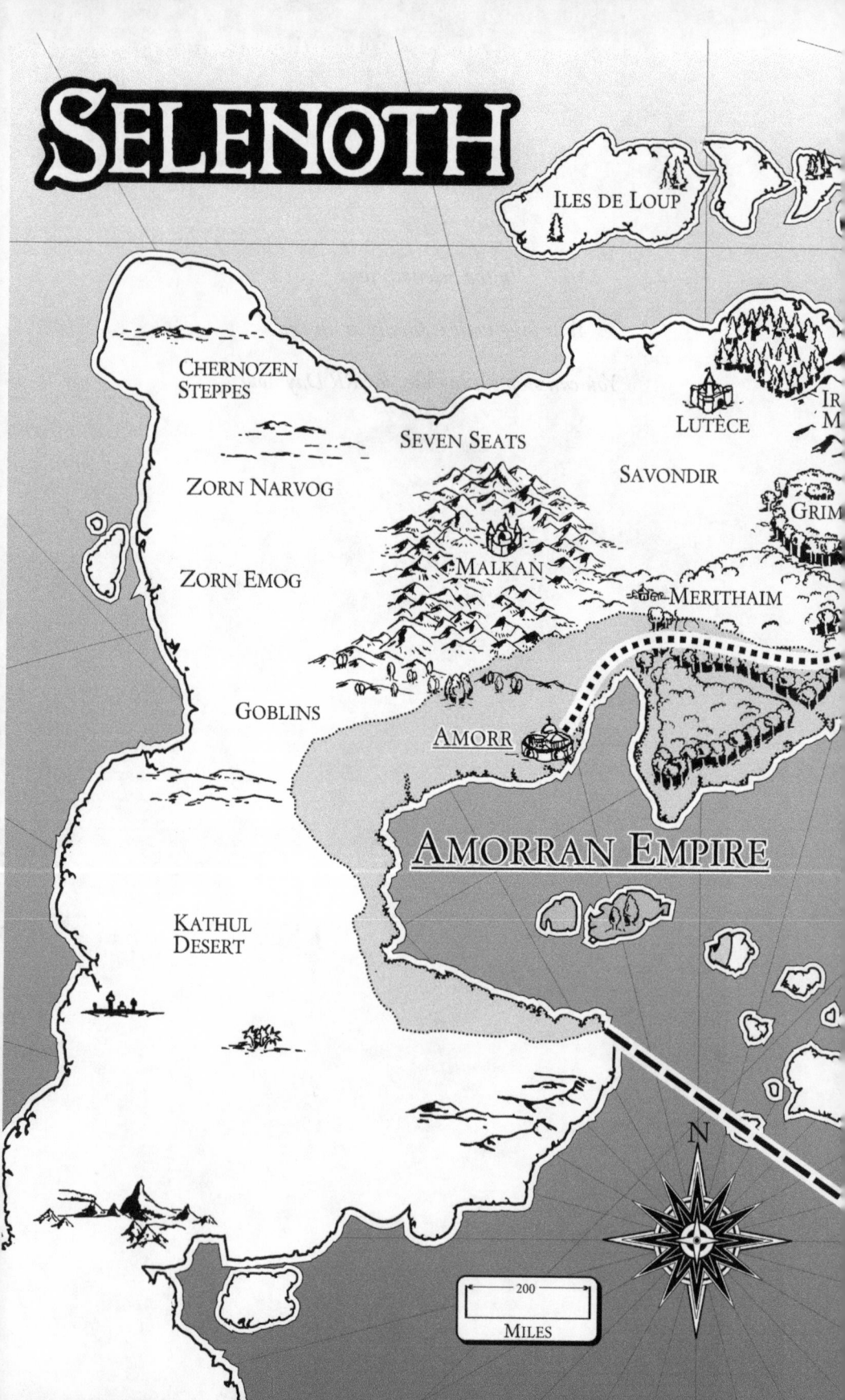

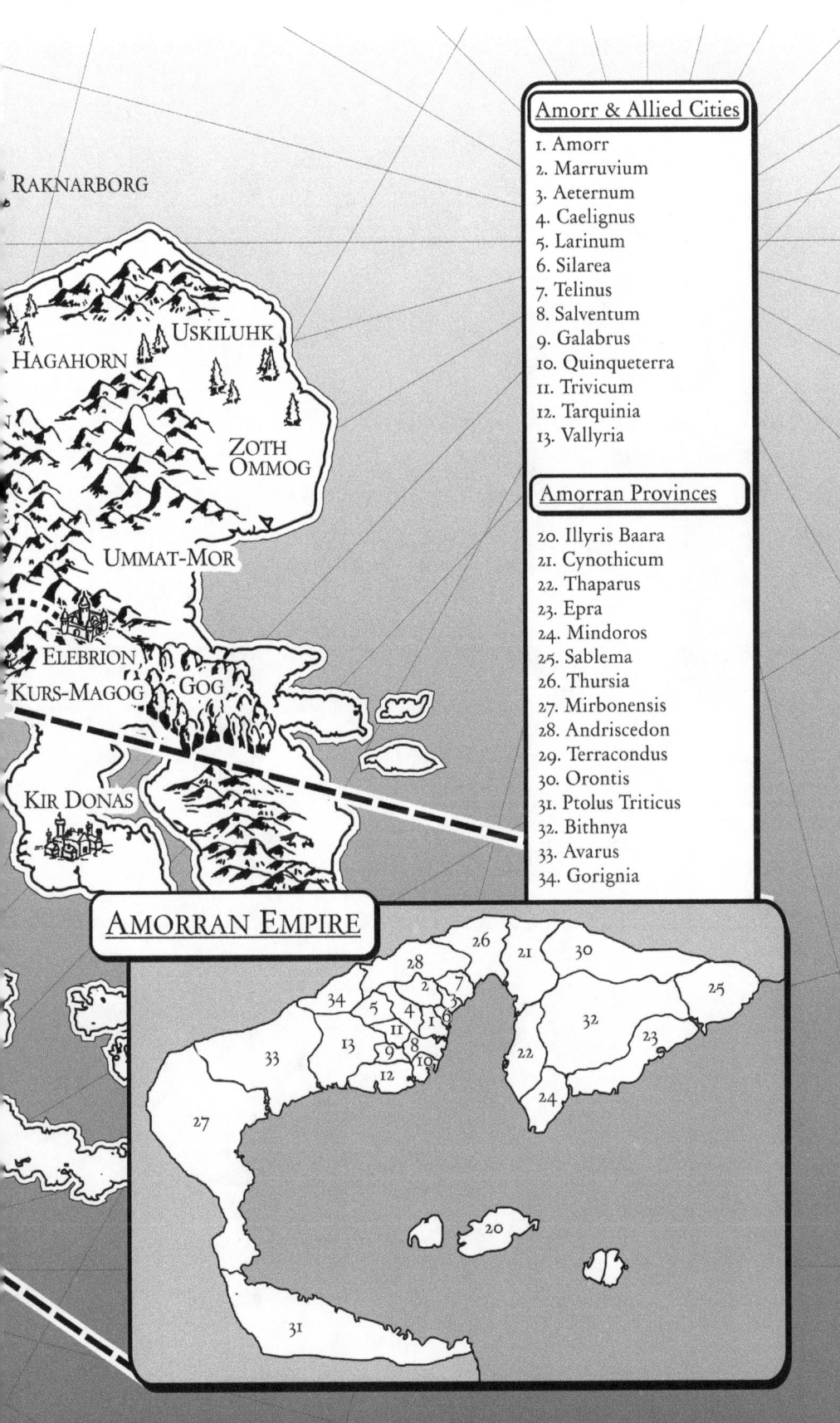

RAKNARBORG

HAGAHORN
USKILUHK
ZOTH OMMOG
UMMAT-MOR
ELEBRION
KURS-MAGOG   GOG
KIR DONAS

AMORRAN EMPIRE

Amorr & Allied Cities

1. Amorr
2. Marruvium
3. Aeternum
4. Caelignus
5. Larinum
6. Silarea
7. Telinus
8. Salventum
9. Galabrus
10. Quinqueterra
11. Trivicum
12. Tarquinia
13. Vallyria

Amorran Provinces

20. Illyris Baara
21. Cynothicum
22. Thaparus
23. Epra
24. Mindoros
25. Sablema
26. Thursia
27. Mirbonensis
28. Andriscedon
29. Terracondus
30. Orontis
31. Ptolus Triticus
32. Bithnya
33. Avarus
34. Gorignia

PROLOGUE

I SABEL DE BORDELEAU was a very unhappy young woman. She was upset with her parents, she was angry with His Royal Majesty the King, and she was downright furious at the lack of justice to be found in what had suddenly, and unexpectedly, turned out to be a deeply unfair world. How could it be, she asked herself, that a young woman had no right to decide for herself how she would live her life? Was she not a viscomte's daughter? Did her blood not run as blue as any other noblewoman's in Savondir? Was she not pretty? Was she not well-behaved? Did she not attend the Mass every Lord's Day and dutifully listen to the priest drone on until midday in the unintelligible language of God? Her questions went unanswered. She frowned and looked down from the glass window of her bedroom at the grounds of her father's estate below. It was early summer and the grass was green. The trees extended their branches invitingly as if begging to be climbed, and the sun was shining in a clear blue sky. It was the sort of day that only last week would have filled her heart with *joie de vivre.*

But last week she was still unaware of how her life had been ruined two years ago. It had been a pleasant summer's day not unlike today when she walked with her parents to the nearby village of Morel. There, in the village square, she had seen an old, bearded man, wearing royal blue robes, surrounded by all the children of the village. In his hand he held a small crystal ball, and, one by one, each child would warily approach him and place a hand upon the crystal as the old man held it out to them.

Isabel didn't understand what the object of the game was supposed to be, as nothing seemed to happen to either the children or the crystal when they touched it. A few of the children appeared to be relieved, most were indifferent, and one boy even looked disappointed. But the little ball just sat in the old man's hand, as harmless as an ordinary pebble. If only she had known then how dangerous it was! If only someone had told her not to touch it!

Her parents urged her forward. The boys and girls of the village, recognizing her, parted before her approach. The old man glanced at her without any sign of interest in his heavy-lidded eyes; he didn't seem at all impressed that her father was the local lord. But the moment she touched the crystal in his hand, his eyes suddenly came to life and focused on her with an intensity that alarmed her.

Unnerved, she withdrew her hand, and she was astonished to see that the crystal was now glowing, radiating a bright white light that shone from the old man's hand like a miniature sun!

She heard children around her gasp. Adults too. The old man was smiling at her as if he approved of what she'd done, but there was something possessive in his expression that frightened her. She retreated from him. Alarmed, she looked back at her parents and saw her mother appeared to be upset. Her father, on the other hand, was smiling at her and she relaxed as he clapped his hands proudly together, approving of whatever it was she'd done. She smiled back at him and returned triumphantly to his side, feeling very much like a swan that had been swimming amidst ducks.

In truth, she was more akin to a rabbit caught unwittingly in a snare.

Two years ago, she had known nothing of the old man or what brought him to the little village on the outskirts of the Forêt Sinistre. Now she knew the man was one of the King's Own, a magicien who scoured the kingdom on His Royal Majesty's behalf, traveling from town to town throughout the year. Such men visited every little village and hamlet across the realm in the hopes of discovering young men and women with a talent for magie. She understood now that she was one of the gifted, which meant that she was also one of the cursed. The very gift which made her special also rendered her, by royal decree, the property of the King. She was to be slave, no, worse, she was to be a brood mare.

Her father explained it to her. Magie was the sole province of the crown. Not only its practice, but even its potential was kept firmly under royal control by L'Académie des Sage Arts. Boys with the talent became magiciens, and scholars, and battlemages, some, in time, would even become the mighty immortels of L'Académie, feared and respected throughout the lands of men. But girls like her would be taught nothing of the arts, indeed, she was barred from exercising her birthright in any way.

Instead, she would be expected to breed with the young men at L'Académie as if she were nothing more than an animal of desirable stock. Not until she bore two children to a magicien would she be free to leave L'Académie and begin to live her own life, to the extent that was still possible.

Unless, of course, she was able to convince her parents otherwise. She knew better than to appeal to her mother. Mother was from a well-respected merchant family and Isabel knew she would never dare anything controversial enough to cause local tongues to wag. But Father was a lord of the eastern march, a lesser one, perhaps, but out here on the borderlands, a mere viscomte wielded more power and influence than a duc in Lutèce. And surely neither the king nor the magiciens of L'Académie would care if one young woman from an insignificant border village was lost to their breeding program. The old man had never come back to Morel. Was it not possible that she had been forgotten by now?

She looked in the silvered glass and saw a tall, pretty girl on the verge of womanhood, with brown eyes, sun-browned skin, and long, straight, brown hair, staring back at her. But the dress the young woman was wearing was too fine, too embroidered, and too womanly to be suitable for a young girl pleading her father's favor. She slipped the dress off over her head and replaced it with a simple, virginal white dress that barely fell past to her knees now. It made her look like a dryad, or an elfille, her father once said. The important thing was that it her look more like a girl and less like a woman.

Now, to find Father. She left her room and ran lightly down the wooden stairs to the ground level. She heard voices in the great reception chamber to the right of the stairs, but saw it was only a pair of young maids gossiping about one of the blacksmith's assistants as they polished the silver. They fell silent upon Isabel's entrance, but smiled and resumed their conversation when they saw it was only her. One of them thought she had seen the Seigneur de Bordeleau near the stables, so Isabel decided to look for him there first.

The stables was to the left of the great house, past the rows of little cottages in which the married servants lived and the orchards that kept the household supplied with apples, pears, quinces, and other fruits. She ran easily over the long green grass, barefoot, and the familiar sensation of the stalks beneath her toes made her feel certain that her kindly father would never send his beloved daughter away from her family and her home, no matter how many kings and magiciens might demand it of him.

She saw her younger brother, Perrin, running towards her. He was four years younger than her; their older brother, Robinet, had been sent to the monastery at Corénaz to study numbers with the monks there, as befitted their father's heir. Perrin was a sweet, happy little boy whose head barely came to her shoulders, but as he drew nearer, she thought he almost looked as if he was upset, or frightened.

"What's the matter?"

"Father yelled at me! He says I have to go to the house! He told me to run!"

"Why?"

"I don't know. He was talking to Simon and two other men. I think something is wrong."

Isabel nodded. "Better do as he told you. Run along home and I'll go see what it is."

To her surprise, he shook his head. "He said if I saw anyone, I should tell them to come with me."

"Oh, you'll be fine. You know the way. Besides, you can hardly get lost from here." She dismissed his protests. "Go, if father wants me to run home too, I'll catch up with you."

He nodded obediently and ran off. She laughed, surprised, and more than a little curious, as to what their father might be about with Simon. She didn't mind seeing him; the hunter was one of the more handsome young men in the village and sometimes she caught his eyes following her as she walked past. She broke into an easy jog, and before long, spotted the young man on horseback, riding away from her father in the company of two riders wearing leather armor and shields strapped to their back. She frowned, disappointed that the young man had left before she had had the chance to greet him.

"Isabel, is that you? You shouldn't be here!"

Her father was running towards her now and he was shouting at her. His face was red and angry, and the shock of his displeasure brought her to a halt.

"Go back to the house right now! What are you doing out here?"

He loomed over her and grabbed her arm roughly, jerking her around and half-dragging her back in the direction of the house. He wasn't a big man, but he was taller and stronger than her, and he was squeezing her arm hard enough for it to hurt.

"You must have seen Perrin. Didn't he tell you to go back to the house?" He didn't wait for an answer. "Run back to the house and tell your mother to bar the doors. Le Chasseur says there a raiding party of orcs about and they may be coming this way!"

"But the king," she said. "I wanted to talk to you–"

"Damn the king!" he roared and he shoved her, so hard that she stumbled and nearly fell. "Run, Isabel, run to the devil-damned house!"

She ran.

Her eyes were blurry with tears as she ran back in the direction she had come, much faster this time. She didn't know of whom she was more afraid, the dreadful goblins of whom she'd heard terrible tales since she was half Perrin's age but never seen, or the red-faced, shouting stranger who looked like her father but certainly didn't act like him. Her bare feet fairly flew over the grass, though whether she was running towards home or away from her father, she couldn't possibly have said.

As ran past the cottages and came within site of the house, she could hear her mother shouting at someone. Alarmed, but doubting that her mother would be likely to administer a tongue-lashing to orcs, she put on a last burst of speed and turned the corner to see her mother gesticulating angrily at the backs of two of the male cooks who were running away as fast as they could on the path towards the village road.

"Isabel!" she cried as when Isabel called out to her. "Oh, praise le bon Dieu! I didn't know where you were! Those wretched cowards came to tell me they heard there were orcs lurking about the woods nearby, but they ran away to town instead of arming themselves! Can you imagine? Come inside, dear, everything will be fine. Did you see your father?"

She nodded as Isabel told her that Father was out near the stables, and that he seemed to be aware there was a raiding party nearby. She wasn't frightened anymore, not now that she understood why her father shouted at her. Perhaps the lily-livered cooks might run away, but her father was a knight with twenty men-at-arms sworn to him and she knew there wasn't an orc on Selenoth that could hope to stand against a true Savondese knight, much less one who was both a viscomte and royal vassal.

They were walking towards the house, her mother's arm around her, when they heard a fearful shout and Daniel the gardener came sprinting around the side of the building away from the stables. He was an older man, with short, stumpy legs and a fat belly, and he was easily run down by the pair of huge green monsters that were at his heels. They seemed to have appeared out of a nightmare! Their appearance was grotesque, with powerful, bulging shoulders and long, apish arms. The monsters leaped upon Daniel from behind, bringing him down to the ground before smashing in his head with repeated blows from the large spiked clubs they were carrying.

Her mother screamed. Isabel stood frozen, too astonished to be afraid, her eyes locked upon the terrible red ruin of the back of the gardener's head. She looked up and stared at the brutish orcs, taking in the tusks that jutted up from their thick lower jaws, the dark green skin which was covered by a few rags of some dirty material so faded and worn she couldn't tell if it was cloth or leather. Their faces were wide and looked to her like a demonic cross between a pig, a bat, and a dog, and while there were sparks of intelligence in their cruel yellow eyes, she saw no sign of either mercy or humanity in them.

And if they weren't much taller than her, they were about three times wider, with muscles that bulged like living armor beneath the paint and smeared tattoos that adorned their skin. Five more appeared as the first two, having dispatched poor Daniel, began to advance towards Isabel, with broad smiles on their grotesque faces.

"Get behind me," her mother whispered, interposing herself between Isabel and the monsters, and finally Isabel found herself able to move again. "It's going to be all right. Don't run."

They're not dogs, Mother, Isabel wanted to say, but she was far too terrified to speak. The first orc waggled his club suggestively and the gardener's blood sprinkled the grass as he took a step towards them. Then he stopped and an expression that might have been fear filled his bestial face. That step was his last, as the pounding of horse hooves erupted without warning behind her. She saw something big and brown flash past the corner of her eye just before her father's lance spitted the orc right under his chin. The monster's blood was dark green, not red, Isabel noted as it sprayed from his throat. Three of Father's men were right behind him, all of them mounted, and the four warriors cut down the half-naked orcs as easily as the monsters themselves had murdered the helpless gardener.

"To the house, now!" her mother shouted and pulled at her arm.

Isabel turned and ran with her. Behind her, she heard her father shouting his battle cry and it was echoed by his men. *"Je suis prêt!"* she heard them shout as they drove the orcs back, away from the house. Just hearing his deep voice restored her courage. *"Je suis prêt!"*

As soon as they were inside, her mother slammed the door behind them. "Where is Perrin?" No sooner had a chambermaid produced her frightened little brother than her mother was ordering all the doors to be barred and the shutters on the ground floor windows closed and latched.

Isabel was quickly ushered into the kitchen, where a makeshift barrier had been assembled from a heavy table and some chairs. Seven of the household staff were gathered there, all of them armed with a weapon, however humble. The five women were mostly armed with kitchen knives, an elderly valet held an iron poker from the fireplace, and the one remaining cook was wielding a large, razor-sharp butcher knife. After the windows were secured, her mother and the two maids helping her returned to the kitchen, clambered over the barrier, and then secured weapons for themselves.

Isabel saw her mother select a little hatchet normally used in preparing the meat; she wanted to ask for a knife or even a rolling pin, but something in her mother's face dissuaded her. Instead, she went and put her arms around a wide-eyed Perrin, who was doing his best not to weep.

"Father is outside!" he whispered to her in a voice full of fear.

"Shhhh," she comforted him. "Be brave like him. Father is with his men. He's a knight in vassal to the king himself. He will kill them all!"

He relaxed a little, trusting in her words. She wished she could believe them too. She listened for the familiar sound of Father's voice, but with all the others talking around her in the kitchen, she couldn't hear anything outside. Her mother was nervously fingering a rosary in one hand while holding the hatchet in the other. Her lips were moving, but Isabel couldn't tell if she was praying, reciting the rosary, or talking to herself.

Then there was a loud thudding sound that seemed to come from somewhere near the rear of the house. Everyone froze and fell silent. She felt Perrin go rigid in her arms.

"Doublet, go and see what that is," her mother ordered the valet. The old man was visibly afraid, so much so that his hands were shaking, but he obeyed nevertheless, climbing awkwardly over the barrier with the help of the cook. They all waited, motionless, listening for a sign that the dreadful creatures were gone, hoping to hear the sound of her father calling to tell them that he'd driven the creatures away.

Then there came another thud, followed by the unmistakable sound of breaking glass. Isabel screamed, and she wasn't the only one to do so. They heard Doublet's voice shouting curses, interrupted by a crashing sound, after which the pounding of heavy feet running through the house was all they could hear. Then a horrible green face appeared at the top of the barrier; it vanished right away, but from the blood-curdling cries that followed Isabel knew it was alerting its fellows to their presence. She glanced around and saw a cupboard just big enough to hold Perrin.

"In there," she held the door open and pushed him into it. "Hide! Don't you make a sound or come out, no matter what you hear!"

No sooner was he safely hidden than the heavy table was torn away as if it weighed nothing. The first orc burst into the kitchen and the cook bravely leaped at him, swinging the big butcher's blade. It caught the monster in the shoulder, but the beast swung its bloody club and sent the cook back reeling, stunned, with a blow to the side of his head. Her mother lashed out with her axe, but the orc caught her arm and simply pulled her back, hurling her into the room behind him. She had barely disappeared from sight than she began to scream hysterically, terrible wordless screams like an animal. All the while, more orcs were pouring into the kitchen, and their powerful clawed hands reached out for the shrieking, terrified women defending themselves with their makeshift weapons.

"Mother!" Isabel shrieked and she picked up the butcher knife that the cook had dropped a moment earlier. She chopped down hard, using both hands, but an orc blocked the metal blade with a chair it was holding, shoved her backward, then smashed the chair into her face. The force of the blow sent her flying backward and she struck the back of her head upon the wall.

Darkness descended and she knew no more.

When Isabel came to her senses, her first thought was that she must be damned and in Hell. A sharp pain seemed to be splitting her lower body in half while a dreadful pressure on her back was smashing repeatedly against her, forcing the breath from her and all but crushing her under its heavy weight. It took her one long moment to realize that she was not dead, another moment for the full force of the pain to hit her, and a third to realize she was no longer a virgin.

The dreadful stench of the monster raping her filled her nostrils, along with the scent of something that she dimly recognized as smoke. For a moment, the shock of realizing what was happening left her paralyzed, and she lay there helplessly on her belly, pinned to the ground, her body rocked again and again by the beast ruthlessly violating it. Then her horror transformed into rage, pure incendiary anger, fury fueled by a boundless hate of a sort she had never even imagined could exist. As the orc thrust itself savagely into her again, she opened her mouth and screamed, as if she was already one of the damned and this was one of the ten thousand torments of Hell.

Her throat-searing cry was met by an answering shriek that was deafening in her ear, and she felt whatever had been tearing her apart abruptly vanish from between her legs, leaving nothing but hollow agony behind. She rolled over and tried to scramble backward, away from her assailant, but her hands slipped in the blood of the dead women lying on either side of her, and she fell sprawling on her back. Only then did she realize she had been stripped naked.

She was not alone. In addition to the huge beast that had been attacking her only a moment ago, there were four more orcs standing in the kitchen. They had been watching the other one violate her; perhaps they were even waiting their turn. Now they were howling and making other strange and terrible sounds, but their attention was not focused on her. They were pointing at her attacker, the naked one whose exposed, half-flaccid green member was slick and red with her blood. They were laughing at her attacker, she realized to her astonishment. They were laughing!

She looked away, more horrified and humiliated than scared. It was at that moment she saw the little body lying in a large pool of blood in front of the broken cupboard door. It was Perrin; she recognized the tunic he had been wearing. But he had no head.

Something broke inside her. Perhaps a dragon slumbering deep within her woke, or maybe a dark angel from some fiery abyss erupted from the void that had only moments ago been her soul. Whatever it was, she didn't care. She no longer knew shame or fear or pain. She was rage incarnate, and there was no place inside her for either grief or sorrow, not with the burning hunger for vengeance that consumed her. She rose from the floor, wearing nothing more than the blood that striped her legs, and she thrust out her hands at the monsters that were staring at her in curious bemusement.

They did not stare long. Sorcerous fire exploded in the room, instantly engulfing all five of the orcs in green-and-blue flames as it blew out the wood-and-stone wall behind them. The monsters howled as the magical flames turned them into running, screaming torches. The soulless creatures burned alive in the fire that consumed them as indifferently as they had slain their victims. She walked past the dead bodies of the servants and ignored the dying orcs as they thrashed about, devoured by the ravenous flames. The fire did not touch her, but seemed to bow down before her as she passed. Hell knew her for its own.

Blue and green flames danced on Isabel's palms and encircled her wrists as she walked through the smashed beams of what had once been her family home's front door. Outside, she saw more orcs and the flames leaped from her hands, again and again, and each time they set more of the monsters alight. She burned the orc that was violating her mother's lifeless body lying on the grass. She incinerated the two orcs that were kicking her brother's head back and forth between them. More flames leaped out from her hands and engulfed the four orcs that were attempting to hang her father's mutilated body on a makeshift cross on the path that led to the village road. Victors no more, the monsters were transformed into screaming candles, turning what was meant to be humiliation into a glorious pyre worthy of a fallen warrior.

She was an angel of death. She was a fiery avenger. She was pure, white-hot anger, and to look upon her was to die. The pain, the humiliation, even the terrible aching grief was gone, all of it burned away by the cleansing flames of her boundless fury. She did not think and she did not feel. She burned with rage and the world burned with her.

A group of orcs rushed towards her, their mouths gaping open, but she could not hear their howls. She heard nothing but the beating of her heart and the sound of blood rushing in her ears. She threw open her arms, now fully wreathed in flames, as if to embrace her attackers, and a great sheet of fire leaped out to envelop and engulf them. She did not exult in their shrieking deaths, she did not rejoice in their writhing agonies, she did nothing more than methodically scour the earth with the purifying fire that cleansed everything it touched.

Then something flew past her. A moment later, a crossbow bolt slammed into her left thigh. She fell to the ground, crying out more in surprise than pain. She looked up and saw a big orc wearing leather armor pointing a sword at her. Behind him, more orcs carrying crossbows were taking aim at her. But the flames had not abandoned her, still they curled and danced about her arms. Even as the orcs loosed their missiles at her, Isabel stretched out her arm towards the orc with the sword, and the fire lashed out at him like a green-and-blue serpent striking.

Three iron-tipped bolts hammered into her slender body in rapid succession, crushing flesh and bones as they passed nearly all the way through her, lifting her up before hurling her back down upon the ground. The flames vanished as she lay there, and so did the pain, but as the light spiraled away from her eyes, Isabel could suddenly hear the anguished howls of the burning orcs again. The sound brought a faint smile to her bloody lips. As Isabel died, she felt their screams of monstrous agony lifting her up towards the clouds, as if the shrieking voices belonged to a choir of angels ushering her into Paradise.

THEUDERIC

IS DUTY to King and country accomplished, Theuderic lay back on the feather-stuffed pillow and exhaled deeply. He eyed the girl with whom he'd been sporting, mildly surprised at the enthusiasm she'd shown. She wasn't unattractive, merely younger, plumper, and more innocent than he tended to prefer when left to his own devices. She was sixteen, he guessed. Her breasts weren't even proper woman's breasts, they were still the soft girlish cones that defied gravity with the easy impunity of youth. He observed her birth was neither noble nor peasant; she had the round, ruddy cheeks and ready smile of a shopkeeper's daughter.

A healthy girl with healthy appetites. He had suffered worse injuries to his dignity in the service of Louis-Charles, the fourteenth of his name. But there was something intrinsically absurd about a nobleman and a battlemage being put out to stud like a prized warhorse.

He shrugged philosophically. Despite the ridiculous position the royal policy put him and the other mages, he couldn't reasonably complain. It was a sensible policy, and indeed, in light of last year's losses suffered by l'Académie, an increasingly necessary one too. After losing no less than six experienced mages, four of them Immortels, in Narcisse de Segraise's failed attempt to ensorcel a dragon, the king would have put every maid in the kingdom to his mages' swords if he believed the Church and the petty aristocracy would stand for it.

"I trust you took no great harm," he told the girl.

"None in the slightest, my lord magus," she said, looking rather like a well-fed cat in cream. She rubbed her belly complacently.

The slight emphasis she placed on his title informed him that the sparkle in her brown eyes had rather less to do with his masculine charms than her own ambitions. A clever shopkeeper's daughter then. She wasn't one of those misfortunates who would moan and bewail her fate for years, but rather, the sort of girl who produced the requisite pair of king's bastards before her eighteenth birthday, then triumphantly settled into a marriage well above her natural station.

He grinned. He liked survivors. She might be no more than a brood mare, but she was a worthy one. And moreover, he reflected with amusement, an eager young mare with a not entirely unsatisfactory ride. Feeling the vague stirrings of desire, he was just about to reach for her again when there was a series of three sharp knocks on the door.

Never mind that. He threw her a rumpled blanket to cover herself and rolled off the bed.

"Who is it?" he called as he slipped a blue robe over his head.

"Leave off the trollop and open the damned door, de Merovech," he heard an acerbic voice call. He recognized it immediately. Besides the king, there were only two men in the entire Kingdom of Savondir who would dare to address a royal battlemage in such a dismissive manner, and the voice was too high-pitched to belong to the king's heir, the Duc de Chênevin.

"Dress yourself," he hissed at the girl. What was her name? He didn't recall.

"Mon seigneur!" she squeaked, frightened at his tone, and began fumbling about the bed looking for the cotton shift she'd been wearing.

Theuderic didn't wait for the girl to cover herself. François du Moulin was not a man who brooked delay. He opened the door and bowed respectfully to the king's chancelier, who was dressed inconspicuously in a nondescript brown cloak and a wide-brimmed hat that concealed his face in shadow.

"Monseigneur." He assumed du Moulin did not wish to be openly identified and omitted the other's title. "To what do I owe this unexpected pleasure."

Du Moulin's dark, piercing eyes flicked over the still-naked girl and a faint smile crossed his thin lips. "I see you've managed to find consolation in the absence of the elf."

Theuderic forced himself to smile. It was hardly a surprise that the king's master of spies knew about his previous attachment. He bowed again.

"I am but the humble stud-horse of His Majesty. *De bon valoir servir le roi.*"

"Your keen sense of duty commends you." Du Moulin glanced again at the girl, who was unsuccessfully attempting to smooth out her shift, run her hands through her hair, and curtsy, all at the same time. "*Deceptae dabunt odorem.* I apologize for the interruption, mademoiselle, and pray that our dutiful servant of the king has gifted you with child. I fear I must claim him for labors rather less delightful, though no less arduous."

"Monseigneur!" she breathed, eyes wide with awe the man who could so readily command a kingsmage. Her ankles weren't bad, Theuderic reflected thoughtfully, despite the legs being lamentably short.

"Come, de Merovech. We have much to discuss and too many ears abound in this place. I shall await you outside." Du Moulin turned and stalked silently from the room, leaving the door open behind him.

Theuderic sighed and bent down to collect his sandals. He slipped them on and blew a kiss to the girl.

"Will you return, mon seigneur?"

"As the king wills it, mademoiselle."

If the fates were generous, he would be back in her embrace tonight. Of course, if they ran according to the form he'd come to expect over the years, she'd bear his brat and most likely another man's before he saw her again.

Du Moulin was outside, looking over the academy grounds in what could only be considered a proprietary manner. Six young mages-in-training were chasing each other back and forth on the grassy quad in front of the bibliothèque, hurling harmless balls of sparks at each other. A pair of maids watched them, giggling and pointing.

"Do you contemplate exchanging seats on the conseil, Chancelier?"

"I imagine d'Arseille would find the notion amenable," du Moulin said. Jacque-Rene d'Arseille, Grandmagicien of l'Académie des Sage-Arts, was a man whose ambitions were not limited to the magical arts. "Nevertheless, as important as His Majesty's breeding program may be to the realm, I suspect my abilities are more wisely focused elsewhere."

"Alas for the talent-blessed mademoiselles. How fortunate that mine are well-suited to them."

"You don't miss your elf? She was a rare beauty."

"She was bony." Theuderic shrugged dismissively. He knew du Moulin far too well to give him anything the man might one day use as a weapon against him. "And, more to the point, she is not here."

"I read the report of your brief. I couldn't help but notice that you said nothing about the young Amorran general's similar attachment when you gave it to the Comte de Ilyois. Was it because you thought it might draw unwanted attention to your own?"

Theuderic didn't like the direction the conversation was taking. He was a head taller than the other man, nearly three decades younger, a battlemage and a combat veteran. He had slain more men than he could count with earth, wind, fire, and steel, whereas du Moulin had probably never once stained his soft, long-fingered hands with anything more than ink. And yet, there was something quietly powerful and frightening about the king's conseilleur that had nothing to do with his ready access to the throne.

"Do you doubt my loyalties, monseigneur Chancelier?"

"I harbor no doubts about them at all." Du Moulin tore his eyes away from the young mages and glanced up at Theuderic. "I am fully aware of how your loyalties are divided. You are an Écarlatean, are you not? And you are close to the widow of the Duc d'Aubonne, the Comtesse de Domdidier, as well."

"I am acquainted with the lady." Dear God, what idiocy has Roheis been dabbling in now? "One might even go so far as to say well-acquainted."

"Might one? Might one also say you were lovers? Speak truthfully now. This is no time for reticence, de Merovech, even on so delicate a matter."

"I am afraid not. The Lady Roheis is charming, to be sure, but regrettably, I have never had the pleasure."

Du Moulin sniffed. "You disappoint me. That would have been most useful. I suppose… no, at this point, an unexpected romantic pursuit would appear to be suspicious."

"You would have me seduce Roheis Desmargoteau?" Theuderic said disbelievingly. "As well ask me to teach a bird to sing, or a fox to hunt!"

"She is the rich widow of a powerful man, she was a paramour of the late prince, and she is known to have a considerable number of questionable acquaintances. Moreover, she is a dyed-in-the-wool Écarlatean. There are growing rumors of instability in the Grand Duchy and she is, at the very least, near the heart of it. What do you know of Saint-Agliè?"

"The Comte? Little enough. I have met him, of course. A diffident man. Not without charm, but always one to keep his own counsel. He seems to have made a strong impression on the Lady Roheis."

"Indeed," du Moulin said, looking thoughtful. "De Merovech, if I were to ask you to choose between crown and duchy, what would you say?"

Did the man take him for a fool? Even if he had been a traitor to the crown, he was hardly fool enough to declare himself one to a member of the Haut Conseil. "I should say what I said earlier, Seigneur Chancelier. One might even go so far as to call it my motto. *De bon valoir servir le roi!*"

"I thought as much," du Moulin sighed wearily. "I ask you about the crown, you answer with the king. So it is with many whose natural loyalties are even less doubtful than your own these days."

Realization struck him. He thought he understood why the Chancelier had come here, had come to him. If he was correct, then it was a deadly and dangerous game du Moulin was playing. To conceal his emotions, Theuderic looked back at the young mages still playing their game on the grass, although one had now separated himself from the others. He was standing over the two maids and juggling three balls of red-golden flames in an attempt to entertain them. Or, to put it more precisely, impress them.

In small and seemingly simple acts are the destinies of kingdoms made and unmade.

"Has Étienne-Henri been implicated in his brother's death?" He still could not bring himself to speak Charles-Phillippe's name, so great was his grief. "As some have suspected."

"No." Du Moulin's voice was decisive. "Much to my own surprise, that is one act that cannot be laid at the Duc de Chênevin's door. The Red Prince's death has been investigated thoroughly. It was the misfortunes of war, nothing more."

"It was the sheerest and most deplorable idiocy!" For a moment, Theuderic forgot to whom he spoke and his rage, suppressed for months, momentarily boiled over.

Du Moulin shook his head sympathetically. "You could not have saved him even had you been there. Do not torture yourself, de Merovech. The prince had Blancas and de Foix with him and neither were incompetents. You were there that day, at the meeting of the Haut Conseil. His Majesty could have no more kept Charles-Phillippe away from the Wolf Isles than he did from Montrove. Once the prince caught the scent, he was drawn to war like a hound after a rabbit."

Theuderic couldn't argue. He had fought too many times at Charles-Phillippe's side to deny that the Red Prince had been cursed with a love for battle that bordered on the fey. Nor was it entirely a surprise that he had been cut down by that curse before succeeding his father. But to have been leagues away, to have been on the wrong side of the White Sea when his friend fell, was almost more than he could bear to contemplate. And more than any other man, du Moulin had been responsible for that absence.

The two men stared at each other. Theuderic was the first to look away. He cursed under his breath and glared at the chancelier.

"Why do you wish me to spy on Étienne-Henri if he was not culpable? He is now but a step from the throne. Surely you do not think him so impatient as to plot against the king when his brother's corpse is barely cold! Or so foolish!"

"You mistake me. I do not wish you to spy upon to the heir to the throne. That would be unthinkable, you understand, and would surely be accounted a crime of *lèse-majesté*. I merely wish for you to become a trusted advisor to him, a valued tool upon which he will learn to rely. The men with whom he has surrounded himself are mostly unreliable non-entities, thugs and clowns and fools, with one notable exception. I wish you to provide the counterbalance to that exception."

"Does this notable exception have a name?"

"Guiheim Donzeau. By all accounts a dangerous man. It is said he is the Duc's wizard, although I found no record of him in the archives here."

"A hedge wizard." Theuderic dismissed the man. "You couldn't have sent a clerk?"

"I couldn't have trusted a clerk. Nor would you have obeyed my summons with the alacrity I require had I sent one."

Theuderic shrugged. Du Moulin wasn't incorrect. Being ordered to attach himself to the cowardly Duc de Chênevin's entourage was hardly the sort of thing to inspire a man to precipitate action.

"What am I to do? Why do you expect him to welcome a known friend of his brother's into his pack of unreliables? He hated Charles-Phillippe!"

"Welcome you? I expect him to embrace you in much the same way a drowning man clings to a rope!" Du Moulin chuckled unexpectedly. "He will welcome you, my dear mage, because the king is going to give him the chance to win his spurs. De Beaumille is too old and the Grand Duc is too busy deciding when is the right moment to rebel against the crown for either of them to be given the honor of commanding the royal forces against the orc incursion."

As Theuderic blinked in astonishment, rapid movement to his right caught his eye. One of the matrons charged with overseeing the young maids had descended upon them and was now gesturing angrily at the juggler. The two girls were giggling as they gathered up their skirts and obediently returned to their dormitory. He shook his head. The king might as reasonably give command of the royal forces to that matron, in fact, based on how effectively she was chasing off the lads, the woman would probably prove more effective.

"Is His Majesty mad with grief?"

"Not in the slightest. His Majesty is well aware of the martial shortcomings of his present heir-apparent as well as his distaste for taking counsel. Those shortcomings must be rectified, in fact, I can say that they will be rectified, before His Majesty will permit the Duc de Chênevin to be formally crowned and recognized as his heir."

Ah, so his first instinct had been correct after all! He was to be, if necessary, the knife in the back that would keep an unworthy king from the throne. His eyes must have betrayed something of his understanding, because du Moulin was quick to clarify the matter as much as he dared aloud.

"Don't assume too much, de Merovech. It is sincerely hoped that Chênevin will rise to the occasion. And it is expected that the mage who stood so steadfastly at the side of the Red Prince will do no less for his brother. I have no doubt you will be able to advise Étienne-Henri well. We may even hope that he will listen to a man with your considerable experience in battle."

Theuderic wasn't fooled. Of course he would advise the prince to the best of his ability. It was his sworn duty, and in any event, only a lunatic would seek to find an advantage in permitting an army of orcs to ravage the southeastern portion of the kingdom. Even the most rabid supporter of the Grand Duc and his coming bid for Écarlatean independence would not think to draw swords against the Miridines until the orcs were driven back to their mountainous wastelands. But he knew du Moulin, he had killed more than a handful of men at the chancelier's command, and he was certain du Moulin would not hesitate to order him to see to the prince's death if it was deemed to be in the interest of the realm.

"I'm not concerned whether he will listen to me or not, mon seigneur Chancelier. My fear is not for the corpse, but for the blade. What assurances will you give that once used, it will not be discarded."

Du Moulin was silent for a moment, and he looked out over the now-empty quad. "I was under the impression that as both kingsmage and vassal, you swore to serve His Majesty even unto death. I should imagine that no matter what sacrifice was deemed vital to the crown, you would not hesitate to make it."

"You have a powerful imagination, mon seigneur." They locked eyes again and this time Theuderic didn't look away. "If you trust me to hold my tongue now, why would you doubt my ability to do so at any point in the future?"

"Hold your tongue now? Concerning what? I have told you nothing you could not repeat before the entire court." Du Moulin affected mild surprise. "Your inferences and interpretations are your own, sieur. Nevertheless, you need not worry about the proverbial knife in the back, at least, not mine. You may recall I am not in the habit of throwing away useful men. Guiheim Donzeau, on the other hand, should be watched if ever he comes to see you as his rival in the prince's confidence. But if you would fear something, fear the prince's generalship, for I intend you to be at his side. If you cannot talk sense into him, you may one day find yourself surrounded by ten thousand orcs. In such an event, there would be nothing I could do to save you."

Theuderic nodded, pretending to be reassured. *But I do not fear orcs or charlatans, or even the foolishness of princes, monseigneur le Chancelier. I fear you, spider. I may be a dagger in your hand, but I know full well there are others. And I know how readily you will cast a bloody blade aside, lest it stain your lily-white hands.*

"I am, as you have so graciously reminded me, at the king's service in all things. When would you have me depart and where shall I go? Is Étienne-Henri even aware of the duty that has befallen him?"

"He is not, but he will be upon my return to Lutèce. I would have you depart upon the morrow; that should give you the opportunity to be sure your seed is well and truly sown."

"You are too kind."

Du Moulin acknowledged his sarcasm with a ghost of a smile and a brief inclination of his head. "Do not the priests tell us not to bind the mouths of the kine? And in truth, the loss of your bloodline would be a loss to the kingdom."

The words cost the chancelier nothing, Theuderic knew. And yet, even so small a gesture, so casual a compliment, reassured him in a way du Moulin's earlier assurances had not. Not that du Moulin wouldn't kill him if his death was determined to be necessary; if the ruthless chancelier was willing to murder the king's heir apparent, he would not shirk at a mere comte and kingsmage. But he would only do so if it was absolutely necessary and Theuderic was determined to ensure that would never be the case.

In any event, forewarned was forearmed. If worst came to worst and it looked as if he'd been chosen to play the scapegoat, he could always flee to Merithaim.

Du Moulin produced a pair of sealed scrolls that had been secreted in his tunic. The wax was the blue one that Theuderic recognized as belonging to l'Académie and the seal was the Grandmagicien's own. He handed them to Theuderic; one was thicker than the other.

"The larger one is your credentials, as well as those belonging to the four mages who will accompany you. Give it to the prince when you are brought before him. They will all be young men, recently raised to the blue, and answerable to you as their superior. I told d'Arseille I wanted the best he had, so I expect you'll find them useful on the battlefield. They should suffice to give you a status that Donzeau cannot contest and ensure you a place in the prince's council."

Theuderic nodded. Du Moulin's plan was, unsurprisingly, well-conceived. Five battlemages was a military asset at which no general could afford to turn up his nose, no matter how suspicious he might be.

"And the other?" He raised the smaller scroll.

"Your secret orders from me to spy upon the prince and report upon his loyalty to his father. Open it once you have been accepted into his entourage and be sure to hide it where it will be found. Like all instinctive connivers, Chênevin is a suspicious man, and his mind won't be at ease about you unless he is convinced he knows your purpose. This will suffice to convince him you are harmless. As far as he is concerned, he has only to wait and the throne will be his."

"His brother was less convinced of Étienne-Henri's patience."

Du Moulin sniffed contemptuously. "I should not be surprised if this small taste of responsibility will be sufficient to inspire him to pray God grant his father a long and active life. It is one thing to desire a crown from afar, but the nearer one comes to it, the heavier it is seen to weigh. In any event, try not to despise him, no matter how much he merits it. All Chênevin truly seeks is approval from men he finds admirable. He'll never get it from Charles-Phillippe now, so see that you dole it out to him slowly, even reluctantly, and soon you'll have all the influence with him you require."

"Will that do any good?" Theuderic said bitterly. He found it hard to imagine.

"See that it does," du Moulin replied.

MARCUS

The afternoon ride through the green rolling hills of southern Savondir was quite possibly the most relaxing thing he'd done in months, Marcus realized, and yet the warmth of the late spring afternoon did nothing to calm the raging fury that boiled within him. It was with no little difficulty that he choked down his rage and maintained a tranquil facade for the benefit of his companions, both Amorran and Savonderic. There was a time for anger, just as there was a time for all things, but that time was not now. Now there were too many decisions to be made, too many decisions for which he did not have sufficient information. And too many decisions that were bound to cost lives, many lives, no matter what he decided.

He was well aware of the fact that he was not up to the responsibility placed upon him. He lacked information, he lacked experience, and worst of all, he lacked reliable advisors. The situation was utterly ludicrous. Here he was contemplating the fate of kingdoms and empires while riding a borrowed horse and accompanied by an imposed bodyguard through a foreign land that had, for most of the previous century, been formally at war with the Senate and People.

On the positive side, Marcus reminded himself, he was alive and he was on the right side of the grass. There was much to be said for the ground beneath one's feet, he found, especially after spending more than a month with it above his head. It was only three weeks ago that Legio XVII emerged from the tunnels that the legionary wags had labeled the Via Pumilia, and there still was not a morning in which Marcus did not find himself lifting his eyes to the sky and giving thanks to God for the light of the sun upon his face. However gray the day might be, there was no cloud thick enough to obscure the light completely.

Decisions. In such circumstances, even to delay a decision was to make one. He wished he had a better grasp on Savonderic politics, as the one thing that had become very clear to him in his recent meeting with the two members of the king's *concilium altus* was that the distribution of power throughout the northern realm was not as clearly defined as it appeared from afar. It hadn't taken him long after Marcus Saturnius's death to learn how little direct control the legate held over the legion, and it was readily apparent that the king of Savondir faced even greater difficulties. Even in a reduced legion of five thousand men, there were far too many details and decisions required for any one man to make them, and Marcus couldn't imagine how much worse the problem must be in a kingdom of more than ten million.

At least in the legion, he knew his officers were more or less loyal. That didn't seem to be the case with many of the king's nobles.

As nearly as he could tell, there were two rival factions that currently had the king's ear. One, led by the Chancelier and supported by the royal general, saw Legio XVII as a divine blessing given to them in a time of need, and was eager to provide its legate all the resources he required. The other faction, which was more amorphous and lacked any leader known to him, seemed to view the Amorrans as a threat potentially more dangerous than the vast horde of orcs and goblins now invading the eastern borderlands. Fortunately, it was the Chancelier who held the purse strings, and though his ally on the concilium was elderly and set in his ways, the Maréchal de Savonne clearly understood the difference between a minor incursion and a major invasion.

Gold, horses, food, and information. That was what he had obtained in the little walled town of Sainte Jorat sur le Lac where he met the royal representatives. Or, rather, he had obtained assurances of them. Once it became clear that he was willing to lead his legion against the orc tribes on behalf of the realm, the councillors were willing enough to make promises. Whether those promises would be fulfilled was still an open question, but he was confident that the general, at least, had understood that without four hundred horses to replace the beasts they had slaughtered and eaten under the mountain, the legion's cavalry would be nonexistent.

Both he and the decurion who accompanied him, Vitalis, rode rather better mounts now than the poorly fed nags Proculus bought from a farmer prior to their journey to Sainte Jorac sur le Lac. The animals were bigger than the Amorran horses to which he was accustomed; they had to be in order to bear the weight of the heavily armored Savonderic knights. Marcus wished the legionary cavalry of the XVIIth had been riding big brutes like these last autumn in the Battle of the Three Legions. If they had, they would have ridden down Magnus's outnumbered cavalry before his uncle's damned knights had sprung the trap on them that was the turning point of the battle.

He sighed, refusing to indulge himself by picking again at that oft-revisited wound. South or east, that was the first question he had to answer, and the one from which all the others would follow. His heart, and the fury bubbling within him, urged him south. His head, his word, and his sense of duty called him east. So, too, did the scrolls which bore stylized signatures and elaborate wax stamps and were stowed away in his saddlebags, but he wasn't overly concerned about the agreements he'd signed. Only the king, and perhaps the Grand Duc, possessed larger armies than he presently commanded, which meant that no matter what the agreements might say, he was at liberty to change his mind at any time.

No doubt that was why the royal councillors and their various priests and scribes had been so determined to try binding him through the web of words that were spun throughout the beautifully inscribed scrolls he now carried. But what the Savonders didn't realize was that Marcus had been speaking for the legion, not himself, and though a patrician's word was his bond, a legate's word was nothing more than one of the thousands of weapons at his disposal in defense of the Senate and People.

Still, he would like to keep it, if possible. If nothing else, it would be one less sin to confess to Father Gennadius.

It was with a mild pang of regret that he spotted a pair of legionaries seated in the shade of a small copse of trees that topped the highest hill in the area. They had surely been gambling, but they were alert enough. No sooner had the sound of creaking wagon axles reached them than they were on their feet, one hand on their sword hilts and the other over their eyes as they peered into the western sun. He sighed, knowing his responsibilities were about to fall upon him and the time for decisions was approaching. He felt the weight of them all the heavier in light of the dark news he now bore.

"Surely your men don't fear an attack," scoffed de Forbonnais, the Utruccan-speaking comte whom the Royal Chancelier had named as royal liaison to the legion. That was his official assignation, but Marcus assumed that in addition to spying on the Amorrans, the cocksure young noble was almost surely a sorceror in the mode of the departed, and deeply unlamented, Comte de Thoneaux. De Forbonnais was likable enough, although his long, flowing brown hair would make him look rather like a woman amongst all the shaved and close-cropped heads favored by the Amorran legionaries. It didn't help that the man's Savonderic accent also made his Utruccan sound a little less than entirely masculine.

"It is our custom to remain on our guard regardless of where we happen to find ourselves, monseigneur comte."

"I'm told you have nearly six thousand armed men," The comte laughed. "Who is going to attack you, mon cher général, our little friends, the birds?"

A few of the men riding behind the comte joined in the laughter. They were supposed to be de Forbonnais's honor guard, knights of one elaborately named order or another, but Marcus had seldom seen a less martial group of soldiers. They rode their giant horses well, that much he had to give them, but their shining armor and brightly painted shields were unmarred by scratches and it seemed unlikely that any of them had ever seen a battlefield, much less fought upon one. Their good humor irritated him, and it was all he could do to prevent himself from turning and biting their heads off.

Marcus shook his head and reminded himself that youthful exuberance and inexperience didn't mean their minds weren't keen, or their eyes were less than observant. He, of all men, should be aware of that. De Forbonnais might affect to be careless, but if the royal spymaster had chosen him as his eyes and ears in the legion, he was probably a capable man, perhaps even a dangerous one.

One of the guards on the hilltop vanished, presumably to alert Gaius Trebonius of their approach. The other one must have recognized Marcus, as he stood at rigid attention while he watched them pass below. Marcus nodded and casually tapped his fist to his chest; the legionary returned the salute forcefully enough for them to hear it, then relaxed his posture.

"Seems Trebonius hasn't let them go slack in your absence, sir."

Marcus glanced at Vitalis. The decurion was calm and reliable, which was one reason why Marcus had chosen him over some of the more senior officers for the embassy from which they were now returning. The other was that for some reason the man had never seen fit to explain to Marcus or anyone else, he spoke fluent Savonnais. His light gray eyes tended to suggest that one of his parents might have hailed from the kingdom, but if he did harbor any exotic ancestry, it was natural that, as an equestrian, he would be inclined to hold his tongue about it.

"I never imagined he would."

Legio XVII might not be a veteran legion in terms of its battle experience, but the long underground march through the eternal night of the Dwarven mines under the mountains had tested them in a way that a dozen battles could not have. The northern sun had already restored the color to Marcus's face, and the simple, but plentiful Savonderic fare had put flesh back on his bones, but like every other man in the legion, he would not soon forget those arduous weeks of darkness, fear, and hunger under the ground. The legion had bonded through its trial by the tunnels; no legion capable of accomplishing such a hitherto unknown feat could feel a need to prove itself any longer, not even a legion with a history measured only in months.

After passing the hill and the trees that covered its backside like a thick green pelt, they turned toward the south and the castra soon came within sight. Marcus smiled grimly, pleased to hear the expostulations and surprised exclamations of the Savondese riders.

"*Sale bleu*, do you intend to found a city here, Amorran?"

"Did I not tell you it is our custom to remain on our guard?" He grinned at the discomfited de Forbonnais.

For all that it lacked the stone walls of the Savondese towns, the legionary castra made for an impressive sight, even to Marcus's experienced eyes. The castra covered a larger area than the town from which they'd ridden, to say nothing of the various villages they'd passed on the way. With weeks to deepen the trenches, build up the earthworks, and replace the palisade with logged trees, the legionary camp had been transformed into a veritable fort. Give the architecti another two months and access to a decent supply of stones, and it would become a permanent fortress, as defensible as any city in Savondir.

But they didn't have two months. Nor could he and his legion remain safely behind walls, be they made of earth, wood, or stone. As much as he desperately wanted to march Legio XVII back south in defense of an Amorr that was under assault from its own provinces and allies, he knew it wasn't possible. There was more at stake than who would rule over the Senate and People with what appeared to be every orc east of the Grimmwalde marching on the lands of Men and Elves.

"What on Earth is that?" Vitalis exclaimed.

For a moment, Marcus thought the decurion was surprised by the various wagons and shoddy wooden dwellings that had attached themselves to the eastern wall of the castra, looking for all the world like some sort of cancerous growth swelling from the lower half of the walls. But they were nothing more than the usual collection of merchants, swindlers, and whores who trailed after the legion and founded a temporary township every time it made camp for more than a few days in succession. It was perhaps a little surprising that the Savondese managed to find them so far from everything that passed for civilization in the north, but then, last year, had their provincial counterparts in Gorignia not shown themselves entirely willing to follow Legio XVII into goblin territory?

Then he realized Vitalis was not looking at the whores town, but at a crude structure erected about a spear's throw east of it. It took him a moment to grasp what he was looking at, and then he swore under his breath. It was a crucis and despite its distance from them, Marcus could see there was quite clearly a man hanging from it, his head slumped down onto his chest.

Marcus resisted the urge to steal a glance at de Forbonnais and the rest of the Savondese party, hoping that perhaps the unfamiliar magnitude of the castra would prevent them from noticing the dying man, but a wry voice from behind him quickly dashed his hopes.

"It would appear your man Trebonius is a bit of a disciplinarian."

"Amorr's legions are well-known for their discipline, monseigneur."

"So I am told." Fortunately, the comte sounded considerably more amused than horrified. Even so, Marcus was embarrassed, both for himself and for Trebonius. "And so I see."

There was nothing Marcus could do about his age, or the fact that he and Gaius Trebonius were both mere military tribunes elected in the last election but one. It was hardly his fault that he had only been born twenty-two years ago, or that House Severus's assassins murdered the rest of the legion's command staff. Marcus had managed to overcome whatever doubts the Savonderic king and his great lords harbored about his youth and callowness, otherwise, he and Vitalis would be returning alone to the legion instead in the company of a squadron of noble northern fops. But those doubts were bound to return sooner or later, and hearing that Marcus's second-in-command had been forced to resort to executions so quickly was only going to strengthen the insidious voices that had opposed the granting of the royal charter he was carrying.

"General Valerius, sir!"

A cheerful call from a legionary carrying one end of a deer hanging suspended from a pole drew his attention, and the man's cry was soon echoed by welcoming shouts and salutes from legionaries outside the camp as they approached the Porta Praetoria and the great scarlet banner that proclaimed the authority of the Senate and People of Amorr as well as the divided gray-and-scarlet banner of House Valerius.

"The general's back!"

"The Valerian is back!"

"Ave, Valerius!"

"Ave, Clericus!"

"Ave, Cavarus!"

The last name was new to him. After he heard it shouted in his direction several more times, including from a ballistarius standing behind one of the scorpios positioned over the open gate, he turned towards Vitalis. His saddle creaked.

"Cavarus?"

The decurion grinned. "They mean it as a compliment, general. The men don't think they should be calling you a priest no more. And you did set us to an amount of marching down underground. Some was for calling you Talpa, others was saying Subter, but the centurions sorted them out soon enough."

Marcus nodded thoughtfully. Being compared to a mole would be a little too undignified for a legionary commander, even if the name was not necessarily inappropriate given the circumstances. "Digger" wasn't the most glorious of agnomen, perhaps, but he had to admit that it did serve to commemorate two of the brighter accomplishments of his thus-far undistinguished military career. He might have no victories to his credit, but twice he had been able to preserve a trapped and outnumbered legion.

"As long as they salute when they address me with it, decurion, you can tell your fellow officers that I have no objections."

"They'll be glad to hear it, general."

Legionaries saluted crisply at the sight of him, their fists slamming against their chest with either a thud or a clang depending on whether they were wearing their breastplates or not. Their faces were red and brown and bronze with color now; the ghostly pallor they had all shared when Marcus departed to meet with the king's negotiators three weeks ago was gone. The northern sun of Savondir might not be quite as warm as the one that shone down on the imperial city, but had clearly it helped his men return to good health. His father would have been pleased to know that, Marcus was sure. Corvus had always loved them as much as they loved him.

Marcus hoped de Forbonnais was marking the way in which Legio XVII greeted its commander's return as closely as he had noted whatever disciplinary lapse led to the wretch on the crux outside. But Marcus was just passing through the gate when he heard an agonized cry from behind them. He couldn't quite understand what was being said, and when he looked back, he saw that the noise was coming from the dying man. Then he realized what language the man was speaking and he closed his eyes, feeling as if he'd taken another hammer blow to the belly, the second that week.

"La fin est proche, est proche," he realized the man was shouting. "La fin est proche se trouve à proximité!"

He did not look back at de Forbonnais, though he could hardly dare to hope the king's man failed to grasp the significance of what they had all heard. This time, the Savonder did not say anything, he continued to walk silently just to Marcus's rear, on his right hand side. It was just as well de Forbonnais did not demand answers. Marcus knew he could not possibly supply them.

Damn that Trebonius! What could possibly be the point of executing a peasant? It seemed he would soon have the opportunity to find out, as ahead of him, he saw a group of centurions walking briskly towards them from the direction of the forum. In their midst of their bemedalled splendor, he saw a horsehair-plumed tribune's helmet.

Marcus reined in his horse and swung himself down from the saddle. Vitalis was quick to follow suit, and to bark orders at some of the legionaries watching nearby to come and hold the reins for the them and the rest of the mounted party. De Forbonnais and his Savondese companions dismounted, but after a burst of rapid Savonnaise amongst themselves, did not hand their horses over to the Amorrans. Instead, half the honor guard stayed with the horses while the comte, accompanied by the other ten men, came forward to stand with Marcus and await the approach of Trebonius and the other officers.

If Trebonius was expecting Marcus to be unhappy with him, he showed no signs of it. His fellow tribune was practically beaming with delight, and against his will, Marcus could feel his anger beginning to abate. It pleased him even more to see that the senior officers, too, appeared to be glad at his return even if the hard-bitten veterans were less inclined to display their pleasure so openly. Titus Cassabus, the senior ballistarius he'd promoted to praefectus castrorum, nodded at him, Caius Proculus, the primus pilus, lifted his unshaven chin, while Sentas Tertius merely raised a skeptical eyebrow in the direction of the Savondese men. Marcus was beginning to understand his father's lifelong love for his legionaries; there was something uniquely powerful about the connection between an army and their general. Theirs was a bond sealed in bloodshed, hardship, and battle.

"Good to see you, sir!" Trebonius saluted, and the air resounded with the crash of fists on steel as the centurions and legionaries followed his lead.

"Likewise." Marcus touched his curled fingers to his chest and nodded to the senior officers. "Gentlemen, I have the honor to be accompanied by Seigneur Girart de Forbonnais, Comte de Ilyois, and our royal liaison by the order of our most gracious host, His Majesty, the king."

De Forbonnais made an elegant leg that Marcus knew would be completely lost on his officers; he was pleased to see their discipline hold as not one of them so much as coughed, although Tertius raised both eyebrows this time, even more skeptically than before. And not even the man's Savonnaise-flavored Utruccan made any of them crack a smile.

"My lords of Amorr, I deem it an unmitigated honor to make the acquaintance of the doughty men who led the now-legendary Deep March, of which the bards now sing! I pray you will not view my men and me as an intrusion amongst you, but rather, welcome us as your friends and allies against a fearsome foe that poses the greatest of dangers to both our peoples."

He made another leg, and without any signal that Marcus could see, his dismounted men did the same, in unison. They looked absurd, of course, but they performed the silly movement with sufficient snap and precision that he wondered, if, with the proper training, they might actually be of some use as an auxiliary horse. He'd have to speak to Arvandus, the senior decurion, to see if that could be arranged. But now that the introductions had been accomplished, he was eager to see the Savonders safely stowed away somewhere in the camp so Trebonius could bring him up to speed on how soon the legion would be ready to march east.

"Monseigneur Comte, I'm sure you and your men will want to see to your horses. If you will follow Gnaeus Vitalis, he can show you where the stables are located; we will see that suitable accommodation near them is provided. I hope you will do me the honor of dining with me tonight."

"You are too kind, Monseigneur General." The proud young man's face hardened. "But while my men are establishing themselves, I must insist on speaking with you and your command staff. We have, I believe, certain matters of considerable import to discuss without delay."

Marcus sighed. De Forbonnais had been a charming companion on the ride south, but Marcus had no illusions that the Savonder was going to be anything but a thorn in his side from now on. And if monseigneur comte was not, like the last Savonderic comte who had been inflicted upon him, a royal battlemage, Marcus would eat the legionary standard. It wasn't as if they had been short of opportunities to speak throughout the ride; clearly de Forbonnais was eager to take the measure of his officers.

"Those matters will keep until this evening, monseigneur comte. My men will see to your accommodations, and if you require anything out of the ordinary, you have only to ask and the decurion will see to it."

De Forbonnais drew himself up haughtily, and for a moment Marcus thought the man was going to be foolish enough to stand his ground, but he merely sniffed reproachfully and bowed deeply while drawing one arm to his torso in what might have been a parody of an Amorran salute.

"As you say, monseigneur general. We shall speak again anon."

Marcus nodded and watched as the Savonders remounted and followed Vitalis along the Via Principalis. A centurion whistled, waved his staff, and soon three decani were leading their contubernii in pursuit of the cloud of dust the Savonderic horses were kicking up behind them. Marcus doubted it was necessary to guard the Savonders inside the castra, but he didn't countermand the order. With more than a thousand leagues now separating them from the northernmost borders of the empire, Legio XVII couldn't be too careful.

"The command tent," Marcus said, his voice lowered so that only the senior officers nearby could hear him. "I've got bad news."

Marcus looked from face to face inside the large canvas tent. With one exception, the praefectus Cassabus, the six older men facing him were shorter than him. To a man, they were plebs, and except for Trebonius, they were all longtime veterans who had served under his father in one of the other two Valerian legions before helping Corvus and Marcus Saturnius build XVII. He had next to nothing in common with them; except for Senarius Arvandus, they were poor, uneducated, and vulgar. He was a consul's son, censor's grandson, and consul's nephew educated as a scholar destined for the Church hierarchy.

And yet, he had come to trust them more than he had ever trusted anyone. He knew them better than his own brother, he knew they were closer to his father than he had ever been, and he could not bring himself to lie to them. Not about something so important. Not about something so close to their hearts. Not even though it would grieve them as deeply as it grieved him.

He took a deep breath and looked away from their grim, suspicious expressions.

"How bad is it?" Caius Proculus, the primus pilus, finally broke the silence. "Has the city fallen?"

Marcus blinked, surprised. His news was bad. It wasn't the end of the world.

"Corvus... is fallen. The Sanctified Father as well."

No one said anything. All six officers were too shocked to speak, too astonished to even protest. But the silence that followed his revelation was qualitatively different than the silence of the moment before. To Marcus, it felt as if a great chasm had opened up before his feet, as if the speaking of those terrible words had unleashed an evil spell that altered the very fabric of the world.

My father is dead. The Holy Father is dead.

His eyes remained dry, but they burned in their sockets.

Trebonius reached out to him and silently squeezed his shoulder. Cassabus was shaking his head back and forth in denial, while Proculus staggered back, fumbled blindly for a chair, and collapsed heavily onto it. Sintas Tertius buried his head in his hands, and a moment later, his shoulders began to convulse as he wept silently.

The sight of his grief-stricken officers was almost more than Marcus could bear. He gritted his teeth, looked down at the earthen floor to give himself a moment to regain control, then cleared his throat.

"Before you ask, no one knows what happened. It seems there was a fire in the palace, in the throne room. Corvus was there, meeting with the Sanctiff. They were found dead there together, burned. An archbishop died with them as well."

"Who did it? Were they attacked?" Proculus was the first to get himself under control.

"There are all sorts of wild rumors flying around. The elven ambassador disappeared at the same time, so considerable speculation centers on that. But unless Lady Shadowsong, Lady Everbright and that cursed de Merovech were all lying to me, it can't have been the elves. There are all sorts of incredible rumors, and it's clear that no one truly knows who was responsible."

"Do you think it was the Severans?"

"It's possible, of course." Marcus thoughtfully worried at the cuticle on his right index finger with his left hand. "But I'd be more inclined to suspect my uncle. House Severus is still in disarray by all accounts and Corvus had nothing to do with Severus Patronus's death. This is the sort of bold,

unexpected stroke that only Magnus would dare. I can't think of another
Senator with the stones to do it."

"That makes sense," Trebonius said. The others looked at him, surprised,
and he shrugged. "I don't know any more about patrician politics than the
rest of you, but if the fire that killed him happened before Lady Shadowsong
met us, then the General was dead months ago, before we met Magnus near
Montmila. We know Magnus must have been planning rebellion before
then, and God knows he's a wily old bastard, so it doesn't seem unlikely that
your uncle would have arranged for something to keep the city occupied in
his absence."

"Killing a consul and a sanctiff would certainly tie down the Senate and
keep it well and truly distracted." Marcus punched his open palm. "To say
nothing of frightening the plebs and eliminating the one general he knew
was good enough to beat him. Dammit, if I hadn't put the horse on the left
wing under that fool Nobilianus, we'd have had him and that murderous
traitor's fat arse would have already been roasted over a slow fire!"

"So what the hell are we doing here?" Tertius shouted. His face was
streaked with tears and Marcus recalled that last year it had taken the man
weeks to get over Saturnius's death. "We shouldn't be in Savonderum, we
should be back there, back in Amorr! Damn the northmen, let them defend
their own bloody borders from the orc. Let's march south and put your
traitor uncle's head where it belongs, on the sharp end of a spear!"

"No one wants my uncle's head more than I do, Vitius Sintas. There isn't
a man here who wants to avenge my father's blood more than me."

It was at that moment that everything became clear to him. Let the dead
bury the dead.

"We're not marching south," he told them. "This news is old. The
fighting at home may already be over, one way or the other. These orcs,
they aren't something the Savonders can stop on their own. There are too
many of them. If we can help the king stop the orcs here, we're doing
our duty to the Senate and People by keeping them out of the empire and
away from Amorr. Every orc we kill, every orc we even force them to field
against us here in the north, is one more that isn't marching south toward
our lands."

Trebonius nodded. Cassabus exhaled loudly and shook his head, but
more in frustration than disagreement. The primus pilus looked skeptical,
but he did not protest.

Tertius stared angrily at Marcus. Marcus didn't say anything more, he
simply met the man's angry, pain-filled eyes, until the centurion finally

looked away. But he didn't manage to do so before Marcus noticed another tear run down his cheek.

"What are we going to tell the men?" Trebonius asked.

"Nothing. They don't need to know."

"Nothing? How can you not tell them the Sanctiff is dead? How can you think they wouldn't want to honor the General!"

"They'll think to honor him by avenging him," Proculus answered Tertius. "And that ain't the worst problem. The men who left their women and children behind is already half beside themselves not knowing what is happening to them. If they hear that things down there is that out of control, some of them is going to crack. We might even start seeing men trying to head south on their own."

"There won't be any desertions!" Trebonius said heatedly. "There hasn't been a single one since the day after the battle!"

"Do you think anyone was about to desert when the general's elf was patrolling the skies, or run off in the darkness under the mountains?" Cassabus said.

She's not my elf, Marcus wanted to say, but he let it slide. "No one is deserting and no one outside of the command staff is to hear about either my father or the Holy Father." He looked from officer to officer, making certain they all understood it was an order. "The families are a legitimate issue. Arvandus, arrange for a squadron to ride south to Gorignia tomorrow, taking letters. Those who can write will have to help those who can't. And send a chest of silver with them, twenty terces for each woman and another ten for each child. They can spend three weeks looking for news of the camp followers. If they can't find them by then, they should return. They'll most likely find the women in one of the Vallyrian castras."

"Are you serious?" The senior decurion looked incredulous. "General, you couldn't be certain of finding them if you sent ten squadrons!"

Marcus shrugged. "They may not. But if we can keep the ranks from getting overly restless for the price of a little silver and eight knights, that's not a bad bargain. The men know as well as we do there is nothing we can do for their families, they just want to see we aren't ignoring their concerns."

"This is why they're not allowed to marry in the first place," Firminus grumbled.

"Camp wife is cheaper than whores," said Tertius.

"Depends on the whore," Cassabus said wryly, drawing a bitter snort from the centurion.

While they were talking, Trebonius had gone to the far side of the tent and withdrawn a flagon, presumably of wine, from the shadows. He handed it to the pilus prior, then gathered five of the stemless wooden goblets from which the Savondese peasantry drank. But before Tertius could pour it, Marcus intervened.

"No, not yet." He held up his hand to stop the centurion. "There are two things that require addressing now. First, we march northeast the day after tomorrow. We will assemble the centurions these evening in the forum and instruct them to inform their centuries accordingly. The duke told me that large raiding parties of orcs are known to have attacked seventeen towns and villages north of the Grimmwalde Gap. The local nobles have assembled a force of two hundred horse and hunted down eight of the warbands, but at least four remain active."

"How big are these parties?" Trebonius asked. None of the men looked surprised that they would be abandoning the castra so quickly.

"About a century. The goblins are mounted. The orcs aren't."

"They can't possibly think we're going to chase down warbands that size on foot," protested Arvandus. "And between my knights and Appius Julianus's, we've barely got more than three hundred horse ourselves! Or we would if we had horses, which we don't."

Marcus grinned wryly at the senior decurion. "No worries, Senarius, the Savondese have no intention of wasting a perfectly good Amorran legion chasing shadows in the forest. They've taken captives, and the interrogations have led them to believe that a much larger force is marching through the Gap. We have been requested to march there at all speed and stop them before they manage to exit the hills and threaten the city of Naeon."

"Requested?" Firminus looked suspicious. "How much larger a force?"

"There are conflicting reports, but the most credible estimate is between twenty-five and forty thousand."

That produced instantaneous responses from the five officers, every single one of which would merit at least a mild penance from Father Gennadius.

Marcus wasn't surprised that Cassabus, was the first to stop swearing and think the matter through. "What sort of forces are the Savondese providing? We beat twenty thousand goblins last year, but twice that many orcs is an entirely different proposition, General. And you know we've four hundred fewer men now."

"I am well aware of that. What's more, instead of two veteran generals commanding the legion, you've got an tribune with no victories and a defeat to his credit, and that with the numbers on his side. Moreover, they've got shamans, blood magicians, and the Immaculate knows what other devilries on hand whereas we don't have so much as a single Michaeline novice. Even you wouldn't take those odds, Proculus."

"I hope you're going to tell us that you didn't," the primus pilus said, unsmiling.

"I wish I could," Marcus said, as he walked over and reached into a leather satchel that one of the legionaries had brought into the tent earlier. He withdrew a scroll that was sealed in purple wax marked with an very large stamp and handed it to Trebonius. "Unfortunately, the request essentially amounts to an order, seeing as how it comes from Gaius Trebonius's new liege lord."

"What's this?" the young tribune said, waving the scroll back and forth. "My liege lord?"

"Impressive, isn't it?" Marcus pointed to the seal and smiled at his friend's discomfiture. That would teach him not to execute the local peasants in his absence. "It is the seal of His Royal Majesty, Louise-Philippe de Mirid, by the grace of God King of Savondir, the Wolf Isles, and the Seven Seats. Break it, Gaius Trebonius."

Trebonius broke the seal and unrolled the scroll. Cassabus whistled at the sight of it; the praefectus could read nearly as well as Marcus and the elaborate script was a veritable work of art that looked more like the product of a monastic scriptorium than a royal bureaucracy.

Trebonius, being a merchant's son, could read as well, although the over-flourished hand of the scribe seemed to make it hard for him to distinguish one word from another. But at least Marcus had been able to convince the cleric to write the scroll in Church Faleran rather than in the Savonnaise the Chancelier originally ordered.

"What is a marquisat?" he asked Marcus, looking confused.

"It's like a miniature province. The king has made you something similar to a proconsular governor, only it's a permanent office. Hereditary, even. So, congratulations, Monseigneur Marquis. You're now a patrician of sorts."

"I don't understand." Trebonius stared at the scroll as if it had turned into a serpent. Several of the other officers murmured their agreement with him. Proculus, in particular, was looking askance at Marcus, as if he thought Marcus had gone completely mad.

"It's entirely sensible on the king's part, gentlemen. We have what is, by Savonderic standards, an unusually large army, and the king is a little nervous that we're going to march on Lutèce and attempt to dethrone him. If it weren't for the orcs, he'd probably be raising his levies against us. But as things stand, he knows he needs us. He's trying to buy our loyalty. In addition to the lands and income he's given Gaius Trebonius, he's agreed to keep us supplied through next winter and meet our payroll for the duration of the summer campaign."

"Can't collect if you're dead," said Tertius sourly. "Maybe that's why he's throwing us in the gap. Figures he can kill two birds with the one stone, getting rid of us and a whole passel of orcs at one throw."

Marcus shrugged. "Men, you want to honor the General. This is how we're going to do it. We're going to honor him by slaughtering these orcs and striking fear into the hearts of every man, orc, and goblin in the north."

"This is madness!" Tertius protested.

"Clericus, you've never even fought the orc before!" Cassabus reminded him.

"Cavarus," Marcus corrected the praefectus. "I hear the men are calling me Cavarus now. And I've decided they may as well, because I've come up with a plan, and as it happens, it is one that may involve a considerable quantity of digging."

The senior officers looked at each other in silence. Then Proculus groaned and pretended to rub at his back.

"Damn their numbers, General! Can't we just face them in the open and die like men?"

The officers laughed, but there was a edge of something that, in lesser men, might have been termed hysteria. Marcus only smiled, located a chair, and then pointed to the flagon, relieved to see that they were with him.

"You'd better pour us that wine, centurion. Trebonius, see if you can locate a wax board and a stylus. This could take a while."

SEVERA

AMORR was a city under siege. Although no enemy armies ringed her walls, or assailed her gates, the city had been formally placed under military rule and every day, her citizens awoke with the knowledge that they were one day closer to spring. Men volunteered for the four new legions that had been voted funds by the Senate, while women prepared foodstuffs, sewed everything from banners to thick canvas sacks, and made do without half their household slaves.

The slaves had been commandeered by the Senate vote and it was an indication of the city's desperation that twelve thousand, enough to make up two full legions, were being trained as legionaries. Six of the Houses Martial were sharing the cost of the two slave legions, with the understanding that they would be disbanded at the end of the war, but neither House Valerian nor House Severus had been permitted to participate. With two of the three Valerian legions in league with the rebellious provincials and the whereabouts of the third one unknown, the Valerians were under extreme suspicion by the Senate and People alike.

Three of her husband's older brothers and no less than eight of his cousins had been taken into Senatorial custody. All of them had served at one time or another with Legio VII, the legion commanded by Didius Scato that Valerius Magnus had so easily co-opted. Sextus had been questioned closely by her cousin T. Severus Servius, a quaestor who had been elected at the same assembly, but in light of his youth, his tribunate, and his lack of personal ties to any of the three Valerian legions, he had thus far been spared the indignity of an arrest.

But it was something she worried about every time she heard a group of men marching up the street to the Valerian domus in which they were now living. Her heart skipped a beat every time she heard the clatter of more than two or three pairs of iron-shod sandals, and she had to endure small agonies daily as Sextus had frequent visitors from both the soldiers under his command and small delegations of those pleading for him to show mercy to them or one of their clients. Her husband, having been deemed untrustworthy of defending a gate or serving in one of the Senatorial legions, had been assigned the ugly task of overseeing the ongoing expulsions of residents deemed insufficiently loyal by the Senate due to their connections in the Allied cities.

It was wearing on Sextus. Severa could see that. The suspicion that his father's treachery cast on him was bad enough, but his staunch Valerian pride did not permit him to show how the constant whispers bothered him. Not even when they were alone would he complain about them, or indeed, see fit to mention them. She was convinced that he had chosen to live in Magnus's own domus as more a gesture of arrogant defiance than anything else, his appeal to his mother's need to be in her own home and its proximity to the Forum notwithstanding.

If Sextus's haughty Valerian pride was up to that particular challenge, his warm and sympathetic nature was almost daily overwhelmed by the cruelty that his Senate-imposed responsibilities demanded of him. She never saw her husband entering the homes of the men identified for expulsion or escorting the families to the city gates, but more than once she overheard the desperate appeals from men who came to plead with him, and saw the confused faces of the children and wives who accompanied them. Where would they go? How would they live? Why had they been ordered to leave the only homes they had ever known when other men, who in some cases weren't even citizens, had been permitted to stay?

Sextus had no answers for them. Both he and Severa knew very well that were it not for House Valerius's loyal allies in the Senate and her own ties to House Severus, they might well have faced expulsion, or worse, themselves. The Senators were frightened. Sextus tried to explain the situation to her one night after he had come home, guilt-stricken and hollow-eyed, fresh from discovering that the man he'd been ordered to evict that day had murdered his entire household, right down to the youngest slave, prior to killing himself. The man's crime, such as it was, was to have married a woman from Quinqueterra some twenty years before. And frightened men, especially rich and powerful men not accustomed to being frightened, were prone to acting recklessly, unnecessarily, and without thinking through all the probable consequences.

The mass expulsion of the provincials at the start of the war was dreadful, but tempered by the fact that everyone, including the provincials themselves, understood that the expulsion was a necessary and merciful act. With the provinces in rebellion and word of Amorran citizens being butchered everywhere from Cynothicum to Bithnya inflaming the populace, most of the provincials had counted themselves fortunate to be permitted to try their chances in winter on the Via Epra. There were no few senators, especially among the auctores embittered by the treachery of those whose cause they had championed, who had favored widespread reprisals. Fortunately for the provincials and Amorr's honor, saner heads, led by Manlius Torquatus, the Consul Civitas, supported by Sextus's uncle Corvus, eventually prevailed, thus preventing an untimely bloodbath. If, as it was said, hundreds had died on the wintry roads, tens of thousands had been spared.

But in the new year, Torquatus had been replaced as Consul Civitas by M. Andronicus Declama and Valerius Corvus was dead, burned by the same mysterious flames that had devoured the Sanctified Father. While both Declama and his surviving colleague, the Consul Provincae, Appuleius Pansa, had served in the legions as tribunes in their youth, neither had ever commanded so much as a single cohort in battle. With one of Amorr's best generals dead and the other a traitor, the Senate found itself lacking both military and spiritual guidance at the very time when it needed it most.

Mad rumors swept through the city, reaching even to the domus where Severa lived despite her relative seclusion. She spent most of her day helping her sisters-in-law care for Sextus's mother, who had been rendered distraught to the point of near madness following the revelation of her husband's treachery and the arrest of her sons. She felt no real sense of duty to her mother-in-law, whose gaunt cheeks and white-streaked hair gave her the appearance of a woman ten years older than she was, but found that she preferred reading to the grief-stricken woman rather than endure the looks and whispers that followed her about on the days she went out in public.

It wasn't that she was ashamed to be the wife of Sextus Valerius. She was, somewhat to her astonishment, proud to bear his name, for all that their Houses had been rivals for centuries. It wasn't as if House Severus was in any better odor, thanks to its own missing legions and her father's ill-conceived attempt to make himself King of Amorr. But the first time she walked through the Starsday market and heard a plebian woman hiss "Valerius Perfidus" behind her, it was all she could do to stop herself from

seizing one of the knives being offered for sale in a nearby stall and plunging
it into the woman's stomach.

She was confident that if the city managed to survive what some were
calling "The War of the Three Leagues" and others "The Allied War",
Sextus Valerius would win an honorable agnomen for himself. But in the
meantime, she'd be damned before she'd listen to anyone try to tar her
husband with his father's treacherous deeds.

Some of the rumors were more nonsensical than others. By far the most
pernicious were religious in nature. If the loss of His Sanctified Holiness
Charity IV had hit the city hard, the fiery death of his successor, His
Sanctified Holiness Pelagianus, along with the still-unexplained murders of
six princes of the Church while gathered in Holy Conclave, had the more
devout among the populace in a state of near-terror.

"It's a sign, it's a sign," a weeping kitchen slave told her one morning
as Severa helped her make bread. "The Unholy Father is coming. Blaesia
said the six Celestials and two Sanctiffs stand for the Twelve Black Apostles!
They have the black skin of a burned man and eyes like those of a cat! And
they will have tongues like snakes and the souls of everyone who hears them
speak will be tarred forever and rejected by the Immaculate on the day they
stand before the White Throne!"

She let out a wail of heartfelt dismay. Severa frowned and kneaded her
dough.

"Six and two is eight," she observed. "Not twelve."

The woman abruptly ceased her wailing, puzzled. "No, it's not." She was
an older woman, of an indeterminate middle age, and was named Julipora
after Julia, Sextus's mother, to whom she was entirely devoted.

"Six multiplied by two is twelve," said Carvilia, one of Severa's sisters-
in-law, who had entered the kitchen unannounced. She was tall, pretty,
and supercilious. Unlike the other two women whose husbands were
imprisoned, she was never seen to shed a tear or publicly lament her fate.
She had born Magnus two grandsons, which she seemed to feel granted her
a certain status in the family that Caerilla and Pompilia, both of whom had
born only daughters, lacked.

Severa shot Carvilia an annoyed look as the realization was enough to set
Julipora off weeping again and babbling about how the hellfire in the palace
had been the devil's retribution for the Lord Corvus's kinslaying. She sighed
and shook her head, which proceeded to cause half her loosely bound black
curls to escape the comb she'd employed to keep them out of her way while
she was occupied in the kitchen.

"Will you do something about that?" Severa demanded, inclining her head towards Carvilia. "My hands are covered with flour."

The older woman's long fingers withdrew the ivory comb and expertly twisted her hair about, pulling her head slightly this way and that, before sinking the comb back into place.

"There," she said. "When you're done with the bread, I was thinking of walking to the Forum. The sun is out and it's not very cold today."

"I was going to read to Mama Julia." Severa wasn't keen on the notion of leaving the domus, but she did enjoy talking with Carvilia without Caerilla and Pompilia around. Caerilla was quiet and mousy by nature and Pompilia couldn't open her mouth without fretting about her husband.

"I'll tell Pompilia to do it instead. I want company."

Severa nodded, seeing that the decision had been made for her, and returned her attention to the dough, working it savagely with her hands. The task at hand sufficiently distracted Julipora to allow the slave to get herself under control, and she surveyed the dough before nodding her approval at Severa. With some relief, Severa decided to interpret the woman's gesture as a dismissal, and after dipping her hands in a large clay jar of water, she dried them and went to her room to change her clothes for the market.

She had barely changed into a wool dress when Carvilia appeared, wearing one fur cape made of wolf pelts and bearing another over her arm.

"You're a Valerian now," her sister-in-law announced. "Wear this. Julia won't mind. She's barely left her bed today."

Severa slipped it over her shoulders. The fur was thick and grey, so dark that it was nearly black. It was heavy, nearly twice as heavy than the fox fur cape her father had given her the previous winter, and she expected that it would be somewhat warmer as well. The clasp was silver, and worked in the form of an ornate letter V.

"How does it look?" she asked, twirling in a circle.

Carvilia nodded approvingly. "It will serve."

"Will Marcipor come with us?"

"No," Carvilia said with a distinct expression of distaste on her long, narrow face. She could not abide Severa's husband's handsome bodyslave. "He's with Sextus. Galerus has said we can have Magnis Tertius and Durus for escorts."

Severa nodded. There was no fear of either of those two embarrassing them by behaving in a manner that did not become their station. Magnis Tertius was mute and Durus had a red face like a slab of beef. But they were big strong men, and she and Carvilia would be safe in their company.

The two slaves were waiting for them just outside the front door, receiving instructions from Galerus, the slave who ran the household. The majordomus was a small, spare man, who still refused to hear a word of criticism directed at his master. Not even Sextus, who publicly disavowed Magnus every chance he got, dared to mention his father in front of the stubbornly loyal slave. It was indeed remarkable, Severa thought, that the little Orontine should prove so firmly devoted to such a faithless man.

Both Magnus and her own father, Patronus, had betrayed the Senate and People. Both men were senators of impeccable patrician birth, and yet the two ex-consuls were shamed by the honor shown by this petty slave. The knowledge stung her, especially in light of how her own brother had followed Magnus into treason. It made her all the prouder of her husband, and all the more determined that Sextus would erase the shadow that her father and her brother had cast upon her and upon House Severus. And yet, there was nothing that she could do about the latter, and there was very little she could do about the former except throw herself into wholeheartedly encouraging Sextus to restore the city's confidence in him and her new House.

And if that meant he had to personally evict every last non-citizen from the city, then she would help him find the strength to do it.

"If anyone is disrespectful to the ladies, you'll shut their mouths, do you understand?" Galerus finished his instructions to the two slaves, both of whom were wearing leather armor and carrying long wooden staves with iron caps on either end.

Carvilia raised a skeptical eyebrow at the glowering majordomus, nearly provoking an untimely giggle from Severa. If it was left up to Galerus, bad-mouthing a Valerian would be a crime that merited being thrown to starving orcs in the arena. The little man seemed to forget, or simply ignore, that Carvilia and the other women were only Valerians by marriage, and didn't possess the stiff necks and self-conscious dignity for which House Valerius was known.

They passed through the gates, which at this time of day were unguarded, turned left, and began to walk towards the Forum. The spring wind was brisk, but the sun shone brilliantly through gaps in the thick mass of innocuous white clouds. There was little traffic on the bricked road, but as they rounded a curve one could see mule-wagons carting heavy loads of bricks to the Portus Antica, the city's older port. The new port stood outside the city walls and was indefensible, so the Senate had decided to fortify its predecessor in the event one of the Utruccan leagues managed to build a navy capable of threatening Amorr by sea.

As she surveyed the people moving below, her heart recognized a tall, armored shape before her mind did. Or perhaps it was simply the familiar way the man was walking. She felt her heart skip a beat, and leap at the sight of a helmeted officer striding purposefully in their direction. He was followed by a small troop of armored soldiers.

"Isn't that—" Carvilia asked her.

"It is!" Severa said as she waved excitedly at her handsome young husband. "I wonder why he's coming back already."

Most days, Sextus didn't return to the domus until after nightfall. For a moment, she worried that something had gone terribly wrong. But as he drew closer, she could see that behind the iron cheekpads that covered the sides of his face, his eyes were bright.

She went to embrace him, but a faint shake of his head and the way his eyes flicked back in the direction of his men warned her off. Instead, she made him a formal little bow.

"Tribune Valerius," she greeted him. "Salve!"

"Salvete, Ladies Valerii," he replied, graciously including Carvilia. His blue horsehair plume added nearly a head to his height, giving the impression that he was towering over both of them. His teeth flashed whitely in a broad smile. "I am delighted to encounter you here, seeing as I am the bearer of good news!"

"Have you word of my husband?" Carvilia couldn't stop herself from clutching at Sextus's hands. "Oh, has the Senate released him?"

"Not yet," he told her. "But I am confident they will so very soon. I come directly from speaking with Titus Manlius. He met with the consuls this morning, and among the subjects they discussed were my brothers."

"Manlius Torquatus, the ex-consul?" Severa asked him. She sometimes found it hard to keep straight all of the various officials with whom her husband was dealing. They all seemed to have similar names. She wondered how her mother had kept them all straight for so many years.

"The same," Sextus confirmed. "The Senate has been having some trouble finding anyone to command Legios XXXV and XXXVI. Last week, I went to Torquatus and pointed out that there are three excellent veteran officers from Amorr's greatest military family who are spending their days idle at the Senate's expense. Even if the senators are reluctant to trust them to lead the legions against the rebels in battle, I failed to see why they shouldn't prove rather useful in whipping the slaves and gladiators into shape."

"Did Torquatus agree," Carvilia asked anxiously.

"Did he agree?" Sextus chuckled heartily. "He cursed himself for not having thought of it himself! Your husband and Volesus both served under Magnus as laticlavii. They have more battle experience than half the generals in the Senate. And Tertius was one of Saturnius's tribunes, and Torquatus knew very well how much Marcus Saturnius demanded of his tribunes!"

The women were silent. Torquatus wasn't the only one to know it. Both of them had sat with Julia through the dark hours of the night, holding her as she wept for Fortex, her murdered son. Severa had never met her late brother-in-law, but his ghost was a palpable presence in the Valerian domus. Corvus had publicly claimed responsibility for his nephew's execution before his own death, but Julia remained convinced that Marcus Saturnius, the late legate of Legio XVII, was truly to blame.

"When can I see Potitus?" Carvilia's customary reserve seemed to have been shattered by the news that her husband might be released. "Is he well?"

Severa eyed her husband warily. Even after only four months of marriage, she knew him too well to believe that his apparent high spirits were solely the result of his brothers' pending release. "And what of you?" she asked him.

"Me?" His expression suddenly went suspiciously blank. "Well, nothing has been settled yet, of course."

"Sextus!"

He laughed and grinned at her like a mischievous boy caught stealing sweets. "Torquatus says I will be tribune laticlavius for Legio XXXV!"

Severa nodded and forced herself to smile back at him, even though the news caused a cold hand of dread to squeeze her heart. These damned Valerians! All they ever seemed to think about was war! It was as if they were fish and battle was the sea in which they lived to swim. Her idiot husband would have been absolutely delighted with the duty he found so onerous if only the strangers he was sent to expel had been armed and permitted to attack him on sight.

"That's wonderful news, Sextus!" Yes, wonderful indeed, she thought bitterly. Her husband was going to be the second-in-command of a legion made up of untrained slaves and criminal scum, men who were bound to be put in the very front of the fighting and expected to provide the lion's share of the corpses. She didn't need to know anything about war to know that for a certainty. As the daughter of Severus Patronus, she knew very well how the pitiless minds of the men who ruled the Senate worked. "Perhaps you and your brothers will even have the chance to face your father in battle."

"We can but hope," Sextus said happily, completely missing her sarcasm. She wanted to strangle him.

Instead, she smiled sweetly and pulled at Carvilia's hand. "You must go to the domus at once, my dear. Caerilla and Pompilia will be ever so excited to hear the good news."

He nodded and took her hands in his. Even though she was still furious with him, or Torquatus, or someone, anyhow, she felt a warmth flood the length of her body. His lips twitched as he bowed in mock formality. "I shall look forward to our next encounter, Lady Valerius."

"As shall I, Lord Tribune Valerius." Despite her irritation, butterflies fluttered in her stomach at the thought of seeing him, alone and unarmored, and she cursed her treacherous body. "I wish you a pleasant afternoon, my lord."

He released her and she stepped aside to permit his men to continue their march towards her new home. At least her sisters-in-law would be pleased to know their husbands were to be spared the strangler's hands or the fatal fall from the Rock of Kings. She watched as they walked past her, their iron-studded sandals clattering against the bricks. How long would it be before Sextus would be facing ten or even twenty thousand of such men, trained for years, experienced in battle, and led by accomplished generals like his father?

"Don't be so worried, little sister." Carvilia took her arm and turned her back towards the Forum. "You've known he would go to battle since he declared for the tribunate. You should be pleased that he'll be serving as laticlavius. That way, he'll be safe with the legate in the command post rather than riding into danger with the knights."

"He's a fool and an idiot!" she burst out. "What if he gets himself killed?"

"They all are, darling. That's why God made us, to make sure someone remembered to feed the children while they're occupied with their heroic endeavors. Do you know, once Potitus took little Titus out to the stables to show him the horses. I saw him in the domus later and I asked him where Titus was. He turned white! He'd completely forgotten him!"

"But Titus wasn't hurt."

"Not in the slightest. Two of the stable slaves were playing with him and letting him ride on their shoulders. He was having a wonderful time."

"How is that supposed to reassure me?"

"I suppose it isn't," Carvilia admitted. Then she threw her head back and laughed. "I'm sorry, little sister, but you have no idea how terrified I have been that Potitus would be killed or exiled by the Senate. And then to hear that he's going to be released? And given command of a legion?"

Severa nodded and gave her sister-in-law's arm a little squeeze. As much as the thought of Sextus going into battle frightened her, it would be weeks, if not months, before the rebels would dare to even think about moving on Amorr. If there was confusion in the city about who was in rebellion and who was not, how much more there must be in the provinces and the other allied cities? And Carvilia was right, there was no safer place in battle than the one right next to the legate, with six thousand armed men to stand between Sextus and the enemy.

"I'm happy for you. And for Pompilia and Caerilla too. Maybe it will be good for Mama Julia too."

"Maybe," Carvilia said dubiously. Her face brightened and she pointed at the merchant stalls they were approaching. "Oh, look, they have a jongleur!"

Both the crowd and the stalls were on the sparse side, even for a chilly Martius afternoon, but there were musicians, food merchants with fresh meat roasting, and the aforementioned jongleur, who was effortlessly keeping three burning brands in the air. He winked at them as the approached, then caused them both to gasp in amazement as he extinguished one in his mouth while juggling the other two in his left hand. He bowed deeply as Carvilia tossed a silver coin in the wooden bucket at his feet, then threw one brand high in the air and reignited the second brand with the third one before returning to his earlier pattern.

"My goodness, could you believe that!" Severa said, glancing back at the slender young man.

"I don't think I'd much like to kiss a man with a burned mouth."

"Sextus can juggle." Carvilia looked at her, surprised. "Well, not things on fire, of course, but he can keep up five balls. He does three knives sometimes, but I don't like him to do that."

"So you meant it literally, then, about him being a fool?"

"He's not a fool!" Severa protested, only to draw an amused smirk from the older woman.

"I'm only teasing you, my dear. Do you see any fur merchants?"

"No, why?" Severa looked around the stalls. She saw men selling wool, she saw men selling cotton, and there was even one colorful, well-appointed stall where silk appeared to be on offer. She saw seamstresses and embroiderers, but she did not see anyone selling furs.

"I don't either. I suppose most of the fur merchants were afraid to travel south after the provincials were sent home." Carvilia made a face. "I thought someone would have gone north to find some, but apparently not."

"If they did, it would probably cost more than you'd want to pay," Severa pointed out.

"There is that. Come, let's see if we can find some roasted chestnuts. I thought I smelled them. Over there."

They made their way past the thinly trafficked stalls. Severa wondered aloud why there weren't more people about. She saw one old woman bickering with a young man over the price of a bag of onions, but that was the only transaction taking place nearby.

"I imagine most of the plebs will be saving whatever coin they can to buy supplies. If there is a siege, everyone will want to be well-stocked. Galerus has been preparing for weeks. I was helping him count the jars of oil just yesterday. Look, the only stalls doing much business are those selling fresh food and firewood or stores that will keep."

"I never thought about that."

"It's not your concern, little sister. And besides, I very much doubt we will ever see a rebel army in sight of our walls. The provincials want to be free to go their own way, they don't want to conquer us. We're hardly helpless. Even if half our legions have gone over to one league or another, we still have more men in arms than any other city or province, and that doesn't even count the six new ones the Senate has formed. They could probably raise another ten or twenty if they wanted."

"I suppose we won't be going to Vallyria this summer."

"No, and that worries me more than a siege," Carvilia said soberly as she looked for the source of the aroma. "Ah, there it is. The air here is unhealthy in the summer and I don't want to risk Titus or Publius catching the Sextilian ague. But if this isn't all settled by then, we may not have a choice."

Severa pointed in the general direction of the Severan estate, which until the New Year had belonged to her father. At such a distance, the house itself was not visible, but the Quinctiline, the great hill atop which the villa sat, was in view, and was generally believed to be safe from the summertime agues. "I can speak to my mother. She is very lonely, I think, since... since my marriage. And I think she would not mind having a young one or two around the place. She often laments how quickly my sister is growing and it would give Severilla some little friends with whom she could play."

Carvilia looked skeptical. "Your father may have married you off to House Valerius, but I can't believe your brother, or your uncle, would give refuge to Valerian women and children. Especially since thanks to our beloved father-in-law, people have been calling us House Varietas."

"So? Aulan is with Magnus, after all. House Valerius isn't the only House Martial under suspicion. There is still no word of *Fulgetra*. I don't see that either Regulus or uncle Pullus are inclined to object, or even notice, if a few more women and children happen to be around. They won't abide our husbands, but then, I suppose Sextus and Potitus will be with the legions." She paused for a moment. "So will Regulus and Pullus, for that matter."

"Aulan is only a tribune, and for all we know, Magnus is holding him as a hostage." Carvilia shrugged. "It's a thoughtful offer, little sister, and one that I would certainly be happy to accept if you can talk your brother into it. But I hope this will blow over before Sextilius and we can spend it in Vallyria."

Severa didn't see how that was possible, but she wasn't disposed to argue about it. They'd spent hours, probably days, over the last three months in anxious discussions about what the Senate, or Magnus, or the Marruvian League, or the Utruccan League might do, and none of it had accomplished anything except to frighten her more. She put out her hand as Carvilia reached out to take a second bag of chestnuts from the vendor.

"I only want one or two. You don't need to buy two bags."

"Pompilia will want some."

"They'll be cold by the time we get home."

Carvilia bought the second bag anyhow. It wasn't as if they would go to waste; even if Carvilia didn't want them, one of the slave boys would. She took one from the proffered bag and cupped it in her palms, enjoying the warmth that radiated from the roasted nut. But as she peeled the hard, cracked covering off to expose the meat of the nut underneath, she noticed an old woman staring fixedly at her.

There was something about the woman that bothered her, something malicious, even though her expression was benign. There was nothing remarkable about her other than her age. Her hair was long, grey and unkempt, her face was lined and sun-weathered, and she wore a stained brown cloak that was faded and showed signs of having once been red. Then the wind blew her hair back for a moment and Severa saw the three white studs that pierced her left ear. Three earrings. Three bones. One for the Maiden, one for the Mother, and one for the Crone.

Inadvertently, she found her hand rising to her own ear, where just a single ring ran through the lobe. So much had happened in the last four months that she had almost completely forgotten the promise she'd made to Saint Malachus, the woman in man's garb, the pagan goddess who hid beneath the guise of an Immaculite saint. Severa had done her duty and she had fulfilled her promise, but Eudiss, the servant she'd been ordered to take into her father's house, was gone. It seemed the woman had left her mother's service not long after the fire that killed Valerius Corvus and the Sanctified Father, and since then, Severa had neither heard anything from the servants of the Goddess nor thought about them. She'd been too caught up in the circumstances of her father's death and her subsequent marriage to Sextus to spare any thought for the fate of a servant in a house in which she no longer lived.

Having seen the flash of recognition in Severa's eyes, the old woman smiled. Then she raised her left hand to her ear and deliberately tapped the bottom stud, followed by the middle one. After which, she nodded significantly and turned away, disappearing behind a row of stalls.

Severa gasped. The woman had touched the second earring. The Mother! She placed both hands on her belly. It was flat, and showed no signs of any life growing within it. Was the woman telling her that she was going to be a mother? Was the woman telling her she was already pregnant? Or was it something more ominous, something darker. What did she mean by the gesture? She started to move forward, thinking to pursue the woman and demand answers from her, but Carvilia caught her arm.

"Severa! Where do you think you're going?"

Severa pointed in the direction of the stalls. "Did you see her? Did you see that old woman?"

Carvilia shook her head. She had, Severa noticed, only a single earring in either ear, and more importantly, both were gold. "Which old woman? I can see a dozen of them."

"The one in the brown cloak!" Severa looked to their two guards, but Durus was still engaged in negotiations with a young woman over an iron belt-clasp and Magnis Tertius was entirely absorbed with staring at the young woman, whose wind-burned face was rather pretty. She didn't need to ask to know that they hadn't seen the old woman either.

"Let's go home," she said abruptly, drawing a look of surprise from her sister-in-law. "There's next to nothing here, and I have to talk to Sextus."

"Is something wrong?" Carvilia asked, more bewildered than worried.

"No, nothing's wrong," Severa told her. But she wasn't entirely convinced that she wasn't lying. She didn't know what the follower of Saint Malachus intended by her reference to the Mother, but she didn't like that the woman's indication that their goddess held some kind of claim to her. She ran her hand over her belly again. Was there perhaps a faint swelling there? Surely she would know if she was pregnant!

Frowning, she took Carvilia's arm as they began the journey home. But even as they walked, she couldn't help surreptitiously squeezing and poking at her stomach with her free hand.

AULAN

ULAN had perfect faith in the eight knights who had come with him from *Fulgetra*. They were hard-bitten killers who had proven themselves on the battlefield and in the streets of Amorr too. There wasn't an order he could give them that they would hesitate to obey. He was considerably less confident in the two Valerian turmae he was presently commanding, especially in light of the way in which the senior decurions had the irritating habit of falling silent every time he approached them.

He shrugged. There wasn't much he could do about it. The men weren't about to abandon a lifetime of regarding House Severus as the enemy overnight, and as the only Severan of his generation with genuine Valerian blood on his hands, he was probably not the man best suited to try winning them over. He would have to trust in the famed Valerian discipline to keep them from running him through with a lance in the back. Fortunately, they all seemed to look on Magnus as some sort of martial demigod, so the fact that the Magister Militum had named him the senior tribune for Legio XV and assigned him the tattered remnants of its horse gave him at least a modicum of credibility.

The sixty knights in the two turmae now accompanying him represented most of the legion's remaining horse. Legio XV's cavalry had taken heavy casualties in the Battle of the Three Legions, thanks to Magnus's unexpected use of a feigned retreat that led them directly onto Legio VII's pikes. One of Aulan's appointed tasks was to rebuild it, but that was difficult in a province wracked by the upheaval of rebellion, where every city and village was uncertain as to whose side to take. He had managed to commandeer twenty-four horses to date, but was yet to find a single equestrian capable of sitting one properly. The natural difficulty of the circumstances was compounded by the fact that they were in House Valerius's home province of Vallyria, and the Vallyrians were generally famed for the toughness of their infantry, not seats of their horsemen.

He could, of course, simply draft a few likely looking farmboys, but it would take weeks before he could trust them not to fall off their mounts, and months before they would be even remotely useful in combat. Considering how Magnus had them escorting him from one village to another on an almost daily basis, he favored quality over quantity at present. Speed was of the essence and new riders would only slow them down. Moreover, he had the conventional patrician's distaste for elevating men beyond their natural station. And, he knew, his men shared it. Equestrians were even more fiercely proud of their status than patricians and the other knights would never truly accept new knights created by circumstance rather than birth.

"Lucarus!" he called out to the one decurion he could trust. "Any sign of them?"

The decurion shook his head. He was unmounted and standing atop a hill that overlooked the path into Cernobus, a prosperous Vallyrian village of about eight thousand, whose elders Magnus was attempting to win over to his cause. Magnus was in the village now, accompanied by one of the tribunes and six knights, two of whom were from a nearby village and acquainted with the influential families here, if not necessarily the elders themselves.

There was apparently some question about whether the loyalties of the villagers were with Amorr or House Valerius, specifically, House Valerius in the form of Valerius Magnus. One of the village elders was said to be a particularly slippery man, and since the invitation had come from him, Magnus was more than a little suspicious that the meeting was a trap. So, Aulan and his two turmae were waiting within sight of the village square where the elders were receiving Magnus. They were also in a position to intercept any troops being sent from Trivicum, which was believed to be still holding firm for Amorr.

There were no full legions stationed in Trivicum, so any troops arriving would almost surely be mounted, and there would likely be no more than a decuria or two at most. They were running no serious risks in Aulan's opinion, as far as he was concerned the only question would be the way in which Magnus would react to any treachery. Would he order the elders slaughtered and the town burned to the ground? Or would he be magnanimous? It was the sort of situation to which his father had always encouraged him to pay close attention, as these were circumstances that granted one rare insight into a man's character.

Magnus would want to set an example, Aulan guessed. But burning the town would be going too far for the man who intended to make himself King of Vallyria, even a rebel who had once been called Veheminus. Killing the elders and taking a few hostages from their families would provide a sufficient warning to other villages that thought to play him false as well as dissuade the villagers from further disloyalties.

"Tribune!" One of the knights pointed to Lucarus, who was looking back at him and beckoning. "The decurion wants you."

Aulan nodded, slid from his horse, and handed its reins to Rufus, the knight to his left. His legs protested as he trudged up the hill; they were tight and could have used some stretching out before being forced to attempt the moderately steep slope. He was breathing hard by the time he approached the summit, but fortunately it was cool and the late afternoon sun was behind him rather than shining in his eyes.

Lucarus was a short, burly man who looked more suited to tavern brawls than battlefields. His eyes were small and deep-set, but there was nothing wrong with them as he squinted towards the east and the faint signs of motion in the distance.

"Looks like the Valerian weren't being so skittish after all," he said.

"How many do you think?"

"Not so many. Ten, mebbe twelve. It's hard to say. The road is muddy, so they ain't kicking up no dust."

"Anything less than a turma isn't a problem." Aulan spat, feeling irritated. "Dammit! I was hoping we'd get out of here without any nonsense!"

"How do you want to play it? Hit them when they ride past or go out and meet them?"

"I don't want to risk any horses. Who knows, maybe we can even convince them to change sides." Aulan glanced back to Cernobus and considered the terrain. He pointed to a tree near a bend in the road in the direction of the town. "I'll take Marinus and his turma to await them there. You wait with Marcus Possidius and his men, then ride out from behind the hill as soon as they pass. I aim to capture them, not kill them. We need information, and if we go riding into town with their heads the Cernobians will deny knowing anything about them."

Lucarus nodded. "Right. You'll give us a sign if you want us to attack?"

"I doubt that will be necessary." Aulan grinned contemptuously. "If they try to break north, you and Possidius ride them down. Try to keep at least one alive, though."

The shorter man nodded and the two of them began to make their way down the hill. The grass was wet and green with spring, and both of them nearly slipped, but they made it to the bottom without serious incident and went their separate ways. Aulan mounted his horse, took the reins from Rufus, and summoned Titus Marinus. The senior decurion obediently urged his big bay over with a resigned expression on his face, but at least there was no insubordination in his voice as he awaited orders.

"Tribune?"

"It appears the Magister's doubts about the good faith of the villagers was well-founded. A squadron of horse is on its way towards the village. You and your men will come with me and we will await them in the road. Marcus Possidius will ride out behind them and block their retreat. Everyone is to keep his sword sheathed. The Magister will want to question them."

"Sir!" Marinus's expression became more lively and he thumped his breastplate in a salute that was almost enthusiastic. He wheeled around to give orders to the three decurions who commanded the individual squadrons and Aulan found himself musing on the observation that discipline was a damned sight more useful than affection. In a matter of moments, the turma was neatly arrayed facing east and waiting for him to take the lead.

They rode slowly out along the base of the hill and onto the road, continuing about one hundred paces until they reached the spot he had indicated to Lucarus. Marinus barked out a command and the turma smoothly executed a revolution that left Aulan and the decurions facing west. The knights were bored and eager for anything that would break the tedium. Aulan could feel it, and he hoped the decurion in command of the enemy squadron wouldn't do anything foolish. In such a state, it would be harder to rein the men in than to stop an unleashed dog that scared up a rabbit, discipline be damned.

It didn't take long before they heard the muted clip-clopping of horses trotting toward them. Fortunately, the wind was in their faces, so it was their horses that caught the scent of the newcomers and began to whicker and toss their heads. Aulan could tell the moment the first rider spotted them blocking the road, as the man immediately pulled up and the squadron behind him came to an immediate halt.

"Shall we go after them?" Marinus asked as several of the riders began to turn their horses around.

"No," Aulan answered, seeing that the unknown decurion had merely glanced behind him before gesticulating angrily at the men who had looked to retreat. A sensible man, it appeared, or else a naïve one. He counted twelve riders in all, and waited as the decurion rode towards him, the blue transverse plume on his helm bobbing up and down. The decurion's horse was a grey of modest quality, his breastplate had the gleam of iron unmarred by combat, and most importantly, his sword remained sheathed. He didn't even have a lance or bow attached to his saddle, although there was a large round shield on top the bag behind his saddle.

"What legion are you with, Tribune?" he called as he approached.

"Legio XV," Aulan answered. The decurion did not look surprised.

"You're with Valerius Magnus, then."

"Your name and legion, decurion?" Aulan saw no need to belabor the obvious. "And your business here?"

The decurion glanced from one side of the formation to the other. He didn't need to count the exact number to know he was overmatched even without Possidius's turma coming slowly down the road behind him.

"I am Sextus Lucretius, with Legio XXXI. I was ordered here to escort Valerius Magnus back to Amorr, as the Consul Provincae wishes to inquire of his recent activities in Vallyria and consult with him concerning the recent uprisings." Lucretius turned back and searched in the pack behind his saddle, and eventually produced a sealed scroll, which he brandished. "This is the summons I was ordered to deliver to the senator."

The seal was marked with the SPA of the Senate and People. Aulan laughed under his breath. He had no doubt that the Consul Provincae, whoever he was, would very much like to consult with Magnus. Preferably in the company of a torturer, a priest, and a strangler.

"Then deliver it you shall," Aulan declared, enjoying the look of surprise on Lucretius's face. "In fact, we shall escort you to Magnus. Fortunately for you, the journey is not far. As we speak, he is here in Cernobus, meeting with the elders of the town."

He smiled as the decurion's eyes narrowed suspiciously, betraying his previous knowledge of Magnus's whereabouts. But to his credit, Lucretius didn't insult his intelligence by pretending otherwise.

"So I was informed," he admitted.

"By whom?"

"My legate, Roscius Coelus. My understanding is that Coelus was told Magnus would be in Cernobus this afternoon by the praetor urbanus."

Aulan nodded. It wasn't as if the responsible elder, or elders, would have written to an insignificant decurion. If the urban praetor had given Lucretius's legate his orders, then a senator was involved, most likely one with ties to Vallyria.

"Very well. Come along then, and tell your men to behave themselves. There's no need for any unpleasantries." He leaned towards Marinus and made a circular gesture with his left hand. "Let's help the good decurion deliver his message, shall we?"

Cernobus was a wealthy village not untypical of Vallyria. Its prosperity was derived from the fields that extended outside the town for leagues that produced wheat and hops. If the land was not so fertile as Illyris Baara, ships were not required to transport its harvests to Amorr and other Faleran cities even closer. It had no walls, but its streets were bricked and prior to the winter uprising there had even been discussion of a proper brick road being built between Cernobus and Priscum that would enable the village's grain merchants to more easily cart their products to the Tarquinian seaport.

Aulan elected to enter the village with Possidius's turma, ordering Lucretius to leave his men under the watchful eyes of Titus Marinus and his three squadrons. The loyalist decurion knew better than to protest. After eliciting a promise that his men would neither be harmed or disarmed, he told his optio, a young man who looked about as martial as a mouse, not to cause Marinus any trouble. Aulan shot Marinus a look that stilled him; he could see the decurion was on the verge of snickering at the thought.

The boundaries of the village proper were marked by two huge buildings that Aulan guessed were used for storing grain. After entering the town, they rode past buildings that boasted fresh stucco and two, sometimes even three levels. The village was clean, the gates well-tended, and the inhabitants they passed were more curious than alarmed at their presence. They found Magnus holding court in the central square. There was no other way to describe it; the big barrel-chested ex-consul was standing in the midst of the townsmen, stalking back and forth like a well-fed lion as he set out his vision for the transforming the Amorran empire into a republic of sovereign and independent kingdoms.

As they approached the square and heads began to turn their way, Aulan realized that whoever had sold out Magnus would not know him from Sextus Lucretius. So, he pointed to the decurion and indicated that the man from Legio XXXI should be kept at the rear of their formation, then pulled up at the corner of the square without giving any indication that he was with Magnus. Magnus glanced over at him, but didn't stop speaking and the powerful voice that had been heard so many times by the Amorran Senate now boomed throughout the open air of the village square.

"Elders of Cernobus, noble men of Vallyria, do not look upon the man who stands before you as a patrician of Amorr. Do not look upon me as an ex-consul and a stranger. I am one of you! I am one of you and I say it is time for the Senate and People of Amorr to cease at length treating with you on a footing of superiority! Look around you! We see Vallyria in a most flourishing state by the bounty of God in arms and men, the Legio Civitas being vanquished in war, the Sidicinians and Campanians allied together, the Utruccans now united in league, and the people of the former provinces preferring their own governance to that of Amorr.

"But since the three consuls do not bring their minds to put an end to their arbitrary despotism, we, though able by force of arms to vindicate the independence of the various peoples of Falerna, will even so make this concession to the ties of blood between us and them, as to offer terms of peace on terms of equality for both, since it has pleased the Immaculate to grant that the strength of Amorr is divided while the strength of Utrucca is united. Here is the plan I set before you. In the new year, one of the consuls will be selected out of Amorr, as before, but the second out of the Falernan kingdoms, and the third from the Utruccan lands. In the place of a Consul Provincae we shall have a Consul Socii, in the place of a Consul Aquilae we will have a Consul Utruccae, and no more will the eagles march against the very lands that supply the legions! An equal portion of the senate will be from all three parties. We must be one people and one republic by the grace of the Most High God and the guidance of the Sanctified Father!

"And that the seat of government may be the same, and we all may have the same name, since the concession must be made by the one party or others, let this, and may it be auspicious to both, have the advantage of being the mother country, and let us all be called Amorrans and citizens and countrymen!"

In truth, it was a bold and compelling vision. Even Aulan, who knew it was nothing but a means to an end for an ambitious man, felt caught up in it. Magnus had the Cernobians all but spellbound, dreaming of a new age where they would no longer be regarded as lesser men and third-class country cousins, but equals and co-citizens. It was not the first time he had witnessed this performance, but nevertheless, its effects, its power to move men's emotions, amazed him every time. No wonder his father, even as Prince of the Senate, had once feared this man!

"A compelling dream," a tall, white-haired man with a skeptical expression on his face called out. "But tell us, Valerius Magnus, who is going to lead us against the might of Amorr that even now approaches this assembly?"

He pointed towards Aulan and his squadrons. Was he the man responsible for the letter to Amorr, Aulan wondered? Or was he merely quicker-witted than most? They would find out soon enough. In the meantime, Aulan had his part to play.

"Marcus Valerius Magnus!" He pointed at Magnus. "The Senate has a message for you."

The men standing between him and Magnus moved to one side or the other as their faces turned towards him. Magnus didn't betray his familiarity with his men, instead he smiled confidently and folded his arms. "Then let the messenger deliver his message."

Aulan glanced back and waved Lucretius forward. The decurion was white-faced and wide-eyed, but he obediently dismounted and walked through the crowd of men that surrounded Magnus. He was a little man and the plume of his helmet barely reached the top of Magnus's head. He bowed respectfully, showing Magnus the respect due a senator and ex-consul, however rebellious, and extended the sealed scroll to him.

"Your name and legion, decurion?" Magnus asked him as he accepted the scroll.

"Sextus Lucretius, Legio XXXI," Lucretius answered.

"Legio XXXI? I am not familiar with it." Magnus looked out at the Cernobians. "Men of Cernobus, do you know this legion?"

"No," came a few scattered answering cries.

"Which House Martial fields this Legio XXXI, decurion? Who is its legate?"

"No House, Lord Valerius. The Senate has newly raised the legion itself. Marcus Roscius Coelius is the legate commanding."

"A Roscius? What is a Roscius?" Magnus spread his hands as if mystified. "Do you mean to tell me that a plebian from a minor House now thinks to command a legion? A senatorial legion? And to what end? Perhaps this missive will further enlighten us." He cracked the seal, unrolled the scroll, and looked it over quickly, nodding once or twice as he read.

"Well, decurion, it seems the Senate demands I return to Amorr with you to face an accounting for my actions." Magnus smiled and held up the scroll before his face, then tore it in two, crumpled up both pieces, and tossed them at Lucretius, who fumbled with them and nearly dropped one, but managed to hold onto it before it fell to the bricks. "Elders of Cernobus, men of Vallyria, that is my answer to the Senate of Amorr! I do not answer to them? Do you?"

"No!" a few more men shouted back. But Aulan noticed that the tall white-haired man and many of the men in his vicinity were silent, looking on skeptically with their arms folded.

"Brave words, Valerius Magnus," the white-haired man said. "Will you say as much to the tribune mounted hither, with the twenty armed knights at his command? Amorr's argument is eloquent, for all that it requires no words. No matter how silver one's tongue, one cannot win a debate against iron and steel."

A frosty smile spread across Magnus's face, and Aulan was struck again by the man's agile mind, his genius for turning any unexpected development to his own advantage. He had seen the ex-consul win over one town council after another, seduce one village after another to his cause. In only a matter of months, he had seen generals voluntarily hand commands to Magnus, seen Magnus wrest an entire legion from an adversary by the force of arms. Surely this man was nothing less than a king, and a thrice-worthy king at that!

And for the first time, he found himself wondering if his father might have bitten off more than his heirs could chew by encouraging the Valerian in his ambitions.

"Your name and legion," Magnus shouted as he pointed at Aulan. "Your name and legion, tribune!"

The man was truly a master of extemporaneous theater, Aulan thought as he stifled the urge to laugh and shake his head in awe. Instead, he kept a straight face and answered truthfully. "Aulus Severus Aulan, Lord Valerius, of Legio XV."

"And who do you serve?"

"Marcus Valerius Veheminus Magnus!" he shouted, thumping his breast-plate loudly. "Ave Magnus!"

"Ave Magnus!" his two squadrons roared, the clash of their gauntlets against their iron breastplates echoing through the square.

It was even harder not to laugh at the shocked look on the face of the white-haired man and his allies. Crestfallen didn't even begin to describe the expression on the man's face as he took a step back and literally reeled in dismay. Magnus didn't hesitate to seize the opportunity, as he pointed at the man in righteous contempt.

"You wanted to know who will lead you against the might of Amorr, Lucius Annius? I tell you this: I am the might of Amorr! I am House Valerius! If the Senate will not see reason, if the Senate will not compromise, then the Senate shall see defeat at my hands! At our hands!"

"You presume much, Magnus," Annius shot back, recovering rapidly. "Perhaps too much. A man who changes sides as readily as a snake changes its skin may well change them again. Valerius Veheminus? I say Valerius Veneficus!"

Magnus's face turned red with rage. He clenched his fists, and for a moment, Aulan thought the big Valerian might charge into the crowd and strike the older man down. But somehow, he mastered himself. "You tempt me sorely, Lucius Annius. You bait me. But you will not taunt me into lessening myself in your colleagues eyes. Would you call me traitor? Would you call me a snake with a poisoned tongue?"

"Here speaks an Amorran who would lead us into war against the Senate, and yet he blushes to be named traitor!" Annius gestured towards Magnus with his hand as he turned his head and addressed several of his nearby companions. "Does the bird deny its feathers? Does the cat deny its claws? Does the snake deny its fangs?"

"I was no traitor to Amorr, Lucius Annius. Amorr was a traitor to me! My son was slain by my own brother, he was murdered by hide-bound traditions no more right or just than those that now subjugate the people of Vallyria! Is it treason to have one's eyes opened at last? Is it poisonous to finally wake from a life of long-dead dreams? Is it snakish to realize that one is swimming in a noxious swamp of lies?"

Magnus's eyes narrowed like a lion readying himself for the kill. He and Annius were staring at each other as if they were alone in the square. "And who are you, Lucius Annius, to speak of treason and snakes when you invited me here today in order to betray me to the Senate and send me bound and delivered to Amorr?"

A gasp went up from the men assembled in the square.

Magnus turned to the decurion. "Tell me, Sextus Lucretius, did you ride here alone?"

"No, Lord Valerius. I came in the company of eleven other knights."

"Are the roads so dangerous these days that you required so many simply to deliver a message to me?"

"No, Lord Valerius."

"I see." Magnus nodded and looked out at the Cernobians. "Were you anticipating possible resistance on my part?"

"Yes, Lord Valerius. We were informed you would have a small bodyguard."

The elders and onlookers began murmuring amongst themselves, and more than a few men pointed at Annius and his companions.

"As I do," Magnus gestured to the four legionaries who were standing several paces behind him. "Where are the rest of your men, decurion?"

"We were intercepted by Tribune Severus en route. My men remain with his other turma outside the town."

Magnus made a gesture of feigned surprise with both hands. A few snickers could be heard from the crowd. "It sounds to me as if my resistance has been successful, wouldn't you say so, decurion?"

"Without question, Lord Valerius."

"Then seeing as your business here is concluded, decurion, I wonder if you might be willing to take a message back to the Senate for me?"

"It would be an honor, Lord Valerius." Aulan grinned at the man's respectful civility. Sextus Lucretius might have fallen into his ambush as blithely as a virgin in a whorehouse, but he was clearly no fool.

"My message to my former colleagues in the Senate is this: Magnus is waiting! If you will not grant independence to all peregrini or full citizenship to the Utruccan people, war and defeat awaits you! Send your slaves and your criminals to march here if you dare; the fields of Vallyria will be watered with their blood!"

As his voice rang throughout the square, the decurion bowed. "It shall be delivered even as you said, Lord Valerius. May I have your permission to withdraw with my men?"

"You may return to Amorr, but your men may not," Magnus told him.

"Lord Valerius, I was told my men would be unharmed!" Lucretius's eyes flashed angrily as he looked over at Aulan, then back again to Magnus. "I demand to share their fate, whatever it might be!"

"You shall, should you return." Magnus glanced at Aulan, his jowled face creased with amusement. "Decurion, you misunderstand me. I mean your knights no harm. I intend for them to take service with me."

"You expect them to turn their coats?"

"The equestrian who is not with me may well one day find himself riding against me. Be advised that the men who captured you today are from Legio XV, a legion that fought against me at Montmila." He turned towards Aulan's formation and extended his right arm, palm upward. "Ave, First Knights!"

Their response came immediately again, punctuated by the metal-on-metal clash of their salute. "Ave, Magnus!"

Magnus turned to the decurion, lowered his arm, and extended it to the smaller man. "Three months pay up front for your men, Lucretius. Six months for you as well as a promotion to senior decurion. You are a good officer, Sextus Lucretius, and there is a place in my army for every good man I can find."

The decurion hesitated a moment, and then he seemed to come to a decision. He took Magnus's forearm and gripped it firmly. The two men nodded at each other, then Lucretius turned and walked towards Aulan. The Cernobians watching were silent, though whether in fear or awe of Magnus, Aulan couldn't tell.

"What of you, Elders of Cernobus? What of you, men of Vallyria?" Magnus challenged them. "Are you with Magnus and Vallyria? Or are you slaves of Amorr?"

The was silence first broken by the younger men. "Magnus, Vallyria," they began to chant. "Magnus, Vallyria." Gradually, more of the older men joined them, until at last one of the elders did. But Lucius Annius remained silent, his arms folded, and his eyes narrow with anger.

Magnus raised his hand and the Cernobians subsided. He nodded in satisfaction. "You have chosen wisely, my friends. I will not let you down."

Then he walked towards Annius. The men intervening moved out of his way, until the two men were standing face to face. They were very nearly of a height, Aulan noted, although Magnus was half again heavier than the Cernobian man. Neither of them spoke, but locked eyes in a contest of wills. Annius's pride was such that he lasted longer than Aulan would have guessed, but finally the white-haired elder looked away.

"I will not stand in your way, Valerius Magnus. But neither will I support you."

Magnus slowly shook his head. "Neither your support nor your opposition concerns me, Annius. You are an elder of this village. Advise me. When a host sells his guest to his enemy and his treachery is discovered, what is his rightful reward?"

"Death," Annius answered without flinching. He glanced over at Aulan and his men. "I am not afraid."

"I should hope not at your age," Magnus said wryly, prompting nervous laughter from the men around him. "I will not kill a man for being misguided in his loyalties, not unless he insists upon standing in my way. Leave tonight, Lucius Annius. Amorr's gates may be closed to you, but

Trivicum's are not. For my part, I will spare you and we will forget this ever happened."

For a moment, it seemed as if the haughty man would reject Magnus's mercy. But discretion proved the better part of pride, and at last Annius nodded briskly. He turned and made his way through the hushed crowd, followed by three of his companions, whose expressions ranged the gamut from shocked to relieved.

"Now, friends, we have much to discuss!" Magnus lifted his arms and smiled beatifically at the men who had chosen to cast their lot with him. But first, I understand there are men who know their wine in Cernobus. Shall we refresh ourselves?"

The assembly broke up in a chaotic manner, as some hurried home to tell their wives of the momentous events and others pressed forward to greet Magnus and assure him of their personal loyalty. But Magnus put them off momentarily with the help of his bodyguard, and beckoned for Aulan to come to him.

Aulan dismounted and approached, curious as to what the great man wanted. Magnus thumped his back and put a beefy arm around his armored shoulders. "Well done, son. Your timing couldn't have been better."

"It was no problem at all. I hope that Lucretius does come back to us. He's sensible."

"He will," Magnus said confidently. "Get his men good and drunk tonight. We need them."

"I saw a cathouse or two on the way in. I imagine between Marinus, Possidius, and me, we can make a persuasive case."

"I have the utmost confidence in you three," Magnus laughed. Then he lowered his voice. "You marked the man who spoke out?"

"I did."

"Tell Lucarus to take a squadron and intercept him five leagues hence."

Aulan nodded, unsurprised. Magnus wasn't one to leave an enemy at his back if he didn't have to. "Just the old man or do you wish there to be no survivors?"

The ex-consul clapped him again on the back. "I think it would best if the decurion were to be thorough, Aulus Severus. I understand bandits are a terrible problem on the roads in these uncertain times."

LODI

I T WAS GOOD to be underground again. After helping Valerius
Clericus and his legion safely escape through the roots of the Tessini
mountains, Lodi had turned to the east and begun his long, laborious
journey back to Iron Mountain. Unfortunately, there was no direct system
of tunnels connecting the realm of the Dikhizhod dwarves to the royal
mountains north of the Grimmwalde, which was a problem considering
that the vast forest had been heavily infested by orcs the last time he'd been
there. So, instead of attempting to retrace his path through the elven lands
of Merithaim, he had traveled south, through the Man lands, and taken ship
at Avarus. He crossed the sea to Amorr, the great Man city in which he'd
been forced to fight as a slave for the entertainment of the tall barbarians,
then found another ship that carried him to Thursia.

The Man ships were a marginally more comfortable way to travel than on
the back of an elven warhawk, and they were certainly faster than walking
on dwarven legs across half the continent. The Man lords might be at war
with each other, but as far as Lodi could tell, their merchants still haggled
and bickered and traded and sailed as if nothing at all had changed. No
foreigners were being permitted inside Amorr's city walls, but the only
consequence was that the trader's markets had moved outside the walls
and prices were duly increased to account for the cartmen who charged
a handsome rate to transport goods the two leagues it took to reach the
imperial city by land.

He lost two days at Amorr waiting for a Thursian ship, but finally
found a captain of a small shallow-bottomed ship who was carrying pig
iron to his home port in support of the rebel provincials there. Lodi

found it remarkable that men would sell other men the very means that
were intended for use against them, but he had spent enough time above
ground in the Man lands that he had learned not to question the various
idiosyncrasies of the tall ones. In any event, it wasn't his concern and he
expected that the men of Thursia would soon find that the orcs advancing
southward amounted to a more pressing problem than whatever their
current differences of opinion with their Amorran brethren might be.

From the port he made his way north, occasionally alone, sometimes
in the company of traders who were pleased to have their small parties
augmented by a dwarf armed with a battle axe. He managed to procure
a crossbow from one Man who was bringing a load of furs south to the
port; it was a cheap and shoddy piece of work, but with a little effort he was
able to add a pair of small wooden plates that better stabilized the nut. It
was probably a fool's comfort, he told himself, but possessing it made him
feel safer nonetheless.

And he needed that comfort, as he spent three days going back and
forth across the border that separated the Amorran empire from what were
theoretically the Elflands. But he saw no sign of elves, indeed, he saw few
signs of anyone in the wooded foothills under which lay one of the arteries
of the great triumph of his people, the Dwarroways. There were scores of
access points to the vast system of tunnels that ran under the earth and stone
of northern and eastern Selenoth.

Built over the centuries, some were boltholes secretly opening into
the Man and Elf lands and designed to provide a means of escape, or
alternatively, invasion. The Dwarroways did not yet reach into Amorran
empire proper, (the one for which he was searching was among the closest),
but they did extend into Savondir, Malkan, Merithaim, and even to the
underground river that flowed beneath the High Elven capital of Elebrion.
Prior to the unexpected rise of the Troll King, Guldur Goblinsbane, that led
to the siege of Iron Mountain, one of the primary subjects of discussion in
the Iron King's Court had been the construction of the first major addition
to the Dwarroways in over a century.

But he could not find the one that he recalled was somewhere in the
vicinity. The system used to locate a Dwarrowdoor in the mountains, which
was where most of them were located, simply did not work in the forests
and he could not seem to find the caves that he knew would be used to hide
the door. Every dwarf who left the safety of the world to walk upon the
bright and hostile ceiling was instructed in the art of the Dwarrowdoors as
well as their locations, but since Lodi had not expected to be traveling in

this area, he was somewhat foggy on the specific details of where it was to be found.

He had a map, of course, but it was of severely limited utility in that it featured nothing more informative than an X marked crudely in the general area north of the line that demarcated the border. But since there was nothing to mark the actual border, not even a natural landmark such as a river, a mountain range, or even a sizable hill, he was left to search the wilderness for a door that was intentionally hidden. His prospects of success, he concluded grimly, were poor. And yet, what were his alternatives? To march northward and hope he managed to evade the various greenskins infesting the forest? Return south and wait for a dwarven party more familiar with the local terrain?

After three days of fruitless searching, he decided to devote two more days to finding the Dwarrowdoor, after which he would attempt to travel through Merithaim and hope that he could somehow avoid any elves, orcs, or goblins. The elves might be less inclined to intentionally slay him out of hand, but then, if they were on the war footing he assumed them to be, they would be likely to loose arrows first and ask questions later. And even if they were sincerely apologetic, apologies had never been known to raise a dwarf from the dead.

He was still searching for the door when he encountered the goblins.

He sensed the presence of danger in the air a moment before it arrived. Perhaps it was the sudden silence in the trees around him. Perhaps it was the sensation of enemy eyes upon him. Or perhaps it was simply the hard-won experience of a dwarf who had survived the great Arena of Amorr by learning to trust in his instincts. Regardless, something made him stop and sniff suspiciously at the air. It was a scent he knew all too well.

Goblins… goblin wolfriders, to be exact. He cursed under his breath, knowing it would do him no good to run or even hide, not with the noses on the shaggy, long-legged beasts that the goblin light cavalry rode. He set his axe down upon a nearby tree, then wound the crank on his crossbow and slipped a bolt into the slot. Returning it, now loaded, to his belt, he picked up his axe and held it in both hands, peering intently into the shadows of the surrounding trees. This was as good a place to die as any other, he told himself grimly, but he vowed that he would not do so alone.

"Come on out, ye cowards," he roared in the direction he suspected them to be. "Fear to face a lone dwarf, does ye?"

A wolf growled behind him, and he whirled around to see a pair of riders emerging from either side of a large oak tree. They were scrawny, ill-favored creatures, with pinched, pale green faces and yellow eyes that stared at him in a frighteningly hungry manner. He could see the ribs on their beasts; it was apparent than neither the wolves nor their riders had been eating well in recent days. Troll, orc or goblin, logistics had never been the strongest aspect of the various greenskin generals. Both goblins were armed with long wooden lances that would serve equally well as spear or cooking spit, and based on the smiles that exposed their sharp, jagged teeth, Lodi could see that they anticipated dwarf for dinner that evening.

Another pair of wolfriders came into view, followed by three more riders. Based on the light leather armor that hung loosely over their thin-chested torsos, it appeared as if he had run into an entire patrol of scouts. Had they been stalking him or was it merely misfortune? He shrugged. It really didn't matter. Against two, he might have had a chance. Against seven, his only hope was that they would run away after he killed their leader.

But their desperate state dashed even that remote hope. Half-starved and probably half-mad with hunger, Lodi knew neither wolves nor goblins would be even remotely dissuaded by the threat of losing two or three of their number. He hefted his axe, wondering if he should charge them or wait for them to come at him. The decision was made for him when the first goblin reached down the other side of his wolf before producing a bow as well as a quiver of short, black-feathered arrows that he slung over his shoulder. The goblin strung the bow in two simple moves, and the expert ease with which it did so caused Lodi's heart to sink.

So, Lodi didn't wait for the archer to nock an arrow to the string. He released his axe with his right and and let the heavy double-bladed head fall to the ground as he unslung his crossbow from a hook on his belt and raised it with lethal intent. The goblin's eyes widened, and two of its comrades shouted, but before any of them could move, the crossbow thrummed and the bolt slammed into the archer's throat. Lodi had actually been aiming at the goblin's chest, but it appeared the weapon had a tendency to shoot high.

He didn't hesitate, but took advantage of the goblins' momentary surprise to charge at them, dropping the crossbow and sweeping up the shaft of the heavy battleaxe to balance it in both hands. He lopped off the front third of the lance that was feebly poked in his direction with a half-swing, then punched the axe's spike right through the skull of the goblin who'd stabbed the lance at him. Its wolf snarled and slashed at him, and he felt a burning pain sear his left forearm as he pulled the axe free of the spasming goblin.

He smashed the butt of the axe against the wolf's muzzle and it leaped away yelping, leaving its rider to die on the ground behind it.

Before he could turn around, however, he felt something punch through his armor as it drove all the way through his left shoulder. Caught by surprise by the unexpected eruption of pain in his back, he uttered a most undwarfish cry. The object—it was a lance—was removed almost as quickly as it had struck, but as the goblin rode past him, its wolf ripped at the back of his left leg with its fangs. Already off-balance, Lodi fell to the ground in agony. But he fought through the pain to roll over, even though he knew there was little point in continued resistance. He planted the butt of his axe on the ground and pulled himself up to his feet, even as a goblin bared its yellow teeth at him and kicked its snarling wolf forward. Lodi supposed he might be able duck under goblin's lance, but he didn't have the strength to lift his weapon and he knew that the wolf would be going right for his throat if its rider failed to spit him on the knotted wood of the rudely constructed lance.

As the wolfrider rushed towards him, he dropped his axe and threw himself to the side, narrowly avoiding the fire-blackened tip that was aimed at his chest. What he would do next, he didn't know; his immediate priority was to avoid impalement. But the expected wolf-attack didn't come. Instead, he heard a pair of crossbows thrum, and heard a goblin shriek in what could have been fear, pain, or outrage. The sound of a dwarven battle cry inspired him with new hope, and he rolled over twice more before daring to push himself up using his right hand.

Four goblins and two wolves were already lying dead or dying on the grass. A fifth goblin toppled screaming from its mount, as its pathetic wooden shield and its shield arm were sheared through in a single axestroke by a powerful black-bearded dwarf wearing full plate armor. Its screaming stopped a moment later with the backswing. Before it had even fallen, the other two wolfriders turned tail and fled, followed closely by the three surviving wolves, one of which was limping badly.

A second dwarf with a long red beard bent over to retrieve Lodi's axe and offered it to him. "We'd better get you under before they come back in strength. They'll want the bodies, if nothing else. Can you walk?"

Lodi glared at the red-bearded dwarf. "Of course I can walk!"

He took one hobbled step, then another. Then he pointed to his left calf, which was bleeding badly enough that he wasn't sure he could walk far without collapsing. The torn flesh was visible through the shredded leather of his boot. "Any chance you could tie that up first, though?"

A black-bearded dwarf wearing chain mail with a crossbow slung over his shoulder had already drawn a knife and was starting to kneel down behind him. In a matter of moments, he had adroitly cut through the back of Lodi's boot, washed out the wounds with a pungent spirit that made Lodi gasp, and bound Lodi's calf tightly enough to stop the bleeding. He also soaked a cloth and pressed it into Lodi's shoulder; Lodi gritted his teeth as the alcohol seemed to ignite the wound with fire.

"This might help," he said, offering the tin flask containing the spirit to Lodi. "We don't have time to do anything more for your shoulder now. Don't look like it pierced your lung, so you'll make it."

"What are you doing here?" Lodi asked. Whatever it was, the spirit was strong enough to make his head spin merely from scenting it. He took a careful sip and blinked in disbelief as it burned its way down his gullet. If nothing else, it would take the edge of the pain in his arm, shoulder, and leg. He took a longer swig, then handed it back to the other dwarf.

"We're the local High Guard. The King ordered the sealing of all the skydoors two days from now, so we've been keeping an eye out for stragglers. We saw you tramping around here yesterday, but lost sight of you before we could find you."

"The skydoors are being sealed?"

"War is on the way, friend. It weren't no accident that those wolfriders were about these parts. The orcs are on the march, the elves are gearing up, and men are already fighting amongst themselves. The king don't want no part of it, so we'll hunker down and go about our business while the skydwellers slaughter each other."

Lodi wasn't sure that was either a wise or genuine option, considering the size of the army he'd seen months ago, and he was astonished to learn that the war hadn't already begun in earnest. It seemed that the vast gathering of orc tribes he'd seen on the east side of the Grimmwalde had barely stirred itself while he'd been trudging halfway across Selenoth and back.

"What's your name, straggler" the big dwarf wearing plate armor asked as the red-bearded dwarf helped Lodi support his weight on his left side. On the other side, Lodi used his axe as an impromptu crutch. "And what sort of piss-poor clan cuts its beards off like that?"

"Lodi, son of Dunmorin, of the South Goloi Vein."

"I heard of them," the dwarf supporting him said. "They own a couple of good mines right near the royal mountain."

"What happened to your beard, Lodi, son of Dunmorin?"

"Was a slave in Amorr until about a year ago."

"Amorr?" The two dwarves looked at each other, puzzled. "Never heard of it."

Lodi laughed, then grimaced. "Big Man city. Long way southwest of here. They shave the dwarves they catch."

"The King knows about this?" Red Beard asked.

"Looks like you're some kind of lodestone for trouble," Plate Armor said with a wry smile.

"You might say that," Lodi agreed. "The King knows. I've been out walking the ceiling on assignment for him."

The two dwarves looked at each other, although Lodi couldn't tell if they were impressed or alarmed. "Anything to do with the war?" asked Plate Armor.

"You might say that as well." Despite the pain from his wounds, Lodi felt as if a heavy weight had been lifted off his shoulders. For months, he had been nagged by the thought that Thorald might not have made it back to Iron Mountain with either the King's shield they'd retrieved from the drake or news of the tremendous orc invasion. He'd wondered if he'd done the right thing by going in search of the one Man family he'd known would listen to him.

If the King was prepared for war, chances were that the younger dwarf had made it back safely, perhaps even with the cursed shield.

"What's the news. What did the Kingsmoot decide? Have we marched up already?"

"There hasn't been any Kingsmoot," Red Beard said.

"No one is marching anywhere," Plate Armor added. "We were given orders to seal off the skydoor three days ago, but Bori spotted you through the glass. We've been following the goblins who were following you since this morning."

"You were looking for me?"

"Not you in particular. We just didn't want to leave a dwarf in the Overlands. From the sounds of it, it may be years before the skydoors open again."

Lodi frowned, and not because of the pain. No Kingsmoot. No army on the march. The sealing of the skydoors. That could only mean one thing. The King of Iron Mountain had no intention of interfering with the orc invasion of the Overland realms of Man and Elf. The dwarves were playing turtle and pulling their head and legs into their massive, earthen shell.

"The damned fool," he growled.

"What's that?" one of the dwarves said.

"This damned wound!" He winced and gingerly prodded at his shoulder. Without knowing anything about his rescuers, badmouthing the king was probably unwise. Then, without warning, he found himself light-headed and staggering. Red Beard swore as he struggled to keep Lodi from falling to the ground.

"Hold your tongue, dwarf, and save your energy!"

"Is he bleeding out?" Plate Armor asked.

"No, he's just weak and swooning from shock, not blood loss. You could take his other side."

"Aye, I could," Plate Armor said as he scanned the forest around them with one hand caressing the wooden shaft of his axe. "But I won't. Them gobbos are still about."

Fortunately for Lodi's sake, Chain Mail was willing to help, and between him and Red Beard, they managed to half-support, half-drag him along with them.

The rest of the walk soon became a painful blur to Lodi. He somehow managed to stumble along with the help of Red Beard until he found himself in the cool darkness of a hillside cave. It had been artfully concealed by a pair of fallen trees, which were somehow raised by the use of a secret lever hidden under a stump. The cave itself appeared to be a nothing more than a simple cave with no outlet until Plate Armor pounded the butt of his axe against the smooth stone wall at the end of the cave, and the wall slid silently back to reveal a downward-sloping passageway lined with lichmoss. If the silence of the secret door was not enough to indicate that it was well-maintained, the scent of oil that filled his nose as Plate Armor slid it shut again, then pulled an arm-sized metal bar down to lock it, was.

"Ain't no one coming in after us, 'cept skins. We're the last."

Lodi was in no position to argue, as he was beginning to dip in and out of consciousness.

"Hey, now, hold on there, friend!" Chain Mail encouraged him. "We're almost there." Lodi tried to stay awake, but it was too much effort and it was with no little relief that he closed his eyes and allowed the cool comfort of the darkness to claim him.

He awoke on the most comfortable bed he'd known in literally years. Except for a short period back home under Iron Mountain last year, he hadn't slept on a proper dwarf bed since he'd been captured and sold into Amorran slavery. The moss-stuffed mattress was soft and sweet-smelling, and for a moment, until he shifted his body, he forgot that he'd been wounded. He hissed as the pain shot through his shoulder, and then, as if in sympathetic echo, his left leg. He'd been undressed while he was unconscious, he realized, and when he gingerly poked at where the point of the goblin lance had emerged, he discovered that his unknown benefactors had also shaved part of his chest. The wound wasn't stitched, but it was packed with some sort of mossy herbal concoction he did not recognize.

His leg, on the other hand, had been threaded together neatly by an expert hand. It was smeared with a fungal unguent that he remembered from the war; the pungent odor it gave off was not readily forgotten. That was good. Ragged wounds of the sort the wolf had torn in his calf were easily infected, and who knew what sort of filthy carrion the beast had been feeding on before biting him.

He sighed, ruefully running his hand lightly over the bare patch on his chest. First his beard, now his chest. If things continued in this vein, the next time he'd probably find that someone had shaved his bloody bollocks. He'd look like a stumpy shaven elf if he didn't manage to change his fortunes soon.

There were footsteps outside the door and then it opened. His visitor was a young, fair-skinned dwarfess with the palest green eyes he had ever seen. She was pretty too, even allowing for the fact that it had been a cursed long time since he'd last laid eyes on a dwarf maiden. She wasn't even thirty yet, he estimated, as she shyly averted her eyes and placed the tray she was carrying on the little table near his head. There were bandages and pack-moss on the tray, and he wondered if the young lass had been his nurse.

"Was it you stitched me up?" he asked.

"Please don't talk to me," she answered without looking at him. Then she quickly left the room and shut the door, leaving him to wonder what he could have done to offend her so.

He looked at the bandages on the table. Surely he wasn't supposed to change them himself. Not that he couldn't, although in the absence of pack-moss he'd learned to get by with the fiery sting of spirits to clean out his wounds, but the pretty dwarfess's strange behavior was at odds with how carefully he'd otherwise been tended.

The door opened again. This time it was an older dwarfess of perhaps 150 years, followed by a grey-bearded dwarf who carried himself with an air of authority.

"Glad to hear you're awake and coherent," the dwarf said in a booming voice. He extended a hand to Lodi, who was unsurprised to discover the greybeard had a firm, confident grip. "You'll have to excuse young Myf, she was not expecting you to be alert yet. I understand your name is Lodi, of the South Goloi?"

"Lodi, son of Dunmorin, sir. As you say, my family mines the South Goloi Vein."

"A rich one, I hope. Silver?"

"Gold, as it happens, sir."

"Ah, all the better!" The greybeard chuckled. "We are honored! I am Morits, son of Morits, who was himself the son of Morits. We are a sadly unimaginative lot, I'm afraid. I am the mayor of this cavern, which is rather a grand way to describe what is little more than a half-buried Man village!"

Lodi eyed the ceiling, which was reinforced with timbers. It was alarmingly close to the surface, even for a high town, if the hazy recollection of his descent was a reliable guide. Well, it held no fears for one who had spent as much time under the sky as he had. He looked at the dwarfess whom the mayor had not bothered to introduce. Not his wife or a local dignatory, then, which meant she was likely a healer. "And is it you, madam, I have to thank for the care I have received?"

"It was our privilege to serve such a brave warrior of the Deep, son of Dunmorin." She smiled and curtsied. "I am Mulma, wife to Bodel, son of Hodel."

"Charmed," Lodi said, feeling considerably more foolish than brave. On the other hand, the sheer number of old scars, from the Amorran arenas as well as seven years of siege warfare, could hardly be denied under his present circumstances. Then his eyes narrowed. The two older dwarves were eyeing him in a suspiciously familiar manner. He had the distinct impression that they wanted something from him, and a moment later, Morits son of Morits confirmed it.

"I trust this is not the first time you have recovered from such grievous wounds?"

"No, sir. I had some bad luck along the way."

"Would you say that you heal quickly, Lodi, son of Dunmorin?"

He looked down at the big pink scar in his side that an orc gladiator had given him on the sands and remembered the long days of sheer agony he'd spent tied to the back of a donkey on the hellish ride that had taken him to the Elflands and purchased his freedom in the end. "Quickly enough. What do you need from me?"

"Do you recall the young dwarfess who was in here previously?"

"The one who asked me not to talk to her?"

The elder dwarfess laughed, and the sparkle in her eyes seemed to take decades off her face. "Yes, that would be Myf. I'm afraid she has some unusual perspectives. The problem we have presently is that she is of one of the Deepest clans. She only came here to deliver some very particular fungi we had ordered from her family. But with the king placing the Heights under war law, none of our dwarves are permitted to leave the cavern."

"We need you to escort her, son of Dunmorin," the mayor clarified unnecessarily. "It seemed likely that you were intending to descend, so we thought perhaps you might be willing to see her safely to her clan."

Lodi stroked his beard, such as it was. The lass didn't sound like an ideal travel companion, but better a silent one than an overly-talkative one. And she would have to pass through Iron Mountain if she was headed for the Heart of Fire, which was where the Deepest dwelled. "I can take her as far as Iron Mountain. Beyond that will depend upon the King. But if I can't bring her further, I vow I'll find someone who can, someone reliable."

"What will depend upon the King?"

"I'm Kingsguard."

Mulma and the mayor looked at each other, visibly startled. "You're Kingsguard?" the dwarfess said. "What are you doing in the Above?"

"In a manner of speaking. I don't do a lot of guarding anymore, but I still do a few odd jobs for His Majesty from time to time." He smiled at the mayor's discomfiture. "I'll take care of the lass if the Bodel-wife here can get me back on my feet, or at least my arse, before the tunnel-train arrives. If you're in the habit of trading with the Deepest, I can only assume this is a shaft terminus."

"Three days," the mayor said, eyeing Lodi with a mix of suspicion and respect. He wasn't the sort of dwarf to appreciate his sense of importance being trumped and Lodi's offhand reference to the King of Iron Mountain had thrown him for a loss. "The next one is scheduled to arrive in three days. After that, with a war on, who can say?"

Lodi nodded and glanced at the bandages on the table. "Well, Madame Bodel-wife, if I have only three days to recover, we had better be sure any blood-rot is cleaned out, or the only thing accompanying your young Myf will be my corpse!"

MARCUS

THE ROAN he'd been gifted by the royal councillor was bigger and more powerful than the Bithnyan ones to which he was accustomed. A stallion, it was even bigger than Fortex's Incitatus. Marcus supposed the larger horses were necessary, considering the heavy steel armor worn from head to toe by the Savondese cavalrymen, but he wondered about their stamina. The big roan was spirited, though, and made for a boon companion on Marcus's morning rides that marked his only escape from the ever-present duties of the legion.

He wasn't alone, of course, although the pair of knights who accompanied him were gracious enough to remain well behind him, in sight but far enough back that he could seldom hear them. It was only an illusion of solitude, but it was a welcome one nonetheless. He had much upon which to muse and this was the one time of day when he could be certain to be free from interruptions that shattered his train of thought.

The sheer numbers of the orcs they would soon be facing was a challenge, but at least it was a known one. There were a myriad of ways in which a commander could address his numerical disadvantage, especially one who had the benefit of knowing his men were better trained, better armed, and more disciplined than the enemy. The orcs might be stronger and more powerful than the goblins his men had faced in Gorignia, but everything he had read, and everyone to whom he had spoken, assured him that he need have no fears for the centuries that threw back the charge of Legio VII.

Of more concern was the unknown threat posed by the orcish devil-magic. Here the centurions who had experience fighting the orc were of little help, none of them having been privy to the discussions of either the generals or the Michaelines to whom the responsibility for negating the enemy magic fell. The Savondese accompanying him were too young to have any experience of it themselves and although he suspected de Forbonnais of being a kingsmage, the young noble wasn't about to admit to being a warmage while surrounded by devout Amorran soldiers who might well be inclined to burn him first and ask permission of their commander later.

Nor was Frontinus of much assistance either. To his disappointment, there were relatively few descriptions of battles against the orc and the scanty references to enemy magic were more allusive than descriptive. It seemed the great strategist had found it wise to be delicate in his description of such forbidden tactics, even those utilized by the soiled and godless enemy.

What was one to make of sentences such as this? *"The accursed enemy's devilries struck fear into Proximus's right, prompting many a legionary to quake and turn white with fear."*

Was it a spell that had been cast upon them? Had a demon been summoned, the sight of which had struck men dumb with terror? Or perhaps it was merely the illusion of a summoning, a false image designed to fool unwary and innocent minds? Or was "devilries" no reference to dark magics at all, but merely a description of the evil antics of the subhuman warriors? Frontinus did not say.

Such tactics as were described were precisely as Marcus had seen his father and Saturnius utilize in his first battle, when Legio XVII destroyed the two goblin tribes. Keen-eyed spotters were assigned to the ballistarius, who targeted the enemy magicians with artillery as soon as they were identified. Large and heavy rocks were an effective antidote to occult weaponry. But what if the orc-shamans were more capable than their goblin counterparts and smart enough to focus their spells on the ballistae first? It was bad enough to be without the priests of St. Michael, but if the artillery was destroyed, the legion would be forced to rely on its slingers and archers. And he could not find anyone to reliably tell him what sort of range these orc-shamans might have.

What he really needed was a test engagement, a limited battle that would allow him to feel out the enemy's capabilities without risking serious loss to his men. But the strategic situation didn't allow for that, not with the main body of orcs only a few week's march to the east. The strategic imperative was clear. He had to sever the tendril, cut it off and destroy it entirely before it could be reinforced. And that would require taking the sort of risk that he was extremely loathe to take.

He sighed. If there was one thing he had learned from Corvus, it was that strategy always trumped tactics. He had no choice but to roll the dice and gamble that his ignorance of the orc would hurt him less than the orc general's ignorance of the legion. But if he had to roll the dice, perhaps he could arrange to see that the dice were loaded, however slightly, and increase the odds in his favor.

A shout came from behind him, drawing his attention. He pulled at the reins, turning the roan around, and saw that a decurion was riding towards him at a gallop from the direction of the camp. Frowning, he kicked his horse into a trot; the two knights of his guard were already moving to intercept the incoming rider. What was it now? It could be anything, but of one thing he was certain: it wasn't good news the decurion was bearing.

"Lord Valerius," the decurion saluted as Marcus approached. "The Primus Pilus sends me to request that you return to the camp immediately."

"Why?" Marcus asked. He couldn't place the decurion's name, but recognized him as an officer of the Second. It didn't appear they were under attack.

The cavalry officer glanced meaningfully at the two knights. They took the hint and kicked their horses into a trot towards the castra. "Two legionaries from the Fourth were out on firewood duty this morning. One of the cavalry patrols came across the two o' them..."

His voiced trailed off.

"And what?" Marcus demanded, his relief that the castra wasn't under attack transforming itself into irritation. "A patrol came across them, and what?"

"One of them was using the other," the decurion said, his eyes cast down and his voice tight with disgust. "In an unnatural manner."

"The filthy swine!" Marcus spat out. The decurion blinked, surprised by his superior's uncharacteristic outburst, but nodded in confirmation.

"I'm afraid so, general. The patrol escorted them back to the castra and Caius Proculus has placed both men under arrest."

Marcus closed his eyes and took a deep breath. The unsettling news would delay the morning's march no matter how he elected to handle the situation. Such a gross violation of legionary law could not possibly be ignored, and the fact that the guilty men had been marched back to the camp and handed over to the primus pilus meant there was no chance that he could look the other way even if he were inclined to do so. Which was most certainly not the case.

He cleared his throat and spat. There had been whispers of men engaging in forbidden behavior during the long march through the dark tunnels of the Via Pumilia, as the underground dwarvenway had come to be known. But they were whispers, rumors, nothing more, and none of the senior centurions had thought it wise to demoralize the legion by conducting what might turn out to be a hunt for an imaginary evil.

Particularly when there had been so many genuine evils with which to be concerned, given the cave-ins and chasms that plagued their route, to say nothing of the occasional cave goblins that roamed the underground depths and had been all-too-eager to attack the stragglers and the unwary.

The unwritten rule of the legion was that an officer would look past violations of the Iron Law so long as the violations were minor and the violator was discreet. It was, for example, customary to ignore illicit vows secretly exchanged with a camp wife, a little interest charged on a personal loan, or the occasional overnight excursion from a castra that happened to be situated near the village of one's birth.

"Very well then," Marcus told the decurion. "We'd better address this straightaway."

He whistled at the two knights and waved them forward. After kicking the big roan into a gallop, he gained on them quickly, with the decurion only length or two behind. As the sun rose higher and the red rays of dawn began to give way to a clear blue sky, the four horses thundered back towards the legionary encampment.

"Make the case for mercy," Marcus ordered Father Gennadius. "If you can." He had summoned the legion's priest, along with its senior centurion and the tribune laticlavius, to his command tent, where they were discussing the correct way to deal with the incident. Proculus, the primus pilus, was eager to subject the two legionaries concerned, Claudius Cerficius Fustus and Quintus Annius, to the proscribed punishment and get the legion on the march without further delay, but Marcus was determined not to let military exigencies dictate justice. So long as they reached the location identified by the scouts before nightfall, there was no need to rush things.

The short, middle-aged cleric, who was already beginning to regain some of the weight he'd lost on their long underground march, shook his head. "There is no case for it, Marcus Valerius. There can be no mercy where abomination is concerned. The law of the Eagles is clear, as are the consequences for breaking it. My sole concern, indeed, I would go so far as to call it my sole demand, is that the men concerned be given the opportunity to confess themselves before being executed. They must die, but I would not see even men such as them damned."

"I don't understand how this could have happened!" Trebonius said angrily. "They are not even contubernales. How is it that they were out gathering firewood together in the first place?"

"I asked Marcus Caecilius that very question," Proculus answered. "Fuscus arranged to trade places with another member of Annius's tent. It was premeditated. If Annius had been whoring himself out, we might have thought to spare Fuscus, but as it stands they are both condemned."

"Who is Caecilius?" asked Father Gennadius.

"Their optio."

"Ah, yes, of course," the priest nodded. "Then he would have been in a position to know the duty roster."

"If they planned this, then they knew the risks they were taking," Trebonius said. He sniffed, his dark eyes narrow with contempt. "Proculus is right, Marcus. Confess them, kill them, and get the men on the move. There are thirty thousand orcs waiting for us four days march to the east. We have no time for trivialities."

Marcus looked at each man in turn. They met his eyes without flinching. All three of them, centurion, priest, and tribune, were in one accord. He closed his eyes, made a silent plea for wisdom, then nodded his assent. "Call the assembly, Gaius Trebonius. Have their centurion bring both contubernii to the fore and see that he informs them of their customary responsibility, Caius Proculus. And Father, please give both men the opportunity to confess and be cleansed."

Father Gennadius nodded as the two officers saluted, then departed. Marcus watched them leave the tent, feeling troubled but knowing he had done as his duty to the legion demanded. Was this how his father had felt when news of Fortex's fatal disobedience arrived? Had Corvus ever known this sick and empty feeling at the bottom of his stomach? If so, he had shown no sign of it while standing before the legion, not even when the executioner's axe struck off his nephew's head.

But despite his best efforts to maintain his equanimity, Marcus found that his hand shook when he poured himself a goblet of wine. He made a few desultory efforts to gather his belongings, then gave up, called in a guard, and told him to summon the centurion responsible for packing the command tent. The men had just arrived and were beginning to go about their business when the horn summoning the assembly was blown. The centurion looked at him quizzically, as if to ask if he and his men should continue with their preparations for the day's march.

"Carry on," Marcus told him. "The sooner they could leave this place of blood shed at his command, the better.

He took his time in walking to the tribunal, lost amidst all the noise and hubbub of men rushing to the center of the camp, many of them trying to finish putting on and buckling their armor as they ran, greaves in hand and helmets under arms. It was a good sign, he thought, that they obeyed with such alacrity. They knew as well as he and the senior centurions did that safety on the battlefield was to be found primarily in iron discipline. But discipline was owed by a commander to his men as surely as they owed it to him. He consoled himself with that thought as he stood below the crudely erected tribunal, watching one officer after another mount the wooden steps and waiting for Proculus to let him know that he should take his place upon the makeshift podium.

At last, the noise of the men taking their places died down. The Primus Pilus beckoned him to come forward as a hush fell over the legion. He took the five steps without hesitation, although feeling more as if he was mounting the gallows than assuming the place of judgment. Nearly five thousand faces looked up at him, but he had eyes for only the two men standing stripped and bound at the front of the legion, both of them flanked by seven armored men. To either side of Fuscus and Annius stood their centurion and their optio, and behind them, their signifer held the century's red standard that was marked with a large III sewn in yellow thread.

As he reached the front of the podium and came to parade rest, his arms behind his back, there was a tremendous clash as the entire legion slammed their fists against their breastplates. The entire legion present, save the two men with their hands bound before them. Fuscus, a balding, unshaven man in his early thirties stood his ground bravely, shameless and glowering unrepentantly up at Marcus. Annius, on the other hand, was a beardless youth younger than Marcus. He was red-eyed from crying and nearly lost his balance when he startled at the crashing sound of the legionary salute. Only Caecilius's stretched-out hand prevented the young soldier from falling over.

"Claudius Cerficius Fustus and Quintus Annius, you have violated the laws of God and Amorr by your shameful actions this day," Marcus addressed them loudly enough for the rear ranks to hear him. "Your crimes were witnessed and you have both admitted your guilt. As you admit to having broken your sworn sacramentum, I pronounce you guilty and sentence you to death by fustuarium, as per the Law of the Eagles."

Annius sobbed aloud and dropped to his knees. Fustus merely stared at Marcus and spat contemptuously on the ground.

Marcus looked beyond them to the two pairs of seven men behind them. It appeared Annius had been popular with his tentmates. Their faces were white, their jaws clenched, and each of the seven bore a wooden club. From that, Marcus knew they intended for their young contubernalis to die as quickly and mercifully as possible. The tent-companions of Fustus, however, were unarmed, and several of them were staring at the man with expressions of savage satisfaction. They clearly intended to draw out the beating and make him suffer before he died. Combined with Fustus's surly and unrepentant manner, Marcus surmised that Annius was not the first to be the subject of the older man's blandishments, although he hoped the youth had been the first to succumb.

"Come forward, Longus Avso," Marcus declared.

There was a moment's perturbation among the two groups of contubernales as the men looked at each other, then one man stepped uncertainly forward. He was tall and young, but with a weak chin that made him look rather like a ferret. A buzzing rose up from the ranks as the men asked each other what Marcus was doing.

"General!" Avso saluted.

"Claudius Longus Avso, you have committed no crime. However, as a result of your self-centered and careless actions, you have deprived Legio XVII of two soldiers on the eve of battle. Therefore, I sentence you to be flogged, one stroke for every blow required to execute the sentence pronounced upon Cerficius Fustus and Quintus Annius. Marcus Caecilius, strip him and prepare him for the flogging!"

Avso reeled in horror, almost stumbling backward, upon hearing the sentence. He knew, as did the assembled legion, that such a punishment might well amount to a death sentence in its own right. The vitis carried by each centurion could open a man's back in ten strokes, and while it wasn't nearly as brutal as the flagrum used on slaves and the very worst malefactors, enough strokes could kill a man. As Caecilius, the optio, grabbed him roughly from behind and began unbuckling his armor, Avso did not protest, but stood there silent and shaking with fear.

Marcus returned his attention to the two condemned men. "Claudius Cerficius Fustus and Quintus Annius, as the legate of Legio XVII, I cannot and will not show you mercy. However, in light of the good reports I have had of your conduct during the war against the Chalonu and Vakhuyu, and at the Battle of the Three Legions as well, I have decided to grant your centurion's request that you die by decapitatio instead of fustuarium."

He gestured and two junior centurions brought out a pair of wooden stumps. A third centurion, a big, powerful man who, in light of the circumstances, bore the ironic agnomen Clemens, came out from behind the platform, bearing the same large axe that had taken Marcus's cousin's life.

The relief on Fustus's face was as palpable as the terror on Annius's. The news that his death would be a speedy one did not appear to cheer the young man in the slightest. But then Father Gennadius appeared, from where Marcus did not see, and whispered something to the young man that seemed to calm him considerably. Fustus resisted momentarily, but his centurion expertly forced his subordinate to his knees, after which the recalcitrant man obediently lay his head on the block. Avso did likewise, with the assistance of the optio, Caecilius.

Clemens hefted the executioner's axe in both hands and looked up at Marcus. Marcus, not wishing to prolong Annius's suffering, nodded in the direction of the younger man. The centurion raised the axe, and it was over in a flash. The centurion shook his dripping axe, then moved onto Fustus, looking up again at Marcus for the sign to proceed. But when Marcus glanced at Father Gennadius, the little priest shook his head. Marcus held up his hand, and Clemens dutifully stepped back.

The ranks began to shift and murmur as Marcus walked down the stairs to the ground and around the platform to where the convicted man was still kneeling with his head on the block. He ignored the blood and the headless body of Annius; fortunately the young man had been permitted to void his bowels beforehand so the smell was less noxious than it otherwise might have been.

"Stand him up," he told the centurion, and the man pulled Fustus to his feet.

"You have not been shriven?" he asked the older man.

Fustus had small, mean eyes and sharp features that were too delicate for his broad-jawed face. He remained unrepentant, as far as Marcus could tell, although enough of his legionary discipline held to prevent him from being entirely disrespectful.

"I did what I did. I am what I am and I ain't sorry." The man shrugged. "You can call me whatever you want. Just get it over with, General. I ain't afraid and I ain't asking for no mercy."

"And I will show you none, Cerficius Fustus." Marcus said. "I respect your courage, Fustus. You do well not to fear me. I will only kill your body. But you would be wise to fear Him who can destroy both your soul and your body in Hell."

The condemned man wrinkled his lip and snorted. "Ain't nobody can kill what ain't there."

"Then you will not reconsider?"

Fustus shook his head. Despite his bare torso, his bound hands, and his disheveled appearance, the disgraced legionary bore himself with the pride of a Senator. "No, General. I won't. But my thanks for making this quick. I'd salute you, but for these."

He lifted his bound hands with a rueful grin.

"I'll take the thought for the deed," Marcus answered gravely, then lightly touched his fist to his breast to return the phantom salute. "Very well, Claudius Cerficius Fustus. Let it be as you will have it and may God have mercy on your soul."

He nodded to Clemens, turned his back on the doomed man, then walked back around the platform. By the time he had returned to the podium, Fustus's head was lying beside Annius's on the bloody ground.

Longus Avso took his two strokes bravely, obviously relieved to be receiving considerably fewer than he feared. Marcus was less concerned that the man had learned his lesson than that the rest of the men had profited by it. As Avso was led away by his officers, Marcus addressed the legion.

"Legio XVII, soon we will fight as brothers-in-arms once more. Together, we have known victory and we have tasted defeat. It is my intention that we will once more stand victorious on the field of battle, and it is to that end that I have enforced the Law of Eagles here today. This is my duty to you, both as your legate and as the true head of your House Martial."

A few scattered cries of "Valerius" met his reference to his House, but for the most part the legionaries were silent, waiting to learn if there were further surprises in store for them.

"In Gorignia, Marcus Saturnius and my father subjected you to Modis Austeris, as you were in enemy territory. I will not do so, for the Savondese are not our enemies. But this does not mean you may relax your discipline, as in a mere matter of days we will be facing a savage and bestial enemy. The orcs make war like a pack of wild beasts, whereas we make a science of slaughter, as the goblins of the Chalonu and Vakhuyu tribes learned to their detriment. Therefore, let it be known that any man who exchanges his duty on the duty roster with another without first receiving permission from either his optio or his centurion will receive ten lashes."

There was little protest at this aside from the usual murmuring; it was apparent that the men were expecting news that was more dramatic or related to the upcoming battle. For a moment, he was tempted to tell them about his father's death, but he resisted the impulse. He was not here to entertain them or win them over, he simply wished to avoid any further incidents of this kind. In the meantime, they had leagues to cover and they were already late.

"We will march inside the hour," he concluded, and without further ado, he turned his back and signaled for the primus pilus to take the podium. Proculus was already bawling out the day's order of march before he had descended again from the stairs.

They had passed the mid-day pause and were more than halfway to the location the scouts had identified for their evening encampment when Girart de Forbonnais rode back from where he had been accompanying the other Savondese knights and requested permission to speak with Marcus. Unlike the mounted Amorrans, the Comte de Ilyois was unarmored, and his scabbarded sword was tied to the saddlebags behind him. In stark contrast to the shaved heads and close-cropped hair of the Amorrans, his brown hair was long and tied back with a blue ribbon.

"I understand there were some unpleasantries prior to the march today," the young man Marcus suspected of being a royal kingsmage said. "I was aware that Amorran discipline was commonly supposed to be harsh, but I had no idea it concerned itself with where its soldiers place *la baguette magique.*"

"Legionary training involves more than distributing sticks to peasants in the hope that they won't piss themselves and run away at the first sight of the enemy," Marcus said sharply. He did not like the royal spy, he had no desire to revisit the morning's events, and he was irritated that the Savondese had only delivered half the number of horses promised for his cavalry.

"My friend, it was a mere comment, not a critique." De Forbonnais appeared to be taken aback by Marcus's contemptuous reaction. "We may not make, how did you say it, 'a science of the slaughter', but we do have a martial tradition here in the realm. And I understand you are seeking information concerning the orcish way of battle. Why do you not come to me? I have some experience in these matters."

Marcus eyed de Forbonnais skeptically, unsurprised that the Savondese man was aware of his actions. "If you had the sort of knowledge that would be of use to me at the moment, I would have cause to burn you as a witch and I doubt your king would appreciate my treating one of his pet mages in that manner."

"Are all Amorrans so grim and legalistic?"

"Are all Savonese so frivolent and corrupt?"

"My, you are in a foul mood today, Lord Valerius. Let me try this from another angle. As it happens, it is not only L'Académie des Sage-Arts that takes an interest in the dark magics of the orc. L'École Militaire de Saint-Michel also devotes considerable attention to the subject, in fact, significantly more than L'Académie. As the nature of L'École's studies are rather more practical than L'Académie's theoretical approach, I suspect they may be more directly applicable to your needs. Not only that, but I believe you can contemplate them in good conscience without imperiling your mortal soul."

"The Michaelines have a school here?"

De Forbonnais laughed. "No, Lord Valerius, these are soldiers, not warrior priests. Young soldiers. They are scions of the nobility, usually the second sons, who are sent by their fathers to the school to learn the art of war. We call them Michelards, and they make up a considerable quantity of what I suppose you would call our centurions, or as is probably more to the point, decurions, since we have no foot-officers in the Militaire Royale."

"Which makes sense, considering that you have no actual foot," Marcus observed. He was still mildly incredulous to have confirmed Quintus Veranius's seemingly absurd claim that the Savondese did not utilize any proper infantry. It seemed their king made do with the annual peasant levy, supported by his battlemages and the heavy cavalry of his nobles. No wonder the Savondese couldn't defeat the orcs on their own! How could any general expect to win and hold ground with cavalry and farmers?

"The king maintains a regiment of royal men-at-arms," de Forbonnais protested. "And then there is the Thauronian Guard, which protects his lands and household."

"A whole regiment! And how many men comprise this Guard?"

"Five hundred."

"So your mighty king has little more than a single infantry cohort at his disposal," Marcus observed dismissively. "It is well for you that the mountains separated our two nations, or one of our proconsuls might have added your kingdom as an imperial province decades ago. Inadvertently."

De Forbonnais shook his head and sniffed disdainfully, but he did not attempt to dispute the point. The two men rode in silence for a time, or as near to silence as it could be with the incessant creaking of the leather saddles, the occasional snorting of the horses, and the dull tromp-tromp-tromp of five thousand men trudging methodically through the green fields of eastern Savondir. The legion followed no road, but by the time it had passed, the iron-shod sandals of its legionaries had torn and compressed the virgin ground into a hard dirt path more than ten cubits wide.

"This École... you are telling me that your military men study the orc magics as well as your mages. Are you telling me that you are yourself one of these Michelards?"

De Forbonnais shot him a sly glance. "I am simply telling you that I am willing to tell you what I know. And that there are others who may be able to tell you more. Lord Valerius, I understand your discomfort with these matters. But you know as well as I do that you would be remiss in your duty to your men if you refused to accept freely offered knowledge that was so hard-won. Everything we know about the orcs was paid for in blood over the years. Do you wish to pay that price yourself when you need not?"

"No. No, of course not. Not when it is so easily avoided." Marcus held up a hand in warning. "But I will not countenance any use of magics or counter-magics, Seigneur de Forbonnais. Not even in extremis."

"I understand. So what is it that you wish to know?"

Still feeling some reservations, Marcus told de Forbonnais about the passage from Frontinus. He recited it from memory. "Now, what do you suppose were the 'accursed enemy's devilries' to which he referred? And how did it strike fear into an entire flank of Manlius Proximus's legion?"

"Am I correct you know nothing about magic?"

"Nothing," Marcus said proudly, if not quite accurately. He had, in fact, picked up a few glimmerings here and there by virtue of being in the vicinity of the Lady Shadowsong for extended periods.

"And I presume you have no desire to achieve a basic understanding of the principles involved."

"None at all."

De Forbonnais sighed and looked up into the sky, where the sun had not long ago passed its zenith. "Well, I've heard there are few things more satisfactory than an enthusiastic student hungry for knowledge," he said with no small sense of sarcasm.

SKULI

THE SOUTHERN SHIPS were gone. They departed two days ago, their hulls and decks crowded with that most precious of cargos, the last of the Dalarn people. From time immemorial, the Fifteen Clans had dwelled upon these four islands, warring amongst themselves and raiding all across the northern coast of Selenoth. Now, the islands were all but devoid of Man.

The ships carried the last of the living Dalarn, but not the last of the dead. For thus it was that they regarded themselves, the warriors of besieged Raknarborg, those who remained behind. They were hard men, scarred men, men who had spent eighteen years fighting a losing battle against an implacable and inhuman foe. None of them had ever known a time when they had not held swords in their hands, few could even recall those days when the grey terror of the Aalvarg had not loomed over their humble wooden huts and palisaded towns like a dark and hungry shadow.

Those huts and towns were gone now, destroyed, their inhabitants either fled or devoured. Even the great stone towers of Raknarborg, though they jutted proudly from the sea to the sky, seemed like saplings before the raging demonic storm that had scoured the Wolf Isles from stem to stern. The Aalvarg numbers were not vast, at least not in comparison with the great cities across the sea, but their fury was far beyond even that of the most rabid berserker and their thirst for man's blood had proven unquenchable.

Skuli Skullbreaker looked out over the grey waters of the sea as the waves smashed themselves relentlessly against the rocks far below. Clouds obscured the sun, but the darkening sky offered a warning of the incipient night to come. He sniffed and shook his head; the mindless futility of the waves reminded him of the attack they'd turned back just the day before. Was it the seventeenth or the eighteenth assault since the day the demonspawn army was first seen approaching the fortress? He'd lost count. But the end was drawing near. It was inevitable. The southerners were gone; they had seen the futility of defending Raknarborg and followed the body of their slain prince back across the sea. Most of his men were either departed or fallen. The Fifteen Clans who had once been the terror of the White Sea were now reduced to two hundred of the walking, wounded dead.

He felt a fierce pride swell inside him at the thought of them. Hjalnek One-Hand. Tjolnir Horse-Bjorn. The Strongbow. What a privilege it was to die in the company of such men; as long as men prized courage, the bards would sing their names in the south. And if no one knew exactly how it was they fell, so much the better. No doubt the songs would tell it better than the grim horror of a warrior screaming in agony as a demon wolf ripped out his intestines and gobbled them up before his dying eyes. Not for the first time, he wondered what hellish god had thought to create such monsters, had burned with such fury that he determined to curse the land with them.

He snorted. Whatever that dark god's intent, it had assured Skuli a place in Glaðsheimr. If ever a man had earned the name of Bági Ulfs, the Enemy of the Wolf, it was Skuli Skullbreaker. The Aalvarg would soon rule over the smoking ruins of Raknarborg, but they would not soon forget the Skullbreaker, not with damn near half their number lying dead in massive piles stacked outside the black stone walls. He didn't think it likely that the beasts told bedtime stories to their whelps, but if they did, he had no doubt that the little ones would quake at the sound of his name for years to come.

He smiled at the thought. It was a good legacy. It was a man's legacy.

His wife, on the other hand, was probably still cursing his name right now. He'd finally ordered her gagged as well as bound after she nearly bit off Asmund Hairy-Arse's finger while he and the Strongbow were carrying her onto the last ship just prior to its departure. He smiled fondly at the memory of her storm blue eyes glaring at him, bright with furious tears of rage. What a woman! She'd expected to die by his side, and while he'd initially been tempted to let her do so, the more time he had spent with the touchy, prideful southerners, the more he'd come to realize that Brynjolf and Fjotra would be in dire need of her wisdom if their people were to live successfully among them.

And now that the sun was sinking into the sea somewhere behind the clouds, it was time to send the final ship away.

He heard footsteps behind him and turned around to see the three men for whom he'd sent walking through the door from the tower steps. But behind them followed a fourth man. It was Steinthor Strongbow. He was limping badly; a wolf had ripped open the tall blond warrior's left leg during the assault before the last one.

"What are you doing here?" he asked the Strongbow. "You should be resting that leg for tonight, not climbing those stairs."

"Speak for yourself." His friend's mouth twisted in a half-smile. "Besides, we'll all be resting in Draugadróttinn's halls soon enough."

"Resting?" Skuli clapped Steinthor on the shoulder. "We'll be feasting, man, and the gods themselves will drink to our deeds!"

He looked at the other three men. Mord Redcheek was his most cunning warleader, and unlike the Strongbow and Skuli himself, he was one of the few men still unscathed by the recent months of battle. The left side of his face was disfigured where an Aalvarg nearly tore it off five summers ago, but the terrible scars were white with time and he moved with the agility of a man half his forty years. Surdaember was the second man, short and dark in comparison with the two Dalarn, and the only southerner still remaining in Raknarborg. Skuli didn't understand why the man chose to remain behind when the rest of his fellows were already sailing for the safety of home, but if anyone did, it would be the third man, young Hakon Hakonsson, who had a gift for tongues and somehow was able to understand most of the strange slurring sounds made by the southerners.

"Is the longship ready?"

The Strongbow nodded. At Skuli's order, he had provisioned the last snekkja that remained from what had once been a formidable fleet of sea reavers, as if for a long season of reaving. But the forty men who would be leaving the fortress as soon as darkness hid them from lupine eyes would not be following the rest of their people across the sea. Instead, Skuli intended that under the command of the Redcheek, the last survivors of Raknarborg would sail around the Isles and venture into the heart of the mountains on Hovedholm, the large island to the west from whence the Aalvarg had first come.

The wolf-demons might have driven the clans from the Isles, but they had not destroyed his people. Skuli had seen to that. Now Redcheek and the best of his surviving men would search for whatever secret lay behind their mysterious appearance, and when they found it, they would destroy it. One day, he vowed to himself and to sea and sky, the clans would return to the Isles. And when they did, they would not drive out the demons, they would destroy them, utterly, every single one.

"Then be off with you, Mord Redcheek, and may the All-Father, the Stormbringer, and the Lord of the Waves be with you!" He stepped towards the Redcheek to embrace the man, but to his surprise, the warleader stepped back and shook his head.

"No, Skuli. I have spoken with the men. To a man, they agree. The longship will not leave without the Skullbreaker."

Skuli stared at the man, astonished. Then he looked at the Strongbow, who was staring off towards the sea with an uncharacteristically innocent look on his face.

"Steinthor?" he growled.

"Yes, my lord?"

His ready deference confirmed Skuli's suspicions.

"Did you put them up to this? Would you truly deny me the honor of dying by your side?"

The Strongbow grinned, exposing the scar under his bearded chin that was only half-healed. An Aalvarg sword had very nearly taken his head off in one of the earlier attacks; fortunately the blade had somehow caught on the buckle for the strap that held his helm in place. The gods blessed the brave, but sooner or later, they had to withdraw their favor so the Choosers could come and claim their champions. Skuli had no doubt that the sky riders were jousting even now for the privilege of claiming his friend tonight.

"The Skullbreaker's Saga is a brave one, my lord, full of one noble defeat after another, but the one thing it lacks is a quest. It seems to me it would displease the gods if you were to deprive the bards of it."

"The Redcheek's Saga don't have the same sound to it," the Redcheek added.

"The thing is, we aren't giving you any more choice than you gave your wife." The Strongbow folded his arms. "My lord."

"The four of you can't make me to go anywhere, least of all on that ship!" Perhaps if the Strongbow had been hale, he and the Redcheek might have been able to disarm him and bear him down, but his friend's mangled leg rendered that impossible.

He reached for his war dagger. To his surprise, he discovered it wasn't there. The scabbard was empty! He looked down at his hip in disbelief, needing his eyes to confirm what his right hand had told him. Puzzled, he went to draw his other dagger, his meat blade, and realized it was gone too!

"Looking for those?" The Strongbow said with a self-satisfied smile and a sidelong glance towards Hakon.

Skuli strove to conceal his astonishment at the sight of his two blades, one long and curved, the other short and serrated, in the hands of the young warrior. Hakon grinned, a little apologetically, and handed them to the Redcheek.

"Tongues are not Hakon's only talent," he said, sounding amused. "Now, are you going to come along or do we have to tie you up and carry you onto the ship?"

Skuli glared at the plotters. In truth, he was more than ready to die. He was wounded. He was tired. He was soul-sick. His life had been one disastrous defeat after another; his only successes had been mitigating the extent to which his people were gradually destroyed. His one great achievement was to have arranged for the retreat of the remnants of the Dalarn from the Isles, sending them across the sea to dwell in humiliating submission to the very fishermen and farmers they had long reaved. What sort of warrior's legacy was that for the Reaver King, the last jarl of the Fifteen Clans?

Death was nothing to fear. It promised a welcome refuge. And, if the bards were right, there would be the warrior's banquet waiting for him, for the Strongbow, and for the best of his men. How he longed to meet the great men of the sagas such as Orvar-Odd and Njal the Grim, to say nothing of his mighty father, Jarl Halfrødr, whose booming laugh he had not heard for twelve long years.

It was the thought of living another day that seemed unbearable. Life meant the need to hope again when all hope had been dead for years. It was peering into the despair of the black abyss, seeking endlessly for a light that was extinguished long ago.

And it was that unmanly fear of living that convinced him he must go with the Redcheek. When had anything ever come easily for him, for the Skullbreaker? Even Death himself must be put off as long as possible, must be fought as if he were just another ravenous wolf slavering after the blood of his people. Only then could Skuli be truly certain that he would be worthy to sit in the company of the Warrior's Banquet, a man worthy to march into Glaðsheimr with his head held proudly high.

Skuli gripped Steinthor's arm and found his eyes were stinging. "I wish nothing more than to die with you tonight, my brother."

"I know." The Strongbow grinned, but his eyes were bright with unshed tears. "But go, instead, and avenge me. Avenge us all, Skullbreaker. And I will serve as your harbinger to let the Hirdfestmáltid know that Bági Ulfs is coming. You will board the ship?"

Skuli nodded.

"Your word on it?"

He nodded again.

The Strongbow squeezed Skuli's arm tightly, then turned and limped towards the stairs without looking back. Skuli watched his friend go and waited until his head disappeared into the darkness of the stairwell before turning to the others. He knew it would be the last time he saw Steinthor Strongbow until they met again in Glaðsheimr. He turned and looked up towards the gray, darkening sky. Soon it would be the killing time.

Give him a good death, Váði Vitnis, he prayed the Aldaföðr. Lend strength to his arm tonight, that the wolves may learn what fear is.

The Redcheek proffered his daggers to him and Skuli reclaimed them with what little dignity remained to him. As he sheathed them, he acknowledged Hakon's skill with a little nod, and the young warrior smiled with pleasure.

"Let us be clear on one thing, Mord Redcheek. This is the first and last time I will accept a demand from the crew. Once I set foot on that ship— what is she called?"

"Ulvdræber," the Redcheek answered. Wolfkiller.

"A good name," Skuli nodded approvingly. "Now listen! Once I set foot on Ulvdræber, any mutiny will be dealt with in the customary manner."

The southerner, Surdaember, slurred something unintelligible at Hakon, who shook his head and answered sharply. Skuli ignored him. It was the Redcheek's response that mattered; half the men chosen for the longship were his.

"Any man who does not obey the Skullbreaker will face my axe. And I swear by the Strongbow that I will die before I raise my hand against you again... once Ulvdræber is kissed by tomorrow's dawn."

Skuli laughed. Not for nothing had he chosen Mord Redcheek to command this last desperate voyage of revenge. It seemed he had chosen well, for the man was a clever one. He hadn't actually planned to leave the ship once he boarded it; that would be bad luck for him and demoralizing for the men. But the Redcheek wasn't about to take the chance.

"For good or ill, I am with you, Mord Redcheek. The night is coming, and with it the wolves. Let us go now, and leave Raknarborg to the noble dead."

He took one last look out towards the sea. Leagues away to the south, were Brynjolf, Dagna, and Fjotra. Would he ever see their beloved faces again? Would he ever have the chance to once more hold them in his arms? It seemed unlikely. They were sailing from a place where Death was coming to a place where Death had reigned for a generation or more. What were the odds they would not meet him face to face?

And yet, for the first time since he had bid his furious wife goodbye, the smallest ember of hope was kindled in his breast. Not even the Aldaföðr himself could be certain what tomorrow would bring. Tonight, the wind was strong and favorable, blowing from the west. Perhaps it was an omen. It was time to leave Raknarborg to its fate.

He strode without hesitation towards the stone stairs that would lead him down to the docks and to the ship that would deliver him to his unknown destiny. Death would have to wait another day.

AULAN

A S HE APPROACHED the building that served as the commander's quarters, Aulan was surprised to see no less than four armored legionaries standing guard outside the door. Previously, Magnus had always been content with two. He noticed the different numbers painted on the shields that were leaned against the brick sides of the building; the guards consisted of two pairs from different legions.

They saluted, recognizing his tribune's helm, but did not move out of his way until the leftmost man, from *Fulgetra*, nodded and said his name.

"It's Severus Aulan. Stand aside."

They moved out of his way, but Aulan stood his ground. "What's this?"

"Assassination attempt. Two days ago."

"Magnus?"

"Yessir. He's unharmed, sir. One of the centurions from the Fourth was killed, but he managed to wound one of the assassins. Magnus killed one, the pilus prior got the other."

Aulan nodded. It was clever. With two legions, most of the officers were more or less familiar faces. But the legionaries were practically indistinguishable, especially when they were wearing their helms with their cheek-guards down.

"Look sharp, then."

"Ave, sir!" The men saluted again, and this time he returned it. He opened the door and discovered two more guards inside the entry hall, but they did not attempt to stop him and merely regarded him impassively. He nodded to them and continued through the hall to the chamber that alternatively served as Magnus's triclinium or his staff center, depending upon his needs and the hour of the day. The floor was tiled in white, with a crude mosaic of a pagan sea god transfixing a thrashing male mer on his trident laid out in black.

As it was barely past noon, the klinai had been pushed to the corners of the tiled chamber and the big Valerian sat hunched over a writing desk that was comically small for his bulk, stamping a wax seal with his signet ring.

"Ah, Aulan, you're back," he said, and he pushed back the chair before rising to his feet. They clasped forearms, and Aulan noticed a long scratch across the older man's cheek.

"I heard there was some excitement in my absence."

"It seems I may have frightened the Senate rather more than I intended." Magnus shook his grey-haired head ruefully. "The bastards cost me a good centurion too. Bad enough to lose the two guards, but losing an officer that way is downright vexatious."

"Are you sure it was the Senate?"

"No, but one has to assume they're the most likely candidates. All of their gear was correct. There are no shortage of those who'd like to see me dead, but these days, most of them are in Amorr."

"Pity you couldn't capture one of them."

"Yes, well, I suspect you'll discover a similar tendency to overreact if someone tries to stick a sword in your eye." Magnus chuckled. "Didn't know I could still move that fast, to be honest. You should have seen the bastard's face when I stepped inside his guard and stuck my blade in under his arm. I vow he died more of embarrassment at being bested by an old fat man than the stabbing."

Magnus patted his belly, and Aulan marked the short dagger that the legatus was wearing strapped to his belt. There was still a good deal of muscle under the fat, though, and Magnus was a big, powerful man who had seen more war than most men of his generation. It didn't surprise Aulan that he'd survived the attack.

"They'll be taking other measures now," he observed. "If they can't kill you, they'll try to pressure you in other ways."

"I know," Magnus agreed. "That's why I've been writing to each of our allies who has had the fortune to meet our former countrymen in battle. I am requiring that they turn over all captured patricians, tribunes, and equestrians from the wealthier families to me."

"Will they heed you?"

"Considering their abject pleas for my assistance in various matters, to say nothing of no less than four requests to direct the campaign on behalf of both leagues, I expect so."

"How many?"

"Probably around sixty or seventy young men, all told, although it's only the Andronicans and Falconians that really matter. Seven or eight of them will give me more than enough leverage to safeguard my sons."

"Even though they've forsworn you?" Letters to that effect had arrived before Aulan's recent departure. Marcus had read them, laughed at the futile appeals to end his rebellion they contained, and as far as Aulan had seen, forgot them entirely.

"The Senate won't give a damn. They're growing more desperate every day. I think they'll leave Julia alone since I divorced her."

"You think they'd try to use the women?" Aulan was genuinely surprised.

"My daughters are safe enough. Their husbands, and more importantly, their fathers-in-law, won't permit any action against them. But I can't fault the Senate if they don't place much weight in my sons' disavowals. I wouldn't. Appius Appuleius won't harm them, but Marcus Andronicus wouldn't shirk at it. He's a cold-hearted bastard for all that he's a weedy fellow. And the fact that Rullianus was chosen as Consul Suffectus Aquilae to replace my late and unlamented brother indicates that the Senate is in a bloodthirsty mood."

"Is there any word on what happened to Corvus?"

"God only knows." Magnus snorted. "In spite of everything, I find myself grieving over the murdering prig. He always was so concerned with being correct and proper... and to think he died slaughtering the Sanctiff! For all that his actions last year were sheer lunacy, he never struck me as mad, but then, perhaps it was belated guilt over executing Gaius Valerius that sent him over the edge."

"Slaughtering the Sanctiff? I heard he died defending him!"

"From a demon?" Magnus laughed and set down heavily in the wooden chair, which groaned under his weight. "And here I thought you were a cynic! You don't genuinely put any stock in that story, do you?"

"You have to admit that there has been a good deal of strangeness of late, Magnus. Two sanctiffs dead and God knows how many celestines as well, and all of them butchered right in the heart of the Church!"

"Yes, well, consuls and senators have been dropping like flies in the first winter freeze too, and no one sees any sorcery in that!"

"Most of the men say it was the elves. It's known that the elven ambassador fled the city that same day."

"At least that's a theory that makes some degree of sense. Demons! I have no idea what Ahenobarbus was thinking when he permitted the damned creatures into the city. Elves, that is, not demons. Pity they didn't fry him instead of poor Sebastius. Souls or no, elves are wicked at heart. It's the magic. Steep a race of men in such sorcery for generations and the results will be no different. The Witchkings proved that."

"Some say you're a sorcerer."

Magnus laughed heartily. "Lesser minds find it difficult to accept their inferiority. It's always luck or magic, never their own incompetence. The petty will always hate their betters, whose mere existence is a reproach. Speaking of which, we have a situation I will require your help in addressing."

Aulan sighed and looked down at the dust of the roads still covering his armor. "Immediately?"

"Never fear, tribune, you'll have time for a hot bath and a whore before I send you out again."

"I was hoping more for a decent night's sleep."

"That too. It's your brother."

"Regulus finally showed his hand?" Aulan perked up. His elder brother had been charged by their father to take charge of the Severan legions. "Don't tell me he managed to find himself a battle and lose it!"

"I wish he had. I knew he was vainglorious, but I didn't know he was genuinely stupid. It seems your brother has declared himself king."

Aulan's jaw dropped open. "He did what? Of where?"

"King. Salventum. He's got *Fulgetra* as well as the City legion supporting him. That Falconius Buteo is a cynical bastard."

"That's sheer madness!"

"It's brainless, is what it is. He can't possibly think anyone is going to take him seriously, can he?"

Aulan was already wondering precisely the same thing. What could possibly have inspired his brother to such overt lunacy. Such a controversial action was certain to put the anti-Amorran alliance of the two leagues at risk; the provinces would find themselves occupied with warring with each other at the very moment they needed to band together against the might of Amorr.

Then a thought struck him. "I imagine he thinks it's what father would have wanted him to do. Or rather, what father would have done."

"That's ridiculous!"

"No, it's not. Not from his perspective." Aulan looked up at the ceiling and tried to put himself in his brother's shoes. "You've always been father's chief rival, just as House Valerius was our House's chief rival. So, with all the rumors flying around about your intention to crown yourself king of Vallyria, Regulus must be thinking that the only way for House Severus to keep pace with House Valerius is to crown himself king in response."

Magnus's lip curled contemptuously. "The arrogant puppy!"

Aulan shook his head. "It's worse than arrogance. It's a complete lack of any sense whatsoever. Regulus has always been a snob. He believes that the power comes from the name, be it Severus or Valerius, not the man."

That inspired a short bark of derisive laughter. "I don't suppose it crossed his mind that it is considerably different for the Vallyrians to accept a proconsul who has been commanding legions for nearly thirty years than for the men of Salventum to accept a boy who isn't even old enough to enter the Senate on the strength of his House name."

"I very much doubt it has. As far back as I can remember, the full extent of Regulus's analysis of anything extends no further than the question of whether he wants it or not."

Magnus swore a very unpatrician oath. "You couldn't have told me this any sooner?"

"How would I know he'd declare himself king? This is a depth of idiocy I didn't even know existed!"

"How is it possible for a son of Severus Patronus to be so stupid?" Magnus groaned. Then he stopped and corrected himself. "I suppose I should know. I fathered Sextus after all."

"I doubt Sextus would be so foolish as to declare himself king the moment he had an army at his command."

"Don't underestimate my son's capacity for foolishness. He would not only declare himself king, he'd stake his crown on a single throw of the dice."

Aulan said nothing, having been there when Magnus led Legio VII into battle on disadvantageous ground against two Valerian legions. At least Sextus came by his predilection for gambling honestly. Aulan had no idea what obtuse Severan root might have produced Regulus's spectacular, and hopefully singular, shortcomings. Neither Patronus nor their mother had ever struck him as being similarly short-sighted; even the nonentity that was his uncle Lucullus was reasonably sensible despite his overly pliable personality.

"*Fossa!*" Magnus swore and tore two of the letters he'd recently written in half. "We're going to have to move faster than I'd planned. If we don't distract the allies and the provincials quickly, your cursed brother is going to break at least one of the leagues apart!"

"How do we distract them?"

"We move on Amorr. Right away. The Senate wouldn't be trying to assassinate me if they weren't frightened; they have no confidence in the new legion they'll be raising, nor should they. Corvus couldn't beat me, but they didn't know that; without him, they're stuck with Declama and Rullianus. Quintus Falconius is an aggressive, thoughtless bastard. He'll come out to meet us so long as the numbers are in his favor."

"You can't take Amorr with two legions!"

"I said move on Amorr, not take it. The distinction is paramount."

Aulan didn't see what the point of moving on Amorr without taking it was, but he decided not to inquire. He knew Magnus would explain himself whenever he saw fit and no sooner. "All right. What about the Consul Provincae?"

"What about him? Pansa is no general. Gaerus Tillius is good, as are two of the younger Cassanians, but the Cassanians won't be given additional commands while Longinus is still in the field. The Gaeran legions will stay in the north, to keep the provincials from joining us."

"And Torquatus? He is no longer consul, but he is still a power in the Senate." To say nothing of being an old friend and associate of one Valerius Magnus."

"Titus Manlius will counsel caution and hiding behind the city's walls. He knows me too well, he'll know I don't want a siege. He may talk sense into the Senate for a while, but he won't be able to keep Rullianus on a leash for long. It won't be hard to draw him out."

"Why are you so certain Rullianus will come out to meet us?"

"He's like your brother. He's young and he's greedy for fame. And how better to achieve it than by defeating the great rebel Valerius Magnus, right in front of the walls of the Sacred City with every last knight and senator watching?"

"You're certain you can beat him?"

"A fame-hungry hothead with green legions and no experienced centurions? Aulus Severus, I've half a mind to leave a legion behind just to make it a challenge! Any one of my cohorts will have more centurions with experience than his entire officer corps combined. You cannot win a battle without good centurions, Aulan. If you learn one thing from me, let it be that. The heart of the legion is its centurions."

As he spoke, Magnus was quickly scratching out a short letter on a small scroll, which he sealed, stamped, then handed to Aulan. "Dine with me tonight. You'll leave for Salventum in the morning; take both of your squadrons from *Fulgetra* with you."

"You're sending me back to my brother?"

"Tell him he's to march on Amorr without delay. The rest of the Utruccan League may or may not come, but it makes little difference either way. The provincial legions are useless to me; worse than useless, given the logistical burden they'll impose. And tell him to put the damned crown away and pretend he never claimed it. This is no time for such nonsense."

"And if he doesn't listen to me?"

"Kill him, if you can. If not, give the scroll to either Buteo or the primus pilus of *Fulgetra*. Then tell them to march on Amorr without delay. I expect you'll find them amenable."

Aulan nodded grimly. He'd expected as much. If he'd learned one thing from Magnus, it was to act without hesitation once the decision was made. He was pleased, too, that Magnus honored him by assuming he would carry out the terrible fratricidal order if necessary. But it wouldn't be, he decided. He was certain he could convince Regulus to listen to reason. Almost certain, anyhow.

"I'll bring the Severan legions to Amorr one way or another," he promised, then saluted the Valerian. How strange it was that events had come to this, that a Valerian should be able to order a Severan to kill another member of House Severus without being struck dead for his presumption! "How soon will you march?"

"That's what I'm about to find out." Magnus cleared his throat and raised his voice. "Opilian!"

Aulan hadn't seen Tarrisinus Opilian in the hall, but Magnus's booming voice echoed off tiled floor and it was only a matter of moments before the tribune of the XVth appeared in the doorway. "Lord Valerius?"

"Get me Gerontius and both praefecti, now. I need to know how our supplies stand, so they'd damn well better be ready to answer any questions in that regard. And send a rider to the legati of V and IX in Larinum. I need them here with their praefecti the day after tomorrow, if possible. No later than the day after that. Tell them we need to move the schedule forward."

"Sir!" Opilian saluted, and with a brief nod to acknowledge Aulan, he exited the room. The sound of his boots thumping through the hall was followed by the exterior door slamming, and then it was quiet again.

Magnus looked thoughtful, then grunted as he rose to his feet and patted Aulan on his armored shoulder. "That's four. But I'll need five. Six would be better. It's your House legions that matter, Aulus Severus. If you can get them to me without killing your brother, he can call himself the King of the fornicating Elves and Dwarves for all I care. But get me those legions!"

Aulan wasn't certain at what point the roads over which they were riding began to strike him as being familiar. But gradually, as the leagues passed by to the monotonous accompaniment of the horses' hooves against the bricks, he began to recognize more and more of the landmarks on either side. A half-ruined building set back amidst vineyards, an inexplicable copse of trees standing defiantly in the middle of a corn field, a certain collection of modest, straw-topped hovels; they struck long-forgotten chords in his memory that made him feel as if he was going home.

How long had it been since he'd last been back to the family villa? At least three years, maybe four. Some of his fondest memories were of summers spent there, playing with his brothers and the children of the household slaves. He wondered how many of them were still there, as Patronus had manumitted a number of the older slaves in his will. The villa was Regulus's now, whereas the grand domus in Amorr remained with the head of House Severus, now Appius Severus Pullus.

His mother and the two youngest children still lived there, of course, as the domus was large enough for several generations of Severans. But she was no longer the mistress there, just as his father was no longer the master of the Senate. And that, he imagined, was the thought that would be sticking in Regulus's craw. Aulan didn't fault him for his desire to salvage Severan influence; he shared it. But Regulus was too impatient, too narcissistic, and too confident in his inflated sense of self to understand that a patron had to earn the trust of his clients, that it was not simply his to claim by birthright.

That was the difference between Patronus and Magnus, Aulan thought. They were both brilliant, accomplished, powerful men but Patronus had drawn men to him through a complex web of carefully constructed dependencies. Magnus achieved much the same results through the brilliance of his successes and sheer force of personality. Men *owed* Patronus, whereas they *followed* Magnus. The distinction was significant.

He wished he'd had the same opportunity to get to know his father that he'd had with Magnus over the last few months. But he'd been too young when his father was still commanding legions rather than Senate factions, and besides, it was easier in some ways for men to make demands of young men who were not their sons. Aulan rather doubted Magnus would so blithely have used any of his own sons as assassins, although to be fair, he couldn't be entirely certain of that.

And then, Magnus hadn't actually told him to accompany Lucarus to kill the old Cernobian, that had been his choice. He smiled at the memory of the arrogant elder's outraged face when he'd realized that the man he thought to betray had betrayed him instead. But the old man had courage, Aulan allowed, and at least he hadn't embarrassed both of them by begging for mercy for himself or for his family.

Somehow, he doubted Regulus would die half as well under similar circumstances. That in itself was reason enough to ensure he was talked round; the thought of Titus Severus weeping and pleading for his life, shaming both his House and their father's memory, sent a chill down Aulan's spine.

If you have to do it, you'd better not let him see it coming, he told himself.

"Do you know which way?" Lucarus called to him. They were approaching a fork in the road; one way led to Amorr and the other to the huge permanent castra that Aulan assumed was presently housing both Severan legions as well as the remnants of the Civic Legion.

"Keep straight on," he told the decurion. "With any luck, we'll be riding that one within ten days."

The men were in good spirits, considering that half of them had been with him when he'd been delivering Magnus's messages to Harius Obsidius, the head of the Marruvian League. Obsidius had enjoyed some early success against Longinus, his father's murderer, but proved too timid to follow it up and thereby squandered his initial advantage. Magnus wasn't overbothered by this, for as Aulan had been charged with explaining, his primary concern was for the Marruvian armies to keep the Amorran legions in the north and east of the empire occupied and away from his flanks when he moved on Amorr.

"Think your brother will be glad to see you?" Lucarus had been unusually dour of late. Aulan put it down to his favorite having been made the camp wife of one of the centurions and subsequently taking herself out of commission.

"He will if we play along with his pretensions."

"How do you expect to do that if Magnus wants him to set aside his crown?"

"Magnus didn't say we had to lead with that." In truth, Aulan hadn't decided yet upon what approach he should take with Regulus. No one knew better than he did how quick his older brother could be to anger when crossed, or worse, defied.

He had been six or seven the first time he'd realized how dangerous Regulus's temper could be. They'd been arguing about something, probably a toy, when he swung at Regulus and hit him in the shoulder. Regulus had promptly hit him back, punching him hard in the stomach. That had hurt, but it was fair enough. What was much more frightening, in retrospect, was the way that Regulus stopped and stared at him while he was doubled over, then deliberately punched him in the face, hard, knocking him down.

They'd only come to blows five or six times after that, and each time, Aulan had been careful not to strike the first blow. Regulus had beaten him, but he'd never again shown the cold, merciless fury of that earlier fight.

He'd have to be patient, he decided, and let his brother show his hand. Marching in and proclaiming Magnus's demands would likely be counterproductive, perhaps violently so, and Regulus was not the sort to differentiate between message and messenger.

"What about Buteo?"

"What about him?" Aulan had not given the Falconian legate a moment's thought since reaching Amorr last winter.

"Well, we're with *Fulgetra*, right? So, he's your senior officer, and you didn't have no orders to go riding off with Magnus, if I recall aright."

Aulan frowned. It hadn't occurred to him that Buteo might take exception to the absence of him and his men over the winter. *Fulgetra* was a Severan legion, after all, and ultimately answered to the head of House Severus. It shouldn't be a problem, since they had been following his father's orders, but Patronus was no longer around to verify them.

"Buteo isn't going to give us any trouble."

"He's not going to give *you* any trouble," the decurion muttered. "We'll be lucky to get away with a flogging."

"Don't be a worrywart. If anything, he'll be happy to have twenty more horse at his disposal than he did yesterday." Not that Magnus or Regulus were likely to leave them at the Falconian's disposal for long. "Just keep your mouth shut if they ask you about Magnus's intentions, and make sure none of the others do much talking either. I don't know what he's really up to and neither do any of you. If anyone starts asking questions, just start talking about the Battle of the Three Legions. That should distract them."

"Aye, I suppose it will at that." Lucarus snorted. "Most of the boys think we was lucky to get away for the winter. Except Rufus, of course."

"Granted." A pila had been driven through Rufus's left leg during the charge that routed Legio XVII, the wound had festered, and despite a belated amputation, the unfortunate rider died three weeks later. But he'd been the only knight lost to Aulan since they parted company with *Fulgetra*, which was better than some considerably less adventurous winters Aulan had spent in the past.

Winter was always a difficult time for the legionaries, and especially the knights, who, being accustomed to greater liberty due to their social rank, tended to go more than a little stir-crazy when trapped in a winter castra far from civilization and its amenities. Particularly amenities of the female variety.

"What about our backpay?"

"Backpay? You all got paid twice! First by my father, then by Patronus."

"The boys figured they was bonuses. You know, for the trouble. Besides, if we're still on the legion's roster, our wages is owed."

Aulan sighed. Lucarus might be a stubborn old cur, but he knew his rights by the Iron Law. "I'll see what I can do. Say, is that a patrol up there?"

The decurion squinted. "Riders, anyhow. Two of them. Could be. Did you make up your mind yet?"

Aulan wasn't sure that he had. He had little stomach for facing his older brother today, and his obligation to report to *Fulgetra*'s legate was as a perfectly adequate excuse for putting it off if he wanted one. Regulus was more likely to be reasonable if he didn't show up with two squadrons of knights behind him; the last thing he wanted was to give his brother the idea that he was after Regulus's ridiculous crown.

But now, it seemed the decision might have been made for him. The riders in the distance had turned around abruptly and were rapidly disappearing. "Dammit!" he swore.

"Should we go after them?"

"And do what?" Aulan shook his head, irritated. Their horses weren't blown, but they were weary after riding across four provinces, whereas the patrol's would be fresh. They weren't about to catch the other knights, nor would they know what to do with them if they did. Lucarus's reaction was nothing more than simple instinct, a predator responding to the sight of possible prey running away. "They'll be back with a century behind them before long."

He was correct, and the speed with which they returned proved to Aulan that they were closer to the castra than he'd imagined. The sun was still high in the sky when they saw the column of infantry marching over the crest of a small hill ahead, flanked by a squadron of cavalry on either side. As the tromp-tromp-tromp of their caligae against the brick became audible, it soon became clear that Buteo had seen fit to send out no less than two centuries against the unknown interlopers.

"Keep your swords in your scabbards and your hands on your reins," Aulan called out loudly behind him. "I don't want any pissing matches today!"

Ahead of them, the two squadrons broke away from the infantry, abandoning the road to ride in a pair of semicircles that would permit a double-envelopment and hold Aulan and his twenty knights in place for the footsoldiers. It was a standard mixed-force tactic and no sooner did the men recognize it than they began heaping derision on the other knights.

"Shut your damn mouths," barked Lucarus, silencing them quickly. Like Aulan, he was tense. They both knew that the encounter wasn't guaranteed to be a peaceful one.

The squadrons kept their distance until the infantry column transformed into a three-deep line and Aulan could spot the transverse crests on the helmets of the two centurions. He couldn't make out who they were, not with their cheek-plates obscuring their faces, and he doubted he could name more than two-thirds of *Fulgetra*'s officers on sight anyhow.

But as tribune, they would surely know his face. He reached back and untied his tribune's helm from his saddle, then rose in his stirrups and held the helmet aloft. "I am Aulus Severus Aulan, Tribune of Legio III, commonly called *Fulgetra!*"

Then he smiled as he saw the lead centurion stop and put up his hand, followed a moment later by a pair of optios bawling and the legionary line coming to a halt.

"Aulus Severus, is that really you?" The centurion took off his helmet and Aulan recognized Nemonius Strabo, from the Second Cohort. "The prodigal finally returneth!"

Aulan grinned and winked at Lucarus. "You see," he said archly. "There was never any cause for concern." But what Strabo told him next abruptly wiped the smile from his lips.

"I'm glad to see you, Aulus Severus, but you and your men will need to surrender your weapons. I'm sorry, but I have orders to arrest you."

He heard more than a few obscenities and vulgarities being uttered behind him, though Lucarus only chuckled bitterly. It was with some difficulty that Aulan managed to maintain a steady voice and shout back at the centurion.

"Orders from whom?"

"The legatus, Appius Mallicus."

The legatus? That made no sense! Mallicus was the laticlavius, the legion's senior tribune, not its commander. Had Falconius Buteo shown himself false? Or had he taken ill and died over the winter. Suddenly Aulan realized that the situation here in Salventum might be much different, and much more difficult, than either he or Magnus had anticipated.

And so he watched, with no little irritation, as Strabo waved his hand to indicate that the two squadrons on their flanks should move in and take them into custody. It was with more anger than fear that he unbelted his sword and scabbard and let them slide down to clatter on the dusty bricks of the road.

MARCUS

THEY KILLED the front two lines with nothing but a pile of sand?" Proculus said incredulously. The big centurion was sitting on the other side of the fire from the old Savondese mercenary captain who was regaling the Amorrans with his stories of past battles against the orc. Fortunately, the captain had roved far to the south in his youth, and although his Utruccan accent was heavy, they were able to understand most of his account.

Believing it, on the other hand, was another matter entirely.

"Stupid they are not, Sièculaire." The old mercenary threw back the last dregs of the wine in his goblet and grimaced. "Too sweet, you drink it much too young! The orc is crude, but he is cunning. Like an animal cunning, but an evil animal, *perfide*! The *belette*, you understand, not the *reynard*."

"More weasel than fox," Girart de Forbonnais clarified. He was there to translate for them, but for the most part his services were proving to be unnecessary. Marcus would have liked to send the supercilious nobleman away, but he had no reasonable excuse. And while de Forbonnais had not managed to produce one of the famous Michelards, he found Capitaine Renier in a tavern in one of the towns through which they had marched, and the mercenary was proving to be a useful font of information about orc-fighting.

The mercenary was there recruiting to add to his small company, the Compagnie du Saint Léopold, but had found himself instead conscripted by the nobleman due to his experience with some of the historical orc incursions into Estmarcher. Much to Marcus's surprise, the capitaine's information was turning out to be a veritable gold mine, particularly as it related to the way in which the orc shamans utilized magic on the battlefield.

"Was there nothing to be done?" he asked the grizzled old man, whose grey hair hung in long and stringy locks that were streaked with white.

"The sand stripped the skin from their bones, *garçon*. They was militia. They had no shields, no metal armors. What was to be done?"

Marcus ignored the minor insult, assessing that it was not intended as such. "They could have been ordered to lie down. When the grit was hurled, was it in a horizontal plane? It would be wasteful to project it en masse. And at what height was it hurled? How thick an area did the projectiles cover?"

Proculus laughed. "Militia? They'd still be scratching their bums and casting about for their blankets until they found themselves scoured clean by the sand, General. I suspect their cavalry would be no better."

"How do you protect your cavalry against such attacks?" Julianus wondered. "Surely the caparisons you utilize do not cover them from head to hoof!"

De Forbonnais stared at his Amorran counterpart for a moment, and the shadows from the dancing flames made the pitying look he gave the decurion a cruel, almost inhuman edge. "We find it is the rare orc shaman who is inclined to test its martial aptitude within range of our battlemages," he said dryly. "Any who are so inclined do not survive the experience."

"Yes, yes, of course, I'd forgotten," Julianus said hurriedly.

Marcus winced. All of their reactions, all of their martial instincts, were out of balance here. They were unsuitable. In two days, three at most, they would be meeting a large quantity of orcs in combat for the first time, and every tactical decision he or his subordinate officers would be called to make on the battlefield were almost certain to be based on incorrect assumptions and irrelevant experiences. Which meant they were almost guaranteed to be wrong.

It wasn't only the orcs. The way the Savonders—Savondese, he corrected himself—were structured militarily was, to the extent that he understood it, entirely insane. Untrained, unarmored, almost unarmed infantry that was only available for two months out of the year was combined with heavy cavalry that was similarly indisposable, although less predictably, since each noble's commitment to his commander varied from one man to the next. Apparently the basic idea was for the infantry to engage the enemy and tie it up long enough to give the cavalry a static target to smash. A sound enough concept, and not entirely dissimilar to the way Fortex had used the Second Knights, but a extraordinarily limited variant.

Especially when, to fill in the many gaps that presented themselves, the Savondese resorted to mercenary companies whose term of service was unlimited, and who provided a heavier, more capable infantry than the peasant levies, but whose commitment only went as far as their employer's coin. Or rather, their ability to spend that coin. It was sheer madness!

He sighed and stared at the fire as if it might contain answers to make sense of the situation. But it was nothing more than superheated wood, glowing red and yellow and white against the night. It burned brightly for a moment and then it was gone. For some reason, it made him think of his father and of Marcus Saturnius. The strategist and the master tactician. Both much better suited to lead the legion into battle than him. And now, both gone. Then a thought struck him. He could not count upon his tactics or his allies. That much was clear. So what did that leave? It left him to rely upon strategy. If only he could get the strategy sufficiently right, he could render the subsequent tactics irrelevant!

"Capitaine Renier, every example you've given us is indicative of set-piece battles. But is a marauding force of the sort we're up against, even such a sizable one, likely to be given to such tactics? Would they even be equipped with proper magiciens?"

"I don't see why they wouldn't use glass instead of sand anyhow," Proculus said dismissively.

"Orcs don't blow no glass, Sièculaire. And you, you talk like a *damné* Michelard, *garçon*. But it's true, these *déchets* are *pillards*, they have no pigs, no materials, and their shamans will be few."

"Pillards?" Marcus glanced at de Forbonnais.

"Raiders." The young noble smiled faintly. "*Déchets* is merely a derogatory term."

"Sounds like a good name for the little shits," Proculus declared as he tossed an empty skin of wine aside and reached for a fresh reinforcement. "Dayshits or peelarses, General, everything we've learned says they're nothing but light foot buttressed by a light cavalry auxiliary. They've got numbers, but nothing else, and you saw at Gorignia that numbers don't signify nothing. If their shamans throw some magic at us, it will meet an iron wall. Fire won't burn a testudo and sand won't crush it. Once they show themselves, Cassabus and his boys will drop rocks on their heads. We should meet them head-on. Ten-to-one or twenty-to-one don't matter. We'll stand, we'll kill them, and then they'll run."

"How do they fight at night?" Marcus ignored the primus pilus. "Do either of you know?"

"They don't," answered de Forbonnais.

"*Pauvre pisse*," Renier said at almost the same time. He spat into the fire, which hissed momentarily, as if protesting. "The pillards are more active than the main body will be, because their wolves can see at night and don't spook so easy. The pigs, they are usually staked to the ground come nightfall."

"And they have no chain of command worth speaking of, from every-thing I've read," Marcus mused aloud. "That alone would preclude any substantive maneuvers after dark."

"Their warleaders are usually the biggest, fiercest members of the chieftain's clan. The warbands can range from ten or so up to several hundred."

"Not the smartest?"

"Who can tell?" De Forbonnais shrugged. "Even if there was a proper general among them, the rabble are such that they would not be capable of understanding, much less complying. The warleaders have teams of overseers who whip the foot into place, usually the heavy cavalry as well. The light cavalry, the wolfriders, run freely as they see fit, as scouts and skirmishers. They're less tractable than our own peasant levies, and even our own foot isn't capable of doing anything more at night than sleep or run away."

Marcus nodded. A plan of attack was beginning to take form in his mind. He closed his eyes, envisioning the map over which he'd been repeatedly poring the past few days. Darkness was the key. With each setting sun, darkness removed virtually all of the orcs' advantages, while costing the legion little more than the ability of the spotters to identify targets for the ballistarii. He leaned forward, seeking to feel the heat from the fire against his face.

It wasn't enough to make them run. They already ran from the cavalry patrols that were active in the north. And despite the large size of the enemy force, it wasn't a proper army, it was more like a massive band of raiders who would sooner flee than face a real fight, even one where the numbers were in their favor. Chasing them back to the main body might relieve the pressure on a few besieged towns and villages, and it would certainly meet the objectives set him by the king's men, but it would accomplish nothing. Within weeks, perhaps even days, the same troublesome pillards would be back, most likely marching in the van of a much larger and more dangerous army.

What he needed was to find a way to apply the legion's peculiar science. He thought back to what he now thought of as the last day of his boyhood, the final moments of his childhood innocence. His father had explained to him the abstract concept of Saturnius's geometries, describing the way the movement of the legion's elements over the course of the battle could be seen as lines and blocks, weapons that were moved into position in order to pierce the enemy units in a manner more deadly than any sword-thrust or crush them more finely than a millstone. It was dangerous, he realized, to apply the tactical concept too literally to strategic operations; to do so meant ignoring terrain, logistics, troop quality, and any number of other vital elements.

But it could be done. And he couldn't shake one of Frontinus's examples from his mind. He pictured the terrified herd thundering down the hillside, blazing brands affixed to their horns, sending the surrounding enemy scattering into the night in every direction. How did it go, exactly? He closed his eyes, and with a little effort, was able to envision the text.

"He tied torches to the horns of all the cattle he had in the camp (and there were many), and when night came he lighted the torches, extinguished all the camp fires, and commanded the strictest silence. Then he ordered the most courageous of his young men to drive the cattle up the rocky places between the enemy and the pass."

Ah, it seemed he didn't remember it quite correctly. The flaming cattle had merely been a distraction, they had drawn the attention of the besieging enemy, they had not frightened him away. But there was a world of difference between well-trained, heavily armored Amorran infantry and a rabble of orc raiders. And then there was the fact that the cattle the legion presently possessed were required for purposes considerably more important than scaring orcs at night.

Then again, one could tie a torch to a legionary as easily as a cow. He smiled, then reached into the fire and withdrew a newly added brand that had only caught fire on one end. As the flames guttered out, he marked three spots on the dirt in front of him, then drew three lines.

"What's on your mind, General?"

Marcus ignored the decurion. Instead, he tossed the brand back onto the fire, then sat back and dusted off his hands. "Capitaine Renier, I wish to hire you this evening, for a single night's ride. You will be well compensated. If Monseigneur de Forbonnais provides you with an escort, do you think you can arrange to locate the prince's camp by morning?"

The other four men sitting around the fire all stared at him for a moment. De Forbonnais was the first to find his tongue. "The hour is late. My men will have been drinking. Is it really a matter of such urgency, Lord Valerius?"

The old mercenary took a long swig of the wineskin, then wiped his mouth and met Marcus's eyes. There was no avid greed in his face, only a wary respect. He nodded slowly, then rubbed his finger against his thumb. "Ten deniers. Silver. Give me two knights as well and I'll take the message, *garçon*. I can hold my wine and neither the night nor the forest holds any fears for Saint Léopold."

"It will hold them for the *déchets*, Capitaine." Marcus smiled grimly. "I will write out the scroll while Monseigneur prepares your escort. But you may tell the prince to keep his men ready for company the night after next. And tell him that as I make a present of orcs to his Royal Highness, I shall expect a similarly handsome present of their ears in return."

Proculus laughed. "A night march and a night attack. Ave, Valerius! We'll give the prince his glorious victory, and all he needs to do is sit tight and play anvil to our hammer."

"Are you mad?" demanded de Forbonnais. "Lord Valerius, there are twenty-five thousand orcs rampaging throughout the March! You cannot intend to attack them without even attempting to join up with His Royal Highness! You have barely five thousand men!"

"Five thousand?" Marcus shrugged in the face of the noble's disbelief. "I think two cohorts should be sufficient. And I'm not intending to attack them, Monseigneur. I intend to kill them. The larger part of them, I expect. If you will excuse a paraphrase of the Sacred Word of Our Lord, their slain will be thrown out, their dead bodies will stink, and the March will be soaked with their blood."

He reached for the wineskin and Capitaine Renier handed it to him. He squeezed a long stream into his mouth, swallowed it, and handed it back. "Their ears, on the other hand, will travel to Lutèce. I understand there is a handsome market for them there."

The men were visibly exhausted as they went about the various tasks necessary to construct the castra. Their movements were slow, and even the shouts of their centurions seemed a little subdued. The sun was already setting, as they had marched nearly ten more leagues than their usual twenty today, not stopping until they reached the borders of the massive forest in which the enemy army was known to be sheltering.

"You're taking a terrible risk, you know, Marcus." Cassabus's concerns were visible on his tanned face.

"Most of which falls on your shoulders. I know. But an attack now will be much less dangerous than it looks." Marcus sought to reassure Cassabus, who would be commanding the detached cohorts. "Surprise is the key. They don't know we're here and they're not looking for trouble to their rear. If for some reason they don't run, if you meet any serious resistance, you're to fall back here at once. Be sure the crews understand they are to leave their machines behind in the event of a retreat. If you're forced to fall back and I see any of your crews has salvaged their machine, I'll have them flogged."

The ballistarius winced, but nodded. War machines could be replaced. This far north of Amorr, legionaries were considerably harder to come by.

"At dawn, we'll feed the men and push north as fast as we can. You'll have a squadron, plus four Savondese guides with mounts, so use them to stay in contact with us. You'll only have to hold for a few hours after the sun rises. Keep the pressure on them so long as they look like running. Once you see signs they're starting to regroup, fall back to a defensible position. Everything I've read, everything the capitaine told us, indicates that they're not likely to counterattack before we relieve you."

"I understand the plan, Marcus. And I understand your reasoning. It's risky, not crazy. But the fact is you're sending me to attack five legions worth of orcs with only five centuries!"

"I know that. And you know that. What matters is that they don't know that. The scouts have found their camp, so as long as they don't see you coming, and I don't know how they possibly could once night falls, they won't know if you're hitting them with five centuries or ten legions."

"I wish I had ten legions. I wish I had two!"

Now it was Marcus's turn to wince. He knew Cassabus wasn't trying to remind him of the legion he'd lost, the legion that betrayed him after the Battle of the Three Legions, but the reminder stung even so. "So do I."

"Why are you so sure we'll be able to push them all the way out of the trees? It's a long way from that big clearing in which they've settled to the edge of the forest."

"That's where the villages are. That's where the supplies they need are. Once you drive them from the camp and they're forced to leave all the goods they've pillaged behind, they'll have no choice but to emerge or starve."

"Or turn on each other."

"I don't care who kills them, so long as someone does it in a manner that permits us to collect their ears."

Cassabus grinned despite himself. "You've turned outright barbarian, Marcus."

"Paying the men is only second to keeping them alive. If the Savondese would pay for their balls, I'd harvest them too."

"Now that, I'd like to see!" Both men laughed. Then Marcus put both hands on the ballistarius's shoulders.

"I would lead the attack myself, Titus Cassabus, if I could. You know that. I trust you more than any other man in the legion and that is why I chose you over Proculus, Tertius, and Trebonius. And know this: I have no fears for you, Cassabus, none at all. Put them to the torch, put them to the sword, and they will flee before you. They have never faced the iron of Amorr. They will not stand before the valor of a Valerian legion!"

Cassabus nodded, his face set like stone. "Well, if this goes well, at least I can hope to claim an agnomen of distinction. Aleator, or perhaps Phreneticus."

"It only looks like rolling the dice or foolishness to those without the eyes to see. You cannot let the men see your doubts."

"Are you hiding yours from me?"

"There is nothing to hide! Do you not trust me?"

"I do, Marcus Valerius. But even the most trustworthy man fools himself from time to time. Are you sure you are not fooling yourself in your desire to strike the first blow against the orc?"

Or in your desire to win a victory that will secure your place with the legion, were the words unsaid, words that Marcus could see in the other's eyes. "We can only surprise them once, Titus Cassabus. Once they know our quality, they will do their best to avoid meeting us directly again, and being more heavily armored, we cannot match their speed. This is our one and only opportunity to take them wholly unawares and prevent them from escaping us. And there is another factor."

"Such as?"

"The money." He smiled and held up two fingers, then crossed his fingers. "The two factors are intertwined. Do you think the crown will be so willing to promise us a silver an ear once they learn how effectively the legion butchers its foes? We can feed the men and keep them paid for months, months, Cassabus! And an opportunity such as this will not come again, not soon, at any rate."

"I see," the ballistarius said, nodding slowly. "It is still a gamble, Marcus, but I can see why you deem it a gamble worth taking. I only wish I were not the one sitting in the pot!"

"I can't blame you." Marcus slapped Cassabus on the shoulder. "Feed your men when they wake, with a double-ration of meat and a half-ration of wine, then see that they are confessed and blessed before you march. I will be at the gate with Trebonius to see you off."

The ballistarius nodded, saluted, and went off to find the five centurions who would be serving under him tonight. He would not sleep, Marcus knew, nor would the other officers. He could only hope that the lack of sleep would not overly hinder the men's decision-making faculties. He should sleep himself, he knew, for tomorrow would be a long and brutal day, but he doubted he would be able to fall asleep no matter how badly he needed the rest. His mind was racing with all the possibilities, all the various outcomes, and far too many of them were bad.

If the orcs stood firm and tried to encircle Cassabus and his five centuries, he would be wiped out. In their heavy armor, his legionaries could not outrun the orc raiders, still less the goblin wolf-riders. The legion would be literally decimated and Marcus would likely find himself facing an open revolt, from the men and the junior centurions if not the senior officers themselves. For all that they had supported his decision to risk the attack, he knew that it was more his right to make the decision that they'd been supporting than the decision itself. He'd failed them once, and badly. His authority might not survive a second such failure.

Perhaps he should prepare for the possibility, set a few spies among the men, and imprison any likely troublemakers. His father had told him that there were always a few instinctive rebels in any unit. Keeping them under watch, or even under guard, might dampen any ardor for insurrection. And yet, betraying mistrust of his men might spark the very unrest he sought to avoid, were it to become known.

He watched the men of the eighth cohort raising the gate for the Porta Decumana. He could see Claudius Didius, their centurion, shouting instructions as the men pulled at the ropes that set the freshly cut beams into place. Although they were tired, Marcus could not see a single malingerer in their midst; no doubt every man in the cohort understood that with the enemy nearby, they were liable to be attacked at any moment. And while a few of them occasionally shot envious looks at the tents of the slumbering men excused from their usual duties, he guessed that most of them had enough experience to know that they wouldn't truly want to trade places with them.

They were good men. Fine soldiers. He had gotten to know their true colors during the Deep March. How could he fail to trust them now? How could he expect them to trust him to lead them in the future if he failed to give them the benefit of the doubt now? It was one thing to hold his tongue about Corvus. That was a family matter, and no man would blame him for his silence. But to set spies upon them would be a violation of confidence from which he might never recover. Even if the men never found out, the senior centurions would know. And necessity or not, such a demonstration of weakness might well plant seeds of doubt in their own minds.

The commander who expects to be obeyed must first show himself worthy of obedience, his father once told him. Was it not true, then, that the commander who expects to be trusted must first show himself worthy of trust? No, he decided. He would set no spies. It would be better to fall to a traitor's blade in the night than sever the sacred bond between legion and legate.

Of course, Marcus Saturnius may well have felt the same before being betrayed by his own centurions. It was a haunting thought for the dead man's successor.

Grant me wisdom, Father, he prayed, not for the first or the fiftieth time today. *Give these, the servants of your Immaculate Son victory in the dark night to come, in His most Clean and Perfect Name!*

He felt like finding Father Gennadius and confessing; being purified and blessed might lift some of the terrible burden he was now feeling descend upon him. But the priest would be fully occupied with the men of Cassabus's detachment, those who were too troubled by sin or fear to sleep. He could wait. He would have to wait.

That should be one of the Iron Laws of the Legion, he thought. Thou shalt wait. Thou shalt wait, and wait, and wait, and wait, until finally, at long last, thou shalt know terror sufficient to turn thy bowels to water.

Now that was enough, he told himself. There was too much to be done before tomorrow morning to permit himself the indulgence of useless worry. Cassabus was right to call himself Aleator. The die was cast, or at least the decision to cast it had been made.

What would you do, father? Not for the first time, he desperately wished he was still simply one of the legion's tribunes, carrying out orders rather than issuing them as its commander. What a perfect fool he had been to harbor ambitions of command! Had he known two years ago what he knew now, nothing, not even Corvus's deepest disapproval, would have convinced him to abandon his studies and place his name before the assembled tribes.

But that die, too, had already been cast. Then, to his surprise, he laughed. Why should failure hold any fears for him? He would do well to fear for

Cassabus, to fear for the men of the legion, to fear for House Valerius and for the fate of Amorr itself, but what was it to him if the legion would not serve him as they served his father and his father's father before him? It was simple vanity that was haunting his thoughts, he realized, and little more than vanity. He came to a decision. If God willed that he failed in yet another battle, then he would take it as a clear sign that he had made a mistake in abandoning the priesthood. He would resign as legate, turn the legion over to Trebonius and the senior centurions if they would let him, and return to the bosom of Holy Mother Church. Where and how, he did not know; moreover, he did not care.

It was with a lighter heart and a clearer mind that he strode towards the half-built Porta Decumana. Already the sun was low in the sky and soon the night would fall. Then steel and flame would shed blood in the dark heart of the forest, and by the time the sun rose again, he would know in which direction his true vocation lay.

LUGBOL

L UGBOL didn't like the way Snaghak was staring at him. The hatred in the shugaba's piggish little eyes was easy to read, but so was the triumph. The sneaky bastard was up to something. That much was clear. Lugbol was of a mind to walk right over and gut the coward, but killing a fellow captain in camp was strictly forbidden. Zlatagh would strangle him with his own guts if he gave Snaghak what he deserved, so Lugbol would just have to wait.

"I have tasted Manflesh! I have raped she-men! I have burned Man cities!"

Lugbol rolled his eyes. Who hadn't? He was almost embarrassed for the big mountain orc, who was boasting of his accomplishments while stalking back and forth in a large circle of about fifty warband leaders listening to their warleader's customary evening rant. As for the burned cities, most of them had held populations smaller than Lugbol's own kai hari gungiyar. If they were the terrible Man cities of which Lugbol had been told frightening stories since he was a small orcling, then he was a one-armed goblin.

"Man-Zarki'agh shaking in their tents! Man-Kings on their thrones pissing themselves when they hear the name Zlatagh! Zlatagh Life-taker! Zlatagh Piss-maker! Zlatagh Maneater!"

That was their cue. "Maneater! Maneater!" the shugaba'ugh obediently chanted, Lugbol among them. He knew that Zlatagh secretly hungered after the praise-name Mansbane, but even the mighty warleader knew better than to risk stepping on the clawed toes of the Great Orc Azzakhar, whose claim to the title would certainly trump Zlatagh's.

Lugbol doubted, however, that any Man-King had ever heard the name Zlatagh, let alone pissed themselves at the sound of it.

Zlatagh was an imposing brute, though, even for a mountain orc. He stood nearly a head taller than most of the shugaba'ugh gathered around him, with a thick chest and heavy muscles that belied his violent speed. A pair of captured iron Man plates covered each powerful shoulder; two cow's horns had somehow been driven through the center of both breastplates, curving upward like two spare pairs of tusks. Zlatagh's own tusks were nearly as large; they were thick, yellowed with maturity, and reached nearly to the tip of his nose. Almost unique among the orcs present, Zlatagh's tusks were unsharpened and unadorned with any bone, paint, or metal.

But that didn't mean they weren't fearsome weapons. Lugbol had seen with his own eyes how the big orc once used them to disembowel a goblin. The goblin had been wearing leather armor too, which made the feat all the more impressive. After Azzakhar commanded Zlatagh to invade the Man lands two moons past, the Maneater had found himself facing three challenges to his leadership, two of them on the very first day. Zlatagh beheaded one with the monstrous cleaver he called Headchopper, blinded the second with his bare hands, and ripped the arm off the third before using it to bash in the skull of the overmatched orc. At this point, only a truly thick-skulled shugaba would dare to cross the giant orc, let alone challenge him.

Nor, beyond personal ambition, was there any reason for anyone to do so. Zlatagh was a good warleader, and the warbands over which he'd been given command had enjoyed an unbroken string of victories under his leadership. More than one hundred Man villages had been pillaged and burned, and the orc encampment was littered with the broken remnants of trophies taken throughout the spring campaign. None could complain that he had not passed the ultimate test of leadership; providing his followers with more food than they could eat and more booty than they could carry. Not a single orc's belly didn't bulge with fat of the last two moons' devourings, and even the most cowardly goblin wolfrider wore decorative trophies of one sort or another by now.

That didn't mean Lugbol was entirely confident in the big mountain orc. Smashing sparsely guarded hamlets and carrying off helpless herds and captives was one thing, defeating a large and well-armed army of the sort that waited for them at the northwestern edge of the Korokhurmagh was another. Zlatagh could boast that the Man chieftains were pissing themselves and afraid to take the field against him all he liked, but it hadn't escaped Lugbol's notice that it was their forces who avoided meeting the mounted patrols that chased them throughout the woods, and that Zlatagh hadn't moved their encampment one step closer to the Man army ever since its presence had been reported by wolfriders fleeing from the metal-clad Mandokki warriors and the huge, fierce, four-legged beasts they rode.

"Who marches today! Who takes the fight to Man!"

"Lugbol!" Lugbol raised his fist and cried halfheartedly, quite happy to be outshouted by other shugaba'ugh more eager to demonstrate their enthusiasm to the big orc. "Lugbol!" In truth, he was hoping to spend the next day or three in the camp, sleeping, squagging, and allowing four of his wounded warriors to recover from their injuries. One of his trophies was a large keg of yellow liquid that looked like piss, tasted like honey, and hit the skull harder than ale, wine, or club. He didn't know what it was called, but he fully intended to drain it with the help of a few select companions this evening. It was a pity no females had been permitted; a few abokhi'ahg would just about make for a perfect way to spend a lazy afternoon. There were a few she-men in the prisoner corral, but Lugbol was more in the mood for some relaxed and drunken squagging than having his ears assaulted by the piercing shrieks of a raped man. Rape was a fine thing when the dead enemy was strewn about, smoke was in one's nostrils, and one's blood was up, but for now it struck him as being more akin to work than pleasure. Especially considering how he only had one good arm at his disposal at the moment.

He watched the Maneater nod with satisfaction as the big orc looked over the shouting captains vying for his attention. Zlatagh laughed, a deep guttural sound, as he basked in the raw power of the moment. Two months of slaughter and victory had given him absolute control over the shugaba'ugh, and it was clear that he knew it.

"The auguries!" Zlatagh cried suddenly. "Bring forward the augurs! What say Gor-Gor?"

As the shouting dissolved into a general cheering, Lugbol saw a pair of heavily tattooed orcs with sharpened silver tusk-caps push into the center of the circle. They accompanied someone; at first Lugbol thought it might be a juvenile Man, but then he caught a sight of yellow-green skin and realized it was a goblin. Nearly half their troops were goblins; they had started out with ten thousand but thanks to the inevitable costs of the campaign, there were about a fifteen hundred fewer of them now. The doomed creature looked wild with terror; he seemed to have a fair notion of his imminent fate. But he was silent and he did not struggle; there was literally nothing that a single goblin could do to save itself, not when surrounded by howling, blood-hungry orcs with arms twice the thickness of his legs.

The augury looked to be the usual entrail-reading. For some reason Lugbol had never quite grasped, Gor-Gor preferred to speak to his priests through the intestines of his lesser worshippers. Goblins were the preferred method of communication, though orcs, Men, and even large rats would do in a pinch. He noticed Gor-Gor never seemed to speak through either wolves or warboars, two martial commodities that were always in great demand.

The goblin broke his silence when one shaman kneeled down before him, then ripped open his stomach with both silver-tipped tusks. As the other shaman held the victim, chanting all the while, the killer began calling out the haruspictic ritual and reached into the goblin with both hands. Then he began walking backwards, pulling the dying goblin's innards out. After taking seven steps, he gave three firm tugs, then finally released the bloody, stinking offal and let it fall with a wet thud. The other shaman followed his example, stepping back and finally allowing the moaning goblin to collapse, dying, to the ground.

Lugbol saw the shaman raise his bloody hands and call out to Gor Gor. The shaman's eyes suddenly rolled back into his head and he swayed back and forth, as if drunk, while looking over the entrails spread out upon the ground. He took a step forward, then another, holding his palms toward the ground with his fingers spread wide. It was as if he was feeling his way through something rising up from the spilled innards. Several of the shaman's tattoos flared into life; a rune on his shoulder blazed red and began to smoke as it burned away his skin, but the shaman didn't seem to feel or notice anything was wrong. With nothing but the whites of his eyes showing, he began to grunt and growl. Gradually, the guttural noises became discernible as words.

"Fire," he rumbled. "Fire burns. Demon wings of fire, burning, burning. Demons, iron demons, and death."

The shugaba'ugh looked at each other, confused. This was not how the ritual usually proceeded. Zlatagh's eyes narrowed and he made as if to step forward, then the big orc stopped himself. Even a warleader would not dare to lay claws upon a shaman in the unholy grip of Gor Gor.

"Death come, death come, on fire and iron, death come to all!" The shaman's voice rose into a shriek and he thrust his bloody hands skyward. Then, he began to shake and shiver, as if Gor-Gor was attempting to rid himself of his puppet. Finally, the shaman collapsed face-first on the ground, where he lay motionless except for his labored breathing. Smoke, stinking of burned flesh, rose from three or four blackened tattoos on his back and shoulders.

"The Hell he say? What does that mean?" a furious Zlatagh demanded of the other shaman. One might have almost thought that he was alarmed. "What was the damn augury?"

Lugbol looked around at his fellow shugaba'ugh. They were agitated and alarmed, with one significant exception. Snaghak, alone among the warband captains, wore an expression that was full of fury. He no longer looked triumphant, he looked downright vengeful. And, for once, Lugbol thought, Snaghak's hatred didn't appear to be directed at him. He stifled a dismissive snort and returned his attention to Zlatagh, who had grabbed the smaller shaman by his tattooed shoulders and was shaking him while shouting in his face.

"I don't know!" the smaller orc pleaded. "I swear, I swear by Gor-Gor's tail, I don't know what happened!"

Zlatagh snarled in disgust and shoved the tattooed orc away from him. Then a groan from the fallen shaman caught the big orc's attention and he whirled around to see the shaman, his skin still smoking slightly, trying to push himself up from the ground. The injured shaman failed the first time with a barely muted cry, then his muscles bulged with effort as he succeeded in rising to his knees on his second attempt. He didn't seem to have known what happened to him earlier, because he suddenly winced and looked down at the burns on his shoulders with an expression of pained surprise.

"You!" Zlatagh said, reaching out and pulling the shaman to his feet. "What did you do? What thing did you see in the guts there? What secrets did Gor-Gor tell you?"

The shaman rolled his eyes and slumped in the warleader's grasp. His initial reply was a drawn-out groan, but when the warleader violently shook him, it seemed to pull him out of his swoon. "I saw death. Everywhere, death."

"Whose death! The Man cities?"

"No," the stricken shaman said. He stared intensely into Zlatagh's face. "Ours. Everywhere, all throughout the woods, I saw orcs dead on the ground, murdered, all of them, by the iron demons!"

"You lie!" Zlatagh shouted instinctively, before driving an oversized fist into the shaman's tattooed face. There was a loud crunch and the shaman crumpled as if he'd been cloven through the head with a dwarven axe.

Whether the shaman was dead or not, Lugbol couldn't tell, but he wouldn't be surprised either way.

Zlatagh pointed at the other shaman, who was cringing behind the corpse of the goblin. "You, read the bloody guts! And tell me the truth or I'll rip your balls out of your sack and feed them to you!"

The second shaman was no fool. He quickly stretched out his hands over the dark green ruin of the goblin's innards and began intoning nonsense about death. His fear was transparent and the augury wasn't at all convincing, but Zlatagh didn't seem to care if any of the shugaba'ugh were buying the shaman's performance or not. As he glared at the shaman, it seemed to Lugbol that all the warleader cared about was avoiding the fateful warning of the first augury.

"He was wrong, O Maneater," the shaman finally quit pretending to read the entrails and pointed to the ground. "The vision was a warning, not a promise of things to come. Gor-Gor has given you many victories, but you have not given him his due! You must give him a sacrifice, and soon, Warleader, or he will smash you with his terrible fist!"

Zlatagh's expression mingled anger with relief as his face flushed dark green with shame. The shugaba'ugh murmured and muttered amongst themselves; the shaman spoke truly. As their warbands had rampaged through Man village after Man village for weeks, as they fled from the mounted patrols that the Men sent out against them, then regrouped to rampage again, Zlatagh had not once halted the campaign long enough to honor the terrible war god or give thanks for the favor he'd been given.

"What does Gor-Gor want?" he asked.

"The war god demands his due! Give him fire and blood and honor. You have captives in the corral. Let them be sacrificed in the morning, then pile their skulls high into an offering to Gor-Gor Blood-bather, Gor-Gor Flesh-chewer. Let their blood be drunk and their flesh be devoured, that every orc in your army will know that they eat by the will of Gor-Gor, that they slay by the will of Gor-Gor, that they triumph by the will of Gor-Gor!"

Zlatagh looked out at the assembled warband leaders to gauge their mood. The shugaba'ugh stared back at him expectantly; Lugbol had the impression that most of them were hoping the warleader would have the sense to heed the shaman's warning. Seeing no signs of challenge or contempt, Zlatagh nodded and raised his fist, still splattered with the blood of the shaman. "Gor-Gor speaks in blood. Zlatagh hears! I will give every Man captive here to the war god. And each shugaba gungiyar shall bring a trophy to cast upon the fires! Gor-Gor has given us victory over Men!

Gor-Gor will give us more victory over Men! I have said this, I, Zlatagh
Maneater!"

"Maneater!" the shugaba'ugh chanted, and their enthusiasm was not
entirely feigned. Lugbol, for one, was content to know that he and his
kors would have at least two days to rest before departing on their next raid.
"Maneater!"

But he was not entirely confident he would get much chance to rest when
he caught a frustrated Snaghak staring at him with a murderous gleam in
his yellow eyes. He didn't know what the orc from lower Gog was up to, but
he knew that it would be unwise, and perhaps even fatal, to let his guard
down as long as Snaghak and his three hundred-strong gungiyar were in the
same camp. He didn't think Snaghak would dare to openly attack him, not
as long as Zlatagh's ban on clan wars was in effect, but he wasn't about to
go out and squat alone in the dark anytime soon. If Snaghak didn't have a
night-stabber or two sneaking about and keeping an eye on his tent, Lugbol
would volunteer his entrails for the next reading.

The kors were singing again when he reached the tents allotted to his
warband, their deep bass voices raised in an old campfire favorite.

> "A Goblin's arse is green and tight,
> "An Elven arse is white.
> "A Kobber's arse is small and pink,
> "A Man's arse is just right.
> "A Kobold's got a furry arse,
> "A Troll's big arse is stone.
> "And you'll damn well leave the bloody Dwarf alone,
> "Save the Dwarf for the cookpot!"

"I want three guards on all four sides," he told Ghurash, his senior
galvebel, who was roasting something on a stick over the fire. Ghurash's
once-powerful frame was now wiry like a goblin's and his mane was streaked
with white, but he was a wily old kor and one of the few orcs with whom
Lugbol could share his doubts without announcing them to the rest of the
tribe. "That yellow-bellied bastard from Gog is up to something. You know,
I had the idea he was waiting for the shaman to do something, point me
out as a traitor or something, right up until the first one went kreara and
started babbling about how we was all going to die."

Ghurash frowned. "We all going to die?"

"Yeah, iron demons with wings made out of fire killing everyone. Like I said, kreara."

"Ain't never heard of no iron demons. Some of the Man cavalry wear iron though."

"They don't got no fire-wings."

The kors came to the chorus and they launched into it with the full-throated enthusiasm of the half-drunk.

> "Save the Dwarf, save the Dwarf,
> "Save the Dwarf for the cookpot.
> "Throw the one you caught,
> "In the fire red-hot,
> "Save the Dwarf for the cookpot!"

"No, they don't... unyi!" The galvebel had been absent-mindedly at one of the burning logs with his stick, and swore as whatever he was roasting caught fire. He lifted the stick off the fire and smashed it into the dirt repeatedly, switching sides with each blow to extinguish the flames. "Want some?"

Lugbol stared at the blackened, dirt-encrusted goblin's foot. "Nah, I think I'll save my belly for tomorrow. There will be Man-flesh a-plenty. Zlatagh is going to give the heads of all the prisoners to Gor-Gor, then feast us."

"Suit yourself." Ghurash tore a strip of black flesh from the foot and tossed it on the fire, then dug out a piece of pale yellow meat with a claw and popped it in his mouth. "You said we have to sacrifice something too?"

"All the gungiyar'ugh are to give up a trophy. I think we'll have to give him the keg."

"The sweet firewater?" Ghurash couldn't have looked more horrified if Lugbol had announced he was volunteering the galvebel for a diplomatic squagging by a squad of dwarves. "You can't mean that!"

"I don't want the kors getting drunk on it tonight when that kob-squagger Snaghak is after my vank. They think they're hard now, but you know as well as I do that they may as well be skwaaks for all the real fighting they've seen. It's one thing to burn down a few Man villages with only a few handfuls of agha'ugh to defend them, it's another to fight real kors with their blood up. And for all that Snaghak is a sack of rank unyi, he's got more siri-kors than we do."

"Squats!" Ghurash said morosely. But he didn't argue.

"See the guards are posted on the perimeter. And set a pair on the firewater too. I don't want any 'accidents'. Tell them if I find it's been tapped tomorrow, I'll skin them. Now I'm going to sleep. Tell the first watch to wake me at the change!"

Lugbol made his way through the camp to his tent, which was in the center of the area allotted to his gungiyar. Twice the size of the others that surrounded it, it was made from tanned boarskin and featured his prize possession, a bearskin liberated from a Man village the previous moon that now served as his bed. He carefully unwound the bandage, which was already filthy and stained even though he'd washed it only three days prior, and examined his burned arm.

That little mage-bitch had damn near cooked it for him. The raid on the village had gone smoothly enough, but then he'd lost twelve good kors to a single Man clan living outside it. He'd nearly lost the arm too, but fortunately, one of Zlatagh's shaman had been raiding with them and promptly cast some sort of ice spell on it that prevented the spellfire from burning the flesh down to the bone. A pair of healing spells had kept the rot demons from eating the burned flesh, and now the angry, twisted scars that ran from his claws to his elbow were growing shiny, indicating that he'd soon be able to use it again.

Damn the little bitch!

Recovering the use of his cleaver arm couldn't happen too soon for Lugbol, because he couldn't count on his galvebels to keep order in his stead much longer. Fortunately, Ghurash was too old to aspire to kai hari shugaba and Korpaghu only opened his mouth in order to eat. Neither of them had any ambition to replace him, and both of them knew that whoever took Lugbol's place would want his own galvebels. So, the two of them cracked down hard on any orc who so much as hinted at the idea that Lugbol was unable to lead the gungiyar's kors into battle with only one arm. Lugbol himself had cracked the pate of one piss-taker who'd called him One-Arm to his face; he might not be clever with his left arm, but it didn't take a lot of cleverness to swing a wooden club.

He flexed his fingers slowly and winced as the thick scabs cracked and began to weep. He didn't have a full range of motion, not yet, but every day he sat, and swore, and sweated as he forced his scarred arm up, then down, then left, then right. Then he would curl and uncurl his fingers, trying to bring the tips of his claws to his palm. Over and over he repeated the exercises, gasping at the pain, but knowing that leaving the arm to uselessly wither and curl would bring about his death almost as quickly as the rot demons would have. There was no place for a one-armed kor in the Maneater's army, except perhaps in the cookpots.

"Boil the dwarf, boil the dwarf!" The kors had come to the end of a particularly vulgar verse describing the violent abuse of an unlucky elf in considerable detail and were launching into the chorus again. Lugbol grinned at their good humor, remembering the days of being a young kor with no responsibilities and nothing more to worry about than what to eat, who to kill, and where something to drink might be found.

He thought about washing the bandage, but decided to leave it for the morning. The shaman had said it was better if he didn't wear it while he was sleeping anyway. He stood up, removed his boar-hide belt, slid his cleaver's scabbard off it, and tossed it to the side. He grunted as he awkwardly lay down using only his left arm, then sighed as he stretched out upon the soft fur of the bearskin rug. It still smelled faintly of the smoke from the fire his kors had set, but that didn't bother him at all. What was smoke, if not the scent of victory?

The flap at the entrance of his tent rustled and Lugbol woke in an instant. Pain flared in his healing arm as he instinctively tried to use it to push himself up; he cursed under his breath, rolled over on his other side, and used his other arm. It was too dark to see anything and he fumbled about uselessly for his spiked club.

"Grun-kor?" a voice said uncertainly. It was one of the younger kors, who only two moons ago had been a mere skwaak with the white line of the battle virgin painted over his nose.

"I'm awake, little brother. Go back to your tent," Lugbol ordered.

"Oi, Grun-kor!" The kor slapped his chest and Lugbol heard his footsteps as he withdrew from the tent.

For a moment, he contemplated lying back down and returning to the dreamless void from whence he'd been summoned. But the thought of the malice in Snaghak's eyes would allow him no rest, he realized, and it wouldn't hurt the spirits of the kors on watch to see their shugaba patrolling the perimeter at night. They'd recovered, mostly, from that unlucky assault on the mage-bitch's house, but being one of the few warbands that had taken heavy losses in an otherwise easy campaign was still a sore spot with many of the more experienced kors. Especially given his bloody burned arm! It was hard to shrug it off as nothing when everyone could see that he could barely hold his cleaver, much less use it.

Damn the little bitch!

He snorted as he slid his scabbard onto his belt and secured around his waist. It could have been worse. One warband had been caught in the open by a full troop of cavalry after ravaging a small farm and lost more than one hundred of its one hundred twenty kors. And a large pack of wolfriders had simply disappeared, although it was entirely possible that they hadn't run into an enemy force but simply wandered off of their own accord. Whenever the orcs got careless about keeping their allies in line, the goblins tended to desert. After the wolfriders didn't return to the camp, Zlatagh damn near chewed the arse off the grun-kor who'd been too lazy to bother paying attention to them.

Outside the tent, the night air was cool. The surrounding woods was loud with the constant cry of birds looking for mates; this time of year the feathered little monsters simply never shut up. Give it up and go to bed, he felt like shouting, but there was little sense in being bitter just because there wasn't a female orc to be found anywhere within a two-week march. Let them have their fun. Someone ought to.

He found the first group of guards standing around a fire on the south side of their tents. They were young kors and he was pleased to see they were alert. They'd heard him coming and their weapons were in hand as they challenged him.

"Who is it?"

"It's Lugbol, your bloody captain!" he snarled back at them.

"Grun-kor!" they said in unison as they put up their studded clubs and stood at attention. "Sir!"

"Seen anything?"

"We saw some kors dragging a gobbo past, but they wasn't ours."

Lugbol nodded. A late night squag or a late night snack, either way, it wasn't his concern. "Look sharp, boys. Just because nothing's happened yet don't mean it won't. And sit with the fire to your backs. Save your night eyes."

They saluted and he moved on through the trees to the second pair. He could see their fire, but he didn't see either of the guards until he was nearly on top of them. There was a sudden rush of motion and then the tip of a spear was pointing at his throat.

"Don't you recognize Lugbol, you damnable idiots!" he cursed them, although he was secretly pleased they were so keen.

"Sorry, Grun-kor!" The spear was lowered, and in the flickering light of the flames he could see the chagrin on the tusked face of the young orc who was wielding it. "Galvebel said we was to be on careful guard tonight. Said some of them damn mountain orcs would be looking to grab us if we didn't look sharp."

"I wouldn't put it past them," Lugbol said gravely, stifling a chuckle. None of the great orcs from the mountains of Zoth Ommog were actually serving in the Maneater's great army of raiders, but they made for a useful bugaboo. "They got nothing but trolls up there. I imagine a couple of sweet young kors would make a right treat for them if they're tired of eating gobbo. And you damn sure don't want a troll's vank up you!"

The two young kors laughed, as he intended. But then something in the distance caught his attention and he turned away from them. Lugbol's warband had been assigned a spot towards the southeastern side of the camp, not far from the perimeter. But there seemed to be more campfires to the south and east than could possibly belong to the Green Talons, the single warband that stood between them and the ditch that had been dug to ring the big encampment. And the campfires were moving!

"What the hellfire is that?" he wondered aloud. And then he heard the first panicked screams ring out.

He shoved one guard back in the direction of their tents. "You, go to the camp and wake Ghurash and Korpaghu! Tell them to wake everyone and get them armed, but wait for my return." He pointed at the other. "You, with the horn, you come with me!"

He didn't wait for any protests, but grabbed the young kor and began running through the trees toward the mysterious, moving fires. Thoughts of the shaman's disavowed augury filled his mind, but he dismissed them with a snort. Iron demons? Fiery wings? It was nonsense. Or so he thought until a burst of fire filled the night sky and exploded in the treetops about one hundred paces in front of him. He ducked instinctively and the kor with him shrieked in terror.

The first burst was rapidly followed by a second, then a third, and a fourth. Fiery debris could be seen raining down from the trees, and several of the branches overhead caught fire. The Green Talon camp erupted in screams of terror, and in the light of the flames above, he could see the shadowy figures of orcs fleeing in panic towards him.

"Grun-kor!" shouted the terrified kor, holding up the horn. Lugbol nodded quickly.

The kor raised the horn to his lips and blew three times, then waited a moment, and blew three times again. The low blasts echoed through the dark forest, over the crackling of the burning trees.

Lugbol wanted to retreat and join up with his kors, but first he needed to find out what foe was attacking them. They were coming from the wrong direction to be Men; was it possible that the dwarves were coming up from below the ground using one of their infernal tunnels? Or it might be elves, as they were in what was sometimes called the Elvenwood, after all.

He saw a burst of light growing brighter and threw himself aside. Unnecessarily, as it turned out, as the huge flaming projectile struck the ground about twenty paces in front of him and ten to his left, bounced once, and then buried itself in the trunk of a tree so hard that Lugbol felt a tremor in the ground under his feet. He stared at it in disbelief. It was a giant spear, bigger than a troll's spear, coated in some sort of pitch and then set alight. The flames burning in the treetops above them weren't magic, he realized, but artillery!

And who the hell dragged artillery into a forest? The spear must have been hurled by some sort of massive crossbow! As he picked himself up off the dirt and retrieved the club he'd dropped, a second flaming spear came flying towards him and transfixed a retreating orc though the back. Pinned to the ground and mortally wounded, the orc howled in agony as the fire rose up from both his front and back.

Crying, shrieking, cursing, and wailing, orcs rushed past him on every side, babbling nonsensically about dragons and demonfire. As Lugbol worked his way through the trees against the tide of retreating kors, most of them naked and with their hands coward-empty, he began to hear the clash of metal on wood, metal, flesh, and bone. He glanced to his side and was a little surprised to see the guard-kor was still with him. The young orc was shaking, and he was gripping his club with knuckles that were pallid with fear, but he nodded at Lugbol all the same. The moving fires were coming closer to them now, and the flaming balls that he assumed were being flung by catapults were now flying over their heads.

Then he caught a glimpse of one of the attackers. It was about the height of an orc, but considerably more slender, and covered from head to toe in metal armor of a sort he'd never seen before. Too short to be an elf, too thin to be a dwarf. A Man, he thought, but different than the sort of men he'd been slaughtering in recent weeks. In one hand it bore a torch, in the other a strange weapon that looked more like a long, thick knife than a proper sword. But the warrior man knew how to use it, as Lugbol saw it stab one orc with the knife, then thrust its torch into the face of a second orc. The orc shrieked, and as it raised its hands to its face, the metal-clad attacker ran the orc through.

Before long a second iron-covered man joined the first, and then a third. They cut down what little resistance offered itself without taking so much as a scratch. They were wearing their torches affixed to their shoulders.

Wings of fire! Iron demons! Lugbol couldn't prevent the dreadful thought from entering his mind. He turned to the guard.

"I've seen enough. Let's get back to the others."

The young kor didn't need any further encouragement. He fled, and Lugbol, with his one arm bound to his side, found it hard to keep the pace. He was panting hard and his side was burning by the time they reached their camp and found Ghurash haranguing several kors who were too drunk to stand in formation while Korpaghu was waving his cleaver and threatening to split the skull of any kor who joined the growing number of orcs in loud and frightened retreat. It was a sight to make a shugaba proud. The warband was standing fast, it appeared to be mostly present, and every single kor there had his weapon out and at the ready.

"Grun-kor!" The cry went up as soon as he staggered into view. The two galvebels whirled around, their relief plain to see.

"What in the name of Gor-Gor's giant balls is going on?" Ghurash demanded.

"Man attack. Not savon'ugh like we've seen before. Iron men. They have artillery that throws fire."

"Didn't think it was squaggin' dragons," Korpaghu rumbled.

"Do we fall back? Or do we try to hold them?"

Lugbol thought quickly before answering Ghurash. His kors were too lightly armored to stand before the iron men and the clubs most of them carried were more likely to splinter on those strange metal helms than do any harm. And there was something else, too. The iron men had attacked at night, and yet they hadn't sought to conceal their assault. They could have infiltrated the Green Talons' tents and killed dozens of kors before the alarm went up, instead, they attacked in the loudest, most conspicuous manner possible. Were they stupid or was it possible that they were just that overconfident?

Comprehension dawned. It was neither.

"They're trying to drive us," he hissed, more to himself than to his galvebels. The savon'ugh army had been camped outside the forest, only a full day's march away, waiting for Zlatagh to emerge and give them the battle they were seeking. Unlike the iron men, the savon'ugh feared the forests and seldom did more than send mounted patrols into them to chase down raiding parties. But the iron men did not fear the Korokhurmagh, and with their fire and their metal, they were seeking to drive Zlatagh out of the safety of the trees, where the savon'ugh would slaughter his lightly armed raiders.

He needed to warn Zlatagh! But already he could hear that the gungiyar'ugh to the north of them were in retreat. By the time he and his kors reached Zlatagh's tent, Zlatagh might be long gone. Lugbol could try to stand and buy Zlatagh enough time to stop what appeared to be a rout in the making, but he could not imagine Zlatagh would be able to get the panic-stricken orcs, to say nothing of the easily frightened goblins, under control before dawn. And by dawn, he and every last kor in his warband would be dead.

To hell with the Maneater, he decided. He didn't owe Zlatagh a damned thing. And to hell with the rest of the shugaba'ugh. His only concern was to protect his kors, and the best way to do that was to get out of the trap that the iron men had set. He looked to the southeast. In the darkness, it was not hard to see the fiery focus of the iron men's attack as well as the extent to which their line was spread out. The southeast was blocked, but due south was dark and altogether devoid of fire. He came to a decision and raised his voice as he addressed all one hundred of his kors.

"Stay close! Stay close! And I mean close enough to bugger the kor in front of you if he stops! We're going to run past them. No torches; use your nose and ears to follow each other. Keep your damn mouths shut, keep clear of the fires, and keep your clubs ready in case we run into trouble!"

"Grun-kor!" they shouted. They didn't really care what the orders were. All they wanted was for someone to give them something to do that would keep their minds off the dark and noise and fire and fear.

"Bring up the rear and keep them moving," he told Korpaghu. "If anyone falls behind, leave them."

"Oi, grun-kor!"

He looked at Ghurash. "If Zlatagh stands, we hit them from behind. If he runs, we fall back to rejoin Azzakhar and the main army."

"We're right behind you, Lugbol."

"Good!" Lugbol took a deep breath and took another look at the advancing fires to the southeast. He thought he could see firelight glinting off the armor of the approaching iron men. Before he could second-guess himself, he waved his arm and broke into a loping stride, leading the gungiyar towards the waiting safety of the darkness.

THEUDERIC

THIS WAS SUPPOSED to be an army? Upon cresting the hill that overlooked the valley containing the prince's camp, Theuderic pulled up his horse and stared in disbelief at the view in front of him. What he saw was about as far from the well-disciplined order of the late Red Prince's camps as was possible to imagine. There were no fortifications, not even a ditch, tents were erected haphazardly without any order or pattern that could be detected, not even from above, and there were horses, cows, sheep, and pigs wandering freely about the fields, grazing and sleeping and relieving themselves wherever they saw fit to do so.

Not a single body of men was at drill anywhere. He saw no sign of any artillery, nor any evidence that any was being built, no sign of any guards or patrols, and worst of all, no indication that any accommodations had been made for keeping the sewage outside of the camp. He glanced at his companions; they might be young and inexperienced, but judging by the bewildered looks on their faces, they were just as surprised by the dreadful state of the prince's army as he was.

He was, however, able to identify the prince's tent, as he could see a bright red ribbon floating from a spire that rose above the largest tent below. After having spent weeks in the company of the Amorrans, and having seen them painstakingly build and tear down their fortifications on a daily basis, he didn't know if he was more offended or simply embarrassed for his liege lord. Or frightened; if Étienne-Henri was so incompetent that he couldn't even command a proper encampment, what were the chances he would be able to defeat an army of marauding orcs?

It occurred to him that the best service he could provide the crown at this point would be to walk into the prince's tent and murder him outright, openly and without remorse. Unfortunately, it seemed unlikely that the king would be inclined to accept any such intemperate action.

"Come, gentlemen. Let us go and meet our new commander."

None of the other mages spoke so much as a word in response. Damn you, du Moulin, he thought, not for the first time.

They rode down the hill and ignored the blandishments of whores and merchants as well as the curious glances of men-at-arms and brawny young peasants who were gathered around a pair of wrestling men. Few seemed to grasp the significance of their blue cloaks; certainly no one saluted or asked them their business. Although the sun had not yet reached its peak, everyone appeared to be more than a little drunk, no doubt courtesy of the wine and ale stews that were nearly as ubiquitous as the whores. A penny a cup, drunk right there on the spot, and if the quality left something to be desired, few were likely to care after their second or third one.

At least the prince, or someone close to him, had enough sense to set guards at the entrance to his tent. Theuderic bristled at the sight of them wearing the red livery of the heir, even though he knew it wasn't meant as an insult to the memory of Charles-Phillippe. But he couldn't help being a little haughty with them.

"We are magiciens du guerre of L'Académie des Sage Arts. We have been ordered to attend the prince by order of the Grandmagicien. Is His Royal Highness within?"

The two guards looked at each other. The older one, an obvious veteran, nodded. "I shall tell him of your arrival, Seigneur. May I tell him your name?"

"De Merovech."

The guard bowed respectfully and disappeared inside the tent. He reappeared a moment later.

"The prince will see you now, Seigneur de Merovech, Seigneurs."

The interior of the tent was not in as much disarray as the camp containing it. It was expensively appointed, and indeed, looked as if Étienne-Henri had simply arranged for the furniture from one of his residences to be transported here. There was a divan and a pair of comfortable chairs arranged around a small table, a large wooden desk with occultic images carved all over the legs, and a proper set of table and chairs at which eight could comfortably dine. It was readily apparent that the prince was not intending any rapid advancements or retreats.

Étienne-Henri himself was seated behind his desk, and he had the good grace to rise in welcome. He was a small man, a head shorter than his brother, but more handsome than Charles-Phillippe had been. Where his brother had been a two-handed broadsword, Étienne-Henri was a rapier. A razor-sharp rapier, Theuderic reminded himself, and quite likely one that had been dipped in poison. He might be incompetent with regards to military matters, but he appeared to have no dearth of cunning where politics were concerned.

There was also a second man in the room, wearing the livery of Étienne-Henri, but olive-skinned and more lethal in appearance. He had a lean, predatory look to him, and he reclined in his chair as if he were a snake coiled about himself. This must be the deadly Donzeau of whom he had been warned, Theuderic thought, although he could detect no sign of sorcery about the man. He noticed that Donzeau, if it was indeed Donzeau, did not see fit to rise from his seat.

"My dear Theuderic!" the prince exclaimed with a smile, as if he was genuinely pleased. "I rejoice that you have come to me upon the very eve of battle! In fact, I find myself more glad to see you than I would be to be visited by all the Immortels of L'Académie!"

The very eve of battle? In all his years, Theuderic had never seen a less prepared military force, not even when he helped Marcus Valerius take the unsuspecting Legio XV by surprise in its own castra. He bit back his first three instinctive responses and forced a smile. "You praise me too highly, your Highness."

"It has nothing whatsoever to do with your talents, my dear battlemage. I am more interested in your acquaintances. Are you familiar with an Amorran general by the name of Valerius Cavator, by any chance?"

"I... I am, your Highness." Theuderic didn't believe it was his place to correct the prince on the Amorran's agnomen.

"Very good. Then we have much to discuss. But not, I think, in front of your colleagues. What are their names?"

Theuderic introduced his four companions, Ambroys, Maussart, Sebastien, and Talbot. Each mage, well-drilled in the proprieties, stepped forward and bowed as his name was announced. For his part, Étienne-Henri nodded at each man, then glanced at the seated man. "I bid you welcome. This is Guilhem Donzeau. He is, for all intents and purposes, my second-in-command, and he speaks with my voice. He will find you quarters; I shall send Seigneur de Merovech to you when I am done with him."

Donzeau uncoiled and rose, seemingly as unimpressed with the prince's announcement of trust in him as with the presence of the five battle-mages. He was of a height with Étienne-Henri, perhaps a little taller, and he moved with the grace of a skilled swordsman. Theuderic would have given much to understand the nature of their attachment, but he knew no more than du Moulin had told him. Donzeau had not been with the Duc de Chênevin on his previous campaign.

"Monseigneurs." His voice was deeper than Theuderic expected, and his bow was just deep enough to avoid any suggestion of insolence. Was there a hint of sarcasm in the man's voice or was it merely his imagination? "Your presence is most welcome here. If you will accompany me, I will find you suitable accommodations."

Donzeau bowed again, this time to his prince, and led the four mages from the tent. Étienne-Henri turned his attention to Theuderic and the false friendliness disappeared from his face.

"So."

Theuderic smiled coldly. "So… your Royal Highness."

"What am I to do with you, sieur mage? Are you D'Arseille's eyes and ears?"

"I am not," he answered truthfully. Du Moulin was not D'Arseille, after all. "I am here for the very reason you mentioned. I was in Amorr last year and I am acquainted with the legion and its commander. Since the Valerian is now an ally of the crown, I expect I may be of some assistance to you with regards to him and his legion. The Amorrans are a haughty and difficult lot, and as they very nearly outnumber the forces of the crown, it is believed some degree of delicacy is desirable. As for what you are to do with me, I suggest that you do what you did not three years ago and listen to me when I advise you on matters military and magical!"

He was surprised when the prince unexpectedly laughed.

"That's the problem with you, de Merovech. You're too damn servile. No wonder my brother valued you."

"Perhaps you should consider doing likewise, Highness."

"Perhaps I will. Very well, sieur mage. Advise me concerning the Amorran general. Would you say that he is a man of his word? I don't mean in terms of loyalty. I just want to know if he is reliable or not. If he says he is going to do something, would you say he is a man one can reasonably expect to follow through?"

"I should say that depends upon the word. What does he say he is going to do?"

The prince selected a half-unrolled scroll from the various documents on the table and slid it across to Theuderic. "Kill a quantity of orcs, apparently. Beginning tomorrow morning, if I have understood the man correctly."

Theuderic blinked. "Your Highness, I intend no criticism, but what I saw in your camp here is not an army fit to meet twenty-five thousand orcs in battle!"

"Of course it isn't," the prince said dismissively. "Do you take me for a fool, de Merovech? Believe it or not, I have learned considerably since that disaster of a campaign in the south three summers past, and I am perfectly aware that I have been set up to fail here by those who have not gotten over their disappointment that it will be me, and not my brother, who will succeed my father to the throne."

"No, Highness, but—"

"This so-called army of orcs was never an invasion force! Do you not understand that? Despite their quantities, they are pillards, nothing more. They never had any intention of meeting us in battle, a battle I was not given the means of fighting in the first place. They ran from the border lords every time they managed to get one hundred horse together and they have run from me. The Haut Conseil knows this. Look at you! D'Arseille belatedly sends me five battlemages when twenty would not suffice for a genuine battle of this size. Perhaps you do not take me for a fool, de Merovech, but it seems d'Arseille and de Beaumille do! If they sent me here to fight, which I very much doubt, then you cannot deny they sent me here to lose!"

He gestured towards the east and shook his head. "And yet, it appears their machinations may come to no avail. Read the scroll."

Theuderic picked it up and read it. He whistled softly. It was indeed a letter from the young Amorran. His eyes met the prince's. Now he understood.

"Hence the question. Can he do as he claims?"

"He can certainly make a credible effort." Theuderic thought back to his short time with the legion. If the orcs were reluctant to meet the lords of the March in battle, they would not even try to stand before the Amorran heavy foot. As to whether the Valerian could frighten the orcs badly enough, and harry them long enough, to drive them a full day's march northwest with only one-fifth their number, that seemed difficult to believe. But then, Theuderic had seen—had helped—the man take a fortified castra garrisoned by an entire legion without suffering a single casualty. "It would not be madness. He is intelligent and careful. If he says he will do it, I think it considerably more likely that he will succeed than fail. It would be reasonable to plan accordingly."

"His men-at-arms must be of exceedingly high quality."

"Without question. Their foot is armored nearly as well as our knights, and they carry great shields that cover them from chin to shin. What they lack in our cavalry's mobility, they more than make up for in numbers and discipline. When pressed, they can march forty leagues in a day, fully laden. And their artillery is equally well-adapted to field or siege."

"How superlative of them. Did you observe any weaknesses?"

"Their weakness is their horse. Their mounts are small and slow, their knights are more lightly armored than their foot, and they are not accustomed to the stirrup, so they usually rely upon spears and swords instead of lances."

"They are not? Strange, that."

"Perhaps. My sense is that they have little use for cavalry, except as scouts."

"The more fool them. That is good to know. But, de Merovech, I expect that you will see this Amorran presents us with a problem. While we may safely assume that the orcs will not be arriving in any shape to give battle, assuming that they arrive at all, as you have observed, we are less than entirely prepared to take advantage of the situation."

Theuderic did not look away as Étienne-Henri stared at him, challenging him to cast the blame where it was due. He merely smiled and shook his head, declining the bait.

"Your Highness, while I will not deny the state of your forces are not what one might wish them to be, the undeniable fact of the matter is that the strategic situation has changed, and it has done so in an unforeseeable manner. You know very well I did not fear to criticize your decisions with regards to such matters in the past, nor will I fear to do so in the future. After all, that is the duty of a kingsmage."

"You show unexpected promise as a courtier, Monseigneur de Merovech."

Theuderic shook his head. "I am not flattering you, Highness. The simple fact is that the levies would be all but useless even if they were in good order. Even your men-at-arms are of limited utility here. What we are contemplating here is a pursuit, albeit a pursuit in which the defeated foe is running towards us rather than away."

"So you believe it is only our cavalry that counts."

"For the most part. Although I suspect the prince may find our services to be of use as well."

"But we have only seven hundred horse! The Count of Jevey might be good for another fifty; he has been promising them for the last week. Even if he finally comes through, though, that is only seven hundred fifty in all."

Theuderic smiled. For the first time since setting his eyes upon the sprawling disorder of the prince's camp, he felt confident of victory. "Your Highness, men have taken kingdoms with seven hundred fifty horse. I believe it will be more than enough to murder a few orcs. Summon your seigneurs and captains, Highness. If you can provide me with a map and a list of the various mounted levies, my colleagues and I should be able to provide you with a tactical plan by the noon hour."

"Monseigneur, it's the third watch." Theuderic groaned as a hand lightly shook his arm. Waking after so little sleep was sheer agony; his thighs were still sore from several days of riding and his shoulder ached for no reason at all. "It's the third watch, monseigneur, you ordered us to wake you."

"I'm awake," he croaked, opening his eyes and confirming that it was still the deep of the night. Above the clearing he could see Arbhadis was the higher of the two moons in the sky, telling him that they were closer to dawn than midnight. With more than a little regret, he sat up and extricated himself from his blankets. He rolled them up, bound them tightly, and then tied them to his saddlepack. After first rooting around in the wrong pocket, he withdrew a small pouch, then made his way over to the fire around which several men were standing. He was relieved to see one of them was Seigneur Roche, the viscomte of the Val-de-Sirine, who was commanding the makeshift company.

"Heard anything yet?"

"Nothing out of the ordinary," said the old viscount, whose belly hung well over his belt, but appeared otherwise fit for action. The ends of his long white mustache fell down past his chin, but his men were the best of a not terribly impressive lot, so Theuderic had chosen the viscomte for the most important role to be played in the next hours. "Think we'll be seeing signs o' them soon?"

"I would imagine so." Theuderic shooed the men back from the fire and emptied the contents of the pouch onto the flames. The fire immediately took on an unnatural green tinge, sparking comments that were swiftly hushed by the more experienced men. Theuderic ignored the reaction; this was an old, familiar working for him and he barely needed to concentrate in order to utter the words of the spell.

"Hear me, Sebastien," he called out softly. "Sebastien, I am here."

There was no response. He tried again.

"Sebastien? Sebastien, if you can hear me, answer me!"

This time, a faint voice came from the flames. "Theuderic?"

"It's me, Sebastien. Have you seen them?"

"They're crossing the river en masse. There's a ford. I've counted about two hundred so far. Mostly wolfriders. Maybe ten orcs."

"Have they seen you? Are they in good order?"

"No, as near as I can tell they're on the run. We're keeping our heads down."

"Good. Stay on the far side of the river. We'll hunt down the wolves. You watch out for the orcs. They are the main quarry."

"Understood. But I will have to put the fire out. I think we'll have to move soon."

"Never mind that. Use the horns if you need help."

"Okay, we will. Good hunting!"

Theuderic laughed and whispered the word that broke the spell. The flames abruptly returned to their normal red-and-yellow shades, sparking some suspicious murmuring among the viscomte's men. It was amusing, Theuderic thought, that very men who were disappointed when the king's mages didn't hurl bolts of lightning at the enemy or summon vast winds from the sky were so often alarmed by a simple method of communication. But one of the first things every mage had drilled into his esoterically-talented head at l'Académie was that it was almost always more effective to use magic as a means of enhancing one's conventional forces and making more effective use of them than as a substitute for them. It was a pity they only had the one firestone, but they were precious and he was fortunate to have the one. He glanced at the viscomte.

"Two hundred goblins are crossing a ford. Do you know where that would be?"

Roche looked over at one of his men, a small man who, unlike the others, wore only a leather jerkin and carried a bow instead of a sword. A huntsman, Theuderic assumed. He'd been careful to ensure at least one marcher lord was in each of the five groups positioned inside the great forest. "The smaller one downstream, don't you think."

"Must be. They can't have reached the bigger one yet."

The viscomte nodded to him. "We know where it is. Shall we ride for it, monseigneur mage?"

"Aye, but slowly. No torches! I'll ride next to your guide and leave a trail of witchlight behind me. But tell them not to tarry; the spell won't last forever."

"And when we see the skins?"

"Tell them not to be surprised when their torches light of themselves." Theuderic had prepared one torch for each of the eighty riders in his group; a single word and all of them would ignite at once. He very much hoped they would encounter this first group of goblins before dawn, as the effect promised to be striking in more ways than one. "Then kill everything they see."

The viscomte nodded and walked off to give last instructions to his captains. It wasn't long before they were all mounted and moving deeper into the dark shadows of the great forest. It reminded Theuderic of the border patrols he'd ridden some fifteen years ago, a frightened young kingsmage with his royal blue cloak resting heavily upon his shoulders. Soon the night sky was gone, obscured by the leafy branches high overhead.

He would have liked to check with his other three colleagues, but Sebastien's group had been pushing the most aggressively to the southeast, making it the most likely to encounter the enemy first. There was a certain risk in dividing their force into five parts, but they had all agreed to make contact through the flames at dawn, noon, and sunset, which would hopefully permit them to avoid any one group being isolated and overwhelmed. As long as the orcs failed to rally and regroup, Theuderic was confident that the prince's men would be able to butcher any enemy they encountered with impunity.

Both the prince and his man Donzeau remained back at the camp. They retained a fifty-horse reserve and were supposed to be getting the men-at-arms and the peasant levies in some semblance of order in case the regrouped orcs were able to drive off the five cavalry squadrons and threaten the nearby city of Vallon-sur-Bois. Theuderic had his doubts about them managing the task; he was not counting on the prince's foot being able to do much more than get trampled underfoot in a general rout. But matters shouldn't come to that, especially since Sebastien's first report indicated that the goblin cavalry was still disordered.

The false dawn was just beginning to pierce the darkness of the leafy canopy with faint hints of the new day to come when two of the horses whickered and Theuderic heard movement ahead of them. His horse threw its head up and broke the rhythm of its easy trot, leading him to conclude that the wolfriders were nearby. As the sound of the wolves loping towards them became unmistakable, Theuderic called out softly to the viscomte behind him.

"Now, Seigneur Roche!"

He heard the marcher lord draw steel behind him. "God, King, and Prince!" he shouted.

"God, King, and Prince!" the greater part of the men echoed the cry.

Theuderic counted to ten, to give the men time to find their torches and raise them clear of horseflesh and anything else that might not take kindly to the kiss of flame. "Fiat lux!" he said, triggering the spell, and the forest erupted before the light of eighty torches blazing into life.

The roar of the flames was echoed, then drowned out, by the frightened shrieks of the goblins. There were scores of them not more than an easy spear's throw away, and they pulled up their wolves in sudden terror at the sight of the Savondese knights in front of them. But the wolves were exhausted from a long night of running, their red tongues lolled from their jaws, and eight or nine of them did not pull up, but instead threw their riders before fleeing into the trees. Theuderic could hear a deep-voiced goblin shouting what sounded like orders, but his troops had no time to do whatever he was ordering, because the viscomte's men, led by Roche himself, rode past Theuderic and crashed into their midst, assailing the goblins with sword and torch alike.

Theuderic stayed behind them, content to observe the skirmishing. The viscomte's scout had drawn his bow and was loosing arrow after arrow in the direction of the goblins' shadowy figures; most of them missed, but the man did manage to send one shaft through the throat of a wolfrider, who promptly tumbled from his beast. It was one of the most confusing fights he'd ever seen, and for a moment, he thought one of the knights had gone down, but when he kicked his horse forward to see if he could help the man, he saw that the knight had only thrown down his torch, preferring to fight in the darkness rather than be encumbered by it.

A snarl was the only warning he had as a wolfrider nearly spitted him with a crude lance. He managed to parry it with his staff before pointing it at the goblin and blowing its head off its shoulders with a highly concentrated wind-summoning. It was a useful spell he'd learned from Abattre, an Immortel who unfortunately died in battle ten years ago before figuring out how to scale up the spell for artillery purposes.

Feeling its rider slump in the saddle, the wolf snarled again and leaped away, disappearing into the black trees. The goblins had a modicum of training, Theuderic recognized, but not enough to present the knights with much danger. Neither their poorly constructed weapons nor their wolves' teeth could pierce the marcher knights' armor, whereas a single stroke of a blade or mace was usually sufficient to cut them down.

"Ride them down! Ride them down!" he heard the viscomte shouting and rode in his direction. Theuderic swung his now-glowing staff like an axe as another goblin rode by and his arms vibrated as if he was chopping wood when the staff struck the creature right in the chest. There was an audible crack, and for a moment Theuderic thought he'd shattered his staff, but then he saw the goblin was clutching at its chest as it fell to the forest floor and painfully thrashed about in the mud in its agony. He pulled up his horse, leaned over, and shattered its head with a single savage, downward jab of the staff's iron-shod bottom. He realized he was smiling broadly. War was a terrible thing, there was no question about it, but he would be lying if he didn't admit that he was enjoying himself.

A flaming wolf shot past him, howling in pain and terror, and he laughed. Someone had obviously managed to set the wretched brute alight with his torch. It would make for a memorable sigil, he thought. The Flaming Wolf! If the viscomte knighted anyone after the battle, he would have to be sure to mention the sight. If that didn't prove popular with the men, he would eat his bloody boots.

The goblins were shattered now, fleeing in every direction, and he could see by the bobbing lights of the torches that the knights were beginning to spread out too far. He was just about to send up the green burst of light they had agreed would be the sign to regroup when the viscomte's hornbearer sounded the recall with two short blasts, a brief pause, and then another two blasts. Almost immediately, the lights began to converge, and Theuderic urged his horse towards the gathering of the flames. The knights moved aside to make way for him, and it was not long before he was at the viscomte's side.

"We didn't lose anyone. But we didn't get as many as the buggers as I would have liked," the older man complained. "Fucking cowards knew better than to try to put up a proper fight."

"It's a start."

"Long fucking day ahead of us if we're only going to kill twenty or thirty at a time, Seigneur Mage."

"True enough. Before we go any further, I'd like to see what's going on with the other groups. We're not far from Sebastien and perhaps one of them will have contacted him."

"Who?"

"The mage with Sieur Hirunel."

"Ah, right." The marcher lord cleared his throat and spat. "Do your witcheries, then. I'll tell the men to wet their throats while we wait."

But before he could even dismount from his horse, they heard a horn being sounded repeatedly in the distance. Four short blasts, followed by four more.

Theuderic and Lord Roche looked at each other in mutual alarm. The horn came from further east than Sieur Hirunel's squadron, which meant that it was the one led by the defrocked priest turned routier, Jean de Cervole. The signals had been agreed upon before they separated. One blast meant attack. Two blasts meant regroup. Three signified retreat. And four was a cry for help, indicating that the squadron was outnumbered and in trouble.

The marcher lord looked away and Theuderic suspected he knew what the older man was thinking. If the orcs had successfully regrouped, they might find themselves facing three or four thousand, perhaps even more. It would be insane to take such a risk on behalf of men who were little better than land-pirates.

"The prince would likely look askance at the loss of one of his mages," he commented.

"He'd look a damn sight more askance at losing two, to say nothing of the loss of another hundred fifty horse. And I'd look askance at me gettin' et by them monsters."

"I can see where it would be tempting to leave de Cervole to their tender mercies."

"Grey-toothed bastard tried to bugger one of my squires two summers ago. If it was just him, I'd leave him for the damn orcs. And half his men are scum too. But they got Joscelin de Courcillon and Michel de Brienne with them. They're good lads."

Theuderic waited. He could hear when a man was trying to talk himself into something he really didn't want to do. And, to be honest, Theuderic wasn't terribly enthusiastic about the idea of riding to the squadron's rescue himself. The idea of galloping into the woods and butchering hundreds of defenseless orcs had seemed dangerous, but viable under the mid-day sun in the safety of the camp. Now, with the dawn threatening to break upon the horizon, it struck him as insanely stupid.

The viscomte sighed. "Ah, well, I never wanted to die in bed and both my sons are grown men. And I expect my wife will sleep better without me snoring. Anyhow, so long as we don't get ourselves ambushed and surrounded, we can outrun the stump-legged sons of whores. I suppose you can scare up a trick or two to give us a head start, Sieur Mage?"

"Without a doubt."

"Good man. You remind me of Amand. What was his name? Estochait, I think. I rode the border patrol with him."

Theuderic blinked. Amand Estochait was an Immortel, and so fat it was hard to imagine him ever sitting a horse. "You knew Estochait?"

"Damn good man with a timely fire spell," the viscomte declared with a faint smile. "So after all these years, here I am, still riding the woods with a damned bluecloak, hunting orcs. Well, shall we get on with it, Sieur Mage, or shall we leave the verdards to bugger the bloody curé in peace?"

Theuderic glanced back at the men. Most of the riders were covered in varying amounts of green blood. He saw no fear in their eyes, only anticipation. He nodded to the old nobleman.

"Keep it close, lads," Lord Roche's voice boomed out through the trees. "You heard the horns. That damned de Cervole has got hisself in trouble and it's our duty to see that he dies the death he deserves, with a rope around his fat neck! We already had goblin for the starter, so let's go kill some orcs for the next course!"

The men roared, more than willing to follow the viscomte into more slaughter and bloodshed. Theuderic laughed, though he wasn't sure if it was the thought of Amand Estochait on a horse or the world-weary expression on Lord Roche's white-mustached face that amused him more. He kicked his horse into a canter, ducked under a low-hanging branch, and wondered what on Earth had convinced him to let the old man talk himself into rescuing the others.

LODI

I T WAS the fourth day of their journey downward and Lodi found himself beginning to fantasize about pushing his pretty young travel-companion off the cart. He would have thought her mute were it not for their single earlier exchange; she responded to most of his conversational overtures with a flat, uncomprehending stare that would have done credit to an orc being lectured on the gods by an Amorran priest. It was maddening to sit so close to her in the darkness, knowing that she was there, smelling the alluring scent of her body, and not even being able to talk to her. For a dwarf who had been away and above for very nearly a year, it was something akin to torture. Even if she had been an older dwarfess, like the Bodel-wife, he might have found her tempting. But the young Deepling was as exquisite as a newly found gold vein rated at more than 20 unsam per tonne!

His one saving grace, the one thing that kept him from giving into the temptation to take her in his arms or make a fool of himself by trying to kiss her, was the fact that he was still in a considerable amount of pain. His wounds were healing, but they were far from fully healed, and indeed, twice each day Myf crushed a bit of glowmoss and checked his bandages in the dim green glow it cast, changing them if she deemed it necessary. Her touch was always light and gentle, and if he closed his eyes he could almost imagine she was caressing him. And yet, despite her tenderness, she never said a word nor evinced even the slightest interest in any of his conversational gambits. By the end of the second day, he gave up trying to break through her reserve and contented himself by lying back on his well-beaten leather pack and calculating how much profit his various veins had produced during his absence.

That was one benefit of being an adventurer in the King's service. It kept one's expenses down. On the other hand, it had led him here, where he was lying on his back in the dark, wounded, bored, and frustrated. At times, he actually found himself wishing he was back in the troll-infested mountains of Uskiluhk, clinging to the side of a windswept cliff and hoping that an angry wyrm wouldn't notice him. At least in Uskiluhk, there was no possibility of feminine companionship, barring an unlikely decision to court an orc. He knew he was only making matters worse for himself, but he couldn't help it. Each time the pitch dark was sporadically broken by strategically placed glowmoss on the walls, he immediately turned to look at Myf. Even though each flashing, blurry glimpse lasted only seconds, it wasn't long before he had her every feature burned into his mind.

Fortunately, after three days of silently riding in the cart without a single stop, the tunnel-train finally came to a stop in a small, well-lit cavern where the wheels were examined, the pulleys were carefully checked, and another six sections were attached to it, including, much to Lodi's relief, an actual passenger cart. Its toilet facilities were the same seat-and-hole arrangement that he and Myf had been using the last three days, but it had proper seats, genuine storage space, and a roof. Also, the prospect of company that didn't leave him feeling alternately infuriated and foolish was a welcome thought.

He was informed by the station-master that they had less than an hour before the train would automatically resume; the tunnel-train waited for no dwarf. Lodi took the opportunity to visit the cavern's tavern and purchase a lunch of fried cave-fish and ale, which was particularly delicious after the dried rat and fungi on which he and Myf had been subsisting on the first part of their downward journey.

He paid and bought a large sack of spiced mushrooms that looked rather more appetizing than the fungi he'd been given by the surface dwellers. He also bought a small tin barrel of mushroom wine, deciding that it would taste better at cave temperature than the ale since the tunnel-train lacked any deep wells in which to keep it cold. When he returned to the train, he saw a pair of fair-bearded dwarves who must have been brothers, so similar were they, overseeing some crates being dwarf-handled onto the train.

From the way they were strapped and restrapped onto the cart, Lodi assumed they must contain something valuable. Certainly the two brothers looked prosperous enough, wearing thick wool capes and shiny new leather boots. They stared at him curiously until one of them realized he was a fellow passenger, after which they came over to introduce themselves. They were Thori and Yori, custom pickaxe makers, and they were traveling down to the capital to deliver more than fifty orders they'd fulfilled over the last year.

Myf was already seated in the corner of the passenger cart, looking out the glass window towards the darkness of the tunnel into which they'd be descending soon. Fortunately, the cart had a glow lamp built into the ceiling, so there would be no repetition of the silent journey through the darkness he'd endured earlier. Three more dwarves clambered aboard as well, a young married couple traveling deep to visit the dwarfess's parents and a rather shady-looking dwarf with a black beard who claimed that he'd been summoned to serve in the army.

Lodi, observing the poor state of his clothes and the way his heavy coin purse hung from his belt, guessed that he'd been hired as a substitute for one of his wealthier clansmen. It was a legal dodge, but it went a long way towards explaining why most of the regular Army units weren't worth a well-mined vein of marcasite. The married couple introduced themselves as Raldri and Raldrizena, while the shabby soldier-to-be announced himself as Orin Sperrylite. Lodi was relatively sure that was actually the name of the dwarf who had paid his new namesake to stand in for him, but he wasn't inclined to press the dwarf on it.

A small crowd of well-wishers, mostly young dwarfs and dwarfesses, had gathered to see Raldri and Raldrizena off. Raldrizena cried prettily, as befitted a young wife, giving her new husband the welcome opportunity to comfort her. She was sitting between her husband and Myf, who sat next to Lodi, while Orin, Thori, and Yori took up three of the four seats that faced them. The seats slid down to provide makeshift beds, and Lodi was deeply grateful to see that there were bars that would prevent one's neighbor from inadvertently rolling over atop one while asleep.

"So, how long is this going to take?" asked Orin brightly. His face was a portrait in comic dismay when Thori informed him it would take two weeks before they would reach Iron Mountain.

Lodi had no idea how the tunnel-train operated, as near as he had ever understood, it operated by virtue of some form of magic that had something to do with the thermal energy generated deep under the deepest mines, where the rocks themselves were said to glow red, and deeper still, flow like water. All he knew was that it was the fastest way to travel safely under the lands belonging to Men, Elves, and Orcs, and it moved continuously, always maintaining roughly the same speed whether it was sliding down deeper, traversing a flat, or climbing a short rise.

There were two tracks, and very occasionally they saw a line of carts traveling the other way. These rare incidents were cause for celebration, as they broke the monotony, if only for a few moments, and it became the custom for someone to share with everyone from their stock of alcohol, be it Lodi's keg of mushroom wine, Yori's rather more expensive spirits made from fermented moss, or Orin's eye-watering rotgut that he vowed up and down was made from crushed quartz.

Only Myf refused to partake on such occasions. At first, her refusal to talk to anyone inspired some annoyance in the others, particularly Orin, but on the third day, when Lodi left the passenger area to use what passed for the facilities, he came back to see that Myf had commandeered his seat and was whispering quietly in Raldrizena's ear, who was now sitting in Myf's seat. He shrugged and sat down next to Raldri, for whom he had a fair amount of sympathy, given that the young dwarf's position was even less enviable in some ways than his own.

The days passed by slowly, but not as tediously as Lodi had expected. With the exception of Myf, they took turns telling stories about themselves, and both Yori's tales of business deals gone awry and Orin's scarcely credible recountings of unlikely get-rich-schemes and risky wildcatting ventures that were inevitably ruined by the peculations of one of his devious partners proved to be reliably entertaining.

His own recollections of the siege of Iron Mountain, his efforts to free captured dwarves from slavery, and his own subsequent enslavement were also very well-received; Raldrizena, for one, couldn't seem to get enough of hearing about the bloody sands of the Amorran arena. Yori and Thori didn't believe him at first, until he lifted his tunic and showed them some of the scars various gladiators had left him as mementos.

Only Orin didn't enjoy hearing about the siege of Iron Mountain. As Lodi described the vicious battles in dark tunnels against goblin sappers, or the desperate stand of the Kingsguard on the terrible day when South Gate was breached and one in three dwarves of the Guard fell that day before the Troll King's forces were beaten back, the black-bearded dwarf's face gradually turned sickly green.

"Buck up, old fellow," Yori encouraged him. "It's not like you've anything to fear. There's hardly a war on!"

Even Myf turned to look at the yellow-bearded dwarf in astonishment. It turned out that he had been so occupied with meeting their manufacturing orders, working day and night for nearly three straight months, that he had no idea the sky doors had been sealed. And it wasn't until Lodi told the rest of them about his encounter with the tremendous army of orcs, some of which was probably, even now, right over their heads, that he truly began to appreciate the situation.

Lodi had to admit, however, that Yori's reaction was not quite what he would have anticipated.

"Thori, do you know what this means?"

His twin nodded glumly. "We could have started the crew on making battle axes three weeks ago."

Yori waved him off. "No, it's perfect! We're going to be right there at Iron Mountain! While there is a war on! They're probably handing out weapons contracts as fast as the king's scribes can scribble them! Don't you see? This is like hitting a pure vein of silver! No, it's like stumbling upon a fountain of gold!"

Thori glanced at Lodi, a worried expression on his face. Lodi only chuckled. It was hardly news to him that whether wars were fought above ground or below, the vultures would always take their pound of flesh. He leaned towards Orin.

"You see, lad? We all does our part, right?"

The mood of the cart was unsettled by Yori's naked greed, so Lodi reached under the seat and pulled out the bag containing Raldri's Grag stones. Grag was one of the more popular Dwarven gambling games, and the five dwarves had been playing it since the second day. They were playing for small stakes, by general agreement, but by the score on the slate toteboard Raldrizena was keeping for them, Orin already owned a small percentage of Yori and Thori's business. Lodi himself was up twelve unsam of silver, while Raldri was modestly down.

"Who's turn is it to toss?" Orin asked. The tosser rotated every round, as he was not permitted to bet.

"Mine," Thori answered, and Orin handed him the leather sack containing the stones with a wink and an expectant grin. Yori was too cautious and Thori was too eager, and the two of them were usually the first two players out. Grag was a simple game; the object was to score as close as one could to thirty-three without going over. There were sixty-six stones in the sack, each with a point value between one and ten carved into each side, which the tosser threw to each player, one at a time. The highest score won; a tie went to whichever player required more stones to make up the total. If the number of stones was the same, both players flipped over the stone of their choice and the lower number won.

Each round required a copper to buy in, and with each stone tossed after the second round, a player could call "deeper", which would increase the ante by one level. There were seven levels; the deepest was diamond, but here on the cart they were yet to go beyond three, which was silver.

Orin gave the sack a good shake, long enough to ensure the stones were well mixed, reached into it and expertly flicked four stones onto the floor with his thumb. Each one landed neatly in front of the player for whom it was intended, from Yori to Lodi. Lodi's first stone was marked with a five; his second was also a five. When his third stone came up five, the others groaned. A run of three meant that the player could force the other players to flip over one or more of their stones. In practice, this usually meant that the other players would cave, which gave the round to the player with the run.

Yori, on thirty, caved immediately. Thori, on twenty-four, also scooped up his stones; it was considered bad form to turn them over and see what one would have had. Raldri eyed Lodi, then shrugged and tapped the floor with his foot. He was only on fourteen, so he had a fair chance of turning over better stones than he had. When Orin glanced at him, Lodi held up two fingers, so Orin leaned forward and turned over Raldri's first two stones, then tossed him a fourth.

Now the young dwarf was on eleven, three less than Lodi. He smirked and called deeper. Orin flipped two more stones at them. Raldri's stone showed a crown versus a six for Lodi, making it twenty-one to twenty. Lodi raised his eyebrow at that, then called deeper himself. Two more stones and it was twenty-six to twenty-four. Raldri stared at his five stones, then held up his hand. He was standing pat, so Lodi winked at him, called deeper again, and tapped the floor. Now they were playing for gold and Raldrizena was clutching her new husband's hand so tight the young dwarf's fingers were bright red. All Lodi needed was anything between a three and a nine and he would win.

Orin tossed the last stone. It landed near Lodi's small toe; an anvil was carved into it. Eleven points. That put him at thirty-five and he was bust!

Lodi clapped his hands once and grimaced in mock disappointment as Raldri and his wife whooped triumphantly. Going deeper down to gold had put him down and Raldri up, which had been his intention as soon as he saw the twins withdraw. Now that he was safely returned from the Overworld, a gold coin or two made little difference to him. But it might spare a young couple a fight or two over money; he'd seen how hard Raldrizena took her husband's petty losses over the course of their journey. They were only four days out from the city, and now perhaps the lad could buy his wife a little treat at the next station.

But you couldn't simply hand a dwarf charity; that would be an insult to his pride and his dwarfhood. You had to make the lad earn it, and if that meant slapping him down a few times in the process to see if he was dwarf enough to get back up, so much the better.

He looked up and saw Orin stifling a grin. It didn't surprise him that the shabby gragsnagger knew what he was doing. The black-bearded dwarf wasn't just slick with the stones, he was damn good with the odds too. Lodi figured Orin would make himself a fortune in the barracks once they arrived at Iron Mountain if he didn't get himself killed in one way or another.

Then, without warning, the cart began to slow. It was a gradual, gentle reduction in speed, with the train slowing to a speed little faster than a walk, until at last it halted entirely. The seven of them sat there, unsettled but not scared by the unexpected silence, until at last Raldri got to his feet and opened the door, went to the rail, and leaned out over the track.

"We're not moving," he announced unnecessarily.

Lodi pushed himself to his feet. He had a bad feeling about this. Everything had gone smoothly, much too smoothly, if the last two decades of his life were any guide. He looked back at the other carts, and by the flickering of their glowlamps, he could see that their passengers were up and moving about in confusion too.

"Better have a look," he said.

"You can't get off!" Yori protested and he reached out to grab Lodi's tunic. "If it starts up again, you'll be left behind!"

"Better me than you, friend." Lodi chuckled as the dwarf released him. "Besides, I got me a feeling that we ain't going anywhere."

"Why do you say that?" Raldrizena demanded, but Lodi had already joined her husband outside the compartment.

"What do you make of it?" he asked the younger dwarf, who was leaning over the rail and peering down into the darkness below.

"Not a damn thing. There isn't enough light to see anything. You'd think they've got an engineer along?"

"Easy enough to find out." Lodi jerked his thumb towards the rear. Go back and see if anyone in the other compartments knows what's up. I'm going to check something."

"What's that?"

Lodi followed the rail around to the front of the cart. Without any glowmoss on the tunnel walls nearby, it was like staring into the mouth of the void. He could sense the huge open space extending for miles before him like a demon's gullet leading down towards its fiery belly, but he could not see it.

His own gut was telling him something, but he couldn't think what it was. Then a thought struck him. He didn't know how the tunnel-train operated, but he knew it operated on heat. Previously, when he'd stood at the fore of the cart, he'd felt a slight heat coming up from the rails on which it ran. Sometimes there was even the faintest of glows in a line that indicated the track. But now, he could see nothing, and he couldn't feel any warmth radiating upward either. Well, there was only one way to check.

He took a deep breath, jumped down from the cart, and kneeled down in the middle of the track, hoping the train wouldn't suddenly spring to life and crush him. But there was little chance of that, for as he feared, the central ridge, a rounded iron tube wider than his leg, was barely warm. There were still some lingering remnants of heat there, but whatever magic or energy that powered it was fading.

He stood up and placed his hands on his hips, looking up at the cart, wondering what under the Earth they were supposed to do. The carts had no form of self-propulsion, and they could hardly drag them along until they reached another downhill section of track. Even if by some miracle they could, unless the track came to life very slowly, they'd run the risk of failing to get on again before the train picked up speed and left them behind.

It wasn't as if they were going to starve. They had sufficient supplies to reach the next station; this close to Iron Mountain there were several stations less than a day apart. What concerned him was what might have caused the system failure. Aside from the siege, when the entire tunnel had been collapsed for ten velkata in order to keep the orcs from finding it and exploring it, he hadn't heard of the tunnel-train going out of order before. It had few moving parts and the technology developed by the legendary Dhorli the Digger had been old before King Svato was born.

"Better not be damn orcs again," he muttered as he climbed back aboard the cart. He'd had about enough of the cursed creatures. He saw Raldri and the two twins were talking in low voices with a strange dwarf outside the compartment. As he slipped under the railing, he grunted, and they turned towards him in near unison.

"This is Khurzo," Yori introduced the stranger. "His brother is the station-master three stops back."

"The rail is cold," Lodi said. "That's why the train ain't moving."

"It's cold?" Khurzo gasped. "That's not supposed to be possible!"

"Jump off and see for yourself." To his surprise, the dwarf nodded and did just that. Lodi shrugged and turned to the others. "Get the lasses to packing as much food and water as they can in whatever we can carry. Then have them make torches from whatever they can find. I got my axe and another knife in stowage. Any of you got any weapons? Or armor?"

Raldri had a long knife, but Yori and Thori were unarmed. "We can open one of the crates, take out the pickaxes," Yori suggested.

"We can't do that? They'll lose a third of their value if they're scratched! How can we say they're new if they're all blunted and banged up?" Thori said.

"We can't sell anything if we get caught unarmed by cave goblins, Thori," his brother pointed out.

"You don't think it's cave goblins, do you?" Raldri sounded nervous. "Or orcs?"

"I don't think anything," he said. "But I know we can't stay here. What we can do is gear up and walk to the next station. It's been a while since we passed the last one, so it can't take us more than thirty-six hours, and probably won't take more'n eighteen. But one thing I learned above is that you don't go nowhere without being ready for trouble."

At first, the twins and Raldrizena resisted the idea of leaving the false safety of the cart. Myf, he was pleased to see, no sooner heard his instructions than she went about the preparations he'd ordered, although she was as silent as ever as she did so. The dwarves on the carts farther back were slow to go about it, judging by the sounds that echoed off the rock walls of the tunnel, but the longer the train sat motionless in the darkness, the more dwarves seemed to decide that they couldn't simply sit there and wait for it to start moving again.

As Myf was tying a second skin of water to the backpack he didn't remember her having, he caught her arm. Her eyes were wide in the yellow glowlight, and for a moment, he almost forgot what he'd intended to tell her. "Look, I know keeping your mouth shut is important to you for Zemtek knows what reason. But I promised those folk that I'd bring you back to your kin and I aim to do that. Now we don't know what's out there in the dark, but if we run into something, and my gut tells me we're going to, you need to listen to me. And that means you've got to talk to me. Can you do that?"

She looked down at the floor. He wasn't certain in the light, but he thought perhaps her cheeks might have reddened somewhat. "We can…

it is permitted to speak to the Skyburned in cases of emergency, and I have been placed in your charge. I am correct in thinking this may be one?"

Skyburned? That was a new one on him. He pursed his lips. "An emergency? I don't truly know, lass. But I seen a fair amount o' brouhahas in my day, and one thing I know is if you wait until you're sure, you'll wait too long."

"I have seen—" she stopped herself. "I know you are a great warrior, Lodi, son of Dunmorin. And you are a good dwarf, even though you are Burned. I will obey you. And I will speak to you since you tell me I must."

He stared at her, and for the first time her innocent emerald eyes met his. Something twisted inside him, something broke, as if a very old scar had finally given way. And he knew, as he looked into her unblinking gaze, that he would die before he would permit anything to happen to her.

"All right, you do that," he said gruffly. Then he turned his back on her and stalked out of the compartment to see how the twins were doing with their damned pickaxes.

By the time the other compartments were packed and ready to leave, more than an hour had passed and even Raldrizena was convinced that the train wasn't going anywhere. Every male dwarf was armed, many of them with the shiny new pickaxes that Yori had mournfully distributed, muttering darkly under his breath each time he ran his fingers over the runes inscribed with the prospective owner's name. They were thirty-six strong, plus another ten dwarfesses who joined Raldri's wife and Myf in the middle of their loose formation.

Lodi, Orin, and another veteran of the great siege took the lead; Boru was forty years older than him, and he had been traveling to Iron Mountain with his great-axe and a full suit of plate armor, complete with helm. They both slung their axes around their backs and carried torches, as did one of every fifth dwarf behind them. Raldri and the twins brought up the rear; Lodi didn't know them well, but he had enough sense of their character that he trusted them to keep the others moving.

"Is this what soldiering is like," Orin asked after they'd been walking for a while. He was panting a little, as they were laboring up an incline that seemed considerably steeper than any they'd climbed on the train.

"You bored?" Boru asked.

"I don't know, I suppose. I mean, we're just going from nowhere to nowhere in the dark."

"Yeah, pretty much," Lodi growled. "Except it ain't so boring when a bunch o' screaming orcs is trying to chop you to bits."

"I suppose boring ain't so bad," Orin said after a moment's reflection.

"No, it ain't," Boru agreed, huffing and puffing in his heavy armor. "Dammit, Lodi, I may have to take this off if we got to keep going up instead of down!"

Fortunately, they crested the rise before too much longer, at which point Lodi called for a halt. He posted one pair of guards ahead and another behind the party; one thing he'd learned about tunnel wars was that the enemy could appear from anywhere, including above or below. After reassuring the grumbling guards that a rotating schedule would be established, he went to find Myf and see how she was doing. She sharing her water with a young dwarf who seemed to be regarding their unexpected jaunt as an adventure and a lark.

"Are you holding up all right?" he asked.

She looked up at him and smiled shyly. "You look very fierce in that armor."

"It beats plate for hiking. I daresay Boru started wishing he was wearing chain before we even hit that hill." He kneeled down and ruffled the hair of the paslido. "You take good care of the lady, now."

"My mama is scared, but I'm not," the young dwarf declared. "I wanted a pick, but they said they was too heavy."

Lodi laughed. "Give it time, little one." He glanced at Myf. "Got that dagger I gave you?"

"Right here." She pulled back her cloak and showed how she'd slipped it into an impromptu rope belt.

"Good," he said. "Things get confusing in the dark. Remember, stay low and strike low, and always slash up, not down."

He nodded to the paslido again and walked back to the front, exchanging words and answering questions without stopping until he'd reached Boru and the two guards.

"Hear anything?"

"Nothing, sir," one of the guards said. He was even older than Boru, but something about the easy way he leaned upon his pickaxe told Lodi he'd seen war.

"Good. Boru, you catch your breath yet? No sense wearing that gear if you're too tired to fight if we get jumped."

"Shut your filthy pyrite mouth," Boru shot back. "Sooner we get going, sooner we get there."

"All right." Lodi took a torch from the old guard and sent the two of them to spread the word that they were about to start moving again. "Tell everyone to stay close, I don't want anyone getting left behind."

They waited and watched the bobbing torch make its way back, then Lodi nodded at Boru and they began their long march anew. The track was entirely cold now and devoid of any hint of life. It was flat for a while, then almost imperceptibly began declining, although not so steeply that it was necessary to lean backward to fight it. The tunnel seemed to be arcing to the left, and for a moment, Lodi could have sworn that he heard mining sounds coming from somewhere overhead. But that made no sense, they were too deep for surface dwellers to be digging down, and too close to the tunnel for it to be a mining operation.

"I can't hear it, but my ears are older'n yourn," Boru said after Lodi drew it to his attention. "This deep, the rocks are alive, and sometimes they talk."

Lodi shrugged. Sometimes the earth really did move, and obviously, that was bound to make some noise. Although there were no visible signs of the next station, he began to feel they were getting close. A faint glow appeared ahead.

"Do you see that?"

"Probably just a waymarker. And not necessarily the last one."

But as they walked on, it gradually became apparent that the glow was too bright to be a mere waymarker. Lodi soon saw that the light was flickering, even as it seemed to be growing in intensity. And then he scented smoke, a more pungent, more powerful scent than the one given off by the torch he was holding.

"That's fire!" he blurted.

"What should we do?"

"I don't know, but we can't go back! Let's go see if we can help put it out. If it gets too big, it could smother us all!" Fire was one of the great fears of the dwarves, it was both their most vital friend and their most lethal foe. More dwarves died every year of smoke inhalation than of mining accidents, getting lost, and cave goblin attacks combined.

He barked word back to the rest and they picked up the pace. But as they drew nearer, the sounds of conflict could be heard. Lodi couldn't tell if it was goblins, orcs, or simple dwarf-on-dwarf violence, but whatever it was, it was definitely no place for paslha and paslidha. He called Raldri forward.

"Pick out ten to stay and guard the others. Fall back about 300 steps and wait one hour, but no more! If one of us doesn't get word back to you then, lead them back to the train and wait there. We'll all leave our food and water here for you; someone will have to come eventually."

"So what's going on up there?" Raldri said, trying, and not entirely succeeding, to avoid sounding relieved that he wouldn't be finding out soon. The clash of metal on metal was more apparent now that they knew what they were hearing.

"Somebody's trying to kill somebody else. We're either going to help them or stop them."

"Okay." Raldri put his hand on Lodi's armored shoulder. "You can count on me, Lodi."

"I am," Lodi said. "Keep an eye on Myf, you'll have to see her deep if I can't."

The younger dwarf nodded; Lodi swatted him on the back and jogged forward to join the makeshift company that Boru had organized into four rows of six. Even in the dim, flickering torchlight he could see that their faces were strained and the knuckles that gripped their shiny new pickaxes were white. Poor lads. It was a hell of a way to go into battle for the first time, untrained, unarmored, and completely uninformed about the enemy.

There wasn't much time for instructions or encouragement, so he kept it simple. "Follow Boru and me and keep it tight, lads. We don't know what we'll find, so be ready for anything. Watch the sides of the dwarf next to you and poke with the flat head, don't swing it and get it stuck. Bash, don't stab!"

He spotted Orin in the second row, his eyes wild with fear in his black-bearded face. "Oi, Orin, you're all right, lad. Stick with me and we'll see it through."

"Just a little sooner than I was expecting, Lodi."

Lodi frowned as half the dwarves burst out laughing even though they couldn't have possibly known what Orin meant. It was nervous laughter, bordering on hysteria. "Keep it tight, lads," he repeated. "Poke and bash, don't swing and stab. Now, follow me!"

He hurled the torch aside and slipped his two-handed axe over his head. Boru was already holding his double-bladed great axe in both hands. Without further ado, he began jogging forward, not looking back to see if the others were following. The sound of battle grew louder as they approached the light, and Lodi could feel a slight warmth on his face from the burning fires.

As they rounded the final curve, he realized that the station, indeed, the town, was under attack. The situation wasn't as bad as he feared, though.

Two buildings at the station were alight, but there was already a team of dwarves busily engaged in putting one of them out with sand, gravel, and water that was being pumped from a reservoir he couldn't see.

He couldn't quite see who their fellows were fighting, as being down on the level of the track, all he could see was the backs of the rearmost dwarves. When they reached the platform, he slid his axe onto it, clambered up, then turned around and extended a hand to help the dwarves following him, pulling them up one after the other while Boru got them back into formation.

He had just gotten back to the front when as something smashed its way through the thin defensive line set up by the station dwarves, felling one dwarf before shoving the dwarf next to him aside. It locked eyes with Lodi as he brandished his axe and then it bared its teeth as it gave an angry, unintelligible war cry.

Lodi nearly dropped his axe. Not because he was frightened, but because he had never, ever seen anything like the creature that stood in front of him, holding a crude iron bar in one hand. It looked like a dwarf, but a dwarf that was encased in some sort of metallic scales instead of skin and its eyes were yellow like an orc or a goblin. Was it armor? Or was it some sort of unholy abomination from the Underdeep?

Whatever it was, it leaped at him, swinging its weapon horizontally at his head. Lodi dropped to one knee and the bar passed over him even as he swung his axe in a vicious plane about two lakets below it. He saw that the creature bled just as red as any other dwarf as the upper half of its body abruptly parted company with the lower half, showering him with its blood.

He rose quickly to his feet, gore dripping from his axe. "Kingsguard!" he roared without even realizing what he was shouting. "Kingsguard!" the dwarves behind him echoed. And then he led them forward into the fray.

STEINTHOR

STEINTHOR STRONGBOW was privy to two secrets. The first belonged to several of the others numbered among Raknarborg's final defenders. The other was his alone. In the meantime, he was greatly relieved to see that the Redcheek's ruse had worked, and he watched as the black sails of the last longship grew smaller as Ulvdræber sailed forth under a dark, starless sky. Soon the longship disappeared into the deepening gloom no eyes, however keen, could penetrate. Even if there were wolves on the shore who had seen Ulvdræber depart, the longship was now safe from any pursuit.

"Fare you well, Skullbreaker," he said aloud. "Fare you well, Redcheek."

He turned back from the arrow-slit from which he was peering and descended down the wooden stairs of the sea tower into the room in the central keep that was now serving as their final staging ground. Armor, shields, axes, and spears were scattered throughout the room, leaned against walls and tables or simply piled haphazardly on the floor. The other four captains were waiting for him there, along with twelve or fifteen other men who were acting as his bodyguard for this, the final battle. All of them were wounded, some worse than others. Horse-Bjorn was drinking from a large mug of mead with his shield arm bound closely to his breast. Ottar the Grævling stood at his side, his face flushed with the iron-fever that would not kill him now. Hrafnkel Half-Giant towered over the rest of them, his head nearly touching the giant beams of the ceiling.

Upon hearing his approach, they turned to him, waiting for his news.

"The Skullbreaker took some persuading, but he went with the Redcheek in the end. Ulvdræber is safely away. I saw no sign of pursuit."

A cheer went up, with two exceptions. The Grævling was lost in his thoughts. The Half-Giant, as was customary, looked vaguely confused.

"Who commands tonight, if the Skullbreaker be gone?"

Not for the first time, Steinthor found himself marveling that despite the man's prodigious strength, he hadn't managed to get himself killed in nearly three weeks of near-constant battle. The Aalvarg aside, it was a miracle that Hrafnkel hadn't broken his massive neck tumbling down a stairwell or falling from a tower. He was clumsy and he was slow-witted, but he could literally rip a wolf-thing in half with his bare hands. Steinthor had seen him do it.

And like the rest of those who remained behind, the giant was badly wounded. He had lost an eye early in the siege, and two nights ago an Aalvarg spear penetrated his thigh. Now he limped worse than Steinthor did, and he needed two men, two strong men, to help him navigate the stairs. The Half-Giant would be among the those who were certain to fall tonight. Knowing he could not retreat, the big man had agreed to meet the final assault on the tower with his twenty-five men. They would hold the line while the others fell back to the keep.

Steinthor had no doubt that Hrafnkel would slaughter many wolves before he fell. But the grey tide was simply too great, and whoever was commanding the wolves seemed to value Aalvarg lives as little as he did those of their enemies.

"I, Steinthor, command, Hrafnkel," he declared loudly. "I promise nothing but death, certain death, a warrior's death. Our plan is simple. Tonight we fight, and tonight we die. Are there any here who object?"

"Strongbow, the Strongbow!" Horse-Bjorn shouted and others were soon to pick up the cry. "Strongbow!"

Steinthor nodded. For years he had followed the Skullbreaker. For one night, and one night only, he would lead the clans. But first, there was something that must be done. He limped into the center of the room, all eyes upon him.

"Hear now the death-song of Steinthor, by some called the Strongbow," he called out to them.

> "The Wolf lies waiting.
> The Moon covers her silver eyes
> In fear and sorrow.
> No more shall I sing.
> Silence will rule over ruins
> Come the dawn morrow

"Never shall they learn,
Fair ladies I have known in love,
From enemies' blows
I backward turned me.
Here shall my body, fallen, lie
Devoured by demons, wolves, and crows.

"Nor shall she taunt me,
Fair Dagna, safe across the sea,
That from swords I fled
Or from wolves I ran.
At Raknarborg I stood among my friends,
The valiant dead.

"Once my courage failed
Before the white-browed jarl's daughter.
To a better man
It was I lost her.
In fear I held my tongue and thus
Dared not ask her hand.

"A lasting sorrow comes
This night to the fair Dagna.
No more shall Steinthor
Hold her in his secret heart.
Wounded and lame, I stand here, doomed,
On this Aalvarg-stinking shore.

"Will it wring the heart
Of the jarl's proud, white-browed daughter,
And the Skullbreaker's wife,
When comes the crow's tale
Of the red end of Raknarborg
And the Strongbow's life?

"Knokkelmanden rides
The Loptrbørn bear him hither
What man here will flee?
Who will run in fear?
I, the Strongbow, will fight the Wolf.

Who here stands with me?

"They come from the North
Mighty flocks of famished ravens
Whom I have fed well.
Once more I feed them.
On my corpse they'll gorge and fatten.
But my spirit,
In Glaðsheimr,
Shall henceforth ever dwell!"

As the last words echoed off the stone walls of the chamber, there was a moment of respectful silence. Then came much whooping and hollering, wooden mugs of mead were raised, and many a surreptitious tear was brushed away.

"Aye, we'll stand with you, you cowardly bastard," Horse-Bjorn blustered as he embraced Steinthor and thumped his back. "Did you really think no one knew you were still besotted with the Skullbreaker's wife after all these years? Fordømme, man, Skuli never forgot how you got there first, but he loved you too far too well to hold it against you."

Steinthor stared at the big warleader, too surprised to speak.

"You knew?" he finally said.

"Who didn't?" Horse-Bjorn laughed loudly. "I suppose there might be a few wolves out there from the outer islands that are still in the dark, but there wasn't a maiden in one of the Fifteen Clans who didn't envy—what did you call her? Ah yes, 'the white-browed Jarl's daughter', the woman who held the hearts of the two greatest warriors left to us in the palm of her pretty hands. Could have been a proper saga in the making there, if only you and the Skullbreaker would have fallen out over her."

"Never once did we speak of it!"

"Sure, and it would have been stupid, considering how we were all fighting for our lives. But men are stupid when it comes to harboring their longships, especially in so sweet a harbor. Believe me, Strongbow, there were women counting their fingers when Brynjolf was born."

"I never touched her, not after–"

"Oh, I know. I know." Horse-Bjorn thumped him on the back again. "But it was a bloody good thing you were away reaving at the time or wicked tongues would have been set to wagging!"

Hrafnkel Half-Giant dragged his huge frame over and lightly placed a massive hand on Steinthor's shoulder. A dark tear-track ran through his dark brown beard under his remaining eye. "Honor to stand with the Strongbow, tonight. We die well, Captain."

Steinthor placed his own hand over the giant's. The sight made him smile; it looked like a child reaching out to his father.

"The honor is mine," he assured Hrafnkel. "We will kill many wolves. Better than dying in bed like a woman or an old man, eh?"

In light of the grim night before them, the mood in the room was surprisingly jocular. The mead helped, of course. This was no time to go into battle sober. He accepted a mug from the Grævling, raised to salute the men nearby, and drained it. If the laughter was a little louder than the jests might otherwise have provoked, and if the protestations of indifference towards death sometimes sounded a little forced, it didn't matter. It was only the way men who lacked true courage found it in the company of their doughtier fellows.

Perhaps they were the bravest of all, Steinthor mused as he quaffed another mug, albeit in a more measured manner. Those who feared death, but feared the contempt of their brothers-in-arms more. He frowned. That didn't make much sense, come to think of it. Well, it probably wasn't worth dwelling on. He wasn't afraid to die, anyhow. He might not be a berserker, biting at his shield and lusting for battle, but he was beginning to feel a little impatient waiting for the wolf to come.

He was just mulling the wisdom of a third mug when he heard someone's boots thumping their way down the stairs from the northern tower. It was young Bosi, he saw, Horse-Bjorn's cousin, who'd been left behind as a result of losing his sword arm at the elbow four days ago. The stump was infected and inflamed, but didn't prevent him from serving as a messenger for the warriors who remained.

"They come," he shouted. "The wolves are coming!"

The men reacted without hesitation, reaching for their spears and shields. Some of the men whose arms were bandaged or missing clamored for help with their armor, and Steinthor helped Horse-Bjorn strap his shield on tightly to his useless arm. The old veteran grinned at him, exposing a line of black and rotted teeth on the left side of his mouth.

"You're a lucky one, lad. A man can't lose a battle that's already lost. If the Choosers turn up their noses at us, I'll see you in the high hall of Hel."

Steinthor nodded, suddenly unable to speak. Horse-Bjorn laughed and stepped to the side as four men, their eyes bright and fey, rushed past them up the stairs.

"Never you mind, Steinthor Strongbow. The Skullbreaker would be proud of you. Not every man could turn a collection of half-dead old men and dying boys into a proper fighting force." He waved to his men. "Come on, lads! With just one arm, I can't hold them off by myself!"

Steinthor nodded at him and looked to Ottar the Grævling and his five men. They alone were still sitting, knowing that there was no need for them to hurry. The Grævling was the most intelligent of the four captains, so Steinthor had put him in charge of their weapon of last resort. Ottar was of an age with Steinthor, approaching his fourth decade, although his grey head made him look older. Steinthor knew Skuli had considered putting the Ulvdræber expedition in the Grævling's capable hands, but a sword-thrust through his thigh had made Mord Redcheek the obvious choice.

"Go," the Grævling said calmly. "Have no fear. If you don't make it back to the keep, I'll see it's done."

Steinthor nodded. He paused for a moment, until he realized he had nothing to say to the man. In a different time, Ottar the Grævling would have likely been his enemy. Now they were brothers-in-arms, to the bitter end. But that didn't mean they had to love each other.

He could hear the familiar howls as soon as he walked out upon the ramparts of the North Tower. The night air was cool and dry. Most of their meager forces were arrayed there; a man could hardly miss the Half-Giant in his position well behind Horse-Bjorn and his rambunctious, half-drunk men. The wind was cold and still blew from the east; the Skullbreaker and Mord Redcheek would be at least six leagues away already. The cries of the wolf-demons filled the night, seeming to come from the north, the east, and the west, everywhere but the vast dark ocean to the south. He could see the enemy fires dotting the land below, although there were far fewer of them than one would expect from a similarly sized army of men.

The Aalvarg had little use for fire, as they neither forged their weapons nor cooked their meat. And unlike a human army, they devoured their dead, which made them particularly deadly opponents in a siege. Even when the nights of the heaviest battles finally gave way to dawn, the only corpses in sight, human or wolven, were on the battlements of Raknarborg. Blood on the ground below and a few scattered remnants of weapons and armor too damaged to be worth scavenging were the only signs there had even been any activity the night before.

The wolf-demons' grasp of tactics was rudimentary at best, which was why Steinthor only stationed a skeleton force on the East and West Towers to alert him in the unlikely event either of them turned out to be the focus of the enemy attack. In fourteen of their seventeen previous assaults, the wolves had stormed the North Tower; one young warrior, dead these last ten or eleven days, had told Steinthor that the bricks on the North Tower protruded more and were therefore easier for the creatures to climb.

He walked over to the ramparts, chipped, blood-stained, and worn down from the repeated attempts to storm them. Four spotters were spread out standing watch across the curve of the tower, all of them young men with sharp eyes. The howls below were rapidly growing louder and closer. He couldn't see the Aalvarg yet, as they were comfortable attacking in darkness and the few torches that were already flickering on the ramparts ruined his night vision. But no matter. They all knew. The wolf-storm was coming.

He turned around and reviewed his front line. The Horse-Bjorn's men were mostly armed with spears and axes, the better to deal with wolves climbing over the walls. He counted six, no seven, big warhammers, as well as two or three makeshift wooden ones made to simply sweep the attackers from the heights. Four men bore torches, ready to light the unlit ones set in the brass fixings as soon as he gave the command. Another twenty stood beside large baskets, in pairs. The baskets were full of rocks and bricks, as what little oil remained was reserved for other purposes and boiling water had proved to be of limited utility against the thick-furred foe. Behind them, on a knee-high platform, were fifteen of the best remaining archers.

The night considerably limited the utility of the bowmen, but the torches let them pick off the occasional wolf, and more than once they had proven themselves useful in turning the tide when the Aalvarg briefly established a hold on a section of the ramparts. One of them now held Steinthor's own bow and quiver; he would join them when the battle was joined.

The men were quiet now, their faces white against the night and set with determination. Even Horse-Bjorn was silent, although he cleared his throat and stepped forward to spit off the ramparts more than once.

Steinthor said nothing. There was nothing more to say. He simply walked along the front of the line and nodded to each man. He knew they would stand, even to the end. The howling continued to grow louder, and now the lower-pitched snarls could be heard as well. The moment was nigh.

One of the young watchmen cleared his throat. "Captain, ah, I think–"

"They climb, Captain, they climb!" A second watcher was less hesitant. "They climb!"

Steinthor sighed. To think that his whole life had been aimed at this night, this very moment. He said a silent prayer to the Hjaldrgoð, asking only for strength enough to prove himself worthy of the Choosers he knew were circling invisibly overhead even now. Then he took a deep breath.

"Watchers, join the line!" he roared with a voice that drowned out the howls. "Fire! Light the fires! Light the torches!"

Two torches tumbled end over end through the air, hurled at the firewood spread out across the entire base of the tower this afternoon. It had been drizzled with the last remnants of their precious oil, so that it would catch easily. And catch it did, as the two torches set the wood alight and quickly spread from one end to another. Several wolves were caught up in the rapidly spreading flames and as their fur blazed, they added their agonized screams to the demonic chorus that filled the night air.

The fire did no harm to most of the wolves, but that was not his object. Between the fire below and the fixed torches that were now blazing, the creatures climbing the tower were no longer cloaked by darkness. Steinthor leaned over the ramparts and looked down. What he saw resembled a mass of huge, gray, hairy spiders as they clambered up the stones, their long, clawed hands reaching out and pulling them rapidly upwards with the help of the purchase provided by their clawed feet. Despite the clamoring of their fellows, they climbed in silence, and several of them trailed long ropes behind them.

"Rocks!" he shouted, urging the men with the baskets forward. They rushed towards him as fast as they could, weighed down by the heavy burden of the baskets they carried between them. By the time they were in position, the lead climbers were more than halfway up the tower, and he could clearly see their bared fangs in their long, wolf-like muzzles. A foul odor rose before them, so musky and so acrid that it nearly made him retch. The smell wasn't unfamiliar to him, but it hit him hard nevertheless.

Then a large boulder bounced off the wall and struck one of the wolves at front of the assault just under its chin. The force of the blow flipped the creature backward and it howled in dismay, its arms and legs flailing wildly in the air. A second stone, aimed more carefully, smashed into a wolf's head and caused it to lose its grip. It fell crashing into the wolf below it; three in all were swept from the side of the tower and sent plunging towards the surging masses.

More projectiles rained down on the climbers. Steinthor saw one wince as it was struck in the shoulder by a brick. It stubbornly pressed itself against the rocks and turned its head just in time to evade a second one, but when third brick smashed into its hand and a fourth crashed into its face, it slowly fell away from the wall, flailing its limbs and screaming in helpless fury all the while.

The hail of stones was brutal. Dozens of Aalvarg were scoured from the tower, and yet for every climber fallen, there were twenty eager to take its place. The foul-scented wave of grey continued to surge higher, as if the ocean was sweeping in over the fortress from the north.

The rocks slowed the attackers down and thinned their numbers a little, but Steinthor knew the Aalvarg would not be dissuaded so easily. He stepped back from the ramparts and found Horse-Bjorn.

"Another five man-lengths," he told the old warrior. "Hit them as soon as they crest."

Then he made his way through the four-deep lines to the archers, where Rennir Longeye was waiting for him with his bow. It was his favorite and his best, its beautiful ash limbs having been artfully carved by his grandfather long before he was born. He picked up a quiver filled with more than twenty shafts and tied it to his belt, then took the bow from Longeye, who had been stringing it. After withdrawing a shaft and attaching it to the string, he took his place in the center of them.

"Remember, lads, it's the hairy ones we're aiming at," he said, provoking an amount of laughter among the men on either side.

Then Horse-Bjorn shouted a battle cry. "Raknarborg!"

In response, the line surged forward to attack the Aalvarg that were finally reaching the top of the battlements. A battlehammer arced high above the press of men before flashing down fast and hard, followed by a second, and a third. They were striking at the hands of the wolves attempting to pull themselves up over the merlons, crushing them between stone and iron. Despite their efforts, a first wolf managed to pull itself atop the stones, where it was instantly transfixed by two spears.

It fell backwards, as did the next wolf to surmount the parapet, nearly cut in half by the Horse-Bjorn's axe. But the third one launched itself forward even as it was impaled, and by entangling the men in front of it, bought just enough time for three more monsters to climb over the wall and throw themselves on the front lines. All three were quickly killed, but they were rapidly replaced as the grey wave smashed into the Horse-Bjorn's suddenly hard-pressed men.

Steinthor pulled the string to his chest and loosed. The shaft flew true and hammered into the throat of a howling wolf standing on the edge of the ramparts. The rest of the archers loosed as well, and nearly ten wolves dropped or staggered backwards, wounded, as at such short range, the arrows slammed into them with enough force for some of the arrowheads to pierce their backs. The moment's respite gave the men at the front just enough time to slaughter the wolves in their midst and reform their shield wall.

In the brief pause, Steinthor saw one man step forward and slash away the rope that one cunning monster had slipped over a merlon before he was killed; with a single blow he likely killed as many attackers as all the archers combined.

The wolves came on, but they seemed vaguely disheartened that their initial attempt to storm the tower had failed. The attack was almost desultory in comparison with the earlier rush, and the Horse-Bjorn and his men fell into a murderous rhythm, smashing the clawing hands, and running through or cutting down any monsters that somehow managed to clamber over the wall. It was hard to tell in the shadows of the flickering torchlight, but as near as Steinthor could tell, only three or four men had fallen, compared to more than one hundred wolves.

The men waited, scratched, bitten, panting, and bleeding.

"Water," he heard someone cry.

"Damn water, bring me beer!" Steinthor recognized the Horse-Bjorn's voice. "Strongbow, looks like they're giving us a breather."

He unstrung his bow, handed it to Rennir, and went to have a look at the situation for himself. At the Horse-Bjorn's command, his men were dragging the dead to the ramparts and hurling them down below, while three of the torches that had been knocked out of their holders were replaced. But the glow from below was gradually fading, and when Steinthor looked down, he discovered why. Not only had a considerable quantity of the wood already burned, but the wolves were methodically extinguishing it by pulling the piles apart and urinating on the flames.

"Pity they're not quite as stupid as they look," Horse-Bjorn said. He had somehow magically transformed his dripping axe into a flagon of ale, which he offered to Steinthor.

Steinthor took a long draught, savoring the cool bitterness in his too-dry mouth. With some reluctance, he returned it to Horse-Bjorn, who drained the remainder, burped long and low, then hurled the empty vessel from the tower.

"Maybe it will brain one of the bastards," he said, wiping his mouth. "Think that's too much to hope for?"

"They'll be coming again soon."

"At least they had the decency to let a man get a drink. Give them that."

"Wish the moons were out to tonight."

But the untimely clouds hid Blood and Bone away. It was as if the gods had turned their faces away, unable to bear watching the carnage to come.

The demonspawn attacked again, snarling and growling in the darkness. The young men with the baskets had replenished their supplies of bricks and stones, but it was harder for them to see the climbers approaching without the fires burning below. They hurled the missiles down blindly, knocking dozens of Aalvarg off the tower and prompting scream after terrified scream from the darkness below. Even so, in less than half the time it had taken the first wave to reach the top, clawed hands began to appear above the merlons and the Horse-bjorn's men moved into action. Hammers once more splintered bones and axe blades flashed red in the torchlight.

But these wolves were wearing armor and more of them were carrying swords and daggers. Some of the weapons were of the crude Aalvarg construction, but more were of Dalarn make, captured over the years. They fought more intelligently too; the men holding the torches were their first targets and the front line rapidly disappeared into the shadows of the night.

Steinthor cursed. They needed more light! He and the other archers were rendered useless without the torches and they couldn't simply loose into the mass of screaming, snarling, struggling combatants. They would hit three or more men for every wolf. The wolves could see better in the dark and judging by the sound of the battle raging in front of him, Horse-Bjorn desperately needed the archers to sweep the walls as they come over. He handed his bow to Rennir and ran over to the Half-Giant.

"We need light! I need five men."

The big man nodded and pointed out the men he was to take.

"Follow me," Steinthor ordered them. He led the five to where the spare torches were piled, then lit them and handed two to each man. "Push forward to the front. Leave your swords sheathed. We fight with fire!"

He charged forward into the chaotic mass, thrusting one flaming torch into the open jaws of the first wolf-demon he encountered. The fire set its fur ablaze, and the howling, panic-stricken beast reeled back just in time to be disemboweled by an upthrusting backswing from an axeman. Two more wolves, their red muzzles dripping with the blood of their victim, retreated before him as he swung his pair of torches in a rhythm that didn't give them an opportunity to attack. One was impaled by a spear jabbed from behind him, the other crumpled as an arrow pierced its eye.

One of the torchbearers had fallen, but his torches were picked up by two of the Horse-Bjorn's men. Between the ten torches, there was now enough light for the archers to see and their deadly shafts flashed past Steinthor's helm and once more swept the parapets clear of the wolves. Seeing this, the Horse-Bjorn shouted his battle cry.

"Slagtetid!"

Their hearts emboldened, his weary men echoed his cry and pushed forward again. They slew, and slew, and slew in a seemingly endless morass of blood and fire.

Steinthor ducked under a slashing dagger and smashed a torch over the wolf-thing's head. But the beast's skull was too thick to crack. Instead, the torch broke in two, and the flaming end slid through a crenel to fall useless downward. Steinthor stared at the broken end for a moment, swung his other torch at the wolf's face to keep its snapping jaws away from him, then stepped in and jammed the jagged wood into the creature's unarmored chest as if it were a blade.

It screamed, fell back and was immediately replaced by a large black Aalvarg that roared as it leaped at him with its claws outstretched. He tried to block it with his remaining torch, but the big beast collided with him and sent him sprawling on his back. The torch flew out of his hand, leaving him defenseless. His armor protected his insides from scrabbling claws that tried to rip them out, and he jammed his chin down towards his chest just as the wolf tried to bite his face off. Despite the noise of the raging chaos surrounding them, he could hear its teeth break on the metal of his helmet, followed by a howl of infuriated pain.

Then the beast suddenly spasmed and slumped motionless on top of him. His arms were pinned, he was trapped under its dead weight and the horrific wolf stench made him fear that he might soon drown in his own vomit. Then a boot came down and kicked the dead wolf just far enough off his chest that he could free his arms and wrestle the limp corpse off him before another of the demonspawn tore his throat out.

A pair of legs was standing over him; it was Horse-Bjorn, he realized, defending him while he was down. He scrambled backwards on his elbows and pushed himself to his feet. Then he drew his sword. The veteran warrior killed another wolf with his axe, bringing it down so heavily that it split the creature's bear-like skull. The man was prodigiously strong, even with just one arm, Steinthor marveled.

But even with the shield strapped to his useless left arm, Horse-Bjorn was vulnerable. Each swing left him slightly off-balance, and a mistimed swipe that missed his target clean caused him to stumble forward. He was only a few steps from the parapet already, and an alert dark-furred wolf that had just climbed over the merlons caught his shield in its claws, twisted, and hurled him high over the merlons. Steinthor heard Horse-Bjorn curse, more in anger than in fear, and then he was gone into the darkness below.

A terrible wail went up from the men close enough to have seen their captain fall from the tower. Steinthor himself killed the dark-furred Aalvarg by punching his sword twice into its chest. He followed that with half-severing its head for good measure. He fended off a rusty, thrusting dagger with his left arm, then chopped off the beast's hand at the wrist. For a moment both he and the wolf stood there and stared at each other. The wolf was stunned by the loss of its hand and Steinthor was astonished that his sword still retained enough of an edge to do such damage.

Then the wounded creature snarled and lunged at him. Without thinking, Steinthor raised his arm and thrust the blade deep into the gaping maw. He found himself gasping as the dead weight of the wolf suddenly dragged his arm down. The sword was too deeply lodged into the beast's skull to withdraw it, so he drew his dagger and fell back into the furiously fighting ranks of the Horse-Bjorn's remaining men.

There were too few of them left to throw back this wave, he saw. The relentless pressure from the Aalvarg was wearing them down and the loss of the Horse-Bjorn had caused more than a few to give into fey despair. Their discipline was all but gone, and he saw two more men pulled forward and hurled from the ramparts by the powerful grey-furred arms of the demonspawn. When the signal flames went up from the West Tower, indicating the wolves were attacking it now as well, he knew the time had come to fall back.

"Half-Giant! Half-Giant!" he shouted as he fought his way back towards the huge man and his men. "Half-Giant!"

"It is time?" Hrafnkel asked him, peering down uncertainly at him. "Do I blow the horn?"

"Blow the horn," Steinthor said. He gripped the big man's thick forearm and squeezed it, wishing he could give the man a more worthy farewell. "Don't let them pull you forward and throw you off the tower."

The big man nodded seriously, as if there was any advice that mattered now. "Go, Steinthor Strongbow, and the gods go with you."

Steinthor squeezed Hrafnkel's arm again. He felt he hadn't properly appreciated the Half-Giant's courage until this moment. And yet, this was not the first or the fiftieth time he had felt Death's cold hands clutching at him, what made him so womanish and sentimental now? Cursing himself, cursing his luck, cursing the wolves, and most of all, cursing whatever evil god had birthed the damnable creatures, he limped over to Rennir and reclaimed his bow, which was already strung.

"Two volleys and then we run for the stairs and down into the keep." He nocked an arrow.

"Can you run?"

"Not really."

"What happened to your sword?"

"Got stuck." He shrugged. "I'll get another one inside."

A horn blew. It was a mighty blast worthy of a true jotun. "Half-Giant!" the men roared as they charged towards the ferocious struggle. The wolves were caught by surprise as the thirty-odd men with whom they were engaged suddenly fell back, giving the archers the space they required. Rennir was the first to loose, but Steinthor and the others quickly followed suit. They sent a second flight of shafts hammering into the foe before the gap was closed by Hrafnkel's screaming men.

He felt Rennir grab his arm as they joined the bleeding, battered remnants of the Horse-Bjorn's men and rushed towards the doorway, as fast as his injured leg would permit him to go. But they needn't have hurried. He looked back and saw, silhouetted against the flames, the great figure of the Half-Giant holding an Aalvarg aloft in his massive hands before snapping the creature's neck and swinging it like a limp, but heavy club. He'd have caught a Chooser's eye with that one, thought Steinthor in astonishment and admiration.

He waited until the last man was through, then stepped down into the stairwell and pulled the door shut behind him. Rennir slid the metal slab into place, barring it, and the two of them began to follow the others down the stone stairs.

"Can you make it down?" the bowman asked him.

Steinthor suddenly realized that his wounded leg hurt and he was very, very tired. It won't be long now, he promised himself. He only needed enough strength for one last task. The West Tower was already taken and the North Tower would only last as long as the Half-Giant and the door they had just barred. Their long defense of Raknarborg was over.

"I can make it," he said.

He leaned on Rennir's arm and together they descended towards the keep. There was nothing left to defend. Now it was time to attack.

THEUDERIC

H E HEARD the sounds of battle before he saw anything. The sun was up and the men's torches had been extinguished and returned to their saddlebags, but the leafy filter overhead created a dappled effect that played tricks on the eyes. As near as he could tell by the bestial roars that echoed through the trees, the orcs were attacking the curé's forces, which puzzled Theuderic considering that all of his men were mounted. Even in a forest such as this, his cavalry shouldn't have had too much trouble disentangling themselves from orcs on foot, unless they'd somehow managed to get themselves encircled.

Lord Roche reined in his horse next to him. "What do you think?" He sounded as if he was similarly puzzled.

"I have no idea. It sounds like they're making a stand."

"That makes no sense!"

"I know." Theuderic shrugged. "Perhaps their captain is fallen and they're trying to defend him."

The viscomte laughed. "Ah, my dear magus, you know nothing of Jean de Cervole or his men. If he's down, they would only delay long enough to cut his throat, steal his purse, and loot his saddlebags. And I can't imagine the old deviant would risk himself or his men for any of the knights."

Then they heard a scream. Then another. The two men looked at each other.

"Was that what I think it was?" Lord Roche said, confusion on his face.

"Those were women's voices!" Theuderic declared.

Without another word, they spurred their horses forward, in the direction of the screams. Theuderic dropped back a little, to let the more heavily armored knights take the lead.

The first thing they saw were the orcs. Dozens of them, big creatures with powerful shoulders and short, but thick, bowed legs. They were hurling themselves at a thin wall of dismounted men who were fighting ferociously in defense of a hastily erected pile of brush that served as an ineffective barricade. Neither the viscomte nor his men slowed down as they charged into the attacking orcs and hit them in their undefended left flank. Theuderic saw Lord Roche behead one screaming orc and trample another; one of his knights drove his lance all the way through the neck of one orc to spit a second one just below his right shoulder blade. The oaken lance snapped, and the knight swung the broken haft down on the bare head of a third orc like a mace, crushing its heavy skull.

Then Theuderic himself was in among the shrieking, dying, and panicking orcs, lashing out with his sword whenever his horse brought him within range of anything with a green skin. They were barely capable of resistance and were trying to flee, but the press of onrushing horses left most of them to be slashed in passing when they weren't run through or trampled. A few were clever enough to stand still behind large trees, then dash for safety when no riders were approaching, but there were not many of them.

The viscomte and his men were already coming back towards him, having turned around after riding through the orcs. Seeing that the wretched monsters were fleeing, Theuderic was finally able to pull up his horse and turn his attention to the men, and, as he saw to his surprise, women and children behind the barrier.

"What are they doing here?" he shouted at one dismounted man-at-arms.

The man, whose weary face was stained with blood both red and green, raised his free hand in a gesture indicating his ignorance. "We came across a band of about fifty orcs shepherding them along. We killed about half of them and drove off the rest, but then we ran into this lot."

"How many?"

"Hard to say. At least six, seven hundred. You interrupted the third crack they took at us. Damn good thing you came along when you did."

"Where are your horses?"

The man jerked his thumb towards the rear. "Behind the women and children. Captain Jean had most of us dismount and kept a reserve of thirty to hit them when they were pressing us hard. I thought that's who you were at first."

"Where are they? Is de Cervole with them?"

"I think so," the man said. But just then, Theuderic heard a familiar voice crying out to him. "Theuderic!"

"Sebastien!" he shouted back. "Over here, at the barricade!"

It was hard to see where his fellow battlemage was in amidst all the confusion of horses blowing, men shouting, women crying, and the wounded shrieking. Unsurprisingly, the women and children outnumbered the men by about four to one. Most of them were naked, or were wearing tattered rags. They were bruised, scratched, and half-starved by the look of it. Many of the women and not a few of the men had dried blood staining their legs. The children had a vacant, dull-eyed stare he had seen before; it was the same stunned look some soldiers wore when they had simply seen too much horror for their minds to accept. And there were scores of them milling aimlessly about, getting in the way of the warriors who were trying to shore up their paltry defenses and arm the male prisoners with sticks that might serve as spears or clubs before the orcs came at them again.

Finally, he spotted Sebastien's royal blue cape as the mage made his way past a pair of men-at-arms bandaging their wounded and trying to catch their breath.

"Sebastien!" he shouted again, and this time the younger mage saw him.

"Theuderic! Thank God you arrived! Things were looking desperate there for a moment." He was looking exhausted and on the verge of collapse. Theuderic could tell he had all but drained himself dry.

"Where is your horse? What are you doing?"

"Captain Jean told me to stay with the captives and help defend them in case the orcs broke through the men he had stationed there. They nearly got through once, not the last time, but the time before. I managed to keep them at bay, but I think I burned down nearly half the forest to do it!"

"You need to rest, Sebastien. You should ride out now, while you can."

"No! Captain Jean said no one leaves. There are more than five hundred villagers here, Theuderic, and most of them are women and children."

"I saw. What are they doing here in the middle of the forest? You said they were captives?"

"Some of them were taken weeks ago. Others more recently. They're from at least six different villages." He paused for a moment and made a face. "Theuderic, I think they were being brought along as supplies."

Theuderic nodded. He wasn't surprised. No army that didn't hesitate to live off its own light infantry would shirk at devouring captives. Mobile food supplies were a logistical advantage. "If we can drive the breeds off, we can escort them out of the forest safely."

Sebastien smiled grimly. "More and more of the monsters keep coming, Theuderic. Thousands of them. At first they were almost completely unorganized, but then a big bastard showed up with a pair of shamans and kicked them into order. The last two waves, they've hit us from two sides; that's why I was helping hold the rear."

More and more of them kept coming. That was the problem. More and more of them would keep coming because that was precisely what he and the prince had anticipated, what they'd expected to be able to use to their advantage. The Amorran pressure on their rear would only increase with time; Theuderic knew enough of Legio XVII and its officers to know that once the attack began, they would be pushing steadily forward, neither dashing rapidly ahead nor slacking off in order to rest. He had seen the Amorrans practicing their revolutions over and over again, one century rotating smoothly after the other, like a slow-moving iron mill that ground flesh instead of flour.

The original plan had called for the four squadrons to use their superior mobility to methodically reduce the fleeing bands of orcs, striking, retreating, then striking again. But suddenly, their mobility was rendered useless by the need to protect the captive villagers. It occurred to him they might abandon the adults, and each take up a child, or perhaps a young woman, and ride out with them. That would require leaving the rest to their doom, but surely saving scores of the youngest ones would be better than sacrificing over one hundred riders in a futile effort to save a few villages worth of peasants. To say nothing of two royal mages.

He had no doubt whatsoever that the king would not countenance the risk. If nothing else, he must convince Sebastien that it was their duty to retreat even if the prince's cavalry captains would not. Courage and honor were for knights, not kingsmages.

"We have to leave, Sebastien. If the orcs are gathering, even with Lord Roche's men there won't be enough to hold them off. We can't force them back, not with the Amorrans driving them in this direction."

The younger mage stared at him, momentarily struck dumb. Then his eyes flashed with contempt and anger. "You run away if you're afraid to stand, Theuderic. I'm not going anywhere. None of us are! Captain Jean said he'd ride down and kill the first man who fled and left these poor people behind!"

Theuderic sighed. An uncharitable thought about the bugger-priest's distaste for leaving children behind crossed his mind, but apparently even the worst of men had their moments. And the fury on Sebastien's dirt-stained face seemed to suggest that it might be counterproductive to speak his mind aloud.

"All right. If we can't run, then we have to disrupt them, break them up and keep them from building enough strength to overrun us."

"How do you suggest we do that?" Sebastien's tone was still hostile, but there was an underlying note of hope in his voice too.

"We kill the big bastard. Go mount your horse and come with me. We need to find de Cervole and the viscomte."

"I'm staying here. They will need me when the orcs come again."

"Go get your damn horse, Sebastien!" he snapped. "If you want to save them, then come with me! I'm going to need someone to distract those bloody shamans and you're the only other mage in sight! I'll meet you back here."

His colleague stared at him for a moment in dismay, then nodded and ran in search of his mount. Theuderic turned his own horse around to see if he could get a better view of the situation now that the orcs had fallen back and most of their wounded had been methodically dispatched.

The trees obscured his view, but he could see that de Cervole had managed to find a slight rise which gave the defenders a modicum of advantage, one that was enhanced by the brush and fallen trees piled up behind him. From the movement in the distance and the flicker of shadows, he could tell that the orcs had not retreated far, which indicated that it would not be long before they would be gathering for yet another assault. He saw no sign of the big orc that Sebastien identified as their leader, nor the two shamans, but presumably they would be further back attempting to either rally the fleeing orcs or rounding up reinforcements.

He went in search of Lord Roche and found him in the company of a filthy fat man with a ring of long, stringy, blood-matted hair hanging down from an otherwise bald head. The fat man's face was uneven, as if he'd been smashed on its left side by a shield as an infant; it gave him a freakish, even frightening appearance. But his green eyes were bright with a keen intelligence that belied his otherwise grotesque persona.

"Seigneur de Merovech, Jean de Cervole. Jean, you will recall the senior kingsmage." The ex-priest nodded at him, unimpressed, and jabbed his finger into the viscomte's breastplate.

"You ride away if you must, Seigneur. I will not stop you. But leave me at least fifty men. I have lost twenty, maybe a few more in that last assault. We can stop them! They have no armor, their weapons are poor. But they are so many, and in the trees, we have no room to maneuver."

"That's why you dismounted your men," Theuderic said.

"I did! And we were better able to defend the poor unfortunates on foot. We cannot simply leave them, n'est-ce pas? Better we should cut their throats before we flee like thieves and cowards. At least have the courage to show them the coupe de compassion, monseigneur le viscomte. Have you the courage to cut the throats of the mothers, the little ones?"

"I've got the courage to cut yours, you filthy excuse for a pig!" The viscomte curled his lip in disgust. "I said nothing about riding anywhere! As if any true knight of the realm would even think to flee and leave those wretched folk to the defense of scum like you and your men!"

"I rejoice to hear it, monseigneur. Then we shall stand together against these beasts, and we shall slaughter these monsters seeking to feed upon the flesh of the innocent." The twisted face seemed to leer, and Theuderic wondered if the defrocked mercenary was actually trying to bait the nobleman.

Lord Roche's face tightened, and for a moment Theuderic thought he was actually going to strike the man. He quickly interceded before it could come to blows.

"My colleague tells me that he has seen what he thinks may be their leader, a large orc accompanied by a pair of shamans. We know from their general disarray that its hold on them must be tenuous. Perhaps their numbers are too great for us to withstand for long, but if we kill the leader, there is every chance their resolve will fail and they will cease to present a danger to us. We must break them apart and keep them from coming at us in strength. The only way I can think to do that is to remove their warleader."

De Cervole nodded. The viscomte scowled, as if to even agree with the man was distasteful to him, but a moment later, he, too, nodded.

"The first attack was hasty and disorganized," the mercenary said. "We would have driven it off easily had we not been taken by surprise. The second two involved multiple groups, attacking in concert, in two different places. I think the mage is right, although who can say if simply murdering the brute will be enough to dismay his fellows. They may be blood-maddened, or by now, they may simply be hungry enough to persist."

"I daresay we've left them sufficient carrion to chew on and assuage their hunger," Lord Roche said dismissively. "They may not find the flesh so sweet, but they'll find it bloody well easier to come by. You've the right idea, de Merovech. Cut the head off the snake and it dies. A mob is always more easily turned than a directed force."

"How do you propose to do it, monseigneur le mage? Can you magic the creature to death?"

"I'll try," he answered de Cervole. "But it would be best not to trust to spells. It's got a pair of shamans, and it may have more at its disposal that Sebastien didn't see. My plan is for Sebastien to keep the shamans occupied and I'll try to kill the warleader. But we will be more likely to succeed if we allocate part of the cavalry reserve to wait until it shows itself, then strike out after it once its orcs have been committed to the attack."

"Damned risky," Lord Roche observed, staring off into the trees. "I doubt they'll be expecting anything like that, not when we didn't try anything similar the first three times, but even so, the chances are that it'll have a second wave of attackers waiting and if it sees us coming, it'll just put them in the way of our riders. If it's smart enough to divide his attackers, it's probably keeping a reserve on hand."

"Perhaps not. From what Sebastien told me, it sounds like it's been rounding up whatever it can find and throwing them at us. It knows the Amorrans are coming behind him and it needs the captives if it's going to feed what's left of its army long enough to break free of the trap and retreat back to the east."

"When do you think they will get here?" de Cervole asked him. "The Amorrans. I think we can hold until nightfall. But if we haven't driven them off by then...."

"The Amorrans won't be coming today. They attacked last night. I know their customs. They'll have built their defenses and be resting behind them now. The soonest we can expect them is probably around noon tomorrow."

The viscomte glowered. "We'd better kill that bloody warleader, then. I'll have the horn sounded. If we can bring in the other two squadrons, we might have enough men to hold them off. De Merovech, I'll give you ten knights to attack with you. De Cervole, assuming it hasn't occurred to you yet, order your men not to give any of their food or water to the captives. The men need to keep their strength up if they're going to be fighting all night."

Theuderic nodded grimly. The old warrior knew whereof he spoke. Each man carried three days supply of food and several skins of water, and it was cruel to deny sustenance to the hapless villagers, many of whom probably had not eaten in days. But it would be wiser to lose a handful of them to starvation than get them all killed because their defenders were weak with hunger. Fighting was thirsty work, and if anyone was going to get out of this cursed forest alive, they were going to have to give themselves every opportunity of success.

He mentally reviewed his available spells. In the confusion of battle, L'étrangleuse Subreptice would be the most likely to pass unnoticed, but it took a little more time than some of his other options. Le Cœur Dilater de Vermouton was the most certain to cause speedy death, as it would cause the subject's heart to rapidly expand until it burst, but it was a wordy spell and would require that he lay hands upon the orc, which struck him as an unlikely and highly risky feat. Micheloud's Marteau du Ciel was devastating, but difficult to aim precisely and was best used against large troop units, not individuals. He sighed. As usual, his best option would be the old standby, Falardeau's Récurer de la Flamme Funeste, for which the sigils had long ago been carved into his staff.

It would certainly suffice to flambée the orc, the problem was that he would need to be close enough to his target for the magical flames to engulf it. That meant he would need to ride with those seeking to kill the warleader in less esoteric ways, which would make it impossible to avoid drawing unwanted attention. Being light infantry, the orcs would likely have archers and other missileers, although the trees would make it difficult to find a clear shot even if the orcs saw them coming.

He saw the defrocked priest ride off, presumably to gather his men, and Lord Roche approached him. The old viscomte had a rueful expression on his face, and Theuderic surmised that he was beginning to regret his hasty decision to stay and fight in what might well turn out to be his last battle. So he was surprised when the nobleman asked him a question.

"Do you wish for me to give the order to leave, sieur mage?"

"With all due respect, monseigneur, I don't take orders from mere viscomtes."

The older man laughed. "Well I know it! But there is many a man who in your position would find it hard to face himself were he to turn his back on these people, and I am aware that your duty to the king indicates that you and your fellow should save yourselves. So go, if you must."

"I would. My fellow is a romantic young fool and will not leave."

"And so he shames you into following suit?"

Theuderic smiled thinly. "Not in the slightest. I don't care about those wretched folk. It makes no difference whatsoever if we are able to save illiterates and farmhands or not. I've seen a thousand such innocents dead before, no few by my own hand. And for all we knew an hour past, they were already dead."

"What about the children?"

"What of them? A third of them will be dead in ten years even if we rescue them all." He shook his head. "I'm here to keep Sebastien alive, monseigneur viscomte. If I can. He may be a fool, but he is a kingsmage, and so here I will remain."

"Cold-hearted bastard, are you?" The viscomte grinned, unconcerned. "Best get back to your fellow, then. They'll be coming before long, and I'm going to send out a pair of knights to escort the wounded."

"You might have them each carry a child," Theuderic suggested. "The older ones might even help with those too badly hurt to hold the reins."

"Just a bastard, then." Lord Roche nodded and urged his horse in the direction of where his men had gathered. "You kill that bloody warleader, de Merovech, and I'll see to it that the jongleurs sing of your noble heart from here to the White Sea. Or drown you in whores, as you prefer."

The latter, Theuderic thought, wondering if he would ever have the pleasure of pillaging a woman's body again. Not that the bodies here were in any shape to stir a man's desires, for all that half of them were naked. As he rode back to where he expected to meet Sebastien, the sight of the people behind the barricade reminded him of the stripped corpses that had been piled up outside the broken walls of Montrove. It was piteous, but it was also revolting.

Still, they were going to fight. Every male villager and most of the women were now armed with clubs and crudely sharpened stakes; one man was even carrying a longsword that looked suspiciously familiar. Others were carrying knives, maces, or other weapons some knight or man-at-arms had given them.

"There you are," Sebastien was already there waiting for him. As his horse stopped and emitted a steaming stream of urine, he noticed that the younger mage wasn't wearing his sword.

"Did you give your sword to them?" he asked suspiciously.

"They need it more than I do," Sebastien answered. He twirled his staff in his left hand. "Besides, I thought the idea was for me to occupy their shamans. Unless you've made considerable progress on that flying spell, I don't see what good a sword is likely to do me."

A large group of horses trotted past them; Theuderic saw it was Lord Roche's men. About twenty of them dismounted to take up positions behind the barricade, other knights took the reins of the riderless horses and rode off with them. Then a smaller group arrived, led by Jean de Cervole.

"Come, monseigneur mages. Your escort has arrived! Follow me to where we shall wait for our oversized green-skinned friend to show itself."

"I thought one of the knights would be leading the charge," Theuderic said, eyeing the former priest with skepticism.

The stringy-haired man smiled wearily, revealing yellowed, crooked teeth. "As did several of them. But your men are more fresh than mine; we have withstood two serious assaults while you have twice routed foes you caught by surprise. I'm getting old, my knees and back are aching, and I need more of a rest than these damned orcs are going to give us."

Theuderic glanced skeptically at the de Cervole's men. They were hard-bitten men, mercenaries with years more experience than most of the young knights, but their armor was boiled leather and poor-quality chain mail. Their captain was the only man among them wearing a proper steel cuirass, and half of them didn't even have proper helms.

Some of his skepticism must have shown on his face, because de Cervole snorted dismissively and shook his head. "Never you mind, monseigneur mage. The boys will get to that bastard and cut it down to size for you. We may not be pretty, but by God, our swords are as sharp as any man's."

A drum began beating, followed by an ominous, guttural roaring that sounded as if it was coming from the trees nearby. Theuderic sat bolt upright in his saddle. A horn blew, and he knew that the battle was about to begin again.

De Cervole reached out and patted his arm. "Relax. We have to wait, let them make their attack. If we move too soon, we won't catch them unaware."

Theuderic nodded. It made sense. "Why are you doing this? It seems... uncharacteristic."

The defrocked priest nodded and rubbed the top of his balding head where once there had been a tonsure. A man might leave the Church, but he would never fully escape its mark. "Have you ever done something that you knew was wrong? Something for which there can be no forgiveness, no return? Yes? Then you know that feeling, the impression that you are on the edge of a ravine, and the moment you decide to act, part of you will plunge into the depths, never to be the same again. You are no more virgin, no more innocent, or your hands are no longer unstained. I have known many such moments myself, and speaking only for myself, I will confess that it was at moments such as those that I have always felt most alive."

Much to his regret, Theuderic almost found he understood. Sometimes he wondered which had been his greatest betrayal of Lithriel, the hunt, the affair, or the silence. Each could, taken by itself, be explained, perhaps even justified. But all three, in sum, rendered him a monster, little better than this ghastly ex-clerical with the teeth and hair of an animated corpse. No, there would be neither forgiveness nor absolution for him. Not if she learned the truth. Elves lived a long, long time, and they did not forget.

There were shouts, screams, and the clash of metal on metal not far away. De Cervole didn't even seem to hear the sounds of the erupting battle, his deeply tanned, deeply lined face was rapt with distant memories. "It is the moment of no return, when doubts become regrets and regrets become pointless. All that is left is to take whatever pleasure is to be had from the deed and then wait to discover what the consequences will be. Perhaps there will be a child. Perhaps there will be a trial. Or, perhaps, nothing will come of it except one more black mark against your soul when it comes time for you to burn in Hell."

"Do you think to expiate your sins by saving these people?"

"He who loses his life shall gain it?" De Cervole laughed, exposing his rotted teeth. "If I saved all these people and a hundred times more, it would not be enough to balance my accounts, monseigneur le mage. No, you mistake me very much indeed if you think I am under any illusions concerning my damnation. My one hope is that the God at whom I have thumbed my nose for so long does not, in the end, exist. I hope, indeed, I pray, if that makes any sense at all, that He does not."

"Then why are you doing this?" Theuderic gestured towards the sounds of the battle. It was impossible to know whether Lord Roche and his men were throwing back the orcs or not. Surely the orc leader must have shown himself by now! "I don't understand."

"I crave that sensation of falling, it seems. Much to my surprise, when one is as thoroughly steeped in degradation as I am, the feeling of taking a step out of the mire is disturbingly similar to the way one feels after that first step into it. It is madness, it is lunacy, it is exhilarating. Perhaps it is only the thoroughly degraded who can find true pleasure in doing good." He reached out and caressed Theuderic's face. "How I once hungered for such beauty. Such a silly, short-lived thing for which to sell one's soul. You would not credit it now, I am sure, but once I was handsome too. I remember the brothers clutching at their rosaries, and mumbling their Notre Dames as I walked by, virgin, but no innocent."

Theuderic's lip curled. "Touch me again, and you'll feel the flames of my bale-fire just before you feel the flames of Hell, priest."

De Cervole laughed. "Peace, monseigneur le mage. You know I am no priest these days. You asked a question. I answered. Ah, the waiting, it is always difficult, is it not? It preys upon the mind, makes one irritable.

Never you mind. It is time, I think. Stay close, and if you see the big one, sear his arse."

Theuderic frowned. He had heard neither the two short horn blasts that were to summon them, nor the high-pitched screams of women that would indicate the barricade had fallen. But de Cervole must have had a better sense of the shape of battle, for no sooner had Theuderic opened his mouth to point out that the other man was wrong than he heard a horn sound. Twice.

The mercenary captain smiled as if he knew what Theuderic was thinking. Then he rose in his stirrups to see that his men had heard the horn, drew his sword, and waved it in a circle around his head. He did not shout, nor order a horn sounded; it had been agreed that they should fall upon the orc in silence, insofar as twenty-two horses could move in silence.

They trotted through the trees as fast as they dared, with one of de Cervole's ragged mercenaries leading them in a direction that should bring them behind the orcs. They emerged into a scene even more loud and violent and confusing than the two previous skirmishes in which Theuderic had already engaged today. There seemed to be at least four times more orcs attacking than when they had been driven off before, they were four and five deep as they swarmed the men-at-arms fighting on foot in front of the barricades.

Theuderic didn't have time to see how well the men were holding their ground. A few images impressed themselves on his mind as he glanced to his right. A large green arm, pierced through the muscle by the tip of a sword. A grimace on the face of a helmed man, although whether it was borne of pain or effort, Theuderic could not tell. The downward swing of a studded club. Bared tusks and a gaping maw.

And then he saw the shamans. There were two of them, both standing near the big orc who was roaring out encouragement to his warriors. Even in the mass of movement amidst the trees, they were not hard to identify, not with the bones tied into their thick manes of dark green hair and the spiral tattoos decorating their faces. Both were narrow-eyed and tense, as if exerting themselves. Theuderic guessed that they were maintaining a spell of some sort.

"Sebastien!" he shouted.

"I see them!"

The two orcs reacted as if they'd been burned when Sebastien unleashed his counterspell. They leaped backwards in unison, crying out and looking wildly about. Were the circumstances not so grim, Theuderic might have laughed, for he knew the feeling well. Having a spell forcibly broken, especially without warning, was rather like having a tightly stretched rope snap free to rebound in your face.

Instead, he decided to take advantage of their discomfiture. He justified the change in plans by observing that the warleader was not yet in range anyhow. *L'étrangleuse* could not be triggered by a single word, but he chanted the three stanzas as rapidly as he dared, then extended his hand at the shaman whose upper body was not obscured by the trees. To his relief, the shaman immediately jerked back and raised his hands to his throat, trying to remove the iron grip of the invisible strangler.

Their charge had been noticed now, and he saw the warleader turn and point at them, his eyes wide with enraged surprise. Theuderic raised his staff, but they were still too far away. And then he saw a third shaman step forward from where he'd been obscured by the warleader, his eyes white and rolled back in his head, and green blood leaking from his glowing tattoos. His hands were raised in either exultation or invocation, and blood dripped from his elbows. Red blood.

That wasn't mere blood magic, it was diablerie. Dammit, that wasn't good. "Sebastien!" he shouted. "There's another one!"

But whether Sebastien was too exhausted to counter the spell or simply didn't see the third shaman appear. Either way, Theuderic would never know. Without warning, the ground shuddered as a huge black fist as wide as three horses appeared out of nowhere and crushed both Sebastien and his mount under it. Six of the mercenaries on either side of the luckless mage were thrown from their horses as either the force of the blow or the sheer terror it inspired caused the horses to stumble or go down. For the briefest of moments, Theuderic had the impression of a giant figure crouching over them, drawing back a horny fist. It was translucent, more sensation than sight. But it was terrifyingly real all the same.

"Gor-Gor!" a guttural cheer went up from the orcs. "Gor-Gor u shaggat!"

Theuderic had heard of the orc wargod before, every royal battlemage had, but he had never truly believed in the power of the inhumanités to actually summon it. How did one dispel a god? Even if it was only a demon, as he suspected, the only priest in the vicinity was about as unfit as a man could be for an impromptu battlefield exorcism.

If you can't kill the summoned, kill the summoner. He could almost hear the voice of the hoary-bearded Immortel instructing the class on les démons et les élémentaux. Which brought another maxim to mind. No plan survives contact with the enemy. Change the plan. Kill the summoner. He raised his staff.

A sparking word and the balefire, called forth from one of the higher levels of the lesser hells, roared forth from the sigils at the end of the staff. It leaped out to engulf the bleeding shaman, which was too caught up in its demonic summoning to see it or even to scream. Caught up in its blood-addled reverie, it burned in silence, without struggle or protest. Its flesh was black by the time its hands dropped to its sides; only then did it take a single step forward before collapsing into the unnatural flames that were consuming its body.

There was a hollow cry, as if from very far away, and Theuderic glanced up towards the treetops, looking for any sign that the terrible fist might be descending upon him. He pulled up his horse and circled around, holding his staff before him warily. There was no sign of the war god, so he was forced to conclude the immolation of the shaman who had summoned it was sufficient to break its link to this dimension. He kicked his horse after the charging survivors.

That was only one threat averted. One shaman still remained but it was well aware of the danger Theuderic posed. Having seen what he had done to its two companions, it was not inclined to stand and fight. Instead, it disappeared behind a cloud of magical smoke and vanished.

De Cervole and his men were already furiously battling the big orcs around the warleader. They were more muscular and better armed than most of those Theuderic had encountered earlier in the day, but they were no better armored. The mercenaries rode down the first bodyguards with relative ease, but then a dozen, a score, and even a few more surged forward and managed to slow their momentum. The cavalry charge slowed, then came to a complete halt as it was transformed from a unitary assault into a melee of mercenary islands held motionless in a boiling sea of orcs.

Somehow, one man-at-arms managed to duck a thrusting pike, then slash his way past two more orcs until only a pair of bodyguards stood between him and the warleader. But one of the orcs he'd ridden past gutted his horse, and the beast collapsed without warning, sending its rider crashing face first to the ground. The man somehow managed to roll sideways and avoid a club that would have crushed his skull, then, instead of trying to retrieve his sword, he pulled at the stabbing arm of one bodyguard and used it to simultaneously get to his feet and throw the orc behind him. As he did so, the other bodyguard swept his legs out from under him, then bent over and bashed out the man's brains with repeated blows of the metal-studded club.

And for a moment, nothing stood between de Cervole and the warleader except the three orcs grabbing at his rein and slashing at his shield. To Theuderic's surprise, the defrocked priest pulled himself up upon his horse's back, then leaped from it over the heads of all three orcs. As he fell towards the ground, de Cervole swung his sword down as well and buried it deeply into the big orc's unarmored neck. The monster screamed, its collarbone shattered, as green blood gouted messily from the mortal wound. De Cervole was immediately swarmed by the three orcs over whom he'd jumped, in addition to four or five surviving bodyguards.

"Mage!" Theuderic heard de Cervole shout in a voice that rang with command, not fear or desperation.

Theuderic didn't hesitate. He channeled another burst of balefire, and it swept over the pile of struggling figures, man and orc alike. The orcs staggered away, shrieking in pain as the hungry nether-flames devoured their green flesh. They fled screaming, six or seven living torches, into the depths of the forest. And after them fled the remaining orcs of the warleader's bodyguard. The warleader itself lay dull-eyed and dying barely a hand's reach from the badly injured man who had dealt it its death wound.

Two of the former priest's men rushed to their captain and were already beating out the flames from his clothes and his red, blistered, half-melted skin. De Cervole had been bludgeoned, stabbed, and bitten, as well as burned, but he was still conscious, if only just. But he, too, was mortally wounded. Theuderic could see a question in the dying priest's agonized eyes. His lips, bleeding and partially burned off, moved almost imperceptibly. But Theuderic understood.

"You killed it. The rest ran. You'll have saved them all, I think."

De Cervole's eyes closed and he seemed to relax. If he was destined for hotter flames than those that had just burned him, he was ready. Theuderic kneeled down, placed his hand gently on the man's shoulder, and quietly spoke the words that Vermouton had first arranged nearly eighty years ago. De Cervole's burned hands involuntarily reached for his throat, his upper body jerked once, violently, and then he slumped back onto the ground again.

"What did you do?" one of his men demanded.

"What had to be done," he replied. Was it mercy to send a man to Hell? He wouldn't have thought so. And yet it felt as if it had been a kindness all the same. He looked at the dying orc, which gazed back at him with yellow eyes of impotent hate. Theuderic smiled coldly, then spat and turned away. Let the creature find its own way to the Devil.

MARCUS

T HE FOREST was much thicker than any the Amorrans had seen before. In certain places where the tree trunks were exceptionally thick, the leaves and branches overhead formed a canopy that concealed the afternoon sky entirely from the view of those marching underneath. But despite the darkness, the mood of the legionaries was exhilarated, and it was with some difficulty that the centurions kept their men in order as they marched in skirmish order through the sun-dappled ground. Each century had a single contubernium designated as ear-catchers; they roamed ahead of the line of march carrying daggers with which to remove the ears of the dead orcs they found and sacks in which to carry them. At intervals, a call went up, as the legionaries marched past, or sometimes over, a corpse that had not yet been deprived of its appendages.

"Oy, Audens! You missed one!"

"Move it along, Opis," an optio barked. "Where is it?"

"Back here, to the right, by that big tree there!"

A tired legionary, his forearm greaves splattered with dark green gore, trudged wearily back towards the marching century, a half-full burlap sack slung over his shoulders. He sighed as the men marched past him, and nodded as one man pointed towards a wide-trunked oak with a large knot on the side. After they passed by, he walked over to the dead orc, kneeled down, and with two expert strokes, removed the green ears. After slipping them into the sack, he stood up and rubbed at the small of his back, then began half-jogging at a pace that would let him overtake the century again.

"How many do you think were killed," Marcus asked Arvandus as they rode along the path through the forest made by the men's iron-soled sandals.

"A few hundred. Ten percent at most."

"That would be nearly twenty-five hundred silvers."

"If we find them all. Which we won't. We'll be lucky to collect five hundred."

"Even so."

Think the king will pay up?"

Marcus snorted. "We just saved his eastern provinces from being overrun. More importantly, we have five thousand swords. He'll pay."

Collecting from the King of Savondir was the last of Marcus's concerns. At the moment, his main difficulty was keeping a smile from his face and his own overheated emotions in check. Corvus never smiled in front of the men, not even in the aftermath of battle when victory was assured, and Marcus was doing his level best to follow his father's example.

It was harder than it had looked, though, as every corpse past which he rode reminded him of the massive weight that had been lifted from his shoulders two mornings ago.

Somehow, he'd managed to force himself to sleep after Cassabus and his men marched forth to launch the risky night assault. The thought of spending the night in prayer and fasting had occurred to him, but the knowledge that the legion might find itself surrounded by ten thousand or more orcs if the attack failed made him decide to snatch some rest while he could. If he was going to be leading his men into battle at dawn, he owed it to them to be at his best and sharpest.

The centurions had their men ready to march before the sun rose, and a bright golden gleam was just beginning to appear on the horizon when the two riders were spotted. He'd been going over the supplies with Spina when Titus Falconius strode over and warned him that news of the battle was imminent. He'd steeled himself to be prepared for anything, a disorderly retreat, a rout, or a desperate call for reinforcements; the one thing he had not expected was complete and utter victory.

He savored the knight's words in his mind. He could still see the man's face, sweat dripping down from his helmet into eyes that were filled with an exultant pride. "General, the enemy is no more. They did not stand, but fled in complete disorder. Titus Cassabus reports no losses and only thirteen wounded, none seriously. He also requests that you bring him some sacks, as he has nowhere to store the ears he has been collecting."

The promise of an ear-harvest was why he'd determined to march the entire legion, less three centuries and two squadrons under the command of Senarius Arvandus to escort the supply train, through the forest rather than around it. They would have linked up with the Savondese army more easily by going around it, but if the enemy was routed, he had wanted to crush as many of them between him and the northerners as he could before they escaped to the east. His plan had not been without risk, given how many orcs and goblins still survived Cassabus's attack, but the silver bounty made it worth taking.

They'd reached the tribune and his exhausted centuries before the sun reached its height. Although several of the senior centurions had wanted to press on and further harry the orcs, Marcus demurred and they'd made their camp early yesterday. If the orcs were going to gather themselves and strike back in force, he wanted them to find the legion whole, behind fortifications, and armed with its war machines. The ballistae were disassembled and being transported on the wagons, but the scorpios were more useful in the heavily wooded forest anyhow.

But he'd ordered an early start this morning to compensate for the slow pace the forest imposed on them even without the mules and wagons. The men were carrying five days provisions too, and the additional weight combined with the uneven terrain further slowed them down.

A decurion on horseback made his way through the trees to avoid the infantrymen and approached him. "General, the primus pilus says there is something you should see ahead."

Marcus frowned. The scouts had spotted a few scattered orcs roaming about, but they'd fled upon catching sight of the Amorrans, and with the exception of a single wolfrider brought down by a slinger, they hadn't engaged in any combat. "Is there any sign of the enemy regrouping?"

"No, General. It looks like there was a battle of sorts. Yesterday, most like."

He followed the man forward, and at the barked commands of their optios, the centuries parted, one after the other in succession, to let him pass through their ranks. The two of them rode some way in advance of the First of the First, with the way marked by pairs of knights and Savondese guides who were serving as the vanguard and picking out the legion's path through the forest. One of the knights, Marcus saw, had a green-stained sack hanging down from the saddle horn to which it was tied; he was pleased to know that the knights did not disdain to do their part for the legionary coffers.

He could see from the brighter light that some sort of clearing was ahead, presumably one of a reasonable size, but before they reached it, they began to encounter the bodies. Orcs mostly, but there were also horses, goblins, and wolves, as well as splashes of red blood that suggested men had fallen here as well. There were dozens of corpses scattered about, with more than a few missing limbs, and not infrequently, heads. In the clearing, which was considerably larger than he'd expected, Falconius was standing with a pair of knights whose horses were tied to a tree well away from the various heaps of dead orcs and goblins that had been piled up by parties unknown; the pungent scent of death that filled the air already had his own horse skittish and tossing its head. He reined it in and looked around, more than a little confused by what he saw. Unlike the scattered bodies they'd previously passed, here it looked as if the orcs had not been running away in a panic, but attacking in what passed for good order. On the other side of the clearing, there were three large piles of green bodies stacked up in front of what appeared to be a hastily constructed fort.

"There must be five hundred dead here!" the decurion who'd accompanied him exclaimed. Marcus nodded and dismounted, then silently handed the reins to the other man.

Falconius and the two cavalry officers saluted as he approached. Their faces were grim. "Ave, General."

"What is this?"

"The Savonners must have ridden into the forest rather than waiting for them to come out," the centurion said. He reached out and tapped a wooden shaft that was holding up part of the makeshift barrier. "That's a spear with the spearhead snapped off, and based on the size of it, I'd say it's a human spear. See how the wood is polished? And the way the bodies are piled up, ain't no orcs did that. I seen some with arrows in them too, and they didn't look like they was no elf arrows."

"They must have been gathering their own dead. Otherwise, they would have left the bodies where they were."

"If it was the Savonners, they lost more than a few," Falconius agreed. "I'd guess thirty, maybe forty all told. Lots of red blood around the barricade, on all three sides too. There's about twenty dead orcs around the back; looks like the goblins rushed the side. Didn't get through, though, because there ain't much blood of any kind inside the barriers."

Marcus looked around, worried by the implications of the unexpected battle. "It doesn't make sense? Why would the king's knights have ridden into the forest? They couldn't have made use of their heavy cavalry in here. It would have made considerably more sense for them to wait and hit the orcs once they emerged from the trees."

"I know. Maybe that prince of theirs ain't got no sense."

"I don't like this. If the orcs have got a chieftain able to get them back in order so quickly, they're more disciplined than we'd thought. It's not likely, but we could find ourselves walking into an ambush. They still outnumber us four-to-one."

"Be a good place to camp if it weren't for the stink and the flies," the big centurion commented idly. "Scouts say there's a river not too far ahead."

"Route the men around this place. And assign thirty men from your century to ear-collection; see that their imaginations don't get carried away. We'll cross the river and set up march fortifications on the far bank."

"No ditch?"

"Too many roots, I should think. Tell Cassabus to have the men clear a site for the overnight castellum. However many of them managed to regroup here, it wasn't enough to attack us. I don't see the risk as being too great, not with the Savondese within a day's march."

"Ave," Falconius saluted and mounted his horse, signaling for the two knights to accompany him.

Curious as to what the Savondese could have been protecting, Marcus pushed his way past the makeshift barrier of brush and branches, and examined the ground behind it. What he saw there made him frown. In amongst the well-trodden ground and the crushed grass, there were were footprints in the moss and dirt that were too small to belong to any Savondese soldier. He kneeled down to examine one of the more cleanly demarcated ones more closely, and saw it lacked the long toes and claws that would indicate a goblin.

Had it been left by a woman? Or perhaps even a large child. Well, they would learn soon enough. He peered towards the west. They might reasonably hope to exit the forest on the morrow and make the acquaintance of their royal allies the day after that.

He glanced around the remains of the forest battlefield again, feeling the violence and desperation that were still palpable here on the stinking, bloodstained earth, written in every rictus and twisted limb. How terrible it was, and yet how glorious to be the victor!

And, he thought more coldly, how profitable. There were nearly a thousand silvers to be harvested here. Falconius's men would need to strop their blades well once their work was done.

The Savondese camp was a bewildering array of sights and sounds, to say nothing of a brilliant rainbow of colors. It reminded Marcus more of a fair than a military encampment, let alone a proper castra. Open tents were erected haphazardly as far as the eye could see, small herds of goats grazed and gamboled freely about, while men, women, and even children went about their business as if there were not still thousands of orcs lurking somewhere inside the nearby forest. And there were banners and pennants flapping everywhere in the breeze, as red pigs, white horses, green lions, blue griffons, and nearly every possible combination of color and animal, real or imaginary, was used to mark its owner.

Legio XVII had finally exited the massive, and to Marcus's mind, woefully misnamed, Elvenwood the previous afternoon. The lines for the march castra were still being laid out when a Savondese detachment arrived, consisting of four knights and six mounted men-at-arms, and bearing an imperious invitation that amounted to a summons from the Red Prince. Thus it was that Marcus, Gaius Trebonius, Arvandus, and the First of the Second's centurion, Cyriacus, found themselves being escorted by an honor guard in the direction of the Savondese army. He'd left Proculus and Cassabus behind to command the legion in his absence; The Savondese equestrians rode well enough on their slow, but powerful steeds, and the burnished plate armor of the knights was a considerable improvement over the black steel breastplates worn by the Amorrans, but thus far, they were the only martial element of note that Marcus had observed.

The senior knight, Sieur Damase de Bruissac, told them nothing about the battle they'd discovered, about the orcs, or the arrival of the legion's supply train. His round face was bland and his incurious eyes were seemingly innocent as he professed complete ignorance of anything but the prince's orders to bring the Amorran commander and the Viscomte de Lechaire to his pavilion. Judging by the pristine state of his armor, the tightness of the leather thong that attached his sword hilt to its scabbard, and his tendency to prattle on about complete inconsequentialities, Marcus was inclined to believe him.

"So I was telling Sieur Pons, he was the son of the baron at the time, before his father was given the west county by the King hisself, I was telling him that what we needed wasn't more footmen, what we needed was more wine! Ha! Oh, he laughed, he did! He was allus one for a good jest, Sieur Pons. What do you think o' that?"

Marcus smiled, a little tightly, and nodded. Other than the king, and what may have been an oblique reference to the one of the members of the king's high council, he had never heard of any of the men that Sieur Damase delighted in describing in such enthusiastic detail.

Fortunately, it was not long before they came within site of the prince's pavilion. The heir to the throne of Savonderum had elected to receive them in front of it, as there was an impromptu court setting arranged outside on the grass, complete with a gilded throne upon which a young man was sitting, flanked by men on either side, engaged in conversation with one of the blue-cloaked men to his left. A considerable audience had gathered, petitioners, it appeared, considering the unexpectedly large number of unkempt women and dirty-faced children in the mob of three or four hundred being kept at bay by armed men.

The families would be those unfortunates who had lost their homes and villages in the orc raids, he surmised, who were now desperately seeking support, if not redress, from the crown. But the crowd didn't consist only of refugees, as towards the front, he could see fatter, more prosperous men, presumably merchants or perhaps influential townsmen who had petitions of their own to present to the prince.

To the right and left of the throne, and slightly behind it, Marcus was surprised to see a pair of heads displayed on spears. Both belonged to orcs, although the one on the left was nearly twice the size of the other. It was an unexpectedly savage demonstration, and for the first time since they'd arrived in Savonderum, Marcus felt a momentary flicker of concern.

Sieur Damase pulled up his horse and raised a hand. "Stop here, monseigneurs." His voice was firmer, more commanding now, and when Marcus, surprised, looked at him, he saw the bland mask was gone, replaced by a harder, more calculating expression. "You will address the prince as Your Royal Highness. You may keep your swords, but please understand that there will be archers with arrows nocked and aimed at you."

"This is how you treat an ally?" Marcus said angrily, but in a low voice so as not to permit the curious onlookers, most of whom were now staring at the Amorrans, to hear.

"Prince's orders," Sieur Damase replied, unapologetic. "Take no offense, monseigneurs. He has learned to take precautions since the death of his brother. This is how he treats everyone, friend, ally, or suspected foe."

The Amorrans looked at each other, but it was clear that they had little choice in the matter. Given the excessively wary nature of the welcome, Marcus wasn't even certain that they would be permitted to ride away safely should they decline to see the prince now. Well, better an arrow in the chest than one in the back, he decided.

Nodding to the others, he dismounted. He threw the heavy red officer's cloak he was wearing behind his shoulders and decided to leave his helmet tied to the saddle. Even without the reported archers, there would be no escaping the Savonners if their prince had treachery in mind.

Nevertheless, he quickly surveyed the audience as well as the men with whom the prince had surrounded himself. There were about forty guards, men-at-arms wearing leather or chain mail, but they appeared to be there mostly to keep the large crowd of refugees, merchants and other supplicants seeking the prince's attention at bay. Ten formed a semicircle on either side of an alley that the other twenty had created that was just wide enough for ten men; the men-at-arms were shoving back those tried to enter it.

At Sieur Damase's gesture, the Amorrans began to walk down the gauntlet towards the throne, with Marcus leading the way. He winced as he saw one woman holding a young child by the hand foolishly try to push past a guard again after being denied; the big bearded man barely glanced at her before knocking her to her knees with a back-handed slap across her face.

As they drew closer, Marcus saw that four of the men flanking the Red Prince were knights, apparently of some rank, and three of the four were bruised or scratched about the face. They'd seen recent combat, then, they might have even been responsible for slaying some of those orcs his men had found in the forest. A fifth man, shorter than the others, was dressed simply in a black tunic and leggings. Three of the four blue-cloaks struck him as being remarkably young, nearly as young as the prince himself.

But the tallest of the four, and the one to whom the prince had been speaking, looked familiar. Marcus stifled a curse as he recognized Theuderic, royal battlemage, elf-friend, and abomination before God. Theuderic's eyes glittered with amusement at Marcus's reaction, but otherwise the arrogant sorcerer gave no outward sign of recognition.

Sieur Damase cleared his throat and startled Marcus by fairly shouting in his ear. "Your Highness, I present to you the Viscomte Trebonius of Lechaire, the Légat Valerius of Amorr, and various officers of the legion. Monseigneur, Legate, you stand before His Royal Highness Étienne-Henri de Mirid, Crown Prince of Savondir and the Seven Seats, Duc de Chênevin and Red Prince of the Sacré Royaume."

Unimpressed by the recitation of titles, Marcus had the feeling he was expected to bow, but instead he smartly nodded his head, once. As his companions followed his example, he saw the prince's lip twitch in a sneer that might have been amusement, or scorn, or perhaps even a combination of the two. But the young man didn't seem prone to take offense, as he languidly lifted two fingers of his left hand to acknowledge their presence before him.

His Royal Highness Étienne-Henri was not a tall man. Marcus guessed the prince would barely come to his nose if he stood up. The prince was also slim and small-boned, but despite his stature he held himself with a self-assurance that would have made Marcus wary even without the hidden archers. He was a good-looking youth, although his clean-shaven face was chiefly distinguishable for a prominent nose and small, deep-set eyes of an uncertain color. His fingers were long and slender, and although he sprawled carelessly on the throne, leaning upon one elbow, Marcus had the impression that he was more striking a public pose than demonstrating genuine aristocratic decadence.

He did not wear a sword, or even a dagger, and his uncalloused hands looked more accustomed to holding a harp, or flute than a weapon. And yet, his expression was confident and calmly predatory; Marcus had the impression that this was not a man who did his own killing, but one who did not hesitate to order others to do it for him. Others such as Theuderic de Merovech.

"It is good to finally meet our brave allies at last," the prince said. He was a tenor, but his voice was not unpleasant and he spoke with an air of confidence. "Monseigneur le General, I am neither unaware nor unappreciative of the assistance you provided the realm in defeating these noxious foes."

"Assistance?" Marcus asked, astonished. Theuderic closed his eyes and shook his head slightly. "That is to say, your Royal Highness."

"Forgive me, monseigneur, but I fear I do not know how one is to address one of your rank. General? Sieur? I am given to understand you may be a knight of sorts."

Marcus recovered himself and smiled. "I am no equestrian, your Royal Highness. Legatus will suffice." He saw Theuderic lean over and whisper in the prince's ear.

"Légat? Nothing more? Is that not a humble title for a man with so many swords at his disposal."

"It is not humble in the least, your Royal Highness. Five hundred senators jointly rule Amorr, whereas there are fewer than thirty legati in all the Empire."

"And only one without."

"As you say."

"I'm told there are no kings in Amorr." The prince stared at him speculatively.

"Oh, kings we have in plenty." Marcus smiled. No few are brought there and exhibited in the arena before they are beheaded. Others come of their own free will, to beg for men and gold. There are many kings in Amorr. But they do not rule. Your Royal Highness. They do not rule!"

The prince, he was not at all surprised to see, frowned at that. He clearly did not like Marcus's refusal to play vassal, but his voice remained calm. "I am told my father offered you a title, and yet, you rejected it. Why?"

"I do not expect my men and I to remain here long, your Royal Highness. God willing, we will march south in the spring. My duty is to the legion and to Amorr. I dare not accept any additional responsibilities that may come with such an honor."

"Seeing as how the greater part of the nobles of this realm appear to consider the occasional rebellion against the crown to be one of their responsibilities, I suspect the Haut Conseil would prefer if most of them would imitate your future absence."

Marcus smiled at the prince's dour expression. "I fear I know little about how things stand here in Savondir, but if they are as unsettled as they are presently in the Empire, I have no doubt you are correct, your Royal Highness. That being said, it seems to me that the orcs are our most pressing concern."

"Oh, I rather doubt they will return soon, not after the licking we gave them." The prince met his eyes, as if daring Marcus to contradict him. "As I was telling Seigneur de Thôneaux, we very much appreciate the assistance provided by you and your men. I should like to reward you, Légat, but if you will not accept lands and title, I understand there is something else I may give you."

He gestured towards the crowd behind the Amorrans.

"I have been informed that you had an amount of trouble with certain parties failing to follow through on various contracts. Is that true?"

Marcus raised his eyebrows. He wasn't surprised that the prince knew about their logistical situation, only that the matter interested the young man enough to mention it.

"I believe that is the case, your Royal Highness."

"It is to be lamented, but I fear this is an all-too-common occurrence here in the north." The prince laughed, a little bitterly, and for the first time, Marcus felt as if the young man was expressing his true feelings. "Allow me a surmise, you paid up front?"

"Only half."

"I am glad to know you're not a complete fool, Légat. I rather expect they were hoping you'd be wiped out by the orcs, so they could then sell the goods to me. I imagine they must have found your survival a disappointment of sorts. How would you have dealt with such faithless providers in your empire?"

"Failing to fulfill a legionary contract is a capital offense, your Royal Highness. Those who fail to deliver are hanged, while those who think to cheat us are excruciated. So perhaps you will understand that I am unaccustomed to anticipating any such behavior on the part of our suppliers."

"I'm astonished you have anyone willing to supply you at all."

"I am given to understand that it's only necessary to hang a few of them to convince the rest of the importance of fulfilling their obligations."

"A sound enough principle, I suppose. As it happens, we have a few of the responsible parties here." The prince lifted his hand. "Don't be shy, do come forward, my dear men. Monseigneurs les mages, if you don't mind?"

The crowd gasped. Marcus glanced to see what had drawn their attention, and did a double-take. He turned around, feeling his eyes widen with disbelief at the sight of the rosy coronas that had mysteriously appeared around the heads of five men towards the front of the audience. No, the appearance of the halos was no mystery, he corrected himself. It was magic.

He whirled around and glared accusingly at Theuderic, but the normally supercilious mage maintained an even expression as he shook his head slightly. So. If the prince knew about their procurement problems, there was no chance he wasn't well-informed about the traditional Amorran view towards the corrupting evil of sorcery. And that suggested he was knowingly flaunting it before them, although Marcus couldn't see what he might hope to gain from it. Perhaps the prince was seeking to test him.

The five men came forward at the prince's command. Three of them were babbling, almost incoherently, as they alternately pleaded their innocence and begged for mercy. One man, a fat, bearded man in a white, freshly laundered tunic stood there as impassively as a pig waiting patiently for the butcher, while the smaller man next to him also said nothing, but shook in fearful silence.

"Enough," snapped the prince. "Silence their lying tongues!"

A mage gestured. Almost as one, the five merchants jerked and clutched at their throats, eyes bulging and mouths gaping open as an invisible noose seemed to pull itself tight around their necks.

"Hanging, the Strangler, it all amounts to the same thing, doesn't it?"

"Marcus!" Gaius Trebonius hissed. Marcus could feel his heart beat faster. The prince was looking at the merchants, a cold, contemptuous smile on his face, but then he turned his gaze to the Amorrans and raised an eyebrow.

"It's rather easier this way, wouldn't you say?"

The wordless choking sounds the dying men were making was horrifying. There was something foul in it that went far beyond the mere use of sorcery; Marcus had witnessed both executions and deaths in battle, but this struck him as open murder. And worse, murder in the false cloak of justice. He glanced at the Red Prince, who was staring back at him with a hint of cruel amusement in his eyes.

"Spare them, your Royal Highness," Marcus said, even as one man dropped to his knees. "They are not Amorran citizens, and as such, they cannot be held accountable to imperial law."

The prince's dark eyes suddenly sparkled with triumph. Marcus had the impression that he had just been tested, and that he had failed the test.

"And, more importantly, they have neither been confessed by a priest nor shriven," he added.

The unseemly sparkle abruptly vanished, replaced by momentary chagrin. "Of course, Légat. You do well to remind me."

The prince raised his hand, his palm open, and as one, all five merchants gasped loudly for air. Three of them were on the ground now, and one, already doubled-over, fell to one knee.

"Forgive us, Highness!" one of the men on the ground managed to cry out, his chest still heaving.

"It is not for me to forgive," the prince said. "You have not sinned against me. Perhaps our Amorran friends, whom you have wronged, would be able to tell us how you wretched thieves might best express the full extent of your repentance?"

"Delivery," Trebonius responded immediately. "With a twenty percent reduction in the outstanding amount owed." Marcus nodded his approval. Vengeance bought neither grain nor wine, and with no access to House Valerius's treasury or credit, the legion would have to husband every king-stamped coin until it returned to the Empire.

"Is that all? Very well." Étienne-Henri addressed the five merchants, but his eyes were on Marcus. "Is this penance acceptable to you?"

As the merchants practically fell over each other in their haste to assure the prince that it was indeed acceptable, and indeed, more than acceptable to them, Marcus nodded again. And he was not surprised when the prince raised his hand and rose easily to his feet; he did not know what the young royal intended, but he was certain that a reduced price transaction would not content a man so casual about ordering five men strangled to death by sorcery right in front of him.

"Monseigneurs, monsieurs, and my good people of the East March, I know there are many here who have suffered. It is neither meet nor just that dishonest men such as these should grow fat by cheating the brave men-at-arms who defend those who have lost homes and fields and loved ones. Here is my sentence: in return for sparing their lives, the Amorrans shall pay only half their outstanding debt upon delivery, and they shall pay half of the amount saved to our loyal and well-loved vassal, the Count de Marchissy, who shall distribute it equally among the common petitioners here."

There was a moment's astonished silence, and then a cheer went up from the crowd. The prince acknowledged it with a graceful bow, then said something unintelligible to one of the knights, who laughed out loud. One knight, presumably the count referenced, looked dismayed; in a single gesture, his liege lord had adroitly saddled him with the burden of hearing the petitioners. He was the only one who showed no signs of recent combat, and Marcus had a suspicion his selection was not a coincidence, but rather, a punishment of sorts.

"Should we offer up the amount we're saving too?" Trebonius had no need to whisper with all the excited shouting behind them.

"Good Lord, no!" Marcus, startled, shook his head. "What do we care for their good will? We've saved their lives, I should think we've done enough for them."

He looked at the prince, who was acknowledging the plaudits of his grateful subjects-to-be with a self-amused smile. The young royal was evidently smarter than Marcus had assumed, which meant that he might make for a dangerous enemy if he was handled improperly. And worse, he was subtle. Which, Marcus reluctantly concluded, meant that the young man would have to be won over, even if that meant coddling his insecurities.

And that was why Marcus found himself, just a few moments later, obliged to accept the prince's invitation to join him in traveling to Lutéce, for what he was assured would be the fete of the century. Viscount Trebonius, of course, was included in the invitation.

"Your Royal Highness, I am, of course, most curious to accompany you and your entourage, and to see the royal capital, as is my colleague, but I would request of you one additional indulgence prior to our departure."

At the prince's gesture, he continued. "I should like to prepare a permanent castra, one that is capable of serving as a stronghold, not only for the legion, but for your forces as well. When the orcs come again, and your Royal Highness, they will come again, they will come in greater numbers and they will not be wolfriders and, what do you call them?"

"Pillards," Trebonius prompted.

"Yes, Pillards. They will not be pillards. They will come with their heavy infantry, their warboars and their trolls. You have won a great victory, your Royal Highness, but all it has given you is time. I wish to use that time to improve the kingdom's defenses here."

"You want to build a castle?"

"No, a castra. A fortification in the style of our march forts, only in a more secure fashion, with stone walls rather than wood. We will require it as a base to anchor the March defense against the next army to come."

"Ah, those sort of walled wooden villages you've built. Yes, I saw one on my way here. Damned impressive, they are, although I don't suppose they can be held more than a few days given how many mouths you have to feed."

"Exactly, your Royal Highness. It would pose no threat to you after we are gone, and it might save your army in the event of a reversal."

"This can be done in your absence?"

"Begun, at any rate. I am not skilled in the arts of fortification. One of the other tribunes is the architectus who will oversee the construction."

"Then again, what is to prevent you from building a castle, then breaking faith with the crown and declaring yourself sovereign?"

"What prevents me now?" Aside, Marcus belatedly thought, from your archers. "Your Royal Highness, may I not remind you that I refused the king's gracious offer of lands? I do not wish for a castle, nor will I break faith with those who do not break faith with me. I am honor-bound, no, I am *duty*-bound, to defend your lands. I ask for nothing more than your permission to permit me and my men to do so in the way we know best."

Étienne-Henri glanced at the even shorter man beside him and grinned wryly. "It seems to me I would have to be a fool to deny you, Légat. As I hope I am not a fool, I will grant your request, with the caveat that you return here before noon tomorrow and join me in my triumphant procession to Lutéce. And seeing as my father awaits us there, I should encourage you to bring along what I hear is your astonishing collection of ears."

The prince grinned openly at Marcus's discomfiture. "Have no fear, Légat. My father promised me no similar bounty. As the exchequer is not yet at my disposal, you may as well collect on them."

LUGBOL

I T TOOK the exhausted gungiyar, swollen to nearly five times its original size, fifteen days to make its way through the great forest and reach the main army. Lugbol scented it well before the shadowed and leafy prison of the trees gave way to the smoke and open spaces of the grand encampment. Despite all his boasting, Zlatagh had not stood fast, in fact, he ran like a sniveling goblin before the winged demons of the night. Lugbol, on the other hand, nearly managed to lead his orcs around the right flank of the winged demons. They turned out to be nothing more than well-disciplined men who were armored like iron turtles and bore shields large enough to cook a large goblin. But somehow, Lugbol's kors found themselves caught between the enemy flank and a small force of reinforcements, causing most of them, already unsettled by the rout of the gungiyar'ugh, to flee madly into the night.

Had they stood, his kors would have easily driven back the iron men, despite their great rectangular shields and small stabbing swords, but as it was, Lugbol lost half of the twelve kors who remained with him, including Khorpaghu. It took him two days to gather together the tattered remnants of his gungiyar; of the one hundred kors he'd led prior to the night attack, only sixty-five remained. Their cowardice made him furious, and he was greatly tempted to flay four or five of them as an example to the others, but to his surprise, the dour Ghurash encouraged him to let it pass.

"Too soon," the veteran warrior growled. "And they held up a damn sight better than any of Zlatagh's water-boweled leg-pissers. Give them that, by Gor-Gor's left bollock!"

"They still ran in the end!"

"So did we, in the end."

So we did, Lugbol had to admit. When Korpaghu fell before the iron men, pierced through the eye, both he and Ghurash took to their heels, running from the terrible swords that licked out suddenly from behind the giant metal shields like deadly dragon's teeth. Perhaps they had stood longer than the others, perhaps they had been a little more brave, but in the end, they had run. That was why they were still alive.

And so Lugbol not only let it pass, but instead praised his kors for showing the wit to remain in the relative vicinity rather than continuing to flee in all directions throughout the Elvenwood. Afterwards, his first thought was to lead them back through the woods to the main army, until he realized that they simply didn't have the supplies to make it there. Or at least for all of them to make it there. Korphaghu estimated that they would need to eat two of their number each day, which would mean returning with less than half the kors in the gungiyar.

"We could draw sticks, if you didn't want to let them fight it out."

"It might work once, after that, anyone that thought they might be next to draw the short one would run off. What was the point of gathering them up if we're just going to scare them away?"

"We could kill all of them that we need first."

"There are lots of dead orcs less than a half-day's march away. We don't need to make more."

"You're thinking we should go back?" Ghurash looked at him as if he'd gone berserk. "To where the iron men are?"

"To where they were. They'll have moved on, I'm sure. We'll send a pair of scouts first."

"Send five. Send ten. If you're wrong, we'll have that many fewer mouths to feed."

However, in the day that it took for the scouts to return, twenty-five more kors from six different gungiyar'ugh entered their makeshift camp. And the scouts came back with nineteen more, as well as the welcome news that the bodies they would require to sustain themselves were freely accessible, with no sign of the iron men except for the violent evidence of their passing. By they time they'd retraced their steps and returned to the scene of the night slaughter, Lugbol found himself the unexpected warleader of more than two hundred kors. And by the time they'd finished butchering the dead, cooking the meat, and stripping the camp of everything of value, they were more than four hundred fifty strong.

They gathered another sixty-eight along the way, although five died of their wounds and four more died in squabbles that turned lethal. Actually, only three of them died as a result of fighting, the fourth one had his skull split by Ghurash when the galvebel found him standing over the body of his victim.

The fact that they were no longer fleeing from a terrifying foe, but returning in good order lifted their spirits, and they marched back proudly to rejoin the main army, defeated but not beaten, their voices lifted in a song that Lugbol's kors taught the others.

> We are the eyes of the infantry
> We walk first and we walk free
> Don't mess with us
> Don't scream and fuss
> We're the best in the damn army!
> We'll beat you hard
> Defeat you hard
> We're the Black Fist Infantry
> We'll break your head
> Then squag you dead
> We're the best in the damn army!

Lugbol couldn't help feeling a surge of fierce pride as the voices of the kors echoed off the trunks of the trees. They might not be the terrible Red Claw Slayers, and they might march on their bare feet rather than sit astride the wide backs of the mighty warboars, but of all the gungiyars that had marched out under Zlatagh's piss-yellow banner, his Black Fists were very likely the only warband returning in good order. More than good order, as it happened, and considerably stronger than before.

The strangely soft mossy carpet of the forest floor gradually gave way to hard-packed dirt, and the tall trees on either side to war machines, huge piles of felled trees, haphazard stacks of the branches that had been stripped from them, tents, and big leather tarps under which various bands of goblins and orcs were sleeping. The familiar stench of the camp came as a relief; it was a sure sign that they were safe once more.

A few scores of younger orcs scurried over to watch them pass, and he could tell they were sqwaaks even without the tell-tale stripe of white clay over their noses. They gawked at the weary, blood-stained kors; this was probably the first they'd seen of the war into which they had been drafted. Their innocence drew snorts and sneers from the kors, but for the most part, their passage went unremarked by the camp dwellers.

A violent game of Skullkick was drawing considerably more onlookers, as two groups of powerful orcs, mountain orcs from eastern Zoth Ommog by the look of them, were battling over a much-abused goblin head. When a big kick sent the skull sailing out of bounds high over the crowd, one of the players simply reached out with two powerful hands and ripped the head off the shoulders of a young goblin standing at the front of the crowd, drawing shrieks from the nearby goblins and hearty laughter from players on both sides.

Lugbol chuckled himself, although he noticed that as the orc punted the head far across the field to the other team, sending it arcing through the air trailed by a spray of dark green blood, the goblins were not laughing.

"Who we going to report to?" Ghurash grunted. The taciturn kor didn't appear to have even noticed the game.

"Whatever general is least likely to blame us for Zlatagh getting hisself good and squagged."

"Best stay away from any of the Zoth Ommoghu commanders, then."

Lugbol nodded. Zlatagh was, or by this point, more likely had been, a son of the cousin of one of the king's younger brothers. That was why he'd been given the command of the raiders, and his failure was bound to make the Zoth Ommoghu look bad.

"Uh oh," he said, seeing a banner ahead that appeared to be moving rapidly in their direction. It was a black pennant, but thanks to the breeze, an outstretched clawed hand could be seen sewn in red upon it. "Don't like that. Looks like Slayers."

The various orcs and goblins that stood in between them and the approaching orcs seemed to vanish, and a moment later, a patrol of the much-feared mountain orcs were seen marching toward them. The Red Claw Slayers were one of the elite heavy infantry units of Zoth Ommog, they were famed throughout the septs for their gloves and boots made from the skin of trolls they'd slain, but ever since the Great Orc Azzakhar summoned the gungiyar'ugh and announced the invasion of the Man and Elf lands, they had served as Azzakhar's personal enforcers.

There were only seven of them to Lugbol's five hundred, but even so, he felt outnumbered. The galvebel who led the patrol was a good head taller than him, and looked as if he weighed half again as much. Even if Lugbol's arm was mostly healed now, he knew wouldn't last much longer against the massive orc than the average goblin sqwaak. And two of the galvebel's kors were even bigger; marked with more white scars than tattoos, they were the survivors of inter-tribal wars far more vicious than anything Lugbol or his Black Fists had ever seen.

The big Slayer stopped and stared at him. Lugbol stopped as well, and raised his hand. The five columns of kors behind him came to a shuffling halt.

"You, Shugaba, you were with the First Raiding Expedition, weren't you?"

"Damn straight, Galvebel!" Lugbol saluted. "Black Fist Kor Infantry, Lugbol, kai hari shugaba gungiyar. Zlatagh Maneater, gran-kor."

The Slayer ignored his salute. "The Great Orc wants to see you immediately. Have your second find quarters for your kors. You'll come with me."

Lugbol glanced at Ghurash, who nodded. "Am I under arrest?"

"I don't know jack, Shugaba. I got orders to bring you to the Great Orc, so do you walk or do I have my kors beat you down and carry you?"

"No, I'll walk!"

"Good." Without further ado, the Slayer turned around and began stalking back in the direction he'd come. The bannerkor and the other Slayers waited until both the galvebel and Lugbol walked past them, then fell in behind them. Lugbol was relieved to see they were acting more like an honor guard than captors.

They attracted stares as they walked toward the center of the camp, past large piles of well-gnawed bones and smaller piles of refuse, but it was only the dread banner of the Slayers that attracted them, Lugbol soon realized. Gradually, he relaxed, as he concluded that if the Great Orc wanted him dead, he would be dead already. No, most likely Azzakhar simply wanted to know where his twenty-five thousand orcs and goblins were.

"Is it true?" the galvebel said unexpectedly.

"Is what true?"

"Zlatagh, the raiding army. It's said he lost a battle, a big one."

"You could say that." Lugbol grimaced. "Has anyone from any other units come back?"

"Dribs and drabs. Yours was the first gungiyar to return intact."

Intact? Lugbol snorted. "If you can call it that."

"How many did you lose?"

"Thirty-four. We got ourselves caught between two enemy units during a night attack."

"Heavy?"

"Very. They was like iron turtles."

"Not savon'ugh, then."

"Don't think so."

The bigger orc growled thoughtfully. "You could have done a damned sight worse, Lugbol-shuga. Most shugaba, especially the sort commanding the light infantry, would have lost the lot. So listen. Keep your chin up when you talk to the Great Orc. He don't like no cowards. He don't take no lip neither, but he hates cowards."

Lugbol glanced at the big galvebel, who was staring resolutely forward. He hadn't expected such helpful advice from a Red Claw Slayer. "Thanks, Galvebel."

The Slayer grunted. Soon they past a pair of guard-kors who had the Slayer claw branded on their knotted left biceps; both slammed their fists against their chests loudly in a manner that indicated respect. Little wonder, Lugbol thought, if this galvebel knew enough about the Great Orc to indicate his likes and dislikes.

They were approaching a giant pale green tent that was decorated with haphazardly placed sigils of some kind that were mostly blue and black. Magical protections, perhaps? But there was no pattern to them that he could initially discern until they got closer and he could see what they were. Lugbol's eyes widened as he realized the rumors he'd discounted in the past were actually nothing more than the simple truth; the marks were not sigils, but tattoos and Azzakhar's royal tent had been constructed from the flayed skins of his fallen enemies. And looming behind it was something even more awe-inspiring.

He must have inadvertently stopped walking at the astonishing sight before him, because the galvebel snorted and pulled at his arm. "Nobody gets to be Great Orc by smelling no flowers. Only reason we're all still here sitting on our arses and eating our gobbos is because Azzakhar's the baddest of the bad-arsed."

It wasn't so much the tattooed tent as the gargantuan pyramid of skulls behind it that caused Lugbol to nod slowly in mute amazement. And fear. He didn't believe there was much danger of his skin being added to the tent, but having his skull added to the bone-yellow pyramid that reached to the sky like an evil offering appeared to be a distinct possibility. He suddenly found himself wishing he'd had the sense to stay in the relative safety of the Elvenwood.

A pair of even bigger orcs stood guard at the tent flap. A strangely familiar scent wafted out from it, and all of Lugbol's senses went on alert. He stood up straighter, his fear forgotten, and sniffed eagerly at the air.

"Keep it in your pants," the galvebel growled. "Of course he's got kwee with him. That's one of the privileges of being the big damn Great Orc. But if you don't keep your head on straight and forget the pretties are about with their quiffings and whiffings, he'll rip off your vank and feed it to his devil-witch."

Lugbol nodded and tried very hard to ignore the effect that the scent of the kwee was having on his body. The guards must have recognized the galvebel, because they nodded at him and pulled aside the big flap. It was high enough that even the taller galvebel was able to enter without ducking, and through it they stepped into a world that seemed entirely different than the stinking, green-stripped encampment outside.

Soft furs of various animals lined the floor of the tent, wolf, bear, fox, and several others that Lugbol couldn't identify. The trophies of the Great Orc's many triumphs were on display, from the cracked granite crown that had once belonged to a rival orc king to the giant troll's skull mounted on a sawed-off spear, it was an impressive collection. There were gilded Dwarf toys and other items Lugbol recognized as having been looted from the Man villages.

But it was the kwee that made the biggest impression on Lugbol, since he had been devoid of female companionship since the Great Orc demanded a one-third levy of every orc kingdom, sept, clan, and tribe in Hagahorn. There must have been a dozen kir'agh there, most of them half-naked, their smooth green skin alluringly highlighted by bright bits of captured man-cloth. Their little tusks were all capped with silver, and he saw their bored eyes brighten a little at his entrance, less from any interest in a small kor from the northern plains than at the prospect of some amusing cruelties to come.

Nor were they the only females. There were also two pretty young gob'agh, and unexpectedly, a female troll as well. It appeared the Great Orc was considerably less limited in his appetites than Lugbol would ever have imagined. The troll was smaller than the few trolls Lugbol had seen, mostly at a distance, but she was still sizable. She was leaning back on a knee-stool gnawing on a bone that was very nearly the size of Lugbol's leg. Except for a delicate iron chain about her waist, she was also stark naked, and Lugbol couldn't help noticing that not only were her breasts larger than his head, but her neck was thicker than his thighs.

For once, his imagination failed him entirely. With some effort, he managed to stop staring at the she-troll and direct his attention toward the large orc sitting sprawled upon a makeshift wooden throne.

The galvebel saluted, then bowed. "The shugaba of the returned gungiyar, Great Orc, as ordered."

"Very good, galvebel. You can go now."

"Great Orc!"

Lugbol stood straight and tried his best not to cringe as the Great Orc sat up on his throne and looked him over with a disturbing level of interest. Azzakhar was even bigger than the Slayers, and he dressed as if he was one of them, in fighting leathers, with only a black iron crown and gilded tusks to denote his royal status. His face was flat and brutish, but intelligent, his nostrils were bigger and his tusks were smaller than Lugbol would have expected. His scabbarded cleaver was hung carelessly off the back of the throne, and he didn't even wear a dagger on his belt, although the height of his blue trollskin boots indicated that one might be concealed there.

But his claws were tipped with sharpened iron, and no orc with powerful hands the size of his could ever be considered weaponless. One white scar ran the length of his left bicep, while a somewhat newer one, healed but dark green, marred the left side of his face. This was no token king held up by his kin of sept and clan, but a true orc king who ruled by the strength of fist and the force of his will.

Behind him was a curtain that partially obscured movement of someone, or something, concealed behind it. Whatever it was, it was moving, but it wasn't until Lugbol heard a squeal in response to a rhythmic grunting that he realized what was happening there. He must have betrayed his surprise, because the Great Orc sat up and laughed.

"Never mind them. Your name is Lugbol," he declared unexpectedly. "I'm told you survived the battle that destroyed Zlatagh and the army I gave him."

"I did, Great Orc. As did most of my kors. Gog Black Fists. Light infantry."

"I heard you brought some stragglers with you too. That's good. Now, how in the name of Gor Gor's giant vank did twenty-five thousand kors manage to get themselves killed?"

"I don't know exactly, Great Orc. We were attacked in our camp at night. No one expected it. They weren't savon'ugh. They wore iron and carried great shields. And they had strange war machines that threw terrible balls of fire. Like a shaman, only not magic. Most of the gungiyars were taken by surprise and routed in a panic."

"Panic!" Azzakhar snarled. "How many of them attacked?"

"I don't know, Great Orc. It was very dark, with the trees blocking the moonslight. I was walking the rounds, checking on the guard posts when the attack came. I think that is why I was able to keep my kors together. We fought our way past them and then we returned here after gathering up the others. None of them could tell me much; some of them never even saw any enemy."

"They fled north, where they were destroyed by the savon'ugh." The Great Orc nodded and ran a clawed finger up and down one of his golden tusks in a thoughtful manner. He seemed to come to some sort of decision then, because he looked back over his shoulder and roared at someone behind the curtain.

"Tain! Get your horny damned hide out here!"

Both the movement and the grunting came to a sudden stop. "Just give me a little while–"

"Stow your damned vank and get your arse out here now or I'll cut it off and feed it to you!"

"All right, all right," a sullen voice grumbled.

"He doesn't actually think with his bollocks, even though you might think so," the Great Orc confided. Lugbol nodded mutely, knowing he was entirely out of his element. He'd felt safer in the forest fleeing from the Iron Men.

It didn't make him feel any less uneasy when the biggest orc Lugbol had ever seen pushed his way through the curtain. General Tain was immense, wearing nothing but a sort of leather loincloth that did little to hide the monstrous vank that was threatening to burst it. His skin was a greenish blue, and his tusks were short, thick, blunt, and unadorned. Lugbol had seen him at a distance before, but never up close, and now that he did, he realized the general was at least one-quarter troll.

"This better be damned important, Azza."

"It is. Lugbol, describe those Men that attacked you."

As Lugbol dutifully described them again, and did his best to answer the general's pointed questions about their armor, he could see that both the Great Orc and the half-orc were excited about something.

"How did they fight?" General Tain demanded. "Not how well, we know they did for Zlatagh."

"They stand in close formation. They must drill a lot, because they stay tight. Their swords are very short, more like long daggers than proper swords. They don't use them to chop either. They hide behind large shields and then the short swords flick out like a snake's tongue. They're not very big, maybe between our size and a goblin, they're smaller than the savon'ugh. But a small group of them chopped us up pretty bad. I lost my second galvebel to them."

"They all wear the same sort o' helms, with metal covering their faces?" General Tain raised both hands to his face, covering his cheeks beyond his tusks. "Open in the middle. Some o' them got plumes like a rooster."

"Like that, yes."

"Amor'agh," the general told the Great Orc. "It's got to be. No other men wear pots on their head and fight on foot with little swords."

"Then we can finally march! The witch said if they come north, then the Stone ain't in the south. So she'll want to head west."

"So we march west."

"No, the main body will go south first. The elves must be destroyed; I dasn't leave them at my back to chew on my arse. They've had their damned birds flying over us morning and night, so they'll know if we move on the Savon'agh."

"Maybe they'll leave us go?"

The Great Orc shook his head. "Maybe, but the alv'agh are weak. Only three cities remain to them now. Merithaim and Elebrion we can smash. The city by the sea could be difficult. We have no boats so they can just sail away."

"Don't need no boats. We smash the two cities and kill all their wizzies at the wizzy tower, they'll be too busy hiding by the seashore and pissing themselves to get in the way of anything we do after. They'll just be glad we're gone."

"How long?"

"Ten days for Merithaim. Four weeks for Elebrion."

"So long?"

"We gots to drag the war machines up the mountain. That takes time, especially with elven sky riders dropping rocks and magic on our heads."

"There is that." He indicated Lugbol. "You got any use for this one? Might make for an officer. He was the only shugaba out of eighty-three to bring back his gungiyar intact. In fact, I'm told he come back with more kors than he left with."

Tain looked over Lugbol, a faint scowl on his face. It was an intimidating sight, but Lugbol remembered the Slayer's instructions and did his best to stand tall and show no fear.

"He's too small to make a regular. Where's he from, Gog? He'd end up squagged, if not potted, the first day. He'd need a pair of enforcers to babysit him, and if we're going to march soon, he won't have time for them to kick his kors into shape."

The Great Orc nodded. "What do you think, Lugbol-shuga? You want in the real army?"

"With no disrespect to the general, Great Orc, I think it would be best to stay with the Black Fists. We took a real licking out there and the kors are just starting to get their spirit back. If I can, I'd just ask to keep the kors we picked up from the other gungiyar, at least those as want to stay on. A lot of them don't got no unit no more, and they got nowhere to go."

The two bigger orcs looked at each other. The general snorted. "Sounds like a right grun-kor to me. He's right, he'll do better with his own orcs, but a proper rank would be useful. That way he won't have to take any murdu from some damned regular with rocks for brains."

The Great Orc concurred, nodding. "You can keep your kors, Lugbol. All of them, if you want. Kick out the whiners and the slackers as you see fit. But the general says you sound like a proper grun-kor and I can't see he's wrong. So, what will it be, the ink or the fire?"

Lugbol couldn't stop the smile that came to his face. He stood taller and he knew what the answer had to be, although he didn't relish the pain that would inevitably ensue. "If it's your hand that'll do it, Great Orc, I'll take the fire."

"If it's his hand you want, then it'll have to be the fire. He does the ink, no one will know if you're a slave or a damn general!" General Tain laughed and then bellowed out some orders. It wasn't long before a brazier was produced, hot and smoking, and protruding from it was a metal rod with a wooden handle.

"You want something to bite down on, Lugbol-shuga?"

"No, Great Orc."

"Ain't no shame in the ink, you know. Most of my officers wear the tattoo."

Lugbol nodded. The general was telling the truth, but not all of it. There wasn't a single officer in the Red Claw Slayers, or in the other elite units, who didn't wear his rank burned into his flesh. The arms of both General Tain and the Great Orc were scarred with the brands of rank, among them, the sigil presently heating up in the brazier.

"I'll take the fire all the same, general."

"Ahr!" The general smote Lugbol approvingly on the shoulder with his meaty hand, nearly knocking him over. "Maybe we'll see you in the regulars yet, little Goghu!"

The Great Orc rose from his wooden throne, walked over to the brazier, and withdrew the branding iron from the flame. The end was glowing and radiating heat that Lugbol could feel on his face; the nearly molten iron pulled his eyes to it and mesmerized him. He could barely hear what Azzakhar was telling him, but he stood as straight as he could, tensed his left arm, and grabbed his left wrist with his right hand. He felt, rather than saw, the general move behind him, then one powerful hand grabbed his right shoulder while the other one supported his left elbow, leaving his left bicep exposed.

The Great Orc stepped in front of him, and for a moment, Azzakhar's yellow eyes met his own. Azzakhar nodded once, and then pain unlike any Lugbol had ever known erupted in his upper arm. The searing agony seemed to tear through his flesh and deep into the bone, but he growled low in his throat and resisted the instinctive urge to pull away. He tried to count, but the pain was too intense. It seemed as if the moment would last forever, that he was trapped in a fragment of a fiery Hell. And then suddenly the pressure was gone, the intensity of the pain receded, and he could smell the stink of his own burned flesh. Sweat poured down from his brow and trickled down his sides, and he found himself breathing hard, as if he'd just sprinted across a field.

"Damn good, Grun-kor!" A big hand swatted his backside. "Taken like a true kor indeed!"

The Great Orc merely nodded, then slipped the branding iron back in the brazier. But when he turned around again, Lugbol could see a satisfied look in the bigger orc's eyes.

"Thank you, Great Orc!" He stood up straight and saluted.

"Grun-kor." The Great Orc returned the salute. "You are hereby ordered to return to your unit, which I am raising to regimental status. Have a banner made accordingly. But before you go, is there anything more you'd like than a scar on your arm?"

"The honor is more than this kor deserves, Great Orc!" Lugbol barked in his best imitation of the Slayers he'd seen. But he couldn't help a sidelong glance at some of the nearby kir'agh, the more curious of whom had been watching his promotion.

General Tain burst out laughing. "The lad's been in the field for months, Azza! Can't you see the poor bastard is starving for ghash?"

Lugbol felt mortified, but he couldn't deny that the general was right. Even so, he couldn't bring himself to ask. No orc worth his sweat begged for kwee; not even here where there was none to be found except by permission of the Great Orc. A proper kor took, he did not ask. He said nothing.

But his silence did not fool Azzakhar. The big orc winked and spread his hand at the kir'agh behind him. "Take your choice with you. You can have her for three days and share her with your galvebels, but not more than two per day. Return her in the same shape you found her or I'll rip off that arm I just branded and rape you with it. And if you'll take my advice, don't pick the half-troll unless you want your bloody vank ripped out by the roots."

The newly appointed grun-kor of the Black Fist light infantry regiment looked at the kir'agh standing, or in some cases, seductively lying, before him. They looked back at him, their interest clearly piqued by the favor the Great Orc had shown him. One of them, one of the smaller kir, had short, powerful legs, a long mane dyed blue, and a challenging stare that he found particularly appealing. He indicated her, and she rose, shooting a triumphant sneer at the rest of the harem.

Grun-kor Lugbol exited the tent, burning pain on one arm and the most beautiful kir he'd ever seen on the other. It wasn't until three nights later, when he lay in his new tent sniffing happily at the fading scent of kwee in the air, that he realized why the Great Orc had given the kir to him for three days. Judging by the increasingly urgent orders being shouted in the camp around him, it would not be long before the Great Orc ordered his sprawling army to take the field at last.

STEINTHOR

THE MOOD in the entry hall was surprisingly cheerful, Steinthor thought as he limped painfully into it. He was sorry that Horse-Bjorn hadn't lived to see the fey scene; it would have warmed his black heart to see so many men spitting contemptuously into the face of death. The Grævling saw him and quickly made his way over to him and clapped him on the shoulder. A rare smile lit up his grey-bearded face.

"Strongbow! You made it! I heard both you and Horse-Bjorn fell."

"He fell all right," Steinthor said regretfully. "Stood over me when a wolf knocked me down, and a moment later, got himself thrown from the tower."

"I'll wager he died happy if he landed on one."

"I don't know about that. He was cursing hellfire the last I heard him. Probably didn't think it was proper heroic, getting tossed like that. Poor bastards just trying to enjoy the feast'll be getting an earful about that for a long time!"

They both laughed at the thought of the Horse-Bjorn bitching and complaining to anyone in Valhalla who would listen to him about the manner of his dying.

"You held them off longer than I thought. For a while, I was thinking we went to all this trouble for nothing. I was afraid we'd have to do it all over again tomorrow night!"

"No fear of that." Steinthor sighed and looked around at the exhausted, bloody men surrounding him. They were doing their best to keep their spirits up, each man bragging about how many wolves he had killed or how bravely one of his companions died. The ale didn't hurt, of course, and he gladly took a big horn from which the ale was sloshing forth from a grinning man whose bleeding face had been badly raked by four claws from cheek to jaw.

The cold ale was like a godsend to his battle-parched throat. It might be the last beer he'd ever drink, but damned if it wasn't the best he'd ever tasted! It seemed life was like love, always sweetest at the end.

And the end was nigh. He drained the horn to its dregs, then tossed it to the floor. The Graevling looked at him inquisitively and he nodded. It was time for one final draught.

"Drink deeply, men," he called as the Graevling's men dragged out the bottom two-thirds of a cask that had been filled with mead. "We'll sour their bellies, we will, damn them if we don't!"

The men looked at him expectantly. Then Egil the Wyrm started stomping his feet. The others picked it up, and then the chanting began. "Død! Død! Død!" Death! Death! Death!

Steinthor knew what they wanted. The mead was laced with hellebore and whatever other evils the Graevling had seen fit to add. Skollvaldr alone knew what the concoction contained, or what it would taste like, and for all that the men were ready to die in battle, it was a hard thing to hold your own death in the palm of your hand, to taste it, and to drink it down.

"Someone give me a damned sword!" he bellowed, and in a heartbeat there were ten or more blades being offered to him. He took the one that looked to have retained the most edge and raised it high in his right hand as he approached the cask and its tainted mead. A wooden cup was bobbing in the weirdly clouded liquid and Steinthor pushed it down into the mead before pulling it back up again, full and spilling over his left hand.

"Død for ulvene!" he shouted.

"Death to the wolves!" they shouted back.

"Død til os!"

"Death to us!" they echoed.

It was now or never, he thought to himself. He raised the cup of death to all of them, to each of them, to every doomed man there and every dead man who had fallen bravely in battle, and he realized, somewhat to his surprise, that he was thirsty.

"Now we are truly the dead," he said quietly, mostly to himself, and he raised the wooden cup to his lips. The mead was bitter and it burned like oily fire down his gullet, but he emptied the cup in a single draught. Ottar the Graevling nodded to him, acknowledging that the irrevocable step had at last been taken, and the approving roar of the men echoed off the stone walls of the hall.

Enflamed by his example, men crowded towards the cask, unafraid and eager to drink from the cup of death. But Steinthor didn't wait to watch. He didn't know exactly how much time was left to him, but he knew there wasn't much and there were still wolves to kill.

"Open the doors!" he bellowed. "Open the gates!"

The great wooden doors creaked open. The Graevling ran to his side and handed him a torch. He looked back and saw that Ottar's men had a large stack of them and were beginning to light them. No sooner had a man drank from the cask and roared out his defiance of the death that would soon claim him than he was pushed towards Steinthor and handed a blazing torch.

Steinthor and the Graevling looked at each other. Neither one spoke. There was nothing to say. Steinthor looked around, saw that ten or twelve men had joined him, and decided that was enough. He pointed his torch at the fires that indicated the center of what passed for the Aalvarg encampment.

"Død for ulvene!" he shouted one more time, and then he plunged forward into the darkness.

The Aalvarg were initially taken aback by the unexpected sortie from the main gate. Their attention was on the two towers they had taken and they were fully occupied with trying to break down the barred and reinforced doors that would give them access to the heart of Raknarborg. The wolves closest to the entrance were not prepared for further battle, and were in fact milling aimlessly about, snapping at each other, and in some cases, even curled up and sleeping.

Steinthor drove his sword through one cringing wolf and set another alight with his torch. It soon became clear that these were not whatever passed for front-line troops, as they were smaller than those on the tower, and many of them yipped and ran before the attacking Dalarn. A few snarling wolves tried halfheartedly to stand, but they were rapidly overrun by the men who stumbled forward despite their wounds and the poison that coursed through their veins.

"How long do you think we have?" gasped one bearded warrior, his left arm hanging uselessly at his side.

"Long enough to get there," Steinthor grunted, pointing at the fires that were their destination. It didn't really matter, but he knew the men needed a destination, and if there was any chance he could somehow kill one of the Aalvarg leaders, he was going to seize it.

He'd asked the Graevling to brew something that would be as deadly as it was slow-acting. It seemed he had succeeded, since he hadn't dropped over dead as soon as he'd quaffed the doombrew, as he'd half-expected. Whether it would be strong enough to sicken the wolves that devoured them or if it would merely cause the monsters to turn away from their corpses, there was no way to know. But either fate was preferable to ending up in an Aalvarg gullet.

A series of howls came from the hills above them. They were answered by the wolves on either side, and almost immediately, the few wolves that had been harrying them fell back. It soon became apparent that the enemy was no longer resisting their charge, but was retreating steadily before it. Steinthor looked to the left and he could see eyes glowing in the torchlight, moving as they loped easily alongside the jogging men. The same was true on the right. They were escorting him to the very place he wanted to go, he realized with grim satisfaction.

The slope of the hill was a struggle. More than one man collapsed, overcome with blood loss, and was quickly seized and dragged off into the darkness. The others didn't even attempt to resist. The poison was beginning to take effect, and just to keep moving required all their remaining strength as their stomachs began to cramp and their heads began to spin. But the fires grew closer, and as the slope began to flatten out, Steinthor began to believe they might actually make it to the top.

The wolves falling back in front of him abruptly parting like water striking a large rock in the middle of a river. To Steinthor's astonishment, he found himself facing a large Aalvarg in fully human form, standing nearly as tall as Steinthor himself despite its bare feet. In the light of the flames, he could see the man-thing was wearing an ill-fitting breastplate, underneath which it wore nothing but tattered rags. It held no weapon, nor did it appear to have any about its hairless body, which was lean, but powerful. It was flanked by others also wearing human shape, but none of them were as tall as it was.

"Sigskifting!" he heard someone behind him exclaim. Skinchanger.

"I permit you to come, warrior" growled the big sigskifting in a gravelly voice. "There will be no more manflesh until we cross the great waters."

Steinthor laughed. It was a cold, mirthless laugh, but it took the Aalvarg by surprise.

"Død for ulvene!" he shouted, and attacked.

In normal circumstances, he might have had the sigskifting, but wounded and poisoned as he was, his reactions were too slow. The big creature easily evaded his thrust and smashed its left fist into the side of Steinthor's head, sending him sprawling to the ground. His men rushed past him, but they were immediately beset on every side, as the wolves tore them to pieces, howling triumphantly all the while. Steinthor pushed himself up to his knees, but before he could regain his feet, a violent spasm gripped his innards and he collapsed again, convulsing.

There was a growl in his right ear and then he was shoved over onto his back, his arms flopping weakly above his head. He felt heat on his cheek and a heavy panting, but his sight was failing and even the fires were growing dim. Then the face of the sigskifting appeared, practically nose to nose. The creature's face was still human, but it was changing, elongating. Mottled fur sprouted from its skin and its teeth yellowed and grew longer. But Steinthor could still just make out words underneath the guttural growling.

"I'm going to rip your throat out and eat your guts, Man! By the time I shit you out, you and all your tribe will be forgotten forever!"

"You'll be shitting naught but blood if you're lucky!" Steinthor spat his last defiance just as the monster howled and clamped down on his exposed throat.

Poisoned blood sprayed from his punctured jugular and his legs kicked frantically in his death throes, but Steinthor didn't feel any pain. His eyes widened, not in death, but amazement, as he saw a bright light descending rapidly from the black skies above. The light transformed into a hand, a slender female hand stretching out towards him, and even as he died, he exulted in the certainty that when Skuli Skullbreaker finally arrived in the Hall of Heroes, he, Steinthor Strongbow, would be there waiting.

SKULI

THE SEA SWELLS were gentle, but the hearts of the men who rode them were heavy. Dawn had broken under a cloud-filled sky, which they all knew meant the friends they'd left behind in Raknarborg were now dead. It was one thing to salute the courage of a man going off to face his fate with a brave heart, but another to realize the emptiness of the knowledge that one would never see his face again. Skuli sat in the prow of the boat, wrapped in the thick wool blanket under which he'd slept the night before. A few fat drops of water clung to it, but for the most part it was dry thanks to the relative calm of the sea. He found himself thinking about the Strongbow, part of him wishing he'd stayed behind to die at his friend's side, but another part feeling relieved to know that he was still alive. And with that feeling of relief came shame.

Someone slapped him on the back. It was Mord Redcheek, his disloyal second-in-command, who'd come forward to join him.

"Don't be looking so gloomy now, Skullbreaker. They died well. And we'll see them again soon enough, I reckon."

"Aye," Skuli said, but his heart wasn't in it. He saw the Redcheek's hands were red and chapped, and he was rubbing them together as if to warm them. "Were you at the steerboard?"

"Not much steering to do. The winds took us clear."

"You'll want some sleep, then."

"Thought I'd see how you were doing first. With any luck, it will be a grey day. I can't sleep when the damn sun is bright on the waves."

Skuli painfully extended his legs and stared at them. They throbbed with a dull, bone-deep pain, but that was nothing new. At the moment, the stiffness from spending the night with his legs curled up actually hurt worse than the still-healing wounds in his chest and shoulder. He grunted and massaged his aching muscles.

"I've had worse. Just need a few days to let it heal. It's not like we're going to be walking anywhere soon."

"We'll want to land in a day or two. Keep the butts full. No sense in drawing them dry if we don't have to."

Skuli nodded. They would want to be sure they were sufficiently provisioned for a south crossing at all times. A thought occurred to him. "Do you think the wolves plan to cross the sea?"

"Would have saved us considerable trouble if they had in the first place. That, or we should have run sooner and left the damned Isles to them at the start."

"We didn't know they were so many. No one did."

Not until it was far too late. Skuli closed his eyes and listened as the sail rustled and the sea slapped against the sides of the longboat as it cut smoothly through the waves. The wind was moderate, but it was mostly an east wind and it pushed them along at a healthy rate. But to where? They did not know with any certainty that the home of the cursed wolf-demons was on the big island, it was little more than instinct that drew them there. If only they knew when and where the wolves had first shown their ugly furred faces, then they would know where to go! But even after decades of unending war and steadily being slaughtered and pushed east, they were as ignorant as their fathers had been.

The Redcheek clapped him on the shoulder. "The men are all glad you're here. Just think what a saga it will make!"

"We have no skald. Who will sing it?" He stared at a gull as it dove down towards the surface, presumably having spotted a fish, but came up with nothing in its yellow beak. "I wonder if that is how they were able to overcome us so easily?"

"Because we have no skalds?"

"No." Skuli shifted his weight and pulled the blanket tighter around his shoulders. With the heavy grey clouds overhead, it would not warm up until the sun climbed higher behind them. Even so, they did not look like rain. "Because we have not the art of writing like the southerners do. You saw how they planned their every move, how they kept track of the enemy numbers."

"They still fled across the sea, for all their art."

"One of their mages told me that an army of Aalvarg once crossed the sea, in his grandfather's grandfather's day. They defeated them, destroyed them utterly. And yet we, who have freely reaved their coasts for centuries, were defeated. There is a reason for that, Mord Redcheek."

"Ah, there's a reason for everything, Skullbreaker. But it will do no harm to think more on it. We're not going to retake our islands tomorrow."

"No. How are we for food?"

The Redcheek laughed. "This is not the first time I've reaved. We've stores a-plenty, dried cod and herring, flatbread, and we'll hunt once we get to land. And we can always eat wolves."

"I've tried it." Skuli grimaced. "Foul and stringy. Worse than they smell. Only good for soup, if that."

The Redcheek laughed again, slapped him on the back, and made his way aft. Skuli stared moodily out over the waves, wondering if he was making a mistake not simply ordering the longboat south, to join Dagna and the rest of his surviving people. At least he knew Brynjolf and Fjotra were faring well; if nothing else, his decision to send them south to the King had proven to be a wise one.

The Dalarn would survive. There were other clans and families who had crossed the sea sooner, of course, but they were scattered everywhere from northern Savondir to the western coast of Selenoth. How many there were, no one could say. Single families had begun fleeing even in his father's time, and he knew of at least four clans that had crossed the White Sea in their entirety after the Aalvarg onslaught had begun in earnest.

Cowards, he had scorned them then. But by now, they might be well established and secure in the south, while the remnants of the Fifteen Clans were entirely reliant upon the dubious mercy of an erstwhile victim and enemy. He snorted, wondering what his ancestors would make of a world in which their longtime hunting grounds had become a refuge for their children's children. If they were looking on, from Hell or Hall, no doubt they scorned him and his generation for weaklings.

Well, he would show them otherwise. He had a ship with a good name and a crew of killers. What more did a reaver king need? He was Bági Ulfs, he had killed many wolves, more wolves than any man before him, and he would kill many more before he fell. And then, he promised himself, I will not slink into the feast, but I will enter with my head held high, so that Halfrødr and the Strongbow will feel no shame to greet me or to welcome me as their comrade-in-arms.

The wind and the salt were stinging his eyes, he noticed, as he ran his hand over his face. How long had it been since he'd been reaving? He'd forgotten how the sea cold penetrated to the bone; it made an old wound he'd taken in his left arm, a slash from an Aalvarg's jaws that had ripped it open from wrist to elbow, ache even though it was nothing more than a thick white line running down his arm.

He heard someone behind him and turned around to see Erlind Two-Dagger clambering over a strut, holding out one of his famous daggers with a blackened strip of fish that still had steam rising off impaled on it.

"Diarf caught 'em last night," he explained. "Thought you might do with a bit o' breakfast."

Skuli nodded his thanks and took the dagger, then gingerly took a bite. Not only was the flesh piping-hot, but he'd once seen a man stab himself through the roof of his mouth when the longship slammed against the trough of a wave. And then there was the issue of picking out the sharp little bones too. The cod was a little undercooked and he had to spit out several bones, but the welcome heat warmed his gullet all the way down to his belly.

The wiry Two-Dagger, one of the Redcheek's men, sat there quietly as he ate, content to stare out in the direction of the islands. They couldn't be seen from the ship, not in this grey weather, but to an experienced seaman, they were obviously there all the same. If the east wind held, it would be three days before they'd come within sight of the Hovedmand, the biggest and westernmost island, and a fourth before they would make land on its further side.

The fish eaten and his hunger sated, he handed the dagger back to Two-Dagger, who leaned over the side and rinsed the blade in the salt water to remove the remains of the fish, then carefully dried it with a small cloth he kept tucked in his belt.

"Don't drop it now." Skuli told him.

Two-Dagger smiled faintly, gave the blade one last polish, and returned it to its scabbard. "The Redcheek always says salt water is bad for the metal, but seems to me blood is just as salty. I think this is not the last time I must clean my knife on this voyage."

He nodded to Skuli, then made his way back to his place in the rear of the ship. A good lad, Skuli thought, and a reliable fighter. Of course, all of them were, or they would not have survived this long. Indeed, there may never have been a crew of such killers in all the history of the Dalarn. He looked back out over the swells and prayed silently to the Aldaföðr, to the

Valföðr, to the Father of the soon-to-be slain, that he would give these men deaths worthy of the mightiest saga.

Behind him, he heard one of the younger men lift his voice in a familiar refrain. He smiled and decided he would take it for an omen.

> Tonight we will the wolfsblood shed,
> Strike them down and strike them dead.
> Is that a dog? No! Nothing more
> Than one more wolf-spawned demon whore!

Unfortunately, on the third day the wind shifted to the north, so it took five days before they reached the western end of the Hovedmand. The weather had held, mostly, and they had put to land twice, once on each of the intervening islands, to hunt and water. The men were in good spirits, especially after Skeggi Hjaltisson managed to bring down a a pair of deer with his bow. They saw no sign of the Aalvarg, although they did twice see the grim sight of a burned-out and abandoned harbor town that had been sacked in years past by the monsters in the distance. Skuli had been tempted to go investigate, but the Redcheek convinced him otherwise. First, if there were any Aalvarg in the villages, they almost certainly would see them approaching from the sea, and more importantly, there would no doubt be similar sites once they reached the main island, where the two largest villages on the island had been situated.

There were eighteen villages marked on the old leather map the Redcheek carried. There were no names, just crude drawings of buildings that mostly looked like houses, except for one that appeared to be a tower of sorts, perhaps even a castle. It was the Redcheek's notion that they might find some clue about the wolves in either the larger villages or the castle—if it was indeed a castle. As the ever-dour Gudrik Glum observed, given its position on the coast, it might be nothing more than a watchtower built to let the nearby villagers keep an eye out for returning reavers.

"We don't want to sail too far north. If they've got eyes in the tower, they'll be able to guess where we're going. We should make land to the south of the big village there." The Redcheek indicated the large house that was closest to the tower. "We can grab a few of them, find one who talks, and figure out the lay of the land."

"Then go overland to the tower?" Gudrik sounded dubious. But then, he usually did.

"Probably not, but we don't know we're going there yet," Skuli said. "First we'll search the village. For all we know, it may be empty. The important thing is that we keep the ship safe. If we lose it somehow, they'll be able to hunt us down and there will be no escape. Mord, pick two skeleton crews of eight men. They will join Surdaembar and Jorund the Skald sleeping at sea every night."

The Redcheek nodded. "You want them to be able to bring back the news of whatever we find. I'll be sure both crews have a good steersman."

"We can't exchange crews if we're going inland," Gudrik pointed out. "Will they both stay with the ship?"

Skuli and the Redcheek looked at each other. Skuli shrugged. "We can decide that when the time comes. We don't know we'll want twenty men going inland anyhow."

Neither of them said it, but they both knew that they didn't know how many men would be left by the time they decided to go inland. Even the initial raids in search of shapeshifters to interrogate would be dangerous and could well prove fatal. But regardless, Skuli was determined to keep Ulvdræber out of reach of Aalvarg claws, even if that meant dooming those left behind on land.

And this time, he would not let them take his death from him.

They spent one more night at sea, taking advantage of a southeasterly wind that brought them closer to the mysterious tower marked on the map. Jorund was convinced that it had something to do with the town of Thjovrer, which featured in two of the sagas he knew by heart. It had been a seaport, and one of the sagas referenced a bay, which could be seen on the map as well. As an obvious anomaly, the tower made for as good a starting point as any, especially since it was something they could approach at night by sea.

The village, on the other hand, they would have to come at from the land. As the wolves were creatures of the night, the chances that the ship would be spotted as it beached were too risky to run. On land, there was still the chance that the damned creatures would smell them, but Skuli had a plan for dealing with that too. He'd ordered the Redcheek to save the blood of the deer Skeggi had killed as well as the scent glands; given the powerful scent of the glands, he figured that crushing them and mixing it with the blood, then smearing the mixture on their hides and the soles of their boots would mask their scent enough to let them approach the village unobserved.

Halldor and Solmund, two of the youngest men, were standing just behind the snekkja's dragon, their youthfully keen eyes focused on the distant shore, looking for signs of the abandoned human habitation. Skuli had just finished wolfing down the last of a rabbit he'd cooked over one of the ship's brass braziers when Solmund suddenly lifted his head and called out a warning.

"I see… rooftops!" the young reaver announced. "And that point there, the land curves in. I think it's the bay!"

"Tell the Redcheek to steer to port and take us out of sight of land," Skuli ordered Gudrik, who nodded and immediately began making his way aft. Skuli threw the remains of his lunch over the side, and gestured at Engli the Black, indicating that he should do the same with the hot coals. The wind wasn't likely to carry the scent of smoke and burned flesh towards the town, but there was no sense taking any unnecessary chances. Aalvarg noses were keen, as many a Dalarn chieftain had learned to his dismay.

He felt the longship shift underneath him, and before long it was apparent that the land was disappearing to their right. The Redcheek came forward, pushing his way past men who were pulling on their armor and digging out their weapons from where they were stowed underneath the rowing benches. The two of them had chosen the men for the shore party days ago, but even those who would be staying on the ship were arming themselves.

"With this wind, it won't take long to make the three vika," the Redcheek said, referring to the distance north they had agreed to leave between them and the village before landing. "It's after high day, do you want to anchor and then land in the morning?"

Skuli had something else on his mind. "I'm wondering if we should send a pair of men north right away. To the tower."

"They might be able to reach it by the nightmark."

"If they withdraw and make camp once they find it, then they can investigate it in the morning and still be back before the sun sets tomorrow."

"Who do you have in mind?"

"I don't. Except I don't want you going and I'm not in any shape for it myself."

"Has wisdom finally broken through the thick skull of the Skullbreaker at last?" The Redcheek laughed. "Two of the older men, I think. Neither Eilif nor Svan the Barkman are wounded, and Svan is good in the woods."

"Tell them. And tell those staying on board that they can have until mid-even before pushing off again for the night. Except for the two hunting parties, no one goes out of sight of the ship."

"I'll see to it. When do you want us back tomorrow?"

"Come to within sight at first light. If we're not there, pull back and return again at day mark. Try again between mid-even and night mark, and if we're not there the following day mark, sail south."

"For Savondir," the Redcheek said, nodding. He looked in the direction of the coast, towards nothing Skuli could see. "I'll get back to the steerboard now; I want to take us in."

Skuli nodded and began digging into his own possessions, looking for the lighter of his two mail coats. He didn't anticipate any serious fighting tonight, but one never knew, and he wanted to be able to move quickly if need be. His wounded shoulder ached as he pulled it awkwardly over his head, but it stopped hurting as soon as he was able to put his arm down again.

He pursed his lips as he debated the wisdom of carrying his axe or his shield. He decided to go with the axe; he'd learned that when fighting by moonlight, especially moonlight obscured by tree branches and leaves, it was better to be the aggressor. While not entirely useless, it was hard to use your shield to block what you couldn't see.

Besides, with any luck they'd be up against unarmed bitches and wolf-pups. Their jaws and claws were still dangerous, but considerably less lethal than edged weapons in the long, muscular arms of the grown Aalvarg males. He slipped his scabbarded sword onto his warbelt, then stood up, keeping his legs spread wide against the rhythmic rocking of the snekkja, and buckled it before slipping his dagger inside the thick leather.

It wasn't long after he sat down again that he felt Ulvdræber turning, although he had no idea what observation had informed the Redcheek's decision. He'd never been a navigator. Gudrik came forward to sit beside him; although he was staying with the longship, he too was armored.

"Mord says you're sending Svan and Eiliff to the tower?"

"North, anyhow. Who knows what's really there."

"You think that's wise?"

"I think it saves us time. And if they run into something, better we lose two than twenty."

Gudrik nodded. He seemed to be wrestling with himself. Skuli looked at the younger man expectantly.

"I'm better than Eiliff," he finally said. "With the bow. Want me to go with the Barkman?"

Skuli stared out past the prow. The faintest hint of land ahead was beginning to appear through the sea mist. He grinned. This was truly a saga of the damned, even Gudrik Glum appeared to have found an adventurer's heart.

"Don't want them putting arrows in anyone. Stay with Ulvdræber and the Redcheek. We need someone with the ship who won't get excited and come after us if we don't come back."

"I'm not afraid," Gudrik insisted. The slight shaking of his hands belied his words, but Skuli ignored that and answered the younger man's real question.

"We all die sooner or later, Gudrik Glum. But today is not your time, not yet. I promise you that."

"You're not afraid." It was a statement, not a question.

"Of course I am." Skuli laughed at the startled look on the other man's face. "But I'm afraid of different things. I'm afraid for my wife, and for my children on the other side of the sea. I'm afraid for the clans, trying to find a place among the southerners. Honestly, having a damn wolf tear out my throat would come as a relief of sorts."

"You don't mean that!"

Skuli ignored Gudrik for a moment, studying the treeline of the approaching coast. He saw no signs of habitation, human or Aalvarg, and a glance to the south showed that they were well out of sight of the village the younger lads had spotted. The shore was dangerously rocky, but a lighter-colored patch slightly to the north promised dirt, if not necessarily sand, upon which the longship could be beached.

The Redcheek obviously saw it too, as the prow gradually edged portside until it pointed directly at what he could now see was largely rock-free shoreline. He patted Gudrik's leg and gave him a reassuring smile. "Wait until you're my age, when everything hurts, you've got scars from your shoulders down to your toes, and then decide if you're still so reluctant to die." He groaned theatrically.

That made the younger man laugh, and they braced themselves as *Ulvdræber* sailed inexorably closer towards a shore that struck Skuli as dangerously steep. He hoped the Redcheek could see it; if the snekkja beached head-on, it seemed to him they'd risk staving a hole in the bottom, or worse, actually breaking the keel. But just as Skuli was about to rise and shout for the men to take the oars and back water in a last-ditch attempt to slow the longship, her sail was abruptly furled and she adroitly arced to port on a path that brought her smoothly up on the shore almost perfectly sideways.

An impromptu, albeit subdued murmur arose from the men at the Redcheek's impressive feat of steering, and then they were leaping down from the starboard side. More than a few of them tumbled to the ground, their legs stiff and cramped from days at sea. Skuli himself managed to stay on his feet, but he couldn't repress a groan as a sharp spike of pain inexplicably ran down his spine, from the back of his head to the middle of his shoulders. He flexed his shoulders and lifted his arms, moving them back and forth until the mysterious pain disappeared.

Someone cleared his throat behind him and he turned around to see Svan the Barkman standing in front of him. The Barkman was a slender, dark-haired fellow with a long braided beard and sad, expressive eyes. He wore no armor but a thick wolfskin coat, and carried no sword. Instead, he had a longbow slung over his back, a large roll of arrows tied together suspended from his belt, and a thick spear that doubled as a staff in his left hand. "The Redcheek wants us to espy the tower, see if it's there?"

"Have a look. Stay out of trouble and don't take any chances. Follow the sea north and you should run right into it. Learn what you can and then come back." He slapped the Barkman on the shoulder. "Be back here at dawn; I'll mark that tree over there."

The Barkman looked to see where he was pointing, then nodded. Skuli nodded back, picked up his axe, then walked over to the big birch and cut four sizable chunks out of the side facing the sea. He made them at eye height to make them easier to see.

"This is where we meet," he called out loud enough to cause everyone's heads to turn towards him. "Unless you want to take a wolf to wife, you damned well better be here by day mark if you get separated. Those with me, keep your mouths shut. Var and Engli, you'll take the lead. Remember, we want to capture a *sigskifting*, so try not to kill any of them until you're sure they can't change."

He glanced back at Mord Redcheek, who nodded coolly. Ulvdræber would be here on the morrow. The trick was to ensure that he and his men were as well. He raised his axe in a salute to the Redcheek, then began walking south. It was going to be a long night, and perhaps a bloody one too, but at least he'd get a break from trying to get to sleep on that damned boat!

It was not long after night mark when they heard the first howls. They were high-pitched, juvenile howls, considerably less frightening than the deep ones that used to come down from the hills above Raknarborg and echo off the stone walls. They had made good time through the forest, and before the sun had set, both scouts detected numerous signs of wolf spoor and even the well-gnawed remains of a recent kill.

They made a cold and silent dinner as the sky turned red, as Skuli dared not risk the scent of a fire so close to the suspected Aalvarg habitation. Engli supplemented his paltry repast of dried meat with a handful of blackberries he'd somehow managed to collect in passing, and their unripe bitterness did more to quench his hunger than the tørkød.

After Var located what looked like a well-traveled path, Skuli decided that they would try an ambush. He had Engli rub more of the musky blood-gland mixture on his soles, then had him walk a good ways towards the ruins of the village they'd spotted from the sea. He decided that they would wait until the Blood Moon had climbed as high into the sky as the Bone Moon before they risked venturing further towards the village.

"I hear something," Halldor whispered in his ear. Skuli had kept the young man near him, partly to keep him safe, but also because young ears are keener than old ones, especially old ones that have long known the deafening din of battle. "They come... quickly, I think!"

Skuli nodded and gave out a soft owl call. He heard a faint rustling down the line in response; the men were ready. There was just enough light from the two moons overhead to see the far side of the clearing he had chosen for the ambush. He couldn't see the eight men hidden behind the trees on the other side, but he knew they were there.

Then he could hear the softly-rhythmic buddadadum-buddadadum of the Aalvarg approaching as their pads drummed against the soft woodland soil. They were coming rapidly indeed, so quickly that even though he was waiting for them, their actual appearance still managed to take him by surprise. First one grey blur, then a second followed by a third, flashed in front of him. He almost leaped out at them instinctively, but restrained himself when, as he hoped, the combination of the clearing and the crushed gland he'd buried towards the far end of it brought them to a halt.

None of the three were in the pure wolf form, he was disappointed to see. No shapeshifters these, for surely one would have transformed itself in order to better follow the trail of scent. All three were in their twisted natural shape, half-man, half-wolf, with long, wiry arms and powerful haunched legs that were an obscene parody of a man's limbs. They were obviously young; the biggest was only two-thirds the size of the average Aalvarg warrior, and they were fixated on the scent with their noses were pressed hard against the ground. As they ran, they made loud whuffling noises that sounded for all the world like dogs.

Skuli was just about to whistle when one of them looked back in the direction from which they'd come and made a sound that could only be described as a remonstrative, but friendly bark. A moment later, two more young Aalvarg appeared, followed, to Skuli's astonishment, by what looked very much like a young woman wearing tattered rags that left her long white legs exposed. *Sigskifting*!

He took a firm grip on his axe, took a deep breath, raised his right hand to his lips, and whistled loudly. Two of the wolves whipped their heads around, then whirled in a circle as men leaped from the trees around them. Skuli himself sprang at the female shapeshifter, whose mouth had fallen open with the shock of the unexpected assault. She shrieked as he expertly swept her legs out from under her with the butt end of his long axe handle, then swung the head at the nearest wolf-demon as it leaped at Halldor with its claws outstretched and teeth bared.

He missed as the metal blade slashed through the air behind the creature, but it screamed in either pain or fury as it impaled itself on his young clansman's sword. The force of its leap, combined with its weight, caused Halldor to stumble back and let go of his blade, but another Dalarn was already on top of the wounded beast and repeatedly stabbing it with either hand, almost as if he was beating a drum. Two-Dagger, Skuli realized, and he glanced down just in time to see the shapeshifter was trying to scramble away into the forest on all fours.

He leaped forward and kicked her thigh, causing her to collapse on her stomach, clutching at her leg and screaming. He dropped his axe and fell to one knee, grabbed both her arms and then lifted her up, twisted his upper body, and slammed her to the ground to knock the wind out of her lungs. Before she could recover, he was on top of her, pulling both arms up as he pressed his left knee into her back. Only when she was helpless and secured did he glance back to see how his men were faring.

Although he could not make out many faces or any other details in the darkness, he could tell from all the laughing and light-hearted cursing he heard, that all five of the other young wolves were already dead.

Halldor, having managed to find his blade in the corpse of the Aalvarg that Two-Dagger had killed, finished cleaning it off, sheathed it, and handed Skuli a long leather thong. He bent the shapeshifter's arms together, looped the thong around her forearms several times, then tied it tightly enough to draw a gasp of pain from her. That way, even if she shifted, or grew claws, she wouldn't be able to cut through the thong.

He stood up, turned around, and looked around the clearing. He didn't see anyone on the ground except the dead wolves. "Anyone hurt?"

"Engli stabbed me!" he heard someone declare reproachfully. He thought it was Alrik.

"You got in the way, you clumsy *snyde*!" Engli the Black sounded entirely unrepentant.

"Are you all right, Alrik?"

"He'll live," the deep bass of Var rumbled. "I tied up his arm."

"How am I supposed to fight with one arm?"

"You didn't fight with two," Engli said, which sparked no little laughter among the men.

Skuli smiled and turned back to the wolf-girl. He stuck his foot under her and flipped her over, revealing a tear-stained face that was unexpectedly pretty, even mottled as it was by the shadows and the moonlight filtered through the leaves above. Had he encountered her in different circumstances, he might well have thought her a young woman only a few years younger than Fjotra. He couldn't tell what color her hair was, but it was neither dark nor light.

He kneeled down beside her and took her face in his well-callused hand. He was mildly surprised to see fear in her eyes rather than the bestial defiance he'd come to expect of her kind. "Can you understand me? Can you talk?"

She blinked and nodded.

"Where is your village. How many of you live there?"

Her answer confused him. "You are... you are men?"

Now it was his turn to nod. And if her first words had confused him, her next ones had him rocking back on his heels in astonishment.

"I am not *sigskifting*! I am like you!"

LODI

THE FLASH of a pickaxe. The grunt of a dwarf being struck. The screams of the wounded. Movement. Motion. Instinct. Action. Watching his foe's chest, trying to read his next action, then either striking first, blocking, or seeking to evade an incoming blow. The smell of blood. The acrid stink of bladders being released in fear, and the deeper, more pungent odor of bowels being released in death. It was all so familiar to Lodi, and to his body, that he might have been battling cave goblins deep below the foundations of Iron Mountain, or men under the sky before the massive crowds of the Amorran arena. As he brought his axe down across the unarmored collarbone of one of the strange scaled dwarf-things, nearly cleaving it to the chest, he felt something tear in his wounded shoulder and knew he would be paying for it afterward. But for now, there was no pain, for his blood was up and the battle-fever was upon him.

"Kingsguard!" he shouted so that his unarmored companions would know where he was. It made no sense, for he was the only Kingsguard there, but old habits die hard and the cry served as well as any other. The station dwarves had been on the verge of being overwhelmed when Lodi and his companions arrived, and the unexpected shock of their charge had initially driven the attackers back.

"Kingsguard!" he heard Boru shout back from somewhere to his right. Lodi began moving that way, as the older dwarf's plate armor was proving to be a godsend. That, and his massive two-blade, which he swept back and forth before him, driving back the invaders and permitting the other dwarves to take advantage of the space created by their foe's fear of the giant axe. A few of them had developed a deadly technique where one dwarf would engage a scaled monster, his neighbor would crouch down to hook the dwarf-thing's heel with his pick-head, then pull back hard on the handle. When the creature lost its balance and went down, the first dwarf would step forward and crush its head with the flat of his pick as his companion defended him.

Between that murderously efficient technique and their two armored axe-dwarves, Lodi's impromptu company finally managed to force the enemy into retreat. There was a strange, wailing call, and then the freakish dwarf-things abruptly disengaged, throwing down their crude metal weapons, jostling, and knocking each other down in their panicked rush to flee. The fallen and the slow were quickly dispatched, and Lodi had to forcibly dissuade a few of the more hot-tempered young dwarves who would have foolishly followed the routed enemy down into the tunnel through which they'd fled.

Lodi studied the hole from which the strange creatures had emerged. It was small, but it didn't look properly bored. It looked smooth, almost as if the stone had been melted rather than drilled. But what in the name of Skála Otek, the Rockfather, could possibly create such a neatly formed tunnel?

"They're going to want to seal that up, I should think," Boru commented as he joined Lodi in front of the hole and ran his hand around the edges. "You ever seen anything like that?"

"Not our problem." He looked at Boru. The dwarf's armor was liberally splashed with blood from the crest of his helm to the toes of his steel boots. He realized he probably didn't look much better, and the blood was going to wash off of Boru's plate a damn sight easier than it was out of the heavy wool jacket that he wore under his chain mail. "What the peklo were those things? They had scales!"

"They're called draktakha. It's said they are devils made by Hublok Otek. We'd heard rumors of such creatures, although this is the first time they've been seen this close to the surface."

The speaker was a bald dwarf with a singed beard, a blackened face, and more than a little blood splattered across his forearms and chest. He started to hold out his hands to them in greeting, then belatedly tried to wipe them off on his trousers, and finally gave it up as a hopeless cause and bowed instead. "I'm Vismi, son of Bismi. I'm the mayor of Hotstone Cavern, and I can't thank you enough for what the two of you and your fellows here did for our clan."

Lodi waved his hand and Boru made a dismissive sound. He understood the dwarf's appreciation, but gratitude was hardly necessary. It wasn't as if the draktakha or whatever the strange creatures were truly called, would have invited them in for mushrooms and moss tea after slaughtering the cavern clan.

"I'm afraid you may have lost a few," the mayor said. "Why don't you see to your wounded and let us know what we can do for you."

"We left about twenty pasla and pasladha up in the tunnel, about five hundred yards back. Can you send a group of your zenha out to them and bring them here?"

"Is that where you came from? A stopped train?"

Boru nodded. "We was marching up when we heard the ruckus. Figured it was no place for the females and young 'uns. We left ten dwarves there to guard them."

"Well, I'm damn glad you showed when you did." Vismi glanced over where some of the dwarves from the train were dragging a body out from under a pair of dead draktakha. "And I'm sorry about those you lost. See to your own; I'll send my own wife out after the families."

Lodi nodded. He figured there was no point in explaining that he didn't even know most of the names of his own fallen. He and Boru walked back towards where two dwarves from the train were standing over their dead companion. They were both bloody, one was wounded, and they both had tears in their eyes.

"It's our brother, Hari," the wounded dwarf said. "We was just going back to see our folks. How are we going to tell them? What do we—"

His voice trembled and broke off as he looked down at the ground, away from his fallen brother.

"You tell them the truth." Boru put his hand on the young dwarf's shoulder. "He died saving dwarves, dwarf wives, and children. He died a hero and Zeme Otek will welcome him into the earth with honor."

Lodi walked past the grieving brothers, patting each one on the back as he did so. There were fewer corpses along the route where they'd chased the cursed creatures, but once he reached the place where they'd stopped the attackers and thrown them back, he saw how brutal the battle had been. They must have slain over sixty of the scaly things, and dozens of dwarves had fallen too, though most of them were Hotstoners. He saw Thori and Yori; they were both alive but Yori was cradling his left arm even though he didn't seem to be bleeding.

"What happened?"

Yori's face was pale and he was wincing with the pain, but there was fierce pride in his eyes as he raised his head and recognized Lodi. "Otekzatra thing caught my forearm with one of those stupid bars. I saw it coming and tried to block it with my pick, but I was too late."

"I killed the bastard, though." Thori said proudly. "We was keeping it tight, just like you said. But his arm... that's why we didn't follow you when you went chasing after them."

"You got there soon enough," Lodi reassured Yori. "Too late is when they knock you on the head. You'll heal."

He started to move on to check on the others, but turned back when a thought occurred to him. "Say, lads?"

"Yeah, Lodi?"

"You may want to gather up those picks. Scratched or no, you'll be able to sell them for four, maybe five times what you were asking. After I tell the king what you all did here, with your picks, half the rich mizera at Iron Mountain are going to want one."

The twins looked at each other, then broke into simultaneous smiles. "You may have a beard for business after all, Lodi Dunmorinson," Thori said.

"If the king don't have nothing for you, come find us," Yori added. "We'll give you a job."

Lodi laughed and turned away. But what he saw next quickly wiped the amusement from his face. A single dwarf lay dead not far from the severed halves of the draktakh Lodi had cut in half just after it broke through the Hotstone line. It was Orin Sperrylite, and his black beard was soaked and matted with the blood that had spilled down his tunic all the way to his crotch. His eyes were open and staring up at the stalactites on the ceiling overhead.

Lodi frowned, kneeled down, and gently lifted Orin's beard. As he suspected, the young dwarf's throat had been ripped open, most likely by a dratakh's curved claw. Cursing under his breath, he closed Orin's eyes, whispering a short, silent prayer to the First Fathers as he did so.

Accept him, Zeme Otek.
Cover him, Skála Otek.
Console him, Roztok Otek.
Release him, Pozar Otek.

Shaking his head with frustration, knowing that the younger dwarf must have been struck down practically within reach of him, Lodi rose to his feet again. He leaned down to pick up Orin's pickaxe, and was surprised to see there was blood on one tip. He snorted ruefully. Hadn't he told the thieving gragtosser to bash, not stab? The unlucky lad may not have fought as well as he tossed, but he had shed zlotakh blood, and that made him worthy of the last line of the prayer, the one only addressed to the War Father on behalf of warriors fallen in battle.

Honor him, Válka Otek.

He heard the rush of several dwarves approaching and saw it was Raldri, followed closely by Raldrizena and Myf.

"Lodi!" the young dwarf cried. "Are you hurt?"

Lodi stared at him, incredulous, until he realized how he must have looked to them, covered in draktakha blood as he was. "I'm fine, lad. Orin didn't make it through, though."

"Oh, no!" Raldrizena cried. Myf didn't make a sound, but she raised her hand to her mouth and her eyes were suddenly bright with tears. Two of them traced a path down on either side of her nose, until she wiped them away and looked at Lodi with a concerned expression on her face.

"Are you really all right? Lodi, you look… dreadful."

"It ain't mine." He shrugged. "Seems they bleed a lot when you chop them in two."

She noticed the two halves of the draktakh for the first time, as her eyes suddenly widened, she raised a hand to her mouth, and he heard her gag three times before mastering herself. It took her a moment to recover. "Did you do that? What is it?"

"The Rock Father knows, but I sure don't." He looked at Raldri. "Orin had a fat coinsack on him. Best you take it off him. He don't need it now."

"I'm not a robber of the dead!"

"I ain't saying you is. But if you don't take it, strangers who never knew him will."

Raldri hesitated, then, at his wife's silent urging, he kneeled down beside their former traveling companion. Before he turned away, Lodi noted with approval that the young dwarf had shut his eyes and seemed to be saying something, though if it was addressed to Orin or the First Fathers, he couldn't tell. In truth, he didn't care, he was just glad to see the younger generation still seemed to have a sense of decency about themselves.

"Come with me," he told Myf. "Let's see if we can find you somewhere that ain't burnt where they can put you up. I want to find some water so I can get cleaned up."

He led her away from the bloody remains of battle and past the smoldering buildings into the town proper. The circle in the heart of the cavern was full of dwarves, most of whom were either in shock or wailing with grief. Twenty or so corpses had been arranged side by side in the center; as they watched, another young dwarf with a red beard was carried in by two older, red-bearded dwarves that looked as if they might be his father and his uncle. Myf looked away as they laid him carefully down by his fallen companions, the pain etched into the older dwarves' faces was simply too much for her to bear.

Then there was a piercing scream and a pretty young divci, distraught, tried to throw herself on the dead young dwarf. One of the older dwarves intercepted her and buried her face in his chest to muffle her heart-rending shrieks. Gods, Lodi thought. It wasn't the battle itself that was so bad. For the most part, you were too busy to do much more than try to bash them before they could bash you. By far the worst part of it was the aftermath, and the sight of hearts breaking one after the other.

"Zemtek, how could you let this happen?" he heard Myf whisper.

"Zeme Otek didn't have nothing to do with it. Better you ask Válka Otek."

"Why were they attacking this cavern?"

"Let's go ask him." Lodi pointed to the mayor. "Maybe he knows something by now."

But Vismi Bismisson knew no more than he had before. He did, however, lead them to a ice-cold rock pool where Lodi was able to climb in and wash off the worst of the now-sticky blood before it hardened, and he even promised Lodi some dry clothes. He also located the town's two tavernkeepers, who readily agreed to put up all of the unexpected newcomers in their establishments without charging them for either room or board.

Once he saw Myf safely ensconced in a room with Raldrizena and several other pasla, Lodi joined Boru, the twins, and about ten other dwarves in the larger of the two taverns. Raldri joined them and used one of Orin's gold coins to buy them all three rounds of ale, and even those who hadn't met Orin mournfully raised their tankards to salute the fallen dwarf's courage and his generosity once, twice, and then again thrice.

"He must have gone down in the initial charge," Lodi, maudlin in his cups, muttered to Boru.

"I didn't see the poor lad," the older dwarf, considerably less imposing now that he was shed of his armor, admitted. "Didn't know him, more's the pity. Earth Father rest him."

"Why didn't he push the damn thing off him? I told them all to poke at the bastards, not swing the bloody useless things. When the hell did dwarves stop carrying axes about anyway?"

Boru snorted. "About six months after the Troll King got hisself spitted."

"They're too damn soft now! We was all carrying axes, half our dead would still be alive."

"Soft? No axes, no armor, and not a single lad ran! You ain't being fair, Lodi. They was a credit to the dwarves, they was!"

"Yeah, they was," Lodi said as he hunched wearily down on the wooden table between his outspread elbows. "I don't know, it just sickens my heart. Maybe I ain't cut out for this sort o' thing anymore."

"You and me both, laddie!" Boru rolled his shoulders and groaned. "I'll be hurting for a sixday and I didn't take so much as a bruise. Getting old hurts."

"Not as much as not getting older!" Boru laughed and knocked his ceramic tankard against Lodi's. "Damn, Kingsguard, we may have lost a few, but we beat those bastards with nothing more than a bunch of young green civilians. That'll be good for a few drinks once we reach the Mountain!"

Lodi frowned. A thought had been niggling at the bottom of his mind ever since he'd seen the draktakha disappearing down the tunnel from which they'd come. It finally formed itself into something he could express in words. "They wasn't near the line."

"Who?"

"The draktakha, the scaly things."

"What about it?"

"If they didn't cause the trouble with the train rail, what did? And if the trouble ain't here, they can't fix it here. And if they can't fix it here, how we going to get to the Mountain?"

The next day, Lodi slept in. That didn't prevent him from waking with a headache that briefly made him wonder if someone had hit him with one of those damn iron clubs. He'd just been thinking of going upstairs and turning in when Vismi Bismisson and a group of locals showed up, seemingly determined to pour all the ale in Hotstone down their rescuers' throats. He didn't remember staggering upstairs, and he apparently hadn't bothered undressing, as he was still wearing the brown wool tunic and trousers the mayor had given him the day before.

He found the urinal in the next room in the nick of time, and took longer than he would have imagined possible "draining the goblin", as his old sergeant used to describe it. He was still standing there stupidly, holding his dwarfhood in his hand, when a bleary-eyed, bushy-bearded Thori stuck in his head and announced that there was a breakfast spread downstairs, and that their presence at the funerals, which would be held at noon, was requested.

Lodi grunted something noncommittal before looking down and wondering if he was going to be done urinating by then. It would have come in handy yesterday, he thought. He could have put out all the damn fires by himself. After finally finishing, then splashing water on his face and running his wet hands through his hair and beard, he wandered downstairs and discovered a decent collection of lizard eggs, blindfish sausage, and flatcakes, all of which he washed down with several hairs of the dog that bit his arse the night before.

He went to find the tavernkeeper, who was kind enough to show where his clothes and armor had been left to dry. The clothes were nearly dry, but the chain mail was tacky, so he borrowed a wire brush and carried it outside, where he could clean it off without making a mess. He was still sitting there, working on some bloody grit in the left shoulder, when a familiar scent made him sit upright in a hurry.

"Good morning, Lodi." It was Myf, looking considerably fresher than any of the dwarves he'd encountered at breakfast.

"Mornin', anyhow," he grunted, returning his attention to his armor. "Don't know about good."

"Raldrizena tells me there will be a funeral today. Will you be attending?"

"Aye. Seems the thing to do."

"It occurs to me you may have reopened your wounds yesterday. Do you want me to look at them?"

He looked up at her, startled. "Gods, no! I'm fine, Myf, you needn't concern your pretty little head about me. Might want to have a gander at Yori's arm, though, make sure they splinted it right."

She nodded obediently, then climbed the steps past him. It took a considerable effort not to turn and watch her enter the tavern, but he managed it and returned to his mail-polishing after making a sound that was half-grumble, half-sigh.

After he finished cleaning the armor, he returned it to the room in which he and the others had been sleeping, found the twins, and arranged for a purchase. His newly-owned pickaxe thus acquired, he went in search of Vismi Bismisson and found him in the funeral plot, where the bodies of Hotstone dwarves were interred to rejoin with the Earth Father. The huge cavern was abundantly lit with glowmoss and earthlight lamps, and festooned with colorful banners bearing clan runes, but the rows of rough canvas bags belied its somber purpose.

"What can I do for you, Lodi?" The mayor was polite, but he was clearly pressed for time.

"I wanted to give you this." Lodi offered him Orin's pickaxe and two silver coins. "That should cover the cost o' havin' it bronzed. Thought it would make a good remembrance for the folks here. You know, for the ones who died, the outsiders."

The mayor accepted the pick, but refused the coins. "We won't have it bronzed, we'll have it gilded. Get me the names of those who died. They'll be buried with our own and their names will be inscribed on this. A fitting tribute to the dwarves who saved Hotstone. Will you want to say a few words?"

Lodi shook his head. "Nah. Just wanted to give you Hotstoners something to remember them by. Seems they deserve it."

The mayor smiled, though his eyes were grim. "Never fear, Lodi Dunmorinsson. We dwarves, we don't forget."

The mass funeral was every bit as horrific and heartbreaking as Lodi assumed it would be. Forty-eight Hotstoners and nine outsiders were given back to Zeme Otek, who would see that their bodies eventually returned new life to the Kamensvet. The zemknez, an elderly dwarf with a long white beard that brushed the ground despite being braided, spoke eloquently enough of bravery and sacrifice, but his words were cold comfort to the bereaved families who had lost their loved ones. Myf and the other pasla wept openly, and even Lodi found he had to swallow hard once or twice when a young widow tried, and failed, to hold herself together when speaking of her fallen husband.

Afterwards, Lodi found Boru, and they sought out the cavern station-master. Fortunately, neither he nor his two engineers were among the slain, but they confirmed what Lodi had already surmised. While they could drag the carts to the platform easily enough, there was absolutely nothing they could do to bring the track back to life again.

"It's possible to walk it," the older of the two engineers pointed out. "I done it a while back, after they cleared the blocking of the tunnel, but afore they had the track hot and running again. Takes a sixday, maybe half that again with the wives and little ones. There's only two declines that'll be a little tricky, but there'll be ropes to assist you. Maybe even steps carved on the sides by now."

"There has to be a better way," Boru said. "Don't you got none o' them carts with the push lever on it?"

The two engineers looked at each other. "Yeah, we got one. That's how we was going to bring the train to the station. But you can't use it to go all the way to Iron Mountain. You'll go too fast on the big declines, jump the track, and probably kill everyone riding."

"I ain't talking about the whole train," Lodi said. "Forget the train. We got to get word to the king. He needs to know what happened here. For all we know, every cavern from the Underdeep to the Nebesvet is in danger from those creatures."

"We could rig up some brakes for it," the younger engineer said. "We never needed them here, but it shouldn't be too hard. It'd let you carry two, maybe three carts safely."

The older engineer had his eyes closed. "Three is no problem. The decline ain't that steep. We could probably do four, but let's leave it at three and keep it safe. You can't take everyone on three carts, though."

"I don't see that we want to anyhow," Boru pointed out. "We got no idea what we might run into anywhere between here and Iron Mountain. Track's dead, but maybe it's blocked by a rockslide, maybe it's been mined, hell, maybe a dragon found it and followed it down to the city! We don't want the families coming with us until we know it's safe."

"You, me, and eight others," Lodi told the warrior dwarf. "If you Hotstoners can help us gear up, that'll be enough to deal with most anything we run across. I'll need to bring the young divci too; she's in my charge, and considering that tunnel, I can't be certain she'd be safer in Hotstone anyhow."

The stationmaster looked as if he wanted to argue, but Lodi quelled him with a stare. "With eleven, we only need two carts. Attach the push-cart to the the first one from the train and leave it loaded. Thori can be one of the eight; the twins will make our lives a living hell if we don't let them unload those damn picks."

He half expected opposition, but found none. Boru shrugged.

"We owe it to them. We'd have lost five or six more if they hadn't been carting their wares along."

There was a brief silence. Then the younger engineer spoke up. "Make it an even twelve. I'm coming with you."

"You can't—"

"I certainly can!" The younger engineer cut off the stationmaster. "I'm fifty-five years old and I'm old enough to make my own decisions, father! If something goes wrong with the push-cart, who is going to fix it? Besides, I've never been to Iron Mountain and I want to see it. What if I'd been killed by one of those *supina pasla*?"

Lodi frowned, not because he had any objection to the young dwarf joining the expedition. In fact, he thought it would be rather handy to have someone familiar with the track machinery along. But the engineer's use of the term "scaly dwarves" troubled him. The bodies of the draktakha had been buried in one of the caverns used for degradable trash; they too would serve the dwarves of Hotstone Cavern in death. But before they'd been disposed, Lodi had taken a close look at one, and there was no denying that whatever it was, it was much more closely akin to a dwarf than an orc or a goblin.

There were minor differences about the beardless faces, the teeth were similar to a kobold's and the bodies were somewhat thinner than the average dwarf's, but it could hardly be denied that if you starved a dwarf, shaved him, bashed him in the mouth with a shovel, dipped him in glue and rolled him in bronzed snake scales, he'd look damned close to a draktakh. Too damned close.

But that was for the king's council to sort out. His job was to see that Thorvald had gotten word to the king about the massive orc invasion of the Elf and Man lands, and to let him know about this incursion by the mysterious creatures of the deep. He regretted that they hadn't thought to preserve one of the bodies, then realized he could simply ask the Hotstoners for permission to dig one up. He looked at the young engineer and smiled. The lad could come in handy sooner than he probably expected.

It took two days to prepare and provision the three carts, which was a day longer than Lodi would have wished, but the stationmaster insisted on affixing one of the cavern's largest glowstones to the front of the push-cart. He argued, reasonably enough, that given the greater-than-usual chance of a cave-in or rockslide blocking the track, it would be foolish to depend on their darksight alone. Barring the two steep declines that would increase their speed considerably, the stone would cast enough light to let them brake before crashing into any unexpected blockages.

The first two days on the track passed quickly, though laboriously. The push-cart was essentially a giant lever, which permitted three dwarves on one side and three dwarves on the other to alternate pushing down, which turned the axle that propelled the iron wheels underneath. This permitted them to move nearly as fast as the thermo-propelled train normally did so long as there was a slight decline, but the going was considerably harder and slower on a flat or an incline. Fortunately, the greater part of the track angled down, as the city of Iron Mountain rose from the shores of the great underground lake nestled at the heart of the mountain.

Every hour, two dwarves rotated off the cart and two fresh dwarves took their places at the levers. It wasn't difficult work in comparison with the mining that was familiar to most of them, the trick was to stay in rhythm. They sang mining songs, and smithing songs, and even fighting songs. Lodi, forgetting himself, taught the younger dwarves one of his old favorites from the siege days, a ribald Kingsguard song, before he spotted Myf standing at the front of the cart behind them, listening to them. But his partners at the lever were already in full throat, so there was little he could do in good faith but join in with them.

> You can bash an orc with a battle-axe,
> Beat a goblin to death with a stick.
> You can crush a troll with a boulder roll,
> Kill a kobold with a mining pick.
>
> The Kingsguard ain't like t'other dwarves
> We got balls like igneous rock.
> We don't got no fears, we don't need no spears
> We beat 'em with a big hard cock!

There were about twenty more verses, most of which involved the various and creative ways the Kingsguard claimed to slaughter the enemies of the king with their unique and oversized weaponry, but Lodi decided against teaching them to the lads. Or rather, Lads, he corrected himself, for as his old Sergeant, Dulin Rockjaw had told his unit after their first skirmish, "once you see'd blood spill, you ain't green no more. Yez still lads, but yez lads with a capital bloody L!"

Aside from Boru, who'd taken an earlier shift, his companions were all decidedly young, but except for the engineer, each of them had broken red ground, and unusually vicious red ground at that. So, they merited due regard, even if the way they delighted in putting particular emphasis in the form of volume on the last three words of the last line made Lodi wary of giving them any additional material.

After his shift was over, Lodi carefully walked across the thick iron bar connecting the two carts and pulled himself up to the platform. Despite the chill air of the tunnel and the wind caused by their movement, he was stripped to the waist, and sweating as he was, he was reluctant to enter the compartment knowing that Myf would be in there. So, he was further discomfited when she came out bearing a pair of scones and a skin of mushroom wine.

"I thought you might be hungry after all that work," she said.

"You may not want to stand directly downwind, lass. It's sweaty work, pushing these carts."

"I can see that," she said, seemingly unconcerned. But she did lean against the side rail, which kept her safely out of the breeze of their passage. "Aren't you going to come inside?"

"Aye, once I dry meself a bit." He raised the skin in salute and took a swig from it. "Thank you for this. I saw you was listening to us sing."

"If you can call it that."

"You know we didn't mean nothing by it."

"By what? I could scarcely hear anything with all the noise from the track. But some of the younger dwarfs are undaunted by the fact that I cannot speak to them and I find their attentions onerous at times. So, I come out here to get away from them."

Lodi's eyes narrowed. "Who's been at you? I warned those hot-peckered louts to keep their poxied hands to themselves!"

She burst out laughing. Her laughter sounded like the sweet shattering of delicate crystal. "They're very sweet and they mean no harm. You needn't be at them. They merely grow tedious after a while."

Lodi growled low in his throat. They was good lads, they was, but if they didn't treat the lass right, he'd bash a skull or two, he would.

They stood there together in companionable silence as Lodi finished the scones and the wine. The breeze had dried him off and he was beginning to feel the chill, so he handed her the wineskin and slipped his shirt back over his head. His beard, he was pleased to see, was finally long enough that he needed to pull it out of his shirt, although it was still embarrassingly short for a dwarf of his years.

"Do you think we're likely to see any orcs or cave goblins?" she asked him unexpectedly.

"No, I shouldn't think so. If anything, we're more likely to run into them draktakha again."

"And you will let me know if we do?"

"Of course," Lodi assured her, puzzled. "Why'd you ask?"

"I should like to be warned when I am to avert my eyes, Kingsguard," she replied demurely. She sniffed twice, rather archly, turned around, and went back into the passenger compartment.

Lodi stood there in the darkness with the tunnel walls flashing by, alone, feeling as if his cheeks had been set afire. He wasn't sure whether he should laugh or leap off the front of the moving cart in shame. At just that very moment, the dwarves laboring on the push-cart burst into song again.

"You can bash an orc with a battle-axe!"

Lodi groaned. He closed his eyes and shook his head. Then, he dug deep within himself to find the nerve to do something that took more courage than facing three orcs in the great arena of Amorr with nothing more than a rusty Man-sword, something that made him distinctly more nervous than climbing down the bare rock face of a cliff into a wyrm's den deep within the troll-infested mountains of Uskiluhk. He took a deep breath, after which he opened the door to the passenger compartment.

Myf was sitting in her usual seat. Their eyes met. And then, her lips turned upward in a faint, but distinctly mischievous smile.

BERETH

IT WAS a perfect day for sky riding, thought Bereth, as she yawned and stretched under the warming rays of the springtime sun. The wind was gentle and from the west, the few clouds that wandered by high overhead were white and harmless, and the sky was a bright shade of azure that practically invited one to leap joyfully into it. The brilliance of the blue reminded her of the cloaks worn by the Kingsguard in a painting by Saeliras that she particularly admired. Then it occurred to her that the painting was entitled "The Last Stand" or to give it its full name, "The Last Stand of the Kingsguard Before the Gates of the Crystal City".

It was only hours after the event so nobly depicted that Glaislael fell to the Witchkings. And with the royal city, both High King Lasgolir and his noble Kingsguard had fallen. She sighed and put the thought aside. It was a rather morbid one in light of the present circumstances. Even so, she found herself looking forward to the thought of leaping aloft and immersing herself in the rich, shimmering blue.

She spread her arms and addressed her singular audience, the sun.

> Shall this cobalt sea
> Be swallowed up by horror,
> That many-legged beast?
> I rise into cloudless skies,
> My hatred my companion
> Astride fearless wings.

She was not discontent. It made little in the way of sense, which was a pity, but it was true to her sense of the morning. There was a practical advantage to the cloudless day as well. The prospect of good visibility was pleasing; a pair of Silverbows that were charged with keeping a watchful eye on the vanguard of the orc army making its way towards Merithaime had not been seen in three days. Her orders, direct from Lord Oakenheart, were to spend the morning searching for them, although he was not sanguine about their prospects.

Bereth was aware that she possessed the sharpest eyes in the ranger wing, and so she concluded that if she couldn't find them, either the Silverbows did not want to be found or they were already dead. It was hard to imagine that a pair of veteran scouts could be taken without so much as a hint of a distress signal, but then, the orc army was so massive that trying to hide from it on the ground was very like standing on a beach trying to hide from the sea. Except, unlike the sea, this vast army was neither advancing nor retreating. It simply sat there, day after day, doing nothing but slowly dwindle as it fed on itself.

Perhaps a different approach would better suit her heart. After all, what did the sky fear from those poor wingless worms who crawled miserably across the surface of the earth? Nothing. Nothing at all.

> Cancer on the land
> Engorged, and still it starves.
> O many-legged beast!
> Will you spare a limb for me
> Or devour yourself entire?

She smiled. That was more properly expressive of her contempt for the foe. The vast army of orcs, goblins, and various and sundry other monstrosities stretched out for leagues along what would have been called its line of march were it still moving. But what had once been a slow-moving river, albeit a stinking, greenish-brown river more than half-choked with filth and sediment, was now a fetid swamp, coated from one end to the other with slimy green algae. Why, she did not know. The wizards did not know. Lord Oakheart himself did not know.

All they knew was that the invading army halted its march two weeks ago. The demonic drums still echoed, the shrieking shamans still enacted their foul rituals, and screaming goblins were still spitted and roasted over open flames when they were not simply torn limb from limb and hurled into the large pig-iron pots to boil. But, with the exception of a few exploratory tendrils that were extruded out to west and south, the savage grotesquerie that she thought of as a gargantuan many-legged beast squatted fitfully in its own squalor. It was an army that fought no battles, an army whose only casualties were self-inflicted as it devoured itself.

Unfortunately, every few days, ragged new columns of goblins would march in, and those that did not bring sufficient supplies with them soon found themselves fed to the ravenous hunger of the great beast.

The reason the vast army did nothing was much discussed throughout the elven camps. One popular theory was that a new troll king had come to power in Uskilukh and the army was awaiting the arrival of its liege. The orc septs were nominally subservient to their trollish masters, and since it was not long since they had last marched south at the behest of the Goblinsbane, the notion was not incredible. It was, however, somewhat undermined by the fact that no one, neither scout nor sky raider, had laid eyes upon a single troll, with or without a crown.

Another theory was that the orcish warleaders feared the high mages of the Collegium Occludum and were attempting some dark ritual, perhaps seeking to raise mighty devils from the pits of the deepest hells, in order to remove the mages from the field before launching their invasion. That made somewhat more sense to her. The archmages of the esoteric college fully merited being feared by any rational being, but then, if the orcs had a means of neutralizing the elven maesters, would they not have done so before gathering their massive army?

Bereth's take on the sprawling migration was rather more straightforward. Orcs were stupid, short-sighted, and their ability to connect consequences to actions did not considerably exceed that of the average rock. One could no more reasonably expect to understand their motivations for doing anything that didn't involve killing, eating, or raping than one would expect to understand the actions of a tree, a stone, or a river. Such an invasion was best seen as a sort of natural disaster, averted if possible and mitigated if not.

She whistled, a seven-note succession that ended in a long, high trill. For a long moment, there was no response. She was not alarmed, however, as it was always possible that her great bird was too far away to hear her. But then she heard his answering cry, a distant shriek from the west that brought a smile to her lips. A small speck appeared in the sky to the west, high over her head, and it rapidly grew larger as Merlian obediently sped towards her. Seeing that he was on his way, she glanced about her campsite to ensure that she had forgotten nothing.

Her tent and her blankets were rolled up and tied tightly under her leather pack, which was secured with a pair of iron buckles. She had enough food

for three more days and water for four; she couldn't count on being able
to find anything edible within leagues of the starving orcs and any water in
the area was bound to be thoroughly fouled by them as well.

The giant hawk arced gracefully towards the ground, his massive wings
fully extended. She reached into a pouch on her belt and retrieved a
desiccated mouse, which she offered to him after he landed and took three
delicate steps in her direction. He accepted the offering with his customary
delicacy, taking it from her palm with a powerful beak that could easily
have severed her forearm.

After swallowing the morsel, Merlian shook his head and ruffled his neck
feathers. That was her cue; she obediently reached up and between the long
quills to scratch the sensitive skin beneath. He gave out a satisfied caw, then
shook his head again. They were well familiar with each other; the great
hawks were long-lived and he had born Bereth safely through the skies for
more than three decades now.

His scent was pungent, but comforting to her, as reassuring as the creak of
the aged leather of the saddle and the shift of the powerful body in between
her legs. She didn't even bother with the reins, but left them loosely tied
around the pommel of the saddle, as she'd left them last night.

She did, however, slip under the thick leather straps that would keep her
on Merlian's back should he shift directions too suddenly or tilt overmuch
and pulled them tight before securing the bronze buckles. The orcs had no
fliers themselves, but they did have archers and mages, and abrupt changes
in course could be fatal to the unprepared. And more than one sky raider
had fallen to a well-aimed spear thrown by a troll, although she doubted
she would have to worry about any such fate today.

Bereth clucked and Merlian leaped into the sky. Her body rocked back
and forth in the usual rhythm as the warhawk's wings beat against the air,
pulling her skyward. Soon he leveled out, facing east, and she gave him his
head for a little while, allowing him to fly towards the sun and the distant sea.
It was so peaceful up high that she found the thought of simply flying away
and spending a quiet day or two fishing and meditating to be seductive, but
her sense of duty quickly reasserted itself. The Silverbows were almost surely
dead already, but until their fate was known, they must not be abandoned.

She reached down and patted the left side of his neck. Ever alert, the
great hawk banked his wings and turned north. It was an easterly wind
today, and cool, coming as it did from the direction of the sea.

Why was the thought of flying away so tempting? She was a little
surprised at herself. It wasn't the first time Ilriathas had proposed marriage

to her. It wasn't the tenth time, for that matter. The heir to Mons Kelethan was a handsome elf, tall, brave, and of impeccable bloodlines. He was barely a century old, some thirty years older than her own sixty-eight, but possessed of a calm wisdom of an elf two centuries his senior. She liked him, in fact, had she been able she would have taken him as a lover four decades ago.

But the price he asked of her was too high. It wasn't that she was overly enamored of her magic. While there were those elfesses who made a fetish of sorcery and devoted their lives to it at the Collegium Occludum, she was not one of them. To her, it was a tool, nothing more. Still, without magic, one could not utilize the spell required to control hawks like Merlian, and she was loathe to even think about giving up this, the freedom to soar high over the lands of Selenoth like some sort of wind goddess.

She cursed whatever perverse god or devil had tied an elfess's ability to procreate to the sacrifice of her magic. She had friends who had cast aside their virginity without a moment's thought for what they were giving up, and she envied their blithe uninterest in all things magical. And perhaps she would have felt the same, had her father not so often taken her up on Gaern, his ancient warhawk, and learned what it was like to feel the sky winds on her face.

For as long as she could remember, she'd dreamed about one day having her own bird, her own sky companion. She'd learned the spells of binding when she'd barely reached half her present height and chanted them to herself as she fell asleep at night. And she had never known such happiness as the morning of her thirty-fifth birthday, when her father had taken her up on Gaern and flown her to the Royal Aerie high above Elebrion, and there shown her the great speckled egg from which Merlian had been hatched. She spent most of the day there, caressing it, singing to it, and telling it of the adventures they would have together.

When the time of the hatching came closer, she would beg rides from every skyrider she encountered; she passed more than one night asleep in the Aerie. On the day Merlian hatched, she'd been initially disappointed to discover that he was a male bird, but the disappointment soon passed as she eagerly awaited the day when he would first take to the skies. And every night, she recited the spells that she would use to let them ride the winds together.

Waiting for him to grow to a size sufficient to carry her was the longest three years of her life. Fortunately, he was large and she was small, and so she was finally granted permission to cast the spell that was now engraved upon her memory and take to the skies.

Bereth glanced down at the trees slowly flowing by beneath her, like a vast bright green river. She would need to pay closer attention soon; it would not be long before she would be approaching the first outposts of the enemy army. She stroked the back of Merlian's neck and smiled. In truth, she could live without magic. But this? Never. Let Ilriathas breed his handsome sons and beautiful daughters on some other maiden, let some other noble-born elfess who did not know the joys of the sky dwell in Mons Kelethan and be called Lady Kelethan and sit near the royal table on feast-days. Let her lay claim to the lovely mountain castle and its famous views, none would ever compare to those she had seen from on high.

A hint of movement far below caught her eye. She frowned, wondering what it might be, and swiftly untied the reins that had been hitherto unneeded. It was a valley of sorts below, with a ridge that ran north to south to the east and a gentler series of hills to the west. There was a lake closer to the hills than to the ridge, and it appeared some sort of creek or little river ran down from the ridge and through the trees of the valley to terminate in the kidney-shaped lake. With a gentle tug on the reins, she caused Merlian to circle about, hoping to get a better view of whatever was moving down below.

It was moving quickly through the trees, too quickly to be an orc. It could be an elf, but then, it could be a deer as well. Or, perhaps, a goblin wolfrider. She urged Merlian into a descending spiral, and reached behind the saddle for her bow and a quiver. She untied the leather thongs that held the former and withdrew three long white-feathered arrows from the latter.

The green expanse of the forest gradually transformed into individual trees and the gaps in the forest canopy became more apparent. She saw a gap in the coverage that appeared to be in the direct path where the creature was headed and caused Merlian to level out. It wasn't a huge opening, but it was just enough to see an elf jogging through it underneath.

"Silverbow!" she cried. "Silverbow!"

He pulled up, drew his sword, and looked wildly about him. He did not, however, think to look straight up. She laughed and slipped the arrows back into the quiver.

"Up here!" she shouted as she retied the bow and slid it behind the saddle. He looked up, started at the sight of the massive hawk circling above the trees, and waved. His clothes were stained and ragged, and his face was dirty, but the white gleam of his smile showed that he was in good spirits. To her surprise, she saw he was not from Elebrion, but was a wood elf.

"Which one are you?"

"Arwis Autumnleaf!" he shouted. "Gelrinas is wounded. I hid him in a tree about a day's march north of here and led the orcs chasing us away from him. Are they nearby?"

"Didn't see them. Do you want me to drop a ladder down to you?"

"No, you need to find Gelrinas before they do! I can make it back to the camp on foot. But I can tell you exactly where you'll find him!"

"How bad is it?"

"What?"

"His wound! How bad is it?"

"Took an arrow through the leg. I removed it and cleaned his leg. He should survive if they haven't found him yet."

"How am I supposed to find him?"

"It won't be hard from the air." He pointed almost due north, towards the direction from whence he'd come. "A bit more than two day's march, you'll see a round lake. A river feeds into it and out of it, and there are three small islands in the middle. Two of them have trees. He's in the tallest tree on the second-largest island. I tied him onto a branch so he can sleep without falling off."

Bereth nodded approvingly. This elf was clever. Orcs and wolves hated water and wouldn't have willingly followed them into the lake. Even if they did, there was a good chance they wouldn't climb any trees when Arwis had left them a trail to follow on the other side of the lake. He would have made it look as if they'd camped there briefly, then continued, leaving them no reason to search the island.

And, of course, both elves would have known that if anyone was going to rescue Gelrinas, it would be a sky raider on the back of a warhawk. A tree was the optimal location for an extrication from enemy territory.

"How far from the outskirts of the camp?"

"Three-quarters of a day. I doubt they'll see you coming." He looked back to the north. "I should leave now. They weren't far behind me. Those cursed wolves are fast and they stick to one's trail."

"Do you need anything?"

She thought he smiled up at her. "If you don't mind, I haven't eaten anything in two days."

"I thought as much." She reached back into her left saddlepack and withdrew a pouch containing a loaf of hard bread, then slipped a pair of apples into it. "Watch out, now!"

She dropped the pouch and it landed with a thud that even she could hear. Ah well, even a bruised apple would ease an empty stomach. He retrieved it and held it up to salute her with it. "My gratitude is boundless. What is your name, angel of my salvation?"

"Bereth, Bereth Mathonwy."

"Then my thanks to you, Bereth Mathonwy. I hope to see you again, so I may thank you more properly." He bowed, adding a little hand flourish that made her laugh, then waved before breaking into a swift and graceful jog.

She couldn't help smiling as she watched him go. There was something spirited about him that she liked. Perhaps if Ilriathas was a bit more like this wood elf, bolder, less deliberate, less consumed by the supreme importance of his bloodline and its continuation, she might be willing to countenance the sacrifice he required of her. But that was impossible. To him, she was nothing more than another piece to be flawlessly arranged in his perfect, aristocratic life.

It was, she supposed, a sincere compliment that he deemed her worthy of bearing his children. Her bloodline was barely noble, nowhere nearly as royal as his own, and the mere fact that he wanted to marry her proved that she was beautiful, for Ilriathas was far too haughty an aesthete to surround himself with anything that was not.

Never mind that for now, she told herself. There was a wounded elf who needed rescue. She directed Merlian north, and pulled back on the reins, guiding him higher into the sky, further from the eyes of the enemy she anticipated would soon be upon her. The hawk's wings beat strongly, but smoothly as he carried her rapidly over the trees and grass and stones below.

It wasn't long before she began seeing signs of the orc depredations. Sizable swaths of forest were blackened and burned, presumably on the part of foraging expeditions sent out to obtain meat of one form or another. Instead of stalking their prey or even utilizing beaters, the orcs would set a series of fires that drove their prey into nets. It was an effective tactic, especially in enemy territory, since it could take years for the flora and fauna to recover.

Although it was not the first time she had seen such abuse of the forest, the sight awoke an anger within her. She curled her lip and shook her head.

How was it that her people had not wiped out these hateful creatures long ago? She thought for a moment, and then spoke into the wind.

> Fire, madness, axe, and pain
> They rape the green land.
> Great spirits of the trees
> Awake! Arise, in righteous wrath,
> And wreak your vengeance upon them!

But the great spirits slumbered on, insensate. Or perhaps they were no more, gone, departed from the world like the ancient races of old. Only the elves remembered them now, the Deathless Ones, the Shadow Walkers, and the Sylvanae. The younger races, Man, Orc, and Goblin, knew nothing of their kind. What she would not give to see the woods awaken, to see the trees rise up and tear their violators limb from limb! But the forest slept on.

She passed over a dozen black gouges torn from its green body before she stopped counting them. Doing so served no purpose except to quantify her pain. And then, she had spotted a gleaming ribbon that worked its way south in a twisting, curving path that might be the outlet of which the scout had spoken. She followed it, and before long spotted the lake with the three islands she had been seeking.

Before descending, she circled it, looking carefully for any sign of the enemy. It looked as if there might have been a pair of modest camps, judging by the two areas where trees had been downed near the water, but no one was there now. It looked safe enough, so she guided Merlian towards the middle island, then towards the more thickly wooded part of it, where the trees grew the highest. But although she circled it twice, and even called out Gelrinas's name, she saw no one and heard no reply.

It wasn't until Merlian landed and she dismounted to investigate the trees more closely that she saw the signs of the struggle. Enough feet to trample the grass had been here recently, and there were small traces of blood, red blood that belonged to no goblin or orc, along the way those feet had been traveling. She followed the blood and bent grass to the water's edge, and saw the marks of clawed and booted feet imprinted on the damp, sandy soil, as well as the unmistakable indications of a boat landing.

She swore bitterly. She could not have missed him by long! Judging by the marks, a mere two day-tenths sooner and he would have been safe. Vexed, she folded her arms and tapped her fingers. Should she go after him and try to see what had become of him? She had a bow and she was a fair shot from Merlian's back, perhaps she could even spare him the rape and torture that were his most likely fate. She knew rescue would be impossible, but mercy might not be beyond her reach. Her other option was to fly south and ensure that Arwis Autumnleaf was not ridden down and captured.

Lord Oakheart would have her bring Autumnleaf to him, on the off-chance that he had gleaned some useful intelligence concerning the enemy's intentions. And for her own sake, she did not wish to fly over the enemy's camp again; the stench alone was sufficient cause to turn away. But she could not bear to think about the atrocities that would be visited upon a brother elf; it would have been kinder if Autumnleaf had simply cut his wounded companion's throat before leaving him behind.

She turned west before she even realized she had done so. Taking a deep breath, she resigned herself to the morbid task before her, and untied her bow once more. This time, she only took out one arrow, but she slung the quiver over her shoulder. She knew that she might not get more than one or two shots before the orcs reacted to her; hopefully Gelrinas's captors would not have reached the main camp before she caught up to them. She stroked the great hawk's neck and urged him on, then rocked back as his next wingbeat, more powerful than the previous one, sent them surging forward.

The signs of the invasion, or infestation, as she thought of it, were unmistakable. Instead of blackened, burned-out scars, the trees had been leveled and the grass all but killed by tens of thousands of orcs tramping about and spraying their stinking urine everywhere. The green carpet below her gave way to sickly browns and yellows, dotted with tents like warts or tumors upon the land.

She took the risk of descending low enough to make out individual orcs, and sure enough, it was not long before the first alarms went up. She could see arms pointing at her, and two or three archers sent shafts up towards her, but none of them came anywhere near her or the hawk insofar as she could tell. They didn't worry her; orc archery was little more accurate than children throwing stones. Her attention was focused on the ground, looking for the small party that would, if she was any judge of things, be bringing their captured treasure to one of the warleaders in the center of the camp.

Then she spotted them. There was a score of armored warriors marching in two lines on either side of about half that many irregulars. In the middle of the irregulars was a supine figure lying on what appeared to be a makeshift cart, only the ends dragged on the ground and left two parallel lines in the dirt behind it. Two big orcs, one on each pole, were pulling it along; it was essentially a stretcher, she realized, only the orcs couldn't bother to carry it in a manner that would give the passenger a smoother ride.

She considered her options. A shot straight ahead and down was difficult, but shooting to the side as the bird moved perpendicular to the target was nearly as hard. She would have to come at Gelrinas from behind due to the stretcher-draggers, as their big bodies would be in the way if she flew ahead and then came back towards him. The problem was that she would probably have only one shot before they understood her purpose and took measures to stop her by shielding his body.

She must make it count, she told herself, if she was to spare the elf the indignities and depredations of his captors. And, she realized, there was only one option if she was to be absolutely sure of her shot. She would have to bring Merlian to a stop in the air, and the best way to do that was to cause him to bank steeply just as she passed in front of the stretcher in a curve tight enough put her directly above her target. That would leave her vulnerable to any archers quick enough to respond, but there were no more shafts being directed her way at the moment so she decided the risk was minimal.

She nocked her arrow and aimed Merlian for a point to the right of the orc party. Just as she passed it, she leaned to the side and pulled hard on the left rein. The hawk obeyed instantly, and for a brief moment she was suspended almost parallel with the ground as the great bird seemed to swoop around an invisible pole. The ground swept past her in a dizzying blur, but the elf on the stretcher was right at the center of her perception and all the world rotated around him. Without thinking, she pulled back the drawstring, and loosed her arrow. Almost as soon as the drawstring snapped, she felt herself being lifted skyward again as Merlian leveled out and began flying back the way they'd come.

She heard the consternation erupt below before she'd even looked back to see if the arrow had hit home. She looked back over her shoulder and saw the two orcs had dropped the front of the stretcher to the ground, and like many of their companions, were staring up at her, gesticulating angrily.

Bereth laughed, as much in relief at the sight of the arrow protruding from Gelrinas's chest as at the furious impotence of the orcs. Even if he wasn't dead yet, he would be soon, before he could face further torture. She toyed with the idea of trying the same trick to kill a few of his captors, but decided against it. The faster she could leave this enfouled, diseased land, the better.

Then, without warning Merlian let out a high-pitched shriek of pain and he unexpectedly pitched to the left. His wings stopped beating, and he held them out, spread wide, as if trying to keep himself aloft. Bereth knew at once that something was wrong. She looked down, and saw a group of orcs jumping up and down, pointing, celebrating. And, to her horror, she saw a pair of cart-bows, insidious machines that were similar to the elven hydra, only they loosed one large bolt instead of three. Both were propped upon upon a pile of logs to permit being aimed skyward. The cart-bows were normally used as anti-cavalry artillery, as its winched cables allowed the bolts to punch right through armor.

Or, as it happened, feathers and flesh. As Bereth urged him on, Merlian fought to beat his wings, but the effort was halting, as if it pained him too much to do so. Bereth looked back and saw a small group of orcs was chasing after her, as if they knew her struggling warhawk could not long stay aloft.

Anguish smote her heart as she realized they were probably correct. Merlian's eyes were pinning, the irises growing rapidly larger, then shrinking again, a certain sign that he was in pain. She wanted to sob and throw her arms around his thick feathered neck, but she knew that doing so would only make it even harder for him to keep flying. Instead, she took a deep breath, set her face, and tried to put her terror and her grief aside for the moment, in order to better calculate what she would need to do to stay alive once she was forced to ground.

Merlian was gliding now in a slow, steady descent. They were still over the ruined earth of the orc camp, or rather, the section that was given over to their goblin slave-allies, and she was low enough that she could hear the smaller monsters jabbering as they halted their activities and came out of their tents to point at the sky. At their current altitude, they would barely make it to the tall green trees that marked the extent of the orc army's deforestation.

"Come on, brave heart, come on, my dear," she leaned forward and whispered to the stricken warhawk. Tears streaked back from her eyes into her hair, as the wind refused to permit them to fall. "Be strong, my darling."

Arrows flew up at her, as did stones from goblin slings, and she was forced to lie flat on his neck to avoid them. She could feel his body twitch as several of them struck him, and she felt his pain in her soul as if it were her own.

He somehow seemed to understand her need to reach the trees, because he stroked his wings twice more, a valiant effort that gave him just enough height to clear the first row of them. Then they were engulfed by a leafy green storm, leaves and branches whipping at her face as Merlian broke through the forest canopy into the shadowed depths below.

Miraculously, the great hawk found the strength to backstroke once, twice more, slowing them down considerably before he abruptly furled his wings and fell to the forest floor. "Merlian!" she screamed, more concerned about her bird than the fact that they were plunging rapidly towards the ground. Somehow, they missed striking any trees, and when they struck, his big body and soft feathers cushioned the impact for her.

"Merlian!" she screamed again. He opened his eyes, only a little, and she rapidly undid the two buckles that held her strapped into the saddle, then leaped to the ground. She ran around him and embraced his head, crying and kissing his beak. But no sooner had she thrown her arms around him than he gave out a whistling sigh and sagged to the ground, his ink-blue tongue lolling from his beak.

"Merlian, no!" she cried. But when she stepped back, she could see the end of the crudely hewn wooden bolt protruding from the left side of his breast. It must have nearly pierced his heart; she wondered at the amazing strength that had allowed her to escape the orc encampment.

Which reminded her, she was far from safe. The orcs would already be after her, the wolves would soon be on the scent of her trail, and though it made her soul-sick to think of the foul beasts devouring her dear hawk's flesh and decorating themselves with his noble feathers, the discovery of his sizable body would be a major distraction to most of the hunters now chasing after her.

She climbed back up to the saddle and retrieved those items that she needed most. Her bow, her arrows, her sword, a pouch of food, and two small skins of water. Everything else she would have to abandon, because there was only one way to ensure the wolves would not easily scent her trail. Fortunately, the trees here were tall enough, and thick enough, that their big branches extended out well past their nearest neighbors.

Bereth kissed Merlian's beak again and plucked a single feather from his neck, then another one from his breast. After one last mournful look back at her longtime companion, she began climbing a nearby oak as quickly as she could.

LUGBOL

LUGBOL lay sprawled on his back, as exhausted and satiated as an orc could be. In addition to gifting him the lovely Meighar for three days, the Great Orc had sent his newest grun-kor a cow from his private herd as a sign of his favor yesterday. They had feasted and futtered and then feasted some more. His belly full and his bollocks empty, Lugbol barely noticed the lingering pain from the brand on his left bicep or the marks that her claws had left on his shoulders, back, and buttocks.

"I wish you could stay another day or three," he told her, following a contented sigh.

"So do I," she said, surprising him.

"Truly? Why? I'm no Great Orc!"

Meighar shrugged and looked off into the distance. "So? I barely see him. He had me once, the night I was given to him by the King of Shadaru. Ever since, he only keeps me around to dole out as a reward to his captains, and gives me to kings he thinks are trouble and wants to keep in line. That way they can say they had one of the Great Orc's kir'agh; some of them are so eager to boast about it they can hardly wait to get the futtering over with. And then, some of them are cruel."

He frowned, suddenly wondering if he had been too rough with her. Somehow, she seemed to read his mind, because she laughed and pulled at his hair hard enough to make him growl.

"Don't be silly. Every kir wants to be properly pounded! It's hardly difficult to feel the difference between enthusiasm and cruelty.

He looked up and down her naked body. Her upper arms and breasts were mottled blue with bruises.

"I was maybe too enthusiastic?"

"There is no such thing." She lightly ran a claw down his chest. "I want to ask you something."

"So ask."

"Will you do something for me?"

"Yes."

"Ask the Great Orc for me. As a gift."

"I can't do that!" He looked down. "I mean, it's not... I don't–"

"I don't mean now! I mean when you do something that brings you to his attention again. Something that makes him ask you for a reward. I know him, Lugbol. He always asks, because he knows most orcs are too afraid to ask for anything from his hand. I mean, look at you!" She lowered her voice in mock imitation of a male orc's. "It's an honor, Great Orc! If I can just cut off me vank for yez, Great Orc, I'd be damnable proud!"

"Shut up! Bloody kwee don't know nothing of honor!"

"Maybe not, but bloody kwee know all about this!" She grabbed him in a manner that made him close his eyes and grunt. He was just about to throw her on her back when he heard Ghurash call to him from outside the tent.

"Grun-kor!"

Oh, for the cursed love of Gor Gor. "What?" he bellowed, hoping the older orc would correctly conclude from his tone that he should squag off and go bother some other unsuspecting kor.

"Got a summons from King Nekheru. He's calling all grun-kors and warleaders under his command to attend him. Now, Grun-kor!"

"What command? We ain't under his command!"

"We are now. His kors made it real clear."

Lugbol unleashed a thunderous stream of obscenities and vulgarities that only made Meighar fall flat on her back and laugh. She watched him dress, with a speculative expression that made him feel both proud and suspicious.

"Well, I should go. You want someone to bring you back to the Great Orc?"

"Go." She fluttered a hand at him. "Go and do something that will make me yours, Lugbol."

He growled low under his breath. By all the gods of the orcs and trolls, she was the finest, loveliest greenskin he'd ever seen. "I'll do it or die trying," he assured her.

"Try not to get yourself killed," she said. Meighar ran her dark green tongue alluringly over her pretty little left tusk. "I would be sorry to hear it."

Damned if she wasn't the sweetest ghash he ever did see. He cursed again, then stormed out of the tent, half-aroused and half-ready to kill the first orc he looked upon. Fortunately, that first orc was Ghurash, and the sight of his sour, tusked face was enough to settle him down.

"Who put us under Nekheru?"

"Who knows? Nobody knows nothing more than what I told you. Didn't you say the Great Orc wanted us back in the Man lands?"

"Yeah."

"Yeah, well, Nekheru's got the command. He's taking an army west while the Great Orc goes south, after the damned Elves."

Lugbol thought about it a moment. The iron Men were bad, but their fire magic didn't seem to be anywhere nearly as dangerous as the hellish forces wielded by the elf shamans. "I don't know squat about Nekheru. Is he good for anything more than squagging gobbos?"

"Cursed if I know."

Fortunately, it wasn't hard to find Nekheru's camp. They weren't the only warleaders being summoned to kiss the crown. Lugbol found himself following a pair of Hagahorn'ugh heavy cavalry kors who weren't any taller than he was, but whose arms looked to be very nearly the size of his head.

"Looks like we won't be doing no hit-and-runs this time," he observed. "Them boys are for straight-up banging heads."

Ghurash nodded, and somehow, although Lugbol wouldn't have thought it possible, his expression grew even more sour.

Ten massive Hagahorn'ugh mountain orcs stood outside the rude barrier of uprooted trees that marked the limits of Nekheru's turf, five on either side of an opening barely big enough for the pair of boar riders to pass through. Lugbol was not a small orc, but these mountain orcs looked as if they had more than a splash of troll's blood in them as most were a full head taller than him and several had a faint bluish cast to their skin. They eyed the two smaller orcs contemptuously, and Lugbol rubbed his new brand to remind himself that for all their size, he had the favor of the Great Orc.

One of the guards had what looked like a galvebel's tattoo on his exposed chest, and he tilted his head as he studied first Ghurash, then Lugbol. His lower left tusk was broken off and capped with a false iron tusk.

"This some kind'o joke?" he demanded of Lugbol in his thick-tongued northeastern accent. "Half-gobbo like you can't be no Gor Gor-damned graborgh!"

Lugbol spit at the bigger orc's feet. "Who you calling half-gob, kobber?"

The galvebel's yellow eyes narrowed, but with suspicion rather than anger. Lugbol exhaled slowly, glad to see that the mountain orc was inclined to think before he split any skulls in his massive, club-like hands.

"You either stupid or you somebody."

Lugbol spit again and wrinkled his lip in a contemptuous sneer. "If I'm stupid, then why am I standing here staring at your shriveled vank, squaggee?"

The big orc guffawed, setting off his subordinates, who pointed at Lugbol and slapped each other on the shoulder, no doubt picturing what would happen if Lugbol tried to mount their officer. Lugbol forced a hard smile and let them have their fun. He knew the galvebel had already backed down.

"Yeah, you somebody. The king told me to look for a pissant what was a sharp bastard. He be you, yeah?"

"Yeah, he be me," Lugbol confirmed. "I ain't no graborgh, though. The Great Orc just made me grun-kor."

"No szhar?" The big orc sounded impressed. He pointed to some of his kors. "You four, come with me. We bringing these little kors to Nekheru; we got orders. You five, you got the gate until I come back!"

"Galvebel!" The remaining guards saluted while the four ordered to escort them fell in on either side of him and Ghurash. He practically had to jog to keep up with the long strides of the Hagahornu, but the galvebel clearly wasn't trying to walk fast because he was chatting cheerfully down at Lugbol as he strode through the milling ranks of Nekheru's forces.

"We ain't been here long, but the food sucks something fierce. All the wood is green and you can't cook a bloody pot without a proper flame, so everything ends up half-raw and tasting like the damn bitter smoke. We thought when we was coming down out of the mountains that we'd be eating dwarves for breakfast and elves for dinner, but all we get is roots and bark and maybe a bit of gobbo in the stew. And now they saying we going after men?"

"Man ain't bad," Ghurash commented. The galvebel glanced at him skeptically.

"When you be eating men? I ain't never had none meself."

"We was in the Man lands," Lugbol explained. "We just came back three, four days ago. Got our voreghs handed to us, but not before we sacked and burned maybe twenty, thirty of their villages."

"Yeah?" You must have got your taste of Man then. What's it like?"

"More tender than gobbo, less stringy. Less froggy, if you know what I mean."

"Damn!" The galvebel nodded eagerly. "I hope we get on the march soon, I could go for some o' that!"

Lugbol nodded. The purposeful pace at which the bigger orc had set them was drawing attention to them now as they made their way towards wherever the king was, and Lugbol was, despite himself, impressed by what he was seeing. The Hagahorn'ugh were not cowardly kor-come-latelies, they were big, they wore armored breastplates and spaulders and vambraces cast in the iron mined from their mountains, and they looked proper hard. They might not be as numerous as the Ommog'ugh, nor as ruthlessly disciplined as elite Zoth Ommoghu units like the Red Claw Slayers, but they were no slouches. Seeing them up close, it was easy to understand why the Great Orc was wary of his newly-come ally. They weren't no ghash'ugh.

And they were certainly nothing like the rowdy, slipshod gungiyar'ugh that Zlatagh had led to disaster the previous moon.

That could be either good or bad. Nekheru would need hard kors if he was going to beat the iron demons and the terrible steel riders of the Szavon'agh. On the other hand, if they weren't of a mind to listen to Lugbol, he and Ghurash were liable to find themselves torn limb from limb and stuffed in the iron Hagahorn cookpots no matter how highly the Great Orc valued him. Once the two armies split up and the Hagahorn'ugh marched on the Man lands, there would be nothing that Azzakhar, or the brand he'd personally applied, could do to protect them from the big mountain orcs.

"Is Nekheru the kral of all Hagahorn?" he asked the galvebel.

"Ain't nobody ever been the kral of all Hagahorn, except of course the Troll Kral. Nah, he's just the clan chief of the Drangahanu, and they's the biggest sept, so all the mountain tribes that matter pays him hubble. They's some that don't, but mostly smaller tribes up north, real vicious bastards that's half-troll, half-goat. He just calls hisself kral so's the Great Orc and t'other southies give him his props."

The clan chief of the Drangahana, Lugbol saw, was standing on a wide, shallow hill of sorts, surrounded by circles of grun-kors, galvebels, and assorted kors sporting inkings that indicated dozens of different tribes. He didn't look tall, but he had the powerful shoulders and bulging forearms of a boar rider, and a square, pugnacious face marked by two comically stubby lower tusks. The sides of his head were shaved, and his white-streaked mane was tied back into a boar's tail. He was listening, with a skeptical expression

on his face, to a big orc with yellowish skin who was energetically waving
his hands as he spoke.

The kors surrounding Nekheru gave way reluctantly, but they gave
way nevertheless as the galvebel and his men pushed through the crowd.
Conscious of the many curious eyes on him, Lugbol stared fixedly ahead and
stuck his chest out. Only a few of the kors here would grasp the significance
of his still-raw brand, but word would spread soon enough that he was, as
the galvebel said, somebody.

Nekheru waved the yellow orc to silence as the galvebel saluted. "Felseg
Kral, this is the little Goghu what you wanted."

The kral nodded and waved off the galvebel. The big yellow orc started
to say something, but Nekheru shot him a warning glance, and he had the
sense to clap his trap and back away. When the kral returned his attention
to Lugbol, Lugbol saw that they were much of a height, although the older
orc was considerably heavier and more muscular. He had a paunch and his
squat legs were bandy with years of sitting on boar's back, but despite his
age, his eyes were still keen with intelligence.

"You're to be Azzakhar's leash on me?" he asked, raising one skeptical
eyebrow. "Who the faszh are you, kor?"

"Grun-kor Lugbol of the Gog Black Fist Infantry, Felseg Kral. And my
galvebel, Ghurash."

"And why the faszh do I need a faszhek grun-kor from anyafaszhek Gog,
Grun-kor Lugbol, especially a grun-kor with one faszhek arm?"

Well, at least Nekheru wasn't threatening to rape him with it, Lugbol told
himself. "Because the kral is marching west into the Manlands, Felseg Kral.
And because not one moon past, the bloody Szavon'ugh fed twenty-five
thousand kors under Zlatagh Maneater their own anyafaszhek vanks. My
Black Fist Infantry was the only gungiyar to fight, to stay together through
the night, and return to the army afterwards, Felseg Kral."

"You think yez some kind of bad-arse kor, Grun-kor?"

"No, Felseg Kral. I just try to look before I stick my vank in it."

Nekheru barked with laughter. "Then yez one kor in a thousand, Grun-
kor Lugbol. So Azzakhar ain't looking to throw my kors into the grinder?"

"I wouldn't know, Felseg Kral. I seen him once, when he give me this."
Lugbol pointed to his arm.

"With the fire," the kral said approvingly. His bulging arms were marked
with nothing more than tattoos and scars, but then, Lugbol hadn't seen a
single Hagahornu zabit sporting a brand. It didn't seem the northerners
were inclined to burn themselves; after taking the fire himself, Lugbol very

strongly felt that the Hagahornu had the right of it. "So what did the looking learn you?"

"They can fight. We thought we was safe because we was in the trees, so their cavalry couldn't smash us and their foot couldn't catch us. We bled them, we burned their villages and we killed their kwee and their kin, but somehow they got behind us and squagged us good. All the gobbos and half the kors who live is probably still running."

"Orcs."

"What do you mean?"

"Orcs," the kral repeated. He gestured around him. "They wasn't no kors. These be kors, Grun-kor. Kors like you."

"Right," Lugbol said as if he meant it. He didn't know what else to say. And what was he going to do, argue with the orc?

The kral chuckled. "I'd half a mind to send your head back to Azzakhar before, but now I see he didn't mean nothing by it, I think it'll serve me better on yez shoulders. I'm naming you Hadvezer. You'll command the scouts and the skirmishers."

"Felseg Kral!" Lugbol blurted, half in shock, half in protest. In normal circumstances, a hadvezer was a warleader of more than one clan. In the present situation, it meant that the kral was putting Lugbol on his command staff, and making him senior to every graborgh, grun-kor, and shugaba in the cursed army!

"Do I keep my kors?"

"How many you got?"

"Roundabout five szazad'ugh, Felseg Kral."

The kral tapped his chin reflectively. "Yeah, Hadvezer Lugbol, you can keep them. Probably best to keep a few Gogh'ugh around in case some thickskull gets it in his head to think he don't have to take yez orders."

"Thank you, Felseg Kral." Lugbol knew very well that the kral had probably just saved his life. No matter what he was called, he was going to need all the muscle he could get to keep the Hagahorn'ugh kors in line. Fortunately, the same thought appeared to strike the kral.

"Oi, listen up, all you sqwaaks and squaggies! This here's Lugbol, of the Black Fist! He's small, he's Goghu, but for all that I'm telling you he's the new Hadvezer for the light infantry! He's a right proper kor, he's fought Man before, and if he's yez commander, you'll damn well do what he say or I'll have yez skin flayed and made into a vest for him to wear! You got that, kors?"

"Oi, Felseg Kral!" the Hagahorn'ugh shouted, with no reluctance that Lugbol could see. But it wasn't enough for Kral Nekheru.

"You got that, kors?" he shouted back.

"Oi, Felseg Kral!" they roared, much louder the second time. Nekheru nodded and turned back to Lugbol.

"Can't say you won't run into nobody who'll give you trouble, what with being Goghu and all. If they do, pull rank on 'em; I'll back you up." The kral snorted, his eyes distant. "Some of the big 'uns need to be kicked in the bollocks once or twice to fall in line. Come back tonight at sunset; you'll be meeting your alulzabit'ugh at the talakhoza."

"How many kors will I have?"

"Counting the sqwaaks, maybe fifteen ezer, four o' them farkhut'agh."

Lugbol nodded. Fifteen thousand, four thousand being goblin cavalry. He was being given command of an army bigger than any he'd ever imagined could possibly exist before being summoned by the Great Orc the previous autumn. It reminded him of when his anya had first told him tales of Mulguth the Mighty, the terrible Goblinsbane, who commanded more kors than any orc could count. And yet, that was ten ezers less than Zlatagh had commanded, Zlatagh Piss-taker, whose body now lay rotting in the Korokhurmagh along with thousands of other orcs and gobbos.

"I'll be your eyes, Felsig Kral!" He saluted, and the kral saluted back. When he turned around to face the crowd of bigger, more powerful orcs staring at him again, he no longer felt the weight of their collective gaze. He was grun-kor of the Black Fist infantry, and damned if they weren't the best in the cursed Hagahorn'ugh army.

He didn't wait for an escort. He simply plowed straight ahead, with Ghurash falling in behind him, and all the Hagahornu kors parted before him as if he was an anyafaszhek troll. The big galvebel was back at the makeshift gate with his orcs. He must have heard the kral's announcement, as he raised his fist swiftly and his fellow guards followed suit. Lugbol grinned and raised his fist in response; it felt pretty damned good.

Once they were clear of the kral's camp, Ghurash finally opened his mouth. "You really want to go back into the Korokhurmagh?"

"They're not going to fight us there. Not when the real infantry are with us. The mandokki will wait for us out in the open once they know we have to come to them."

"If you say," the galvebel said. He sounded dubious.

He was disappointed to discover upon their return that Meighar was already gone. Korpaghu reported that a pair of the Great Orc's guards had

appeared not long after Lugbol's departure to collect her. He was just about
to order an assembly when behind him, he heard a familiar voice calling his
name.

He turned around to see a most unwelcome sight. It was Snaghak, the
bastard orc he'd hoped was rotting deep in the forest with Zlatagh. No such
luck, it seemed.

"What in the name of Ordogh's bunghole is yez ugly face doing here,
Snaggletooth?"

Snaghak held up one finger to his left nostril and blew. A long string of
green-yellow snot flew out and landed very near Lugbol's left foot. It was
a damned good shot, Lugbol was reluctantly forced to admit. "I heard the
Black Fist was taking in all sorts o' kors."

"Don't want you, Snaggletooth."

"Didn't think you did, Grun-kor." He jerked a thumb at a hulking orc
behind him who looked vaguely familiar to Lugbol. "See, I was just talking
to Unbaak here, and he don't much like how yez calling the shots around
here."

"That so?"

The big orc blinked slowly. He wasn't a mountain orc, and compared
to the Hagahorn'ugh kors he looked almost underfed, but even so, he was
clearly capable of tearing Lugbol limb-from-limb.

"Yeah," Unbaak said. "Yeah, you punk-arse, me say."

Right. Lugbol glanced to both sides. There were far too many of his
orcs paying witness to let the challenge pass, and while he was loath to
kill one of his own kors, there was no way he could hope to beat down
Unbaak, especially not with an injured arm. Well, Snaghak left him little
choice. He gestured to a kor he saw wearing a crossbow slung across his
back.

"You, yeah you, point that at the big one there."

The kor hesitated for a moment, then shrugged, wound the crank,
slipped in a bolt and aimed it at the big orc's unarmored chest.

Unbaak blinked stupidly, a perplexed expression gradually making its
way across his broad green face. Snaghak, on the other hand, exploded
with rage, just as Lugbol had hoped.

"I knowed you was tricksy, but I never knowed you was yellow, you
bloody ghash!" The former shugaba was nearly frothing at the mouth in his
fury. "You may be grun-kor, but you think one single kor in the gungiyar
is going to follow you anywheres if you have yez kors kill'im instead of
fighting the challenge, you stinking coward?"

Lugbol merely smiled. The Law of the Orc was less an iron-clad set of rules than time-honored traditions violated with impunity by those with the power to do so, and bent as far as possible by those without it, but there was one law that was always kept by every orc, in every clan and every tribe. And that was, in times of war—defined as when the gungiyar'ugh were gathered and the hadvezer named—no challenges were permitted to the warleader on pain of death.

"You would be right, if yez big friend there had challenged me when I was just a grun-kor, Snaghak. But I ain't no grun-kor no more. I'm hadvezer now."

"Murdu!" Snaghak snarled. "You ain't no hadvezer!"

"Go ask the kral of the Hagahorn if you don't believe me."

Ghurash stepped forward, twirling a spiked club he had somehow acquired without Lugbol noticing. A circle of kors had begun to gather now, sensing the prospects for some afternoon entertainment.

"Best watch your filthy faszhek mouth," the normally taciturn galvebel said loudly. "I was there. He's grun-kor of the Black Fist, but now he's hadvezer for the whole bloody light infantry too."

Triumphant whoops and blood-curdling howls erupted from the orcs who heard Ghurash's announcement, prompting even more of them to rush out of their tents and inquire as to the cause. Lugbol looked around and saw nearly one hundred of his kors had gathered around already; even some passing heavy infantry had heard the commotion and had stopped on the outskirts of the mob to see what was going down.

"You want me to pincushion this big faszhan, Hadvezer?" the orc with the crossbow asked with a smirk. Unbaak, already pale with fear, promptly wet himself, sparking shrieks and screams of mocking laughter.

"That depends on our friend Snaggletooth here," Lugbol said, staring down the former shugaba. "If he'll take me on, right here, right now, I'll let the piss-legger live."

"Fight, fight, fight!" The gathered orcs began to chant, delirious with anticipation. Snaghak's eyes narrowed suspiciously.

"Yez just trying to trick me."

"No trick. What, you gonna yellow out now?"

"Yez gonna say I challenged you, then hide behind yez damn hadvezerek to kill me, yeah?"

"What sort o' yellow ghash is you, Snaggletooth?" Lugbol wrinkled his lip contemptuously. "You put yez stupid pal here up to challenge me, and now yez gonna let him die because yez too damn yellow-bellied to fight an orc with one arm?"

"I ain't too yellow nothing! You swear to Gor Gor and the Great Orc hisself that yez'll fight me fair, one-on-one, and it ain't no challenge."

"It ain't no challenge," Lugbol agreed. "You beat me down, you still ain't grun-kor and you sure as hell ain't hadvezer."

It was a moot point, he knew. Snaghak had no intention of leaving him alive, and even if he did somehow survive a beat-down, the kors would never follow him after so many of them saw it happen.

"Swear it!"

"I swear it by Gor Gor and the Great Orc Azzakhar," he vowed. "And by Kral Nekheru," he added, just in case word got back to the Hagahornu leader. It couldn't hurt to kiss the kral's green arse if he survived the fight. "That enough for you?"

Snaghak still looked suspicious, but he nodded slowly. Lugbol glanced at the orc with the crossbow and made a gesture with his hand. The orc slipped the string and removed the bolt, prompting a cruel laugh from the crowd as Unbaak began to shake and shiver with the afterfear.

"Who's the punk-arse now, you fazhek fraud?" someone shouted at him, and the big orc cringed. Lugbol almost felt sorry for him; the poor brute was too stupid to know how Snaghak had been using him. For that alone, Snaghak deserved to get his head stove in.

"So, how you wanna die, Lugbollocks?" Snaghak seemed to be recovering from the unexpected shock of Lugbol's promotion and was returning to his usual brazen self. "Clubs, claws, or blades?"

"I was thinking I'd just beat you to death with my big ol' cobber," Lugbol said, grabbing himself. "Seeing that yez too damn tight-arsed to squagg and yez teeth are too damn snaggled to risk my vank."

The Black Fists roared their lusty approval of his open contempt. Snaghak flushed dark green with fury, which was exactly what Lugbol wanted. The shugaba might be a sneak and a backstabber, but he'd earned a reputation as a good fighter, and he'd made for a fairly even match even when Lugbol had been healthy.

"I'll kill you for that," Snaghak hissed. "Think I'm a faszhek gobbo? I'll rape your corpse and fry your vank for my dinner tonight!"

"Better invite some friends then, Snaggie. This big ol' vank'll feed at least five." His kors fairly screamed with laughter, but Lugbol resisted the urge to throw more wood on the fire as Snaghak looked more than ready to leap at his throat. "Jaws and claws, Snaghak. Just jaws and claws. Now throw the faszh down or run like the bitch yez be!"

Snaghak snarled and leaped at him, leading with his left shoulder in an attempt to knock Lugbol down. Anticipating this, Lugbol dodged right, but slashed to the left with his right hand, raking his outstretched claws across Snaghak's ugly face. He raised his hand, and the watching orcs shouted at the sight of Snaghak's blood dripping down his forearm.

Snaghak growled, but the pain of the three deep scratches carved in parallel across his left cheek seemed to calm him rather than enrage him. Lugbol reminded himself that the other orc didn't get to be shugaba of the Long Marchers by being stupid and prone to spiraling out of control. They circled each other slowly, each looking for an opening to exploit. Lugbol lashed out with his left foot, but it was a half-hearted feint and Snaghak simply ignored it. His angry yellow eyes never left Lugbol's face.

"Just kill the bastard already," he heard Korpaghu shout, and he hurled himself forward, slashing and clawing at Snaghak's face. But the other orc ducked his windmilling swings and smashed his shoulder into Lugbol's bad arm, then threw two punches at it in rapid succession. He didn't even try to hit Lugbol's face, and he didn't have to, as the pain that erupted in Lugbol's arm nearly took his breath away as it flared all the way up to his shoulder. He somehow managed to kick Snaghak off him with his left foot, but sensing an advantage, Snaghak closed in again, avoided a jab, grabbed Lugbol's shoulder with both hands, and snapped at Lugbol's arm with his tusks.

But before Snaghak's jaws could close on the injured limb, Lugbol head-butted his enemy. Green blood spattered all over his forehead, blinding him momentarily. Snaghak shrieked and stumbled back, both hands covering his face. Lugbol was staggered himself by the force of the blow, but he wiped at his face and threw himself at his bloody opponent with a snarl that was echoed by the watchers. His own blood up, Lugbol barely felt the fiery pain in his arm as he smashed his left fist into Snaghak's jaw, then threw a right to his cheek, and another left that harmlessly clipped the other orc's ear before finally buckling Snaghak's knees with a powerful right uppercut.

As the dazed orc started to crumple, Lugbol reared back and hit Snaghak as hard as he could on the side of the head. Snaghak went down heavily, as if he'd been struck with a club, and Lugbol was on him in a flash, straddling his limp body and pinning down his arms with his knees before smashing fist after fist after fist into the now-unconscious orc's bloody face. Then there was a loud crack, and a sharp new pain flowered in his hand.

"Gordammit!" he swore viciously, before awkwardly pushing himself off of Snaghak, cradling his left forearm in his right hand. He'd either broken his hand or his wrist and it hurt like an anyafaszhek. "Son of a whore can't even take a beat-down without being a pain in the arse!"

He rose unsteadily to cheers and an incipient chant that quickly grew louder. "Black Fist, Black Fist, Black Fist!" Lugbol nodded, and turned in a circle to acknowledge the chanting kors, and not without effort, raised his broken, bloody hand above his head.

Ghurash stepped forward. "Yez ain't gonna to let the bastard live, is yeh?" The galvebel fingered the Man dagger he wore at his belt meaningfully.

"Don't be stupid," Lugbol said wearily. "Be a piss-poor grun-kor if I dasn't do it meself."

He walked over to Snaghak, lying prone and helpless in his own blood. He almost felt sorry for the arrogant shugaba, who had never known when to shut his trap or leave well enough alone. Then he looked up at Ghurash and shrugged, wincing as the movement caused his shoulder to twinge.

"Don't bring it if you don't got it."

And with that, he stomped down hard on Shagrat's exposed throat, crushing the defenseless orc's airpipe under a horny, callused heel with an audible crunch.

BERETH

S HE AWOKE to the harsh, grunting sound of orcish being spoken. Three orcs were arguing loudly amongst themselves as they approached the split-trunked oak tree in which Bereth had been sleeping. They didn't seem to be paying much attention to where they were going, so as she yawned silently and rubbed at her eyes, she decided that it was mere bad luck that had brought them here so close to her.

She'd leaped from tree to tree, initially heading west rather than south in an attempt to hide her trail from her pursuers, most particularly the goblin wolfriders whose mounts could not only follow her scent, but easily outpace her on the ground. Once she felt she'd gone far enough to escape the likely extent of their pursuit, she climbed down in order to make better time. No matter how agile the elf, it was much faster to run over the dark mossy floor of the forest than it was to balance on the branches of the trees, ignoring the annoyance of having your face constantly whipped by twigs and leaves, and occasionally having to stop and climb either up or down in order to find a branch that extended far enough to reach another tree.

Only well after second Moonrise did she finally stop running and climb into the forked embrace of a slumbering forest giant. She tied herself to a branch, curled up in her cloak and fell into an exhausted, fitful sleep, only to be woken by the guttural sounds of the orcs arguing below. Or complaining, she realized as she listened to them. It was hard to understand them, as they spoke in a dialect different from any other she'd heard before.

As near as she could tell, they were angry about being sent on a pointless chase after an elf who they wouldn't be permitted to eat anyhow. Her eyes narrowed as the conversation turned more optimistic, as the smallest of the three orcs pointed out that even if they couldn't kill her or eat her, there were other entertainments to be had. He then began expounding on his plans for her, the full extent of which Bereth never learned. It was her own fault, though, as she rather rudely interrupted his oration by loosing an arrow that entered his left eye and partially exited the rear of his misshapen skull.

His two companions didn't notice at first, but continued for three or four more steps before turning around to see what had happened to him. It was almost comical to see how they looked back, then down, then stared stupidly at each other for a moment before awareness of what had happened finally dawned on them. As the bigger one roared defiantly up at the trees, Bereth put a second arrow right down his gullet, and the razor-sharp point came out the back of his neck as he slumped, choking and dying, to the ground. The third orc was a little more clever, as he didn't waste any time shouting or looking up at the trees, but instead began running as fast as his stumpy bowed legs would allow.

Bereth raised her bow, but there were several branches obscuring her line of sight, so she was obliged to put an arrow through his thigh rather than a more lethal location. But she knew it would be enough to slow him down, so she untied herself and climbed down from the tree without hurrying, then strolled in the direction that he'd fled. He was limping badly and bleeding profusely, so it wasn't difficult to catch up with him.

At the sound of her footsteps behind him, the wounded orc whirled around. He was about a head shorter than her, but he was probably three times her weight. He wore a metal breastplate and had several dark tattoos on his arms, that, combined with the large rectangular cleaver he was drawing from its goblinskin sheath, told her that he was what passed for a proper soldier, not an irregular. The arrow piercing his left thigh was hampering his movements, but between the big blade and his bulging arms, there was no doubt that he could chop her in half if he could get close enough.

"Yar!" he shouted as he took a step towards her. She calmly put a second arrow in his throat, then stood there and watched him die. She retrieved that arrow easily enough, as it very nearly went all the way through him, but the one in his thigh was a little tougher. She walked back and recovered the second arrow, but not even putting her foot on the dead orc's head and tugging hard was enough to pull the first one out of its skull. She gave it up with a sigh; that still left her with eighteen arrows, although three of them were now fouled, like her hands, with dark green orc's blood.

She wiped them off as best she could on some leaves, followed by some moss, then slipped them back into her quiver. It was tempting to use a little of her water to at least rinse off her hands, but she knew she'd better save it for drinking. Perhaps she'd stumble across a creek soon. In any event, it was time to move on. If they were still looking for her this far west, they probably weren't going to give up the chase easily and although orcs were undisciplined, three regulars would be missed well before sunset.

Still stiff from her makeshift bed, she took the time to stretch her arms and legs before breaking into an easy jog heading south. With any luck, she'd be spotted by one of her fellow raiders before the end of the day.

The sun was just approaching its apex when Bereth heard the howls in the distance. Wolves. She cursed under her breath and took one last bite out of the apple she'd been eating before tossing it into the stream at which she'd stopped to wash her hands and catch her breath. She debated wading through the water to try to break her scent trail, but the stream seemed to be meandering more west than south and the water would only increase her pursuers' worrisome advantage in speed.

If they lost her scent here, they'd simply send a pair of wolves running along each bank until they picked it up again, and gained even more ground on her. Best to simply run straight south as fast as she could and hope someone spotted her from above before they caught her.

And so, she ran. She wasn't tired, but it soon became apparent that something in her left knee wasn't quite right. Had she twisted it without noticing when poor Merlian struck the ground? She tried not to favor it, but the more she tried not to do so, the more conscious of it she became. It wasn't exactly painful, it was more of a discomfiting pressure, but it prevented her from properly stretching her left leg out as she ran and put a sort of hitch in her stride.

Again and again, she looked to the sky above the forest canopy and saw nothing. Every time she sensed motion overhead, her heart leaped, hoping that it was the familiar shape of a warhawk soaring above her. But time and time again, it was only birds, or occasionally, a squirrel leaping from one tree to another. At first, she felt despair, especially as the howls of the wolves grew louder, although they were still too far behind her to see. But the despair rapidly turned to irritation, then anger.

Where were they? They knew she was out here. Surely Arwis Autumnleaf had reached their forward base and told Lord Oakenheart that he'd seen her, and where she was heading! Why didn't the High Guard commander have sky raiders out looking for her, as she'd been ordered out to find the wretched Silverbows? And where was Ilriathas? He came up with one excuse or another to inflict himself upon her nearly every evening, surely he, at least, would have missed her. He probably wouldn't have gone looking for her himself, given his other responsibilities, but he might at least have sent out a hawk or two.

She fumed as she ran. If an elf was so besotted with her as to propose marriage more than a dozen times, how could he possibly not notice her failure to return to camp by nightfall? The howls were getting closer and she knew she didn't have much more time. Should she climb a tree and attempt to keep running? Or should she try to find some defensible ground and make a last stand?

She looked back and saw a green-and-grey flash behind her. It looked like her choice was made for her. She nocked an arrow, waited until the wolfrider cleared a large tree, then loosed the arrow at his chest. She didn't wait to see if she'd hit, instead she looked upward to locate the biggest, most branch-laden oak she could find. There was one about twenty paces to her left, so she ran towards it as fast as her injured knee would allow.

It was a snarl that saved her. Somehow, the wolves must have gotten past her and circled back to cut her off, because she heard the sound and instinctively ducked to her left just as the wolfrider shot past her, the tip of his lance barely missing her right shoulder. She had a clean shot at the goblin's back, but without knowing if there were others, she didn't dare take the time to draw and nock an arrow.

A second lancer appeared, but this time she was ready. She let him come at her, then ducked under his lance and jammed her bow into the wolf's slashing jaws. It snapped in two, but did something to the wolf that cause it to break its stride and start thrashing and snapping wildly at nothing in particular. Its rider pulled desperately on the reins, but to no avail.

She regretted the loss of her bow, but admittedly, it wouldn't have done her much good in the belly of a wolf pack. She reached the tree she'd picked out and leaped at the huge trunk, using her right leg to propel herself up to the lowest branch. She pulled herself up to it just in time to avoid having her legs skewered by a third wolfrider who was standing in the saddle and stabbing up at them with his lance.

A quick count revealed there were at least ten of them approaching, and several appeared to be pulling shortbows from their saddlebags. Goblins might not be crack archers, but considering she was barely off the ground, they didn't have to be. So, she grimly clambered up the giant oak, knowing that it wouldn't be long before some of them started climbing up after her.

Assuming, of course, none of their archers managed to pin her to the trunk first.

A shaft flew past her and struck a branch above her. She had no choice but to keep climbing, until finally she was high enough that none of their wild attempts were coming anywhere near her. That being accomplished, she stepped out on a branch that reached out to entangle itself with one from a neighboring tree and adroitly changed trees. But any sense of relief was short lived, as she could see there were already two goblins well off the ground and rapidly climbing the first tree.

She looked down at the branch on which she was standing and wondered if she might be able to saw through its thickness before the goblins could reach it, but one look at her knife's sharp, non-serrated edges convinced her otherwise. What else did she have? A sword, some food, some water, and a few rudimentary magic spells, none of which would permit her to blast a goblin from a tree.

But one of them might help someone find her, if only they were looking. She hadn't dared send up a signal previously, for fear that it would lead her pursuers to her first, but that was a moot point now. She reached into her pouch, withdrew a small sack containing an amount of red powder, and poured about a third of it into her hand. She closed her eyes, concentrating to remember the words of the spell, then spoke them quickly and hurled the powder skyward.

A burst of red light shot skyward, forcing her to shield her eyes against it. She heard unintelligible shouts from below; the goblins had obviously grasped what she intended, though what they planned to do about it was beyond her. She continued moving from tree to tree, and sent up three more magical beacons before the spellpowder was exhausted.

Her options appeared to be exhausted too. It sounded as if more goblins had arrived, as the first two were following her path through the trees, while judging by the cries, others had marked the trees from which her spells were shining into the sky and were climbing them. Her hands began to shake with fear as she realized there was nothing more she could do. She had a sword, she had a dagger, and she had her arrows, but the chances that none of the climbing goblins was carrying a bow didn't strike her as very likely.

Despite herself, she began to cry. Silent tears made their way down her face as she realized that her terrible decision to go after the unlucky Gelrinas had not only gotten Merlian killed, but sealed her own fate too. Why didn't she turn back after seeing he was gone? He was as good as dead already, now she had thrown away her life, and her hawk's life, for nothing!

A shadow passed by overhead. From her vantage point, she couldn't see what it was. Was it just another cursed bird? Or had someone seen her signals? Could it be she wasn't high enough for them to see her through the leaves and branches? She put a hand to her lips and gave out a piercing whistle, followed by another, then she began to climb to the very top of the forest canopy.

She had nearly reached the top of the tree when a black-feathered arrow whirred past her shoulder. Whipping her head around, she saw a grinning forest goblin sitting precariously on a thin, swaying branch with his back to the trunk, holding a shortbow in his left arm. He must have anticipated her and climbed higher once she started throwing out the spell-beacons; how else was she going to escape, after all, but from above?

Calmly, deliberately, he nocked a second arrow and raised his bow. But before he could aim it, there was a soft whirring sound and he convulsed unexpectedly, arms flailing, dropping both bow and arrow to clatter their way down through the leaves and branches below. He jerked twice more and then sat still, his head slumped on his chest, just above the bright yellow-feathered arrow now buried in his heart.

Yellow feathers? She only knew one elf who insisted on dying his feathers yellow! She looked up to see the familiar face of Ilriathas, Lord Kelethan, as he drew back the string on his silver bow again and sent a second arrow down into the trees beneath her. There was a scream, followed by a crashing sound as a second goblin plunged towards its death on the forest floor far below. His warhawk, a black-headed giant nearly half again the size of Merlian, was perched with its huge wings spread on the very top of a taller tree nearby.

"Bereth!" he cried. "Are you hurt?"

"No!"

He held up a knotted rope that she assumed was attached to his saddle. "Can you climb?"

"I'm up here, aren't I?" She couldn't help it. There was something about Ilriathas that inevitably sharpened her tongue.

He merely grinned, shook his head, and tossed the rope down. It tangled on the branch above her, and she pulled herself up to grab it. But before she could start climbing it, he held up his hand. "Hold on tight, let Ebon pull you clear."

At his urging, the huge hawk beat its powerful wings and pulled her up and out of the treetops. The rope swayed back and forth, but with the aid of the knots she easily climbed up it until Ilriathas was able to reach over and pull her bodily up into the saddle in front of him. He held her close for a moment, and she let him, allowing herself to relax against his strong, lean body in a moment of pure relief.

He pushed her back and examined her closely. "What happened to your face?"

"Trees," she said, wondering how bad she looked for him to comment on it. "I tried to break my trail by going west through the branches, but some orcs stumbled upon me. I think the wolfriders must have found the bodies and picked up my trail from there."

He nodded. "That would explain why you're so much further to the west than we expected. Elrithas sent out ten raiders looking for you this morning, but no one thought you'd do anything but run straight south."

She was glad to hear she'd been missed after all. Elrithas was Lord Oakenheart to those less highborn than Ilri. "You did."

"You've never done anything straightforward or sensible in your life, Bereth. I didn't see any reason you'd start now."

She hit him on the shoulder and then put her head against his chest again, stifling a sob. "Why didn't you come sooner? They almost got me!"

"I thought you were already dead until I saw that first red light go up. I came as fast as I could. Bereth, don't cry!"

She couldn't help it. "Merlian's dead, Ilri. And I couldn't save Gelrinas. The orcs already had him."

"Shh, it's not your fault."

"It's not my fault? I put an arrow in him! And then... and then they shot poor Merlian with... with a ballista!"

She was crying too hard to say anything more. For once in his life, Ilriathas had the sense to keep his mouth shut. He simply held her close in his arms and let her weep as the giant hawk bore her south, to safety.

Her face was healing, but it felt like a map of the northern mountains as the little cuts and scratches inflicted on her by the trees scabbed over, creating ridges and peaks on her cheeks and chin. They itched, too, and it was hard to resist the temptation to pick at them.

She pulled on her flying leathers with reluctance. She didn't know what Lord Oakenheart had in mind, but she'd been summoned to him and told to be armed and armored. So, she buckled her belt with its two scabbards, sword and dagger, ran her hands through her unbraided hair, and went to see him.

The elf lord was in his tent, poring over a map with two of her fellow sky raiders. He looked up when she entered, and she was surprised to see him frown at her.

"You don't look ready to fly, Bereth. Your hair is loose. And where is your bow?"

"I don't have a hawk," she protested. "How am I going to fly?"

"You're still a raider, aren't you? You'll fly with Lassarian on Mellt."

"I don't know if I'm ready–"

"I don't care if you think you're ready or not, Bereth. You cost us one very valuable bird in a foolish attempt to save an elf who was already lost to us. You very nearly cost me an equally valuable raider and put twelve other elves at risk in the process. So don't tell me that all that effort was in vain or I'll send you back to Elebrion today!"

Her mouth fell open. How could he be so unfair? Didn't he know that Merlian's loss hurt her more deeply than it could ever bother him? She blinked back tears and stood at rigid attention.

"I'm sorry, my Lord. What are your orders?"

"That's better." The intimidating anger vanished from his face. "We're seeing some indications that the Great Orc is finally preparing to make a move. We want two captives for interrogation, regulars, preferably officers. That's why I'm sending two hawks, and two elves per hawk. We can get in and out faster if the rider stays in the saddle."

"And having a spotter always helps," Lassarian added. He nodded to Bereth. "I'm sorry about your bird."

"Thanks," she said absently. "Who is the fourth?"

"The Collegium is sending over a proper mage. He's called Daeledeth, and he's familiar with both *than* and *gwaed ludrith*. We've had reports that their shamans are less hapless than would be desired and I don't want to risk losing two more birds. We have few enough as it is."

She looked down, all-too-aware of the implicit criticism in his words. She felt a pair of strong hands on her shoulders and looked up to see Lord Oakenheart looking closely at her. "Bereth, you must be more careful. Lord Kelethan was beside himself when you didn't return and the Silverbow told us you'd gone after his wounded mate. You don't have anything to prove, so stop taking these risks! Focus on your orders, on the mission."

But I do have to prove myself, she wanted to say. To you, above all else! But she nodded obediently instead.

Daeledeth turned out to be a tall, quiet elf, more scholar than sorcerer, although his calm demeanor favorably impressed the three sky raiders. He arrived with the morning courier from Elebrion, bearing messages from the King and various other personages in the capital. The easy way he unbuckled himself and dismounted from the messenger's hawk was also a good sign; not every scholar at the Collegium had experience with sky riding.

Rhian, whose hawk the mage would be riding, explained to him their basic plan, and warned him of the orcish shamans. Daeledeth smiled faintly upon hearing the warning, which gave Bereth some confidence that he would be able to deal with them if necessary. Since Lord Oakenheart had scouts flying daily over the giant abscess the orcs had carved in the forest, they had a very good idea of where the various orc tribes were located; they didn't know their names, but they did know the banners. The idea was to fly high over the outskirts of the camp, then drop down unexpectedly in one of the camps on the northwestern side that belonged to a tribe of regular infantry. Fortunately, there were clouds in the sky, not many, but more than likely enough to mask their approach from above.

The irregulars were much easier to capture, stationed as they were on the periphery of the army, but they seldom knew any more about the intentions of the orc high command than Lord Oakenheart did. In fact, they usually knew considerably less than the elven commander did about what was happening inside their own camp.

Bereth braided her hair as Oakenheart gave Rhian and Daeledeth some final instructions. Her own orders were simple; put an arrow into any orc or goblin who threatened hawk or rider, leap off the hawk and bind the hands and feet of any orc stunned by the mage so that the hawk could safely carry them, and not to take any undue risks while trying to fulfill the first two tasks. Above all, the three of them were to make sure that the mage was returned safely to the Collegium or consequences most dire would befall them all.

Two other warhawks were already over the targeted section of the orc encampment. They were spotters charged with identifying the probable officers and they could provide additional archery if required. But Lord Oakenheart made it clear that they should only be summoned in the case of the most dire emergency; he wanted to draw as little attention to the captured prisoners as possible. Given the poor communications among the orc tribes, news of the capture might not even make it to the Great Orc if it was accomplished in a sufficiently circumspect manner.

She felt a slight ache in her heart as Lassarian pulled her up behind him in the saddle. His Mellt was about the same size as Merlian, but was a more fidgety bird with a more pungent odor to him. She had two bows and more than fifty arrows stowed about her; hopefully she wouldn't need many of them. It was far from the first time that she'd ridden skyward on another bird, but it hurt to think that this would be only the first of many such flights. It would be at least seven years before she could possibly raise another hawk from its shell; there were lengthy waiting lists and she was not of such rank as to jump the list.

A sky raider without her hawk might be a raider still, but she didn't feel like one anymore. Even the familiar rhythmic surge as the warhawk leaped into the sky and bore them aloft on his powerful wings felt different without the reins in her hands. They flew at a normal altitude for some time, then the other hawk began to climb and she knew that they were approaching the orc-infested lands. At such heights, it was cold, and both she and Lassarian withdrew the leather hoods and masks that would keep them from getting overly chilled. Before too much more time had passed, they spotted the scouts far ahead, circling above a medium-size white cloud that shielded them from any onlookers below.

At this height, of course, it hardly mattered, as even if they were seen, a warhawk was indistinguishable from a much smaller bird at a lower altitude. And there were no shortage of eagles, vultures, and birds of prey to be found soaring over the nest of abomination below, looking for carrion.

Rhian flew wing-to-wing with one of the scouts, then broke off to inform them of what he'd learned. "They've got three likely targets!" he shouted over the wind. "One shaman, two officers. We want to bag the shaman if we can; the mage here will take him out first."

"Do they know we're here?"

"They don't think so!"

Lassarian nodded. He didn't seem nervous, and Bereth probably wouldn't have been if she'd been flying Merlian either. They practiced dive-landings and live extractions on a regular basis. But her stomach was already tightening; a steep vertical was terrifying when you weren't the one telling the bird when to pull up. Not that a bird would ever fly into the ground, but every one was different and no two birds ended a dive alike. She found herself rather desperately praying that Mellt preferred to pull up sooner than Merlian had.

She tugged at the two sets of straps that would be keeping her in the saddle and pulled the looser one tight. She checked Lassarian's; both of his needed tightening as well. She pulled out an arrow; it was one of the green-stained ones from three days ago, and tucked it under her arm with the bow. She could feel that Lassarian was already taking deep breaths to prepare himself, his body was rigid with tension. It relieved her a little to know that she wasn't the only one who was scared.

After all, there were one hundred thousand orcs and goblins waiting below, all of whom would simply love to kill and eat them, if not worse, given the opportunity. And no elf knew better than she how vulnerable they would be so close to the ground.

She could see Rhian leaning back and shouting instructions into Daeledeth's ear. It would be worse for the mage than any of them, and they needed him to be able to cast his spells as soon as they leveled out, if not sooner.

"I hate this!" she shouted into Lassarian's ear.

"So do I!" he agreed. "Just hold onto that bow! Now get ready!"

She leaned forward, tucked her head against his back, and put both arms around his waist, holding her bow and the arrow alongside her left forearm. Lassarian's leathers were too thick to make them uncomfortable for him, and besides, that would be the least of his concerns in a moment.

With her eyes tightly closed, she couldn't see Rhian give the signal. But Lassarian abruptly leaned forward onto the warhawk's neck and she heard Mellt furl his wings. Then they were falling, plunging like a stone dropped off a precipice and she screamed into Lassarian's cold, leather-clad back as her stomach seemed to leap violently up her throat and out her open mouth. The wind howled in her ears, her heart raced, her muscles flexed tightly as if bracing for a blow. Lassarian was so rigid he felt more like a statue than an elf, only the motion of his breathing against her face and chest made it clear that he was alive. Down, down they fell, until it felt to her as if the torment would never end, that this was some sort of cold bottomless Hell into which the damned were doomed to fall forever.

Falling, falling, falling. It was too long! They had fallen too far! She cringed, wondering if she would even feel anything, striking the earth at such speed.

Just as she felt she couldn't possibly take it anymore, Mellt stretched out his wings and a strangely warm sensation swept through her body as she was abruptly thrown backward. The great bird had come out of his dive considerably closer to the ground than she would have dared and was hurtling over the stripped and barren plain not far over the heads of the gaping, astonished orcs. It was with some difficulty that she pulled herself forward, then released Lassarian and concentrated on nocking her arrow before looking for a target. She saw Rhian and Daeledeth were two hawk-lengths ahead of them, and observed a faint purple aura swelling around the mage's head as he focused his power.

Lassarian pointed out the two big orcs standing on either side of a grotesque figure wearing some sort of horned cloak. Presumably the shaman. Dozens of tents and scores of orcs flew beneath them, and she quickly scanned the ground to the left side of the hawk looking for archers or any ballistas of the sort that killed Merlian. She spotted one about one hundred fifty paces away, although its solitary crew orc was lounging against it and paying no attention to the commotion erupting nearby. She put an arrow through his neck anyhow.

After nocking another arrow, she saw that Daeledeth must have cast his spell, because both the big orcs and the suspected shaman were down. She loosed her arrow at the closest orc, then slipped her bow over her shoulder and unbuckled the saddle straps.

"Going in," Lassarian said tersely. He had his own bow in one hand, and was guiding Mellt with the other. The hawk backstroked on command, extended its legs, and no sooner had it touched ground than Bereth was out of the saddle and off its back, leather thongs in hand. First she bound the shaman, slashing off a piece of cloth and stuffing it in his tusked mouth for good measure, then she tied up the nearer of the two officers. As she pulled his heavy arms behind his back and rapidly wrapped a thong around his wrists, she could hear the steady thrum, thrum, thrum of Lassarian's bowstring as he methodically shot down any orc who looked like approaching.

Then there was a crackle and an explosion not far away. Bereth looked up and saw that Daeledeth had hurled a lightning bolt just in front of a large tent from which orcs had been pouring out. Now there was a crater, around which about twenty orcs were lying motionless where they had been flung, and the tent was burning. She finished tying up the officer, glanced at the other, and without thinking twice, drew her dagger again and drove it into his throat, then pulled back hard. A gout of green blood erupted in response.

Satisfied, she wiped off the blade on the furry rag that covered the first officer's groin and ran over to Mellt. She leaped up and caught Lassarian's extended hand; he pulled her up the side of the giant bird and into the saddle. Mellt took two hops, grasped the unconscious shaman in one talon, then leaped into the air. Bereth saw Rhian was already descending upon the other orc, so after buckling her straps she slipped the bow from her back and began scouring the area, searching for targets.

A tightly compact group appeared to be charging forward from the east, so she dropped the leader with an arrow through his leg, which caused them to spread out and slowed them down a little. She cursed; she'd been aiming for his throat but the jerking motion of the hawk as it climbed had thrown her off. She loosed two more shafts at two other orcs, both scoring hits, although she couldn't be certain that she'd hit anything vital.

Rhian was right behind them, his hawk having swooped down and seized the orc in both talons without so much as touching the ground. Daeledeth pointed his fist and a second lighting bolt erupted amidst the orcs at whom she'd been shooting. Bereth looked on enviously as more than a dozen orcs went flying through the air. It was a neat trick, that. She consoled herself by putting an arrow through the face of one that had survived the sorcerous blast and was struggling to survive.

They were safely off the ground and out of the range of any orc archers when something went wrong. The other hawk abruptly stopped beating its massive wings and started coasting. Then, for no reason that either Bereth or Lassarian could see, the hawk began turning in a slow circle, as if it was going to head back towards the section of the encampment they had just escaped.

Both of them could see that Rhian was shouting and pulling on the reins, but to no avail. "Something is wrong!" Lassarian shouted, in case she hadn't noticed, and he pulled Mellt around in a tight wingtip turn.

"What is he doing?" she shouted back.

"I have no idea!"

"Did it get hit?"

"I don't see how!"

And then, without warning, the other hawk furled its wings and began to fall from the sky.

FJOTRA

S PRING WAS very different in Savondir than it was across the sea in
the Wolf Isles. There, in the north, spring crept upon you slowly,
Fjotra thought, rather like a fox stalking a vole. The snows receded
little by little, the brown earth eventually poked through its white covering,
and as the weeks passed and the days lengthened, the dormant grass was
gradually resurrected by the pale sun that shone stubbornly down upon it
until the reluctant blades finally consented to show their color. In Savondir,
matters were rather more hurried. It rained relentlessly for ten straight days,
then, for absolutely no good reason that Fjotra could see, the sun appeared
in all its blazing glory, dried the damp ground in a single day, and caused
the world to explode with greens and yellows and pinks and purples and
reds all gloriously resplendent under the bright blue dome of the sky.

This sudden transformation was disconcerting, but happily, it did make
it possible for her to comfortably venture out of doors considerably earlier
in the year than she had imagined possible. And, of course, it was vastly
more pleasant to stroll through the royal gardens outside the king's palace
than to worry about being snatched and devoured by wolf-demons every
time you ventured outside the village stockade. Even after spending the
entire winter in the safety of Lutèce, Fjotra still occasionally found herself
jumping at shadows from time to time, particularly on windy days. And
her insistence on always carrying two daggers secreted about her person was
the despair of the ladies-in-waiting, who seemed to regard her as some sort
of wild animal that required breaking before it could be properly tamed.

Fjotra wondered if she might be in love. But she did not know that she
was in love, at least not in the Savondese sense, because Dalarn history
was sadly deficient with regards to the softer and romantic aspects of

relationships between a man and a woman. She only knew that she found itself very hard to tear her thoughts away from her prince and the penetrating green eyes that seemed to pierce her to her core every time she dared to look at him.

Fjotra did not wonder if she was at war. This she knew, with all the certainty of a warrior with a hundred bloody battles to his name. She was at war with the ladies of the court, several of whom were waging an ongoing campaign against her with all the viciousness of an Aalvarg pack hunting down a helpless fleeing child.

She had gone through three attendants already, breaking the arm of one who had tried to forcibly tie her into a corset, blacking the eye of another who had surprised her after sundown, and scaring off the third for no reason that anyone had happened to explain to her yet. And yet the ladies of the court remained, for the most part, kind and very patient with her, in part because she was unofficially affianced to the heir to the throne, but mostly because the queen made it absolutely clear that Fjotra was in her favor, despite being a wild northern girl.

The king might rule the realm, but there was no question that it was Queen Ingeborg who ruled the court. She was, she informed Fjotra, of Dalarn descent herself, albeit many generations back, courtesy of a reaver lord who had settled down on the northern coast to establish what gradually turned into a county, then a marche. Her hair was still fair, although it was streaked with grey, and while her eyes were brown, her face betrayed the high, haughty bones of her northern ancestry. And she and Fjotra were much of a height; few of the ladies and only about half of the men were taller than either of them. The king himself was a big man, however, rather like an inflated version of his elder son, the brave prince who had all but died in Fjotra's arms. It was that, Fjotra imagined, that so bound the queen to her, more than the fact that she was to marry the queen's second and considerably less favored son. Indeed, the queen seldom talked about Étienne-Henri at all, and when she did, she sometimes left Fjotra with the impression that she was attempting to warn Fjotra away from her handsome, but inscrutable son.

But what was there to warn her of? Fjotra already knew the man who had somehow stolen her heart was as capricious as a bird and more deadly than a snake. His eyes could be hard and cruel, then transform in a moment into mischievous playfulness, depending on his mood. But he was smarter and more focused than anyone she had ever known, with an energetic ambition that she found captivating after a lifetime in the company of tall, grim,

and silent men who spoke of little more than war and death. While she
had been attracted to the charismatic, commanding presence of the late
Charles-Phillippe, the smoldering intensity of his younger brother made
her chest feel tight, and drew her to him like a lodestone summoning a
helpless needle.

It was true, she had to admit, that Étienne-Henri was arrogant, occasionally insecure, and nearly two fingers shorter than she was. But he was also
dangerous in a way she had never seen before, despite having grown up
amongst warriors in a land riven by war. He could make the bravest lords
and the haughtiest ladies of the court quail before him by simply fixing his
eyes upon them and raising one dark, supercilious eyebrow, less because he
was now the Red Prince than because there was absolutely no telling what
he might do next. He was, she thought, capable of almost anything. It
was no wonder that men speculated what sort of king he might one day
become, and sometimes, if sufficiently careless or deep in their cups, even
dare to lament the loss of his elder brother.

No one speculated about what sort of queen she would be. As far as
she could tell, the consensus of the court was that she was young, strong,
healthy, and capable of bearing even more sons than Queen Ingeborg had
produced. She would also provide her husband with a plausible claim to
the northern isles, although that claim was considerably less attractive now
that they were known to be inhabited by ravenous demons so terrible that
they had driven out the once-feared reavers. But Fjotra knew that the ladies
of the court also considered her to be an uncouth, ill-mannered catastrophe
who would likely prove a continuing embarrassment to the future king and
crown alike if the royal marriage was permitted to take place.

She looked down at her embroidery. It was no longer an utter disaster,
and she even managed to go for extended spells now without sticking the
needle into her long and clumsy fingers. The design upon which she was
working was even recognizable as what was referred to as her brother's
shield, although she couldn't imagine him fighting with the bright, ornately
painted thing if there was a more stout one of oak to be had. But she hated
doing it, she wasn't any good at it, and if the queen hadn't informed her that
it was required of her as a royal lady of the court, she would have happily
used Lady Margreith, her disdainful instructor, as a pincushion instead.

She sighed and dutifully returned to her task. Learning how to dance,
on the other hand, she actually enjoyed. She still wasn't sure how she felt
about learning how to ride. The huge beasts terrified her, especially their
large yellow teeth, and although she'd been repeatedly assured that they

had absolutely no interest in feeding on her flesh, she still found herself trembling in their overpowering presence. Once safely on a horse's back, however, she did rather enjoy the sensation of flying over the ground with the wind in her hair.

If she would never be a good rider, at least the grooms at the king's stable didn't laugh at her behind their hands the way the court ladies laughed at her needlework. As if any one of them knew which end of a knife to hold, or had ever even swung an axe in anger!

She heard footsteps on the marble outside her chamber and looked up, assuming it was Lady Margreith coming to check on her progress. But it was one of the younger girls, an orange-haired girl with bad skin who was the daughter of some count or another. Despite her best efforts, she still found it almost impossible to keep all of the various names and titles straight, let alone remember the myriad of complicated relationships between the various families, clans, and counties.

"Lady Fjotra, are you receiving?"

Fjotra stared at her blankly for a moment before realizing that the girl was offering her a perfectly reasonable excuse to abandon her embroidering. "Yes, I am. Yes, certainly!"

The girl returned a few moments later escorting one of the last people Fjotra expected to see at the moment, her mother. The two of them had fought bitterly the last time her mother had come to the capital, as her mother was entirely opposed to the notion of her marrying Étienne-Henri, or, as she usually referred to him, *den lille slange*, "the little snake". While they had not actually come to blows, it might well have done. Fjotra was still angry, and it was with some difficulty that she restrained herself from saying the first six or seven things that sprang to her mind.

"Mother," she finally said as politely as she could manage, rising from her seat. She did not say anything about being glad to see her, for she was most certainly not! The orange-haired girl adroitly made herself scarce, although Fjotra had no doubt that the little spy would be doing her best to listen from a position just outside the room. Having grown up in small, fortified villages, Fjotra was well-accustomed to being careful with her words, knowing that anything she said in a normal voice might well be overheard. But today, she did not care that if the girl was listening or not, knowing that few southern eavesdroppers would be able to understand her conversation with her mother in their native tongue.

"Fjotra," her mother said with equal civility. But there was an undertone to her voice, as if she was keeping herself firmly under control. "I know you are upset with me. I do not regret my previous words, because I only want what is best for you—"

"Yes, and I want what is best for our people!" Fjotra heatedly interrupted. "Never mind the fact that I love him! You and father sent me and Brynjolf here for a reason, mother, and this is exactly what father—"

"Your father is dead, Fjotra," her mother interrupted. "The Skullbreaker is dead."

Caught off-guard, Fjotra paused and studied her mother's face. It was an older, lined and wind-reddened version of her own, but the years had also refined the bones underneath and she was still, if not precisely beautiful, a very striking woman. Her blue eyes were dark, but otherwise calm and dry, but Fjotra knew her mother too well to trust that they belied her terrible words.

"What? He's not dead! Why would you say that?"

"A longship sailed north, across the sea to the castle. They saw smoke rising from the walls of Raknarborg and Aalvarg moving freely about the shorelines. And they saw no living men. Raknarborg is fallen and with it, they are certain, the Skullbreaker. He would not have fled and left his men behind."

Fjotra slowly nodded. No, he would not have. She felt a strange, twisting pain in her heart, even though her mother's news was not at all unexpected. But there was some news that no amount of preparation could reduce the sting.

"Your eyes are dry," she said accusingly.

Her mother smiled grimly. "I did not marry a milksop whose fate was to die in bed. The night before he forced me to take ship without him, he sang me his deathsong. Though it was not a song unworthy of a man destined for the Feast Halls, I was not ashamed to weep then. But you, I see, you do not weep now."

"No, I do not. And I will not! I will believe my father is dead when I see his body."

"Fjotra—"

"I said, I will believe my father is dead when I see his body! And no sooner!"

Her mother nodded, in understanding if not agreement. "Very well. All the same, I thought you should know."

"Have you told Brynjolf?"

"Not yet. I thought we should... I thought perhaps we might tell him the news together."

Fjotra's anger, having risen abruptly, died even faster. "Yes, we should do that. Do you know where he is?"

"No," her mother shook her head, then brushed a trace of gray hair back from her face. "I was hoping you might."

"I expect he's probably with my betrothed at the field near the stables. You know he's been trying to learn *la joute*?"

"To do what?"

"That game where they ride the big animals, *les chevaux*." She used the unfamiliar Savondese word since there was no Dalarn equivalent. "The game where they ride at each other with spears and try to knock the other off."

"By the Aldaföðr!" her mother gasped. "Can he be so foolish? He has scarcely recovered from his injuries!"

Fjotra realized her mother had misunderstood her. "No, he's not actually riding against the others. He is too big and he doesn't sit on the back of the animal well enough yet for it. They have a device made of wood that they use for practice. That's what he rides against. He tries to hit the target and then duck the branch that swings around. If he doesn't duck low enough, he'll take a knock on the back of the head. But they all wear helms, so it is harmless."

"Even so." Her mother sounded dubious.

"It is a stupid game. But my prince insisted that he should at least learn to play it like the others. The men respect him for it. And he seems to like it well enough."

Fjotra's mother was a jarl's daughter and she had survived many a desperate battle to the death with the Aalvarg. As such, Dagna had learned how to keep her emotions under control from her earliest youth. A momentary flash of concern, a scarcely audible sigh, and a slight pursing of her lips were the only signs of concern that she betrayed. But Fjotra knew better.

"It's perfectly safe, mother. For all the noise and shouting they make, I've yet to see anyone seriously injured."

"Yes, I suppose after a lifetime of always half-expecting to see one's men die the moment they leave your sight, I am going to have to get accustomed to the idea that we might actually be safe here in the South."

Fjotra grimaced. "Well, there is talk of an invasion of some sort of strange green men, *gobelins*, I believe they are called. But no one seems to be particularly concerned about it, as it seems they do this sort of thing fairly often and cause no serious trouble. At a banquet before you came to court, my lord prince gifted his father with two thousand of their ears!"

"No wonder your father thought well of these southerners," her mother said, and she smiled faintly for the first time. "They are not quite as soft as we had always believed them to be."

"If we'd only had a few hundred warriors mounted and armored in their fashion, that might have been enough to drive back the demons."

"And if we had wings, we could fly over the sea." Her mother sighed. "Come, Fjotra, whether you believe it is true or not, we at least must tell your brother that Raknarborg has been taken by the demonspawn. If he is now the lord of the castle, it will fall to him, and to his sons, to take it back one day."

"Very well, mother." Fjotra sighed. "Let us go and see him together. I will show you where they ride."

The two women watched as Brynjolf, his eyes intent on the strange wooden device, kicked the enormous beast on which he was sitting into a trot that gradually increased to a thundering gallop. Fjotra held her breath as her brother adjusted himself in the big leather seat, trying to keep the point of the giant stick he was holding under his arm from wavering too much. But the stick seemed to have a mind of its own, as the end of it fairly danced up, then right, then right some more, then suddenly down to the left as Brynjolf fought to keep it under his control. The watching noblemen fell silent too, abruptly abandoning their jests and jeers in mid-sentence as they turned to watch her brother's rapid, but ungainly approach.

It looked to her as if he was going to miss the wooden, shield-shaped target entirely, as the point of the stick continued to creep up, and up again some more, as he rode closer to the target. But at almost the very last moment, Brynjolf's shoulder twitched, the white-painted point dropped, and it struck the target soundly, if not squarely, causing the entire device to whip around and send the wooden branch on the other end hurtling directly at the back of her brother's armored head.

"No!" she heard her mother shriek, and Fjotra couldn't help but gasp herself as the branch fairly whistled through the air as it rotated on the cylinder to which it was attached. But Brynjolf was already leaning forward on the animal's thick neck, ducking his head just low enough to cause the branch to pass harmlessly over him without even brushing his helm. The Savondese broke into applause and cheers as Brynjolf reined in his *cheval* and caused it to turn back in a broad arc, raising his stick in a triumphant salute.

"By the Aldaföðr, he has his father's courage," she heard her mother breathe. "Thank the gods for that!"

"Brynjolf! Brynjolf!" she shouted. His head whipped around at the sound of her voice, and after handing the reins to one of his companions, he slipped ungracefully from the back of the big beast and removed his helmet. His fair hair was dark with sweat, but his eyes were bright with pride and self-satisfaction.

"Did you see that?" he demanded. "Did you see me, Mother?"

"We saw you," she assured him, stifling a smile. But her blue eyes grew dark again as she reached out to embrace him. "Brynjolf, I bear bad tidings. Raknarborg has fallen. You must now rule our people. You are now their jarl."

"The Skullbreaker is dead?" The sheer disbelief in his voice tore at Fjotra's heart. "Was he actually seen to fall?"

"Raknarborg burns. Aalvarg roam its ruins. There can be no doubt."

"Father had longboats. He will have taken to the sea before the end."

"Then he would already be here by now." Anger flashed in her mother's eyes. "Brynjolf, do not let yourself entertain false hope. You cannot be a leader of men and lie to yourself. Lie to others, if you must, but never lie to yourself!"

Her brother glanced at her. When she met his gaze without blinking or looking away, he nodded and a faint smile appeared on his lips.

"Fjotra doesn't believe he is dead either!"

"Your sister has taken many strange notions into her head of late."

"Mother!" Fjotra clenched her fists and reminded herself that whether her father was dead or not, her mother was already grieving his loss. "Mother, you may well be right. But what is the harm in waiting for confirmation of our fears? Whether Brynjolf is named jarl or not, there are none here who will challenge his rule now that he is recognized as the prince of the isles by the king himself!"

"It is not wise for you to stake your right to rule upon the favor of a southron, Brynjolf. Their whims are passing and their hearts are fickle."

"Are they indeed?" Mother and daughter whirled around to see the Red Prince was only a few paces behind them, and judging by the expression on his face, well within earshot. "I surely hope that you, my beautiful princess, do not imagine yourself to be nothing more than a passing fancy of mine."

"My Lord Prince–" her mother began to apologize, but Étienne-Henri interrupted her by taking her hands.

"Fru Dagna," he said, surprising all three of them by addressing her mother with her Dalarn title, "my father informed me of the most noble castle's fall. Please accept my sincere condolences on this saddest of days. While I regret that it appears I shall not have the opportunity to meet your husband, I have heard many a brave tale of the Skullbreaker and I held him in the highest esteem. You may rest assured that he shall be honored by the court as if he were my own father."

Her mother's suspicious eyes softened, just a little, at her betrothed's gracious words. "I thank you, Prince Étienne. You are very kind."

Fjotra stifled a growl. While she was pleased to see her fiancé's uncharacteristic sensitivity to her mother, she did not think she could endure the idea of the entire royal court going into mourning for weeks for a man who was neither known to them nor dead. It was absurd! It was ridiculous! And moreover, did it not make a mockery of the many brave warriors who had actually given their lives in the defense of fallen Raknarborg?

She was just about to launch into a passionate argument against the prince's magnanimous gesture when the sight of her mother actually embracing her betrothed and kissing him on either cheek silenced her. The day before, she would have sworn to both her gods and the lonely southern god as well that such a thing would have been utterly impossible.

"Mother must actually believe he's fallen," murmured her brother in their native tongue.

"The Skullbreaker would never fall to the Aalvarg," she said firmly. "He would never permit them to have him."

"That's true, he did vow as much." Her brother frowned. "But let us not argue with Mother, and certainly not today."

"Let's not."

Her mother took her leave of the prince and approached them both. "I must return now, to prepare the necessary rites for your father's spirit. Fjotra, will you at least wear the mourning clothes for him?"

Fjotra ignored her brother's meaningful glare. "Of course, mother. Whatever you require of me, I will do."

After all, what difference will it make when he returns, she thought. But she was careful not to show any sign of her indifference.

"You were his pride and joy," her mother told them, reaching out to both her and Brynjolf. "He was so proud of both of you, with the way you found a place for our people here, safe in the very lands he used to raid."

"We will be worthy of his legacy, Mother," Brynjolf reassured her. "And if the Aldaföðr wills, the Skullbreaker's grandson will rule over these lands."

"A worthy legacy indeed," Dagna said, staring at Fjotra with tear-filled blue eyes. "If the Aldaföðr wills."

BERETH

BERETH watched in horror as the warhawk ridden by Rhian and Daeledeth dove towards the ground. It didn't seem to have been wounded or hurt, its bizarre behavior was almost as if it had lost its mind. Rhian was shouting commands and frantically pulling up on the reins to no avail while the mage seemed to be in some sort of trance. Then Bereth remembered being told that the Collegium elf was a specialist in *gwaed ludrith*, blood magic. The orc shamans used it to drive their own soldiers mad with battlelust, and sometimes even to demonically possess them. Perhaps Daeledeth was trying to break a spell....

Where there was a spell, there had to be a spellcaster nearby. She scanned the ground. There! An orc wearing filthy robes, as if in mockery of his elven counterparts, was standing with his head thrown back and his hands outstretched, as if calling the hawk to the ground. With an arrow already nocked, it was a simple matter to loose it and put it through his outstretched neck. She saw the fletchings appear in the center of his throat, then they all but disappeared beneath the first fountain of dark green arterial blood.

The shaman threw up his arms and fell backward; the spell broken, Rhian's hawk shrieked in avian fury and spread his wings. The speed of his descent was such that he nearly bounced the captured orc in his talons off the ground before managing a sweeping turn just over the heads of a platoon of orcs. The platoon angrily, but harmlessly, hurled curses and clods of dirt at them, before they climbed into the sky again on the strength of his powerful wings.

Bereth shot two orcs from the platoon on general principle, then stowed her bow as Lassarian followed Rhian higher into the sky.

"Nice shot," Lassarian shouted. "How did you know it was magic?"

"I didn't!" she shouted back honestly. Then again, what else could it have been?

Once at altitude, they pulled level with the other hawk. Rhian patted his heart, then gave her a thumbs up, while the mage acknowledged her with a wry smile and a little bow from the waist. The scouts who had been waiting in the clouds above descended and fell in with them, one on either side, not that they had proved to be any use in the emergency.

Whether it was the shock of the cold air high in the sky or simply the spell wearing off, both orcs soon woke and began thrashing about. But on command from their riders, the two hawks simply tightened their talons a little until the orcs stopped struggling; it only took three repetitions before the shaman learned his lesson. The officer required two further rounds of squeeze-and-relax before he likewise gave in to the inevitable.

Lassarian laughed and shook his head before leaning back and putting his mouth against her ear. "Not the smartest bastards, are they?"

No, smart they were not. And yet, they could afford to trade twenty-for-one and still come out ahead. The loss of the Silverbow yesterday was almost as grievous a loss as all the losses she and her fellow raiders had inflicted upon the cursed greenskins; throw in the loss of Merlian and even though she'd killed at least 12 orcs and one goblin herself, the end result was still probably to the Great Orc's advantage. True, they were probably well ahead on the basis of Daeledeth's lethal lightning bolts and the capture of the shaman, but things could have so easily gone the other way. How long could they survive this slow bleeding? The High King had to know he couldn't win a war of attrition against a foe boasting such numbers.

It always seemed to take less time returning than it did flying out. The aerial sentries saluted them as they flew in, and three trumpet blasts were sounded by their earthbound counterparts as they approached to land. Mellt held up his captive in one talon while alighting carefully on a single leg, while Rhian's hawk unceremoniously dropped the other orc before landing normally on two. Fully armored regulars leaped upon the orcs immediately, slashing through the thongs binding their legs and pulling them roughly to their feet before literally dragging them off to be interrogated.

The orcs were surprisingly subdued, but then, being ensorcelled, bound, hauled away and frozen at high-altitude was liable to dampen even the fiercest spirit.

"You did well," Lassarian complimented her as she undid the strap buckles and retrieved her gear from the saddlebags. "That was some quick thinking back there."

She nodded absently, then shook her head at him. "You pulled out of that dive awfully late. You should be more careful with him."

"You're probably right." His grin disappeared and his eyes darkened with pity that was hard to bear. "Well, if you ever need a lift."

"I'll know who to avoid!" She winked to take the sting out of her words and swung herself down from the saddle. "See you around, Lassarian."

"And you, Bereth." With a brief wave, Mellt took to the skies again in a brief explosion of wind and feathers.

She walked in the direction of her tent, her stomach rumbling. She hoped the mess chefs would provide something edible this evening; the mushroom-stuffed quail she'd eaten the night before hadn't sat well in her stomach. She'd cried herself to sleep, with the salt from her tears burning wherever they crossed the scratches on her face. She didn't know if she'd ever felt so bereft, or alone, even though she knew there was still a place for her in the raiders.

Several of them greeted her as she walked by, as did various members of their support staff. Their forward base had been here long enough for a variety of amenities to spring up, although unfortunately nothing like the hot bath for which she would cheerfully murder an entire squadron of goblins. It was evident that word of her loss had spread throughout the unit, as they spoke to her in soft, subdued voices that indicated their sympathy without forcing her to acknowledge it. It insensibly angered her, and yet she loved them for it.

She had nearly reached her tent when she heard someone calling to her. She recognized the voice and sighed. It was Ilriathas, of course, and he was bearing a bouquet of flowers, *liliaugwyn*. She smiled faintly at him, took them from him, and permitted him to put an arm around her. For a moment, just a moment, she put her head on his chest, and for once, the safety and comfort that he offered was welcome.

"I have something else for you," he said. "If you want it."

Without opening her eyes or looking up at him, she shook her head. "If you propose marriage to me again, Ilri, I swear to you that I will gut you right now and leave Mons Kelethan without an heir."

"I spoke to the King."

She had to admit, ready access to the crown was one benefit of being a High Lord of Elebrion. "About what?" She scarcely dared to hope.

"Your egg."

"My—my what?" She pushed away from him and looked up at his face. His green eyes were sincere as ever. "My egg?"

He nodded. "I couldn't secure one from the next clutch, but you're to have the second pick of the third clutch. It's been arranged."

"Oh, Ilri!" Impulsively, she pulled him down to her and kissed him on the mouth. Then her eyes narrowed and she pushed herself away again. "That must have cost you considerably."

"It's nothing."

"*Cachu adar!*" she swore, knowing that he lied. She knew very well how much an egg right was worth. He might well have given up a village, or even an entire demesne, simply to let her move up so many clutches. "Ilri, I'm not going to marry you just because I'm in your debt!"

"Obviously." He shrugged. "How fortunate I am to be able to wait for you to come to your senses and give up your maiden sorceries."

She stared at him. "You didn't even ask me first."

"You can always change your mind between now and when the egg hatches." He smiled. "I might even make a profit."

"No, but be honest with me. You can't tell me this isn't exactly the moment for which you've been waiting for ten years!"

"I would never take advantage of you that way, Bereth! I love you. And I know you! I know you're not ready to give up all this. Riding the sky is part of who you are, at least right now. But yesterday, I thought I'd lost you forever. It just about killed me."

She frowned at him, skeptical. "Well, all right. You can't blame me for being suspicious."

"Haven't I proved my innocence in that particular regard?"

"Yeah, and in an admittedly impressive manner. It must be nice to be that wealthy."

"I find it's really more the influence and the royal connections that matter," he said, mock-pretentiously. "Gold only gets you so far."

She smiled faintly. "Far enough. Will you come tonight?"

"I'll fly you there myself if you'll let me."

She thought about it for a moment. When a hawk died, it was customary to burn his body on the Brig Brenin, the only peak higher than Minith Eleb, on a bonfire lit by the sorceries of his rider, or if the rider had been killed too, by a fellow sky rider. But since Merlian's body was lost, and by now, probably butchered, cooked, and devoured, she had only the one extra feather to burn. She could burn it in the camp tonight and save her fellow riders the not-inconsiderable trouble of saddling up their birds and taking the time to fly to the mountain and back in the dark.

She tried to explain that it wasn't necessary to Ilri. But overcome by her emotions, she suddenly found that she couldn't talk. Breathing hard and biting her bottom lip, she reached into her jacket and pulled out the two feathers, then held them out to him imploringly, her eyes filled with tears.

He understood, of course. Cupping her hand gently in his, he leaned forward, closed his eyes, and inhaled the fading scent of the feathers. Then he looked at her, and with great solemnity, offered her a *certhbas* in Merlian's honor.

> "Harthwch a dewrder
> "Dim'mwy hela yr awyr
> "Mae'r wylais wynt"

The grief was suddenly more than she could bear. He took her in his arms as she cried against his chest. He held her as long as she needed, until she cried herself out. She finally pushed herself away, her nose running, her face red and blotchy, feeling both embarrassed and resentful that he should see her this way. She wiped at her face and tried to apologize, but he shushed her.

"Let us honor him properly, Bereth. Let us grieve with you. You are not alone."

"But–" she waved her free hand indicating the camp. Somehow, he understood her. He tapped one of the feathers still clutched in her hand.

"He will be burned on the mountaintop tonight, with a feather from the breast of every warhawk in the High Guard. Leave it to me."

"All right," she managed to say. "Will you?"

"I will come for you before sunset," he promised. Then he kissed her on the forehead and walked away. She watched him go, wondering how it could be that she simply could not find it in her heart to love him. He was so good to her, he was, as her mother often reminded her, literally too good for her. And he loved her, there was no doubting it. Why, then, when he kissed her did she feel nothing inside?

It was three days after the High Guard gathered on the Brig Brenin to honor Merlian and half the camp was staring at the two distant specks in the sky that were rapidly growing larger. They all knew something was brewing by the speed with which the morning patrol was returning. Also,

they were returning early. Bereth glanced at Lassarian; Lord Oakenheart
had assigned her temporarily to the rider of the big warhawk and they had
been having what could either be considered a late breakfast or an early
lunch together discussing her new partner's patrol of the previous evening.
He hadn't noticed anything out of the ordinary, but as the camp began
stirring with unusual activity, they both fell silent and looked to the north.

"They're flying hard," she said, unnecessarily.

Lassarian nodded and threw back the remaining contents of his silver
flagon. He winced; he'd been complaining that the wine was sour. "Two to
one they're on the move."

"Two to one what?"

He simply raised an eyebrow. She laughed and shook her head. "Mellt
has a better chance, Lasri. And he smells better too. When is the last time
you took a bath?"

The tall elf wrinkled his nose and sniffed at his leathers, then recoiled.
"Gods, you're right. It's those bloody night patrols. About the time I start
feeling capable of anything more than eating or sleeping, they've got me in
the air again."

She cringed a little inside; losing Merlian had put more pressure on the
already overworked riders and hawks alike. But she forced a smile. "It
doesn't look like you're going to be any less busy now."

"Nor you," he waggled a finger at her, then reached out, took an apple,
and tossed it to her. Then he took two more for himself. "Better save that.
They'll be giving everyone their orders tonight and who knows when we'll
be able to get away to eat."

She nodded and stowed the fruit away in a pocket of her leather flight
coat. This high up the mountain it was cool enough, especially with the
wind coming from the north, that she habitually wore it hanging open
about the camp. "What do you think the Lord General's plan will be?"

"Same thing it always is. Harry them from above, use the cavalry to cut
off any deep thrusts, and use the infantry to destroy them. Then hope that
they get bored dying the death of a thousand pinpricks and go home."

"That many orcs, they can take a lot more than a thousand pinpricks."

Two hours and one very cold immersion in a mountain stream later, she
was standing in between Lassarian and another raider, listening to Lord
Oakenheart give them their flying orders. As Lassarian had predicted,
Prince Hoelion wasn't going to try to stop them cold, merely make their
march south unpleasant.

"The most important targets are their shamans, their officers, and their mounts. And by mounts I mean the boars, don't bother with the wolves. The goblins are no match for our cavalry, but their warboars are not only heavy enough to defeat our cavalry if they can catch it, they're heavy enough to break our infantry line. They're going to be protected, of course, but I want to know where they are at all times. We can pick off a few from the air here and there, but our real focus is going to be taking out entire corrals any time they get sloppy or careless."

"What about their magic," Lassarian called out. "Have we seen any more of whatever it was that happened to Rhian's bird?"

Their commander looked back and nodded to an elf wearing the gold-threaded robes of a Collegium magister. The magister stepped forward and answered for the prince. "It is our considered opinion that it was a form of daemonology. The hawk was most likely possessed, temporarily, by some sort of demon summoned and held captive, then forced into the bird by the demon's summoner."

"If the bird was possessed, how did it get away?" another raider asked. They had all been briefed on the orc's new defensive tactic already.

Because I killed the summoner, Bereth wanted to say, but she held her tongue. If the bird was already possessed, then how would killing its summoner have banished the demon possessing it? She recalled enough daemonology from her weeks at the Collegium Occludum to know that wasn't likely.

"I'm afraid we can't be certain," the magister admitted. "While we have conducted several successful experiments inserting a demon into a hawk from similar distances, I regret to say we were unable to test the effects of actually killing the summoner due to a lack of the volunteers required."

As the other raiders laughed, Lassarian nudged her. "Why not?" he murmured. "We brought them a shaman, didn't we?" She grinned. He might dare the devils to excess, but he was good company and he made her laugh.

"Our assumption is that the demon had no interest in the hawk, but was under a compulsion. The compulsion being broken by the summoner's death, the demon was free to abandon the bird." Bereth nodded. That made as much sense as anything else she'd heard bruited about.

Lord Oakenheart cleared his throat and the magister bowed to the assembled raiders and returned to his place. "Today you're going to stay high. Is everyone clear on that? We don't know what other tricks they have in store for us, but considering that they've shown us one, we have to conclude there will be others. You are to withdraw at the first sign a bird has been possessed and make no attempt to either kill the possessing shaman or rescue the bird's rider. Bad enough to lose one; we can't risk losing more."

There were some rumblings and grumblings amidst the raiders, but they all knew that the prince was right. The raid to obtain prisoners had caught the orcs by surprise, but now that they were on the move, they would be keeping a wary eye on the skies.

"Remember, those of you who are flying second seat, your primary job is to be the general's eyes. You're not there to hunt orcs. If you don't have a *gweldbel* crystal, see the Magister here and get one. Stay attuned and let your rider know that you're in rapport so he can show the prince-general what he needs to see if he calls upon you."

A raider raised a hand. "Commander, what is the point of hitting them now? Even if we bloody their nose, they're hardly likely to give up right away."

"They've already taken one bloody nose from the Men of the West. We're going to give them another one. This war isn't going to be won by a single battle, that army is too big. Prince Hoelion is going to bleed them, and slow them down, until they're too weak to even think about climbing Minith Eleb."

"What if they go for Merithaim instead?" another raider asked.

"Then we will adjust our plans accordingly. But according to the prisoners who have been interrogated, and whose information has thus far proven accurate, Elebrion is the Great Orc's objective. It is our duty, and it is our honor, to ensure that he does not get there!"

"*Byth y corachod ymlath!*" most of the raiders, knowing a cue when they heard one, called out in response. The elves will fight!

"*Byth y corachod yn sefyll!*" The elves will stand!

"*Byth y corachod futhugoliaeth!*" The elves will triumph!

They were arrayed in triads of three. Her triad was typical, three birds and five elves. Tywyllas, as the triad leader, flew alone, Rhian carried a mage whose name Bereth did not know, and she flew with Lassarian. Aside from the four hawks of Prince Hoelion's escort, were nine other triads, which represented a disturbingly large portion of the High Guard. They would act as the prince-general's eyes when needed, allowing him to swiftly give orders to his officers, all of whom were accomplished adepts capable of hearing his orders, and in some cases, reporting in to him, through the *gweldbel* crystals. It was the only way their paltry numbers could even think to engage with the massive number of orcs marching towards them.

And that was the other, even more important reason the prince-general, who flew a huge tawny-feathered hawk named Fflyd-Adenyth, had ordered more than thirty hawks and ten mages aloft with him. If, through some unfortunate turn of fate or unexpected enterprise of an orc commander, either the infantry or the cavalry was cut off and found itself unable to retreat, Prince Hoelion could rapidly summon sufficient archery and spellcraft to create an opening for them.

She knew their squadron of sky cavalry must have made for an impressive sight. But there was a time, long ago, when the lords of the High Guard would have ridden dragons.

The prince-general could have used a dragon or two now. Seen from on high, the orc army on the move was an awesome and intimidating sight. What she knew was all disorder and chaos closer to the ground looked almost organic from her current height. The army spilled out from the forest like a flooded lake overflowing its banks, a rising dark green tide so large that it seemed impossible anything could stand before it. Smaller rivulets stretched out before it, growing longer and thinner as the lead units spotted the seven small white stones that were the elven regiments that had ridden north two days before. The largest regiment, nearly twice the size of the others and forty White Oak Knights strong, was in the fore, commanded by the Horse Lord, Malchderas.

She couldn't see their infantry anywhere, but she suspected they were concealed behind a line of hills lying to the south.

Bereth slipped her bow from where she'd tucked it in the saddle and quickly strung it with a brand new string.

"You brought that? I thought you were supposed to leave them behind?"

"Didn't say we had to," she reminded Lassarian. She held up the translucent red crystal hanging suspended from a silver chain around her neck. "I'll feel it if the prince wants me. Until then, well, I can hardly miss, can I."

He snorted. "From this height, you could probably kill one with an apple core."

"No, their skulls are too thick." Then she frowned. Actually, bringing along a bag of rocks or two wasn't a bad idea. With such a mass of orcs below, she could probably kill nearly as many as a bolt hurled by a mage simply by emptying out the sack over their heads. She made a mental note to cadge some sacks from the quartermaster next time.

Two of the larger rivulets reached out for the closest white stone, which abruptly transformed its shape into a small triangle and leaped forward at a much faster pace. The rivulets tried to shift from columns into lines, but before they could manage the trick, the white wedge smashed though the left rivulet once, neatly turned, then smashed through it again before slashing through the right one. She saw intense bursts of red and golden light erupt in the midst of the forward edge of the giant lake, as the mages in the cavalry hurled spells so hellishly powerful that it actually arrested the flooding for a few brief moments.

She knew that hundreds of orcs were screaming and dying under the lances, swords, hooves, and spells of the royal knights, but from her present vantage point, it looked more like living art, like a painting come to life. The death and destruction taking place before her eyes simply did not seem real.

Now the other white rocks had similarly taken more lethal forms and were moving too, slashing repeatedly through the disintegrating ends of the rivulets. Their movements almost seemed choreographed, they *were* choreographed, she corrected herself, through the orders being given by the prince-general, whose distinctive bird she could see below and in front of her. Flanked by two warhawks on either side, the giant Fflyd-Adenyth soared serenely over the battle raging furiously below.

Although the huge army's central advance had slowed down, the southward motion of both its flanks was unimpeded, and particularly on the left, a sizable force began to angle inward, moving at a rapid pace nearly equal to the elven cavalry. Wolfriders, she knew, goblin light cavalry that was normally no match for the powerful horses and magically reinforced armor worn by the knights. But there were hundreds of them, thousands, and they did not need to defeat their bigger, faster, and heavier counterparts, they only needed to entangle them and slow them down long enough for the orc infantry to come to grips with them.

Three sharp horn blasts echoed through the sky, accompanied by a bright green flash from below. That was their sign to descend and engage. Only four other triads would be making the attack with them; blue referred to the other five that would be remaining on high, and yellow indicated everyone. Red, which she devoutly prayed never to see, meant an immediate retreat to camp.

"See, I told you this would come in handy," she shouted at Lassarian as she felt about the saddle for her quiver. She'd brought two of them, each holding forty arrows. She hoped they would be enough.

"You said nothing of the sort!" he protested. He was fumbling awkwardly around the saddle, looking for the roll of sky darts he'd stowed in one of the pockets. She retrieved them for him and received a pat on her leg by way of thanks. Like most sky riders who weren't particularly good archers, Lassarian preferred the lethal, iron-tipped darts that were half the length and three times the weight of her arrows. Thrown from above by a descending raider, they could crush even an orc's heavy skull, or pierce both a wolfrider and his wolf alike.

Sky darts also left one hand free to guide the raider's hawk, which even a confirmed archer like Bereth had to admit was an advantage. Their horizontal range was considerably shorter, but on days like today, that was unlikely to matter. And three could be hurled in the time that it took to nock and loose a single arrow.

Tywyllas held up a fist, indicating that they should follow him and await his signal to dive. Lassarian and Rhian both pumped their fists, acknowledging it. Bereth tightened her straps, then checked Lassarian's as well. Her stomach tightened and her palms began sweating, so she consoled herself with the thought that at least this time they wouldn't be flirting with the ground. Also, there weren't likely to be any shamans worth worrying about in the middle of the goblin cavalry.

It didn't really help. She looked at her hands and saw they were actually shaking. She closed her eyes, closed her hands tightly around her bow, and tried to clear her mind. One deep breath. Then two. Then a third. She felt Mellt's wings beat one, twice, three times in powerful strokes, then felt him angle to the left, drifting in the wake of two of the preceding triads.

Down below, the goblin cavalry was arcing in towards Lord Malchderas and his regiment, who had reformed into a wedge again, as if to charge. Only they were not moving, they had come entirely to a halt despite the fact that they had enemies to fore and right flank. The other elven regiments were continuing to pursue the scattered central elements, but they were starting to fall back before the forward elements of the orc left wing that were now beginning to angle in to the center could come anywhere close to them.

What could the Horse Lord be thinking? Then she realized that he was probably acting on orders from the prince-general and waiting for their aerial attack. She glanced back, and sure enough, saw that the elven infantry had emerged from behind the hill and was marching north, towards what was now the goblin cavalry's right flank. Despite the apparent chaos, it was evident to her that the battle was proceeding more or less to the prince-general's plan.

Unfortunately, the knowledge did not make her feel any less stressed about the imminent skydive. She saw the first triad leader lower his arm; his hawk furled its wings and fell, and was promptly followed by the other two hawks in the triad. The second triad waited a ten-count, then did the same.

"Hold on!" Lassarian shouted unnecessarily. She already had both arms wrapped around his waist. Then Tywyllas brought his arm down and they were falling, falling, falling, towards the battlefield below.

This time, she managed to keep her eyes open, although she had to squint against the force of the wind. She saw a pair of fiery explosions erupt at the very front of the onrushing goblins as the first triad's mage hurled two fireballs, and then she was suddenly engulfed in a sea of screams and bloodshed and madness as the peaceful detachment she'd known above abruptly vanished as they hurtled down towards the ground.

The first triad had blunted the tip of the goblin cavalry's charge, but hadn't even slowed it down. The grey river of wolves simply flowed at first around, then over, the dozen or so bodies that lay strewn about the point of impact. Then the second mage struck just as the second triad pulled out of its dive and swept over the goblins about thirty *lathaid* above their heads, detonating a thunderbolt so powerful that it not only sent a score of wolves and goblins flying through the air, but actually cracked the earth.

That was enough to disrupt the elongated wedge and divide it into two, as wolves shied away from their howling, snapping brethren whose fur was on fire and goblins that were running every which way like shrieking torches. And yet, they were only slowed, they were far from stopped, as the two sides of the shattered wedge continued charging forward, wolves slavering, goblins shouting in fear and rage.

Bereth braced herself for the moment when Mellt would spread his wings as Tywyllas brought his hawk out of its dive and began rapidly hurling darts, one after another, into the teeming mass of cavalry below. She focused on one big goblin who was standing near the place where the second mage had struck; he was mounted on a wolf nearly twice the size of the others and was clearly attempting to get a group of riders milling about to rejoin the attack.

She felt Mellt's wings unfold and leaned back, rolling with the force of gravity pushing her down rather than fighting it, then flexed her stomach muscles to sit up, nocked, pulled and loosed the arrow at the big goblin all in a single motion. She didn't see if it struck, and then her vision was blinded momentarily by a bright flash as the mage on Rhian's hawk incinerated the wolfriders almost directly in front of them.

"*Anfon gyd i uffern!*" Lassarian swore savagely. Bereth blinked, seeing mostly stars and all but useless, until her sight returned to normal. They had already swept past the goblin cavalry by the time she could see properly, so she turned in the saddle and loosed an arrow that struck a goblin in the back and sent him sprawling, arms flying high, from the back of his wolf.

"Are you all right?" Lassarian shouted at her as he urged Mellt to regain the altitude for a second sweep. "What the devil was he thinking?"

She didn't say anything, as she was lining up a long shot at a goblin below. Missed! The arrow flew just wide. The fourth triad targeted the northern of the two prongs that survived of the original wedge, while the fifth one focused on the southern. But Tywyllas didn't lead them on the second pass she'd anticipated, as the sound of horns from behind and below were echoed by the one sounded by Lord Malchderas's standard bearer.

They could not have had a better vantage point from which to watch the royal elven cavalry smash into the reeling wolfriders. As they soared over the heads of the embattled goblins, the heavily armored elves spitted goblins on lances, slashed heads from shoulders, crushed lupine bodies beneath silver-shod hooves, and left a wide trail of green, gray, and red devastation in their wake.

As Lord Malchderas's regiment plowed over and through the near-helpless light cavalry, the elven infantry was rapidly advancing. They were armored less heavily than the knights, but they were armed with halberds that would allow them to impale a wolf or cleave a goblin with equal ease. A few of the wolfriders saw them approaching, but the few officers who realized their danger were unable to redirect their undisciplined riders and Bereth, after asking Lassarian to guide Mellt close enough to bring one goblin officer within range, put an end to his efforts to reform the southern flank by putting an arrow through his left eye.

"Devil of a shot!" Lassarian praised her.

"Your darts are probably better for days like these," she admitted. An arrow would kill, but it wouldn't cause a goblin's head to explode like a green grapefruit being struck by a dwarven warhammer. "But nothing beats a bow for precision slaughter."

"Can't argue with that," Lassarian called back as he guided the hawk back into formation. Tywyllas gestured angrily at them, but made a gesture of acceptance after Bereth raised her bow.

They were almost directly over the infantry now. Their conical white helmets gleamed blindingly in the sun, and rays of light reflected from the polished steel of their large halberd blades. They advanced in grim silence except for the occasional shouts of their captains, tall, haughty, and utterly merciless. They were a sight to stir emotion in any elven breast, and Bereth felt her own swell with pride. Their white surcoats were embroidered with the Sun-and-Mountain of the High King; they were the *catrodau brenhinol*, the royal regiments of Elebrion and in more than a thousand years, they had never been defeated in battle. Six banners, each denoting a regimental insignia, fluttered brightly in the breeze.

"*Gatrawd, atal!*"

Less than fifty *lathaid* from the goblin right flank, they came to an abrupt halt. Even above the din of battle, she could hear the dull thudding sound of eight hundred wooden butts striking the earth at precisely the same time.

"*Gatrawd, paratoi eich gwaywffyn!*" Eight hundred halberds were lowered, their deadly, gleaming spear-points aimed at the foe. A few scattered shortbows loosed arrows, but to little avail. Bereth and the two other archers immediately responded, by the time she'd loosed six arrows, any goblin who still had a bow was unwilling to show it.

"*Gatrawd, ymlaen llaw!*" The regiments advanced in line, two hundred wide and four deep. The surviving goblins in the front were doing their best to wheel about and attack the elven right flank, but they were still in so much disarray from the aerial assaults and the crushing charge of the heavy cavalry that it was obviously a hopeless task. Even reduced as they were, their numbers were simply too great to quickly put in order, and lacking Bereth's vantage point, very few of the wolfriders could have had any idea what was happening.

"*Gatrawd, codi tâl!*" Twenty *lathaid* from the teeming mass of the confused enemy, the elves responded to the shout with a thunderous roar and broke into a run. As they crashed into the wolfriders, the first rank speared, the second rank raised their blades and chopped. They moved forward methodically; it was more butchery than combat and Bereth did not see a single elf fall.

The cacophony was horrendous. Wolves screaming, goblins shrieking, elves shouting, the clash of metal on metal, and the duller, more ominous thudding of metal on flesh and bone all combined to create a terrible music that was simultaneously horrifying and enthralling. But before long, Bereth saw the rear ranks of the wolfriders begin melting away, falling back and turning tail for the north and east. There were no horns, or whistles, or any sign that it was purposeful, but the rout was on and the goblin cavalry fled before the dripping halberds of the infantry.

Lord Malchderas rode up with his regiment in three neat columns behind him, and as far as Bereth could tell, not a single knight missing. The infantry had suffered five or six wounded, but there were no tall white-surcoated bodies on the ground amidst the hundreds of slaughtered wolves and goblins. There were three dead goblins for every wolf, for like Bereth herself, the infantry were trained to focus on the rider, not the steed. There were dozens of wounded goblins too, who cried out and shrieked in their bestial tongues, but they were ignored. The elves knew, as did the goblins themselves, that there was no need to finish them off. Their cruel masters would devour them soon enough.

Then a booming sound echoed across the battlefield. First one, then twice, then a third time. It was the war drums of the Great Orc. As the last of the defeated goblins disappeared to the right flank of the massive army, the almost-countless battalions of the orc infantry approached in a line that from the ground must have looked as if it stretched across the horizon. As the drums boomed out, again and again, the orcs advanced behind banners made of bone and topped with skulls.

Even from above, it was a fearsome sight. The first line went twenty-five deep, each rank comprised of big, crudely-armored orcs carrying thick stone-tipped wooden spears that were three times the diameter of an elven spear. Their shields were triangular in shape, made from scrap metal beaten flat over hardwood and painted with clan and tribal runes. Their bulging muscular arms were strong enough to drive one of those stone-tipped spears right through elven mail as if it were made of silk, not steel.

The second line was only fifteen deep, but what concerned Bereth was what she saw between them. There were at least 20 large ballistas on rollers, each angled at the sky, being pulled by teams of ten bare-chested orcs and the occasional blue-skinned troll. The crews were heavily armored, presumably against arrows, and Bereth squinted in a futile attempt to spot any obvious openings she might be able to target. To either side of each ballista, a pair of orcs dragged sledges containing huge bolts of the kind that had slain Merlian. It was evident that the Great Orc had devoted no little thought to the threat posed by the elven High Guard.

She wasn't the only one concerned about the approaching artillery. She heard four horn blasts and looked up to see a purple burst of light in the direction of the Prince-General's quintad. Fall back. She felt Mellt begin to rise and arc away from the approaching artillery and saw that the other triads were also retreating.

She could hear shouts coming from the infantry below and saw they were reforming and turning their backs on the great mass of the approaching orcs. Victorious once more, the *catrodau brenhinol* began marching south, their long legs setting a pace that would soon leave the orcs far behind. Wolfriders might have caught them, but the enemy light cavalry was shattered and Lord Malchederas's heavy cavalry still held the blood-soaked field littered with dead and dying goblins.

They rose about one hundred *lathaid* then circled around, lazily holding a position where they could still strike if ordered. She rather hoped they would not, though. The orcs were too obviously prepared for them.

"What is he waiting for?" she asked Lassarian anxiously. The cavalry commander was still calmly holding his ground, his oversized regiment arrayed in perfect order, lances high, behind him. Were it not for their blood-spattered surcoats and the corpses surrounding them on every side, they might have been on review in Elebrion's central square.

The drums continued to boom and the orcs marched on. Now she could hear the roar of their angry shouting. The slaughter had enraged them, and the sight of the small body of elven horse responsible only seemed to inflame them further. But just as they were approaching within what Bereth considered to be the effective range of the orc bows, Malchederas's standard bearer raised and lowered the Sun-and-Mountain banner and the knights kicked their horses into a gallop, riding east across the face of their furious foe in one last mocking gesture of defiance before turning south and abandoning the field to the Great Orc.

She could feel Lassarian shaking as he laughed. She didn't see much humor in it, though. For as the big warhawk rose higher into the reddening sky, she looked down and saw that despite all of the casualties inflicted upon it over the course of the afternoon, the massive army below looked every bit as imposing as it had before the battle began. And as it marched inexorably southward over what had been the battlefield, with the hooves of warboars and the booted feet of orcs tromping carelessly over the broken bodies of the slain, it would soon appear that no battle had been fought at all.

BESSARIAS

THE AGED ELF rose carefully from the chair that he had placed to face the morning sun. A mild jolt of pain shot through the underside of his too-slender thighs, which brought a thin smile to his lips. Not that there was anyone to look at his legs underneath his robes, not anymore, but if there had been, they would have been surprised to be informed that there were still any muscles there to ache.

The pain was a blessing, though. It was one more reminder that he was, against all his expectations, still alive. He could still feel the magic all around him, feel the force of the life emanating from the grass underneath his bare feet, feel the exuberant spirits of the wind as they danced about his face and ran their invisible fingers through his white, thinning hair. It called to him, the magic of Earth and Sky, tempting him to open himself up to its sweet, siren song and let it fill him, heal him, and rejuvenate him with the mighty power of Nature herself.

But it was not the prospect of renewed youth and strength that he found hardest to resist. Even the daily pain and indignities that age inflicted upon him now were little more than petty annoyances. After more than 600 years, he was content to do little more than sit in the sun, potter about the little garden he maintained, and if he was feeling particularly energetic, read a section or two of the three scrolls he had permitted to accompany him on his final journey into the unknown.

He saw movement near the center of a white flower and leaned over to peer more closely to see what sort of insect it was. It was a little black-and-yellow bee, its legs and hairy belly marked with clumps of pale yellow pollen, and it crawled about the carpels as if it was looking for something. What that might be remained a mystery, but after a short time the bee gave up its futile search and rose into the air.

"I wish you well, little friend," the elf told the bee solemnly. It buzzed off, first to his left, then circled around again towards his right before disappearing behind a tree. He smiled, and traced the path the small insect had taken in the air with his finger. The dance of the bees was not impenetrable to him; centuries ago he had cracked the code of their voiceless communication, but now he lacked the wherewithal to comprehend it. That he could no longer fathom their purposes did not perturb him in the slightest; he still took pleasure in seeing them go about their vital business in their striped uniforms.

How sweet life had become as his last days drew nigh. At last he understood, truly understood, the fierce urgency that drove the race of Man to build its empires, and sow its seeds, and send its armies tramping incessantly in every direction, north, south, east and west. Even the furious rage of the Orc made sense, burning all the brighter and the more intense for the shortness of its years. More importantly, it had given him insight into the roots that underlay the decadence of Elvenkind, the insidious weakness that had reduced the great race that ruled all Selenoth with a cruel and haughty hand to its present straits.

There, too, lay temptation. It stirred in him, the desire to wake up his people, by force if necessary, and compel them to again take up the greatness that was their ancestral right. It lay within his power, if only he would reach out his hand and accept the mantle that fate offered him. But no, he would not forswear himself, nor would he forsake the God for whom he was walking, ever more haltingly, this painful path that would soon lead him to the grave. He smiled again, pleased that he had once more mastered the seductive ambitions that fluttered, unwanted, through his mind.

O Grave, where is thy victory? O Death, where is thy sting? At this point, so near the end, he feared the little bee's sting more than that of the Black Harvester. Not that he had ever feared it much; an accomplished necromancer, he had spoken with the dead on too many occasions to be persuaded by the fear-filled fancies of those who declared that there was but one life, after which came either the Void, the Eternal Slumber, or the Ever-nothingness, depending upon the philosophical school.

He found that he was rather looking forward to this next adventure, to walk through the one-way door and discover what lay waiting on the other side. Not for him the eternal battles of the savage Men of the North, or the endless orgies of rape and slaughter of the even more savage Orc. His idea of Heaven was to experience Truth, to see it in its fullness instead of the mere glimmerings he had been fortunate to glimpse from time to time over the last six centuries.

And if he was also vouchsafed the opportunity to discuss what he learned there with the likes of dear Father Waleran, so much the better. Though the years had passed, it seemed as if it had only been yesterday that he'd been sitting in front of the fire with his old friend, drinking that wretched Man wine as they plumbed the unknown depths of Creation with their minds. Smiling, he closed his eyes and turned his face towards the sun, drifting off as he recalled a long-ago argument with the Man who had preceded him through the last door so many years ago.

Even if he hadn't closed them, his eyes were too dim with age to have spotted the distant speck in the Western sky that was growing larger as it approached his solitary domain.

"Bessarias! Bessarias!"

He blinked against the blinding brilliance of the sky, and raised a hand to shield his sun-dazzled eyes. Someone was shouting at him. Why were they shouting?

"Bessarias, wake up!"

It was a voice he recognized. A female voice. He rubbed his eyes, and sat up to see Caitlys Shadowsong standing over him. She was wearing her flight leathers, and behind her loomed the giant figure of her warhawk. "Why are you shouting, my dear? And why are you calling me by my former name. I left it behind when I came to this place, as I expect to leave everything else behind, if God is willing."

"Don't be such an old fool, Bessarias." There were very, very few elves in Elebrion, and none at all in Merithaim or Kir Donas, who would dare to speak to him in such manner, but the princess of the House of Shadow was one of them. She was of the royal blood, a Collegium-trained sorceress in her own right, and perhaps more importantly, since her return she had taken on the responsibility for seeing to his provisions here on his isolated aerie. One need not be overly polite to those one can starve at will, however lofty their past reputations. "I come at the High King's command. He requests the honor of your presence and he requests it at your earliest convenience!"

"That hardly sounds like a request."

"It isn't. He's being unnecessarily polite to an addle-pated sorcerer in the hopes that you'll stop killing yourself and take up your magic again to aid your people in their hour of need."

Bessarias sighed. "And what is it this time, Caitlys? Orcs, Dwarves, or Men?"

"Don't make light of it. There are over one hundred and fifty thousand orcs gathered under a single Great Orc, and most of them are moving on Elebrion!"

"Most of them?"

"Does it matter?"

"Not necessarily," he said. "I merely found it interesting that you thought it important to inform me some of them were not involved in the march south. What are the rest of them doing?"

"That's the part you found interesting?" Her face was a portrait in perfect exasperation. "The scouts say about twenty thousand were marching on the Man lands to the West."

He smiled. "You see? That is interesting. Tell Mael he should investigate the reason behind the division. I imagine he will find it profitable."

With that, he nodded pleasantly to her, closed his eyes, and leaned back again in his reclining chair.

A moment later, he felt two small fists grasp the lapel of his robe. Unperturbed, he opened one eye. She shook him roughly before pulling him towards her so that her pretty nose was very nearly touching his own.

"Bessarias, if you don't get up and find something warmer to wear so you don't freeze to death on the way, I swear by the Wyrms of Mount Pelinothassas that I will get on Vengirasse's back and he'll carry you to the High King in his claws!"

She released him and he fell back.

"There was a time, my dear, when no elf would have dared to lay hands on me so rudely."

"That was when you were Magistras Gnossi of the Collegium Occludum. And that was before I was born! Without your magic, what are you, Bessarias? A withered husk! A desiccated corpse! Don't you understand? We need you as you were! We need the sorcerer, not this time-withered follower of a dead Man-god!"

"You sound disturbingly like Mastema," he told her. "Are you certain he didn't put you up to this? He usually wears the body of a cat, his preference is for grays, but he has been known to take other forms."

"I haven't spoken to your damned familiar!" Caitlys snapped. "And he certainly didn't put me up to it. Aren't you listening? The High King did!"

"Ah, yes. Of course, it is a matter of long-standing tradition that the Magistrae of the Collegium do not answer to any of the seven kings."

"You're going to try to hide behind the Collegium when you won't even do magic anymore!" she shrieked. A murderous look entered her bright green eyes. "Get dressed, Bessarias. Now!"

He sighed. "Is there nothing I can say to convince you to leave me here in peace?"

She bared her teeth and he raised his hand.

"Very well, my dear. But I assure you, it will serve no purpose. The king will in nowise be inclined to heed my words. Neither he nor his father ever has before."

"Things change, Bessarias. Given enough time, even kings may change their ways."

Or given sufficient desperation. He smiled. The lady had a point, he had to admit. Did he not know an exceedingly prideful sorcerer who had changed his own? He reached out for his staff, once a thing of might, now nothing more than a support to help him walk, and grunted as he rose unsteadily to his feet. "Very well, Lady Shadowsong. As a humble servant of the High King, I shall mind the summons, and perhaps we shall see if this miracle of which you speak has, in fact, taken place.

Mael, High King of Elebrion, was visibly shaken by the sight of Bessarias's appearance upon the sorcerer's entrance. Unlike Caitlys, the king had not laid eyes upon him for decades and was unaware of his rapid descent into decrepitude. The Elven king now towered over the ancient sorcerer, whose back was stooped with age.

"What in the Nether Hells have you done to yourself, Magistras?"

"I merely go the way of all flesh, Majesty. I highly recommend it as an efficacious antidote to overweening pride."

"Overweening or not, the pride suited you considerably better, Bessarias. Now, as your king, I command you to stop this nonsense and restore yourself to a reasonable state at once. You cannot possibly expect to serve the Three Kingdoms in your current condition, and I have need of you and your particular powers."

Bessarias glanced at Caitlys, who had accompanied him to the chamber in which the king had received them, which appeared to be the heart of the High King's martial preparations. Even the guards had been excused; this was not a conversation to which even the most loyal ears could be privy. The king's niece-by-marriage had closed her eyes and was shaking her head slowly in dismay. She, at least, understood that he was not to be commanded.

"Perhaps you do and perhaps you don't. That is not for you to say, my dear Mael. You may bluster, and you may issue orders to your heart's content, my friend, but you know perfectly well that you do not command the Collegium or its members. Perhaps more to the point, you may not tell me to do anything at all. I'm too old and too near death to be impressed by your splendid crown and your royal visage. Let us talk, rather, as one friend to another, of these troublesome orcs I am told are of concern to you."

The High King looked at Caitlys, who shrugged. "I can't help you, Majesty. I only managed to bring him here by threatening him with an involuntary ride under the bird."

"At least you're not in a hurry to commit suicide, at any rate," the king said sourly. "Very well, old friend, let us talk of these orcs. They trouble me indeed. One might even say the problem they pose is vexing."

He beckoned Bessarias towards the large oaken table in the center of the room, upon which was displayed a map of eastern Selenoth. Scattered around the map were a number of figures carved from wood and ivory. It did not take a military genius to see straight to the heart of the problem; the squat wooden pieces considerably outnumbered the eight slender ivory ones.

"You hardly need me to perform basic mathematics for you. It would appear there are around thirteen, no fourteen, of them for each of yours. Difficult, I suppose, but hardly odds you have not faced before."

The king smiled grimly. "That would be true were you not incorrect by an order of magnitude. Each of those ivory figures represents a company of knights, not a regiment."

"There are only eight hundred knights in all of Elebrion?"

"Other than the twenty-four in the Kingsguard, yes. And we have another three hundred combatants of one form or another, raiders, scouts, and sorcerers."

Bessarias shook his head. "I warned your father after the war with the Witchkings. We'd lost so many knights, we were down to five thousand then, half the number of when your grandfather ruled over the Seven Kingdoms. How could you let it come to this, Mael?"

The High King's white face flushed momentarily and he looked away. "Our numbers always seemed sufficient," he said stiffly.

"Sufficient? For what purpose? You relied upon the Magistrae and fear of the Collegium's magic!"

"Yes, well, it seems that is no longer enough to dissuade this particular orc."

"Why not?" Bessarias eyed the king suspiciously. "Mael, don't tell me you tried to bluff them!"

"The Council of Magistrae agreed! What else were we to do?"

"What did you do?"

"I sent out three mages in the robes of the Magistrae, with an honor guard of 33 knights under the command of Prince Lelwithas, to confront them. I thought... well, the scouts told me they slew more than five hundred orcs, including more than thirty-five gwrachod, before they fell."

Bessarias sighed. Now he understood why he'd been summoned. There was one thing, and one thing only, that he and no other mage or magistras of the college could do. There was a single spell he had reserved for himself, one that he had arrogantly refused to share with his fellows of the college. And he knew very well that it was a secret that remained kept, for the unleashing of the power held locked within the *calengalad* was not a spell that one could cast without leaving evidence behind. A considerable quantity of evidence, as it happened, as Dasaltha-Muran still testified mutely today, hundreds of years since he'd cast the spell. Dasaltha-Muran, the ruinous waste now better known throughout Selenoth as the Glass Desert.

"I have given up my magic. You can see that, Mael. I am hardly going to break my vow and take it up again so that I can re-enact my greatest crime. Of all my sins, and over six hundred years there have been many, that was by far the worst! And you ask me to repeat it?"

"It may not be necessary—"

"If it wasn't necessary you would not have dragged me here. No, Mael. I warned you a century ago that we could not proceed in this manner. How many children have been born in the last year. In the last decade! You ask me to forswear myself on behalf of a people who are too sunk into decadence and self-absorption to marry, let alone bear and raise knights who will defend the kingdoms in the years to come? There is nothing to save! We are a dead people and you reign over a barren white kingdom of bones!"

"How many children did you have, Magistras?" the High King, his face coldly furious, replied.

"I, too, am to blame. I do not excuse myself from this charge. There may have been a few elves more decadent than me, but certainly none more arrogant or self-absorbed. At least you and the Queen fulfilled your duties in that regard. It is as a king, not an elf, that you have failed, Mael."

"What was I to do?"

"Whatever was necessary. Your responsibility was, is, to the Elven race, to all the peoples of Elebrion, Merithaim, and Kir Donas. To protect them and ensure they not only survive, but thrive! But if a people does not thrive, they will not survive long." He pointed to Caitlys. "How old are you?"

"Eighty-seven," she said, her voice wary.

"And yet you remain a maiden untouched, more wedded to your magic than you will ever be to an Elf."

"How dare you!" Her green eyes flashed with feminine rage.

"How dare I speak the truth? Had you married at your majority, you might have born one, two, even ten sons by now. Not all of them would be old enough to bear a sword yet, but what about your cousins, your aunts, to say nothing of your nonexistent sisters?"

"That's not fair–"

"It is the truth! Look at your young sorceress there, Mael. In her virgin womb, in the virgin wombs of every sorceress in the kingdom for the last five hundred years, is your army. Did you ever drag them here to your castle and make of them the demands you now make of me? Did you ever tell them, even once, that it was their duty to their king, to their people, to their very race, to give Elebrion the warriors she would one day need? Or do you think to make warriors of them now, to see virgin bellies never swollen with child raped with spears and swords instead?"

The High King looked at his niece and sighed. "What's done is done, Bessarias. There is no point in engaging in recriminations of past errors. See, I will admit it. You were right. Does that give you joy, to know that your proclamations of doom are upon us at last?"

"Even now you seek to shirk your duty! You inquire as to my feelings? The only feeling of mine that needs concern you is my answer! It is no. Absolutely and unequivocally no! All the abuse of my accursed powers will buy you is time, and what use is a few more years to a king who has wasted *centuries*? No, Mael, the Collegium will not save you again from your misrule this time; humble yourself in the sight of the Most High God, and perhaps the King of High Kings will grace you with wisdom. I have a higher allegiance than you, and I will not betray it as you betrayed our people!"

If the king's face had been crimson before, it was deep scarlet now, filled with pure, unadulterated rage.

"I could have your head for that!"

Bessarias laughed. "Then take it! Look at me. Look at this broken body! Do you think I fear death?"

"I have not betrayed our race!"

"Have you not?"

The furious High King locked eyes with the decrepit Magistras, and it was the king who looked away first. There was a long moment of silence, and when the king finally spoke again, his voice was subdued.

"If you will not serve me with your magic, then perhaps you will consent to serve me with your wisdom, Bessarias. Our need is dire and I do not exaggerate the danger. The day that you foresaw long ago is now upon us, and so perhaps you will also be able to see an answer now, one that I cannot."

"Wisdom?" Bessarias snorted dismissively. "I have none to give. But I will do for you, and for our race, what conscience allows, Majesty. And my first counsel to you is this: do not give into despair. Elebrion is not the Elves. If the Elves must flee the White City, then you must be at the fore of their flight. Fly to Merithaim, or to Kir Donas, and even further beyond if need be. To preserve and protect your people is your first and foremost duty, High King. Do not let pride or shame tell you otherwise. Ignominy is not death, it merely feels like it to one who knows nothing of death's merciless touch. You were right to say that what is done is done. There is no need to dwell upon the past. All that matters now is what you do next."

The High King nodded absently. His eyes were unfocused, as if he gazed upon something distant in time as well as space. Then he blinked, and stepped forward to take Bessarias's hands in his own. "Forgive me, Magistras. You speak truths that are hard to hear."

"The truth usually is." When the king released him, Bessarias stepped back and bowed, to the crown, if not the younger elf. "As you have need of me, I shall be at your service for whatever days remain to me, High King."

Mael nodded curtly and turned to Caitlys. "Take him to the Crown Prince's chambers. My son will not be needing them now that he is in the field."

"As you wish, Majesty." She offered her arm to Bessarias, a little coldly. "My lord Magistras, if you will come with me?"

Angry or not, Lady Shadowsong had not forgotten her place as a lady of the court. They walked slowly from the chamber together. Bessarias looked back over his shoulder and saw the High King staring silently at the little ivory figurines as if he could multiply them by the sheer intensity of his gaze.

BERETH

FOR THE NEXT two weeks, there were no more major battles. Instead, the High Guard found themselves flown ragged in an seemingly endless routine of patrolling and skirmishing. The only engagement permitted by the Prince-General was a surprise attack conducted by all ten regiments of the royal archers in the late afternoon when the daily march was coming to an end and the enemy had grown tired and careless. They poured hundreds of arrows into the massed enemy before the Great Orc responded by sending out his wolfriders to drive them off, but the attack was brief and to little avail. By Bereth's estimate, between the wooden shields of the infantry, the metal armor of the elite troops, and the occasional shaman's spell, eight in ten arrows were wasted.

She had been soaring on the back of Mellt over the chaotic mass of orcs and goblins below when the attack was launched with orders to ascertain how effective it was. And, although it pained her as one whose useful contributions were now essentially limited to spotting and archery, she had to admit that the royal archers' attack was ineffective. In fact, even aside from the risks that had been run, the attack had not been worth the number of arrows that loosed and lost, and which now would require replacement.

Most of their patrols were without incident, and involved little more than flying back and forth around the perimeter of the enemy army, keeping track of the various tribal banners and seeing if any targets of opportunity presented themselves in a sufficiently low-risk manner. Bereth herself killed one orc shaman she'd spotted surreptitiously separating himself from the march as he disappeared into a nearby woods with a tall officer, presumably intending to slake their illicit appetites.

But before they'd managed to do so, Lassarian landed Mellt on a sturdy tree branch nearby, she climbed down low enough to obtain an unobstructed shot and put two arrows through the shaman and one through the officer. Neither of them turned out to have much of value on their bodies, but she did find a tattered skin covered with crude orcish runes on it. The next day, she was informed that it was a duty roster belonging to the Split Rock River warband, which unfortunately told Lord Oakenheart little more than the fact that such a warband existed. And, presumably, was in need of a new captain.

But every shaman they could kill now was one less to imperil their own mages come the inevitable day of battle. Such opportunities were rare, however, as the sky hunters were themselves hunted from the ground. Rare was the day that bolts were not launched into the air at them, more as a warning not to come any closer than as an actual attack. No more attempts at possessing a hawk were made, though whether that was because the elves were keeping their distance or because the first attempt failed was impossible to say.

It was out of boredom, more than anything, that she began to sport with Lassarian. She wasn't particularly attracted to him, and he knew as well as anyone that she would neither bond with him nor grant him the Seventh Pleasure. But it passed the time, she found his devil-may-care attitude to be contagious, and it amused her to reach around and start caressing him when they were flying close enough for Rhian, or whoever was flying lead in the two-hawk patrol at the time, to see them.

He would curse at her and break formation, but she could tell by the way he relaxed and leaned back against her that he wasn't going to tell her to stop. They never spoke about it back at camp, nor did he treat her any differently than before, but once or twice she saw Ilriathas staring strangely at Lassarian, as if he might have some inkling of what was going on up in the sky.

Well, it wasn't Ilri's affair anyhow, she reminded herself. He didn't own her simply because he'd bought her an egg and it wasn't as if she was doing anything wrong. She didn't see him often now, as he was seldom in the camp, being mostly engaged in other aspects of the defense preparations back at the White City.

It was becoming increasingly clear that the preparations would be needed, because try as they might, they could not spot any obvious weak links in the Great Orc's defenses. The crude boar corrals were erected each evening, with one ballista pointing at the sky in each cardinal direction and at least one goblin shaman assigned to the night guards, who were, for orcs, uncommonly vigilant. They learned why one clear morning, when Mellt flew over a corral that was just being dismantled, and they saw two orcs that had been flayed of every fragment of their green skin being impaled upon a pair of spears. Given that the impalements were taking place in front of at least a battalion that was being actively harangued by a large officer wearing the armor of a boar rider, it wasn't hard to guess what had happened.

"I've never seen orcs that disciplined before," Lassarian commented as they circled above the bloody scene below. "Do you think they fell asleep or something?"

Bereth nodded thoughtfully. "No wonder we haven't been able to get at their damned boars. And if we can't, the Horse Lord won't risk his cavalry against them. The prince-general will have no choice but to fall back inside the walls."

Two days later, however, Bereth noticed a moderately sized pond that was not only in the path of the enemy's line of march, but was near a large embankment that would readily serve as two sides of an oversized corral.

"Lasri, look at that," she pointed it out to him. "Doesn't that look like the sort of place the orcs would put their boars for the night?"

"Yeah, so?"

"So that pond is where the boars will be watered. The stream to the west is where most of the army will drink because it's moving and fresher. But can you imagine the boarherds bothering to do that with a closer supply right there?"

"What about it? They always make a couple of goblins taste the water, so poisoning it wouldn't work even if Lord Oakenheart would agree to it." Lasri's voice dripped with disdain. As was the case with most elves, the thought of intentionally fouling and defiling the Land as if they were no better than orcs or men was abhorrent to him. Moreover, while poisoning the water supplies might be an effective tactic against some armies, it was known that the orcs would simply make do in the absence of water by drinking the blood of their allies.

Considering that every previous orc invasion had been eventually turned back, it was strongly felt that poisoning the waters for years in return for reducing the number of goblins by one-quarter was not a reasonable exchange. But poisoning one specific body of water might well be worth it, particularly if it could whittle down the number of warboars available to the Great Orc. But how to do it? It was possible that the orcs wouldn't bother to check that particular pond, but that seemed highly unlikely considering the heightened level of discipline to which those watching over the boars were subjected.

What if the effects of the poison could be delayed a little? A smaller dose wouldn't work, she knew, because anything that was sufficient to harm one of the huge boars, even over time, would outright kill a goblin. She shrugged and decided to ask one of mages about it when they got back to camp.

It took her nearly until sundown to find a mage who was willing to talk to her. She hadn't met him before, but he was easy to spot as he was the only elf in the vicinity who wasn't wearing either armor or flying leathers. He listened to her with polite indifference at first, but as she described the problem, his eyes gradually brightened with interest.

"You need a way to keep the poison inert until it can be undetectably administered to the beasts," he commented. "It's not a delay, to be precise, although I suppose you could describe it that way if you insist."

"It's not a delay?"

"Let us call it an effectual delay. To be more precise, the poison will not be a poison until it is transmuted. Would you prefer to trigger the transmutation at the time of your choosing? Or would you prefer the spell to be linked to the heavens? I would recommend basing it upon the rising of Little Sister."

"You can do that?"

"Most certainly. The moons are a most potent and reliable triggering element. There are those who utilize certain stars and occultations, and there are advantages to that approach, but as your only real concern is that the beasts can safely be assumed to have drunk their fill, it should admirably serve the purpose. What poison did you have in mind?"

Bereth confessed that she didn't know what her options might be, but to forestall what looked like a long-winded lecture on various poisons, she suggested that they find Lord Oakenshield and let him make the decision. The High Guard commander immediately grasped the strategic benefit to be gained, and approved her plan to magically poison the pond without hesitation.

It took the mage, whose name was Terfielon, until sundown to complete his preparations. Bereth, who was exhausted and so emaciated from day after day of flying that she could count her ribs when she took her blouse off, took advantage of the delay to sleep. She was much refreshed by the time Rhian and Lassarian flew her and Terfielon through the night sky and landed next to the small body of water.

"Is this it?" The mage wasn't dubious, he simply wanted confirmation.

"Yes, I'm sure," she called back, running her hand along the rock wall that would so tempt the boar herders, as it would save them time erecting their nightly corral. She estimated that they could probably fit 350 boars in the area, perhaps 400. That wouldn't account for even one-in-ten of the Great Orc's seven thousand, five hundred-strong heavy cavalry, but it would be the first real blow inflicted upon his army since the march began.

It was hard, she thought, to defeat an enemy who devoured more of its own soldiers in a single day than it lost in week of skirmishes. Despite nearly devoid of elven casualties, even Lord Malchderas's remarkable victory had accomplished little more than save the orcs the trouble of chasing down their smaller allies in order to make stew of them.

Terfielon had brought a small wicker basket of sorts, and he kneeled down by the pond before withdrawing several bottles, each of which he examined closely before turning to the others to dismiss them.

"This will take me some time to prepare. I can't cast the spell until Elder Sister rises and I'd prefer not to work with the three of you looking over my shoulder, or asking questions."

Lassarian glanced at her and raised an eyebrow. Bereth narrowed her eyes and shook her head. Was he mad? They were on a mission, and roving nights scouts or a scavenging party could catch their scent at any time.

Rhian stretched and yawned. "I was on patrol last night and this afternoon, so I'm going to take a nap. Go far enough away so I don't have to listen to you two, will you?"

"What?" Bereth stared at him. "You knew?"

"You were hardly subtle about it, my dear. Now do go on and wipe that damned smirk off Lasri's face."

"Just because we got friendly a time or two doesn't mean we're going to run off to the shadows every time we happen to—"

The mage interrupted her with an unexpectedly vulgar invitation for all three of them to be alternatively raped by boars, cooked by orcs, or devoured by wolves, as they saw fit. Rhian shooed them off with a gesture and Bereth took Lassarian's hand as he led her, stifling his laughter, away from the irritated mage. The handsome raider managed to keep it in until they were on the other side of the rock wall, when he burst out into a fit of laughter.

She didn't see what was so funny, but the sight of him laughing made her laugh, until Lassarian finally got himself under control.

"Oh, I'm sorry. It was just that I didn't expect Lord Magister stick-up-his-arse there to have such a filthy mouth on him! I think he may have missed his true calling as a sergeant in the *catrodau brenhinol.*"

"He wasn't very nice."

"Unlike me," Lassarian murmured as he pulled her to him. "I can be very nice indeed." He kissed her hard, forcibly, urgently, and she let herself melt into him. He meant nothing to her, well, not precisely nothing, but she knew very well that theirs was just a wartime affair, the inevitable product of time and proximity. But he was tall and forceful and sure of himself, and he inflamed her senses in a way that Ilriathas, Lord Kelethan, for all his noble heart and staunch loyalty, never had.

"Stop," she said suddenly, trying to pull back from Lassarian. "Stop!"

"Now why would I do that?"

"Listen!" she hissed. Something in her voice broke though his focused passion and she felt him tense as he leaned back from her and cocked his head. "You hear that?"

It was a soft, distant sound, but the repetitive nature of it was unmistakable. Something, or rather several somethings, was running. Then she knew what it was.

"Wolves!" they both said at the same time.

"We should warn Rhian and the mage," she said.

"We can't let them get away," he said as if he hadn't heard her. "No time. And if they catch our scent then turn around to head back north, that might ruin your plan. The orcs might suspect something is up."

"My bow is back on Mellt!" she said, panicked. The two hawks were tethered on the banks of the pond.

"Relax," he urged her, running his hands over her backside, then squeezing her hips. "You have your daggers. I have a sword. What more do we need?"

"Depends how many there are. Shhh!"

"I make two," he said after a moment of silence.

"Me too." She pointed to the northwest. "That way. With the wind, they'll have our scent soon."

He nodded and pointed east. "Go that way, just a little ways. Stay close enough that you'll be able to see me. I'll climb up on the wall and jump them from behind."

"How do you know they'll go after me? They might scent you."

Lassarian chuckled. "You're female and you haven't bathed in three days. They've been without their she-gobbos and dodging orcs for months. I could probably stand here waving my magic wand at them and they'd ride right past."

She sighed, then couldn't help laughing. It was pathetic, but no doubt he was right. She watched as he clambered easily up the rock wall, then drew her blades and began jogging in the direction he'd indicated. She could just about see him in the light of the larger of the two moons when he waved and abruptly disappeared. For a moment, her heart leaped into her mouth, then realized he'd probably dropped to his belly so the goblins wouldn't spy him as they approached. If she looked carefully, she could just barely see a glint of light reflecting from metal that was probably his drawn sword.

Bereth still couldn't see the wolfriders, but she could hear the beat of the wolves' paws getting louder. Then they must have caught her scent on the night wind, because there was a howl that sounded disturbingly close followed by the footfalls picking up their pace. She finally caught a glimpse of them less than a half-bowshot beyond the rock wall, ghosting towards her like some sort of nightmare.

The gray fur of the wolves and the sickly yellow-green skin of the goblins made them hard to see, but they came into focus as they approached the rock. The wolves were sizable, but thin, and their ribs were showing. The goblins weren't much better, which no doubt was why their faces were gaunt and stretched into rictus grins of bestial excitement. Whether it was lust or hunger that drove them, she could not tell, but even in the darkness and at a distance, their desperation was palpable in their every movement.

And, as Lassarian anticipated, desperation made them blind to their danger. He rose silently to his feet as the pair of wolves approached his position, then leaped lightly down from the rocks, swinging his sword as he dropped on the right side of the closer wolf. His timing was perfect; the fall gave his sword additional force and his sword sliced cleanly through the neck of the beast, eliciting a scream from its rider at the sudden appearance of this deadly apparition.

The scream caused the other rider to veer to its left, away from its companion, who was tumbling side-over-side, its feet still entangled in the rope stirrups on the headless wolf's body. Before it could disentangle itself, Lassarian was already on top of it, and with a quick slash followed by a back-handed thrust, the goblin's throat was opened before its mouth was filled with elvish steel. Lassarian placed his boot on the dying goblin's chest and jerked his sword out of its head.

The goblin circled around, its yellow eyes filled with uncertainty. Lassarian beckoned to it with his free hand, but his long sword dripping blood was enough to dissuade it from attacking. The wolf growled and took a step towards her, but the goblin took one look at the daggers in her hands and clearly decided it was in over its head. It yanked at the crude leather reins to pull the wolf's head around and kicked the beast into a galloping retreat.

"Dammit!" Lassarian swore, watching helplessly as the wolfrider disappeared into the darkness, fleeing to the dubious safety of the north.

"Do something!" Bereth shouted.

"Like what?"

Neither of them noticed the momentary flicker as a dark shape briefly obscured the risen moon. Bereth sheathed her daggers and stomped over towards Lassarian, who was cleaning his sword on the rags worn by the goblin he'd killed.

"We'd better hope they weren't part of a larger force. What if they come back here before that mage is finished with his cursed spell? The other moon ain't risen yet."

"Oh, no!" Bereth hadn't thought of that. She'd been thinking about the orcs being warned off the water. The idea that they might actually be in danger tonight didn't cross her mind. "We'd better go tell him to hurry up, if he can!"

"Watch out!"

They both jumped at the sound of a voice calling out from above them. A moment later, a pair of thickly wet thumps were accompanied by a cracking sound as something, two somethings, struck the ground right in front of them.

It was a goblin and his wolf. Or rather, the corpse of a goblin and his dying wolf. The beast, bleeding from three massive puncture wounds in its side, bared its teeth at them and tried to push itself up, but whimpered in pain as its broken forelegs couldn't bear its weight.

"Kill the poor thing!" Bereth put her hand over her mouth in horror.

"You kill it. I just cleaned my damn blade!"

"Put it out of its misery, will you!"

Grumbling under his breath, Lassarian drew his sword and flicked it across the dying animal's throat. Blood spilled out darkly onto the ground as the wolf tried one last time to rise, then finally collapsed into death. Still grumbling, Lassarian walked over to the body of its former rider and wiped off his sword for the second time that evening.

"Satisfied?"

"Was that so hard? You saw how much pain the poor brute was in."

There was a rush of strongly-scented wind, the loud ruffling of feathers, and then Rhian landed his big hawk on the rock wall above them. "Tough bastards, they are," he called down to them. "I can't believe the cursed thing survived the fall."

"You're the bastard, Rhian! You nearly hit us with them."

His high-pitched laughter echoed off the rocks. "I wish I could have seen your faces when that goblin hit the ground. Lassarian leaped farther than I've ever seen an elf jump at the Queen's Games. And he did it backwards!"

"How did you get here so fast?"

"Awyrllid must have caught their scent. He was so agitated that he woke me up. Considering the two of you weren't likely to be on your guard, I thought we'd go and see what was out there. Not much of a plan, Lassarian. You shouldn't have killed that first one right away."

"It would have worked if the other one went for Bereth like I thought he would."

"They're goblins and scouts, my thick-headed friend. In my experience, they're not generally known for standing and fighting to the death."

"Well, he didn't get away, anyhow," Lassarian said in a surly voice. "Come on, Bereth, let's see how that blasted mage is getting on with his spell. It can't be too much longer before second moonrise."

It was nearly a full day later when they returned to the watering hole, this time as the fifth in a full wing of flyers. The prince-general himself was flying lead, in the hopes of seeing if their plan had come to pass. The last patrol to return had reported that a large group of boar riders had been seen in the vicinity of the pond, but as ordered, they'd retreated before the orcs got too near and became suspicious about the lingering eyes in the sky.

The mage, Terfielon, was on one of the other birds, but Rhian and Awyrllid were finally getting some much needed rest. Bereth was a little worried about Mellt being overworked, but Lassarian reassured her that his hawk was in fine fettle.

"If he doesn't fly everyday, he starts to get bad-tempered. He's the happiest soldier in this war."

Even so, it was hard for Mellt and the other birds to keep pace with the prince-general's giant, with its wingspan that was a third again broader than any of the four hawks escorting him.

They were flying high above the clouds, in case there were any more surprises in store for them. Only this morning had Bereth heard that two nights ago, the orcs had moved four ballistas under cover of darkness and hidden them on a hilltop over which they knew the elven scouts would be flying upon their return from the morning patrol. Thinking that they were safe, the patrol had been flying low over the treetops and only an instinctive reaction on the part of one bird had saved both hawk and rider. Even so, one of the large bolts passed through its left wing, and even with the assistance of the other hawk, the wounded bird had barely made it back to camp. And while it would live, the High Guard would have to do without the hawk until it mended.

"Look!" Lassarian shouted, pointing ahead. There was a veritable swarm of black birds intermittently visible through the clouds below them, their cries echoing through the skies. "That looks like a good sign!"

It did look rather like a sight Bereth had often seen before a battlefield, as crows, ravens, vultures, and other carrion eaters waited impatiently for the slaughter to begin, knowing that they would eat well by evening.

"They might only be there because of the camp!"

"Not that many. We haven't seen flocks like this since the Horse Lord butchered the goblin cavalry!"

The prince-general had noticed the birds too, and he raised his arm, giving the signal to descend with caution. They followed him in a gentle arc towards the ground, and Bereth slipped her bow out from the saddle and selected an arrow from her quiver. She didn't bother to nock it yet, she just wanted to be prepared in case the orcs had placed artillery, or worse, a shaman, on top of the rock wall near the pond.

The smell hit them as they emerged from the clouds, even before their eyes took in the extent of the carnage below. Whatever lethal hellbrew of toxins Terfielon had concocted caused the boars to vomit and void their bowels before expiring, and there were scores, no *hundreds*, of dead animals below. Bereth choked at the dreadful odor; she couldn't fathom how terrible it must be on the ground. She could feel Lassarian heaving, and it was only with an iron effort of will that she managed to keep herself from spewing the contents of her stomach.

One elf didn't succeed, and he broke formation to tilt his hawk to the left and send a thin rope of vomit down to splatter amid the stinking morass of death below. The orc encampment stretched out to the north, east, and west, but there were less than a score of boar riders standing up on the rock wall, staring in helpless horror over the lifeless corral. Bereth could only imagine the horrific scene that must have ensued last night when Little Sister rose and awakened the poisons already lodged in the bellies of the beasts.

Around the periphery of the corral were a surprising number of smaller bodies. There were only a few near the pond itself; the lethal spell had not struck until well after both beasts and riders had drunk their fill. Although their main target had been the boars, it looked as if about half the riders had also been afflicted.

"Mother of Hell," Bereth swore under her breath. She had seen carnage before. She had flown over Iron Mountain during the great siege and witnessed the vast piles of corpses that were swiftly stripped of flesh and turned into boneyards. She had witnessed dozens of violent skirmishes and more than twenty full-fledged battles, but never before had she seen the cruel and implacable face of death so clearly. It seemed to mock her and her elven mortality, reminding her that no matter how many years an elf might lead, one day she too would find herself silenced by the grave.

"Two hundred..." Lassarian was counting.

A pair of orcs in black metal armor were approaching the corral, and one pointed up at them. One of the other sky riders waved down at them with mock-friendly cheerfulness, but Bereth was too shocked by the devastation below to put the arrow she was already holding in her hand to her bow. It was strange. She had killed hundreds of greenskins before, and more than a few wolves, although she had never slain a boar. And never before had those deaths bothered her in the slightest, let alone appalled and upset her. But whether it was the sheer scale of the slaughter or her own culpability for it, she simply could not cope with the thought of taking another life, not today.

"Four hundred and twelve boars," Lassarian said proudly. "I'd guess around one hundred twenty riders. It's too hard to count them exactly, they're not as big. And do you see that one there? Doesn't that look like it might be a shaman?"

Bereth dutifully looked to see where he was pointing. And, she had to admit, the crumpled figure lying in a pool of yellowish filth did seem to be wearing the sort of headdress that she'd seen shamans wear before.

"It's a pity that mage couldn't have concocted something that made them die in their sleep or something. Or at least something that didn't make such a horrific mess. Then they might have eaten the boars and we'd have gotten two-for-one."

"God, Lasri, do you have to talk about eating right now?" Bereth clutched at her stomach. The smell was really getting to her. "Can you take Mellt up higher?"

"Why?" Something in her voice made him turn around. "Dammit, Bereth, you're as green as an orc yourself!"

He pulled back on the reins and Mellt obediently beat his wings and took them higher. The cool air helped, and more importantly their increased height combined with the wind of their passage took most of the dreadful stink away. Her eyes were still watering and her stomach was sour, but at least she could finally breathe freely now.

"How can you be so cheerful?" she demanded. "That was one of the worst things I've ever seen, and you were practically gleeful?"

He looked back at her again, but this time there was no sympathy on his face. He glared at her angrily. "Damned right I am, Bereth. And you know why? Because every cursed boar that died there last night, every whorespawn orc, is one less that we have to kill once they enter our lands. You've seen what they've done to the forests up north. What do you think they'll do to ours? Every boar that we killed is one that won't be fed on the ground-up bones of dead elf children!"

"I know, I know, I know," Bereth admitted. "Lasri, I'd do it again, I would. It had to be done. We should do it again and again, if they give us the chance. But just because what we're doing is necessary, that doesn't make it any less terrible. And it doesn't make it any easier for me."

"You should be proud of yourself. This is like something out of the legends! Not even the Feysie Sword was supposed to be able to kill four hundred foes with a single blow."

"They've still got more than seven thousand boars left. The Horse Lord has less than a thousand horse. It's not enough."

"No, but it's a start!"

"They won't fall for it again."

"So think of something else!"

She nodded. He was right. The orcs wouldn't fall for the same thing twice. They'd have their shamans carefully testing every spring and watering hole, and probably riding ahead to do it. And that would not only slow down the daily march a little, but might even give the High Guard the chance to take out more of the Great Orc's most dangerous assets if they were careless enough to get too far out in front of the main body of troops.

And there were other ways to catch the orcs by surprise. She remembered the rock wall from which Lassarian had jumped. What if a mage could summon a rock elemental, or even two or three, and keep them bound until the boars were pegged down for the night? How many could the elementals kill if goaded into a fury before the Great Orc's shamans managed to dispel

them? Or perhaps it would be possible for their mages to reverse the
orcs' possession scheme, and to seed their herd of boars with a few raging,
murderous demons from one of the deeper bits of Hell.

None of these tricks would be enough, in itself, to stop the Great Orc.
But it was clear that there were many ways of bleeding his army without
meeting it in battle, many, many ways.

MARCUS

T HE TWO AMORRANS sat on the ribbon-strewn pavilion in front of the four equestrians who had accompanied them, and behind a pair of young women who had distractingly low necklines on their colorful dresses. One was wearing pale green, the other light blue, but Marcus doubted Gaius Trebonius could have told him what color the dresses were if he asked him. The tribune's eyes were locked on one deliciously freckled white bosom as its owner leaned forward to whisper something into her companion's ear.

Trebonius started as Marcus elbowed him savagely in the ribs. "What?"

"The combat, the whatever-they-call-it, is about to begin."

Trebonius's gaze had already begun to drift downward, but as the trumpets blew a fanfare, he shook his head and looked out at the strange little arena before them. A pair of men were at each end of a narrow lane, one mounted and heavily armored to such an extent that the Amorrans couldn't figure out how he was expected to fight, the other dressed more or less like a well-appointed slave and clearly charged with assisting him prepare for the combat. Both of the armored men were armed with a giant lance that was comically long and thick; it looked more like a battering ram than a proper spear.

"Is this some sort of ritual before the real games start?" Trebonius asked.

"I don't see how they're even going to scratch each other wearing that much armor," Marcus commented. "No wonder their horses are so big!"

They had seen Savondese knights before, but the knights had invariably been wearing either leather armor, chainmail, or at the most, a steel cuirass. Of course, the cavalry they had seen was border cavalry, whose lords did

not outfit them in the expensive style of the royal knights, which entirely
encased the man from head to toe in shining steel plate. Whether their lords
could afford to do so or not, Marcus guessed that the real reason was that
the border knights had more need for speed and freedom of movement than
the additional protection afforded by the plate. After all, even the heaviest
armor couldn't be expected to save one from an elven arrow aimed at an
eye-slit or a chain-covered joint.

"No, these are the real games," Vitalis said. The half-Savondese decurion
was visibly excited to finally have the chance to see the combats of which
he'd heard since he was a boy. "All the contestants are free men-at-arms, and
most of those who ride today will be the flower of the Savondese nobility.
They don't fight to the death here."

"Really?" Marcus and Trebonius said in chorus, legitimately surprised.
Marcus was rather glad; he did not approve of the vulgar and violent arena
games, but they were a familiar aspect of daily life in Amorr. "What do they
bet on, then?" Trebonius added.

"You can't gamble," Marcus said in a low voice as he leaned towards
his second-in-command. "It's not good for the men to see their officers
gamble."

"Why on Earth not?"

"If they know you for a gambler, you run the risk of them thinking you
don't know what you're doing if you lose. And they'll think you're gambling
with their lives."

Trebonius glanced back at the knights behind them. None of them were
paying attention. "But we do gamble with their lives!"

"They don't know that! That's the point."

"Your father's advice?"

"Saturnius, actually. But I expect Corvus felt much the same way. I never
saw him place any bets when he took me to the games when I was a boy."

"When you were a boy?"

"Once I decided I had a vocation, I no longer attended. My tutor taught
me that it doesn't behoove a man of God to take pleasure in such a base and
violent past-time."

"Says the legate with two thousand pairs of severed ears," Trebonius said,
grinning, but then a thought struck him. "Wait, I don't understand. The
primus pilus is one of the biggest gamblers I know! How come he can
gamble if we can't?"

Marcus grinned, keeping half an eye on the young woman in the blue
dress below him. She had taken a deep breath, for some reason, and he

found it distracting. "Because centurions aren't proper officers. They're men. Or rather, the men consider them to be a higher form of themselves. They can imagine one day becoming an optio or a centurion. They know some of them will in time. We, on the other hand, are different creatures altogether. We aren't bound to the legion for twenty years. It's not our family the way it is theirs. They'll never sit in the Senate, or command a legion, or hold office, and they know it. So, quite naturally, they don't trust us."

"Even though they obey us."

"Did you trust every officer who gave you orders?"

"I don't trust the officer who gives them to me now!" Trebonius cackled and Marcus mock-shoved him. The young tribune turned and indicated a group of women who were standing off to the right of the pavilion. It was hard to know with any degree of certainty at such a distance, but on the basis of their attire, it appeared their affections might be negotiable. "Is that why you never go to the second city?"

Marcus knew the tribune was referring to the small army of merchants and camp-followers who made a living by following the legion around. Legio XVII had lost their previous whorestown when they'd traveled through the dwarf tunnels, but already a motley collection of Savondese volunteers had replaced the larger part of it. The women were taller, fairer, and spoke a different language, but for all intents and purposes, life outside the castra was the same as it had always been.

"I have my reasons," he said, his tone making it clear he had no intention of entertaining further questions. Trebonius stared at him for a long moment, then shrugged and pointed at the mounted gladiators. "It looks like they're ready!"

The loud buzz of conversation filling the crowded wooden stands abruptly stopped as a herald wearing the royal crimson stepped out onto the red dirt track that served as the arena sands and blew a fanfare. To the Amorrans' mystified amazement, the herald was followed by a strange little man wearing a bizarrely colorful outfit and a strange green-and-yellow hat who first capered stupidly about, then abruptly bent over and exposed his bottom at the crowd.

This provoked a gale of laughter from the Savondese around them, and the two young officers, astonished, looked at each other, wondering what the northerners could possibly find so funny. The little man wiggled his bottom, then stood up and capered off, which met with further cheers and applause.

"Either there is something we're missing or they are a very stupid people," Trebonius concluded. Marcus wasn't so sure. He'd seen what passed for humor in the Amorran arena, and at least the Savondese version was considerably less bloody and cruel.

An official-looking personage now stepped out onto the track. He was holding a staff with a bit of ribbon tied to the end, although neither Marcus nor Trebonius understood what it signified. He turned to one gladiator and raised it; after the gesture was acknowledged by the dipping of the massive lance, he turned and saluted the other rider. The crowd seemed to hold its collective breath as he then stepped back from the track, away from the pavilion and raised it a third time.

The people in the stands erupted when the staff struck the earth, followed by the slow thudding of the hooves as the knights urged their steeds forward and the giant horses gradually built up speed. The beasts were ponderous, and they were far from quick off the mark, but they were big, powerful creatures, and soon the thudding transformed into rhythmic thunder. And just as they were hitting their full speed, the two gladiators came together with violent force.

Encased in metal or not, there were most certainly brave men inside those shining turtle shells, Marcus found himself thinking. Neither gladiator slowed, and each man aimed his lance at the breastplate of his onrushing opponent. There was a tremendous metallic crash, accompanied by a sharp crack like a tree falling, and then the warrior who had been riding from the left reeled and fell heavily to the ground like a knight pierced through the skull by a crossbow bolt. The other gladiator swayed a little as the other's lance struck his painted shield and shattered, but he managed to stay in the saddle and gallop on.

Somewhat to his surprise, Marcus found himself on his feet and shouting, although he wasn't entirely sure for what, or for whom, he was shouting. Trebonius was standing right beside him, one fist raised, screaming in triumph as if they were in Amorr, watching an underdog score an unexpected kill.

"Damn, but that was better than the arena!" one of the knights behind them enthused.

"Can't feel good hitting the ground that hard."

"Ah, he's fine. He's fine! Look, he's getting up already." True enough, several young men had come out to help the downed gladiator get back on his feet in his heavy armor as another man caught his riderless horse and passed its reins to the assistant who had come galloping down on a much smaller horse. The crowd cheered politely as the defeated man raised a hand to them, but they cheered much more loudly as the victor rode past in returning to his starting place and dipped his lance to them.

The crowd noise mostly subsided, but now its blood was up, the discussions were louder and more animated, and the sense of energy and anticipation filling it was palpable to the Amorrans. Marcus found himself wishing he'd had the foresight to bring a skin of wine with him, or even water, as he had the impression that his throat was going to be well-parched by the end of the day's games.

"Say, isn't that lord high-and-mighty's boy?" Trebonius pointed to a young man wearing the prince's red, who looked vaguely familiar. He was walking down along the front of the stands, peering up into it as if he was looking for someone.

"That's His Royal High-and-Mighty to you, viscomte," Marcus corrected him. Neither of them had found themselves overly impressed with Étienne-Henri or his courtiers on the long ride to Lutèce. The Red Prince was sharp enough, and he could be amusingly witty at times, but his sly arrogance and pompous bearing grew quickly grew tiresome.

"Think he might be looking for us?" Trebonius glanced down at what they were wearing. In an attempt not to stand out, they were both dressed in tunics and pantalons cut in the Savondese style that one of the prince's men had given them. They also wore ridiculous blue floppy hats made out of a strange, soft material that were apparently now in fashion, although they only did so under advisement, to protect themselves from the hot spring sun.

"Get his attention and see."

Trebonius dutifully stood up and waved his hat, prompting the young man to gesture to them that they should come down from the stands. They left the four knights where they were, with strict admonitions not to get drunk, not to pursue any woman whose virtue was not for sale, and not to start any fights.

"Shouldn't you have told them not to get into any fights?" he asked Trebonius.

The tribune grinned. "And you're worried they won't trust us if we gamble? They're soldiers in a strange city on a festival day. Chances are one in three that some fools will attempt to start something with them. You can't tell them not to defend themselves." He reconsidered. "Well, you can tell them, but they won't listen. Didn't your father say to never give an order you know won't be obeyed?"

Marcus had to agree that Trebonius had the right of it. The prince's man greeted them. "Seigneur Valerius, Viscomte de Lechaire, did you not know you are guests in the royal box?"

The two Amorrans looked at each other. "No," Marcus answered. "The prince suggested that we should see the combats, so we made our way here after breakfast."

The young man was too polite to say anything about their faux pas, but he did blink several times and stare at them with a fixed smile before managing to decide what to say. "His Royal Highness will be pleased to have you join him now, I'm sure. If you will come with me?"

Trebonius chuckled and Marcus shook his head. They'd argued over whether the Red Prince's suggestion had been an invitation or not, and it appeared Trebonius had been correct. They made their way towards the center of the stands, and right in the middle was an elevated area large enough for twenty or thirty people, accessible by a wooden staircase that was guarded by no less than ten armed guards wearing the king's livery.

"You can hardly expect me to have assumed we were to sit here," Marcus muttered in a low voice.

"My mother always told me patricians had beautiful manners and I must emulate them if I was to advance myself. I rather look forward to returning to Amorr one day and disabusing her of the notion."

"You do recall the fate of my dear cousin?"

"Even he never spurned a prince's invitation," Trebonius pointed out accurately.

Fortunately, Étienne-Henri was in far too festive spirits to mind, or even notice, that they were attending upon him. He greeted them effusively, with kisses on both cheeks, his dark eyes sparkling with good humor. Marcus did his best to smile broadly as he tried to surreptitiously wipe his cheeks dry with the back of his hand.

"My friends, my friends, how pleased I am to see you are here after all! Have you seen the jousts before?"

When Marcus admitted they had not, the prince cheerfully launched into an explanation that was sufficiently detailed to reveal that he was not merely an enthusiast, but had taken part in what was apparently called "the lists" from time to time himself.

"Today, however, I do not ride. As the combats are being given in the honor of my victory—what do I say, I mean, of course, to say our *mutual* victory—over the miserable *verdards*, it would not be proper for me to take up the lance this day."

Marcus found himself forced to silently re-evaluate the arrogant heir to the Savondese throne. He might not be worth a damn as a general or much inclined to take the field, that much Marcus had gleaned from their conversations on the road, but it was clear he was no coward. Armor or no armor, there was no man alive who could ride headlong towards a lance aimed at his chest without possessing an ample quantity of courage. Marcus certainly had no intention of trying it himself, as it seemed a good way to break one's back even if one escaped impalement.

The fanfare blew and the herald announced that one sieur whose name Marcus didn't catch was riding against another sieur whose name meant absolutely nothing to him. He did, however, now grasp that these riders were no slaves nor even common soldiers, but equestrians, and even lords, and he gathered that the king himself had been a champion of the lists in his day.

Bets were flying back and forth between the various men in the room, and even some of the ladies were getting involved, wagering kisses against gold, or in one case, a silver necklace against a fine dagger. Trebonius looked at him with pleading eyes; it hadn't escaped Marcus's attention that this was very nearly the last place they needed to worry about their knights seeing anything they did.

"If you must, viscomte," he said, laying particular stress on the tribune's strange foreign title.

Trebonius beamed and immediately stuck his head out the open side of the structure, attempting to survey the two knights, although how he was going to make a determination between the one and the other, Marcus could not imagine. Did the size of the horse matter? Was it the size or the skill of the man that counted more, and how could the latter be ascertained? One could hardly come to a conclusion based on the way the men sat their mounts; he had seen overstuffed saddlebags that rode a horse more easily than the heavily armored knights.

It wasn't long before the crowd was roaring and the two horsemen were galloping towards each other, lances high. This time, both men stayed upright following their collision, although one shattered his lance while the other merely broke the tip of his. Marcus was a little confused by the shouts of triumph and disappointment, until one of the prince's men explained that there were bets on broken lances as well as certain desirable strikes of one sort or another.

Then three women entered the already crowded box, and Marcus caught his breath. All three of the women were fair, but the tallest one, the second to enter, had skin so pale and unblemished that she might have been a half-elf. Not since Caitlys departed for Elebrion had he seen female beauty that struck him so hard.

She wore a dark blue dress that starkly contrasted with her fair skin, and when she glanced at him, he saw that it very nearly matched the color of her eyes. Her cheekbones were high, but her face was wider than an elf's, and her jaw was shorter and stronger. Her deep-set eyes were wide, and her pale lips were full and slightly parted. She was nearly as tall as Caitlys, but her shoulders were broader and her breasts were larger than the elf maiden's, although set rather higher than most of the bovine Savondese women who serviced the legionaries.

Her eyes passed over him, unseeing. Then she must have seen someone for whom she was looking, for her eyes all but disappeared as she smiled broadly in unaffected pleasure. Marcus whipped his head around to see who she was so happy to see, and he felt a cold hand of jealousy grip his heart as he saw that the beautiful fair-haired girl was looking at the prince. What was she to him? Was she one of Étienne-Henri's lovers? Or worse, his mistress?

Marcus tried not to watch as the tall girl made her way to the prince's side, and courtiers and nobles alike parted before her like water under a proud keel. Étienne-Henri favored her with a nod and a wry smile; Marcus relaxed a little at the prince's seeming indifference to her.

An elbow dug into his ribs.

"Are you crazy? Stop staring at her like a starving dog!"

"Who is she?" Marcus ignored Trebonius's hissed demand. "She's beautiful!"

"She's the northern girl, the one they call the Wolf Princess. That's the prince's future bride!"

Marcus bit back the curse that very nearly leaped from his mouth. The beautiful girl—surely she was half-elven—was affianced to the little Savondese princeling? For the first time in his life, he understood the purpose of the Ninth Commandment; hitherto he had felt no more need to be cautioned against coveting wives than against coveting oxen or donkeys. He shook his head, though whether it was in disgust, dismay, or simply denial, he did not know.

"Did you not see her last night?"

"No!" Marcus wondered how he could have missed her, and then he remembered he had left before the dancing, being concerned to ensure that the chests of silver he'd received from the king were safely secured and placed under legionary guard. The queen had been absent during the banquet as well, so presumably the princess would have entered with her, after his departure.

He shook his head regretfully; while the evening had been well-spent in the company of three knights from L'École Militaire, who had answered many of his questions relating to the battlefield tactics and maneuvers he could expect to see from the orcs, he would have liked to have had the opportunity to be properly presented to the lovely northern girl. Then he laughed. Who was he, once very nearly a priest, now a soldier who lived like one, to moon over another man's promised?

He did his best to put her out of his mind, which was somewhat easier than it might have been given the excitement of the spectacle before him. Trebonius lost his first bet when a knight wearing yellow and black was adjudicated the loser for reasons that neither of the two Amorrans understood, but he collected both a silver coin and a kiss from a pretty red-haired young woman when a knight with three wolves heads painted on his shield managed to unhorse a knight whose sigil was a blue rose.

"What sort of soldier goes into battle under the symbol of a flower?" a jubilant Trebonius demanded. "It only stands to reason that the wolf-rider would defeat him!"

The unruly young nobles found their new viscomte's enthusiasm for the lists to be amusing, and the obvious fact of their being strangers seemed to pique the interest of some of the ladies as well. Marcus had to extricate himself politely, but firmly, from the embrace of one plump young woman, who, as near as he could tell, was under the impression that Amorr was located to the west and was comprised of a collection of barbarian tribes.

He was somewhat relieved to be called over by the prince, whose face betrayed his irritation at the importunities of a young man with the appearance of a messenger. However, not even the obvious royal displeasure was sufficient to dissuade the young man, as he was clearly unmoved with the Red Prince's protests.

"My dear general, it seems your presence is demanded elsewhere. At once, if I am given to understand this ill-mannered messenger boy of the Maréchal correctly."

"Has the main body of the orcs been spotted?"

"No, nothing like that." Étienne-Henri sipped at his silver goblet and shook his head. "I expect he wants to discuss with you what level of supplies and so forth you'll be able to bring back to the marches with you. It's not like you and your men are going to carry it all in your saddlebags, after all.

I told him to arrange the wagons and drivers you'll be needing the day we arrived here."

Marcus stifled a smile. He knew the prince was not entirely unaware of the importance of logistics, but he had never expected to be anticipated on the subject.

"I shall be sorry to miss the bouts to come, but as you know, it is a matter of some import." He turned to the messenger. "Where am I to meet Monseigneur le Maréchal?"

"He said I should bring you to Notre Dame des Eaux, on the Rue du Divin, at your soonest convenience."

Marcus looked at the prince, who spread his hands and shrugged indifferently. He thought quickly. If there was a plot unfolding, it seemed improbable that Étienne-Henri was involved, as the prince could have had him and his men killed at any time during their travels here. Or, if he so desired, he could simply poison Marcus's goblet or have one of his courtiers slip a dagger into him right here at the games. The press inside the royal box was such that even a murder might well escape notice until one or more bouts had passed.

In any event, making eyes at the prince's betrothed was sure to be the fastest way to find himself on the wrong end of a sword. Marcus had no wish to upset the young man who was his most important ally in the kingdom, and furthermore, the beautiful northern girl's presence was too unsettling to permit him to concentrate on, much less enjoy, the spectacle. He decided to take his chances and assume the meeting was nothing more than it seemed.

"Will you excuse me, then, your Royal Highness?" He fished into his unfamiliar vestments and withdrew a small purse half-filled with silver and shook it. "By your leave, I shall leave this with my tribune to place wagers on my behalf."

Étienne-Henri smiled, amused, and looking rather like a hungry predator suddenly scenting crippled prey. "You are too kind, Légat. Let us pray La Fortune will favor your man! Go to de Beaumille, see what the old man requires, and in the meantime, rest assured we shall watch over the dear comte like a shepherd with his most cherished sheep."

Marcus smiled back, knowing full well the chances of Trebonius returning to the palace with so much as a single copper coin were negligible. He did not care if the sheep was well-shorn, so long as it remained in good health. It was a small price to pay for bonhomie.

Marcus bowed, made his excuses to the courtiers and ladies in his immediate vicinity, whispered instructions to Trebonius, and followed the messenger out the box and down the wooden steps. Judging by the excited stir that followed his passing the purse of coins he'd given to Trebonius, any bad feelings that might have been caused by his abrupt exit appeared to have been preemptively allayed. By the time he'd reached the exit, the prince's lordlings and petty parasites were already eyeing the remaining Amorran like weasels staring at an unaccompanied chick.

He was still having problems getting the lovely princess out of his mind as four royal household guards followed him, the young messenger, and the two decurions he'd dragged out of the stands to accompany him through the streets of Lutèce towards the palace that had replaced the Citadelle des Enfants as the royal residence. He'd left Vitalis and the other knight to rescue Trebonius from the prince's courtiers, if need be, but mostly because he didn't think two more men would make much difference if he was walking into a trap.

La Citadelle, as the name suggested, had once protected all the children of Lutèce from the largest Dalarn raid recorded by the royal chroniclers, although now its massive walls enclosed the royal library as well as the city arsenal. Its two towers were just visible over the trees and building tops to the west, but then his escorts turned right onto what they informed him was la Rue du Divin, so called for the three famous churches, each larger and more ornately decorated than its predecessor, culminating in the cathedral of Notre Dame des Eaux, which his scholarly instincts suggested to him had probably once been a pagan shrine to a long-forgotten Savondese river goddess. But the citadel's defenses had not been required for many years, as the open courtyards, visible behind gates that were, more often than not, also left open, were ample testimony to the safety and security the people of Savondir's capital city had known for generations.

How much longer would that last now that there were two foreign armies established inside the realm, a rebellion brewing in the south, and a massive orc-and-goblin army on the march to the east? He shrugged. The king could simply return to La Citadelle if need be. It was a formidable fortification, and one that would provide a challenge even to his own architecti, although he had no doubt they could take it if need be.

The messenger's steps slowed and finally came to a halt as they approached the marble-covered building. The dark grey structure lacked the something of the grandeur, as well as the size, of the great cathedrals in Amorr, but it nevertheless captured something of the glory of the triumphant God who had conquered both the waters and the dark spirits that once ruled over them. He could see there was a statue at the top of

the steps, and when he shot an inquiring glance at the messenger, the man
indicated that Marcus should precede him. The seven men followed him up
the wide, granite staircase, and he noticed, as he walked up the steps, that
the stone was lightened and worn away in the middle from many previous
footsteps over many years.

Upon reaching the top, he peered at the statue that was set inside a
fountain. It was a statue of a woman, and although he assumed she was
nominally supposed to be the Holy Mother, her stone robes were rather
too water-logged and clinging to hide her curves, which might have done
credit to a camp whore. Most of the symbols were conventional enough,
but there were a few he did not recognize, and several that he guessed had
nothing to do with the Church proper.

"Why the waters?" he asked the messenger.

"Mon Seigneur?"

"The Lady of the Waters," he said, indicating the statue of the woman,
looked as if she had water pouring out of both her sleeves; presumably there
were some sort of pipes cunningly concealed in the stone. "Why is she of
particular significance to Lutèce?"

The man looked uneasy. "I don't know much about such things, Seigneur
Valerie. Perhaps you could ask one of the priests?"

Marcus nodded. The maréchal was nowhere to be seen, presumably
he was inside. He signaled the equestrians to stay where they were and
mounted the three broad steps in front of the huge double doors alone; the
wooden doors, too, were carved with animals and people, and symbols of
dubious theological antecedence. They were well-oiled, and made virtually
no noise when he entered.

It took a moment for his eyes to adjust to the darkness, as there were
only four windows on each side of the sanctuary, and all eight were made
of a heavy stained glass that obscured more light than they let in. There
were no pews or benches, the sanctuary was merely a large open space with
an altar on a platform at the far end and four wooden confessionals on the
right side near the front of the sanctuary. Stairs on all four corners led to a
wooden balcony that ringed the huge room on three sides, constructed in a
manner that did not obscure the brightly colored paintings that decorated
the ceiling with parables, scenes of Scriptural accounts, and other religious
iconography. Most of it was more or less recognizable to him, but it was all
painted in a style that was somewhat alien to his eye.

The confessionals were screened more heavily than was the Amorran
manner, heavily enough that it was impossible to see if there was anyone

in them or not. And yet, the sight of the familiar structures was enough to inspire him with a wave of homesickness combined with guilt and remorse; it was as if the consciousness of his many sins, too many of them unconfessed and unforgiven, suddenly landed upon his shoulders with a palpable sensation of weight.

He heard footsteps behind him and recognized one of the members of the royal Haut Conseil. But it was not the conseilleur he had expected to see, nor the man he had been told would be awaiting him. Instead of the white-mustached Maréchal de Savonne, it was the smooth-faced Chancelier, François du Moulin, who was emerging from the shadows at the other end of the sanctuary.

"Should you wish to avail yourself of the confessional, General Valerius, I understand Father Alain makes himself available to all who seek absolution here from the ninth bell until the twelfth."

Marcus smiled faintly at the older man. "I fear I have much to do and little time to do it, Monseigneur Chancelier. My sins will have to keep for the present. Do you think to add to your own?"

"My own?" Du Moulin affected to look surprised.

"You lured me here under false pretenses. But if you think to kill me as a threat to the throne, I assure you, you will be making a dreadful mistake."

"I am unarmed, General. You have the advantage of me. And I doubt that sword is your only weapon."

Marcus smiled, unamused. "Please don't insult my intelligence, Chancelier. I would be astonished if there were less than two crossbows aimed at me right now. And I should not be surprised if there were not one or more swordsmen in the confessionals there as well."

He undid the buckle of his belt, and held up the well-worn leather, with his scabbarded sword hanging from it. "I would not shed blood on holy ground, monseigneur. Not even yours." He dropped the belt, and the sword, to the marble floor.

Du Moulin laughed. But it was a genuine laugh of good humor, not a superior one. "Three crossbows, but only one swordsman. He's very good, you see. Warin, you may come out now, if you please!"

The door of the third confessional opened and a slim man of modest stature came out, looking rather sheepish. He looked more nondescript than dangerous, and the sword he was wearing looked slender and toy-like, but Marcus had learned better than to judge a man by his appearance. The most dangerous swordsman in the legion was a balding veteran of fifteen years service, who gave up more than a hands' worth of reach to Marcus, but was an absolute demon with a blade.

Warin ducked his head twice, first to du Moulin, then to Marcus. "Will that be all, monseigneur?"

The chancelier looked at Marcus. "That remains to be seen. I expect so. You may wait outside."

The assassin bowed again, then walked past du Moulin and into an annex on the other side of the sanctuary, where he disappeared from view. The chancelier watched him go, then turned back to Marcus and spread his hands apologetically.

"Did you find the combats much to your liking?"

"As it happened, I found them rather artificial and of limited utility in war. Though admittedly more civil than our own games."

Du Moulin smiled, although no hint of amusement touched his eyes. "The king was most impressed by the ease with which you defeated the orcs. Am I correct in understanding you lost less than twenty men?"

Marcus ignored the question. "I am pleased to have been of service to His Majesty. Now tell me, Monseigneur Chancelier, why you have arranged to bring me here under false pretenses?"

"This world is corrupt, besmirched, and fallen, my son. A man of responsibility often discovers that there is no right choice before him, and that he must choose between two evils. This does not mean he does not sin when he chooses the lesser, it means that the evil is not in him, rather, it is in the world around him."

"You must take that up with God, monseigneur, not with me. You have lied to me, set assassins to lie in wait for me, and now think to lecture me on philosophy. And of those three offenses, it is the third I find the most grievous, and to which I take the most exception. If you would speak with me, speak plain!"

"Ah, so the priest and *philosophe* is now the plain-speaking soldier? Very well, I will speak plain, if you please. I do what I must, General, in the interest of crown and throne, and I do so without apology. My intent was not to deceive you, but rather, the eyes that have been upon you since you came to this city in the company of the heir to the throne, while in possession of the largest army in the land. I do not fear you, my sole concern is with those who seek to turn you, and your army, against king, crown, and throne. They are silent now. They hide behind the king's shield while the danger from without threatens the whole realm. But once the danger is gone, they will emerge, as they always do, whispering their promises, and offering their enticements."

"And you wished to warn me of this?" Marcus snorted. "Chancelier, I fear I have considerably more pressing concerns on my mind. It is my dearest wish that I should survive to be troubled by such dangers!"

"I do not seek to warn you. Rather, I seek to understand if you will prove amenable when they come calling."

"I have heard of your rebels. In the southwest, yes? The Grand Duchy? They have nothing to offer me."

"No? They cannot bring back your father, they cannot restore the peace of your empire, but they can offer you an army. And they will! Hundreds of horse and mounted men-at-arms, all armed in the knightly style. The right to make legionaries of the serfs belonging to other lords, if only you will help them conquer their lands. Can you truly say that there would be no appeal for a general in such things? Especially should he be in desperate need of additional troops as he prepares to take his depleted legion home, to where his nemesis lies waiting?"

Marcus blinked. He had not considered any such thing, indeed, he had not thought much beyond the battle that was soon to come. "No, I cannot," he admitted slowly. "Are you making a preemptive offer?"

"Of course not. It would be irresponsible, and false, and anyone but a complete innocent would see right through it. General."

Marcus instinctively bristled at the insult implicit in du Moulin's words, but he controlled his temper. The Savonder was right. He would not have seen past the bait, he was, in Savondese terms, an innocent when it came to their alien politics.

"You have an evil mind, Chancelier."

"Is evil born in the hearts of men, or are its seeds planted there by the prince of this world?"

"Both, of course." Marcus snorted. "I presume you don't actually wish to bandy theology with me, Chancelier, although I am certainly capable of accommodating you if you wish."

"It would be a pleasure, General, had we only the time. Believe it or not, I was once like you. I, too, was intended for the Church. I, too, might well have taken vows. Beware, my son, even the most sacred duty can prove corrupting over time. The more wholly you devote yourself to your duty, the more it will corrupt you."

"You serve a man. I serve Amorr itself!"

"Come now! Are you so poor a *philosophe* that you have failed to discover that the crown is more to be valued and higher and holier far than mother or father or any ancestral House, and more to be regarded in the eyes of God as well as men of understanding?"

Marcus discovered, to his dismay, that he was beginning to like the man. But that instinctive liking was tempered by the knowledge that it was du Moulin's intention for him to feel that way.

"I am duly warned, Chancelier. You may set your mind at ease. As I told you at Sainte Jorac, I will serve His Royal Majesty so long as Legio XVII is welcome in His Royal Majesty's realm. House Valerius is loyal to its friends and does not truck with whisperers."

"I am pleased to hear it. And, of course, if they do come whispering in your ears, I should be most glad if you would let me know."

"Said the man who whispers in the king's ear." The chancelier only chuckled.

"Mon cher General, I could hardly meet you in the open, nor could we speak frankly in front of an audience. I assure you, the maréchal was entirely willing to play the stalking horse and the young man who brought you here is indeed in his service."

"Then why the assassins?" Marcus did not mean to betray his outrage, but he could not help himself, the words came out rather more heated than he intended.

"You are young. I did arrange for you to be deceived. And you Amorrans are rather famously violent. You cannot blame me for taking precautions."

Marcus nodded. It was sensible enough. He certainly didn't have any trouble imagining Magnus, or even Falconius Buteo, taking murderous exception to a similar deception. A thought struck him.

"What about Theuderic, the mage. Is he one of yours?"

"Theuderic? Ah, yes, the kingsmage, who is also the Comte de Thôneaux. No, he is one of d'Arseille's men, my colleague on the Haut Conseil, the Grandmagicien of l'Académie."

"And the liaison, de Forbonnais?"

Du Moulin nodded complacently. "Yes, of course, as you must have expected."

Good, Marcus thought with satisfaction. At least he had spotted the chancelier's spy. It seemed he was not *quite* as innocent as the Savonder imagined.

"As long as I am here, I have some questions for you. Can you tell me anything about Amorr? Has the Senate purged House Valerius over Magnus's treachery?"

"My sources have suffered in the wake of the expulsions last winter, as you can imagine, but I am given to understand that while there is an amount of suspicion concerning your cousins, your mother and your siblings remain untainted. It is generally believed that your uncle intends to make himself king of Vallyria and as many allied cities as he can win over. It is said that he has eight legions sworn to him, but that number strikes me as an exaggeration."

Marcus nodded. Eight was impossible, especially since he was in possession of one of the three House legions. Four was the most he could imagine. "Does the Senate know the legion is here?"

"They must by now. Before that, the general belief was that you'd surrendered it to your uncle after being defeated." The chancelier chuckled at the expression on Marcus's face. "It rankles, does it?"

"More than you can know."

"I imply no criticism, General. Considering what you have accomplished in the King's name since your arrival, I shudder to imagine the general who defeated you. I imagine he must give the Senate many a sleepless night."

Marcus grinned despite himself. "I have no doubt of that. Have they found my father's killer?"

"No. Nor that of the Sanctified Father."

Marcus nodded. He wondered if he would ever know the truth of Corvus's death. "That is all I need to know. And before I go, Chancelier, will you not tell me the real reason you arranged for us to meet this way? A man of your subtlety is seldom given to confessing the truth on the first question."

Now it was the chancelier who smiled. "You flatter me, Marcus Valerius. Very well. In truth, I wish to know your opinion of Étienne-Henri."

Marcus's first instinct was to dissemble, but after quickly rethinking the wisdom of attempting to deceive a man who lied as readily as he breathed, he decided that if he was going to set himself at odds with du Moulin, it would have to be over something more significant than his opinion of a man to whom he owed nothing.

"He is clever. Those who are inclined to underestimate him are likely to be surprised, I think. He is ambitious, he is anxious for glory, but he is not eager for the throne. From what I have seen, he respects his father, he both loves and envies his late brother, and if I am not mistaken, he seems to fear one of his younger brothers. He keeps to his own counsel, for the most part."

"I noticed you hesitated to answer…" The chancelier's voice trailed off suggestively, but Marcus declined to take the bait. The older man smiled a little, and continued. "I understand it is not uncommon for men who have fought together to become close."

"We did not fight together," Marcus corrected him. "Nor have we become close. We traveled here together, that is all. The Crown Prince is not a soldier. Nor, in my estimation, is he a leader of men. But I do not think you need question his loyalties."

Du Moulin nodded, as if in agreement. "Charles-Phillippe would have been a great king, but I sometimes wonder if Étienne-Henri would have proven restive under his rule. Under his father, no, he will wait his turn. Which brother does he fear?"

"The one closest to him in age. He never mentioned his name, and there was something in the way that he avoided even speaking it that caused me to notice. He has considerably more fondness for the youngest."

"That makes sense. The Comte d'Ainme was closer to Charles-Phillippe than to him, and some have even said that the comte shows considerable promise as a general."

"I could not say."

"No, of course not. Just one more question, General, and then I will take my leave. The orcs. Can you win?"

"I will certainly do my utmost."

"That's not an answer."

"No, it is not." Marcus paused, and looked up at one of the stained glass windows. "In my considered and educated opinion, I do not see how we can, monseigneur. We will buy you time, and reduce their numbers. But do not rely upon us to turn them back."

Du Moulin closed his eyes and took a deep breath. When he opened them again, Marcus saw, for the first time, the merest flicker of genuine emotion flash across the chancelier's face. Was it fear? Was it doubt? Was it resignation? Whatever it was, it vanished in an instant as the older man mastered himself. He smiled tightly, and gave Marcus a formal little bow.

"I thank you for your candor, General. And I will fervently pray, every morning and every night, that your considered and educated opinion is mistaken."

"*D'accord*, Monseigneur Chancelier." In this, at least, they were agreed.

Then light shattered the dim gloom and both Marcus and du Moulin whirled around, startled, as both doors to the dark sanctuary abruptly burst open and the urgent clatter of boots echoed over the marble floor. The tall figure with a rigid military bearing cast in silhouette soon revealed itself to be Antoine de Beaumille, the Maréchal de Savonne, followed by no less than ten of his men, all wearing the royal blue-and-gold livery. Behind them, Marcus's two decurions trailed, as well as the young messenger who had found him at the tournament.

"Du Moulin, the king has summoned the Haut Conseil at the palace, now!" the elderly soldier roared. "General Valerie, you'll be wanting to ride back to the Eastmarch at once! The damned verdards are on the move!"

BERETH

BERETH lay back in the pink-veined white marble of the tub and sighed with pleasure. It was the first time in more than a month she'd had a proper bath, and this morning was the first time she'd been able to sleep in since the day she'd flown to the High Guard's forward encampment north of Kurs-Magog. Perhaps she should have returned sooner, perhaps she should have let Lord Oakenheart send her home after losing Merlian, as he'd threatened.

No, she decided. As awful as the assault on her senses had been, she had done the right thing in helping the High Guard cut down the number of boars the king would have to face in the field. On her flight back to the city, she had seen the defenseless estates, the vineyards and the cultivated lands, that would be devastated even if the city walls proved impervious to the Great Orc's rage. And if they were not, well, that was something that did not even bear thinking about.

She had done the right thing. And yet, the thought of the one orc who was too lost in its grief to shake its fist at them, to even bother looking up at them, troubled her. Did it—did he—like her mourn the loss of a faithful steed? Whatever pity she momentarily felt disappeared in the flash of anger at the reminder of her beloved hawk and the knowledge that she would never ride through the sky on his back again. She looked down at the water and shuddered. It was grey, and there were bits of flotsam floating in it; her mother would not be pleased with the sight of a thin crust of filth lining the sides and bottom of the tub. With another sight that was more regret than pleasure, she pushed down the lever that opened the drain, then stood, letting the water drip from her before banishing the last drops from her skin with a murmured spell. Her minor gift for hydromancy served little purpose in the High Guard, but it was occasionally useful at times.

A clean white robe had been left there for her, and she slipped her arms inside it, then ran her hands through her wet hair and tucked it behind her ears. She could have banished the water in her hair as well, but she'd learned decades ago that doing so tended to leave her hair brittle and dry.

"Are you hungry?" she heard her mother call from downstairs.

"Not particularly." She descended the circular staircase carefully; even with her feet being dry, the marble was slick under them and she had fallen on these very stairs more than a few times over the years. Her mother was seated in what she called her "interior veranda", an open room adjacent to the kitchen with a large window that overlooked one of the four artificial lakes inside the city walls. Her parents were not rich; her father Eulenarias was a royal adjudicator of the second rank, and her mother was presently occupying herself with painting flowers, although it took her about three years to complete a single painting. Bereth thought the paintings were rather good, but her mother absolutely refused to let anyone outside the family see them.

"It's so good to have you back again," her mother told her for the third time this morning. "It's just not the same without you here."

Bereth smiled at her mother. She was a pretty elf of two hundred fifty, but except for a few very faint lines around her eyes, she might have been no older than Bereth. Her dark golden hair betrayed her Kir Donassian origins; she lacked the true alabaster of the High Elf, but were she a little more fair, they might have passed for sisters.

"I wish I didn't have to, but I can't stay more than another night or two."

"Of course you can!" Her mother smiled sympathetically, but she had the good sense not to mention Merlian. "I worry about you, Bereth, and I know perfectly well that you're not telling me everything."

Bereth shook her head and snorted to herself. She wasn't mad. Of course she hadn't told her parents more than the barest details. If they'd had any idea how close she'd come to providing an early lunch to a goblin cavalry patrol, they'd put chains on her feet and ensorcel every door and window in the residence.

"You don't understand, mother. There is no running away from this. This army, it's bigger than anything I've ever seen before. I can't believe no one is doing anything here. It's as if no one is aware that we're all in mortal peril."

"When you live as long as we have, darling, you eventually learn that there is seldom a need to panic. Very often, if you simply ignore the problem, you'll find it goes away on its own accord before long."

"The Great Orc is not going away, mother. He's coming here and he's bringing over one hundred thousand orcs and goblins and sky knows what else with him!"

Her mother yawned behind her hand. "I know, darling. He's not the first, and I find it hard to imagine he will be the last. But these things have a way of sorting themselves out."

"Like what?"

"I don't know. It's always something different. There was the time that a large army of Men marched all the way to the lower slopes of the mountain. Everyone was very excited, I was only a child, but I remember it very well because my mother and I were flown from our family estate here to the city by a sky rider. It was very exciting!"

"I can imagine," Bereth said dryly.

"Yes, well, I suppose you can. In any event, I remember my mother was absolutely terrified and everyone was convinced that we were in dreadful peril because it was said these awful Men possessed engines of war that could destroy the walls. But then one of the princes dispelled the supports for one of the bridges that crossed a gorge while the army was crossing it, and that was enough to send the Men running home."

Bereth sighed. "Those particular Men were southerners and they were unfamiliar with magic. That's not the case with the Great Orc. He has a considerable number of mages, both orc and goblin, and they've been utilizing spells and tricks that not even Lord Oakenheart has seen before. And he's more than a thousand years old!"

"You're missing my point."

"Which is what?"

"Every invasion is different, of course. But regardless of whatever the particulars might be, it's nothing that the King and his commanders haven't seen before. That's one of the advantages of being long-lived, darling. It provides a certain familiarity in any given situation. You're so young that it's not surprising that you can't see that yet."

"Lord Oakenheart and the Prince-General are hardly young, mother. And I can assure you, they are very concerned about the possibility we won't be able to stop them."

"If the High King can't, the Collegium will," her mother's confidence was unshaken. "Indeed, I've even heard that Bessarias has been summoned from his seclusion. Perhaps that is why."

"Who is Bessarias?" Bereth had never heard of the elf. "He's a mage?"

"He is the greatest magister in the history of the Collegium. Do you mean to tell me that in all of your flying about, you've never seen the Glass Desert?"

"There's not much to see. It's out in the wastes of Kurs-Magog. It's just flat patch of sand and brush, pretty much like any other."

"Yes, I suppose the Mother always claims her own in time."

"I don't understand."

"Well, I have never been there myself, but I imagine that if you dig a little beneath that sand, you'll find that underneath it lies a vast sheet of glass. It's said that as a young magister, Bessarias created a spell that broke the very fabric of Creation. It turned the sand to glass for as far as the eye could see."

"*Danneth uffernyn!*" Bereth's own sorceries were barely sufficient to light a candle if she concentrated hard enough; she couldn't fathom possessing such incredible power.

"Language, dear. He disappeared for decades about a century ago, and some said he was dead, but it seems he was only in retirement. Or perhaps he simply preferred more solitary studies; I imagine the scholarly life can become rather tiresome when one is constantly at the mercy of students who wish to pester one."

Bereth nodded. She wasn't particularly interested in hearing about yet another acquaintance of her mother's she'd never even met. She let her mind wander, thinking about which birds and riders would be returning from the morning patrol about now. She had no intention of doing much more than bathe and sleep while she was on leave; that would give her a reserve that would make the inevitable exhaustion of the brutally repetitive sky patrols easier to endure. Then a name caught her attention and she began to listen more closely.

"And so naturally I thought of you, given the close attention he has paid to you over the years."

"Wait, did you say something about Ilri?"

"Why yes, weren't you listening? It seems Lord Kelethan sold his stables recently."

"His stables! So that's where he found the money," Bereth mused aloud. Her words didn't escape her mother's notice.

"The money for what?"

Bereth sighed. "He bought me an egg."

"An egg?" Her mother frowned for a moment before comprehension dawned. "He bought you a warhawk?"

"Not exactly. I suppose you could say that he allowed me to move up a few clutches. I'll still have to wait another year or two."

"Bereth, you can't possibly accept that sort of gift from Irliathas! Are you affianced? Did he propose marriage to you?" Her mother had half-risen from the divan on which she was sitting and her eyes were flashing as if she was angry.

"What? I don't understand!"

"Iliriathas had more than one thousand horses in his stable. He's been breeding them for decades; no one could believe he sold most of his prize mares. And ten of his finest stallions! And now you tell me that he did this for you?"

"Mother, I'm not affianced to Ilri. Or to anyone. And he didn't propose marriage, I mean, not anymore than he always does."

"Bereth, you cannot treat him so lightly! It is cruel to toy with his affections as you do. Would it be so terrible, to be married to such an elf? He is young, he is handsome, and you have told me yourself how brave he is!"

"And he is wealthy and influential at court, Mother, I find it difficult to imagine that somehow slipped your mind!"

Her mother's pale face reddened ever so slightly and the tips of her long ears twitched. For an elf as normally self-controlled as she was, Bereth knew this indicated a severe state of irritation. She rose gracefully to her feet and turned her back on her daughter, and walked over to the window to look out over the placid waters of the lake.

When she turned around, she was calm again, but there was something icy about her expression.

"Your father and I have tolerated this High Guard nonsense long enough. You are young, that is true, and one has to make allowances for the stupidity and selfishness of youth. We were willing to accept that you had won a place in the Guard, and that you had important contributions to make. But you have no more place in the Guard, Bereth, not anymore."

Bereth glared at her mother in silence. She was too angry, too furious, to find the words to even begin. It was with some difficulty that she prevented herself from raising her voice.

"I am not the first sky rider to lose her mount," she hissed from between her teeth. "And the High Guard is my place!"

"No, your place is here, in a civilized home, not gallivanting across the northern wastes treating orcs like pincushions! You should be providing your father and me with grandchildren, not playing at being a proper sorceress. You've never had the aptitude or the interest!"

"Is that what this is all about?" Bereth shouted at her. "You regret giving up your precious sorcery to have me, so now you want me to be miserable by making me give up the one thing I love most too? Well, guess what, mother. I already lost it! I already lost him! They shot him and they murdered him and even though he was dying he still gave everything he had to save me and I killed him and it was my fault!"

She burst into tears and covered her hands with her eyes. A moment later, she felt her mother's arms embracing her, pulling her in, and holding her tight.

"Shh, it's all right, honey. It's all right."

Bereth didn't know how long she cried, but her mother's green tunic was soaked through with tears by the time she finally stopped. She wiped at her eyes and then at her nose with her hands, then stared at her mother in silent, rueful apology.

"Never think that I regret giving up my magic for you, my dear, darling daughter." Her mother smiled, and a dreamy look entered her eyes. "The truth is that I gave it up for your father. That was more than a hundred years ago, and I can still remember my very last spell, knowing perfectly well that it was going to be the last one I ever would cast."

"What was it?" Bereth asked, genuinely curious.

"That is absolutely no business of yours," her mother replied archly, stoking her curiosity even more. "But I will say this. For all that I loved, truly loved, both spellweaving and spellcasting, I have never once regretted my decision."

"Truly?"

"Truly." Her mother frowned unexpectedly and a thoughtful expression appeared on her face. "I had debated over whether to tell you this or not. Your father didn't think anything would come of it, but now that I know the extent of Lord Kelethan's interest in you, I really think you had better know."

"Know what?" Bereth asked, suspicious at the mention of Ilri's title.

"Your father was helping one of the Lord Magistrates with some research into the legal archives a few days ago. This magistrate had been charged by the High King to delve into some rather arcane areas of law, most of which were related to the king's ancient rights concerning his subjects. Specifically, his right to demand additional subjects from them."

"I don't understand."

"I'm not sure I do either. But as your father explained it, as subjects of the king, we all have duties as well as rights. And one of those duties, as a royal subject, is to provide the realm with future subjects."

"Children," Bereth said. "But why is the king concerned with old laws like that? Surely he isn't going to demand that every elfedd drop what she is doing and immediately provide him with children? Does he plan to father them himself?"

"I rather doubt the queen would permit that." Her mother smiled. "No, your father said the Lord Magistrate was primarily interested in the laws as they related to marriage. It seems that some of the older lords have been pressing the king to announce a decree ordering certain elves to marry."

"He can't do that?"

"According to your father, he absolutely can. Whether he will, though, is an entirely different question. He's never been inclined to listen to those ancient blowhards before, that much is certain."

"Why are you telling me this. Do you think I might be one of those he orders to marry?"

Her mother shrugged. "It's possible. I don't know. But I don't think so. Your father suggested, on the basis of one of the documents, that the king might be thinking of ordering all of his knighted nobles to marry as a condition of their vassalage. It's no secret that he's worried about the number of knights he can put in the field. If that's the case, you would do well to consider accepting Lord Kelethan's offer."

"Why?"

"Because Ilriathas will definitely be required to marry and he is the best offer you're ever going to get, even if you live to be five hundred. Among his other advantages is the fact that he happens to love you."

"But I don't want to marry him! I don't want to marry anyone!"

"The stars do seem to be aligning, my dear. What I don't understand is why you're being so stubborn. Is there someone else?"

"No!" Bereth protested hotly. Too hotly, it seemed, as her mother's ears twitched and her finely plucked eyebrows rose with suspicion. "I mean, not really. No one serious."

Her mother sighed and shook her head. "Let me guess. He's dashing, he's frivolous, he's amusing, and he's someone you know perfectly well is never going to demand any kind of commitment from you, or make any sort of impression on your heart."

Bereth stared at her mother. Short of adding a physical description, she could hardly have described Lassarian better. "How did you know?"

"Because you're doing exactly what *morwynion ifanc* have done for generations. You're putting off any chance of developing the sort of real relationship that frightens you by hiding behind impossible ones you know will never go anywhere."

"If everyone does it, what is wrong with it?"

Her mother smiled grimly. "Once you start down that path, it's hard to know when to leave it. There are seven-hundred-year-old sorceresses in the Collegium who fully intended to marry one day, but with every year that passed, they found it harder to change their ways and fewer elves who were interested in them. I have friends like that. It's a lonely way to live, Bereth, and it doesn't get easier with time."

"So what are you saying, I should just marry Ilri even though I don't love him?"

"I am saying that if you marry Lord Kelethan, you will come to love him in time. It is the Mother's great gift to us, to compensate for the sacrifices we must make and the burdens we carry. Love is a choice, Bereth, it's commitment, not magic. That flutter of excitement for which you are waiting is ephemeral; even when it comes, it disappears again in the blink of an eye."

"And if I don't intend to marry him, I shouldn't accept his gifts?"

Her mother made a face. "Normally, considering the extravagance and the expense, I would say yes, most certainly. But this is different. The nature of the gift he's offered you is such that it precludes you marrying him. So, he's making it clear that he intends to wait for you, the young fool."

"He's a fool, I'll grant you that, but why do you call him young when he's already past his first century?"

"Males age much more slowly than we do, darling. And motherhood ages an elf; I expect I learned more wisdom in your first year than in the one hundred I'd lived before."

"I don't understand."

Her mother laughed. "I learned how many of my ideas about the world were utterly and ridiculously wrong. When you have children of your own, you will understand too. Now, does Ilriathas know about this other elf?"

Bereth blushed. This was simply not a conversation she wanted to be having with her mother. "Ah, no, I don't think so. It's nothing serious, I swear!"

"And yet it is serious enough that you're not comfortable telling him about it. That should tell you something right there, my dear. Now, I very much recommend you put an end to the affair at once, or else decline Lord Kelethan's gift. Males can be very possessive, especially of those they do not actually possess. You're playing with fire there, Bereth."

It was true. Bereth wanted to tell her mother how it was different at the camp, and in the sky, how the combination of fear, exhaustion, and the knowledge that every patrol might be her last gave her the sense that anything was possible and everything was permissible. But how could she tell her that and not drive her mother mad with worry? And even she knew it was foolishness, a short-sighted madness that stemmed from being constantly drenched in battle, blood, and death. It was easier to stop thinking and lose herself in momentary pleasures than face her fears... or the terrible things she had done.

So she simply nodded dutifully and avoided meeting her mother's eyes. What she would do about Lassarian, she did not know, but then, if this war had taught her anything, it was to not worry overmuch about a tomorrow that might never come.

As it turned out, her worries were groundless. The next day, one of the prince-general's captains appeared at the door of her parents' home with orders from Lord Oakenheart seconding her to the prince-general's staff and instructing her to proceed immediately to Tir Diffaith, the great fortification that demarcated the wasteland of Kurs-Magog from the lands of Elebrion proper. The orders surprised her, both the staff transfer as well as the implication that the prince-general intended to make his stand at the Tir rather than continue with his plan for a more aggressive mobile defense.

Both her mother and father were there to see her off, as were several of their friends. Her father held her close for a long moment, but said nothing; his eyes spoke sufficiently of his love and concern for her. Her mother wept, rather more prettily than she herself had the day before, Bereth noted, before embracing her.

"Now take care of yourself, and do mind your behavior, darling. Even if you must fight a war, you can do so as a proper *firain*, not a *brwnmerch*." She smiled sweetly at her daughter's astonished expression, and blew her a kiss.

Feeling somewhat dazed at her mother's unexpected choice of words, Bereth took her leave, bearing considerably more in her saddlebags than she had arrived with. The captain, a well-bred elf of moderate height, took them from her, nodded to her father, then climbed the stairs that led to the garden where his rather small, dark-feathered hawk was chained to a post. Bereth felt her eyes prick slightly at the sight; it was the very same post to which she had chained Merlian so often in the past.

"I hope you took the chance to rest rather than recreate while you were here," the young captain said. "I'm Cangenhelas, by the way. I should warn you, the prince is liable to run his attaches rather ragged."

"Nothing but sleep, bathe, and be lectured by my mother," Bereth assured him. "And thank you for coming to fetch me. Do you have any idea why the prince-general wants me on his staff?"

The young elf grinned as he expertly leaped up and caught the saddle horn, then swung himself gracefully up to the saddle. He couldn't be in more than his sixth decade yet, and his bright-eyed smile made him seem even younger. "I can't remember his exact words, but it was something to the effect of, 'bring me that damned *elfonwy* who came up with the idea for the witch-brew, that's the first useful idea anyone in this damned army has had since the Great Orc marched!' "

"He sounds lovely," she said dryly as she handed her bags up to him. She wondered how long she'd be able to stand him shouting at her before she broke down and started crying.

"Oh, he's not so bad. He barks at everyone. You just have to not take it personally." After stowing her saddlebags with a grunt and a mildly accusatory glance at her, he pointed to the chain. "Mind releasing that?"

She eyed the hawk uncertainly. Merlian would never have permitted anyone else to approach his feet so closely without at least considering a swipe with his talons, but every bird was different. Figuring that the captain must know his bird, she crossed her fingers, bent down, and unhooked the chain from the iron band around its right leg.

The hawk hopped once and gave out a loud, crow-like caw, which startled her and sent her stumbling back. The captain laughed, but not unkindly, and leaned over to extend a hand to her. She took it and clambered up the side of the bird, pleased that he hadn't insulted her by tossing down a rope ladder. She might not be of the High Guard any longer, but she was still an experienced sky rider and it warmed her heart to be treated like one.

Cangenhelas clicked and shook the reins, and that was enough to inspire the hawk to leap skyward. His movements were neither as graceful as

Merlian's nor as powerful as Mellt's, but they quickly climbed into the sky above Elebrion even so, and she knew a moment's regret as she looked back at the white buildings and the spotless streets below. Tir Diffaith would be more comfortable than the forward camp at which she'd been living for the last three months, but there would be no hot baths or refined food for the foreseeable future.

Then again, she wouldn't be subject to a daily inquisition by her mother, so there were some benefits to living in a war zone.

They flew rapidly away from the capital mountain, and once they were clear of city walls, Cangenhelas let his hawk drop and they flew down along the angle of the slope, just over the treetops, then leveled out just before they reached the foothills. They flew over luxurious villas, ripening vineyards, and meticulous rows of plants that Bereth couldn't possibly identify. A flower farm caught her attention, and she waved to a young *elfonwy* who was on her knees amidst the riot of color, presumably weeding, who waved back.

It made her angry to think how all of this beauty and hard work would be destroyed, the vineyards burned, the houses leveled, and the flowers trampled and torn, if the prince-general could not hold at Tir Diffaith. The situation must be dire if the royal commanders were seeking her advice; what did she know about military matters behind ambushes, archery, and sky raids?

Gradually, the pretty villas gave way to farms and the small fields were replaced by bigger ones where the grains were grown. Gradually, those too gave way to forests, although the occasional building or temple could be spotted in clearings as they flew by. Some elves found flying over the forests to be tedious, but Bereth always enjoyed it.

"Look down there," Cangenhelas called back to her.

She looked down. There was a long double column of elven troops marching below, clad in the seldom-seen green-and-white of the Elebrion militia, followed by an even longer line of ox-drawn wagons. A few officers, wearing royal white, rode to the sides of the column urging it along. It was the first time in her lifetime that she could recall the militia being called out, and it was a worrisome reminder of how dangerous the situation was shaping up to be.

And all too soon, they were past them. She didn't like to think how long it took to fly over the Great Orc's army in comparison. The militia would help, a little, but they were far too few to make any substantive difference, especially in light of their lesser capabilities. Perhaps that was why the prince-general had decided to make his stand behind the triple walls of Tir Diffaith, where he could make better use of the relatively inexperienced reinforcements.

They passed two smaller parties also on the march, one regiment of about one hundred horse wearing the colors of one of the eastern lords, and two regiments of foot marching haphazardly behind an unfamiliar blue-and-yellow banner. A levy of some sort, she guessed, although she had no idea whose it might be. But if they looked undisciplined, at least their shields gleamed bright silver in the late afternoon sunlight.

Finally, as the sky was beginning to take on a rosy hue and the faint circle of Elder Sister could be seen low on the horizon waiting for her turn to shine, the towers of Tir Diffaith appeared in the distance.

The great eastern fortress rose from the floor of the narrow valley that provided a natural passageway out of the wastes of the Kurs-Magog. Unlike the shining white quartzite walls of Elebrion, it was built from dark ironstone mined from the north by dwarves, then reinforced with spells cast by generations of archmages who specialized in *Thaearhudau*, the magic of earth and stone. It was considered an esoteric art at the Collegium, and rather looked down upon by those who felt it was too dwarvish in nature, but as Bereth recalled from the lectures through which she'd been forced to sit, there was always an archmage-in-residence at Tir Diffaith who was responsible for maintaining its magical defenses.

The fortress was deemed impregnable, and indeed, it had never fallen. Even when the orcs had taken Arathaim and Kir Kalathel, they had bypassed Tir Diffaith, a decision that had ultimately proved fatal to more than one orc king. It was less intended as a defense than a deterrent, and indeed, more than one orc army had turned back upon seeing the imposing sight of the fortress's three walls, the arms of the twelve massive trebuchets that could throw massive one-tonne boulders further than any war engine, and the seven towers upon which eagle-eyed elven archers were stationed. There were more ballistas than she could easily count, and she could see at least three piles of the giant bolts they fired stacked strategically where they could be easily distributed.

The tallest tower, in the center of the fortress and three times wider than any of the others, was where they were headed. It was called the Nyth Tower and it was where the warhawks landed and were launched. It had nests for as many as ten of the big birds, although in times of war, the tops of several of the other towers were converted so that the greater portion of the High Guard could come and go without risking any peril from below.

But the problem the prince-general faced was apparent even as they approached the fortress. The vast battlements were being patrolled by a total of four elves, and with the exception of a crew working on one of the giant trebuchets, the walls were otherwise unoccupied. All the forces the High King had thrown against the Great Orc, including High Guard as well as the royal horse and foot would barely suffice to serve the great complex as a skeleton garrison.

There were already six hawks tethered near the landing site marked out in black granite tiles. Two of them she knew; it would have been impossible not to recognize the prince-general's monster, and the other belonged to Lord Disglarion Greenwood, who commanded the largest infantry force besides the High King's own. Cangenhelas brought them in rather faster and lower than she would have, but he was good with his bird and they landed without incident. There were two elves in plain brown tunics waiting to meet them, and they had a chain attached to the hawk's leg ring before either Bereth or the captain managed to dismount.

"Welcome to Tir Diffaith!" one of them called cheerfully as he led the warhawk, its head bobbing a little uneasily, over to a tethering post. "Captain, the prince wants you to go directly to the smaller meeting room. He's there with the rest of the staff."

Cangenhelas groaned and the other elf laughed.

"What's wrong?" Bereth asked.

"I suppose a walk will help stretch our legs after a long day in the saddle. Do you see that tower there?"

She nodded. It was the second tower to the left.

"That's where we have to go."

Ah. She groaned herself. Down the stairs, over, and then up again. Surely it would have been easier to simply fly over there!

"We're not allowed to do that." Cangenhelas shook his head, seemingly reading her mind. "The prince is very clear on that."

It took them longer to walk down the first tower, exit it at the level of the battlements, then walk along the walls to the other one than she would have expected. A pair of guards saluted Cangenhelas and confirmed that the prince and his advisers were in the room towards which they were headed. Unfortunately for her aching legs, the map room was more than halfway up the tower and she was beginning to breathe hard by the time the captain finally exited the winding stone staircase.

"Ah, good, you've arrived," the prince-general looked up from the ensorcelled map he was perusing when they entered the low-ceilinged room.

He was a tall, imposing elf, and the top of his head very nearly touched the wooden beams above. "Thank you, captain."

"Not at all, your highness."

The prince-general turned his attention to her. He looked very much like his cousin, the High King, but whereas King Mael's expression was inclined to arrogance and cruelty, his was more relaxed, almost serene. His eyes were the pale gold of the royal family, and his hair was long and entirely white, as befitted the highest of the High Elves. There were elves who were known to bleach their hair, or even use sorcery to whiten it, but considering the purity of his blood, Bereth had no doubt that it was natural.

"I have decided you will be my newest advisor, Bereth mer Eulenarias. I believe I have met your father. We hunted together once, many years ago. He was a fair shot with the bow, although I understand you are even better. He is well?"

"Yes, your highness. Thank you very much. I last saw him just this morning."

"Well and good." He smiled and gestured towards the other elves, most of whom were at least a century older than her by the looks of it. "I suppose you may wish to understand why I have requested your transfer from the High Guard?"

"Yes, your highness. If it please your highness."

He raised a skeptical white eyebrow at her formality and sniffed in an amused manner. "I expect you are innocent of Balalwyf?"

"Your Highness?"

"One of the great tacticians of King Iomgywn's day. And may I presume you know nothing of Linden?"

"Nothing whatsoever, your Highness."

"That is as it should be," he said approvingly, which mystified her. "It is meet that *elfonwyth* should study poetry and painting, not war. You see, every elf in this room can recite Balalwyf and Linden and Crewaldus, to say nothing of a dozen other great philosophers of war, be he elf, Man, or Dwarf. And every elf in this room therefore knows that the answers we seek are not to be found in them, or in our collective centuries of experience in battle."

"Why not?" she asked, too intent on understanding him to address him properly.

"Because the weight of numbers involved makes it perfectly clear that we cannot defeat them in battle. Indeed, even to run the risk of meeting them in the open field is enough to flirt with complete disaster. We are too few."

"What do you expect from me?"

"Ideas!" he said, with a cheerful sparkle in his golden eyes. "New ideas, the sorts of things that would not occur to us, ossified by our knowledge of the way things are supposed to be."

"Like the poison spell," one of the elves wearing a blue tabard with a silver cat head on it added. "Poisoning water supplies is nothing new, but the use of a time-delay to evade the goblins testing it was clever. It's not just the idea itself that's useful, you see, but the fact that it opens up whole new lines of tactics."

"The problem is that we have little time, very little time," the prince-general said. "We need to come up with some new ideas to whittle them down, quickly, before we're forced to fall back behind the walls."

"Whittle them down to what?" she asked.

"About two-thirds their present numbers."

She frowned. That seemed strangely specific. "Why that particular quantity?"

The prince-general glanced at one of the other elves towards the back who was rather less splendidly adorned than the rest of them. "Ah, Lady Bereth, the art of war has been transformed to a science of sorts, if you take my meaning. According to my calculations, which you must understand are very precise, we can quite reasonably estimate how long our garrison can be expected to hold out against various numbers of besieging forces."

"Really?" Bereth asked, too surprised to correct the elf's misunderstanding of her rank.

"Oh, most certainly! The details are considerable and complicated, but the basic concept is very simple. We might expect to hold out indefinitely against a single orc, for example, whereas an infinite number would be expected to overwhelm even these eminently well-fortified walls in a single day. Once the principle is accepted, it is but a matter of time to work through the relevant variables involved. And in fact–"

"In fact, Valrond has worked through those variables in significantly more detail than we have time to discuss," the prince-general interrupted. "To summarize, if we cannot reduce their forces to the extent suggested, then Tir Diffaith can be expected to fall in seventy-two days."

"Give or take two days on either side," Valrond added.

The prince-general looked towards the ceiling and sighed. He clearly found the other elf a trial. "We have a few ideas. But we are hoping you might be able to produce some better ones."

Bereth stared at the royal elf in shock. Was he serious? How was she supposed to come up with a solution when elves five times her age, with fifty times her knowledge, had not? For a moment, she didn't know what to say; she felt so self-conscious that she thought she might faint, and she swayed upon her feet. But then her courage returned to her, and she nodded quickly.

"I will do what I can. Will you have support from the Collegium?"

"I'll have the High Guard flying every magister and mage here, in their beaks and talons, if necessary. How many of them will we need?"

She thought about it for a moment. "All of them," she said.

SKULI

THE ABANDONED VILLAGE was now occupied by about twenty bitches and thirty pups of various ages, the girl they'd captured said, although none of the pups were older than the striplings they'd killed. More importantly, she told them it was also home to twenty-six women and girls, all of whom had been kept as slaves for years. The news was both welcome and sickening to Skuli; on the one hand, there was nothing to stop them now from rescuing the women and bringing them south across the sea to safety. On the other, the knowledge that the wolf-demons had been keeping Dalarn women captives for all these years shamed him deeply even though he hadn't known about it and thanks to the heroics of him and his men, the women of his own tribe had escaped their dreadful fate.

He did not ask why there were only women and girls being held captive. He knew very well how the demonic creatures made use of the Dalarn men and boys. Well, they would avenge the Strongbow and many more of the dead and devoured very soon, once Two-Daggers was in place and gave the signal.

He'd left the girl behind with the wounded Alrik, bound, gagged and tied to a tree. She had answered their questions freely, and indeed, seemed inclined to view them as her rescuers, but Skuli had not survived as long as he had by placing any faith in strangers. He'd also warned Alrik that if the girl was freed, raped, or gone when they returned, he would personally skin the young warrior before offering him to the sea gods. Alrik was also under strict orders to cut the girl's throat if he so much as saw a fox or a dog in the vicinity. She might be *sigskifting*, she might not, but regardless, she would not be giving any warning to the demon bitches of the village tonight.

His plan was for them to hit the village from north and south at the same time, with a smaller group remaining on the inland side, to the east, to cut off any attempts to retreat in that direction. Skuli was with the northern group, but Engli the Black would lead the attack. The girl had told them that the Dalarn women were kept in three large huts, so he and Var All-Strong would go directly to the huts and keep the women safe while the rest of the men were slaughtering their captors.

"Bastard's taking his time about it, ain't he," growled Engli.

"Be patient. It's a south-southwesterly wind, so he had to swing wider than we did."

"I still don't see why we don't attack from the west, set fire to all the buildings and drive them into the sea. We're going to lose more men this way."

Skuli sighed. The Black was a ferocious fighter and he was well-respected by the men, but his approach to battle tended to be as single-minded as it was bloodthirsty.

"We'd also run the risk of burning those women and children to death, Engli."

"Then why'd you tell Two-Daggers to light the roofs?"

"Because we can't fight the beasts in the dark. You know that. We need something to see by. That doesn't mean we don't want to save the women if we can."

"Doubt there's much to save." The Black spat. "Only one reason them wolves been keeping them around, Skullbreaker, and you know it. Might be a kindness to kill them."

"We're going to need all the women we can get if we're ever going to take these islands back."

Engli snorted. "You won't live to see it. Neither will my son's sons."

Skuli shrugged. No, they wouldn't. Nor would Brynjolf and Fjotra. But their grandchildren might. And he'd be damned to Hela's deepest, coldest hell before he'd give up his people's claim to their own damn isles.

An owl hooted softly. Armor creaked as the men, already on edge with their weapons drawn, tensed as if to move. But it was only an owl.

"Damn me, but Two-Daggers is taking his time," he heard someone curse softly behind him. Was it possible the other men had been ambushed, taken in silence by surprise in the dark? No, surely they would have been alerted in the ruckus that followed. Just as Skuli was giving serious thought to the idea of starting the attack on their own, he heard a sharp whistle that sounded vaguely like a seagull. That was it!

"I still say that don't sound like no bird," The Black grumbled. Skuli stifled a laugh as they moved forward as quietly as armed men could, and the popping of his aging joints reminded him of the futility of attempting to achieve complete silence. But there was no sound or movement from the village as they emerged from the shadowy cover of the forest and caught their first sight of its dilapidated walls. They slipped swiftly through the gaps. Then the stars appeared to fall, as one flaming arrow arced high into the sky before plunging down onto a rooftop, followed in rapid succession by five, six, seven, eight more arrows. Not all of them landed on rooftops, and half of those that landed failed to ignite the thick-matted straw of the roofs, but enough caught fire to give them the light to see by.

A long, low howl signified that the alarm had been raised, but Skuli had already entered and exited two empty huts before he saw his first Aalvarg. It was little more than a pup, and the teeth it bared at him were thin and needle-like; he beheaded it with a single stroke of his sword. He dispatched two of its litter mates with equal ease when he heard their outraged mother make a sound that was halfway between a howl and a scream. Maddened by grief and fury, she charged directly at him, but the All-Strong stepped forward to drive his spear through her throat and out her back before she could reach him.

Skuli reversed his sword and plunged it into her eye, bringing the thrashing of her transfixed body to an end. As the All-Strong pulled out his spear, Skuli quickly killed the two remaining pups.

"If we could've got at them small like this, we would have beat them," Var commented as he kicked at one small, furry, lifeless body.

"Come on, let's see if we can find those women."

Enough rooftops were now burning toward the center of the village that they could easily see where they were going. Skuli's leg prevented him from running, and the wolf corpses littering the streets indicated that the others were advancing more quickly. The shrieks and howls and snarls had crescendoed, interspersed with the occasional oath of one of his men, but thus far he had yet to hear the sort of scream that indicated a serious wound had been suffered.

An adult bitch ran past him before he noticed she was near, but apparently she hadn't seen them coming either, as she ran into the swinging butt of Var's spear without even attempting to avoid it. She crumpled to the ground, and the All-Strong crushed her skull with two brutal downward thrusts.

Skuli looked in the direction from whence she'd come in case others were following her, but it appeared she'd been alone. Now, where were the damned women? If his dim recollection of captives was any guide, they'd be staying where they were, and would likely make his task more difficult by attempting to hide. He tried to make sense of what he was seeing and match it to the landmarks the girl had described.

"The big building must be that one!" Var pointed with his spear.

So two to seaward meant his right. The flames were rising higher into the night sky now, and he could smell the scent of smoke even though the wind was blowing in the opposite direction. But before they could cross the street, five adult Aalvarg, followed by three younger ones, emerged to their right. They were on all fours and their ears were flat to their heads with fear as they fled something Skuli could not see. Egli, he assumed. The Black often had that effect on men and wolf-demons alike.

"Let them go," he placed his sword in front of the All-Strong's chest before the younger man could intercept the fleeing Aalvarg. "Leave them for the others. They'll run right into them."

The house in which they suspected the women might be had a wooden door, but when Skuli pushed on it, he felt something blocking it. It moved a little, which made him suspect that it was not barred, that there was a barricade behind it. He waved for the All-Strong to join him, and between the two of them, they managed to force the door open wide enough to see that there were indeed women inside.

"Dammit!" The All-Strong cried unexpectedly as he leaped away from the door. Skuli stared at the other man in confusion, then ducked as he detected movement in his peripheral vision and just missed being stabbed by a sharpened stick. Someone, presumably the women, began to shove the door shut again, but Var managed to shove his spear into the gap, cursing all the while.

"You all right?"

"Bitch just scratched my neck." Var irritably wiped at the right side of his neck and the back of his hand came away bloody. "Open up, you god-accursed wenches! What's the matter with you? We're here to bloody well rescue you!"

Somewhat to Skuli's surprise, his appeal was met by the opening of the door. A middle-aged woman with dark hair and a dirty face, wearing a patchwork sack dress, stood barefoot before him, still holding her stick in her hand. Her eyes were wide with awe.

"You are men!" she declared. "Real men, not shapeshifters?"

"Damn near the last ones on these islands. How many of you are in here?" He could see there were more than a few young ones among them as they began to emerge at the sound of his voice."

"Seventeen. No, nineteen."

"Any of the male creatures around?"

"No." Her face twisted with hatred. "They left us with their bitches and pups two months ago. I don't know why."

"I do." He took her arm and tried to pull her outside, but she resisted. The fire was spreading and it was getting warmer fast. "Come with us, we have a ship. We'll bring you across the sea, to where you'll be safe. Are there any more of you?"

"Yes, but I don't know where they all are. I think they are probably together in Sigrun's cottage."

"Go out, go, go with my friend!" Skuli snapped at the other women. They were slow to move, presumably because they were afraid of him. "Go now! I'm a man, I'm not one of the damned Aalvarg!"

"It's all right." The middle-aged woman reached out and touched two of the younger children to reassure them. "These men have come to help us. Go with the big one."

"Where do you want them?" The All-Strong had already picked up one little girl, who was still staring at him, wide-eyed, in apparent disbelief.

"Bring them to the edge of the woods, where we waited before the attack. Stay with them. I'll see if I can find the others."

"I will show you," the woman said. She raised her stick. "I am not afraid."

Skuli laughed, but in approval, not contempt. If this one still had spirit after what she must have been through for the last few years, maybe there was hope for the Dalarn after all.

"Let's go then." This time, she didn't resist, as the others were already outside. "I'm the Skullbreaker."

"I am Dagrid."

She led him past several rows of the town's ramshackle buildings, to a weathered wooden house that was a little larger than the others. More importantly, its roof was not thatched, which was presumably why the other women had taken shelter inside it. Dagrid rapped on the door with her stick.

"Sigrun! Sigrun! Come out! There are men, true men, here to save us!"

Skuli could hear the sound of something being pushed away from the door, then it opened to reveal the dirty face of a pretty, young Dalarn woman with dark, unkempt hair. Her blue eyes were anxious as she looked Skuli up and down, as if searching for something.

"You're not one of them!" she exclaimed.

"No," he smiled grimly, sheathing his sword. "Some have even called me Wolfsbane. How many are you?"

"Eleven in all. I am the oldest. But where will we go? If we leave, they will hunt us down and kill us!"

"Not where we're taking you. We have a longboat, not far from here. We're taking you across the *Hvit Sjø*, to the southlands. All that remained of the clans have left the Isles. We are the last men."

The pretty woman stared at him, as if she scarcely dared to believe him, but then she took his hand and kissed it. "How we have prayed to the gods that you would come, Wolfsbane!"

Skuli blinked and stepped back, startled by the depth of feeling that her words stirred in his breast. He had thought he was ready to die, he believed that he was more than ready for the great feasting hall where the Strongbow and so many of his brothers-in-arms already dwelled, but something in the young woman's gesture awoke his desire to live, not only to save his people, but to avenge the tens of thousands who had fallen. Dagrid had already pushed past him to go inside and gather the others.

"Follow us," he told her as a fair-haired young girl peeped out cautiously from behind her. "The others are waiting."

It did not take long for the women and children to join them outside, although several of them cried out in fear at the sight of the flames that were rapidly advancing towards them, leaping from roof to roof. Nor were they reassured by the anguished howls of dying wolf-demons, as the flames devoured them or they were cut down by the vengeful warriors. Skuli, led them, sword in hand, through the burning village, with Dagrid bringing up the rear. It was not long before he caught sight of the All-Strong and the others on the edge of the forest. Engli the Black was there too, his blade still red and dripping with wolf-blood in the light of the flickering flames, but there were also more women and children than there should have been, at least ten more than the twenty he'd been expecting to see.

"She's not one of us!" a young blonde woman shrieked in a thick accent that Skuli could barely understand, pointing at a naked dark-haired woman who was standing behind a similarly unclothed young girl with her hands protectively placed upon her shoulders. "She's a shapechanger!"

"She's lying!" shouted the dark-haired woman. Her accent was, if anything, even thicker. "She's the *Awlferg!*"

Engli looked at Skuli in confusion. He looked from one woman to the other as if trying decide which one to stab. Skuli knew he had to act quickly, before his men decided to kill them all just to be on the safe side.

"Just wait!" he ordered. He waved the middle-aged woman forward. "Which one of these is the shapechanger?"

"Her." She pointed decisively at the dark-haired woman.

"She's lying!" the woman spat back.

Skuli sighed, and much to his own surprise, found himself thinking back fondly to those simpler days of being outnumbered and surrounded by hordes of slavering wolves. At least then you didn't have to think about who merited killing and who didn't. His instinct told him that Dagrid was telling the truth, but his experience of the demonically cunning *sigskifting* made him wary of trusting anyone.

"What do you think?" he asked the All-Strong. He didn't bother asking the Black, knowing what his answer would be. And while the big warrior wasn't known for his wits, he did have a way of cutting straight through to the core of things.

The All-Strong didn't answer. Instead, he grabbed a torch from young Olæif and held it close to the face of the girl he'd carried out from the village. She blinked at the brightness of the flame and instinctively jerked her face away from it, but aside from the puzzled glare she shot at the big warrior, her reaction was entirely normal. Var nodded, then thrust the torch toward the face of the dark-haired woman's daughter.

Even Engli leaped back at the horrific transformation of the girl in the face of the flickering flames. She snarled like a beast and her jaw was distorted by the bestial fangs that erupted from her mouth as she recoiled violently from the torch. But the Black was the first to react, as he punched his blade under the chin of the girl's mother just as her fingers began to elongate. Var jabbed at the girl again with the torch, but this time he put his weight behind it and smashed it into the demon-pup's monstrous face like a club, then followed it up with a thrust of his sword that shattered her breastbone and killed her instantly.

It was hard for Skuli to tell who was more terrified, the Aalvarg, their former slaves, or his warriors. The panicked wolf-pups were showing their true forms even as their shapeshifting mothers tried to drag them off into the safety of the dark forest, the real women were screaming and begging frantically for their lives, and the men were slashing wildly at every Aalvarg within reach, no matter its size or age. In a matter of moments, most of the pups and bitches were down on the ground, dead or dying.

"Alive!" he shouted. "I need one alive!"

The explosion of violence was over nearly as soon as it started. Skuli, who hadn't managed to do more than shove Dagrid down at the base of a tree and stand guard over her, looked around to assess the damage. Hjort One-Ear was standing over the corpse of one bitch, viciously cursing her as he attempted to staunch the bleeding on his left forearm from a deep gash she'd inflicted upon him. Engli was covered in blood from head to toe, but none of it was his own. Dagrid had gotten to her feet and was attempting to comfort the women, who were in shock at the sight of the fallen *sigskifting* all around them. Several were on their knees, keening over the body of an older woman clad in a ragged dress.

"What happened here?"

"Sorry, Skullbreaker." A chagrined Olæif indicated the dead woman with his bloody sword. "She was running toward me and I thought she was a shapechanger."

"Never you mind that," Skulli told him and slapped him on the shoulder. "But will someone please tell me if we managed to capture any of the cursed things alive?"

"I got one," he heard the All-Strong call from behind him. "Don't nobody do nothing!"

Skuli turned and saw the big warrior holding what looked like a young girl by the hair with one hand, and the edge of his sword to her throat with the other. Behind him crept a *sigskifting*, mostly in its woman form, except for its rage-filled yellow eyes. Its mother, he assumed.

"After I caught the pup, I told her *mor* to come along behind me. I said you'll spare the little one if she tells you what you want to know." The pup, frightened, was trying to pull away from the All-Strong and reach her mother's side, but the All-Strong's grip on her long, brown hair was unyielding.

"If you will spare her, I will tell you everything I can." The bitch was having some trouble talking, and Skuli realized that her teeth were still in the process of returning to their false human shape. He'd seen the dreadful process once or twice before, though usually the other way, from man to wolf, and it took some doing to restrain his instinct to kill both of the surviving Aalvarg at once.

"Hasn't there been enough killing tonight?" Dagrid said quietly.

Skuli snorted, causing a few of the men to laugh. "They don't call me the Skullbreaker because I'm in the habit of allowing my enemies to live, woman." But as the bitch's lips began to draw back in a snarl and she shifted her weight in readiness for a desperate bid to free her pup, Skuli raised his free hand.

"Just this once, I will make an exception for you, wolfling, but I want to know everything you know about that ruined fortress to the north of here."

"*Hrrahgrijawah*," she growled incomprehensibly.

"I don't know what that means."

"It's what we call the Black Tower. We don't go there. It's where she lives."

Skuli glanced at Engli, who shrugged. Neither of them knew what she was talking about. "Where who lives?"

"*Giavuhlensmor*. The great devil mother. She is dead and she is terrible and she devours all who go to her."

"She's dead, but she still eats... what?"

"Anything. Everything. But mostly, she devours men. The *kowahring* tell us she will grow strong and live again, and lead us across the sea to a land where there are deer and rabbits and better things to eat than men, but I think they lie. She is still dead. And the deer are no more."

Skuli was thoroughly confused. He knew the creatures were not natural, and that someone, or something must have created them with the aid of either some very evil magic or a very powerful demon, but he was having trouble grasping what a devil mother might be, and just how awful a monster it must be for creatures as foul and bloody-minded as the Aalvarg to describe her as terrible. And yet, he thought it was very likely that it might have something to do with the origins of the wolf-things, given the way they called it 'mother'.

The Black appeared to be thinking on the same lines. "I think she's talking about their priests. Maybe the devil mother is their god?"

"Or their maker."

"You let her go now. I tell you more, but first you let her go!" The Aalvarg mother was insistent. Skuli looked at the women, but only Dagrid had the courage to speak.

"She wasn't a bad sort, as they went."

He nodded to the All-Strong, who released the little shapechanger. No sooner had he done so than the bitch snarled at her pup, and with a frightened whine, it fled into the darkness of the nearby trees.

Skuli was still interrogating the bitch when Two-Daggers and the rest
of the men arrived. They had two young girls with them, who Dagrid
confirmed were exactly what they seemed. Unfortunately, despite his best
efforts, he was unable to get much more out of the Aalvarg that made any
sense to him or anyone else, and the women, half-naked and in shock, were
badly in need of some warm clothes and a fire. Olæif had gone to fetch
Alrik and the first girl that they'd captured, while Egli bound the captured
Aalvarg's hands behind her back and stuffed a wadded rag into her mouth.

"Don't think this'll hold her if she changes, Skullbreaker," the Black said
as he tied a second rag around the creature's head to prevent her from
spitting out the gag. "We should put her in chains, maybe some silver too,
once we get back to the ship."

Skuli nodded. He wasn't concerned with the captured Aalvarg, as he was
too occupied with thinking through the various possibilities suggested by
its account of whatever strange monster lived in the black ruins to the north.
Could it be that this being was actually connected to the first appearance
of the Aalvarg in the isles? And could it perhaps be possible that they could
somehow harm the Aalvarg by destroying it? For the first time in his war-
torn life, Skuli felt that he might finally find an answer to why the cruel
gods of his people had permitted the cursed wolf-demons to descend upon
them.

This sounded like exactly the sort of thing he'd dreamed of finding when
he'd set off from Raknarborg. What better way to end the Skullbreaker's
saga than by seeking revenge for all the Dalarn people who'd fallen to the
Aalvarg over the last three decades? And yet, how could he permit himself
and his men to continue their voyage of the doomed now that they were
burdened by twenty women, most of them young and fertile, who must be
brought across the sea to safety? Even finding space for them on *Ulvdræber*
would be difficult; it was simply not going to be possible to bring them
along on a hunt for some sort of demon goddess.

That was something to worry about tomorrow, he decided, and he raised
his hand in a signal to the men that they would return to the landing now.

THEUDERIC

THE RIDE toward the northern coast of Savondir had been an arduous one, but not unwelcome, thought Theuderic, shifting his weight in his saddle as his horse trudged up yet another hill upon the deeply-rutted dirt road. It was good to get away from the increasingly crowded camp of the Red Prince, as more peasant levies and noble retinues belatedly appeared to fulfill their annual military obligations, at least in part, accompanied by daily reinforcements for the small army of whores, merchants, and charlatans who preyed upon the amateur soldiery like vultures.

The landscape had grown gradually more hilly, and the trees a little more sparse, but what more than anything reminded Theuderic that he was back in the north was the red soil. It was more clay than dirt, and much to the annoyance of the travelers, it stuck to everything from their clothing to the horses' shoes. Every evening, he and his three companions would sit by the fire, sullenly picking off the little reddish clumps that had been kicked up by the horses and somehow become firmly attached to their cloaks, tunics, and pantalons.

They traveled sullenly, and for the most part, silently, as none of the three men-at-arms assigned to him by Étienne-Henri had proven to be particularly voluble or much interested in him or in the mission to which they had been assigned. This was a relief to Theuderic, as he had half-wondered if the heir to the throne, or perhaps his dangerous companion, Donzeau, had ordered them to kill him once they were sufficiently far from the prince's camp. But surely an assassin would feign at least some degree of sociability, if only to be able to get closer to his target without inspiring any alarm.

Theuderic spent the first night on the road sleeping sporadically with one eye open, his hand on his drawn dagger, but neither the pair who were sleeping nor the man who took the first watch ever made so much as a single movement in his direction. It wasn't until the afternoon of the next day, when he noticed the youngest of the three surreptitiously sketching a tree on his chest, presumably to ward off the evil eye, that he realized they were considerably more afraid of him than he was of them. That knowledge allowed him to relax a little, and although it didn't make the journey any more sociable, it did permit him to sleep more soundly on the journey's second night.

Although they rose early, rode quickly, and did not stop for the evening until the sun was beginning to descend in the west, Theuderic found himself enjoying the temporary respite from his military duties. Now that the long-feared reavers had finally been tamed, the north was at peace, and neither the peasants tending the flocks and fields nor the villagers in the towns they rode past appeared to be aware that a massive army of orcs was marching westward. When they stayed overnight in a small inn in the village of Droyure, Theuderic allowed himself to indulge his curiosity by asking the innkeeper if he had any concerns on that score.

"They ain't never come north afore," said the grizzled old man, whose white-streaked whiskers grew down both cheeks to meet at his chin. "Not in t'ree, four hunnert years. We never worried about t' greenskins none, 'twas t' damned rovers coming over t' White Sea t'at kept us awake at nights. It's allus rovers been afflictin' us."

"I understand that henceforth, the rovers are unlikely to be an issue," Theuderic assured him.

"And a damn good t'ing, I say!"

"A damned good thing indeed," Theuderic raised his mug of bitter ale in cordial salute. And perhaps the old innkeeper was right and the orcs would turn back, or be turned back, before they reached the northlands and ravaged it as well. But he was not sanguine about their chances for survival if the monsters did come this way. They might be farmers hardened by generations of battling a half-fertile land, but this was clearly not a land of warriors. In comparison with the men of the borderlands, they were soft, weak, and unprepared.

In the interest of bonhomie, he had purchased a local whore for his taciturn companions, which he now realized was a mistake, as the wooden walls of the inn proved to be rather thinner than he would have preferred. He was beginning to regret having declined the whore's gracious offer to go and find a friend for him, but upon further reflection, decided he had made the right decision to abstain for the evening. While the young women of Droyure were not entirely unattractive, they appeared to wear scent derived from whatever fertilizer had been most recently used on the nearby fields. A kingsmage was expected to maintain standards, after all.

It occurred to him that the engagement of his companions was presenting him with the perfect opportunity to ride off and leave them behind. In three weeks, four at most, the matter would be settled one way or another. He need only lay low for a month or so before riding to Lutèce and joining the royal army that would no doubt be gathering there under the command of the king himself. They would ask him no questions and they would trouble him for no explanations, as they would be far too delighted to know that at least one kingsmage survived the terrible battle that had claimed the life of the Red Prince, the border lords, and the brave southerners. Oh, it was certain that du Moulin would have his suspicions; the chancelier might well be in possession of six sworn attestations confirming that Theuderic had been nowhere near the battle before he even reached the capital. But the damnably clever man would never denounce him publicly, instead, he would hold Theuderic's secret in reserve, waiting for the time it would provide him with the leverage he required.

It was better to be at the beck and call of du Moulin than to feed one's flesh to the orcs. After all, he was only here because du Moulin had ordered him to spy on the prince. The coming battle would not turn on his presence. Nor would it turn on his mission, be it success or failure. He ran through the Oxonian logic in his mind.

Whether fleeing on the eve of battle is a sin?

First objection. It would seem that fleeing on the eve of battle is a sin. For that which is not just is a sin. Now it is written in praise of the just man: "The just, bold as a lion, shall be without dread." Therefore it is a sin to dread battle, especially to such an extent that one is tempted to flee from it.

Second objection. Further, nothing is so fearful as death, according to the Philosopher. Yet one ought not to fear death nor those who mete it out. "Fear ye not them that kill the body," nor anything that can be inflicted by mortals: "Who art thou, that thou shouldst be afraid of a mortal man?" Therefore it is a sin to fear death in battle, and, fearing it, flee.

Third objection. It is written: "He that feareth the Lord shall tremble at nothing." Therefore, it is a sin to fear to risk one's life in battle.

A SEA OF SKULLS

On the contrary, It is said of the unjust judge that "he feared not God nor regarded man."

I answer that, since fear is born of love, we must seemingly judge alike of love and fear. Now it is here a question of that fear whereby one dreads temporal evils, and which results from the love of temporal goods. And every man has it instilled in him by nature to love his own life and whatever is directed thereto; and to do so in due measure, that is, to love these things not as placing his end therein, but as things to be used for the sake of his last end. Hence it is contrary to the natural inclination, and therefore a sin, to fall short of loving them in due measure. Nevertheless, one never lapses entirely from this love: since what is natural cannot be wholly lost: for which reason the Apostle says: "No man ever hated his own flesh." Wherefore even those that slay themselves do so from love of their own flesh, which they desire to free from present stress. Hence it may happen that a man fears death and other temporal evils less than he ought, for the reason that he loves them less than he ought. But that he fear none of these things cannot result from an entire lack of love, but only from the fact that he thinks it impossible for him to be afflicted by the evils contrary to the goods he loves. This is sometimes the result of pride of soul presuming on self and despising others, according to the saying of Jobe: "He was made to fear no one, he beholdeth every high thing": and sometimes it happens through a defect in the reason; thus the Philosopher says that the "Orcs, through lack of intelligence, fear nothing." It is therefore evident that fearlessness is a vice, whether it result from lack of love, pride of soul, or dullness of understanding: yet the latter is excused from sin if it be invincible.

Reply to Objection 1. The just man is praised for being without fear that withdraws him from good; not that he is altogether fearless, for it is written: "He that is without fear cannot be justified."

Reply to Objection 2. Death and whatever else can be inflicted by mortal man are not to be feared so that they make us forsake duty and justice: but they are to be feared as hindering man in acts of virtue, either as regards himself, or as regards the progress he may cause in others. Hence it is written: "A wise man feareth and declineth from evil." And surely death in battle is an evil worthy of declining!

Reply to Objection 3. It is also written: "When you are persecuted in one place, flee to another." Therefore, when one is in fear for one's life, it cannot be a sin to preserve it by fleeing the danger, even if the fear which inspires the act of flight is, in itself, sinful.

And thus I prove it is the good, right, and moral thing to flee on the eve of battle. *Quod erat demonstrandum!*

Theuderic knew it wasn't death that he feared; he had risked his life in battle far too many times to believe himself a simple coward. It was more the thought of utter defeat, or rather, experiencing the sort of life-shattering, soul-killing defeat from which a man could never hope to recover, even if he survived physically unscathed. He had never known such a defeat himself, but he had seen it more than once from the perspective of the victor. He recognized the guilt, the despair, and worst of all, the shame he had seen in the eyes of the defeated, even in the eyes of those who should never have seriously believed themselves to be capable of victory in the first place. In many of those grimy, blood-stained faces he had borne witness to the dispiriting wounds that catastrophic defeat inflicted on the souls of those who had rebelled against the Crown, or against their rightful liege lord, and it was not something he ever wished to experience himself.

And yet, even as he reached the inescapable conclusion that flight was the only rational decision for a reasonable man in his position, he knew that he would never go through with it.

For better or for worse, he would, at the very least, see through this futile search for nonexistent magic-killing clerics and return to the Red Prince's side. Perhaps he would be fortunate, and the orcs would arrive sooner than anticipated, or perhaps Étienne-Henri would send him away again before the battle began. He sighed, very much doubting that fortune was reserving any such happy fate for him, rolled over on the hay-stuffed bed, and attempted to ignore the laughter, curses, and other noises coming from the adjoining room.

They arrived at the Abbaye de Pergaud just before noon on the sixth day of their ride. It stood outside the little town that had grown up around the abbey over the years, and the crumbling state of its walls testified to the relative peace of the region. A pair of priests came out to meet them; they wore the dark red robes of their order, which was devoted to the first martyr, Saint Étienne.

Theuderic found himself musing on the irony of the Red Prince's namesake. He found it hard to imagine a less likely martyr than the prince. Even if the young man did acquit himself well in the coming battle and resisted the temptation to flee the field before his men were overwhelmed by the monstrous green tide, it would be for the sake of his pride, and not for any love or fear of God.

"Blessings and salutations, strangers." The taller of the two priests called out to them as he made a gesture of holy benediction. "Do you come in the peace of Our Risen Seigneur?"

"We come in the name of the King and in the service of His Royal Highness, Étienne-Henri."

The priest nodded. If he was impressed by Theuderic's words, he managed to hide it well.

"We do not often see servants of the Red Prince here. Still less often are we visited by royal magiciens. But you are welcome here all the same, Seigneur...."

"Theuderic," he answered the priest's implied question. "We shall not trouble you long. I am here to speak with several of the monks I am told reside here in the monastery, men who do not belong to your order, but are sworn to the service of Saint Michel."

This time, the priest's eyes flickered, and he glanced at his companion before replying.

"It appears you have traveled a long way, Seigneur Theuderic. Am I correct in assuming your visit is of some urgency?"

"To the Prince and to the Realm," Theuderic assured him. "Are they here?"

"I think it would be best if you were to speak first to the Abbé. Would you prefer to see him at once or may I first offer you and your men some refreshment?"

Theuderic smiled. The priest's unexpected evasion was almost certain assurance that his travels had not been entirely in vain, and it was a good sign that while the Étiennite clearly preferred to warn the abbé of his arrival, the priest had nevertheless left the matter to his own discretion. If Michelines were not here, it was likely that the abbé would know where they were. He decided there was no reason to rush matters, and besides, he had always found it best to honor the proprieties when dealing with men of influence, particularly those of a religious persuasion.

"I should appreciate the latter, Monsieur. I would prefer to make myself presentable before intruding upon His Révérence."

After following the priests into the abbey, they were given over to a pair of young novices who escorted them to a pair of simple rooms that apparently served as a guest chambers. The rooms were small and contained little more than a pair of cots and a table each, but the ceilings were high and the air was fresh thanks to the small windows that looked out over the nearby fields of wheat, sugarbeets, and what promised to eventually transform into a golden field of mustard.

Theuderic ordered the cleanest and quietest member of his entourage to share his room, and thanked the novice who brought him a large bowl of water and a clean cloth with which he could wash the dust of the journey from his face. He was pleasantly surprised to discover that the water had recently been heated, and he sighed with pleasure as he splashed it repeatedly over his face. Another novice arrived with a bowl of fruit and a loaf of bread, which he shared with his companion in silence.

He had barely finished his second apple when the tall priest knocked at the wall next to his open door, flanked by a new pair of novices.

"Seigneur Theuderic, the Abbé will see you now, if you are ready."

"Excellent," Theuderic replied, standing aside to permit the novices to clear away the water bowl and the remains of his repast. As they departed, he retrieved the leather satchel which contained his credentials in the event they would prove necessary.

"Have you any need to visit the middens first?"

"I believe that can wait, Monsieur."

"Very well. If you will follow me?"

As Theuderic followed the priest through the twists and turns of the abbey, he noted a distinct absence of the tapestries and artwork that decorated the churches and cathedrals of Lutèce with which he was more familiar. It seemed they lived a humble life here, these religious in the north, and he wondered if this was an indication that the abbé might be inclined to cause him some difficulties in accomplishing his mission. A letter bearing the seal of the royal heir would serve to command obedience from any knight or noble in the kingdom, but it might not impress a man more accustomed to addressing the King of Kings than one of his mortal subjects.

The abbé received him in a large chamber that appeared to be reserved for formal receptions, with tapestries displaying familiar scenes from the Writ and well-padded couches that would comfortably seat old men with weary bones for hours on end. On either side of the room, three monks knelt in seeming prayer, although Theuderic suspected that at least two of the six men were armed. The abbé himself was a short man of peasant stock, although his keen eyes belied an otherwise stolid appearance. He did not smile as Theuderic entered the room, but nodded civilly enough as Theuderic was introduced by the tall priest.

"Révérence, I present Monseigneur Theuderic, a royal servant of His Majesty the King, in service to His Royal Highness, the Red Prince. Monseigneur Theuderic, the Revered Father Loic, Abbé of the Abbaye de Pergaud and the brethren of Saint Étienne."

"Révérence," Theuderic said, bowing rather more deeply than he ever had to Étienne-Henri.

"Greetings, my son. What brings a royal battlemage to this little band of religious brothers so far from the wars and intrigues in the south?"

"Necessity. A great battle will be fought very soon. The prince will be outnumbered, both in terms of men and magiciens, by the armies of the Great Orc."

"A battle? How soon is soon?" The abbé looked concerned, but not surprised.

"Weeks. A month at most."

"So soon! This is distressing news, my son, but I can offer nothing more than my prayers. I'm sure you know I have neither fighting men nor magiciens to give you."

"I am not here to make a request, Révérence. I am rather here to demand—in the name of the Red Prince and the defense of the realm—the services of certain priests I have been told are resident here in this abbey."

The abbé nodded. "You are aware that the Order of Saint Michel was suppressed throughout the realm some years ago, by the order of the King's father?"

"I was not. Was it really?"

"It was, I assure you. In fact, the banishment accomplished at the behest of the grandmaster of your own order."

Theuderic nodded. That made sense. No Immortel, still less the Grand Magicien, would tolerate priests who could, supposedly, negate all his formidable powers with little more than a word and a prayer. And, it occurred to him, that might have even been the original cause of the rift between Crown and Sanctum which he had journeyed to Amorr to help mitigate.

"Theological history is not my forte, Révérence. And while I do not hesitate to take you at your word, I fail to see how these matters affect my mission in any way."

The abbé graced him with a benevolent smile. "Do you not, my son? Then you are blessed with a soul devoid of an instinct for politicking, whatever other sins might weigh upon it. My question to you is this: how can I release to you men who are under my protection—if we assume, for

the sake of argument, that your information about their location is correct—
when their very presence in this realm is forbidden? Do you carry any
document promising immunity or containing any other sureties of their
safety?"

"No, Révérence, I am afraid I do not."

"This place is a sanctuary, magicien. Not even the King's royal hand
reaches so far. If even men who are guilty of murder, blasphemy, and worse
crimes find protection in The Immaculate's house, how much more shall
blameless men of God who have committed no crime do so?"

Theuderic frowned. He could see the abbé's point. This was one place
where the King's writ simply did not run. It did not matter that the letter
he carried was in order, stamped and sealed by the Red Prince himself. And
assuming that it was true that the Michelines had been suppressed—and
he had no reason to doubt that they had been—they were then, in the eyes
of the law, criminals with the right to claim sanctuary within the abbey
grounds.

"What assurances can I give you, Révérence? All I can promise is that
these men will face no peril that my colleagues and I will not share. No,
I can also promise you that if we fail and the orcs prevail, then you will
have accomplished nothing. Instead of fighting in company with the king's
finest mages and men-at-arms, they will be forced to stand with old farmers
armed with rusted pikes and young boys carrying pitchforks. What you
offer them is not sanctuary, but an even more certain death!"

"I should not like to do that. Are you willing to pledge their safe return
here after the battle?"

"I am." Theuderic smiled. "Subject to our mutual survival, of course."

"Of course. And do you truly believe a handful of men could make a
difference in a battle of such magnitude."

"I know the Prince is in dire need of every single man who can bear a
blade, Révérence. And if these priests can truly do what is said of them,
each man will be worth more than one hundred men-at-arms."

"Then we should not discount them. Our Lord and Savior only required
twelve, after all. So that is the salient question, is it not? If they can do what
is claimed of them, or not."

The abbé's surreptitious glance at one of the hooded monks on his left
did not escape Theuderic's notice. Perhaps not a bodyguard, but one of
the Michaelines he sought? He looked the man up and down, but aside
from the monk's broad shoulders and the unremarkable brown robe he wore,
there were no useful details that Theuderic could glean.

"Are you suggesting you will consider releasing them to me if it can be shown that they can be of service to the Prince?"

"I will, on two conditions. First, they must consent to go with you. Second, I wish to see that they can provide you with the services the Prince is expecting. Am I correct in assuming that you know little more about their abilities than I do?"

"I only know what I have been told, Révérence. But the King's ban on their order suggests that what I have been told is true."

The abbé nodded. "And yet we need not rely on logic when we possess the wherewithal to determine the truth, my son. Have you a particular artifice that you favor, when you wish to do someone harm?"

"An artifice?" It took Theuderic a moment to understand. "Do you mean a spell? A *magic* spell?"

"Indeed."

"Here?" Theuderic was incredulous. "Right here in the chapel?"

"Where better?" The abbé gestured at the carved tree mounted on the wall, from which the Immaculate was suspended in his holy agony. "Are we not men of faith? Do you truly believe my faith in the Almighty God is any less than yours in your own sorceries? Where better to test those iniquitous powers than right here, in the House of the Holy?"

"Will you promise that I will not be punished if you are harmed?"

"You will be held blameless, by God and man, should your magics injure me in any way. My word on it."

"How can I question the word of one who speaks for both God and Man, Révérence?" Theuderic bowed slightly. "You are prepared?"

"I am." The abbé crossed himself. "Do your worst, magicien."

Theuderic nodded. The fireball was not the problem, what concerned him was the second spell he would have to cast to put out the magical flames before they burned the naive priest to cinders. There was no source of water nearby upon which he could draw to inundate the fire, and any of the wind spells at his command would run the risk of setting the entire chapel alight.

"At least you need not fear the flames of Hell, Révérence."

Theuderic smiled, raised his hands, summoned his power… and discovered that it simply did not rise inside him as he expected. He could sense it within him, but somehow, he could not access it. It was as if something had been severed; his inability to call it forth did not feel the way it did when he had exhausted himself. Nor was it as if he did not know the spell, for then the sensation would swell inside him, sometimes to the point of discomfort, as if the magic must find a way out of him before he burst.

"I can't... it isn't there!" he finally exclaimed. "I mean, it is there, I can feel it, but I can't reach it!"

"Praise be to God!" the abbé raised his hands in thanksgiving, and perhaps just a little relief.

Theuderic stared at the holy man, astonished. Then he turned toward the monk in the middle and pointed at him. "You!"

The hooded man glanced at the abbé, who nodded and bade him to stand. Slowly, the man rose to his feet, then slipped back his hood to reveal a strong, bearded face, bronzed by sun and lined with age, and dark eyes that did not fear to meet Theuderic's.

"You are a Michaeline."

"For my sins, I am a priest sworn to Saint Michael, my lord." Theuderic was impressed that the man did not hesitate to admit his membership in the banned order. "His Révérence has been kind enough to provide shelter here to me and my brothers in our time of need."

Theuderic's heart rejoiced, but he forced himself to remain impassive, as befit a Kingsmage.

"Your brothers? How many are with you?"

"Eight now. Once, we were eleven, but one returned to Amorr and two others elected to join another order when ours was named anathema by His Majesty the king."

"Sanctimonious, more like," muttered one of the other hooded monks, but he fell silent at a gesture from the first Michaeline.

"What are your assurances worth, Kingsmage? Will your liege ignore his own grandfather's dictate? Will he resist the pressure from l'Académie?"

"I can assure you that his Royal Highness cares nothing for the opinions of his late ancestors." Theuderic smiled scornfully. "What is your name, warrior-priest?"

"Emil, my lord."

"Then think on this, Brother Emil. By the time this war is over and the last orc has been chased back to its mountains, your order may well be restored. The king who banned you is dead. I expect his Majesty will think well of those who stood with his son against the devilish sorceries of the orcs." He spread his hands. "When war stalks the land, even those who hate and fear powers like yours must see the value in them."

"And what of your colleagues?" The abbé stepped forward and placed a hand on the Michaeline's shoulder. "It is said that your Grandmagicien, what is his name?"

"D'Arseille."

"It is said that Seigneur d'Arseille is powerful in the councils of the king."

Theuderic shrugged. "It is not d'Arseille who has the king's ear. It is the Chancelier, du Moulin. Of this, I can assure you. And if he sees utility in the Order of Saint Michael, if these priests can prove their worth to him, it would not surprise me if they found themselves restored by royal decree."

The hooded monks murmured amongst themselves, which Theuderic took to be a good sign. His impression was confirmed when, after Brother Emil whispered something to the abbé, His Révérence nodded and pointed to a monk standing unobtrusively near the entrance.

"Bring the Kingsmage his staff, Brother Onfroi."

As the man slipped out of the chamber, Theuderic raised an inquiring eyebrow at the abbé.

"You are not a man of God, Kingsmage. I will not ask you to swear an oath upon the Holy Writ."

"Is it not written in that Writ that one must refrain from oaths, and take a man's yes for yes, and no for no?"

"As I have said, you are not a man of God." His Révérence was smiling but his eyes were cold. "Therefore, you will swear to these men, before me and the Immaculate, that you will not permit them to be turned over to the king or his officials, and you will do your utmost to see that they return safely here once the orcs are defeated. And you will do so on your staff, which I am given to understand is of some value to your kind."

Theuderic nodded slowly. An oath, of course, meant nothing to him. As a Kingsmage and a nobleman, the only vow that mattered was the one he'd made to the Crown of Savondir. But he could see that the abbé was a formidable man, and one he would not wish to have as an enemy.

And so, he bowed.

"I will do as you command, Révérence. And then, with your leave, we will depart this evening."

"Say rather tomorrow morning, my son. There are preparations to be made, prayers to be prayed, and who knows? Perhaps even you might wish to confess your sins whilst you are among us."

It was an amusing thought. Theuderic couldn't help laughing out loud. "I'm afraid there's no time for that, Your Révérence. The orcs would be here before I even came close to finishing."

BERETH

THE SKY was grey and full of clouds, but it was worrisomely barren of birds. Not of all birds, exactly, as a large flock of starlings were whirling about to the west in one of their strange cabalistic sky-rituals, but of the sort of birds she was expecting. She had seen crows, buzzards, kites, and even a stork today, but since noon, not a single warhawk had arrived.

She heard someone emerge from the tower steps out onto the roof and call out to her. She turned and saw it was Lord Oakenheart.

"There won't be any more coming," the elf lord told her as she stared at him, ashen-faced. She looked up at the sky in disbelief; it was empty of anything but clouds. Where were the hawks that were supposed to be bringing at least twenty more of the Collegium's spellcasters she and the prince's command staff had decided were required for their plan of attack.

"He said he'd bring them all! He said he'd bring them in his bird's beak if he had to!"

The commander of the High Guard laughed mirthlessly.

"Prince Hoelion is not the king, Bereth. The Council has decided we cannot afford to risk everything on a single throw. The High King supports their decision."

"They're cowards!" she cried.

"Essentially. They may be powerful sorcerers, but they're also old and set in their ways. I expect half of them are more frightened of being flown out here than they are of the Great Orc or his shamans. One hundred thousand orcs is a difficult concept to fathom if you haven't seen it from on high. But falling off the back of a flying bird? That's all too easy to imagine."

"So what are we going to do?"

He laughed, genuinely amused this time. "What choice do you think we have, Bereth? What we will do is follow the king's orders to the full extent of our abilities. We will kill as many of them as we can, then we will hold these walls and trust that Valrond got his cursed calculations wrong. They're mostly theoretical, after all. Personally, I don't believe a word he says. What is the last siege he saw with his own eyes, Glaislael? That was centuries ago!"

"Do you really think he is wrong, my lord?"

"How would I know? I don't know a cursed thing about sieges. But as long as orcs don't sprout wings, I don't see why we can't keep them out. Our magecraft is considerably stronger than theirs. And the High Guard rules the skies."

"We are too few," she muttered, looking at her feet.

"Yes, we are. But it's hardly your fault–"

"It's not going to work." She looked up at the too-empty skies in despair. "We won't have enough mages to do half what we were intending. And if we don't have the traps, we may not be able to extricate the horse, let alone the foot, my lord!"

The tall elf smiled, a little indulgently. "I think we need not fear overmuch for them. Even if we cannot spring most of the traps you envisioned, the Lord Commanders are well-versed in safely extricating their elves from the battlefield. Nor is the High Guard entirely helpless. A few timely fireballs thrown in the right place would permit forces much less disciplined than ours to retreat without meeting much in the way of resistance."

"Lord Commander!" They both looked up to see a skyrider circling over their heads. "The Horse Lord sends his compliments and asks if you would send out as many squadrons as you can spare to cover his retreat!"

"Retreat?" the elf lord frowned. He glanced at Bereth. "They must be under more pressure than we expected."

He cupped his hands around his mouth. "Retreat?" he queried loudly.

"The Great Orc has sent a large cavalry force around them to the west. He's trying to cut them off before they can join us here."

Lord Oakenheart held up his hand for a moment and looked down at the stones of the tower, thinking furiously. Then he held up his hands, palms together, to indicate a positive response, and waved both hands at the elf on the hawk. The skyrider raised a fist in salute, the giant bird beat its wings, and rapidly grew smaller as it flew north.

"What are we going to do?"

"Stop that cavalry from cutting off Malchderas and the infantry. There must be a considerable quantity of them if he fears being unable to reach these walls."

"Warboars?"

"I should think so. I doubt wolfriders would concern him overmuch."

Remembering how easily the Horse Lord had slaughtered thousands of them the last time she'd been in battle, Bereth couldn't argue with his conclusion. "I'll go find Lassarian. Is he here?"

"No, he was on patrol this morning." He smiled at her. "Will you not ride with me? I could use your bow, and Ilriathas tells me there is no use in attempting to persuade you to stay here."

"I don't have enough arrows." She only had the one quiver.

"Go to the armory. Take those with the biggest heads you can find. I'm going to tell the Prince-General the news; if he's amenable, I'll send two squadrons to reinforce the patrols and everyone else will fly northwest to delay their flanking action."

"Thank you, Lord Commander!" She'd never flown with him before, much less in battle. "I am honored."

"Just don't fall off," he said wryly. "Lord Kelethan will murder me if I let anything happen to you. Now go. Get your bow and meet me at the aerie."

He turned away and preceded her down the stone stairs of the tower, taking them two at a time. But when he turned off to enter the central building, she continued to make her way down to the armory underground. It was a long way down the circular staircase by the time she reached the bottom, and her legs were already aching with the awareness that she would have to mount all of them again soon. But the torches flared to light as she walked through the open door that connected the staircase to the tower warehouse, and the two young elves set to guarding it had obviously heard her coming, as they were standing as straight-backed and motionless as if they were on public review. They'd probably thought she was an officer come to inspect them, she thought, and she nodded at them as she passed.

The elf in charge of the armory was considerably older, with the almost imperceptible stillness and distant air that tended to come with great age. He did not smile, but his eyes seemed to focus as she approached and bowed respectfully to him.

"I am Bereth mer Eulenarias, a rider with the High Guard. I am in need of three quivers, preferably shafts with heads that can pierce boarskin."

The ancient elf nodded indifferently and waved her through. He gestured vaguely towards the back of the large, low-ceilinged chamber, and she saw a pair of flames erupt off to her right. "Over there."

"Thank you," she said. The master of the armory only grunted and closed his eyes, returning to his reverie.

She made her way past wooden crates and boxes, past stacks of round painted shields made of oak and larger, more rectangular shields leafed in steel. There was row after row of metal breastpieces and vambraces for the infantry, piles of boiled leather armor for archers and militia, and a huge array of bows that caught her attention, and for a moment, made her forget what she'd come for. She ran her hand over one massive walnut bow, exquisitely carved, that must have belonged to a great elf lord now vanished into the depths of time. It would have too much pull for her, indeed, it might well be more than Lassarian or Ilirathas could manage, but it was a beautiful weapon and she marveled at the skill of its maker. It was a weapon for a hero, and as she knew all too well, there were no heroes to be found in Elebrion these days.

Unfortunately, the bows were followed by large bundles of rods, which upon further investigation turned out to be pikes and spears. There must have been more than twenty thousand of them, she quickly calculated, ruefully reflecting upon the much smaller number of militia she'd seen marching towards the fortress while en route herself. How easy it would be to turn back the orcs, as his fathers had done so many times before, if only King Mael could send out even half as many elves as the Great Orc was hurling against them! Then she shrugged and patted the comforting rough surface of a nearby pillar. The magically-reinforced walls of Tir Diffaith were strong enough to break the Great Orc's army like waves crashing harmlessly on stone.

Finally, she came to the arrows. There were thousands, and they came in five different varieties. There were green-fletched needle-nosed arrows for target shooting, red-fletched arrows with small two-barbed arrowheads for hunting, red-and-green fletched arrows with heavier, three-barbed heads that would serve well for goblins, orange-fletched shafts that were the conventional elven war arrows, and yellow-fletched arrows with wicked heads made up of four sharpened edges specially designed to punch through leather armor or thick boarskin. There were also purple-fletched arrows, but after drawing one out, she swiftly slipped it back into the bundle when she saw the white, crumbled substance that was coating the arrowhead. Poison could be effective, but in the heat of battle, when one rapidly drew and nocked one arrow after another without looking, it was much too easy to scratch oneself without even realizing it.

She gathered six bundles of the yellow-feathered shafts and stacked them neatly on the stone floor, then went in search of quivers in which to carry them aloft.

She found them nearby; there was a surprisingly wide variety of embroidered and painted quivers adorned with the signs and sigils of various lords and families. A few of them she recognized, but most were unfamiliar to her. She made a face as she examined one age-yellowed quiver on which had been painted, in cracked and fading colors, a spread-eagled goblin with its hands and feet pierced by spikes. Some old traditions were better lost to time. She selected three plain leather quivers more on the basis of size and the fact that they had long straps that would make them easier to secure to Lord Oakenheart's saddle, when a gaudy quiver half-full of black-and-red fletched arrows caught her eye.

Unlike the other decorated quivers, it was neither painted nor embroidered, but was encrusted with garnets and opals. They were arranged in a design that suggested flames, and when she drew out one of the long shafts, she gasped aloud at the unmistakable sense of an old magic radiating from the heavy, black-iron arrowhead on the end. She examined it more closely and saw that it was inscribed with a spell all along the length of the arrow, from the head to the fletching, while the iron head was stamped with sigils she did not recognize. The script carved into the wood was hard to read, but she was able to make out two words: *laddais* and *nraigh*.

She whistled softly in astonishment and withdrew another arrow. It, too, was carved with the same spell, although the sigils on the head appeared to be different. She quickly confirmed that the rest of the arrows were also imbued with magic; they were weapons from an age long past, dragon killers from a time when the great beasts still filled the skies with lightning and fire. She began to slip the quiver back on the hook from which it had been suspended when it occurred to her that she might do very well to have an arrow or two that was capable of defeating even dragon armor. After all, trolls had been spotted in the orc camp, and who knew what further surprises the Great Orc might have in store for them. She selected two of the arcane arrows, hesitated, and then withdrew a third.

She carried the quivers and the three arrows over to where she'd stacked the yellow-fletched shafts and spent a few moments filling all three of them. She thought momentarily about putting one dragon-killer in each quiver, but thought better of it and put all three in the same one before slipping the quivers over her shoulder. She was just feeling her way back towards the lights at the entrance when she placed her free hand on a rough canvas sack and felt something sharp nearly pierce her hand. She stifled a cry and felt at the sack, wondering what was inside. It felt like a small orb, but with four spikes protruding from it. Caltrops!

Would they work on boar hooves, she wondered? Then it occurred to her that a warhawk could carry a considerable quantity of them, and, more importantly, being struck by one falling from the sky might well slow down a boar, or its rider. And any that didn't strike home might very well end up embedded in a warboar's hoof. She shifted the quivers to free her other hand, and worked one of the insidious little devices out of the bag. The spikes weren't long, not much longer than her index finger, but the orb gave it just enough weight that it might do to crack even a boar's thick skull. It probably wouldn't pierce a metal helmet; she thought the spike would probably break first, but it might well stun the rider badly enough to knock him off his mount.

She grunted as she withdrew a sack; there seemed to be about one hundred caltrops inside. With some difficulty, she managed to get her arms around it and carry it out to where the old elf was sitting, still lost in his thoughts. Or, more likely, his memories.

"I see you found what you needed?" he commented idly as she dropped the heavy sack of caltrops to the floor with a loud crash.

"Yes, and thank you," she said. "Guards!"

The taller of the two guards entered the chamber and eyed her warily. "Is there a problem?"

"No, I just need you to talk to the master here and bring as many of these to the aerie as you can. Right away!" She pushed at the back with her foot. "I'll send more help down, but in the meantime, you and your companion out there must bring up as many as you can."

The guard's expression didn't change, but she could all but feel the affronted disapproval radiating from his body. "On whose authority, *merchogion?*"

"On the Prince-General's," she snapped. "Is that sufficient?"

The guard stiffened. "It is. But we are under orders not to leave our post."

"Very well," she said, realizing that he wasn't trying to be difficult. "Those orders are superseded, by me, Bereth of the High Guard, on the authority of the Prince-General and Lord Oakenheart. Once you've delivered two loads each, you will return here and resume your previous orders. Will that do?"

"Admirably, Bereth of the High Guard." He gave her a very slight bow as she kneeled down to remove a caltrop from the sack, then rose and shouldered her quivers again. "Good luck today."

She smiled at him and held up the caltrop. "Pray that this is it."

Lord Oakenheart's warhawk was a large brown bird that was nearly as large as Ilriathas's Ebon, and after she explained her idea about the caltrops, the Commander of the High Guard immediately ordered them distributed to all twenty-one of the birds that would be flying to delay the enemy's flanking movement. After the first two guards staggered up to the top of the aerie tower, each bearing three bags, he ordered seven more guards to go to their assistance. Soon each hawk had a heavy bag of caltrops tied to its saddle, in addition to its riders. Each bird bore two elves, half of the passengers were mages, and the other half archers like herself. One mage, an older elf who looked tremendously unhappy to find himself being strapped into the saddle, suggested that the mages might heat the caltrops with fireball spells as they were dropped, which would further discomfit any orcs that were struck. Some signals were quickly arranged, and then Oakenheart gave the command to leap skyward.

Bereth held tightly onto her bow even though it was lashed to the saddle along with the three quivers she'd taken from the armory. Her own quiver was slung around her shoulder, though she'd left her sword back in the quarters she'd been given. If they were somehow brought down by the orcs, all she'd need was the knife at her belt to cut her own throat. Not that the knife would spare her any indignities, orcs being orcs, but at least she need not participate in the festivities alive.

Rising up from the highest tower of Tir Diffaith, the warhawks were soon at a safe altitude and beating their wings as they headed due east. It would be an all-too-short flight, she feared, as the enemy was desperate to seize the opportunity to take out once and for all the elven forces that had been harassing them for weeks. This wasn't their first attempt to encircle the infantry, but it was the first time the orcs had tried it since they'd known that both elven foot and horse would be falling back to the great fortress.

"Where are the scouts?" she shouted at Lord Oakenheart.

"Scout!"

"What?"

"Just one. I sent Elrian out as soon as we got the word."

"I don't see him!"

"I know." She could feel him slump a little in the saddle. "We should see him by now."

The terrain below was mostly barren scrubland, intersected by the occasional stream. It was the border of the Kurs-Magog, the great wastelands inhabited by only the most barbaric orcs, goblins, and occasionally, men. The ground was rough, but flat, and the Great Orc's cavalry would be making good speed over it.

"There they are!" The lord commander pointed one black-gloved hand at a swelling dark mass on the horizon below. "They're too close and they're coming too fast. They're going to beat the *catrodau brenhinol* to the walls."

"There must be five or six thousand of them!" Bereth's heart sank as she quickly estimated the number of boar riders moving west at a rapid trot. "How can he have so many?"

Lord Oakenheart raised his arm, signaling that the sky riders should fall into attack formation. Bereth clutched at his arm, astonished.

"What are you doing?" she demanded. While it was normal for the High Guard to approach and immediately attack, they almost never did so without first scouting the enemy forces for artillery, shamen, or other ground-based threats. "We should do a flyover first!"

"We should," the lord commander agreed grimly. "Especially since Elrian is missing. But there's no time for that now. Ready the caltrops."

She shook her head as she looked out at the approaching enemy cavalry below them. She didn't see any artillery or even any wagons being drawn that might contain a scorpio or some other device capable of harming a warhawk or its rider. She didn't even see any obvious shamans in the dark, teeming mass moving over the ground. They must have something, though, to have brought down the scout, unless he had inexplicably flown north for some reason rather than back to Tir Diffaith.

Regardless, they were committed now. The other hawks had moved up to form a line with them, with one exception; the skyrider carrying the mage who would cast the flame spell had dropped down below and behind them. She turned her attention to the saddlebags and fumbled at the heavy sack lashed to the saddle. The weight of the caltrops had tightened the knot, and it was hard to unpick, but with the help of her dagger, she managed it, and grunted as she pulled the now-open sack up onto the saddle in front of her.

"Are you ready?" Lord Oakenheart called as they swept towards the front line of the trotting warboars. It had been decided that they would use the first line as their mark. If that would spare the frontmost orcs and their mounts, it would also have the benefit of ensuring more of the wicked little objects struck something on the way down. The tall elf raised his hand, and just as they passed over the first orcs, a red light flashed from his hand and the hawk banked hard to the north.

As one, the line of warhawks parted, nine breaking south, the other nine following the lord commander's lead. There was a searing sound that ripped through the sky, and as Bereth began emptying her canvas sack, she saw a massive fireball erupt horizontally, completely obscuring her view of the enemy. She could feel the heat on her exposed face as the caltrops plunged through the fire, down towards the unsuspecting heads and shoulders of the orcs below.

The sack was considerably lighter, but it wasn't empty yet, so she grasped it by the two corners, lifted it and shook it. That nearly did the trick, but the spikes from one caltrop had somehow gotten embedded in the canvas, so she had to reach in and draw it out with her hand. The fireball was already fading by the time she hurled the little spiked ball down towards the ground, and as she watched, the first caltrops began to land amidst the enemy like a hellish rain of hot metal.

Starting about the sixth or seventh row back from the front, the cavalry formation abruptly began to disintegrate. From above, it looked almost as if a giant pillar had been dropped into a still body of water, as first the long hole appeared, followed by violent ripples that flowed towards the rear of the formation. Although they were still high above the orcs, Bereth could hear the outraged screams of the injured pigs and the enraged shouts of their riders over the continuous thunder of the thousands of unshod hooves.

There were more than a few riderless boars, their riders having fallen, either senseless or dead, after being struck on the head. As Bereth watched, one stunned orc tried to rise, only to be trampled into green ruin by the next wave of riders who were unable to avoid him. Other riders slumped wounded on the backs of their mounts, arms and wrists and even shoulders shattered. There were a few fallen boars, their skulls caved in by one or more caltrops, but far more were wounded, both from being struck by a falling caltrop or stepping on one that had failed to hit anything. The injured boars caused further havoc among the enemy, lashing out in helpless fury at their riders and nearby boars alike with their deadly tusks.

A horn blew, and was quickly echoed by others, and the huge mass of cavalry came to a gradual halt as the various warleaders attempted to maintain a degree of order before their orderly formations devolved into complete chaos. But before they could get their shattered squadrons properly arrayed again, Lord Oakenheart had passed the northernmost edge of the enemy and given the signal to launch the second phase of their attack.

Bereth, having spent too much time watching the devastation unfold, hurriedly untied her bow and slid the drawstring into place, then slipped an arrow out of her first quiver just in time before the hawk went into a steep, headfirst dive.

It was always much harder as a passenger, she thought, even as she leaned forward against the lord commander's leather-armored back and tightly shut her eyes against both the rushing wind and the sight of the rapidly approaching ground. She counted, one, two, three, four, five, six, seven, and was just beginning to worry that Lord Oakenheart wasn't going to pull up in time when she heard the giant warhawk spread its wings and smoothly ease them into flight path parallel to the ground at a height barely higher than a warboar's head.

She opened her eyes and discovered she had already nocked her arrow without thinking about it, and as they sped across the face of the enemy formation, she loosed it, burying it in the throat of a standard bearer little more than a stone's throw away. Without waiting to watch him fall, she was already drawing another arrow; she managed to loose seven more shafts before they were past the front line. Even though they were flying fast, at such close range she could hardly miss. The others were right behind them, and arrows, lightning bolts, and fireballs ripped into the front ranks of the stationary cavalry, felling scores of orcs and boars alike. The enemy seemed to be in shock, as not a single rider charged forward even though the warhawks were well within reach of the ground. The audacity of the aerial attack, coming so quickly on the heels of the caltrop bombardment, seemed to have paralyzed the orcs.

But the shock of the twin attacks didn't last very long. No sooner had the sky riders completed their reckless low sweep than the horns began blowing again and the crack-snap of crossbows began to be heard. Bereth looked back as the big warhawk began beating its wings to gain altitude again, and was relieved to see that none of the bolts that had been fired appeared to have struck home. However, she could also see, to her dismay, just how little damage their attack had done to the formation; at most they had, one way or another, taken two hundred orc-and-rider pairs out of commission. Still, the High Guard had not only slowed the Great Orc's flanking movement down, they had actually managed to arrest it entirely, if only for a short time.

"Where are the gwrachod?" Lord Oakenheart shouted at her. "They must have brought some along!"

Bereth frantically scanned the huge formation, trying to spot any signs of horns or staffs or any of the usual accoutrements of an orcish magic-user. Too many of the boar riders had brands and tattoos marking their faces and bare arms for the skin markings to be of much use, but then she saw movement in the middle of the formation and saw riders making way for four of the troll-drawn wagons being brought forward from the rear. Following the wagons were smaller orcs riding smaller animals than the big boars on either side. Wolves, she realized, and the riders were not orcs, but goblins. The deference both wagons and riders were being shown as they were ushered towards the carnage in the front lines suggested they were the gwrachod for whom they'd been looking.

"Down there!" she yelled into his ear as she grabbed his shoulder and pointed with her bow.

He nodded and immediately urged the warhawk higher. He also pumped his left arm three times, paused for a moment, then repeated the gesture. which was the High Guard's order for the riders carrying archers to disengage and provide cover for those bearing mages as they attacked their orcish counterparts.

"Wish we had more caltrops!" she shouted. She could feel him shrug; it might have been wise to hold onto a sack to disrupt the shamans, but the Lord Commander could hardly repent the damage they'd been able to inflict on the orcs already, and without loss. The next stage of the air-to-ground battle would be considerably riskier now, though, and the need to slow the orc's advance meant they couldn't simply withdraw, as they usually did once the enemy was able to marshal its magic against them.

The nine warhawks bearing mages arranged themselves into three formations of three. In the present circumstances, attacking an unscouted enemy, Bereth knew that they would take a cautious approach. On the first attack, two mages would be responsible for defensive spells, while the third, usually the most powerful, would attempt to kill or incapacitate as many of the magic-users as possible. Once the gwrachod were sufficiently distracted, she and the other archers would descend, first to attack any artillery that presented itself, after which they would take out the remaining gwrachod.

Only then would they return their attentions to the rest of the formation, concentrating first on officers, particularly the commanding general or warleader if they could identify him. There were simply too many orcs to even try to kill them all, but Bereth figured that if they could kill another thousand riders, there was a reasonable chance their surviving officers would abandon the flanking attempt and scatter to avoid the hell falling on them from on high. Orc or elf, a warrior who was helpless to respond was much more inclined to break and run than one who was able to fight back, even by proxy.

A cry arose from below as the first squadron swooped down towards the gwrachod struggling to push through the press. Crossbow strings snapped as a flurry of wooden bolts were fired up at the descending warhawks, but the sky riders knew well their margin of safety and the bolts lost momentum and began to fall back to the ground before ever endangering hawk or rider. Bereth had just enough magecraft to see that one of the mages was maintaining an arcane shield of sorts. The other one, she guessed would be alert for a diableric assault on the bodies of the birds or the minds of the riders.

Orcs leaped out of the canvas-shrouded wagons, and judging by their colorful attire and ornamental headgear, they were indeed the gwrachod she'd suspected. They brandished wooden staves and ivory bones and other fetishes aloft, and the air above them fairly crackled with the mystical energy of the magic they were wielding. As near as she could tell, there appeared to be perhaps twenty orcs on the carts, plus another fifteen or twenty goblins riding wolves.

"Too many!" she shouted at Lord Oakenheart.

He shook his head and reached back to reassure her by patting her thigh. Then he pointed to the three descending squadrons. The mage on the back of the leading hawk had risen in the saddle and was holding both hands up toward the white clouds above. He threw head back, shouting something, and then three bolts of lightning abruptly flashed in the blue sky, accompanied by a rapid series of thunderclaps detonating.

Bereth blinked and looked away, her eyes momentarily blinded by the bright burst of light. But when her vision returned to her and she looked down, she was surprised to see that instead of being three craters where the carts had been, the orcs were untouched.

"Big hoodoo!" Oakenheart shouted at her.

She nodded, astonished at the power being exhibited by the gwrachod; to not only deflect, but *disperse* three direct lightning bolts was something only a magister could do. Were they mutually augmenting each other's power? Or were they drawing on an external power source that they had somehow managed to hide from the High Guard's most talented mages?

The same thought had clearly struck the mages in two of the attacking squadrons. Six of the nine warhawks abruptly pulled out of their dive, their great wings beating powerfully as the lead squadron arced north and the second squadron broke south. But the third squadron continued its descent, grimly intent on taking out the orcs' magic users before they could demonstrate similarly effective offensive capabilities.

"What are they doing?" she shouted fearfully. She could feel the Lord Commander's shrug, but she saw him shake his head too and knew that he was equally concerned for the fate of the three warhawks and their riders.

The force of the wind was too strong for the lone archer, but the two mages in the squadron abandoned all thought of defense as they hurled one fireball after another at the gathered gwrachod straining to hold up their magical shield below. The first four fireballs splattered against the invisible protection, sending fiery plumes arching in every direction above the orcs, but the fifth one penetrated the invisible barrier and exploded just in front of the first wagon, incinerating one gwrach where he stood and setting three or four others on fire. The flames also seared two of the blue-skinned trolls pulling the wagon, who shrieked and bellowed like animals as they beat at their scalded hide.

Bereth shouted in anticipation, but the weakness in the barrier was only momentary and subsequent fireballs detonated harmlessly against the restored magic shield. The three warhawks were just beginning to pull out of their dive, and the archer had risen in his saddle as he began to nock an arrow when the beleaguered orcs struck back. Or rather, the trolls struck back.

One of the oversized creatures had ducked under the yoke of the third wagon and ripped off the leather cover, revealing that it was filled with long wooden poles, crudely sharpened at one end. The troll withdrew one and handed it to an even bigger companion, a monster with massive arms who looked as if he might well outmass the boars that flanked him on either side. The troll hefted the heavy pole, adjusted his grip, and then stepped forward and hurled it upwards as if it was a javelin. The oversized spear flew up and caught one of the warhawks in the side, just behind the wing, and the bloody tip burst out through the breast as the huge bird was spitted in mid-air.

The dismayed cry of its riders and the shriek of the hawk itself was drowned out by the terrible roar that erupted from the watching orcs below. The hawk crumpled and its wings furled like a man clutching at a wound. The two elves were strapped into the saddle, but the mage lost his grip on his staff as the bird turned over and began to plunge limply to the ground. The staff fell from the sky, rotating end over end, and the rest of the High

Guard watched, helpless, as the dying bird bore its doomed riders down toward the unforgiving ground.

The squadron's archer loosed his arrow and the shaft flew straight and true. It struck the troll in the shoulder and caused him to take a step backward, but his tough blue hide was too thick for the arrowhead to bury itself completely in his flesh or do any serious harm. With a snarl of pain, the troll ripped the shaft out and snapped it in twain.

Ignoring the blood running down his side, the troll raised his mighty arms and roared defiance at them. His triumphant shout was echoed by the newly emboldened orcs, and rose to a fever pitch when the stricken bird struck the ground, killing mage and skyrider instantly. The orcs rapidly swarmed their fallen enemies; Bereth couldn't help crying out in horror as both elves were swiftly beheaded and their heads mounted on spears that were thrust up mockingly towards the sky as the orcs howled in bestial triumph.

"Eumelltithio i fagddu!" Lord Oakenheart swore bitterly. He held up his hand, and the High Guard rose higher into the sky, seeking the safety that came with altitude.

Encouraged by the elven retreat, the orc officers began shouting at their riders, whipping beasts back to their feet, and ordering those who had dismounted to clamber back astride their boars. A deep horn resounded, and was answered by a series of shouts, horn blasts, and whistles as the various warleaders and clan chieftains indicated that they were ready to resume the march.

"We have to stop them!" Bereth shouted.

"The risk is too great!"

"They'll cut off the infantry if we don't stop them!"

"I know!" She could feel him sigh deeply, and he shook his head in frustration. "We can't throw away two-thirds of our mages for nothing!"

Bereth thought frantically. They needed to break the gwrachod to stop the cavalry, but they couldn't get close enough to break through the spells of the magic-users without putting the warhawks at risk from the trolls. She made a mental note to be sure to kill the orc commander if she saw him; whoever he was, he had adroitly leveraged his forces to negate the usual elven advantages.

Then she remembered the dragon arrows. They were forged by long-dead magisters of the Collegium, infused with the arcane magic of the ancients. If they could penetrate dragon scales, they could surely punch right through the toughest troll hide. She only had three of them, but three might well be enough. She pawed at the Lord Commander.

"I can kill them!"

"Who?"

"The trolls. The big ones! With these!"

She withdrew one of the dragon arrows and passed it forward to him.

"Where did you get this?"

"I've got three! If you can get me close enough, I can take them out."

He ran his hand over the shaft thoughtfully, taking in the runes inscribed into the ancient wood. "It will be risky."

"You said we had to stop them, at any cost!"

Lord Oakenheart looked down at the mounted horde beneath them, now moving rapidly again in the direction of the fortress. The High Guard could withdraw safely and the Prince-General would not blame them; protecting the mages was their foremost priority and they had already lost one. And it was not impossible that the infantry would be able to fight its way through to safety, although it would certainly take heavy losses in doing so.

He handed the arrow back to her over his shoulder. Then he patted her thigh.

"Don't miss, mer Eulenarias," he said. She nodded grimly as he began a mildly complicated series of gestures that indicated to the other skyriders in their oversized squadron how they were going to attack. Two of the hawks bearing the two most powerful mages would distract the gwrachod with fire and lightning. Oakenheart would circle behind one of the remaining hawks, at which point the mage on the fifth hawk would cast a cloaking spell over them. The fourth and fifth hawks would remain on high, as the other squadrons aggressively faked attack runs until the trolls were dead.

From this, Bereth gleaned that his intention was to dive as low as possible, as fast as possible, then soar across the front line of the cavalry, giving her the best possible shots at the chests of the big brutes. She winced, not looking forward to the steep plunge towards the earth, nor flying so close to the crossbows carried by many of the orcs below. At least she'd be too busy with her bow to spare any thought for the risks they were taking; it was small consolation, but just enough to keep her from wetting herself in fearful anticipation.

"Ready?"

She checked her straps, took a firm grip on her bow and quiver, and slid her arms around the Lord Commander's armored waist, gripping him with her forearms. She squeezed twice, to confirm.

She felt him shift as he gestured to the others, and the two warhawks furled their wings and fell. Their own bird arced to the right, and as it made a tight circle, her trained senses tingled as the cloaking spell was cast upon them. Then, without further warning, they were dropping, and she shut her eyes tightly against the brutal force of the wind, seeking to prevent her eyes from watering. She did not want blurry vision once the great warhawk leveled out and they began their dangerous pass.

Her stomach dropped and the wind roared in her ears like a waterfall. They were falling, falling, falling for what seemed like an eternity, but just when she thought she couldn't take it anymore, she felt a sensation of heat on her face, heard bestial squeals and screams, and the roar of thunder ripping through the sky. She could somehow sense the great moving mass below them, and scent the horrid stink of thousands of monstrous beasts as they fell towards it.

That was all the warning she received before she was hurled back against the saddle as the warhawk spread its wings to end its dive. They arced gracefully to the south. She opened her eyes and saw a hellish scene of smoke, fire, and confusion; at least two or three of the fireballs thrown to cover their dive had penetrated the orcs' magical defenses. They were speeding right over the helms and horns of the boar riders, seemingly so close that one would have been able to leap from the back of its mount and pluck a speckled brown feather from the belly of the giant hawk, and almost unthinkingly, she slipped the arrow onto the string and pulled it back to her ear. She didn't know if the concealment spell had held, she didn't know if they'd been seen, and she didn't hear the snap-crack of the crossbow bolts being fired up at them. She was too busy seeking her targets.

Where were they? But her eyes were keen, even for an elf, and she quickly spotted the first troll, who had just removed another huge javelin from the wagon behind him and was turning back towards them. But he did not see them; he was staring up at the sky. Even though they were so close she could hardly miss, she waited until his chest was fully exposed, then loosed. She didn't wait to see if the shaft struck home, but nocked the next one, aimed, and loosed again. Before the first troll even hit the ground, dying, two were mortally wounded, one in the heart, one in the throat, and the third was dead before it struck the ground, a black-feathered shaft sticking out of its left eye. As she'd hoped, the dragon-banes were more than a match for mountain troll hide.

But she didn't stop there. The gwrachod were fully occupied with their sky-riding assailants and their green skin was not too tough for her conventional arrows. By the time Lord Oakenheart pulled up on the reins and directed the giant bird to ascend the sky to the safety of the heights, she had killed four of the cursed magic-users.

"We did it!" she exulted, as the great bird beat its wings and climbed higher. But the Lord Commander didn't respond except to grunt and send up a magical light that flared green, telling the waiting squadrons it was now safe to begin their attacks. The circling birds brought in their wings, one by one, and dove towards the increasingly defenseless foe.

But it wasn't until they reached their usual altitude and leveled out that she stowed her bow and saw blood on the saddle in front of her.

"Commander?" she asked, puzzled. "Are you hurt?"

Even as she spoke, he slumped back on her breast with a wordless groan. She reached forward, and felt a thick wooden bolt, slick with blood, under her hand; it had pierced his armor just under his ribs on his right side. She couldn't help crying out in alarm, but she still had the presence of mind to remember that she had the materials for a simple healing spell in her saddle pack. Heedless of the blood on her hands, she frantically dug through it until she found the sachet of dried herbs used as a trigger.

Tearing it open with her teeth, she poured half of it over his wound, then put it back in her mouth so she could grip the bolt with both hands. They were slippery from the blood, and it took her three tries, but the bolt finally came out with a terrible wet sucking sound. She couldn't have removed an arrow driven equally deep, but fortunately, the crossbow bolts favored by the orcs were headless and barely tapered; not unlike the orcs who used them, they were dependent upon brute force to inflict damage. Blood gushed out a hole that would have fit four of her fingers, but there was no foul stink forthcoming, which gave her hope that the damage wasn't too great. She poured the rest of the herbs directly into the wound, then placed both her hands over it and spoke the words of the spell known to every sky rider with even a modicum of magic.

> Gods of earth and sky and stone.
> Heal this flesh, restore this bone!
> Rhwymo a benditho a gwau,
> Gwella a selo a chryfhau!

She could feel the heat under her hands as the bespelled herbs flared, searing and mending the torn and bleeding flesh. Lord Oakenheart cried out; the spell was not a merciful one. Bereth had never experienced it herself, but she was told it felt like being kissed by fire. It seemed to be working already, as blood was no longer pouring out of the hole in his armor. When she probed lightly with her fingers, there was nothing more than a deep divot where the wound had been. Oakenheart even stirred and tried to push himself away from her, but she held him fast.

"Must stop them," he gasped.

"We will. But we have to get you back to Tir Diffaith, my Lord. That bolt went deep and the skin will rupture if you move very much. It's just a cantrip, it stopped the bleeding but it won't have healed anything inside."

"Lord Commander!" Dantelys, one of the sky riders from their squadron, had noticed their erratic flight and caught up to them. He was flying just above them, to their right, and could no doubt see the blood. "You're wounded! Is it grave?"

Lord Oakenheart waved a dismissive hand and tried to respond, but he was too weak to shout and his answer went unheard in the rush of the wind.

"I'm taking him back to the castle!" Bereth cried, pointing towards the west. "He says you have to stop them!"

"We will!" the elf promised. "Don't let him fall!"

Bereth waved as the other hawk abruptly turned and descended towards the other three birds waiting below. She reached around her wounded commander, her arms on either side of him and took up the slack reins. Fortunately, the big hawk responded at once to her initial touch and began speeding homeward as if he knew his master was in peril.

She looked back to see if the great green-brown mass below was still in motion. It was, but its front was uneven now and its movements were uncertain. Great gouts of black smoke were rising from its center, where the wagons of the gwrachod burned, and a tentative pillar of flame was answered at once by a pair of lightning bolts, followed by a massive thunderclap. The orcs' magic was failing, overpowered at last by the more formidable arts of the High Guard, and soon their cavalry would be all but defenseless. She turned her back on the battle and set her sights on the distant mountains.

"Stay alive, my Lord," she urged her commander. "You must stay alive! We are going to need you in the days ahead."

LUGBOL

LUGBOL growled and slapped at one of the forest's infernal insects that was busily engaged in biting his left bicep. He crushed it under his horny palm, felt a pop, and looked down to see he'd smeared his own dark green blood along with the remnants of the bug that had bitten him across his upper arm. He shook his head, knowing that the bite was going to start itching momentarily, then slapped fruitlessly at another one that had just bitten his calf.

"I don't remember them being this bad before," he complained.

"They had all the dead to feed on then," Ghurash replied. Even though it had been less than three weeks since they'd fled the dark shadows of the Korokhurmagh, already the denizens of the forest had all but picked the thousands of dead bodies clean of flesh. They were rapidly approaching the western edge of the great wood and soon they would be encroaching on the true Man lands, not merely the pillaging the small villages and hamlets that had been carved out of the trees by the lesser tribes and clans.

The Hagahorn'ugh had been cocky and full of contempt for the martial abilities of the Szavon'agh as they passed through the burned-out remains of the villages overrun by Zlatagh's army, but they gradually fell silent and their mood turned grim as they began to come across one large-skulled, thick-boned skeleton after another. There were few Man skeletons, and the bones of those they encountered were eagerly snatched up and divided among sqwaaks and younger kors seeking clubs or remains to decorate their armor.

More than a dozen fights broke out over the Man bones, the worst of which began when a boar rider commandeered a large thigh bone another kor had intended for a club, then cracked it open and sucked out the marrow. By the time Lugbol and Karnuhg, one of the cavalry grun-kors, managed to put a stop to the fracas, four mountain orcs and two Black Fists were dead, and another Hagahornu was so badly wounded that he ended up in the cookpot that evening.

The kral chewed him out for the needless death of his orcs, of course, but Lugbol had the sneaking suspicion that the older orc was secretly impressed at how Lugbol's veteran kors managed to more than hold their own against the bigger mountain orcs. In fact, knowing that Lugbol, being Goghu and half the size of his Hagahornu officers, could never pose a threat to his rule, Nekhuru had proven increasingly inclined to give his new hadvezer more responsibilities as they marched through the forest toward the Man lands. In addition to commanding the light infantry and the goblin cavalry, Lugbol was now serving as the liaison between the farkh'agh and the various shugaba'ugh and grun-kors whose kors had the annoying habit of feasting upon their fellow marching companions whenever they couldn't find adequate meat to sate their appetites.

Two large goblins, wearing the ornate headgear favored by their shugaba'agh, approached him now, escorted by a nervous-looking body-guard of twelve lightly-armored yellowskins carrying pikes. Lugbol groaned. Given the angry expressions on their hook-chinned, hook-nosed faces, he had a pretty good idea of why they were coming to see him, even though they were attached to units outside his command.

"What you want, little farkh'agh?" Ghurash demanded of them.

"We want yez bloody hadvezer to help us!"

"Or what?" the orc snapped, looming dangerously over both of them. They might be big for goblins, but the grun-kor could still easily snap their necks in his powerful hands and all three of them knew it.

"Or there won't be none of us left to do no more fighting for yez."

"Or maybe we'ze start sneaking about and slashing throats," added the other shugaba, darkly.

"Hold up," Lugbol broke in. "There ain't no need for that kind of talk. Yez been having trouble with some of the kors?"

"Hadvezer!" Both goblins had the sense to thump their chests as they addressed him. "It's more the koruts, sir. They been riding up behind the march and grabbing stragglers. Between us, we'ze lost eighteen in the last two days!"

"Why are you talking to me? I ain't yez commander."

"No sir, but we heard you made yez kors stop chowing on yez farkhut'ugh. So we thought maybe you could tell them to leave our goblins alone too."

"I got no swang with the cavalry, except maybe the wolfriders. Yez wants to do something about the koruts, yez gots to talk to the kral or to Hadvezer Boghrul." He wasn't optimistic about their chances. Boghrul One-Eye, the senior cavalry commander, was so ornery and sour-faced that he made the Hagahornu kral look like a flirtatious young kwee by comparison.

"We tried that," one of the goblins said. "Well, the farkh'a afore me did. Boghrul smashed his head in, then had him spitted and roast for his grun-kors' supper."

Lugbol nodded. He could see why the two farkh'agh were reluctant to request a second hearing with the hadvezer. And while Nekhuru wasn't likely to harm them, he also wasn't going to upbraid one of his most senior officers for what, from the orc perspective, was no more a crime than picking a berry from a bush. The idea that the berry might protest its ill-treatment wasn't so much as irrelevant as ridiculous.

On the other hand, Lugbol was fairly certain that they were going to need the clever farkh'agh for more than their ability to keep orc bellies filled with bloodbread and the occasional serving of fresh meat once they exited the woods and encountered the Man army that was sure to be waiting for them, so he figured it would be a good idea to keep them from deserting en masse if he could.

"I can't do squat for yez, understand? Yez ain't my kors. But I can tell yez that the way we kept our farkhut'agh out of the cookpots is that I told their shugaba'agh to make damn sure they was keeping my kors happy with whatever meats and berries they could find, right? Ain't nobody likes eating that bloodbread yez is carting around; tastes like faszhek tree bark. But yez hands over a deer or some rabbits, that'll be enough to keep them from eating goblin for a day or three, especially if you make the bread from the squeezings instead of cutting yezselves."

"How we supposed to hunt for critters when we'ze doing everything we can just to keep up with the march?" one of the goblins demanded. "It's all very well for the wolfriders to run down some meat; they gots to keep their wolves fed anyhow. But we can't be expected to do more than we'ze already doing!"

He had a point, Lugbol had to admit. Except for a few of the officers, the goblin infantry was weighed down by the strange devices called krobb'ugh, which were a sort of miniature wagon that rolled on a single wooden ball and was dragged behind the goblin to whom it was attached by a wooden rod that served as a yoke. The wagon, or drag-pack, was made of rigid leather, and could be turned into a backpack by removing the yoke. Most of the

krobb'ugh were filled with the root-flour from which the goblins made the
bloodbread that fed the army; but while the bread kept their bellies full
enough, it wasn't enough to satisfy the average orc's appetite for flesh of
one sort or another. And since a full krobb weighed more than the average
goblin who was dragging it did, there was no way the infantry could both
march and hunt.

He sighed. "All right. I'll see what I can do. But I ain't promising yez
nothing, understand?"

"Hadvezer!" they chorused, thumping their chests appreciatively.

"Get off with yez," he growled.

They complied, nodding and smiling, and departed with an observable
spring in their steps that indicated rather more optimism in his ability to
help them than he felt himself.

"Boghrul ain't gonna do squag-all for them, not on your say-so." Ghurash
shook his head. The galvebel's tone was as sour as his expression.

"No, he ain't." His fellow hadvezer wasn't exactly stupid, but the big orc
didn't tend to think much beyond executing his orders to the best of his
formidable abilities. "But I ain't going to talk to him about them."

Ghurash's frown further distorted a face that was already frightful.

"Going outside the chain of command is a good way to get yourself kilt,
Lugbol."

Lugbol shrugged. "Maybe. But at least I won't have to get bit by these
damned bugs no more."

"Want me to go with you?"

"Nah." Lugbol shook his head as he stared off into the darkness of the
surrounding forest. "No point in both of us getting ourselves stripped and
spitted over a few damn farkhut'agh."

But when Lugbol made his way through the towering bodyguards who
surrounded Kral Nekhuru like a squad of walking mountains, it soon
became apparent that this was not the time to share the concerns of the
goblin infantry with him. The felsig kral was in a temper, standing over the
unconscious body of a large boar rider, and rubbing his fist in a manner
that indicated that he was the party responsible for felling the bigger orc.

"Lugbol, how did you get here so fast?"

"Felsig Kral?"

"I sent a grun-kor for you as soon as I heard from this fashzek moron!"
There was an audible thud as the stocky kral kicked the motionless kor at his
feet. "It seems his idea of rekkey was to go off hunting meat and he scared

up a whole herd of them big Man deer. We still don't got no idea where the Man armies are, but at least we got plenty o' fresh meat for a feasting."

His disgust was palpable. The kral knew as well as Lugbol did that while full bellies were good, knowing where the cursed enemy was lurking about was a damned sight better.

"Don't know about no armies, but my farkhut'agh spotted a Man village not far from the edge of the trees. They said there wasn't no more than two, three hundred living there."

"Was they seen?"

"No, Felsig Kral. I ordered them to stay away until night fell, then ride around it and count the fires. But the chief Man might know where the armies are if we put him to the question."

"You talk Man?" The kral's beady eyes widened a little.

"No, Felsig Kral. But lots of gobbos trade with the Northmen, and they know most of the Man tongues. We can find one who talks whatever these Men talk."

The kral nodded. "Do that. Besides, two or three hundred Men will make for a good feeding before we get stuck in good. You know how to ride?"

Lugbol stared back at the kral in disbelief. Ride? On the back of one of those massive, evil-eyed, sharp-tusked boars that would just as soon rip your arm off as let you mount it? He swallowed hard before responding.

"Sure, I can ride," he lied.

He wasn't sure if the kral believed him or not, but the orc's twisted smile seemed to suggest that he'd said the right thing.

"Don't worry, Hadvezer Lugbol, we'll find you an itty-bitty one." The kral laughed. "Find yez Man-talking gobbos and meet me at the first corral. I've had me a hankering for Man flesh since the Great Orc told us to ride west, and I got the notion I won't have to wait much longer!"

It was with more than a small amount of dread that Lugbol approached the pen containing the hulking war boars, followed by the pair of wolf riders he had commandeered from their clan leader. How well they actually spoke the Man talk, he did not know, but their shugabah had assured him, on pain of being torn limb from limb, that their language skills would be good enough for the kral's purposes. He wrinkled his nose; just when he was convinced that the stink of the massive beasts couldn't possibly get any worse, he took another step toward the corral and discovered how wrong he was.

The orcs guarding the entrance to the boar pen didn't seem to notice it, though, or perhaps their senses were simply deadened through long exposure to the animals. They were some of the few orcs in the camp who did not wear any armor, Lugbol noticed, which puzzled him until it occurred to him that no amount of armor would save an orc from either a stomping or a tusking by a ill-tempered boar. The beasts' wicked tusks were nearly the length of the swords worn by the goblins accompanying him, only considerably thicker and sharper. And, of course, they not only came in pairs, but had all the mass of a half-ton brute behind them rather than a spindly goblin arm.

Nor did the boar herders seem to bother carrying any weapons beside the occasional dagger. Instead, each of them held a big three-pronged fork sharpened at the end of each prong, which Lugbol felt was much more likely to tickle a boar than seriously threaten to harm it. As they came closer, though, he saw that each wooden fork was set into a heavy lead casing at the other end, which could either deliver a stunning blow to an orc or a wake-up call to a recalcitrant beast.

One of the guards held up a hand, indicating that he should stop, then turned and bellowed over his shoulder to someone inside the corral.

"Oi, we gots dat one wot wants da little bugger!" he shouted.

For a moment, Lugbol felt relieved that at least the boar riders didn't seem to be intending to put him at the mercy of one of their more evil-tempered giants, and then he caught sight of a herder leading what was, admittedly, a smaller beast than most in his direction. What apparently passed for a little bugger was still a powerful monster that not only dwarfed him, but was obviously capable of stomping him into a bloody mush as easily as he crushed a gobfly between two fingers. He swallowed hard and sternly reminded himself that he was a hadvezer, marked with the fire by the Great Orc himself, and neither pissing himself nor shrieking and running away was an option.

But from where he was standing now, the back of the beast, highlighted by the shaggy mound atop the boar's powerful shoulders, seemed as distant and impossibly attainable as the highest mountains of Zoth Ommog. He swallowed hard. If he could survive the branding iron and the iron fire demons, he would survive this.

"Hadvezer!" a hoarse voice barked, pulling him out of his thoughts. "Dis here's Malkosta. Dey said you wain't no rider and I can sees you ain't. But she's a little sweetie, don't care where she goes, and if you treats her right, she treat you right."

Malkosta eyed him with her beady little eyes and grunted. Lugbol smiled weakly and hoped it was a sweet grunt that promised a mutually affectionate relationship for the rest of the day. He gingerly reached out to stroke her snout and was pleased to discover that she didn't try to bite him. At the herder's prompting, he grasped the thick corded leather that hung down from the saddle with his good arm, inserted his right foot into the bone-and-leather stirrup, and with an awkward lunge combined with a desperate tug, somehow managed to propel himself into the saddle without help from the herder.

"See, yez a natural, Hadvezer!" the herder praised him a little too enthusiastically, and he belatedly realized that the older orc was a little intimidated by his rank. Lugbol was, after all, almost certainly the first hadvezer he'd ever encountered so directly. He watched, feeling helpless, as the herder half-climbed up the side of the beast to slide the pair of straps that were meant to keep him on the boar's back over his thighs before tugging them tight with a grunt and a grimace. "Mind you don't lean over too far; they'll help keep yez balance, but they won't keep yez on if'n you tries to do a header."

Lugbol looked down at the orc and did his best to nod confidently, as he imagined an actual boar rider might have done after accomplishing a simple act he'd done a hundred times before. But in truth, he felt almost intoxicated by the sudden change in his perspective, the feel of the awesome power of the beast beneath him, and the way the herder, the guards, and the wolfriders were all literally looking up at him. He suddenly understood the swaggering arrogance of the cavalry, who tended to strut about on their bandy bowlegs as if they were a head taller than a trollslayer.

"Let's move out," he growled at the wolfriders, who backed up their wolves to either side in order to give him room to pass. A little nervously, he kicked softly with his heels at the hairy sides of the boar, which the beast didn't appear to feel at all.

"Hold up, Hadvezer!" The herder was reaching up and proffering him a thick, sharpened club of some kind, which he realized when he took it was a boar goad. "If she's feelin' lazy, reach back and give her a little jab with this, that'll wake her up."

Lugbol examined the goad, which was carved of bone and made for a more sturdily constructed and fearsome weapon than most of the actual armaments carried by his kors. It was decorated with various runes and carvings, none of which made any sense to him at all, but gave him the impression that it had been previously owned by a boar rider of some renown. He waved it in appreciation of the gesture and was glad to see the old orc bare his rotting tusks with pleasure at being acknowledged.

A thundering sound caught his attention and he turned to see the kral, followed by about thirty of his best korut'ugh, riding rapidly in his direction. The kral's boar was nearly twice the size of his own, a massive brute with silvered tusks big enough to impale a goblin. His own boar sniffed the air and snorted, apparently excited by the approach of so many of her kind. He pulled the reins in firmly, hoping that she wouldn't spill him from her back right in front of the kral, as the massed boar riders halted before him.

"Hadvezer Lugbol!" the kral cried, with an amused smile creasing his leathery green face. "Wherever did you find that mighty beast?"

His koruts roared with laughter. They towered over him on their bigger boars, but it was the ease with which they sat their saddles high on the beasts' shoulders that struck him most. He suddenly realized, with a sick feeling in the pit of his stomach, that he was almost certainly going to have a very difficult time keeping up with the korut'ugh, should the kral decide to ride hard.

Fortunately, he soon discovered the kral was apparently in no hurry to reach the Man village and they proceeded to plow their way through the forest at a slow, comfortable pace that put Lugbol at his ease. Or would have done, at any rate, if it weren't for the various branches that occasionally threaten to dislodge, if not outright impale, him. He soon learned to keep one eye out for branches approaching at head or chest level, always ready to duck a thick outreach of oak or fend off a prickly, but flexible pine limb with a leather-armored forearm.

He wasn't the only one feeling under assault from the trees. The koruts clearly did not enjoy riding through the forest, and their bitter complaints very nearly drowned out the guttural rumblings and protests of their beasts. Fortunately, it was not long before a bright glow began to penetrate the leaves and branches obstructing their way, heralding the western edge of the Korokhurmagh and an unobstructed path towards the unsuspecting Man villages of the Szavon'agh.

The sun was almost blinding as they emerged from the forest, and Lugbol was forced to shield his eyes with his hands against the sudden glare from the cloudless sky. But the open horizon energized his companions, as they kicked their beasts forward into short, exuberant gallops before reining them in again.

"Leave 'em be," the kral waved off one angry gran-korut who had risen in his stirrups, and, judging from his expression as well as the veins popping out of his neck and forehead, was about to engage in what promised to be a epic series of full-throated recriminations of the undisciplined riders. The officer's jaw snapped obediently shut and he slumped back in his saddle, but given the fury still smoldering in his yellow eyes, Lugbol would take the over if given the chance to bet on the number of skulls thumped by the gran-korut that evening.

But now that they were clear of the forest, the kral elected to pick up the pace as well, and Lugbol lurched uncertainly as his boar suddenly broke into a spine-jarring trot in order to keep up with the bigger beasts. He felt his upper body tilting awkwardly to the left, and for a moment he feared that despite being tightly buckled on, he would fall off and be trampled by the iron-hard hooves of the boars behind him. But before he had tilted too far toward the ground, he managed to reach out with his right hand and grasp the bone that served as a pommel at the fore of the saddle to pull himself back upright. His heart pounding, he closed his eyes and took a pair of deep breaths before daring to glance around to see if any of the other riders had noticed.

None of the koruts appeared to have been paying any attention to him, but he heard high-pitched laughter to his right and realized that the two goblins riding a little behind him had seen the whole thing. He glared at them, which only seemed to amuse them all the more.

"Haegach!" Lugbol started as the kral bellowed at the big graborgh commanding the left wing and made a circling motion over his head with his gauntleted left hand. "Ride wide and stay out of sight!"

"Felsig Kral!" the graborgh shouted, then raised a horn to his broad-tusked mouth and blew three short blasts. A ragged cheer went up from the koruts on the left, and then the ground began to shake and thunder as about one hundred riders kicked their beasts into a full gallop and began to separate themselves from the rest of the herd.

"Where are they going?" Lugbol asked the kral once the riders had gotten far enough ahead that it was possible to hear anything but the pounding of the hooves on the turf.

"They'll ride around the village and wait on the other side." The kral emitted a guttural bark of amusement. "Hu hu hu! When the Szavon'agh sees us coming, their first thought will be to run toward their armies. But there won't be nowhere to run, not with Haegach and his koruts betwixt them and the river."

"The river?"

"Yeah, a big one about a day's ride past the village. The farkhut'agh scouts say it's too deep and too fast for the boars to swim, and there ain't no fords, but there's three or four bridges we can ride over. Got to figure they'll be guarding all of them, so we'll just see which one is easiest to take, then swamp it with the farkh'agh before we cross."

It seemed not even the big mountain kors were more contemptuous of goblin infantry than the boar riders. Lugbol was only surprised that the kral didn't plan to order the gobbos to hurl themselves into the river and make a bridge of their drowned bodies over which his koruts could ride. Using them as a lightly-armed shock troops against the iron-armored Szavon'agh was almost kind by comparison.

They rode slowly at first, at a jarring, but not too frightening trot. The kral smiled at him, but there was a challenge in his eyes.

"Well, Hadvezer? I think they've got enough of a head start. Are you ready for a proper ride?"

"Always, felsig Kral!" Lugbol was pleased that he managed to keep his voice from cracking. He took a firm grip on the pommel and offered a brief prayer to the god of war that death would come speedily should he tumble from the back of his little boar. But much to his surprise, what had been a treacherous and unpredictable ride suddenly transformed into a relatively smooth, rhythmic motion that was easy to follow. The cool wind rushing over his face and sweaty torso felt incredibly good after the sweltering heat of the forest, and much to his surprise, he realized that he was starting to enjoy himself!

He looked back and saw that the two wolfriders were keeping pace with the boars, loping along fearlessly in the midst of the much larger creatures. It seemed that the boars were too big, or perhaps too mean, for the wolves to regard them as prey, and the wolves were too small to inspire any concern in the tusked behemoths.

They hadn't ridden very long before they discovered the grassy terrain over which they were riding transformed into long strips of plowed earth from which rows and rows of small green plants were sprouting. These must be the fields of Man-food of which the scouts had spoken, which meant that the walls of the Man-village should soon be coming into view. The fields were soft, and their progress slowed a little as the boars' hooves sank deep into the exposed dirt and trampled the growing crops. Although there were footprints and other signs of recent activity, there was not a single Man in sight.

They must have seen us coming, Lugbol concluded. Soon after they rode through the second field, this one planted with something that was taller than the previous field, they spotted the walls of the village. The walls weren't very high, but they were made of stone and therefore could not be burned. However, even at a distance Lugbol could see buildings outside the wall that butted up against it, structures that could be easily climbed by even a kor with limited use of one arm like himself.

Without warning, Nekhuru suddenly reined in his huge beast and raised an arm. The cavalcade abruptly halted; fortunately Lugbol's boar was paying more attention to its companions than to its rider, as it stopped of its own accord before Lugbol even had the chance to tug on the reins.

"They're coming out," a korut on his right observed.

And, sure enough, the gates of the village were opening, disgorging a small group of what appeared to be unarmed Men carrying baskets hanging down from their shoulders. They were led by an older Man with white hair and a white beard, who carried nothing, and held his empty palms out before him to show he was defenseless as he strode toward the waiting koruts.

"Graborgh, with me!" barked the kral. "Galvebel, bring four of your koruts. And Hadvezer, you too, and the farkhut'agh with you!"

The eight orcs, accompanied by the two goblins, rode toward the approaching Szavon'agh at a slow trot. The kral ordered them to halt again when they were a stone's throw away from the Man party, which as far as Lugbol could tell, consisted of four vank'ugh and two kwee'agh. The latter two were visibly trembling at their proximity, though there was no way of knowing whether it was the fearsome warboars or their savage Hagahornu riders that terrified them more.

"Felsig Kral!" the graborgh protested when Nekhuru adroitly slipped out of his saddle and grunted an order to stay at his giant boar.

"Stow it," the kral growled, before waving at Lugbol and the two goblins. "Well, tell those damned farkh'agh to see what it is they want."

"Tell 'em we want ghash!" snarled one korut as Lugbol clumsily dismounted, and the Manfolk flinched as the other riders laughed. He wondered what he was supposed to do with the reins, but shrugged and dropped them to the ground, hoping that his boar wouldn't take the opportunity to run off and leave him there holding his vank right in front of the kral and the whole cavalry wing. Fortunately, it seemed content to snort at the air and nose at the ground rather than abandon its present company.

The Man with the white hair stiffened a little in alarm as the two goblins moved toward him, but relaxed when they started making noises that he appeared to recognize. After a moment, he responded with a long string of sounds that made no sense at all to Lugbol.

"What he say?" the kral demanded.

"He say we be welcome and they give us lots of nice things, shiny things, good things to eat."

"Good things to eat?" The kral moved closer to the Man, who quaked a little as the shorter, but much more powerful orc cocked his head and sniffed curiously at him. "Better than Man flesh?"

His arm shot out and the Man's eyes briefly bulged with panic before the kral crushed his throat with an audible crunch. The two kwee'agh shrieked as the kral lifted their leader's lifeless body above his head and shook it as if it were a war banner.

"Kill! Squag! Eat! Burn!"

The koruts roared, and even the boars, seemingly sensing the excitement of their riders, echoed their cries with bestial bellows. Lugbol grinned gleefully and managed to grab the smaller of the kwee-agh before the onrushing riders reached them. He pulled her in close, laughing at her screams as he shielded her from the grasping hands of several koruts with his body as they rode past him towards the nearly defenseless Man village. He already knew the taste of Man flesh, and he had other, more pressing hungers to assuage.

SEVERA

S EVERA folded her hands in a desperate attempt to control herself. She was sitting in the midst of several thousand of the absolute worst scum of Amorr, seated amongst thieves, killers, slaves, rapists, and gladiators, and yet, her fear was not for herself or for her two sisters-in-law, who sat on either side of her, but for the tall young man who was striding out confidently onto the sands of the arena in the company of his brothers.

A group of ten centurions, hard-eyed and encrusted with medallions, stood with their hands on their swords, in two lines of five. A pair of draconarii, one behind each line, held aloft a crimson standard, each representing one of the new city legions, Legio XXXV and Legio XXXVI. Between the centurions stood four fighting men with shaved heads, each holding a different weapon, but the same round, metal-edged wooden shield. She wondered what they were doing there in the midst of all the soldiers.

Sextus looked wonderful in his gleaming armor, she had to admit, as the blue plume of his tribune's helm made him look even more imposing than he already was. The Valerians were a tall breed, and Sextus was the second-tallest of the four brothers who were marching toward the oversized thugs waiting for them, bulging muscles tight with adrenaline, at the center of the arena. To her alarm, the greater part of the crowd began to jeer and shout at the sight of the Valerians, cursing them with a raw and vituperative enthusiasm that she had seldom heard before.

"Kill the traitors," she heard someone several rows behind her shout. "Gut them on their own swords!"

"Throw them from the Rock!" bellowed another loudmouth.

"Animals," she heard Carvilia snarl under her breath. Her beautiful sister-in-law was never inclined to think well of the plebs even in the best of circumstances, so it was no surprise that she didn't take well to hearing them call for the death of her husband. "Cursed animals, that's all they are. I hope Potitus decimates them!"

"Why do they still call them traitors?" Tender-hearted Pompilia was doing her best to control herself, but the horrible insults and dreadful threats being directed at the Valerians had her on the verge of tears. "Both the Senate and the Consuls themselves said the boys were not to blame for Magnus!"

Severa leaned back so that she could see past her sisters-in-law and their bodyguards, and looked first to the right, then to the left. The stone seats were a sea of angry, filthy conscripts from the plebs, far too many of whom were shaking their fists and venting their spleen at the four officers below them. She shook her head, and for the first time, wondered if they themselves could be in any danger. It wasn't likely, considering that they were surrounded by armed house guards under the command of Durus, but even a well-trained group of twenty men would be easily overcome by a blood-maddened arena mob.

"I don't think the plebs care any more about what the city fathers have to say than a baby squalling for its milk does," Caerilla's wry tone surprised Severa, though not as much as her obvious sympathy for the crowd. "They're frightened, they don't know who is to blame, and our husbands will serve as well as anyone else. Better than most, to be fair, since it can't be denied that they are related to Magnus."

"Sins of the father." Carvilia sniffed disdainfully. Severa hadn't known her before her marriage to Sextus, but she had the distinct impression that her sister-in-law had never thought well of their mutual father-in-law, even before he'd turned traitor. "Stop sniveling, Pompilia. Our men will send this trash to the devil in less time than it will take your eyes to dry."

A white-robed senator stepped out of the entrance, flanked by a squad of fascitors and followed by an aeneator carrying a massive horn. Severa recognized him, it was Andronicus Declama, the Consul Civitas and the man most responsible for the rehabilitation, however precarious it might be, of the four Valerian brothers. He, at least, was greeted by a mix of cheers and respectful grumbles, as the crowd momentarily left off its shrieking in anticipation of the event to come.

When the consul reached the men in the middle of the arena, the centurions saluted him in unison, crying out as they thumped their gauntleted fists against their armored chests. The noise resounded throughout the stands, and was echoed by the shouts of the spectators. But when the four Valerians threw out the patrician salute, it was met by relative silence, even as the consul responded in kind. And when the four fighting men imitated the centurions as well, the crowd roared, and they shouted even louder when Declama, who Severa's father had always described as an astute politician, tapped his chest to acknowledge them, soldier-style.

"Does he think he's an actor?" spat Carvilia.

"At least he's distracted the plebs from shouting at our husbands," Severa observed.

Carvilia nodded, unimpressed.

The aeneator pressed his lips to his horn and puffed out his cheeks. The massive blast echoed off the stone stands and silenced the crowd. Declama raised his hand theatrically and began to speak.

"Men of Amorr! The brothers Valerius have been accused, not without reason, of treason against the Senate and people of Amorr!" He paused for a moment as the crowd shouted in anger. "As you surely know, the Senate has investigated this matter and absolved them of any responsibility for, or any knowledge of, the traitorous actions of their father, the senator Marcus Valerius Magnus, who has shamed both himself and his sons by his failure to faithfully perform his duties."

The crowd raged, displeased, and Declama permitted them to rage a little longer before he raised his hand again.

"Men of Amorr! Your consuls understand that in matters such as these, it is not enough for us to provide you with assurances, that mere words do not suffice to prove your doubts are not unfounded! Therefore, we have decided that the Almighty and Most Immaculate God shall decide whether these men are innocent or guilty, and you shall witness with your own eyes the truth of this matter, in a trial by combat!"

Severa gasped. Sextus had told her that he and his brothers would be putting on an exhibition today, but he had left her with the impression that it was merely going to be a demonstration of the importance of legionary discipline to the new conscripts. She looked at Carvilia, and when her wide-eyed sister-in-law shook her head, Severa realized that she hadn't known either. Had Sextus even known himself? She squinted at him, but his face was mostly hidden behind his tribune's helm and she couldn't make out his expression.

"Men of Amorr! You who will serve our city in Legios XXXV and XXXVI. You have chosen your champions! Are you content with them?"

As the crowd roared its approval, Severa realized, with horror, that the four beastly fighters chosen to face her husband and his brothers had been selected from this vast collection of criminals, miscreants, and slaves in order to fight for them. Which surely meant that the four men were some of the most formidable killers to be found in all of Amorr! They might even be professional gladiators!

She shivered as she leaned forward to take a closer look at the four men. While only one was as tall as Caerilla's husband Volesus, the shortest Valerian, all four were well-muscled and at least ten years older than Sextus. The oldest villain, who carried a large, vicious-looking spiked club, appeared to be more than twice her husband's age.

"Oh, Saint Michael, defend my husband," she prayed fervently under her breath. "Grant him victory and keep him from harm, in our Lord and Savior's most holy name!"

The consul raised his hand again to quiet the crowd.

"Lucius Pedanius, Clodius Aper, Staberius Rufus, Trebius Gallus, are you willing to represent the legions before God and Amorr in this Judicium Dei?"

"Aye!" the four men shouted. And the legions whom they represented cheered, until another gesture from Declama quieted them.

"Valerius Volesus, Valerius Potitus, Valerius Tertius, Valerius Sextus, are you willing to represent House Valerius before God and Amorr in this Judicium Dei?"

Severa watched Sextus and his brothers unsheathe their gladiuses in such smooth unison that it seemed as if they must have been practicing all morning. The sun glinted off their upraised blades. "Our House is Amorr!" they cried as one.

There was considerably less cheering than there had been for their foes, but neither were there too many jeers, which for some reason comforted her a little. Their initial contempt for the sons of Magnus notwithstanding, the crowd seemed to be open to the possibility that the Consul Civitas was telling them the truth.

The consul nodded to the centurions, who promptly fell back into a loose circle surrounding the two sets of combatants. Declama then turned and walked back to the door through which he'd entered, followed by the fascitors and the aeneator.

As he crossed the sands, the noise surrounding Severa began to crescendo, rising from a rumbling murmur to a rolling thunder of excitement. The four gladiators—for at this point Severa had concluded that all four men were almost certainly trained gladiators—were waving their various weapons and shifting back and forth in a threatening manner. One man was armed with a spear, the second with the spiked club, the third with a long Northern sword, and the fourth with a double-sided hatchet. Three were clad in leather armor, while the man with the club had an iron breastplate strapped to his chest. But all four wore legionary helms and three of them carried the same round buckler. The spearman, alone of the eight combatants, carried no shield.

Their activity didn't appear to impress her husband or his brothers. All four of them simply stood there, motionless, with their swords drawn and their long rectangular shields resting on the ground. Then a horn sounded and both sets of men fairly exploded into action.

The furious action was strange to Severa's eyes and she found it hard to comprehend exactly what was happening. As the four Valerians raised their shields and leveled their swords, the four gladiators broke apart. The man with the mace leaped forward and Caerilla screamed as it crashed down toward Volesus's head, only to bounce off the top of his shield with a loud, metallic crash. Two Valerian swords licked out like snakes before the man could fall back, and one of them, Tertius's, came back with blood on it.

It wasn't a bad wound, little more than a scratch to the man's left shoulder, but it was enough to make his three companions a little more wary of approaching the brothers. The spearman and the hatchetman moved wider, circling around either side of the Valerian wall as the other two continued to threaten the four brothers from the front. But no Valerian broke off to engage either man in single combat as Severa half-expected, instead, Sextus and Potitus smoothly rotated to present their shields to the two men while continuing to step forward in line with Tertius and Volesus. She held her breath as the spearman jabbed his long weapon at Sextus, but her husband blocked it easily with his shield and did not try to strike back.

The fighter with the hatchet waggled his weapon and feinted, once, twice, at Potitus, but the tallest Valerian didn't even react. He continued his rhythmic march forward in time with his brothers, although he was now walking sideways.

Frustrated, though not intimidated, the two fighters facing Tertius and Volesus fell back before the inexorable Valerian march, sparking a small chorus of jeers from their supporters. Severa didn't know much about combat, but she had seen enough gladiatorial matches to understand that the four Valerians weren't giving their opponents any openings to attack. They simply ignored every feint and gesture, forcing the two men before them to retreat toward the stone walls of the arena as the other two jabbed and postured ineffectually, all the while shouting contrary instructions at each other.

Finally, the man with the longsword waved his weapon above his head in a circle, a gesture which his partners on the sides seemed to understand. They quickly moved to try to get at the backs of the two Valerians on either side, but to no avail, as Sextus and Potitus rotated further and continued to march while walking backward. The effortless ease with which they adjusted their formation seemed to unsettle the swordman for a moment, as a look of consternation crossed his face, but then he snarled and shouted a command at the others.

"One, two, three!"

The crowd roared in approval as all four men leaped to the attack at very nearly the same time. The man with the hatchet was a half-step behind the others, and the delay cost him dearly as Sextus first smashed the spearman's thrust away with his shield with enough force to half-spin the man around, then turned to his right and stepped forward to sink his gladius deep into the exposed side of the hachetman as the man's hatchet rebounded harmlessly again from Potitus's shield. The man dropped his weapon and staggered away from the fray, clutching at his side with both hands as blood spilled from between his fingers. The wound appeared to be a mortal one, but Sextus made no move to finish off the man, and instead continued to follow his brothers, matching them step for step as they pressured the two fighters facing Tertius and Volesus.

With her eyes only for her husband, Severa hadn't seen what transpired with the attack on her two brothers-in-law at the fore, except that none of the four combatants appeared to have been injured in the exchange. But for the first time, she heard Volesus bark an order, and immediately Potitus swung around to add his shield to the pair that were moving forward, while Sextus continued to protect their backs against the spearman.

The two fighters looked at each other. Now there were three shields in the pitiless metal wall that was threatening to pin them between it and the stone walls of the arena. They had two options, attack or run. But while the swordsman chose the former and charged forward with his long sword over his head, the man with the mace ran along the wall to the right of the advancing Valerians in a desperate attempt to escape from the closing trap.

The swordsman was a dangerous and experienced fighter. He slashed at Potitus's face, then smashed his buckler into Volesus's shield, knocking it aside to create an opening into which he could thrust his sword. Before he could take advantage of it, though, Potitus recovered and moved his shield to cover Volesus's exposed side. Instead of flesh or armor, the vicious thrust met with black Amorran iron and was shunted harmlessly aside.

Tertius, on the other side of Volesus, had not been inactive. When the swordsman reached forward to stab at his brother, he stepped with his left foot and thrust low with his gladius. The sharp legionary blade punched right through the swordsman's leather armor. As Tertius closed in, leaned forward, and put his weight behind the sword, it sank nearly hilt-deep into the man's stomach. The terrible blow was rapidly followed by two more blades driven into the mortally-wounded gladiator, Potitus's into the side of his neck and Volesus's under his right armpit.

The crowd groaned with the shock of the lethal violence, and Severa gasped, as for a moment, the swordsman's body was held suspended on three Valerian blades. Then Potitus and Volesus withdrew their gladiuses and he slumped to the sands, lifeless. Tertius, his blade more deeply embedded, was forced to put his foot on the body and exert more than a little effort to pull it out. He extricated his red-stained blade to the sound of cheers from the fickle crowd, and they cheered even louder when Tertius raised it in a bloody salute to them. Next to Severa, Pompilia was breathing out something between a prayer and a sob as she placed a hand over her mouth in both relief and horror.

Returning her attention to Sextus, Severa saw that it was the spearman's last chance to attack a Valerian on equal terms. The man must have realized this at almost the same time she did, as he took a deep breath before rushing toward Sextus again. She reached out blindly and found Carvilia's hand, squeezing it as if somehow doing so would lend strength to her husband's arms.

Desperate to finish off Sextus before his brothers could come to his aid, the spearman attacked without restraint, jabbing the wicked point at her taller husband one, two, three times. The fourth time, however, Sextus stepped forward and brushed the spearhead aside with his shield before twisting it upward and driving its iron bottom into the man's face with the full weight of his shoulder behind it. The man fell to the ground and dropped his spear as he instinctively covered his shattered nose with both hands. But Sextus was on him like a fox leaping after a mouse, breaking the man's left leg below the knee with the bottom edge of his shield before crouching down and holding his gladius to the writhing man's throat in a menacing manner.

The man with the mace twirled it slowly as the three other Valerians approached him from behind their wall of shields. Then he tossed it to the side, slipped his shield from his left arm, and dropped to both knees in the sand, stretching out his empty hands to either side in an obvious gesture of submission. The three Valerians stopped and raised their swords, then Potitus and Tertius each turned outside to salute the northern and southern sides of the arena, while Volesus kept a watchful eye on the kneeling gladiator.

All around Severa, the crowd rose to their feet, stomping and shouting in celebration of the defeat of their four champions. She looked back and forth, bewildered, but there was no doubting the sincerity of their enthusiasm.

"The plebs are fickle," Carvilia shouted in her ear. "Never forget that, little sister! They hate as easily as they love, and they love as easily as they hate!"

Severa nodded. She had no doubt that the people would have cheered every bit as lustily if it were Sextus and his brothers lying dead upon the sand. No, she thought, they would have cheered even louder to see a patrician House Martial brought down in blood.

A centurion approached the wounded spearman and helped him to his feet. The centurion said something to the man and was greeted by an angry response, punctuated by the man spitting in the direction of the Valerians. The centurion called out to Sextus, who bent down, retrieved the man's spear, and then, to Severa's utter astonishment, drove the point up under the man's chin with one hand, killing him instantly. Sextus released the spear, stepped back, and watched as the dead man toppled over onto his back.

"Why did, what… did Sextus just kill that man?"

"Look," Carvilia pointed. Severa, still sputtering with horror, followed her finger.

A second centurion was speaking to the last survivor, the oldest and wariest of the fighters. He was standing now, and he had removed his helm to reveal a head that was entirely bald. But whereas his companion had reacted with anger to whatever the first centurion said, he was nodding vigorously, perhaps even eagerly, Severa thought. To her surprise, to everyone's surprise, the centurion unhooked his own red cape and placed it around the other man's broad shoulders. Another centurion removed his own cross-plumed helmet and stepped forward to offer it to the man, who took it in both hands with a deep nod of appreciation, then set it on his head.

The arena fairly shook as the plebs roared their approval.

But that noise was as nothing compared to their response to Valerius Potitus embracing the man. Her tall brother-in-law threw both arms around the veteran gladiator, thumping his leather-armored shoulders as if they had not been trying to kill each other just moments ago. And when Potitus stepped back and returned the salute of his newly-appointed centurion, the men who would soon be serving under both of them shouted as if they intended to wake the dead. A chant began as Volesus and several of the centurions went to congratulate the man.

"Valerius, Valerius, Valerius!"

Flanked by centurions with one arm around the newest addition to their ranks, Volesus raised his hand to address the men in the stands. It took them a little while to settle down, but the eldest Valerian waited patiently until he could be heard.

"Men of Amorr, we stand before you, justified by Man and God."

He waited again as the crowd cheered.

"Men of Amorr, the Senate has ordered me to serve as legate of the Legion XXXV, and my brother, Valerius Potitus, to serve as legate of the Legion XXXVI. In like manner, the Senate has ordered you to serve in those legions in defense of our city. Men of Amorr, will you defend your city?"

"Ave!" came the response. Another chant began as the plebs began stomping on the stone seats. "Ave Valerius, ave Amorr! Ave Valerius, ave Amorr!"

"Many of you know how to fight. Some of you even know how to kill. But what you have seen today is how Amorr's legions make war!"

The crowd cheered again as the three other Valerians drew their swords and raised them in celebration of their victory, then turned to acknowledge all four sides of the arena.

"Lucius Pedanius, your chosen champion, is now with us. He will serve the city as a centurion in Legio XXXVI. Men of Amorr, will you stand with him!"

"Ave!"

"Men of Amorr, will you stand with us?"

"Ave!"

"Men of Amorr, Legions of Amorr, will you make war on the enemies of Amorr?"

Their reply was as thunderous as it was delirious. "Ave! Ave! Ave Valerius!"

Followed by his fascitors, Andronicus Declama was marching imperiously back out into the arena, no doubt sensing the chance to make another speech like a shark smelling blood in the water, when Severa felt Pompilia pulling at her sleeve.

"Come, sister. Drusus says it's time to go!"

Carvilia and Caerilla were already moving toward the exit, escorted by the Valerian house slaves. She went to follow them, then looked back at the sands and saw her tall, handsome husband standing like a triumphant demigod before the roaring plebs, his sword unsheathed and his arms outstretched as he basked in the public adulation. For the first time, she felt as if she understood what it meant for him to be a Valerian, and what it meant for her to have married into a family devoted to the arts of war.

And yet, the majestic sight did not fill her with pride. It filled her with stark terror.

BESSARIAS

BESSARIAS stared at the word before him. Could they possibly be true? The elderly elf frowned as he re-read a line in the sixteen-hundred-year-old manuscript for the third time. No, his eyes had not misled him, nor had he somehow mistaken the familiar crabbed handwriting belonging to a magistras now dead for more than eight centuries. The words were undeniable, even if the message they conveyed struck him as impossible. There were thirteen of the Ageless. That was not news to him, or to any member of the Collegium who had spent sufficient time studying the Elder Ages. But this unexpected revelation, this was something very strange indeed.

And the Ageless walked unknown among the mortal races, wearing the faces of the sons of Men. They also hid themselves among Orkes and Goblines, and Dwarves, and even among the wise.

He felt a moment's pang of guilt at the realization of how clearly he could make out the tiny letters. Drawing upon his magic for the first time in decades had been the very last thing on his mind, but here, deep in the bowels of the High King's librarea, surrounded by dusty tomes and faded, age-cracked scrolls infused with centuries of High Elven sorceries cast by the greatest of their mages, doing so had been as effortless and unintentional as squinting. It was very far from the first time that an elf had done so.

However, it was, he thought with modest self-reproach tinged with sardonic amusement, likely the very first time an elf had fallen to his knees and repented of doing so since the great building had been constructed.

He was genuinely remorseful for his lapse, and yet he couldn't help feeling relieved that he could now read all but the most faded texts clearly, without the aid of the magnifier to which he'd been forced to resort twenty years ago. He felt better too; his back was straighter, and unless he was mistaken, his gnarled hands would even be able to hold a quill properly again.

It had been but a moment of thoughtless weakness, but it appeared his body had no sooner been afforded the opportunity than it had drunk deeply of the mighty well of magic embedded in the very marble and mortar of the ancient building. And he knew very well that having slipped once, it would be all too easy for him to do so again.

"Give me strength, Almighty Father, Magistras of Magistrae, Archtext and Archmagus and Primordial Word. Let me rely upon Thy Will, not mine!"

But still the lure was there, swirling in the dance of the candle's flame before him, the motes of the dust swirling around the shelves, and the gray-brown leather of the book before him. Always, the tempting magic was there, and it whispered to him seductively, like a long-spurned lover who refused to give up hope of an eventual reconciliation.

Scowling, he put the newly revived temptation firmly behind him and returned his attention to the astonishing sentence before him.

It was a thin reed, the thinnest of reeds, upon which to confirm his suspicions. And yet, there it was, right in front of him.

"Even among the wise." In context, that almost certainly meant his former colleagues at the Collegium. Or, to put it more precisely, their predecessors. Although his kind was long-lived, the elves were not truly immortal and few chose to continue living beyond eleven or twelve hundred years; the weariness of age, combined with the inevitable risk of accidents over the course of the centuries, meant that none of the great magisters who had originally contributed to the book still lived.

He knew about the Ancients, of course. He had even devoted a year or three to studying them, flattering himself with the idea that he might be the one to unravel their mystery. But as the legends about them inevitably turned out to be little more than the source of scores of myths about dragons and demigods and various deities worshipped by the younger races, sorting the few kernels of scholastic wheat from the mountain of historical chaff rapidly became tedious and he had soon turned his attention to more intellectually rewarding pursuits. The Ancients had once ruled all the known world, not merely the great continent of Selenoth, but they had disappeared without warning or explanation, supposedly leaving only thirteen of their number behind. Some scholars said they were immortal, others, more skeptical, believed they had merely been long-lived creatures akin to the elves; one heretical school even insisted that they had been nothing more than the elven architects of a Golden Age, of which the Seven Kingdoms, now Three, were the diminished, latter-day descendants.

But to the best of his knowledge, no one, not even anyone who subscribed to the immortal theory, had ever suggested that their last remnants had walked secretly among the elves, let alone among the magisters of the Collegium Occludum!

A troubling thought occurred to him. It was nearly two hundred and fifty years ago that his former master, the Magistras Daimonae, one of the greatest scholars ever to dwell among the Collegium Occludum, died unexpectedly when a simple summoning spell went horribly awry and he was torn limb from limb by one of the minor netherlings he had summoned. In the months following that shocking death, Bessarias reviewed the incantation dozens of times, and checked it against several of the compendiums of daemonic nomenclature right here in this very building. He had found nothing amiss. He had never seen any sign that his master had done anything wrong or made any mistake, nor had any of the other mages who investigated the affair.

Nor, until today, had he ever had any reason to even begin to suspect that the information on which the spell was constructed was incorrect. But what if it had been wrong. Worse, what if the summoning had been intentionally deceptive? Was it possible that it had been written in such a manner as to summon a different netherling from the abyssal realms, a much more powerful demon, than the one it purported to call? The suspicion defied belief, and yet, was that truly less likely than the great Dolmitrathal making a mistake worthy of a tongue-twisted acolyte?

He placed the tome back on the wooden table. If he was correct, and the incantation had been written in a misleading manner, then whoever had written it was either insane or knowingly culpable of, at the very least, putting the lives of other elves, novices, mages, and magistrae alike, in danger. And it was just barely possible that the author had intended it as an almost undetectable instrument of murder! But given the age of the manuscript, which preceded his master's death by eight centuries, the author of the incantation could not possibly have intended to kill the Magistras Daimonae, unless... his finger traced a single word.

Ageless. It was known to be one way of referring to the Thirteen, to the immortals who walked unknown among the mortal races, even among the wise.

No. It was impossible. His aged mind was merely wandering, leading him on tangent after fruitless tangent. Perhaps he was addled by his earlier slip from self-discipline and abstinence, perhaps he was mildly intoxicated by the long-denied sensation of magic coursing through his blood. Why had he sought out this particular spellbook in the first place? He tried to recall his previous line of reasoning, the one that had led him from the palace to the library so urgently this morning that he had risen early and omitted to break his fast.

Ah yes. It was the idea of a pattern, a strangely nebulous shape arising from the ebb and flow of history, that had caused him to wonder if perhaps there was something more to this unexpectedly sizable invasion that was troubling the High King than the violent ambitions of a single orc. But, alas, if there was, he had been unable to find it, much less any connection to either the unreliable incantation or the death of the 327th Magistras Daimonae of the Collegium Occludum.

He picked up the parchment upon which he had scratched some dates. Each marked an invasion or a war that struck him, in one way or another, as being somehow outside the customary range of mortal events. The rise of the Witchkings, for one. The fall of Glaislael for another. However, he had not been able to find any mathematical patterns or significant correlations, not with the phases of the two moons, with the slow-shifting patterns of the global ley lines, or with what little was known of the history of abyssal politics.

There seemed to be neither rhyme nor reason to any of it, and yet, he could not shake his growing suspicion that there was something more to these occasional kingdom-shaking events than sheer happenstance or the ebb and flow of ambition as it surfaced periodically amongst men, goblins, orcs, and trolls.

A familiar presence loomed behind him. He found himself smiling inadvertently, knowing who it was without needing to turn around.

"Kilios," he said, before slowly pushing himself up from the book-strewn table.

He looked up to see the elven mage who had once been his closest friend, and dismay wrenched his heart as he took in the beautiful features of the elf, unchanged since he had seen him last except for his eyes, which were sightless and white again.

"Oh, my dear friend, what have you done to yourself!" he whispered in sorrow. "How could you reject the martyr's gift?"

"You know I never asked for it. I found that I saw more truly with my seer-sight and took measures accordingly, old friend." The blind mage smiled ruefully. "I had heard the greatest among us was once more in our midst. But never mind my eyes, Bessarias. How is it that you have become so aged and infirm?"

"I have done naught but accept the inevitable. I suppose I am unique among our race in my inaction."

"Well, perhaps not quite so unique as you would have us think, Magistras." The blind elf, whose lack of physical vision did not inhibit his ability to see in the slightest, cocked his head a little as he smiled at Bessarias. "I see the magic still flows in you, although what should be a mighty river is now little more than the barest trickle."

"You see too deeply, my friend." Bessarias spread his hands with chagrin. "I cannot hide my shame from you. A moment of weakness, the habits of a lifetime; it seems my discipline is regrettably less than perfect. I have loved my sin too well and too long, I fear, to give it up as entirely as I should."

"Sin? Why call it sin?"

"What else can one call it? We exert our will upon Creation and change it to suit ourselves. We are unnatural creatures, ruled by selfishness, narcissism, and pride. There is no logos in us, nothing of the natural order or the divine, for all that we flatter ourselves as being one with nature and her gods."

Kilios smiled. "But if we are created as aspects of nature, then surely anything we do is part of the natural order! Does that not logically follow?"

"Don't play pedantic games with me, old friend. You cannot simply define away concepts that make you uncomfortable."

"How am I doing that?"

"By artificially limiting your definition of 'unnatural' to 'that which is not of nature', which of course precludes any action by any being or creature intrinsic to this material plane. But I used the word in the established context defined as something 'contrary to the laws or course of nature', which, as you know perfectly well, is precisely what we do when we utilize magic to move an object or resist the ravages of time."

Kilios laughed. "It is good to see your mind has resisted those ravages, even though your body has not! I will not bandy words with you, Bessarias. Having seldom come out the better before, I do not imagine I shall be able to do so now, particularly not on matters to which you have devoted considerable thought. Very well, I will grant you that we are unnatural creatures ruled by pride. Why should it trouble you?"

"Because it means that in the grand struggle between the Perfect and the Fallen, between the Good, the Beautiful, and the True and the Inverse, we find ourselves taking the latter's side. That is not my wish, and I expect that if you shared my perspective, it would not be yours."

"Indubitably," the blind elf said with a faint smile. "Of course, since I do not share your axioms, the same logical syllogisms and shared values inevitably lead me to a different conclusion."

"And it is that which gives me hope, Kilios. It is merely a matter of providing you with the essential facts of the subject, which is why I am assured of your eventual agreement, over time."

"Time, my unnecessarily aged friend, does not appear to be on your side, if you do not amend your perspective."

Bessarias laughed with the sheer delight of crossing intellectual swords with the younger elf again. "To the contrary! We are of the infinite, and time is the least of our concerns. What is a year, or even a century, in the context of true immortality!"

Kilios shrugged. "You and I have both spoken with the dead, Bessarias. At no time has any departed soul ever told us of Paradise, or Purgatory, and yet the hells of which they speak are manifold. Nor have they instructed any other sorceror in this Collegium in such matters. I'm afraid I do not understand why you have taken these fantasies of short-lived men to heart. Even if one of them came back to life, or was resurrected in some way by some dark magic, what of that? It could merely have been a necromancer's reanimation combined with a demonic possession of the corpse, or some other similarly pedestrian marvel."

"You can no more see the light of my faith than you can see the light of the sun, Kilios. You are twice blind."

"You wound me." The blind mage laughed, then grew more serious. "I know the king did not bring you here idly, Bessarias, and I know you must have a reason for coming here rather than to the Collegium. So tell me, what are you doing and how can I be of assistance."

Bessarias tapped on the scattered pile of ancient manuscripts and scrolls in front of him. "To put it one way, I'm attempting to establish a pattern. To put it another, I'm trying to solve an accident that may have been a murder. And I have the faintest impression that the two things might be connected, although I have no solid grounds to believe they are."

"On second thought, perhaps I would prefer to hear you wax profound on human religion," said Kilios wryly. "I should have known you'd be up to something impossible. Age has not rendered you any less chimerical, Bessarias. Let's start with the pattern, since I'm rather better with history than murder. What does this pattern concern?"

"Wars, essentially. Not the pedestrian warlord wants someone else's land, or gold, or wife sort of conflict, but the major wars, the epochal conflicts that have had significant effects on entire races. The rise and fall of the Witchkings being perhaps the most recent example, barring the present migrations of the orc tribes."

Kilios picked up one of the parchments upon which Bessarias had been scrawling and sighed. "The irony is that while my blindness doesn't prevent me from reading this, your execrable writing does! But if I'm interpreting your hieroglyphics correctly, you've marked twenty-seven wars going back over a period of, what is it, five thousand years?"

"Six thousand. Six thousand, one hundred and thirty one, to be precise."

"Ah, that's what passes for a six in your mind. Interesting. Now, assuming that you've more or less correctly identified the relevant examples of the sort of war that concerns you, I can see why there appears to be some sort of periodic distribution here, but given the time frame concerned, I don't see why it can't simply be happenstance. After all, the average is two hundred twenty seven years between each event, and given how many have taken place over the centuries, they have to happen sometime."

"Yes, but notice that there are no abnormally short or abnormally long intervals. If we were talking about four or five of these events, that might be possible, but not across twenty seven of them, not unless there is an external factor preventing outliers."

"What sort of external factor?"

"It could be anything! A religious calendar. An astrological conjunction. Structural environmental limitations."

"A religious calendar?" Kyrios said incredulously. "What sort of religion goes centuries between events, how would these events inspire large-scale wars, and who could possibly practice such a religion?"

"The Thirteen."

The blind mage snorted. "The Thirteen? They're a myth, Bessarias! None of the historical accounts are even remotely credible, and every single reference to them are far in the past!"

"I read human accounts of them when I was at the monastery. They're strikingly similar to our own. Some of the Witchkings' manuscripts are also suggestive in this regard."

"And I'm sure there are tales of immortal creatures told around the campfires of the orcs too. For the most part, legends are just that, tales concocted by a storyteller with an imagination. Besides, I can tell you right now that there is one possible external factor that doesn't require a hidden cult of immortals manipulating all the races of Selenoth. You already mentioned it, in fact."

"Environmental limitations?"

"No, astrological conjunctions. Although, not actually astrological as such. It would be more correct to say lunar conjunctions."

"I already did the calculations and ruled it out."

"Ah, but did you account for the *lleuad aur*?"

Bessarias paused and slowly shook his head. "The third... Kilios, that's brilliant! If the pattern was established more than six thousand years ago and it concerned lunar conjunctions, then it had to have involved the third moon before it was destroyed. Shall we work out the calculations?"

Three hours later, Bessarias was exhausted and Kilios was rubbing at his eyes as if they were still functioning and fatigued. They were both frustrated; the first three events very nearly fit the three lunar conjunctions recorded in the historical sky charts, although they tended to lag the wars by a period of a decade or less rather than precede them. But the twenty-four events that took place following the destruction of the third moon, called Golden Moon by the elves, simply didn't show any relation to the dates of what would have been the triple conjunctions had Selenoth's third and smallest moon not met with its fiery fate in the Fifth Millennium.

"How can this be?" demanded Kilios. "We must be missing something."

"Obviously," Bessarias snapped. "Removing the *lleuad aur* from the equation has to change the results. And yet, the pattern continues somehow, different than before."

"Have you considered how the cycles of these conjunctions might intertwine with the ebb and flow of the ley lines throughout the continent?"

Bessarias stared thoughtfully at the space before him, his fingers tracing invisible patterns in the air. "I don't see how the latter would be relevant, though it's intriguing to contemplate how these particular conjunctions could have amplified certain arcane phenomena throughout history. But I think it would be very difficult to work out the extent to which the obliteration of the third moon disrupted the celestial choreographies."

"Think about the gravitational influences, Bessarias. With the third moon's mass vanishing, the planetary alignments during the conjunctions could have shifted dramatically. These alterations might have caused variations in tides, fluctuations in magical currents, and even fluctuations in the potency of our spells over time."

"You're onto something, Kilios. The very foundations of our magic could have been altered. They probably were altered. But to quantify these changes, we would have to recalibrate our astronomical instruments, perhaps by tapping into the residual energies left behind by the third moon's demise. Without knowing precisely what the differences were before, we can't even begin to comprehend the way in which magic itself has been transformed."

"Different than before!" The blind mage snapped his fingers. "That's what we were missing! We're using the wrong calculations for the bilunar conjunctions!"

"Yes, Kilios, that's why the dates don't match."

"No, I mean, we have to recalculate the positions of the first and second moons on the basis of their modified orbits rather than their original ones. Remember, the loss of the Golden Moon's mass didn't just have an effect on the tides and the stability of the land, it changed the orbits of the first two moons as well!"

"So we need to determine when the two moons would have had a conjunction with the non-extant third moon, were it still there, but in their current post-trilunar orbits instead of their theoretical trilunar orbits."

"Exactly!" beamed Kilios, a broad smile creasing his face that stood in stark contrast to his expressionless milky eyes.

It took them nearly an hour to work out the mathematics of the revised equation, and when Bessarias finally finished confirming the fact that there had been a hypothetical trilunar conjunction only five years after the final defeat of the Witchkings, he leaned back in his chair and ran an aching hand through his thinning white hair.

"That's it. You were right. The pattern is real. It has to be. There are only six pseudo-conjunctions that have no corresponding war within ten years, which is a coincidence far too improbable to satisfy even a determined skeptic."

Kilios puffed out his cheeks and pursed his lips as he loudly exhaled. "So we have a correlation. But I don't understand how it's causal. Wars take place for a lot of different reasons, most of them rather stupid, but a lunar alignment with a nonexistent moon isn't one of them, at least, to the best of my knowledge."

"Exactly." Bessarias handed Kilios an old scroll that had gone untouched over the last few hours. "That's why I was seeking to learn more about the legend of the Thirteen. I've developed a hypothesis, you see, although I'm fairly certain you're not going to appreciate it."

"I've already got sufficient evidence to have you declared senile, my friend. And given the apparent relevance of the lunar-war connection, I'm genuinely curious to hear what your explanation is."

"I appreciate your humoring an old elf." Bessarias cleared his throat. "Let us assume a small number of immortal beings. Not gods, not spiritual beings from another plane, but material creatures, virtual demigods for all intents and purposes, undying, resident on this earth, and with much the same sort of petty concerns and objectives that we have. They're rather like us, actually, only longer-lived."

"And presumably more powerful."

"Indeed, if they happen to go in for magic. Certainly they are more knowledgeable where historical matters are concerned."

"Naturally."

"But there are only a small number of them. Probably more than thirteen, perhaps less, but regardless, their immortality makes it difficult for them to settle serious differences. Perhaps they try to set up as a council where the majority rules, or perhaps they appoint an arbitrator to decide differences of opinion. This might even work for a time, until one loser realizes that he needs more allies. So he seeks them among the mortal races, among us, among Men, even among the orcs. His peers now have no choice but to respond in kind."

"Thereby leading to a system where conflict among the immortals is settled by proxy wars." Kilios shook his head. "It frightens me, Bessarias, how even now you can turn chaos into order. Had you suggested this to me yesterday, I would have thought you deranged with age. Now, I find myself wondering if we would do well to endow a new magistral seat dedicated to an entirely new domain of study!"

"Historical Erevnarchaio-paremvasication?"

"That's rather a mouthful, don't you think? But let us imagine, for the sake of argument, that these argumentative immortals settle their differences through proxy wars. Why only once every 200 years? What is the connection to the lunar conjunctions?"

"Who can say?" Bessarias spread his hands. "Ritual would be the most straightforward answer. Even the High King metes out justice on certain occasions at times, not always when the need for it happens to arise. In the Amorran lands, sentences are commuted and prisoners are freed on the first day of spring, while traitors are held until their public execution at the winter solstice. It could even be that such customs are a pale shadow of their traditions."

He pushed himself to his feet with a groan. "Enough. Already the letters are swimming before my eyes."

"Shall we continue tomorrow? I am at your service if you have need of me."

Bessarias smiled and put one wrinkled hand on the blind mage's shoulder. "The king will have need of you soon, I think, Kilios. You needn't assume or accept anything, but if you would do one thing for me, continue digging deeper into this pattern and these conjunctions. I cannot see the connection myself, but I am certain that there is something in it, and something that may prove to be far more historically significant than anything I have ever done."

"I confess I am beginning to think you may be right, Bessarias."

"Time will tell. But I do not have much more time. Therefore, this is a task I must leave to you. In fact, I charge you with it! Look to the anomalies and the accidents, Kilios. My old master... it will not be the only such–" Bessarias suddenly reeled and would have fallen had not his colleague caught him.

"Do take your hands off me! I'm perfectly well!"

"No, you've been at this all day and you need to rest, my stubborn old friend. Come, let me help you back to the palace."

"Oh, I suppose you're right. Do you know, I think I forgot my lunch!"

Bessarias reluctantly took Kilios's offered arm and the two masters of magic, one ancient and decrepit, the other adroit despite his blindness, slowly made their way together through the great maze of the towering library's bookstacks.

THEUDERIC

T HEUDERIC rolled over, his lower back aching from the combination of all the riding he'd been doing lately with the hard-packed ground on which he'd been sleeping. He hadn't expected any royal appreciation for tracking down the wayward priests of St. Michael and bringing them back with him, much less a reward, but he strongly felt that at least one day of proper rest and relaxation would have definitely been in order. Unfortunately, events had conspired against him. The orcs were on the move again and the Red Prince was determined to make them pay a toll in blood for crossing his rivers. He pushed his wool blankets off and sat up, squinting blearily at the rosy-hued light entering the tent through the loosely-tied entrance. Amis was snoring, but his movement had woken Maussart, who sprang to his feet with an ease that made Theuderic want to curse the younger mage.

"Aren't we late? The marquis said we should ride at dawn!"

Theuderic yawned, stretched, and arched his spine, trying to see if the ache was inclined to go away quickly or not. "It isn't dawn until the sun's up," he growled. "We don't need to leave with the foot, unless you're planning to walk."

He grunted as he pushed himself up to his knees and rolled the two blankets into a tight bundle, then found the cord he kept to bind them and slipped it over them before pulling it tight. He indicated to Jocelyn that he should do the same. "Always best to keep your baggage stowed in times like these. You never know when they're going to tell you to ride off God knows where, so unless you want to leave it behind when you're in a hurry some day, don't even walk outside without stowing it."

As the younger mage complied, he plucked his vest off the ground, then buttoned it before sliding his cape over his shoulders and tying it. There were times to lay low, and there were times to advertise one's status. Today, they would do well to remind the men of Savondir that the various devilries of the bestial foe were no match for the King's Own. "They're not going anywhere without us. More to the point, the ride to the bridge won't take but an hour, and the orcs aren't expected to reach there until noon. If they were ahead of schedule, someone would have been sent to waken us. Now, go see if you can find us something hot to drink before this morning chill sinks into our bones!"

Maussart nodded obediently and disappeared from the tent in a slither of fabric as his blue cape followed him outside. Theuderic was disappointed to see that the sky outside was grey and overcast. He wondered if he should wake Amis, as the older mage would not be accompanying them today, but when he turned around, he saw the man was already awake and was stroking his white-shot beard as he contemplated the canvas above him.

"Any advice?" he asked Amis, more to be polite than out of any expectation of learning something useful. Though it was going to be his first time going into battle with three untested young mages, he'd seen sufficient combat over the years that he wasn't overly concerned.

"Don't get distracted. Keep them out of trouble; remember, it's better to pull back too soon than too late. And don't neglect to bring down that damned bridge! You and the lads will be fine regardless, I expect, but it will demoralize the levies if the footmen don't make it back safely."

Theuderic nodded. He would see to the bridge himself, otherwise, he'd limit himself to keeping an eye on the others and making sure they weren't caught off-guard by any unexpected sorceries. "Would you like some tea? I sent Maussart in search of some."

"No, I plan to get back to sleep after you lot ride off. I just wanted to have a word with you before you go. Spells prepared?"

"Of course." Theuderic tapped his iron-bound staff, which was practically glowing due to the powerful incendiary spell he'd charged it with the night before. "I doubt we even need the Amorran mines."

"Don't get cocksure, de Merovech. No point in exerting yourself when a simple spark will do. And be sure the damned bags are waxed!"

Theuderic nodded. He wasn't liable to be overconfident when facing the orcs these days, not after having seen the terrible ruin of poor Sebastien and his horse. In fact, he had been wondering if there might be a way to utilize the Michelines to provide an early warning of any demonic summonings by the verdards' sanguinistes. Even if the range of what he thought of as their anti-magical net was limited in its ability to actually suppress magic, their ability to detect magic, particularly magics of the blacker sort, might extend considerably further. A moment or two of warning might make all the difference in the world, especially if there was a mage standing ready to deal with any such incipient threats.

He knew from painful personal experience that it didn't take much to interfere with a successful summoning. A single syllable pronounced incorrectly, a poorly drawn Star of Salomon, impure salt, or a lapse of concentration could ruin even the calling of a minor spirit of the air from the wind. He couldn't even imagine what painful and sordid rituals must be required to dredge up something like the orc war god from whatever hell it presumably inhabited, but he was reasonably certain that a blast or two of sorcerous balefire, even if it didn't incinerate the summoner, would prove to be a distraction sufficient to interrupt its summoning.

"Anything else?"

"Don't give them too many instructions. You'll be tempted to keep giving them just one more word of advice. Don't. Keep your mouth shut. The more you talk, the more you'll make them nervous."

"How many is too many?" After all, he would have to provide them with some basic direction once they arrived at the bridge, it wasn't as if they could hope to perfectly anticipate the enemy's actions.

"Three is ideal. If they ask you questions, keep the answers short. And if they start babbling, tell them to shut up. Novices respond well to calm and quiet. They mistake it for confidence."

"I am confident!"

Amis yawned. "So much the better. Now go away. I'm going to follow my own advice. Try not to get any of them killed."

"Your confidence inspires me," Theuderic said, grinning, as the older mage grunted and rolled over, turned his back to Theuderic, and audibly farted. "I'll take that as a sign to be on my way, then."

Theuderic exited the tent, his saddlebag over his shoulder, his belt, sword, and staff in hand, and immediately found himself shivering in the brisk morning air, which was rather colder outside than he'd expected. He swore, pulled his cloak closer with his free hand, and wondered if he should root around in his bag for his gloves. At least the thick cloak was warm. He had always considered it to be foolish to wear the royal blue of the Kingsmage in battle, since the distinctive color made them obvious targets for the foe, but then, being an obvious target did tend to remind one to stay well back from the front lines. And in situations like today, it would be wise to remain well outside the range of the verdards' crossbows.

"Seigneur Theuderic," he heard Maussart call. He looked up and saw the younger mage was headed his way with Ambroys and Talbot in tow, carrying a steaming kettle in one hand and a pair of wooden cups in the other.

"That's not necessary," he said, accepting the mug with a nod before holding it out to be filled. "Save the titles for when there are ladies who need impressing about." The tea wasn't sweetened, but the warmth was a godsend, and before he'd finished the mug, he was already beginning to feel reasonably human again.

"Fill that up again, Jocelyn, and listen, both of you. The bridge we're riding for is the only one over the River Waut that the marquis left standing, because we don't want the enemy marching any which way he wants across the countryside. We want to draw him here, where the prince will be ready for them."

"Will he be?" Talbot sounded doubtful. He was a thin-faced, blond young man, and had taken Sebastien's death very hard. The previous night, Theuderic and Amis discussed whether or not it would be wiser to leave him behind, but as Amis pointed out, if the young mage was going to prove himself unfit for the field, it would be better to learn that now, in a minor skirmish, than in the middle of a proper battle when something vital might depend upon him.

"Of course he will!" Theuderic lied without hesitation. "The Amorrans and the Eastmarchers have been preparing for weeks. We'll send the king twice as many ears as last time. Now, where are those archers?"

"I was told they'd meet us at the horses," Ambroys said.

"Good." Both Amis and Theuderic had demanded an escort of two mounted archers per mage from the Marquis de Cherdrefin. No one wanted to risk losing another promising young mage through carelessness. The archers would give them eight more pairs of eyes to scan for distant dangers that might escape the attention of a mage intent on unleashing a spell.

The plan was to not only draw the invaders in the direction of their fortified positions, but also buy the recently arrived royal reinforcements one more day to rest and familiarize themselves with the ground on which the prince-or to be more accurate-the Amorran centurions-had chosen to give battle. There were some nobles, overly impressed by the Amorran's engineering, who argued they should fight from behind the high wooden walls of the southerners' castra, but experience won the day as the Marquis de Ponchaux, a local noble, backed strongly by the Amorrans and Theuderic himself, managed to successfully explain that doing so would only encourage the orcs to march right past them and wreak bloody havoc in the more populous heartland of the realm.

There were no guarantees that the orc's warleader would consent to meet them on their preferred ground, of course, but armies, unlike fortifications, were capable of movement, and with its significant numerical advantage, no one seriously believed that the orc would be overly concerned about the additional challenges presented by a few hills and ditches. As long as the prince came out to fight, the orc would know it had to deal with him sooner or later, and orcs were not renowned for their patience. Both de Ponchaux and the Red Prince were convinced that the orc would come directly at them, as quickly as possible, once it knew exactly where the Savondese army was. It would attempt to shatter them quickly, with one terrible blow, which would then leave the whole of the Eastmarch, as well as the cities of Vallon-sur Bois and Lonclieu, defenseless before it.

"Now, here are your assignments. The marquis's men will hold the bridge. The orcs will bring up archers to the far bank on either side, and they have a lot more than we have, so it will fall to us to keep them from overwhelming our own bowmen and raking the footmen on the bridge from three sides. You've prepared the spells I directed?"

They all nodded, and Ambroys held up his staff, an ancient black length of oak that barely had any surface left uncarved. It had reportedly belonged to his great-grandfather, a formidable Immortel.

"Very good. The river flows south, and we'll be defending the west bank, so Maussart, you'll take the northern side. Ambroys, the south. I'm told there is a stone wall that runs along the top of the embankment, but I don't know if it will be tall enough to hide behind. If not, you'll need to stay back where they can't see you, then crawl forward when the archers call for you. Stay low, let loose with no more than two blasts, then crawl backwards out of sight again. Remember, you're not there to clear the banks, you only have to take some of the pressure off the archers."

"What about me?" Talbot asked.

"You've prepared the *De la Croix*?"

"It's ready," the younger mage confirmed. It was a lightning spell that Theuderic suspected might prove particularly useful should the orcs attempt to swim the river.

"Good. You'll be with me in the church. The marquis said there is a bell tower there with clear sightlines to the bridge and the river."

"Is it close enough?"

"Only one way to find out. If it's not, we'll come up with an alternative." He looked at each of them in turn, and while he saw no little trepidation in their faces, he was pleased to see neither cowardice nor terror. "Don't exhaust yourselves. Always keep something in reserve. If you are fatigued, fall back to the church and either Talbot or I will take your place."

"How much warning will we have before the mines go?" Maussart wanted to know.

"Very little. When the horn sounds three times or you see a green flash in the sky, both of you hit the orcs on the bridge as soon as the men are clear with whatever you have ready. Be careful, don't hit our men! Then hurry back to your horses, mount up, and ride hard back to camp. Don't wait for me or for anyone else; your sole duty is to get back here safely."

Theuderic didn't mention that it would fall to him to ensure the mines ignited properly and the bridge was destroyed. He intended to wait as long as possible for the men fighting on the bridge to extricate themselves from the orcs and get clear of the explosion, but he knew he would have to choose between killing a few stragglers and permitting the first two or three ranks of orcs to cross behind them.

The plan was for de Ponchaux to retain a reserve of ten men-at-arms, who would advance after the bridge was blown to deal with what everyone anticipated would be a fairly small number of orcs on the near bank, all of whom would presumably be half-deafened and in disarray from the detonating mines. But Theuderic knew from bitter experience how seldom a reserve was actually reserved for its intended purpose. If the orcs pressed the men on the bridge too hard, too fast, the temptation to throw ten fresh men in as reinforcements would almost surely prove irresistible to the marquis.

He would cross that bridge when he came to it, he thought to himself with a smile. The three mages noticed his expression, and he was further amused to see how it visibly relaxed them. He was tempted to give them further instructions, then recalled Amis's words to mind and made do with a confident nod before leading them to where their horses had been saddled by their waiting escort.

The eight archers who would accompany them were all older men, hunters, if not poachers, by appearance. Their leader was a bald, bearded man who was less clearly impressed by their royal status than concerned about their relative youth.

"Damn me," he said as Theuderic approached, and spat something dark and viscous onto the ground. "Fifty thousand orcs and the King could only spare us a journeyman and three novices?"

"Your name, monsieur?" Theuderic was unconcerned by the apparent affront.

"Regnaut de Sorel. Yours?"

"Theuderic de Merovech, Comte de Thoneaux. Do allow me to present my colleagues from l'Academie, the seigneurs Massault, Talbot, and Ambroys."

The older man's expression didn't change, but his tone was a little more respectful when he replied. "A right proper comte, is yeh?"

"I am indeed. But that is neither here nor there. Rest assured, monsieur, my colleagues may be young, but they are trained battlemages and they are entirely capable of delivering a significant quantity of destruction to the foe."

"Trained, yeh says?" Regnaut raised a skeptical eyebrow.

Theuderic nodded, and the two men shared a look of mutual comprehension. "Exactly. Trained. And it is my dearest hope that you, and your men, will help them survive the experience required to temper that training. We have already lost one of our colleagues."

The archer unexpectedly smiled and pointed at Theuderic. "You was the one with de Roche, wasn't yeh. The mage what saved the people from Chevigny and Merne."

"If you are referring to the villagers we freed from the orcs, that was more our late colleague's doing than mine, but yes, I rode with the viscomte."

Regnaut nodded approvingly to his men. "This is the wizard old Gille was talking about! He can flame-broil a whole passel of orcs with that there stick!"

Theuderic sighed. While he could certainly flame-broil an orc or three, not even the most formidable Immortel had one-tenth the abilities imagined by the average peasant. During his time on the border, he had learned that this gap between expectation and ability usually led, sooner or later, to profound disappointment.

"We shall certainly do our utmost, my dear Regnaut," Theuderic promised, as he indicated that his companions should mount their horses.

"And if you would do us the kindness of keeping us alive, we should appreciate that as well."

The ride to the river was neither overly long nor unpleasant, as the temperature rose with the sun, and by the time they came within sight of the little abbatial village of Rouvillier, all four of the mages had removed their cloaks. Both abbey and village had already been abandoned; on their way they had encountered the very last die-hards to flee trudging slowly cross-country, weighed down by the sum total of their meager earthly possessions on their backs.

The marquis had chosen to defend this particular bridge rather than any of the four or five alternatives that had crossed the fast-moving River Waut prior to their demolition due to the minor fortifications that supposedly abutted it. However, Theuderic was skeptical that a minor abbey was likely to afford them much in the way of protection. His suspicions were confirmed when they rode around the outskirts of the village to the edge of the Waut, then along the river bank toward the bridge. The wall of the abbey extended nearly to the bank, leaving only a gap in which perhaps ten men could walk side-by-side, but while a square, four-level guard tower overlooked the bridge some thirty paces to its north, it was so close to the opposite bank that Theuderic knew he dared not risk taking up a position there.

The marquis's men-at-arms were already on site, having set out for Rouvillier the previous afternoon. Only a few were presently sitting watch on the bridge; they were dicing while two or three dozen men were on the other side of the river chopping down trees and demolishing a modest two-level structure that would have provided the enemy useful cover were it allowed to stand. The rest of the marquis's two hundred men were taking naps in the mid-day sun on the near bank, their weapons and shields beside them, on either side of the bridge itself. The embankment was steep enough to make reclining comfortable, though it was not so steep that a sleeping man would be in danger of rolling into the deep and fast-flowing waters.

Theuderic could have wished for steeper banks, as that would have made it more difficult for the enemy's archers to attack both the men on the bridge and his mages from a variety of angles, but if the orcs succeeded in swimming the Waut en masse, they would all have to retreat, and quickly. The marquis would not be foolish enough to try to hold the river bank despite the small advantage of the slope it afforded.

He looked around, but didn't see the marquis himself. Theuderic presumed de Poncheaux was wherever he had selected for a rallying point, most likely in the central square of the abandoned town.

He saw Maussart looking up at the tower, then across the river and knew that the young mage was reaching the same conclusion he had already reached. They might as well ride home as take shelter in the corner tower for all the good it would do them, because they would be literally a stone's throw away from where the enemy crossbows would be firing up at them. The tower was a strong point, being a solid stone-and-mortar structure, but it was too obvious, too close, and too exposed for them to utilize it despite the excellent line of sight it would provide to the bridge and the east bank alike. That was the problem, Theuderic reflected wryly. If you could see the enemy, all too often that meant the enemy could see you. Even if the orcs didn't possess any artillery, the tower would be a death trap for anyone who dared to expose himself at the windows.

The wall along the southern side of the bridge was rather more encouraging. Theuderic urged his horse next to it, then dismounted and measured himself against it. The stone wall was thicker than the length of his fingertips to his elbow, and rose very nearly to his waist. It would provide excellent cover for Ambroys, against missiles and magic alike. He urged his horse forward, toward the bridge, and was disappointed to see that there was no similar wall on the northern side, just a series of evenly planted oak trees. The trees were old enough, and thick enough, to offer a bare minimum of cover, but there was no way, short of lying flat on his belly, that Maussart would be able to keep himself completely out of sight from enemies on the far bank.

No, it wouldn't do at all. Nor was that the only problem presented by the town.

"The church is too far off," Talbot said, pointing at the only building that stood higher than the guard tower.

Theuderic looked to the north and saw that while the bell tower was in an excellent place to oversee the bridge and the northern side of the far bank, it had to be more than one hundred paces from the near end of the bridge. The bridge itself would block any view of the bank to the south of it, and the distance would dissipate the effects of any spells cast from it, with the possible exception of the lightning spell he'd ordered Talbot to prepare. He was confident he could still set off the mines from that far off, but his ability to assist Ambroys, and in particular, Maussart, would be severely hampered.

"Let's find the marquis," he said, and walked his horse up the slight incline that led toward the bridge. An inquiry of a grizzled old man-at-arms confirmed his earlier suspicions concerning de Ponchaux's whereabouts, and he led the others on the cobblestone-paved road that led directly from the bridge into the empty town.

No sooner had Theuderic spotted the tall nobleman at one corner of the square, poring over a map spread out on a pair of wooden benches pushed together to serve as an impromptu table, than a cry went up.

"The mages! The king's mages!"

He glanced back and saw that Maussart was grinning broadly, Ambroys was doing his best to look the way he imagined a royal battlemage should, and even Talbot was sitting up straight in his saddle for once. He shook his head. The same men who praised them so enthusiastically now would condemn them just as bitterly later, once they discovered the king's mages could not win their battles for them.

"De Merovech! It's about time you arrived!"

Theuderic dismounted from his horse, handed the reins to one of the marquis's men who had come forward to take them, and bowed to the Marquis de Ponchaux. The marquis, who was very nearly of an age with him, snorted and reached out to clutch two handfuls of the blue cloak on his shoulders.

"Some of the men were grumbling and beginning to fear you would not come. But I knew you'd never be able to resist the chance to slaughter a few more verdards!"

"It's good to see you too, Ansoult." He smiled at the nobleman. They had ridden together on border patrols twice, when Theuderic was a little younger than Talbot and the marquis was merely his father's heir rather than lord of nearly one-third the Eastmarch. They had only encountered one small band of goblins during their time together, but it seemed the marquis remembered their youthful patrols fondly. "It only seemed right to make them pay a toll for setting foot upon your lands without permission."

"Pay a toll!" the marquis repeated, delighted. "I shall have to remember that! Well, we'll make them pay one in cursed green blood for crossing that bridge today! Or, rather, for not crossing it, if things proceed in due course."

"When do you expect our visitors?"

"It will be some time yet. One of their patrols found us not long before you arrived; we chased them off but were careful not to catch them. I've got six riders out on wide patrol now, plus a pair of picket riders stationed within eyesight. We'll have plenty of warning even if they're riding hell-for-leather."

Theuderic nodded, satisfied. "And the mines?"

"Already in place. Waxed and waterproofed, as directed. What do you think of these dispositions?"

Theuderic looked over the hastily sketched map, then turned back towards the bridge and pointed toward the bell tower, the top of which was visible even from the square. "That's too far away. We need to be closer, but not so close as the abbey tower would leave us."

"Yes," the marquis grimaced. "I don't know what the old abbot must have been thinking, back in the day, to place it so close to the river with windows instead of arrow slits."

"In my experience, abbots are seldom experts when it comes to siege-craft."

"How about the roof over there?" The marquis pointed.

Theuderic turned around and shielded his eyes. There was a two-story building about halfway between the church and the bridge, set back a little ways from the river, and he could see a ladder coming down from the roof on the side near him. He estimated the distances to both the bridge and the far bank, and decided it was about as good as he could reasonably expect.

"That should suit us. I'll set one mage behind the south river wall, with three of the archers. The other two will be with me on the rooftop, covered by the rest of them." He glanced back at Regnaut. "I want you with Seigneur Ambroys at the bridge. Be sure he keeps his head down. Take your two best with him, send the rest of your men with Seigneur Talbot to the roof now, and have them prepare shelter, waist-high, that will withstand arrows, on the river-side edge."

"I do hope you've got a trick or two up those sleeves," de Ponchaux said, as the archers dismounted their horses and began to lead them toward the building selected. "Beyond the usual, of course."

Theuderic nodded slowly. "I think we can arrange for a surprise or two. Let's go to the bridge."

They made their way back to the bridge, the marquis regaling him all the way with the various minor victories he, and the other border lords, had won while hunting down the shattered remnants of the previous orc incursion. Even so, despite the thousands slain by the Amorrans, and later, by the cavalry with which Theuderic himself had ridden, more than ten thousand orcs and goblins still rampaged within the borders of the Eastmarch, plaguing the surviving villages and slaughtering freeholding farmers too far from the protection of a noble or a town militia.

"Grain is going to come very dear this year," de Ponchaux observed. "I've had my men buying up everything they can get their hands on. If we survive this next wave of invaders, I daresay I'll make a fortune!"

Theuderic looked at the nobleman, surprised.

"Oh, don't be so surprised at me playing merchant, de Merovech. I couldn't afford to keep my men-at-arms mounted and armored so handsomely if I didn't ensure there is always more gold flowing in to my coffers than out. Out here near the borders, we can't afford to play at being court fops worrying about whatever rags the ladies tell us is the latest fashion."

"Are you saying I'm a court fop?"

"God, no!" The marquis snorted. "I suppose it looks obscene to profit from the misfortune of others, but then, I doubt there is another nobleman in the realm who has done more than I have to try and stop these damned verdards. Where is the cursed king? I don't understand why he hasn't sent the Royal Guard, or called up his own levies. Why, even the Maréchal du Royaume is still lazing about Lutèce!"

"It is the Grand Duc," Theuderic said in a low voice. He didn't know if the rumors of insurrection in Ecarlate had reached the hard-pressed marchers, and he didn't wish to dishearten de Ponchaux's men with the knowledge if they lacked it. "He has returned to the duchy and surrounded himself with others of dubious loyalties."

"And yet the kingsmage stays true," the marquis said, his eyes distant and thoughtful. "Well, that does tend to blow away a considerable amount of smoke, I suppose. Dammit! What is that bastard Ecarlatean thinking—no offense, you understand!"

"None taken," Theuderic said wryly. He had long ago decided to serve the realm, and the House of de Mirid that ruled it, rather than his oft-rebellious relations, should he be put to the test. Although history was not one of his stronger subjects at l'Academie, it had not escaped his attention that the periodic sallies at independence on the part of his fellow Ecarlatean nobles seldom accomplished more than hangings and humiliation at the hands of whatever de Mirid was sitting on the Savondese throne.

"I suppose we won't be seeing more in the way of reinforcements, then."

"None beyond those arriving with the Red Prince."

The marquis shook his head. "A damned lot of good having the de Mirids off their backs will do them in the west, if they trade the verdards for him.

Well, that's trouble that will keep for tomorrow. What shall we do about this cursed bridge?"

They had reached the river bank and the entrance to the stone bridge, which was just wide enough for seven men to stand shoulder-to-shoulder. It was solidly constructed, which was why Theuderic was glad to see that mines had been emplaced under the supports on both sides. The hell-powder was prepared as he'd been told, inside two large sacks of tarred and waxed burlap that would not soak through easily if splashed or if the river should run high. He half-stepped, half-slid down the steep bank, using his staff as a support, then licked his index finger. After tracing a rune on the stuffed sack, he placed his hand on it and intoned the words of the spell he'd prepared. Light flared between his fingers, and when he withdrew his hand, the shape of the rune was outlined in black, as if the sack had been branded. Then, he climbed back up the embankment, slid down the other side, and did the same to the second sack.

"Nearly pissed myself when I saw that magelight flare," the marquis observed, unembarrassed by his admission. "Thought you'd set the damned things off and we'd all be blown to Kingdom Come."

"Set your mind at ease. It's not the first time I've used this spell. Now let's go across and I'll prepare the other two." Theuderic walked across the bridge, and the nobleman followed him. But as they reached the far side, the marquis stopped and placed a hand on Theuderic's arm.

"What's the matter?"

"Riders. I want to see if they are ours." He whistled loudly, and the men on both sides of the bridge looked at him. "Let's get these trees across the river. Even if they're our scouts, who knows how much time we'll have; the orcs can't be too far behind them. Pile them along the treeline to the north, and on top of the bridge to the south."

Theuderic had already cast an optic spell, summoning water from the air to give him the eyes of an eagle. He saw four mounted men, all wearing de Poncheaux's livery, riding fast, but not hard. "They're yours, Ansoult. Four of them."

"Four? Dammit!" the marquis swore. "There should be eight!"

Theuderic frowned. One of the men was looking backward at something behind him, but even with the assistance of the spell, Theuderic could not see what it was. Wolfriders, he presumed, but that wasn't necessarily the case.

"All of you, get those cursed trees across the river now! Can you see what's after them?"

"No, in fact, two of them have turned back for some reason. I think the other four must be behind them."

The marquis wasn't listening, he was bellowing at his men, waking up those napping on the river banks and urging those on the east bank to climb the embankment and cross the bridge. Theuderic grinned and shook his head, knowing that it would be at least a bell or more before they could reasonably expect to see any action. A squadron or two of wolfriders wasn't about to try to storm a bridge guarded by a strong infantry force. After releasing the lens spell, he descended the southern side of the bridge and set the ignition spell on the emplaced mine, then did the same on the northern side. As he clambered up the bank, somewhat impeded by his heavy cloak, the marquis appeared and offered him a hand. Theuderic was not too proud to take it.

"Let's go get something to eat. We brought supplies for a decent lunch; there is a wine from one of my neighbor's estates that I think you'll find worth the drinking. I find that a man fights best on a full belly, so long as he's had time to digest it first."

"You have a unique perspective on combat, Ansoult."

The marquis laughed. "I've been doing this for some time now, and I've learned that one can only prepare so much. Some fools would have the men slaving away on fortifications until the very last moment, then have them go into battle exhausted and half-starved. Let the enemy do that! After an hour or two of the old bash-and-smash, we'll see who still has something left."

They crossed the bridge behind two pairs of men carrying the trunk of a moderately sized oak and found themselves amidst a crowd of those who had been sleeping on the west bank. Theuderic had to admit that his old friend's men looked remarkably bright-eyed and energetic for soldiers who had been marching and chopping down trees since yesterday. Considering that they knew they would soon be facing an enemy army that heavily outnumbered them, they were also in unexpectedly high spirits. He could see, from the easy way the marquis moved among them, slapping backs, exchanging friendly jibes, and laughing uproariously at their jokes, that this was a regiment of veterans who trusted its captain and rewarded his faith in them.

Seeing them made the decision he'd been contemplating an easy one. Better to let a few orcs across than allow such men to die. They would clean up the detritus. They had earned that right, and Savondir would have need of them on the day of the real battle. His observation of the marquis and the man's relationship with his soldiers reminded him that he had his own men to lead, even if there were only three of them. He found Ambroys with Maussart; the two of them were overseeing the construction of an impromptu wooden wall using the trees that had been felled on the other side.

"Cut off those two branches, there," Ambroys instructed a shirtless young soldier armed with a saw. "No, the two that stick up!"

"It's hardly necessary," Maussart protested.

"You won't want them obstructing your vision," Ambroys argued.

"Leave them to it," Theuderic told them both. "It's not the first time they've built fortifications."

Both mages turned around, their faces anxious with anticipation of the incipient battle. "Are they in sight?" Ambroys demanded.

"We saw the sergeants rousing everyone and ordering them to assemble," Maussart added unnecessarily.

"Relax. It will be nothing more than a few scouts at first. Then the first regiments of cavalry will appear. After them, the foot, most likely goblins or lightly-armored skirmishers. Unless they're under the command of an orc captain, they'll likely do nothing but sit on the other side and lob the occasional rock at us until someone forces them to attack. They could sit here for days, depending upon how long it takes for the warleader to whom they report to pay attention to them and get up off his fat green arse."

They walked together to the square, where bread, meat, cheese, and the promised wine were provided to them in the shadows cast by the nearby buildings. Theuderic shook his head and snorted at the memory of past meals he'd eaten before battle, most of which he seemed to recall had been devoured hastily under pouring rain or freezing winds.

"Don't get used to it," he muttered under his breath.

"They come!" He looked up and saw Talbot was at the near edge of the roof, pointing excitedly toward the east.

"I'll be right up," Theuderic called back to the younger mage. He gathered up a handful of cheese slices and accepted a proffered skin of wine from one of the marquis's men. "Where are you going?"

"Shouldn't we take our positions now?" Ambroys looked confused.

"It's just the scouts." Theuderic shook his head and vowed never to accept a teaching assignment. Hadn't he just told them as much?

However, once he clambered awkwardly up the ladder to the roof, holding the precious wineskin precariously in his teeth, he realized that he'd been wrong. He didn't need the optic spell to see that there were more than a squadron of scouts riding in pursuit of de Ponchaux's retreating patrols. Judging by the amount of dust the riders were kicking up behind them, it very well might be the entire goblin cavalry.

"Monseigneur Marquis!" he shouted down to the square. "Your guests are arriving!"

"How many?" the nobleman called up to him.

"Five to seven hundred! All mounted!"

The marquis didn't reply, but snapped his fingers at one of his men, who picked up a horn and sounded it, three times. Theuderic was impressed by the alacrity the men displayed in rushing to their assigned positions, many of them carrying meat or bread in their hands as they ran towards the river. Archers were clambering up the ladder behind him, and when he turned around, Theuderic was surprised to see that the marquis himself had also joined them on the roof.

"I thought I'd have a look for myself."

"As you see fit, of course. Is there any chance they'll try to swim the river?"

"More likely they'll try to rush the bridge. I've got my best men there, and they'll put up a barricade as soon as our riders cross, but if you can keep their archers from hitting my men on the bridge from the sides, I'd appreciate it."

"Of course." Theuderic walked over to the side of the roof, looked down, and was pleased to see that both the younger mages had not waited for his orders, but were already heading for their positions. Mentally commending them, he finished off his cheese and took a long swig from the wineskin. It was rather good, he decided.

The first two riders crossed the bridge, and the marquis climbed down to meet them. The other six were riding well ahead of their pursuers, but it looked as if one of the riders might be wounded. As the enemy drew closer, Theuderic could see several of the goblins at the fore whipping their wolves with sticks to try to decrease the gap, but the longer legs of the horses kept the wolfriders at a safe distance behind. That didn't prevent two or three of the goblins from nocking arrow to string and loosing a wild shaft in the general direction of the men they were chasing, but not even a wood elf could have made such an impossible shot.

About thirty lengths separated the leading pack of goblins from the men by the the time they reached the bridge. It was hard to resist the temptation to invoke a wall of fire, but Theuderic knew it was too soon to reveal the fact that the men were supported by magecraft, especially when he hadn't identified the enemy's capabilities in that regard yet. The archers, however, felt no such compunction, and no sooner had the second group of horsemen crossed the bridge than a horn sounded and three dozen shafts were loosed from the river banks and the roofs of the nearby buildings. Four goblins fell, and a fifth reeled on the back of his wolf, pierced through the shoulder, but managed to hold on and turn his wolf around.

As the wolfriders retreated, leaving their dead behind, the men on the bridge hastily drew up the wooden barricades that had been suspended from ropes on the sides of the bridge. They were crudely hewn barriers standing chest-high, and thick enough to be impervious to arrows, rocks, and other missiles. They were cut to span the width of the bridge, so that one or two men were sufficient to hold them in place while wedges were hammered in to secure them more firmly.

"Shall we join in?" one of Regnaut's men, a balding, yellow-haired man with a red face, asked him.

"Save your shafts."

The main body of the goblins halted well out of range of the archers, and parted to permit a small group of ten or twelve to ride through and survey the situation from a safe distance. It would have been easy to strike out at what was most likely the goblin commander or a trusted lieutenant, but this was not a hastily assembled raiding force that would vanish without a leader holding them together. Killing him now would accomplish nothing.

The small group of goblins rode twice up and down the river, keeping their distance as they surveyed the defenders and looked for a way to cross the river without having to force the bridge. They did not find one, of course, as the river was high and there were no fords nearby, so it was not long before they gave up and rode back to the others. After a brief conference, two wolfriders loped off to the east, presumably to inform the orcs of what they had learned, while others, presumably clan chieftains and warleaders, began issuing orders.

"Will they wait for reinforcements or will they attack now?"

"They'll attack now, even though they shouldn't," Theuderic answered Talbot.

"They shouldn't? Don't they have the three-to-one numbers that's required to attack a fixed position?"

Theuderic chuckled. "That ratio assumes equivalence between the troops. Look at them! They're goblins, they're underfed, they're armored in leather that's worn thinner than your tunic, and to top it all off, they're cavalry. They've been doing nothing but raiding and pillaging, and murdering defenseless villagers without the sense to flee in time. Whereas the marquis's men are well-equipped, well-fed veterans who are led by an experienced commander they trust. If he decided to stand firm, they couldn't force this bridge with three times their numbers even if we weren't here."

"So why will they attack if they can't succeed?"

"Well, they don't know the quality of the enemy they're facing. But mostly, they'll attack because there are fifteen thousand orcs on their tail who scare them a lot worse than a few dozen men guarding the only easy way across the river."

"That makes sense."

"Always try to understand the perspective of your enemy. If you succeed in that, you can anticipate what he'll do four times out of five. And even if you can't anticipate his action, understanding how he thinks will help you recognize what he's doing almost as soon as he does it."

"Looks like they're going to try to soften them up first," Regnaut commented.

The goblins had divided into three groups, with about half in the middle being loosely arranged into a long column with seven riders in each line. The other two were moving to the north and south of the bridge, and drawing short bows from behind their crude saddles. Their plan was readily apparent; the mounted archers would loose at both unprotected flanks to whittle down the number of men on the bridge, then the three hundred riders would attempt to hammer their way through the survivors still holding the bridge against them.

Theuderic smiled and withdrew a strip of hide on which he'd carved three sigils. "Watch this," he told Talbot. "It's very impressive to hurl fireballs and summon lightning strikes, but most such spells are too inaccurate to use further than a stone's throw away. The elves solved the problem by a simple expedient; deliver the locus of the spell more accurately, and the spell naturally follows suit."

"How does that help?"

"With a little help from our friend Regnaut here, I shall demonstrate. I assume you have a modicum of fletcher's glue somewhere on your person?"

The old poacher, grinned, exposing yellowing teeth, as he produced a little clay pot from a pouch at his waist. "Allus keep some about. Never know when you need to repair a shaft."

"Would you be so kind to affix this just behind the head of one of your arrows?" He winked at Talbot. "We'll have to give it a little time to dry, of course. We wouldn't want it falling off in flight, after all."

"So, you're going to invoke the spell when the sigil reaches its target, just like you've done with the mines!" Talbot said, looking excited.

"Well, it's not precisely the same procedure, as I'll use a very different spell, but the essential principle is the same. All the mines require is a little spark that wouldn't do much more than tickle a goblin's arse. But you know, I was told that in ages past, elven archers would have entire quivers full of arrows with various sigils carved into the shafts. I thought this might be a good time to put the concept to the test."

He had learned rather a lot from Lithriel, although unfortunately, the secret for which he'd betrayed her had turned out to be worse than useless. Now that had been a bitter lesson, and not only for him! He wondered where she was now. He found, rather to his surprise, that he still missed her. That white skin, those long legs…. He shook his head and forced himself to focus on the matter to hand.

Regnaut was running his thumb and finger back and forth over the hide tightly wrapped around the shaft he'd selected. "She'll hold nicely now," he assured Theuderic. "Where do you want me to put her?"

"The rider leading the southern contingent. Ambroys is alone on that side and I suspect a little disruption would help him."

"That's a long damned shot."

"You just need to get it as close as you can. Too near is better than too far."

"Aye, I can do that." The archer drew back his big bow, sighted, adjusted his aim, and then loosed. Theuderic watched the shaft speed toward the goblin. It was, indeed, a little low, but that was no matter. For, just as the shaft struck the ground at a flattish angle and began to skip under the wolf, Theuderic gestured and spoke the syllable that completed the spell.

The archers cheered as a massive ball of fire sent the wolf and rider flying in two different directions, both aflame, and the sorcerous fire engulfed at least a dozen other wolf-and-goblin pairs. They could hear screams and shrieks and howls, as at least four wolves and one goblin on the periphery of the blast were set alight, and their panicked flight set off a confused reaction in those around them, as in an attempt to avoid the flames, they retreated in literally every direction.

"Loose," the Marquis shouted. A horn blew, and dozens of bowstrings snapped, as the archers behind the wall rose and sent three volleys into the frightened, milling wolfriders before a single goblin managed to loose a single arrow back in their direction.

"Now that there's a pretty trick, monseigneur mage." Regnaut nodded approvingly at him. Theuderic shrugged.

"They didn't really take much damage. See, they're already regrouping." He turned to Talbot. "Keep an eye out. They know we've got at least one mage now, and they'll be hunting for him. Be careful not to expose yourself, but give the group coming toward us a little taste of the storm."

The young mage nodded and glanced at the archers. Four of them nocked arrows, then indicated they were ready. Talbot took a deep breath and stepped forward, held out both hands, and invoked *Gaston's Coup de Tonnerre*. It was one of the least accurate lightning spells in l'Academie's conventional repertoire, but it was powerful, and given the fact that the target consisted of more than one hundred wolfriders in a loose skirmish formation, it could hardly miss.

The blue sky was torn asunder by a mighty boom. Even by day, the momentary flash was blinding. The archers, having closed their eyes, quickly loosed their shafts, then stepped back from the edge with Talbot without waiting to survey the damage. They heard goblins screaming, a few arrows clattered harmlessly against the nearby buildings, and two passed high overhead, but it was clear the attackers had not actually spotted from whence the magical attack had come.

Regnaut edged forward with his bow. He loosed a shaft, then slipped back, smiling. "That stopped them in their tracks! Twenty, mebbe twenty-five are down, and the rest of the buggers are looking about to figure out what hit 'em. One more should send them scurrying."

"I think we can provide them with a little encouragement in that regard," Theuderic said. He edged forward so that he could see, then conjured an illusory wall of fire that rose twice the height of a man from the ground. Had Talbot been more experienced, Theuderic would have had his colleague summon a warm breeze at the same time to add verisimilitude, but he did not want to exhaust the younger mage. Fortunately, the goblins were sufficiently alarmed to be taken in by the false flames, just as he'd hoped, and they promptly turned their wolves around to withdraw in a disorderly fashion. Once it was clear they were not regrouping, he closed his fist, and the wall of fire abruptly vanished. Not so much as a blade of grass had been burned.

"Think they'll notice it weren't real?" Regnaut had come forward and now stood by his side.

"Someone will have." Theuderic glanced at the older man and winked. "That's why the next one will be real."

Neither Maussart nor the archers stationed above and behind the bridge were as successful in driving off the main group in the center. The mage didn't dare risking using any fire spells so close to the mines, and indeed, the hail of arrows that thudded into the hastily erected barrier that protected him was forcing him and the archers with him to keep their heads down. The wolfriders kept up a steady rate of fire as they approached the bridge, and while most of their shafts flew wildly off-target, the sheer volume of them was sufficient to render Maussart useless.

The leading wolfriders were bearing crude lances; unlike horses, wolves were entirely willing to assault a line of spears. But the barriers behind which the Marquis's men were shielded confused them, and the charge slowed, then stopped entirely only twenty paces from the bridge. A brief argument ensued, until the leading goblin gestured angrily and six or seven goblins dismounted reluctantly, then, after more furious gesticulations, they finally ran howling at the wooden barrier.

No sooner had they hurled their weight upon it, however, than the two soldiers bracing it stepped back, letting both big panels fall to the stone. Even before the Marquis's man sounded the horn, the infantry on the bridge was surging forward, and the dismounted goblins, taken off-balance and off-guard, were swiftly dispatched with sword and spear. However, the soldiers were too disciplined to rush beyond the safety afforded by the bridge, and they resumed their positions rather than proceed to attack the enemy.

The goblins, on the other hand, were not so circumspect. The lead wolfrider kicked his wolf forward, and its angry howl was echoed by a deafening chorus of howls, barks, bays, cries, and curses. But the first goblin's lance shattered upon a steel shield, and a moment later, he was run through, with one blade taking him in the side as another punched through his unarmored throat. His wolf, more fortunate, escaped with nothing more than a deep slash in its flank, and it fled along the river bank yipping in pain and terror.

The front line of men staggered under the initial onslaught, but for all their ferocity, the goblins were too poorly armed and the wolves were far too small to threaten a speedy breakthrough. The front line's shields blocked, or nearly as often, broke, the goblin lances, while their armored greaves protected their lower legs from snarling, snapping lupine jaws. At the same time, the second line's spears thrust past the first line to slash and puncture goblin flesh. Several goblins, and one wolf, were impaled, and their thrashing, mortally wounded bodies impeded their fellows, who crashed heedlessly into them.

"I believe they are sufficiently occupied for it to be safe. You can loose on them now," Theuderic ordered, and the archers on the rooftop were quick to comply. They sent shaft after shaft into the mass of wolfriders just behind the melee, and rapidly helped turn what was initially little more than general confusion into an all-out panic. The mounted goblins behind the growing pile of dead and wounded drew their shortbows and tried to hit the soldiers on the bridge, but between the confusion, the fact that the first three lines of wolfriders were actively engaged, and the soldiers' shields, the few arrows that hit anything mostly wounded their fellows.

"Theuderic!" Talbot cried, seeking his attention. He'd been charged with keeping a watchful eye out for shamans, and he pointed to a shimmering green aura around the head of a goblin who had ridden up behind the beleaguered central group attacking the bridge, apparently with the intention of helping them somehow.

Theuderic nodded to indicate he'd seen the shaman and cast *Escoffier's Interrompue*, which he'd been holding prepared for just such a moment. The deceptive spell, which was more counterspell than spell proper, acted as a sort of magical constriction on a spell in the process of being cast by another magic-user, and it caused the green aura to disappear immediately. As he'd anticipated, instead of giving up on the spell, whatever it was, the shaman clenched his fists, stubbornly attempting to force his way past the counterspell by the sheer force of his will. A moment later, the magical pressure inside the shaman's skull grew too great for mere bone to bear, and the goblin's head abruptly exploded in a spray of yellow-green blood and white bone. The headless goblin slumped to the ground, dead, as his nearby fellows screamed and leaped away from him in horror. Theuderic chuckled. It was an evil little spell, harmless enough to a *vauderiste* trained to recognize it, but brutally lethal to the careless and the unwary.

"What was that?" Talbot stared at him, more in dismay than admiration.

"An object lesson in why it is unwise to be overly determined when one meets resistance."

"Looks like they're giving it up as a bad job," said Regnaut. There was much shouting, and whistling, and sounding of horns below. The goblins were beginning to withdraw in a rude semblance of order, their hurried attempt to rush the bridge having failed.

"They'll be back soon enough," Theuderic assured him. "And the next time, it will be orcs."

FJOTRA

FJOTRA did not object, in principle, to learning about the gods of her new people. She had known from the time her father, the Skullbreaker, sent her to marry the heir to the southern kingdom, that she would have to learn many different new ways. The language was different, but she was young enough to learn it without difficulty. The food was considerably more abundant and flavorful, and her palate did not take long to adapt to the various meats and breads and sauces that were much to be preferred to the salted fish and charred game of her home islands. The clothing was lighter and more comfortable, and she adored wearing silk and cotton dresses in the place of the crude leather and canvas clothes that had been worn by Dalarn women since the coming of the Aalvarg had made raising sheep for wool and growing flax for linen impossible. Even the weather was much more gentle than it customarily was in the windswept Wolf Isles.

But despite the best efforts of Father Francois, who took great pains to talk her through the nonsense, she could make neither heads nor tails about the gods of the southerners. They worshipped a god who was both dead and alive, who was both father to himself and son to himself, and also took on a third form that was nevertheless the same as the other two. It wasn't that the idea a god had different forms was foreign to her; the Aldaföðr had a hundred names, from Arnhöfði to Völundrómu, and each name represented a different aspect of her people's greatest god. But despite his many aspects, he was merely the first among a host of gods, and Fjotra particularly venerated Valfreyja, the beautiful goddess who was queen of the Choosers of the Slain.

In Valfreyja, Fjotra understood her duty to be beautiful, to be a mother, and to stand beside a strong and victorious warleader. Hers was not the battle, hers was to send her husband and sons to war without tears, without fears, and to await the word of their death-greetings with the stoicism that would bring them honor. Thus would she best serve her people, as she had been commanded by her mother and her father alike.

What did a divided god who could not decide if he was alive or not offer her? What guidance could he give her? How could he, being a male god, provide her with any example at all, especially when he was useless in war and was more akin to a helpless victim like Baldur the Beautiful than a war god like the Thunderer or Tyr One-Hand?

She sighed as she looked out the window and saw the rotund figure of Father Jean-Félix making his clumsy way through the garden of the manorial grounds. It appeared it was once more time for something the southerners called her Cat Kiss Me, although it never seemed to involve anything more than the priest lecturing her about gods. But both Etienne-Henri and his mother had made it very clear that the soft men in the black dresses were to be treated with the utmost respect, although she had been repeatedly assured that they were not, in fact, trollmands or hekser.

So, she made her way downstairs in time to receive the priest in the large sitting room that served the manor as an unofficial reception chamber. When Flannery, the tallest and prettiest of her ladies, showed him into the room, she rose politely from the chair she was sitting, smiled at him, and offered him her left hand, which he dutifully raised to his lips without showing even the slightest sign that she held any interest for him beyond his duties.

"Do you care for any refreshments, Father?" The priest's face was a little red with the effort of his walk, but he declined Flannery's offer.

"No, although I anticipate that I will need one once we're done here." He sat down heavily in the chair next to Fjotra and sighed even more deeply than she had a few minutes ago at the sight of him.

"I will confess, your Highness, that this entire endeavor strikes me as futile and almost certainly pointless, but the King has made his wishes clear on the matter. Therefore, I shall continue to instruct you until such time as you are decently baptized and sufficiently within the bosom of the Most Holy and Immaculate Church to marry his son."

"I am very thankful to you for your help, Father."

He smiled faintly at the small victory denoted by her address; two previous visits had largely been devoted to her questions concerning why she should call him "father" when everyone knew perfectly well that her real father was the Skullbreaker.

"Your willingness to be instructed is only exceeded by your astonishing refusal to understand anything I tell you, your Highness. Now, do you remember what it means when we talk about the importance of baptism?"

"Of course. I have to take a bath. I have already told you, many, many times, that I am happy to take the bath. Even if it is outside, in front of everyone. We Dalarn do not fear to let others see us naked."

"It's not just about the bath–"

"Did you know that some of our bravest warriors are even known to fight naked, when the battle-madness falls–"

The priest held up a chubby hand to stop her. "Forgive me, your Highness. But do allow me to interrupt, if you please."

"As you wish."

"A baptism is more than a bath. It is a symbolic demonstration of a spiritual metaphor. The cleansing of our body represents the cleansing of our soul by the Immaculate, which is necessary if we are to be able to enter into the presence of the Highest and Most Holy."

"The god," Fjotra said, to confirm her impression was correct.

"Yes, the Highest and Most Holy God. The Creator."

"Like the All-Father?"

"Yes!" the priest said, pleased. "In fact, one of the names with which we address Him is God the Father."

"And his son is the Immaculate, yes?"

"Exactly!"

"So the Immaculate is not a god, he is one of the god's servants?"

The smile vanished from the priest's face.

"No, not His servant, His son. The Immaculate is the Son of God, the only begotten Son of God!" The priest's rosy cheeks somehow seemed to be getting even rosier, and although his tone remained calm, he was speaking a little louder than was really necessary, seeing how close he was sitting to her. "He is not a servant, like us."

"But did you not tell me that we are children of the god? So how can the Immaculate be the only son, if he is our brother?"

"Heaven help me!" The priest looked up at the ceiling and made a prayerful gesture with his hands. "Let's not trouble ourselves with the specific nature of the familial relations right now, your Highness. The important thing for you to understand, and to affirm, is that both the Highest and Most Holy and the Immaculate are God."

"Ah, yes, the *treenighet*. Or as you say, *la trinité*, yes?"

"Exactly. If you are to be baptized, you must confess that you believe in the only begotten Son of God, born of the Father before all ages. God from God, Light from Light, true God from true God, begotten, not made, consubstantial with the Father, and through him all things were made."

"Yes, I remember. That's two. What was the three? I forgot."

"The third is the Holy Spirit, the Lord, the giver of life, who proceeds from the Father and the Son, who with the Father and the Son is adored and glorified."

"Ah yes, the ghost! I think I would like to choose the ghost, if I am to choose one."

"*Sacrebleu!*" The priest put a hand to his forehead, as if he had suddenly developed a headache. "Your Highness, you do not choose one. There is no need. We worship all three."

"So there are three gods! The Aldaföðr, his dead son, and the ghost!"

Father Jean-Félix closed his eyes. Fjotra thought perhaps he was praying, so she closed her eyes as well and respectfully bowed her head. She sat there in silence for a long moment, then cracked open one eyelid to see if the priest had finished yet, but he was still muttering to himself, so she waited until he was finished before saying 'Amen'.

"What did you just say?"

"Amen. You were praying, yes?"

"In a manner of speaking." The priest sighed. "Perhaps we should contemplate addressing this matter in another way. The primary concern of the Archbishop with regards to the matter of the royal marriage is the faith in which any children which happen to result from the marital union are raised. Are you willing to swear that you will raise the Prince's children in the True and Purified Faith, as revealed in the Sanctified Writ and by the Most Holy and Immaculate Church?"

"Yes, Father."

"And you are willing to, as you say, take the bath."

Fjotra nodded eagerly. "Yes, of course, Father."

"And I know you're perfectly capable of repeating the words flawlessly, even if the understanding eludes you entirely," he said, more to himself than her. He held up a finger. "However, I will caution you that you must repeat only the words that the Archbishop tells you. No additions or caveats or similes, you understand?"

"Yes, Father." Then she frowned and shook her head. "No, Father. What is a caveator similee?"

The priest smiled, a little ruefully, and reached out to pat her hand. "Never you mind, my child." He pushed himself up from his chair and gave her a little bow. "Your Highness, I congratulate you. I have come to believe that you may be the most perfect heathen to ever walk this Earth, and that includes every elf, dwarf, orc, troll, and goblin in the East. Nevertheless, you are as God made you and I believe your heart to be rather more innocent than most."

"So we are finished already?"

"I believe we have accomplished absolutely everything that is presently possible, your Highness. And it is even possible, given our Savior's admonition that we are to become like little children, that you walk closer to the Light than me or any of the princes of the Church. Understanding is good, but obedience is better."

Fjotra wasn't entirely sure what the priest was telling her, but she could tell from his tone that she had passed the strange tests and won the Church approval she required to marry her betrothed. "Wonderful, Father! I thank you so much!" She stood up and threw her arms around him, happy and grateful that her ordeal was finally over.

He extricated himself from her embrace, looked at her and shook his head. "All the beauty of the angels." And then, much to her surprise, he laughed.

LODI

THE APPROACH to Iron Mountain was much like it had been when he left it more than a year ago, with one significant exception. The big stone gates were closed, something he hadn't even seen during seven years of the great siege; the Troll King's army had never burrowed deep enough to necessitate the closure of most of the underground entrances to the city. Indeed, had it not been for their ability to bring in supplies and reinforcements from the other dwarf kingdoms, Iron Mountain might well have fallen. A squad of heavily armored dwarves, their faces obscured by their iron helms, were positioned at various points outside the gate, and judging by their postures, they were alert and taking their responsibilities seriously.

"Looks like we ain't going to tell them anything they don't already know," Boru commented. He, too, had taken note of the unusually heavy guard.

"Someone got the wind up."

"Think they been attacked here as well?"

"Don't think so." Lodi looked around the platform upon which the city guards were standing and above them at the gate. He saw no discarded weapons, no suspiciously dark stains on any rocks, and for all that the mighty gates were closed, there were no marks or abrasions on them. And while the guards looked alert, their plate armor gleamed brightly under the glowstones. They did not have the look of dwarves who had seen combat.

"That means other caverns have been hit."

"Most like."

The two older dwarves were riding in the first cart, and as they drew nearer to the circular terminus that passed in front of the large stone platform, one of the dwarves on the pushcart stood up, stretched his back, and then spread his hands. Lodi nodded and held up two hands and gestured to indicate that they should stop working the lever and let the little train coast to a halt in front of the platform. It didn't escape his attention that four of the guards were armed with crossbows, and at least one bolt was aimed straight at his breast. There was a loud screech and a hissing sound as one of the dwarves on the pushcart applied the brakes, and two axe-bearing guards stepped forward to take up positions closer to the front two carts.

A broad-chested dwarf whose helmet sprouted a pair of small, thick horns emerged from a shadow where Lodi had not seen him. He was of middle years, judging by the thickness of his beard and the curve of his chainmail-covered paunch.

"Who ye be?" he barked at them from behind his faceplate. His voice echoed against the walls. It sounded authoritative, but Lodi heard the underlying uncertainty in it. Militia, without a doubt, and he pursed his lips in thought. Where were the regulars? Surely the king hadn't sent them off to aid the elves!

"Well?" the militia officer demanded again. Boru nudged Lodi.

"Best be telling 'em something."

"I am Lodi, son of Dunmorin. Kingsguard and Royal Envoy to the Skydwellers. Now open the damn gates so we can get these carts inside!"

The officer raised his hand and Lodi breathed a sigh of relief when he saw the crossbows lowered. There were few things more terrifying than a loaded crossbow pointed at your chest, especially if you knew the dwarf with his fat finger on the trigger was untrained and inexperienced. But still, he didn't order the gates opened.

"I'm sorry, Kingsguard, but I am under orders to keep this gate closed."

"I'm sure you are. Open them anyhow." Lodi stepped off the cart and onto the platform. He wasn't wearing his armor, which meant that the militia dwarves could see at least a few of his scars. "Do you understand the concept of initiative, vodnekh?"

"Narednekh, Kingsguard. Of course I do!"

"Then why are you showing no signs of it, narednekh?" Lodi asked him as mildly as he could manage. "I am the last dwarf to come down from the sky lands before the doors to the Deep were closed. I have been traveling for months. As you can see, I have been wounded. I have killed sotakha, zlytakha, and draktakha in order to bring my news to the king, and it will not bother me in the slightest to break a stubborn paslo's head as well if that is what is necessary for me to do my duty to the king and complete my mission."

There was a long moment of silence as the horn-helmed dwarf looked from one of his companions to his left, then a second to his right. The second guard shrugged, at which point the narednekh seemed to reach a decision. He reached into a leather pouch at his belt, withdrew a silver whistle, and blew two short, then two long blasts that nearly pierced Lodi's eardrums. Almost immediately, the stones began to groan and a seam appeared in the gates before them.

"If the captain has my balls for this, perhaps you'll carve me a new pair, Kingsguard." The milita officer saluted, which Lodi wasn't sure was necessary, but he returned it anyhow.

"Don't worry about your captain, narednekh. I'm headed straight for the palace. Can you give me a guide?"

"The palace?"

"To see the king," Lodi explained patiently.

The dwarf's eyes widened, but he nodded vigorously and pointed to a young dwarf whose beard barely reached his belly. "Uhrbo will take you there."

Lodi turned to Boru. "You've been here before. See that the others get situated and leave me a message with the Kingsguard in front of the palace to tell me where you are. I'll look you up when I can."

The other dwarf squeezed his shoulder, and they clasped forearms. "I hope to see you again, son of Dunmorin, but if I don't, know that it was an honor to fight by your side."

"I'd say the honor was mine, but to be truthful, I was mostly trying to stay out of the way of that oversized axe of yours!" Lodi slapped the other dwarf on his broad shoulder. "I've stood by the side of many a warrior in my day, but never a better one. Fare you well, Boru."

He started to call out to Myf, but saw that she had already dismounted, and their scanty baggage had been unloaded by two of the younger dwarves. He beckoned to the militia officer, who sighed audibly before dutifully approaching.

"What else, Kingsguard."

"There's a body on the last cart. See that it gets—"

"A body! Do you mean a dead body?"

"Yes, of course! What else would I mean?"

"How did he die?" the officer demanded suspiciously, dropping a hand to his sword. Now it was Lodi's turn to sigh.

"Get that fat hand off your blade, shut up, and listen," he explained. "It ain't a dwarf. Nobody knows what it is, which is why we brought it here. You need to have two of your men put it on a cart and take it to the palace. A cavern uptrack was attacked by about six-score of the cursed things, so maybe the king's mages or engineers can figure out what it is and where they're coming from."

The naradnekh nodded, subdued more by the shock of what he was hearing than by Lodi's command. Lodi nodded back, satisfied, and slapped the fat dwarf on his armored shoulder before picking up both his and Myf's belongings and slinging them over his own.

"Stay out of trouble, lads," he told his recent companions. As a chorus of goodbyes and farewells answered him, he took Myf's small, soft hand in his own without thinking. Startled by his own boldness, he would have released it as quickly as he'd taken it had she not responded with a gentle, but unmistakable squeeze. Smiling to himself, he strode forward in what he seemed to recall would be the closest track station with the direct route to the palace.

Myf's eyes were wide with wonder, and she openly gawked at the massive mansions that were carved into the bedrock below the mountain that gave the royal city its name. The gilding that adorned the homes of the rich and powerful was cunningly inlaid to maximize the illumination provided by the complicated intertwining of earth magic and artifice that could only be found here in the heart of Iron Mountain.

"I've never seen such wonders!" she gasped, almost delirious with gold fever.

Lodi smiled. He, too, could feel the familiar greed-song pulling at his dwarven heart, and it was all the stronger for how much time he had spent in the bright Skylands.

"Breathe easy, lass. It's all a bit much the first time, but ye'll get used to it soon enough."

They had the cart to themselves, which pleased Lodi since it allowed him to stare at the pretty young pasla as she took in the sights of the passing city without attracting undue attention. More importantly, it allowed them to avoid the inevitable condescension that the city dwarves customarily directed at tourists, travelers, and others regarded as rustics, whether they came from above or below.

"Everyone is so rich here!"

"Don't be misled by what you see passing through. The caverns nearest the palace, sure, that's where all the great clans live. The Rock-fellows, the Redshields, the Highmountains, you can't hardly throw a stone in these parts without hitting a dwarf whose family owns a gold mine."

Her eyes narrowed and she surprised him by frowning. "I have been told they do not properly reverence Provni Otkovi here."

Lodi sighed. It was hardly a surprise that her traditional upbringing in the Deep would cause her to revolt against the many things in the royal city, but he'd been hoping the marvels and wondrous sights would keep her distracted until Lodi had the chance to speak with the king. He consoled himself with the thought that it was better for her to share her misgivings with him than stew in silence.

"I daresay you're correct, lass." He decided that truth would be the wisest course of action. "Most dwarves honor the Provteki, more or less, though perhaps not as seriously as they should. City dwarves tend to favor Skála Otek and Pozar Otek, but I'll admit, Hublok Otek probably gets less respect than he deserves around here."

"And you, Lodi Dunmorinsson? Do you honor the First Fathers?"

He smiled. There, at least, he was on sound footing.

"I'm Kingsguard, lass. I've walked with Valtek as my shield for longer than you can imagine, under stone and sky."

She blinked a little at his use of the familiar for Válka Otek, the War Father, or perhaps at his reference to the forbidden sky.

"Sometimes I forget you are Sky-burned," she admitted. "But I have seen that your heart is true stone. I am certain you do not serve Nahotakh."

"The sky holds no temptations for me, Myf. I swear it." He shuddered at the memory of the one time he had been forced to ride the sky on the back of one of the cursed Zlytakh birds. It would be most unwise, he decided, to tell her of that particular incident. "But a Kingsguard must go where the king orders him to go, and it's better to kill zlotakha in their homes than in ours."

She nodded slowly. It appeared to be an idea that had never occurred to her before.

"Yes," she agreed. "To mine a vein, you must go to where the metal is, you cannot wait for it to come to you. But how is it that you came to travel so far under the sky if you guard the king? Does he not need his guards near him for protection?"

Lodi laughed. He couldn't help it, although Myf looked a little hurt by his response.

"Look around you," he said, still smiling. "What enemy could hope to harm him here? No, the dangers to the dwarves lie elsewhere, in the lands of the Sotakha, the Zlytakha, and above all, the Jedtakha. The Kingsguard are not merely the king's shield and axe, but his eyes as well. Which, you see, is why I must speak with him now and tell him of the things that I have seen on my journeys."

"Such as the scaled monsters that attacked the way station?"

"Among other things, yes, certainly. But nothing and no one has attacked Iron Mountain since the great siege."

Her eyes narrowed as she studied his face, but she didn't say anything.

"What?" he said, finally.

"You were here then, weren't you." It wasn't a question. "You fought in it."

"Aye, lass, I did. Seven years, I did."

"That's a long time." She was silent for a moment, then made a face. "Was it… was it like back there?"

Lodi didn't have to ask. He knew she was thinking of what had to be her only previous experience of battle. "It was worse. Much, much worse."

"That's hard to believe." She was looking out over the vast expanse of the mighty cavern of the city. "You would never know it."

"They never made it here," Lodi said proudly. He thought back to the claustrophobic confusion in the dark, to the vicious battles waged in the tunnels against the goblin sappers, who under the whips of their orc overseers dug nearly as quickly through the earth as the dwarves did. They dug, they fought, and they died in the thousands, but more than a few dwarves, and even a few Kingsguard, died at their teeth and claws.

"Lodi?" He shook his head, belatedly realized that he hadn't been listening to her. "Lodi, are you well?"

He wanted to tell her. He wanted to tell her of the way terror gripped your bowels as you crawled through a space barely wide enough to accommodate your elbows, and barely tall enough to let you worm your way forward in the pitch black darkness. He wanted to tell her of the way you had to stop periodically, and listen for the tell-tell scratching and clawing of the goblins as they made their way through the earth. He wanted to tell her of the way you protected your head with your armored left arm, while thrusting forward blindly with your right. But he couldn't.

"It was mostly the armor," he said, not really realizing that he'd spoken aloud.

"What?"

"Nineteen times out of twenty, when we'd encounter them in the tunnels, we'd win. But, you see, it wasn't because we were smarter, or because we were stronger, it was really because we had good steel armor right here." He tapped his left forearm. "See, they'd poke their spears forward at us. We both used these little spears, not too long, of course, because you had to be able to crawl with it. Maybe about like this?"

He held up both hands. Then he made a jabbing motion several times with his right hand.

"You're crawling on your belly, and of course you can't see anything at all. It's pitch black. So, the moment you hear something, you cover your head with your one arm and thrust with the other. Once you feel the spear bite, or you feel something hit your gauntlet, you just keep stabbing it forward, as hard as you can, until you feel something give. Usually they'd start screaming, which was awful, but sometimes, they wouldn't make any noise at all. For some reason, that was even worse."

She shivered. "That... that sounds horrible!"

"It was, but you get used to it." He shrugged. "I think a dwarf can get used to anything. Skaltek saw to that, I suppose."

"Skála Otek," she corrected him, primly. "You must not be so careless with the names of the First Fathers, Lodi. Perhaps that is why they have seen fit to test you so severely."

"Test me?" He laughed. "Seems to me I've been well-blessed, by Válka Otek at least. Perhaps not so much the others."

"Do you forget that I tended your wounds? Do you forget that I have seen you after working the cart without your tunic? The scars you bear are not the signs of their love or approval, Lodi."

Lodi was saved from having to reply by the deep horn that signified the carriage's arrival at the palace. He shouldered his bags and the larger of Myf's two, then rose to his feet.

"Here we are, lass. Ye'll be able to tell your folk that ye met the King of Iron Mountain his own self!"

Her eyes widened as they stepped out of the carriage onto a silver path lined with semi-precious stones. Pairs of axe-wielding guards, their carbonized armor polished nearly as brightly as the path and ornamented with gold, helped visitors resist any sudden temptations to dislodge shiny souvenirs. They were not the only visitors, but as Lodi observed a little ruefully, they were the only pair not dressed suitably for their splendid surroundings.

"Should o' thought o' that," he muttered to himself. But although he'd been to the palace many times, this was the first time he'd entered by the side entrance, which was primarily utilized by visitors, since before the siege. Back then, the path was simple fire-glazed stone and the guards had worn leather armor.

Fortunately, Myf was too entranced with the riches that literally lay before their feet to notice that her canvas workdress was not up to the glamorous standards of the other pasla present. And judging by the surreptitious glances being shot her way by the young guards, her pretty face more than compensated for her homely attire.

They followed the others along the silver path; Lodi was impressed by how few scratches and other marks it showed until he saw an old, stooped long-beard standing aside the path holding what looked like a broom, but with bristles that glowed and smoked. He whistled softly. Pozarlids, the masters of the mystical forge fires, did not come cheap, but he had to admit that the effect they had achieved here was stunning.

A captain of guards, gloriously armored in silver chain, was standing before the open wooden doors, which were carved and inlaid with carbonized iron smelted from the armor of Kingsguards fallen in battle over the centuries. Lodi snorted, thinking of how little of the iron was contributed during the last war; no one was wasting armor on decorating doors with the Troll King at the gates. He'd gone through three breastplates himself, and lost another one on a night raid above ground.

"Lodi, he's asking for our passes." Myf pulled at his arm. "Do we have passes?"

"We don't need them, lass." Lodi scowled at the captain. "We're here to see the king, laddy, so stand aside!"

"Who in the name of the Seven Fathers do you think you are?" demanded the younger dwarf. Four of the guards, their attention caught by their captain's tone of voice, whipped their helmed heads around and shifted their grips on their axes.

"I'm Lodi, son of Dunmorin, of the Kingsguard!" Lodi flicked his finger hard against the captain's silver breastplate. It stung, but made a satisfying ping that he felt served well as an exclamation point. "You tell that to your boss, and your boss's boss, and then keep going until you get to the King! He'll tell you to bring me to him; he's only been waiting ten months and more for my return!"

At the mention of the word "Kingsguard", the captain blinked and the guards involuntarily stepped backward. Even Myf was staring at him, her lovely jaw agape with surprise. The captain, with the quick wit of a survivor, came to the conclusion that any scarred and short-bearded veteran who wasn't afraid to roar at an officer of the Palace Guard very well might be someone whom the king would, in fact, consider a priority, and stroked his beard as he regarded Lodi with what appeared to be a newfound respect.

"My apologies, Kingsguard. I intended no disrespect."

"Think nothing of it laddy." Lodi was feeling generous. "How about you have one of your shiny lads escort us somewhere this poor lass can get a nice cool drink while you see about scaring us up an audience with the dwarf himself?"

After a brief consultation with two of his guards, an accord was reached, and Lodi and Myf were escorted into the massive palace and led to a sparkling chamber of iridescent stalagmites through which a sinuous river slowly flowed.

It was a natural pub of sorts, although a more spectacular one than anything Lodi had ever seen outside of Elebrion, the White City of the Elves. A dwarf wearing glittery cloth in the place of armor brought them a crystal flask of what he initially thought was mushroom wine.

"Oh, Lodi, that is very good!" breathed Myf after she tasted it. "What is it?"

Lodi took the flask from her and sampled it himself. He blinked with surprise at how sweet it was. And how strong.

"I don't know, lass, but I will tell you to be careful about how much you drink."

"But it tastes so nice!"

"That it does, that it does."

Although, truth be told, it wasn't even a patch on a half-decent ale. Lodi dwarfully resisted the temptation to tell the pretty pasli to drink her fill and turned his attention to the dwarf who was waiting on them, whose beard was even shorter than his own.

"Got any real drink in this place?"

"Worthy of a Kingsguard?" the short-beard replied archly. "Dark ale, darker ale, and deep ale, sir."

"Just a sergeant, lad, just a sergeant. I ain't no toff."

"Deep ale, then?"

"Aye, the deepest."

He turned back to see Myf was smiling at him.

"Just a sergeant?"

"Mm."

"Just a sergeant who walks into the king's palace and barks orders at the guards?"

At a loss for words, Lodi was wondering if another grunt would suffice for an answer when he was saved by the entrance of a familiar beard.

"Lodi! There you are!"

Lodi whipped his head around. It was Thorald! Lodi breathed a silent prayer of thanks to the First Fathers that his young companion had survived the perils of the Elvenwood and made it safely home. The courageous young dwarf looked very well, he had to admit. Thorald's luxurious brown beard was arranged into two thick braids decorated with silver rings, and a medallion stamped with the king's seal was embedded in his black leather brigandine.

"Lad," was all he could manage to get out, huskily, as they embraced. "Oh, lad, It's good to see you!"

"Well, you've certainly seen better days, old friend," Thorald told him as he stepped back and eyed Lodi's scarred cuirass and much-mended tunic. "Was it men, elves or orcs?"

"Pack o' wolf riders, in the end. Damned near did for me too." Belatedly, he remembered by whom he was accompanied. "Sorry, lass."

Myf nodded demurely, although her eyes sparkled with amusement. She smiled at him, then glanced in Thorald's direction before looking back at him.

"Ah, right," Lodi cleared his throat. "Thorald, this is Myf. She was caught skyside when the gates closed right after I made it back. I'm takin' her home deep to her folks."

Thorald's eyes lit up. It was clear the younger dwarf liked what he saw, Lodi observed to his displeasure.

"Vodnekh Thorald Thoraldsson, at your service, tesnik."

"She won't be needin' none o' your service, laddy. She's of the true deep, and they don't truck with no stranger talk." Lodi did his best to keep any disgruntlement out of his voice, though he wasn't entirely sure he succeeded.

He felt a small hand upon his.

"No, Lodi, it's all right. As long as I am with you, I am permitted to speak to other paslid." She winked at him. "Though only if I have your permission, of course."

Lodi harrumphed. "It's not like this lad has anything to say that you need to hear, lassy."

Thorald grinned. "It's good to see you're as cheerful as ever, my friend. Myf, my sympathies to you. I, too, have endured long days and even longer nights in the company of this old graybeard."

"Are you of the Kingsguard as well, Captain?"

"No, I am just one of the King's many household dwarves. I am no warrior like old Lodi here. But did he ever tell you about the time he went into a live dragon's cave?"

"Thorald," Lodi protested, trying to stop the younger dwarf, but Myf's interest had already been piqued.

"What?" The pretty pasli turned and glared at Lodi. "You never said anything about a dragon!"

"It was more of a wyrm, actually," Lodi said uncomfortably, which did nothing to distract Myf from further pursuing the subject.

"I cannot believe you went into a dragon's cave, Lodi. Was the dragon actually inside?" She glanced accusingly at Thorald as if the whole thing had been his idea. "Did you go in there with him?"

"I have far too much sense and I am far too young and handsome to do anything that foolhardy, tesnik. No, my job was merely to keep watch in case the vicious beast returned while Lodi was busy rifling through its treasures."

Lodi sighed. If Myf's outrage was any guide, he was going to be hearing about this particular misadventure for a long time to come. And judging by the twitching of Thorald's lips behind his beard and the amusement in his eyes, Thorald was not going to stint on the fertilizer either.

"It weren't no problem, lass. Don't be lettin' him fill your mind full of fancies. I got out in plenty o' time."

"But what were the two of you doing there in the first place! Were you so gold-sick that you couldn't help yourselves?"

"It weren't our idea!" protested Lodi.

"In truth, we had our orders," Thorald confessed. "A certain item had gone missing, and it turned out the dragon–"

"Wyrm," Lodi corrected.

"The dragon had stolen something of great… sentimental importance. So we were sent to retrieve it."

"By whom?"

"By the dwarf who is waiting to see Lodi now."

Lodi, seeing that Myf was ignoring the crystal flask, took it from her hand and took a large swig from it. It was still too sweet, but it burned nicely going down the gullet. He passed it to Thorald, who raised it in a toast to the other two dwarves, then took a respectable pull at it himself.

"Now that's a good sweetwater!" he exclaimed.

"Vodnekh Thorald, are you telling me that the king himself is waiting to see Lodi?"

"Yes, that's so."

"Then why are we still sitting here?" Myf had turned as white as a flour mushroom. "And how can we go before the King dressed as we are?"

Thorald laughed. "Our royal appointment isn't for another half-turn, tesnik. And as far as the King is concerned, he'll be delighted that the Kingsguard isn't actually bleeding on his carpets for a change."

Lodi winced, thinking about the strange corpse he'd ordered sent to the palace. He hoped it wouldn't leak too much. In the meantime, he could see that Myf would be in need of a little extra courage to face the King of Iron Mountain, so he took the flask from Thorald and handed it to her.

"Have some more of this, lass. There's nothing wrong with what you're wearing, but a little fire in your belly won't hurt."

SKULI

THEY'D FORCED the captive Aalvarg to retain her human form by augmenting the iron chains in which she was held with silver necklaces commandeered from the crew. Now she led them toward the ruined fortress to the south, as Skuli had decided to sail wide of it, then approach it from the north. That way, any survivors of the massacre two nights ago would not only have no means of following their tracks, they would have no reason to believe that the Dalarn warriors hadn't simply sailed south with the rescued women and children to the mainland.

It was with a skeleton force that Skuli made his way down along the coast, having left the captives in the care of Mord Redcheek with strict orders to leave them behind and sail for Savondir if he did not return by nightfall. That was the safest course of action, although he knew perfectly well that the Redcheek would put to sea once the sun began to set, then return to the landing in the morning to see if anyone had made it to the rendezvous over the course of the night. Himself, the All-Strong, the Barkman, and Hrolf Half-hand he selected because they were among the oldest of the crew and did not fear death. Hakon Hakonsson he chose for his wits and Gudrik Glum because the youth wore him down with his persistent begging.

He wasn't concerned about the possibility that they would miss their sunset deadline. They'd put in only an hour's march north of the castle, and the six of them had made good time over ground that had been lost to the monsters since Skuli was still a boy. They passed through the overgrown remnants of two burned-out villages, but saw no sign that either of them had been inhabited by humans or wolves for more than a decade. Now they were approaching the ruined fortress, as its broken, fire-blackened walls dominated the southern sky.

The Aalvarg pulled up abruptly and tilted her head back, wrinkling her nose as she sniffed loudly at the air.

"What is it?" Var All-Strong jerked the chain that held her arms bound behind her, prompting an instinctive growl.

"The Mother. Her den is near, behind that hill."

Skuli nodded. The ground ahead was rising, and the hill was thickly wooded with tall trees that obscured even the ruin's highest remaining tower. A few dark stones could be made out through the leaves, but if one didn't already know the castle was there, one might easily fail to see it.

"We'll wait here, then." He beckoned to the Barkman, as the bowman was his keenest-eyed man. "Svan, you and Gudrik go and see what lies ahead. Go softly and make sure you are unseen. The creature says this Mother is unguarded, but perhaps she lies."

"Skullbreaker." The Barkman, nearly invisible in his tattered brown leathers, gestured to the young man and set off up the hill. Skuli slapped Gudrik's shoulder as he walked past, his face set with the determination not to show the fear he was almost certainly feeling.

"Keep your mouth shut and your sword sheathed, boy! You'll be fine."

The frightened young man nodded, no doubt regretting his earlier request to join Skuli's little band of raiders. Skuli watched the two men make their way up the hill until they, too, were lost in the leafy green leaves of the springtime forest. Then he turned to the captive wolf-demon.

"Now, whatever shall we do with you?"

She bared her teeth and hunched her shoulders. Skuli had the impression that if she were in her wolf form, she would have lowered her ears. "I do not wish to face the Mother. Free me or kill me. I do not care."

"Why are you so frightened of this Mother? What is she?"

"I do not know. But our pack leader, who knew no fear, squatted and marked the earth when my mother asked about her. He said she was more terrible than death."

Hakon snorted. "What do you bet it's just an old statue from the castle they worship as a goddess."

"I'll take that bet. A whore when we cross the sea?" the All-Strong said, as he glanced quizzically at Skuli while quietly unsheathing his sword.

"A whore and a room at an inn!" countered Hakon.

Skuli, seeing no need to be unnecessarily cruel, nodded at Var.

"Done," he said, as he drove the sword between the Aalvarg's shoulder blades hard enough that the tip burst out the creature's throat in a fountain of bright red blood. The wolf-demon made a choking noise, but was otherwise silent as her knees buckled, then collapsed and died, bleeding from mouth, throat, and back, as the All-Strong withdrew his blade.

Hakon spit on the corpse. "Pity we didn't kill the pup as well, Skullbreaker."

"We'll come back and take care of her one day."

The young man flashed a grin in response. It was good to see the men's spirits had largely recovered from the shock of losing Raknarborg and retreating in the face of the death of so many of their fellows. Var All-Strong had just finished cleaning off his sword when the sharp crack of a snapping twig alerted them all to the fact that someone was coming. Skuli held up a hand, and it wasn't long before Gudrik and Svan the Barkman came within view as they descended the wooded hillside.

Something is wrong, Skuli thought, as he took in the wild look in Gudrik's eyes and the barely concealed alarm on the Barkman's face. Both of them were pale, and breathing hard for reasons that had nothing to do with physical exertion. The Barkman was the first to notice the dead Aalvarg, and he nodded in callous approval.

"Good," he said. Then he took a deep breath and shook his head.

"What is it?" Skuli didn't understand why both the inexperienced young warrior and the veteran woodsman were acting so strangely.

"I can't... it's difficult, there are so many... you'll just have to come and see for yourself."

Gudrik didn't say anything at all, but he looked less glum than distressed and overwhelmed. Skuli shrugged. Whatever it was, it wasn't immediately dangerous, so there was no reason for them to not climb the hill and see it for themselves.

"Let's go. Svan, you lead the way."

They ascended the hill in single file, their weapons sheathed in order to leave their hands free. Skuli's left knee ached, but there were plenty of trees and down-hanging branches to grab as he made his way up the rise. By the time they neared the top, he was getting short of breath, and he was glad to stop when the Barkman held up his hand, and pointed to what lay on the other side. Unlike the others, he didn't gasp aloud, but he did find himself swallowing hard.

Before and below them stretched out a large and open field. It was mostly an unhealthy yellow-white in color, with green weeds rising up in patches

here and there. It took Skuli a moment to realize that the field wasn't dirt
or dying grass, but consisted entirely of bones, human bones by the looks
of them. And with the exception of a few objects that were identifiable as
skulls and jawbones, all of them were crushed and fractured into shards.
The terrible detritus was more than the remnants of a village, or even a
tribe, it was the broken, sun-bleached remains of an entire people. His
people.

"Aldaföðr damn them," he whispered. "Damn them to the deepest, most
icy hells!"

Now he understood why the Barkman couldn't even try to describe the
sight that lay before them now. It was too harrowing for words. The most
frightful battlefield he'd ever seen, even the hopeless weeks of their last stand
at Raknarborg, paled in comparison to the mute testimony of the story told
by the silent field of shattered bones.

He pointed to the two youngest men. They, at least, must be spared
whatever fate he and the other three would face.

"Hakon, Gudrik, you will stay here. I want you out of sight, here in
the trees. You must witness whatever happens and then get word back to
Ulvdraeber. Don't interfere, don't make a sound, just watch, and leave as
soon as you see what happens to us. And you will tell the Redcheek to set
sail at once."

"We will not leave you, Skullbreaker," Gudrik vowed. "We swore to share
your fate."

"This is not the time to prove your mettle, Gudrik Glum! I am your jarl
and you also swore to obey me!" He glared at both of them until they both
nodded in obedience.

"If the lad wants to go down there with you, I don't object to staying
back." The Barkman held up his bow. "Might even prove more useful from
a distance."

"Shut up, Svan," the All-Strong growled. "Don't you want to see what
sort of creature could do that? I wouldn't miss this for the world!"

"Then Hakon, you must make sure Jorund sings how brave I was when
he composes the Skullbreaker's saga. And how handsome!"

Skuli snorted. "Come with me, both of you. And you too, Hrolf. Our
deathsong will be the envy of all the warriors in the halls of the gods."

The grey-bearded Half-hand nodded, but then turned and gripped
Gudrik Glum's shoulder. "You stood until the end at Raknarborg, lad. You
sailed with the Skullbreaker. You need no man's approval. Don't forget
that."

Gudrik Glum nodded quickly. They all pretended not to notice that his eyes were bright with unshed tears.

Slowly, they made their cautious way down the hill. Skuli had the uncanny sensation that he was literally descending into the grave; the scale of death was so vast, so far beyond anything he had ever experienced that it made him feel as if he was already dwelling in a dark and horrific afterlife. Only the warmth of the sun on his face and the uncertain footing of the grassy ground beneath his booted feet convinced him that he was still alive.

Once they reached the cursed field, the bleached bones crunched and cracked under their feet no matter how lightly they tried to tread. It was as if some potter god had chosen this place to dispose of the broken failures of his kiln, only the clay was human. Skuli frowned as he peered at the black ruin that towered overhead now that they were on the south side of the wooded hill that had previously obscured it, wondering if whatever demons or monsters had created this obscenity was sleeping somewhere within.

"This is strange," commented the Barkman. He was holding up a piece of bone that was flat and gently curved. "These are all from heads. There isn't an arm or a femur anywhere that I can see."

"Ain't none of it chewed neither," added the All-Strong. "No teeth marks."

And then, much to their collective horror, the bones began to shake and rattle. It was the most terrible music Skuli had ever heard, as if a thousand skeletons were dancing on stone and gnashing their clattering teeth.

"I think we should retreat to the hill," urged the Barkman, as he nocked an arrow to his bow. Skuli ignored him, but drew his sword, as did the All-Strong and the Halfhand.

About one hundred paces ahead of them, the earth began to swell, and something black and massive beyond belief began to emerge from beneath the shattered bones. Even at a distance, the evil smell of rotting death swept over them, as a massive creature erupted from the ivory mound like a maggot bursting out of a swelling wound. It was incredibly, unthinkably huge, bigger than anything Skuli had ever seen on land; only some of the whales they saw when far enough out at sea were bigger. It had the bone-white head of a horned snake, the four legs of a crouching predator that ended in claws longer than a sword, and its body was black and streaked with what looked like giant cobwebs.

"*Mørkets mor!*" the All-Strong swore.

It was, indeed, the Mother of all Darkness. He heard the Barkman's string loose, and an arrow sped toward the empty eye socket of what Skuli suddenly realized to his horror had to be a dragon's skull. The arrow shaft smashed itself to splinters inside the skull to no noticeable effect, except that a moment later, flames ignited inside both the empty sockets where the creature's eyes should have been. But it wasn't until the jutting protrusions on the monster's back began to rise and the tattered remnants of a set of giant leathery wings were extended that it became apparent that whatever this thing was, it was not alive in any natural sense.

"I don't think we can kill it," the Barkman said, sighting along the arrow he had already nocked to replace the first one. "Looks like someone already did!"

"It doesn't seem to know it's dead," Hrolf Halfhand pointed out unnecessarily.

Indeed, what Skuli had initially taken for cobwebs were actually strips of the monster's leathery skin that were rotting and hanging down from its body. As the dead thing moved, he could see, in various places, flashes of white bone through gaps in the skin and the underlying flesh. The stench was abominable, and Skuli found himself gagging as another wave of it wafted over him. Never, in all the sagas and all the skald's tales, had he ever heard tell of anything like this obscene monstrosity. It was clearly dead, and it was just as clearly moving toward them, apparently of its own volition.

Dødes trollmann! He realized there must be a sorceror around somewhere nearby, a master of the dead, wielding the huge, half-rotten carcass like a weapon with unholy magic. And while they couldn't kill the undead monster, they could certainly kill the sorceror who controlled it. And Skuli had a pretty good idea of where the *trollman* must be. The problem was how they were going to make their way into the ruined castle without the vast obscenity adding their broken skulls to its considerable collection. Perhaps if one of them could distract it, the other three could get past it, and hopefully, eliminate the puppet-master before his grotesque puppet stomped out the life from the distracting party.

"We need to get to the tower," he hissed at the Halfhand. The grey-bearded warrior nodded and began moving to the left of the creature.

But Var did not respond to his urgent orders. The All-Strong was staring up at the monster, wide-eyed with awe, and without a speck of fear. To Skuli's astonishment, the big warrior dropped his sword and raised his empty hands high, although it was impossible to tell if he did so in praise, in supplication, or in submission.

"Var, what are you doing? Var!"

The All-Strong didn't seem to hear him. His gaze was locked onto the monster's fiery eyes as if he had forgotten where he was, or worse, as if he had forgotten who he was. Skuli cursed, realizing that the man had been somehow ensorcelled by the demonic beast. He shuffled forward, unseeing, in dark communion with the undead, unholy thing, toward what end Skuli could not imagine.

"Svan, stop him!"

The Barkman obeyed instantly. There was the sound of his bow loosing, and a moment later, the dark feathers of his arrow blossomed in between the All-Strong's shoulder blades. The big warrior, his heart pierced from behind, stumbled forward two steps, then fell heavily to the ground on his face. His left arm twitched, once, twice, and then he was still.

Skuli didn't have time to mourn his brave companion. He leaped forward, pointed his sword squarely at the monster looming over him, and shouted at it.

"Name yourself, monster, that the skalds may sing songs of my victory this day!"

Broken skulls crunched as the beast shifted its weight the giant dragon-skull tilted as the great fiery eyes focused on him. The flames seemed to expand, to grow, until they surrounded him, warming him in their dancing embrace. He groaned and swayed as an insensate, but tangible pressure gripped his skull in a powerful, but invisible fist. He could hear a harsh voice whispering at him, a snarling, guttural voice that spoke words he did not know, a speech made of sounds he could not distinguish between one and the next. He saw nothing but fire, he heard nothing but the growling grumble, and he felt absolutely nothing at all.

Somehow, though, he managed to separate himself from the all-engulfing flames that did not burn. This is a spell, he told himself. This is what took hold of the All-Strong. Rage filled him at the thought, fury and outrage, and above all, hate. The berserker spirit came upon him, and although it was not enough to break free of the dark enchantment, it allowed him just enough awareness, just enough freedom, to reach out with his left hand and run it down the wickedly sharp edge of his sword.

PAIN! Suddenly, he could understand the voice that neither of his two surviving companions could hear. *WHO ARE YOU, MAN, THAT YOU CAN BREAK MY HOLD ON YOUR MIND?*

Skuli smiled grimly. Now he was entirely free of the ensorcelling flames. He could hear the voice in his head, but the terrible grip, the sensation of being overwhelmed, was gone.

"I am Skuli, called the Skullbreaker." He gestured around the barren field of bone fragments. "It seems we have something in common, *Giavuhlensmor*."

That night, they burned Var the All-Strong on a proper warriors pyre. They did not put the longship to sea, as there were no more devils to fear, no more dangers that could possibly be any more deadly than the one they had faced that day. And, in fact, for the first time in decades, they did not need to be concerned about the possibility of an Aalvarg attack in the night.

Even so, Skuli ordered guards posted. One simply never knew what evils might be lurking out there in the dark.

"Skuli, you understand how mad you sound." Mord Redcheek's voice was low, but there was a savage edge to it. "You tell me that you somehow spoke with this damnable thing, even though it isn't alive and neither Hrolf nor the Barkman heard it say anything, and then for some reason it spared your lives and let you just... come back here?"

Skuli nodded, and restrained an ironic smile. Even in the firelight, he could see that the huge scar on the side of his second-in-command's face was a deeper shade of red and his eyes were filled with suspicion. Skuli could hardly blame Mord for wondering if he'd gone mad or been possessed by an evil *trollånd*. If he'd come back alone, or if the other four survivors hadn't supported his story, Skuli had no doubt that the Redcheek and the rest of the crew would have bound him, gagged him, and kept him that way until they'd safely sailed south across the White Sea.

"Not some reason. For a reason you and I can easily understand."

"What's that?"

"It wants to sail south with us. It wants to cross the sea."

Mord blinked. He shook his head, as if trying to get water out of his ear. Then he blinked again.

"This thing which Gudrik Glum swears is bigger than ten walruses. This thing that Hrolf swears is bigger than a whale! This thing that all of you swear is *utuktig* dead! And you're going to tell me it very nicely asked you for a *morutukt* passage on *Ulvdraeber*?"

Skuli spread his hands. "I can only tell you what is true. And yes, it very much wants to cross the sea, and it knows that the Aalvarg cannot help it do so."

"How does it know that?"

"Because it created them, if I understood what it told me."

Mord inhaled sharply and looked away from the fire. The expression on his face was more troubled than angry, but Skuli could see that he had managed to shock the scarred, battle-hardened warrior.

"Skuli, I don't want to make you think I think you're stupid, but you do realize that this... this monster or whatever it is, may be the cause of all our suffering, do you not? I don't understand how you can even think to, to do whatever it wants, or to assist it in any way!"

Skuli spat into the fire, nodding. "That's because you haven't spoken with it. It's very persuasive."

"Are you saying it bespelled you, like it bespelled the All-Strong?" Mord regarded him skeptically. "Aside from the nonsense you're talking, you sound like yourself."

"No, that's not it. I mean, it gave me two choices. Either I could agree to cooperate with it and help it cross the sea, or it was going to kill us, then go to the landing and slaughter all of you before you could sail away. I thought that was a credible threat, considering the way we were standing on the bones of those it had killed before." He shook his head. "There were thousands of them, Mord, tens of thousands. You can't possibly imagine it unless you've seen it, and by the gods, I wish I hadn't!"

"Then what are we doing here? Why don't we leave, right now?" The Redcheek gestured toward the flames that were devouring the canvas-shrouded frame of the All-Strong. "And how did it even know about us, or the landing? Did you tell it?"

"It's hard to explain." He shivered, remembering the way he'd fallen into the endless depths of the empty sockets and been swallowed whole by them. "It must have gotten it from me or Var. It doesn't speak aloud, it doesn't even have a tongue. It talks inside your head, so I think it must be able to hear what you're thinking. I was so surprised to hear its voice in my head that I know I wasn't thinking about you here, or the ship, so either Var told it somehow or it pulled the knowledge out of my memories."

He pointed to where a group of girls were sitting, braiding each other's hair in the firelight, as behind them, several of the young men were sharing their allotment of beer with the girls' mothers. "I wasn't trying to save myself or the others, but those girls, they deserve a chance to live. And the people will need every young woman hale and well if they're going to grow strong again."

"That still doesn't explain why we don't leave now." Mord glanced over at the dark silhouette of *Ulvdraeber* that could be barely made out against the darkness of the sea, her sail furled, her broad belly resting easily on the gentle incline of the ground where it lay beached. "We could be out to sea before the red moon rises. We've done our duty by the All-Strong, let the creature contend with nothing more than his ashes when it comes and finds us gone!"

"She would have known if I lied. And so I did not lie." It was true, he had not lied, not to her nor to the Redcheek. But neither had he told them the whole truth.

"She?"

"The Aalvarg call her *Giavuhlensmor*, the Great Devil Mother. She has something to do with that foul race, but I don't know what. She said she didn't create them, not herself, although they seem to believe she did. She doesn't think much of them, which is why she wants to take advantage of us coming here."

"Since the wolves can't abide the sea. Of course. But if she's as big as you say, we can't carry her on *Ulvdraeber*. Why does she want to cross the sea?"

"To kill elves, I think. It will make her whole again, or so she seems to believe."

Skuli didn't bother trying to explain what he was pretty sure was his own severely garbled interpretation of what the monster had told him. While she did harbor an extreme animus for the elves, against whom she and her kind had once warred many centuries ago, what she actually required for sustenance was merely sentient life that was not unnatural like the Aalvarg. And while she could die, at least temporarily, she'd refused to do so and held her rotting corpse together through the sheer force of her will, augmented by her magic, because a rebirth would cost her all of her memories and most of her power. The thousands of Dalarn who had been brought to her by the wolf-demons had strengthened her, but had not been nearly enough. A full recovery would require hundreds of thousands of lives, and the only place she could find enough of them was across the sea.

And while Skuli did not grasp what she sought beyond resurrection and restoration, it didn't appear to have much to do with the race of man or even the race of elves. She'd spoken of her brothers and sisters, of an ancient war between them, and how she now dreamed of being reunited with her own kind. None of it made much sense to Skuli, whose mind had been reeling under the brutal assault of strange inhuman images and emotions, but he had extracted a promise from her that the Dalarn would not be molested by her in any way, not even to meet her needs. As awful and as alien as she was, Skuli had not sensed any untruth in her. He wasn't even certain that she could lie, given the mind-to-mind connection, and so great was her contempt for them that he couldn't imagine that she would deign to deceive a creature so small and obviously inferior.

"So we're going to have to build a bigger boat for the cursed Jotunspawn? That could take two months!"

Skuli shook his head. Among the images she'd showed him was a large vessel that had been abandoned years ago in a harbor town after the villagers fled the depredations of the Aalvarg. It was whole, she assured him, and it was large enough to bear her immense weight. The town was less than a day's sail north from the fortress, and Skuli thought that with the addition of a mast and a tow rope from *Ulvdraeber*, it would be able to carry her across the sea. The voyage would take at least three times longer than usual, he estimated, but even with the women and children, they still had enough supplies to reach Savondir safely.

But he knew that before he could convince the crew of the necessity to transport the terrible living corpse, he needed to convince the Redcheek.

"It's necessary, Mord. I'm not asking you to like it. But we absolutely have to do it."

The Redcheek nodded. He stared into the fire at the All-Strong's burning body before turning his head to face Skuli. "It would be easier to believe it's actually you talking if Var hadn't fallen, especially not to the Barkman's arrow. Or maybe if I had seen this thing myself."

Skuli laughed. "Oh, that won't make it any easier. Just ask Gudrik Glum. He's half-convinced that he's gone mad."

"He's not the only one! There is nothing about what you're suggesting that isn't mad. Skuli, you know I would follow you into the frozen hells to beard Hela herself. By the Valföðr, we are all sworn to follow you to the death! But I have stood beside you, and fought beside you, and never have I known you to be this fey. Not even when the Aalvarg broke the gates of Flekkesvær and we lost half the town falling back into the mountains."

The Redcheek stood and put his hand on Skuli's shoulder. "How can I be certain that you are not enchanted, that this draugatroll is not wearing your face and speaking with your voice?"

Skuli sighed. He did not blame his old friend for his wariness. Steinthor would have taken him at his word with never a doubt or question, but Steinthor was now with his fellow heroes in the Halls of the Slain. The Redcheek had a more subtle, more suspicious mind, and therein lay the danger. He held up one finger.

"One more time," he said. "Trust me one more time, Mord Redcheek. Ask me no questions. Do not speak of your thoughts about this to the others. I am the Skullbreaker, the last jarl of the Isles, the same man you have known all these years, and my voice is my own. Do as I say and all will be well. This, I vow to you by the name of Steinthor Strongbow."

As he expected, invoking the name of the Strongbow was enough for the other man. The Redcheek's lips tightened, almost imperceptibly, and Skuli saw the pain of loss flicker in his eyes. Then it was gone, replaced with a savage smile.

"How he will laugh when I tell him about this madness when we join him in the Halls! Very well, Skuli, I will hold my tongue. But I know there is something you are not telling me."

Skuli nodded. There was indeed. But he, too, held his tongue.

BERETH

I wish you'd have left with the Lord Commander," Lassarian said as they looked down from the ramparts at the orc encampment below. With the first pickets established just out of bowshot from the walls, the vast collection of tents and firepits and garishly-dyed leather banners seemed to stretch out to the horizon. The wolves of the goblin cavalry gamboled and played to the north, while the thousands of boars that had escaped poisoning were corralled to the south. Even from a distance, the howls and growls and shrieks and screams of their besiegers carried to the high walls of the fortress.

Bereth only shook her head. There was nothing she could do for the wounded elf, but if her bow might be able to help the Prince-General stave off the orc assault, she had no choice but to lend it to his service.

"You know Ilriathas will be furious with you."

"Ilri seldom gets what he wants with regards to me."

He stared at her for a moment, then laughed. "You truly have a heart of ice. Perhaps we ought to send you out to sneer at the Great Orc. For my money, he'd go running off north with his tail between his legs."

"Orcs don't have tails."

"You have no poetry in your soul either."

"That's an awful thing to say!" Bereth felt genuinely wounded, offended, even.

"You're also predictably contrary. If Lord Oakenheart understood you better, he'd simply have forbidden you to accompany him and had you on the back of that giant bird of his in a heartbeat."

"That's ridiculous." In truth, Bereth suspected Lasri was right, but she wasn't about to give him the satisfaction of knowing that. Annoyed, she changed the subject.

"What do you think they're doing there?"

"Where?"

"There!" She pointed towards the middle rear of the great sea of orcs. Some sort of large wooden structure had been assembled, what looked like one side of a building, or perhaps a wall that was intended to hide their activity from the eyes of those they were besieging. It was flanked by a pair of large bolt-throwers that were not aimed at the walls of the fortress, but at the sky. Two others covered the approaches to the north and south. "It almost looks like they're planning some sort of surprise that they don't want us to see."

She indicated the bolt-throwers. "I think we'll have to wait to find out what it is. The Prince-General isn't going to be willing to sacrifice a skyrider or two to find out."

"So, perhaps we don't tell him."

"We?" She snorted. "I'm not flying out there with you! If they went to the trouble to build four of those machines, they've probably got gwrachod and gods know what other defenses prepared. It would be suicide!"

"Not if we do it after dark." He raised his eyebrows suggestively. "You know they don't see in the dark like we do. We'll fly out the far side, circle around, and come in from the west, behind their rear. We'll stay high, ride the wind, and they'll never hear us coming or going."

"What about the moons?" She wasn't really worried about the artillery even if they were silhouetted in the silvery light of the Daughter, but the orc mages might prove dangerous if they were spotted.

"We'll go out between moon rises." Lassarian pointed at the sky. "The Mother will be dark and low to the north for an hour before the Daughter rises. Even if they saw us flying out, they'd not see us coming back in from the west. You must come with me, Bereth. I can't fly alone."

"Scared of the dark?"

He ignored her mocking tone. "No, the Prince-General has a squad of guards, and a mage, watching over the birds on the tower in case the orcs target them with some sort of *gwaedhud* that is new to us. If I fly out alone, they'll demand my orders and stop me. If you come with me, I'll tell them that I'm flying you back to Elebrion. Everyone knows Lord Oakenheart and Lord Kelethan both want you out of this, so no one will stop us."

"How do you plan to explain it when you don't take me there?"

"I won't have to explain it. I will take you back to the city, right after we have a look at whatever it is they're up to out there."

Her eyes narrowed. "Are you sure you're not just trying to get me out of the way too?"

"You don't need to treat every elf trying to keep you from killing yourself like an insult, Bereth."

"It is an insult to any sky rider! I'm a raider, and I've earned the right to share the same risks everyone else takes! How would you feel if you were in my place?"

"I don't know, let me see…." His left hand wandered behind her and began to make its way down towards her backside. She reached behind her, withdrew an object, and jabbed down with it.

"Ouch!" The hand vanished hastily. "Did you just stab me with your knife?"

"Did I do what?" She slipped the arrow back into the quiver slung over her shoulder. "You know, I do hope that wasn't one of those poisoned shafts."

He was staring in disbelief at the back of his hand. There was a red mark, a definite puncture mark, marring his white skin.

"I cannot believe you just did that!"

"Do you remember if the poisoned ones had green fletchings or were they yellow?"

"Bereth!"

"Don't worry, if your hand starts to turn black, I'll just cut it off for you."

"I ought to have Mellt throw you off the next time you fly with me," he hissed angrily.

"Mellt would never do that! He likes me. He's a sweetheart."

"I suppose he wouldn't," Lassarian grudgingly conceded. He licked the back of his hand, then recoiled. "It wasn't really one of the poisoned arrows, was it?"

She laughed. "None of them are poisoned, you idiot. You know I never use them."

"I suddenly begin to suspect that I don't know anything about you."

"Oh, stop sulking! You had it coming and well you know it."

"It's not as if it's the first time–"

"What happens out in the field stays out in the field, Lasri. And it's over now, so forget about it."

"Easy for you to say," he complained, as he held out his hand and examined the tiny wound.

Then they were both silent as they contemplated the movements, or rather, the relative lack of them among the great army beneath them. It struck Bereth as more than a little strange that the orcs didn't seem to be doing much, if anything, to either storm the walls of the great fortress or prepare for an extended siege. As far as she could see, there were no trenches being dug, no ladders or siege towers being built, and besides the mysterious, well-guarded construction being assembled, there were no signs of any activity that might even bear the smallest chance of surmounting the massive walls.

"They can't possibly think they're going to starve us out," she commented.

"Even orcs aren't that stupid," Lasri agreed.

"I think you're right. I think we had better take a closer look at whatever it is they're doing out there. And the sooner, the better."

"I thought you said it was too dangerous!"

"It might be more dangerous to let them build whatever it is they're building. And you don't need the excuse of flying me back to Elebrion, because the Prince-General himself told me that he wanted me here."

"I don't follow," Lassarian said, looking confused. "How is not being permitted to fly you back going to help us get past the guards on the tower? I still don't have any orders. And they know who you are now."

"Exactly!" she said. "The Prince-General told me that he wanted to hear my ideas. That's an order. And in order for me to tell him my ideas about whatever that thing out there is, I have to go and take a look at it. So, you'll be following his orders by taking me out there tonight, because otherwise I can't do what he wants."

"I don't think that's what he intends."

"Come on, Lasri! You know he won't care who followed what orders if that thing turns out to be something important, something that we need to destroy before they can finish building it!"

"I'm not concerned about that, I'm concerned about what he's going to say when we come back and tell him that it's nothing."

"Then that's even better! You don't think he and his generals aren't worrying about what the Great Orc is up to, and why his orcs aren't trying to climb the walls or dig under them already? He's got *gwrachods*. He's got trolls. He's got this vast army that has marched all this way and they're doing nothing but sit there as if they've got nothing better to do!"

"He must be up to something foul," the male elf admitted. "That orc didn't come all this way just to turn back at the sight of the walls, like some of them did back in the day. Ever since the fall of Glaisleil and Kir Kalithel, they've known we can be beaten. And whatever his plan is, it's got to have something to do with that monstrosity out there."

"Monstrosity?" Bereth glanced at Lassarian's face. His tone of voice was uncharacteristically harsh, and there was a look of loathing in his eyes.

"Can't you feel it?" He shivered. "There is something strange about that… that thing. I don't know why, it's just a sense that I have. I don't think it's a weapon or a siege tower or anything like that. I don't know what it is, but whatever it is, I'm almost certain that it's evil."

Bereth squinted, trying to see what about the activity in the distance might be causing Lassarian to react so strongly. Even with her keen elvish eyesight, it was hard to make out any details, but she did note a surprising number of large, well-armored orcs surrounding the site. She didn't see any goblins in the vicinity, but there did appear to be a fair number of orc shamans around despite the fact that they didn't seem to be working any magics. And as she watched, she saw the huge figures of a team of trolls dragging a pile of felled and bark-stripped trees toward the thing being built.

"Maybe a golem of sorts?" she suggested. "What if they are building something of earth and wood, then summoned an earth elemental to power it?"

"That would be one giant golem!" Lassarian shook his head. "No matter how big it was, our mages could dispel it in an instant. Before it took two steps, it would be reduced to nothing more than a pile of dirt and logs. A golem wouldn't ever get near the walls, and besides, how would a creature of wood break through stone?"

"Especially magic-infused stone like this."

She leaned forward and looked down at the massive black slabs that had been seamlessly melded together, leaving a smooth, almost glassy surface that, even to her limited senses, fairly emanated sorcery. How could the orcs, even with their stinking *gwaedhud* and sinister *diafolhud,* possibly hope to counteract the spells that had been cast by some of the greatest mages of Elvenkind? Despite the fears and esoteric formulas of the siege master, it was obvious to even the most casual observer that Tir Diffaith was impregnable, as the centuries had proven time and time again.

Even so, she couldn't shake the feeling that Lassarian might be right, and there was something deeply ominous about the quiescent behavior of the army that was now encamped before those mighty walls. There had to be a reason for the focused activity to its rear when the rest of it was lazing about in apparent indifference to its presumed objective. She shook her head. There was only one way to find out.

Lassarian jumped as she swatted him on the backside. "I'm going to go to my quarters and get some sleep. You should do the same, if we're going to fly out between moon rises."

"Go to your quarters?" He grinned suggestively at her.

"Don't be obtuse. Will you come and wake me up when the sun starts to set?"

He nodded. They both knew that she was the sounder sleeper of the two. Then the smile disappeared from his face as he looked out again over the vast gathering of orcs and goblins below.

Bereth stirred as someone knocked three times on the door. She was lying on her side on the soft, feather-filled pallet, and she rolled onto her back, sighing, as the visitor knocked again, even more loudly, as if his previous attempts had failed to wake her. She begrudgingly opened her eyes and blinked, then called out before he could knock a third time.

"I'm awake, Lasri! Just wait."

"This is Captain Diadwyfas. I'm here with orders from the Prince-General, Bereth mer Eulenarias."

Diadwyfas? Bereth recalled a tall, cold-eyed officer she'd seen in the company of the Prince-General once or twice since she'd come to Tir Diffaith, but she'd never met the elf and he wasn't of the High Guard. She was vaguely under the impression that he was the commander of the Prince-General's bodyguard, which made her wonder why he would have orders for her.

"Give me a moment," she called, as she threw off the blankets, rolled off the pallet, and picked up her flight leathers from the stone floor. She donned them as as quickly as she could, shivering as she did so. Her quarters were freezing, as the big, high-ceilinged chamber had room for at least eight elves to sleep comfortably, but besides her bow, her daggers, her three quivers full of arrows, her bag of personal effects, her bedding, and a magelight that cast a soft reddish glow, it was, like most similar rooms throughout the fortress, entirely empty.

After tightening the ties on her jacket, she pulled on her boots, slung all three quivers over her left shoulder, then picked up the bow. She eyed her bag uncertainly, but decided to leave it unless her orders took her back to the city. Only then did she open the door to the elf captain.

He was, to her surprise, fully armed and armored, lacking only a helm to be ready for battle. As she began to greet him, she was distracted by a faint booming noise that the thick wooden door had been keeping out. It seemed to be coming from far away. "What's that sound?"

The elf smiled sourly. "That's why I was sent for you. The orcs are stirring."

"Ah, that would be their drums, then. Are they attacking the walls?"

"No. Or at least, not yet." He eyed her up and down. "Good, you're ready to fly?"

"Where to? And with whom?"

He began walking toward the stairs, clearly expecting her to follow. "The Prince wants to send out a pair of hawks to see what shenanigans the orcs are getting up to now. One with a mage, to deal with the *gwrachods*, and one with you, since he seems to think you're our best chance for making sense of whatever it is they're doing."

"Lucky me." It seemed she and Lassarian weren't the only ones to be concerned about the structure, or whatever it was, being assembled by the besiegers. As they entered the circular staircase and began to climb it, she noticed that the noise was getting louder. It wasn't just the drums anymore either. It was a growing cacophony of orcs shouting, trolls roaring, goblins shrieking, and the gods knew what else adding to the din. She grimaced, knowing that even in the darkness of the night, an active encampment was much more likely to notice a pair of warhawks flying overhead than a slumbering one. "Do you know who else has been sent?"

"I was sent for you. That's all I know."

Bereth shrugged. She'd find out soon enough. They continued to mount the winding stone stairs until they reached the top of the tower; not for the first time, Bereth cursed the fact that she'd been assigned a chamber three flights down. As they stepped out onto the torch-lit battlement, the roaring sound of the orcs below seemed to shake the very stones of the fortress beneath her feet, although now that she was outside, the ability to hear the direction from which it was coming somehow made it less terrifying.

"Bereth!"

Lassarian called out to her. He was already ready to fly, though he was barely recognizable in the flickering torchlight as his face was already darkened by a concealment spell.

"You're to ride with me!" He took her hand, but instead of drawing her toward Mellt, who was chained to a ring behind him, pulled her towards one of the other birds. Another sky rider she knew well, Lalflenddas, was standing there with his face similarly obscured, and beside him was the mage Terfielon.

He favored her with a unenthusiastic nod and raised his ungloved hands. "Prince-General's orders."

She stepped in front of him, pushed her hair back, and closed her eyes as she held her face up to him. She felt his hands on either side of her face and heard him mutter something unintelligible, then felt a pleasant warmth flow forth from his hands onto her skin. As he took a step back, she held up her hands and saw they were still white.

"Just the face," he said. "Won't you be wearing gloves?"

She held up her bow. "Not if I'm using this."

"You won't be needing that," said Diadwyfas. "Bring it with you, of course, one never knows, but tonight you're to stay high and scout."

"Why risk two birds?"

"The Prince-General wants a mage up there in case you run into difficulties."

"Magical difficulties," Lassarian explained unnecessarily.

"Yes, thank you," Terfielon said sarcastically. "Also, as long as we keep both birds reasonably close together, I believe I can keep us sufficiently well-cloaked, both materially and magically, as to allow a closer look at that edifice about which they are raising such an infernal ruckus."

"Given how they've got it at the rear of the encampment, if we're going to get a closer look at it, we'll have to fly north from here, then circle around behind them," Lassarian said.

"Why bother," Lalflenddas objected. We can just fly high above the clouds, directly toward it, then drop down once we've reached it."

"What clouds?" Lassarian glanced upward at the clear starry sky. "Besides, they'll see us leave here, heading in that direction, they'll be on their guard."

"Doesn't sound like it," Bereth observed, but neither of the two elfs was listening to her. They were staring at each other angrily, until finally Lalflenddas turned to Captain Diadwyfas.

"Who has command?" Lalflenddas wanted to know.

"She does," the captain answered, much to Bereth's surprise, as he indicated her with his chin.

"Why me?"

"Why her," echoed Lassarian.

The captain shook his head, though whether it was with contempt for their questions or the Prince-General's orders was not initially clear to her. His words, though, filled her with trepidation.

"Because she's the reason you're being sent out there tonight. The Prince-General wants to know what that thing they're building out there is. Once you get a good look at it, don't get ambitious, don't get tempted into trying to do something about it, just fly back here as fast as you can." He held up a finger in warning. "Don't take any risks! Just see what you can see and report back. If any clever ideas happen to strike you along the way, you can tell them to the prince himself."

Bereth nodded. It also occurred to her that the Prince-General probably assumed that, having lost her bird, she would be more careful than the two other riders. Under no circumstances would the mage have been given command.

"Well, commander, whatever shall we do?" Lassarian's ironic tone did not escape her, but she ignored it.

"Mount up. We'll take lead, Lalflenddas." She looked up at the sky. It was still dark, and the Mother was barely above the horizon, as if she, too, was intimidated by the unholy commotion of the gathered orcs. "We have time to circle around to the south and approach from the east. Even if they see us leave, they won't be looking for us to come from that direction."

The three elves accompanying her nodded and made for their hawks; the two riders first grasping the reins hanging down from the great beaks before crouching low to release the tethers that held them bound to the post rings. She felt a hand on her shoulder and turned around to see the green eyes of the elf captain staring into her own.

"Be careful, Bereth mer Eulenarias. The magister said there are dark and powerful spells being cast tonight. Fly fast, stay high and stay silent."

She nodded, firmly, the way she'd seen Ilri and Lord Oakenheart do it. It made her wonder, for the first time, if perhaps either of the two elf-commanders had ever felt the sense of trepidation that presently was making her feel as if she had bathed in ice. She turned and walked over to Mellt, reached up to take Lassarian's hand, and lightly leaped up onto the warhawk's broad, feathered back. After stowing her bow and her four quivers, she strapped herself in, tugged on the leather bands to test them, and slapped Lassarian on the back.

Mellt let out a cry as he felt his master urge him skyward, then flung himself aloft. Launching as they did from the tower heights, it was barely necessary for him to beat his wings to maintain altitude, but Lassarian urged him higher all the same. It was likely that the Great Orc had set scouts to watch the comings and goings of the sky riders, but anyone watching them would see them departing for the south, and presumably, assume that they were taking messages to reinforcements being gathered in that direction. If only there were truly such reinforcements to be had!

"How far out do you want to fly before we circle around?" Lassarian leaned back and shouted in her ear. The sound of the crazed besiegers was already fading in the distance, but Mellt was flying fast and the cool night wind made it hard to hear.

"Far enough that we can't see them beside their fires. If we can't see them, they certainly can't see us."

Lassarian nodded and glanced upward. The risen moon would orient them, but until the fires of the orcs were within sight again, he would have to use the stars to estimate their position relative to the object of the mission. Her mission, she corrected herself. It was her responsibility to not only ensure that they achieved the goal that had been set for them, but that they returned safely to Tir Diffaith.

For the first time, she began to understand why Lord Oakenheart, who was magnificent with a bow, seldom carried one on any of the raids he led. The narrow focus that was required of the archer was detrimental to the elf in charge. She needed to keep her wits about her and pay attention to all the various directions from which danger could strike.

"At least we didn't need an excuse to fly out tonight," Lassarian called.

She nodded. "How did you hear about it? Did you volunteer?"

"It would be more accurate to say that I was volunteered. Captain Diadwyfas asked if I was the rider with whom you usually rode, then told me to wait for you there with Mellt. He didn't phrase it as a request."

"Don't whine. It's exactly what you were planning for us to do anyhow."

"Somehow, it's always more fun when it's your own idea." He glanced back at the hawk flying behind and to their left. "Besides, that mage is a tedious bore."

"I thought you liked him?"

"I did, before I found out he didn't like me." She laughed at that, and he snorted. "I don't see what you're laughing about. He doesn't like you either."

Bereth strongly suspected that Terfielon didn't like anyone, but after a long look back to the north betrayed nothing but the silvery orb of the Mother, she decided they had gone far enough and could risk the turn to the northeast. She told Lassarian as much, and felt the shifting pressure of his legs as he communicated his wishes to Mellt. The massive hawk responded instantly, banking his wings and bringing them around in a smooth 135-degree arc.

They maintained a watchful silence as the pair of hawks sped toward the great encampment. If they had calculated their directions properly, it should not be long before they would catch sight of the enemy fires to their left, which would then serve as a useful line to which they could orient themselves. And indeed, not too much time passed before Bereth's keen eyes, accustomed to the night's darkness, spotted the first flickering white flames off in the distance to the northwest. She patted Lassarian's leg and pointed; he responded by guiding Mellt a little more to the north, flying more or less in parallel with the line of fires that demarcated the edge of the enemy camp.

Soon they were able to hear the terrible sounds of the orcs carousing, or worshipping, or, for all she knew, engaging in competitive poetry recitations. Although there were a few elfs, particularly at the Collegium, who had mastered one or more of the orcish tongues, Bereth had never seen any point in learning to distinguish one set of guttural shriekings from the next. At this distance, the noise was more of an unpleasant accompaniment to the much louder sound of the wind rushing past her ears.

The line of fires seemed to go on and on. Although she had flown over the entire army many times, at night its size seemed even more massive than when one could see, and count, the individual figures that comprised it during the day. The thought of flying over it, even under the protective cover of darkness, made her stomach feel tight, and she closed her eyes for a moment to control herself before her hands started shaking.

"There are a cursed lot of them, aren't there," she heard Lassarian say. He wasn't shaking, but she could feel how taut with tension every muscle in his back and shoulders was. Somehow, knowing that the male elf was nervous too made her own fear more manageable.

"It's all right," she reassured him. "We'll be in and out before they even know we were there."

"That's the idea. Promise me one thing, Bereth."

"What's that?"

"The next time I come up with an idea like this, tell me it's stupid, will you?"

She laughed and promised nothing. Someone had to scout, and the truth was that she and Lassarian were probably the most expendable members of the High Guard now. If it weren't for the Prince-General's misplaced faith in her imagination, she'd surely have been sent home already. Her one bow wasn't going to determine if Tir Diffaith stood strong or somehow fell to the Great Orc.

"There!" Lassarian called out as he pointed toward the northwest. "There it is!"

She could just make out the object, jutting up from the ground toward the sky, ahead of them and to their left. It was illuminated by what must have been a series of huge bonfires, because even as far away as they were, they could see the red light shifting and flickering as the flame was reflected off what she assumed must be wood. She glanced off to her right, looking to see if the Daughter was showing any sign of rising yet. It wasn't, which was a relief, as the main reason she hadn't wanted to come in from the north was the way in which the two hawks would have been silhouetted against the Mother.

She returned her attention to the object of their flight. Whatever the structure was, it was really quite large, she realized. The shape almost suggested a siege tower, as it was very nearly as high as the walls of the fortress, but it was much broader at its base than a tower would be, and, of course, it had been built much too far from the easternmost wall to be of any use. Nothing, not even a century of trolls, would be capable of dragging a wooden structure that large that far.

The dull booming of the drums was incessant now, and as they drew nearer to the edge of the camp, she began to be able to distinguish at least three different types of noises. There was a slow, deep rumble, as if tens of thousands of orcs were chanting something over and over and over. There was also the louder, more usual sound that one heard whenever a sufficiency of orcs were gathered together on the battlefield, which Bereth tended to think of as an anticipatory howling. And then, there was also the higher-pitched, and unmistakable, sound of goblins screaming, although whether it was in fear or in pain she could not tell.

She was tempted to tell Lassarian to urge Mellt higher, but when she spotted the first picket of guards, it became clear that amidst all the noise and chaos of the encampment, no one was paying any attention. All three guards had their backs turned to the east and were obviously occupied with whatever was happening at the huge wooden construct. As they sailed silently over the guard post and into the enemy camp, it became clear that the fires, tents, and rude lean-tos were mostly empty, as the greater part of the army had gathered in the vicinity of the what now looked to her as if it was some kind of crude ziggurat.

What was of such interest to them? Was it possible that the Great
Orc had unexpectedly died and his replacement was being crowned in
whatever passed for a ceremony among the orcs? Could they possibly be
that fortunate? She knew that more than one orc invasion had suddenly
retreated from the elf lands in centuries past, when the leader who was the
driving force behind it died, in battle, of disease, or by treachery.

Both the orcs and goblins appeared to be gathered more or less by clans
or warbands. There were no banners or totems being displayed, but to
the extent that she could distinguish one mass of greenskins from another,
the different groups appeared to be of similar stature and similarly clad.
Here there were a group of small, unarmored goblins, there was a rather
more formidable group of thick-thewed orcs wearing black leather armor.
Whatever the occasion was, it had some form of official imprimatur to
impose even such a small modicum of discipline on the unruly creatures.

But as they came closer to the center of the scene, a sense of dread filled
her and she saw a large circle of wailing goblins being held forcibly on their
knees by giant armored orcs, most at least a head taller than the average orc,
which she recognized as belonging to one of the Great Orc's elite warbands.
At first it looked as if a mass execution might be underway, perhaps because a
goblin tribe had tried to desert, or, alternatively, turned in sheer desperation
to mutiny before being hurled against the impregnable walls of Tir Diffaith.

Then she noticed how, at the center of the circle, the surface of the
wooden ziggurat appeared to be covered with a greenish, mossy substance,
except the moss was moving! No, she realized, the moss was actually the
green skin of goblins, stripped naked, and either chained or tied to the
wood somehow, and the greater part of the shrieks and wails that they'd
been hearing at the fortress since earlier that afternoon was being produced
by them. Most of the ziggurat was now covered with goblins thrashing
helplessly against their bonds, and she could see from the openings that
the rough construction had left that there were even more goblins bound
hand-and-foot inside.

More armored orcs were forcing a line of goblins to march at swordpoint
up the ramp that wound its way around the ziggurat, and she could see
from the pattern that the orcs had nearly completed what struck her as the
strangest, most obscene architecture she had ever seen in her life.

"It's an altar!" Lassarian leaned back and shouted into her ear. He had
slowed the hawk considerably, so the wind was no longer so loud, but the
cacophony beneath them was now so deafening that it was almost hard to
hear him. "That whole thing down there is one giant altar!"

He pointed as the warhawk began to turn and circle high above the circle created by the kneeling goblins. On the south side of the ziggurat, where they had previously been obscured from her view, stood a collection of orcs of obvious importance, judging by their headdresses, robes, skull-topped staffs, and other accoutrements. There were about two dozen of them, they were facing the ziggurat, and judging by the way they were gesturing and gesticulating, they were engaged in some kind of spell-casting.

Her sense of dread, already filling her with fear, turned to horror. This was not just ordinary battle magic. This was more than mere *gwaedhud*, the blood magic she'd seen and learned to avoid, it was the darkest of all magics, *diafolhud*.

She looked over at the two elves on the other warhawk. Terfielon was studying the gwrachods below, nodding slightly as he followed their movements. He glanced up and saw that she was looking at him, and flashed three signs at her.

Magic. Very Bad. Danger.

She held up a fist to indicate she understood, then flipped her hand in an arc to indicate a question. He responded by holding his palm flat, then bringing his fingers and thumb together to form a circle.

Stay. Watch.

She nodded and held up her fist again. While every instinct in her body was urging her to flee for the safety of Tir Diffaith, she trusted the mage to let her know when it was time to fly away. She could detect the swelling power of the orc magic, but Terfielon's much more refined abilities would almost certainly alert him to that power being aimed at them before any spell was cast.

"I think that's the Great Orc right there!" Lassarian shouted into her ear again. He pointed at a small group of orcs standing behind the gesticulating gwrachods, flanked by no less than two trolls on each side as well as a squad of big, armored orcs. One orc, in particular, was so big she initially mistook him for a troll, but to Bereth's eye, he seemed to defer to the smaller orc beside him. She'd never actually seen the Great Orc before herself, but as she watched the calm, collected way he took in all the noise and chaos around him without letting it visibly affect him, she imagined she could see a glimpse of the cold mind that had wielded its forces so ruthlessly throughout the campaign.

It was sorely tempting to take out her bow, order Lassarian to take Mellt down just a little lower, and put an arrow through the Great Orc's heart. But with so many shamans around him, and so much dark magic filling the air, the chance that they would survive the attempt was remote. And besides, there was no guarantee that the orc general's death would dissuade his lieutenants from continuing the siege in his absence.

Once the last screaming goblin was bound to the ziggurat, the big orcs that had been binding them filed away and took up positions behind the Great Orc and his generals. There was a relative hush as the shamans stopped their magical theatrics and turned to face the Great Orc, who indeed proved to be the smaller of the two orcs that had attracted her eye. The shaman with the biggest and most ornate headdress handed the orc general an object that appeared to be a horned skull on a pike of sorts, after which the orc turned to face the assembled horde, raised it high, and shouted something that could be barely heard over the wails of the hundreds of bound goblins.

Whatever he shouted appeared to meet with the horde's approval, though, as his words were met with a thunderous roar that drowned out the goblins. Then the orcs began chanting a single guttural phrase, over and over, accompanied by the rhythmic stamping of their feet. The mood of the horde was palpably anticipatory, and even from the safety of her seat on the warhawk's back hundreds of feet overhead, Bereth could feel that matters had taken an ominous turn.

"How many of them do you think there are?" Lassarian shouted.

"Goblins?" Bereth had already counted the number on their knees in the big circle. "One hundred sixty-nine!"

"What about in the big bonfire down there?"

Bereth looked down at the ziggurat filled with thrashing, shrieking goblins. Lassarian was right, she realized. It was more than an altar, that was why it was built of wood. The whole structure was itself being offered as a sacrifice. But to what? Or worse, to whom. Her heart sank as she realized what the orcs were doing.

"Two thousand, two hundred," she shouted back.

"What?"

"I'll bet there are around two thousand two hundred goblins in that thing!"

"How can you know that?"

Bereth didn't bother to answer, as a moment later, the next actions of the orcs confirmed her suspicions. At a command from the Great Orc, the orcs holding the goblins captive in the circle raised their swords and the chanting stopped. A second command, and one hundred sixty-nine swords flashed down to behead the captives in a spray of green blood.

"*Gwaedhud*," Lassarian commented.

"No," she corrected him. "Not blood magic. Hell magic. Look!"

Below them, the killers had sheathed their swords and were dragging the headless bodies, the blood still fountaining from them, so as to make a closed circle of blood that surrounded the wooden ziggurat. The chanting began again, but it was lower, deeper, and almost submissive in tone now. Somehow, that made it even more terrifying.

"It's a summoning," she told him. "They're calling up something very, very big. And very, very bad."

Thirteen thirteens. The size of the sacrifice, and the fact that the summoning circle was constructed of lifesblood, suggested evil on a scale she'd never seen before. She waved at the other warhawk, which like Mellt was soaring silently over the ziggurat in a circular pattern. When Terfielon finally noticed her trying to get his attention, she made the question gesture. Wasn't it time to leave? *No*, he signaled. *Watch*.

He was probably right, she was forced to admit. But she was sure she knew what was coming next, and as inured to death and violence as she had become, she really didn't want to see it, much less hear or smell it.

She wasn't the only one who knew what was coming. The goblins knew it too, and their wailing intensified as the Great Orc returned the horned skull staff to the lead shaman, who raised it high above his head as all his fellow shamans dropped to their knees and raised their hands. Then the shaman threw his free hand forward, casting an incendiary spell that sent red-yellow flame arcing over the circle and into the ziggurat. The wood, apparently ensorcelled, erupted as if it had been sun-dried for years, and the flames rapidly ascended the structure like hungry demons scrambling out of a lower hell, devouring the thrashing, screaming goblins as they climbed.

Bereth looked away. Mercifully, the intense heat of the fire meant that the horrific screams of the victims did not last long. But the smell of the rising smoke was ghastly, and when she leaned over to see what was resulting from the mass sacrifice, she could feel the warmth of the towering flames on her face. She worried that the lighter underbellies of the hawks might reflect the light cast by the mighty bonfire, but none of the orcs appeared to have been looking toward the skies.

Instead, they were, almost to an orc, focused intently on the heart of the burning ziggurat. The shamans were back at their spell-work, waving their arms dramatically and calling out to the flames, their bodies bobbing and weaving as if the fire was an animated intelligence capable of responding to their beseeching. In contrast, the Great Orc and his generals stood motionless before the great fire, with their gleaming armor flickering red and gold in the light of its flames, as if waiting for something to respond to all the frantic activity of the shamans.

At first, Bereth thought some of the internal structure of the ziggurat was collapsing as the beams holding it upright burned away. But then she realized that there was something moving inside the flames, swirling and twisting as it slowly took form. It was impossible, it was unthinkable, but the flames seemed to be coalescing and winding around each other, coming together in the shape of a massive being of pure fire.

"What in the name of *y gwir hardd da* is that?" Lassarian looked back at her. For the first time in all their skyriding together, she saw his eyes were wide with genuine fear. "That's too big to be an elemental!"

Alarmed, the elf urged Mellt higher, and Bereth heartily agreed with the decision. She saw that Lalflenddas was quick to follow suit

The fire swirled and spun around the monstrosity, gradually forming a torso, then four pairs of muscular arms, then legs, and finally, a head from which sprouted leaping horns of fire. The orcs were roaring and howling in ecstatic triumph at first, but when the terrifying inferno opened its eyes and began to turn its mighty horned head back and forth, surveying the vast army arrayed before it, they abruptly fell silent, though whether it was out of respect or sheer terror, Bereth could not tell.

The demon, for surely the being was a demon, though from which hell she did not know, stepped forward out of the raging bonfire. But the circle of blood halted it in its tracks, as its summoners had intended, and it threw back its head and roared.

To Bereth's horror, the fiery eyes met her own, and she saw something akin to awareness in them. It could see them! Somehow, it could see them! Abject fear turned her blood to ice.

"Fly!" she shouted at Lassarian.

He didn't need any further encouragement, and immediately urged the warhawk to head for home. A powerful stroke of Mellt's wings sent them forward, just in time to avoid a blast of fire that shot upward from below. She looked for the others and screamed when she saw a second column of fire soaring toward Lalflenddas's hawk, but the flames battered uselessly against the magical shield that the mage somehow conjured before it could reach them. A moment later, both hawks were safely beyond the bounds of the circle in which the terrible fire demon was trapped below.

The walls of Tir Diffaith were not far away. They sped through the night sky for the safety of the fortress, without any concern for the orcs below seeing them. Terfielon cast a spell that caused a green light to burst momentarily behind them; Bereth didn't know what it meant, but she guessed it was a signal of some sort to the elves who were waiting and watching the sky for any sign of them. Her surmise was correct, she gathered, because by the time they landed, the Prince-General, Lord Melchederas, and three mages were already at the top of the tower waiting for them. Behind them, the massive bonfire still raged, although Bereth could not make out the hell-beast, or demon, within the towering flames.

"What happened out there?" The Prince-General looked as calm as ever, but the sharpness of his voice betrayed his anxiety. "They said there was a summoning of some sort!"

"A summoning," Terfielon said, his face ashen. "I should say so! They called up a cursed great *arglwydd uffern*, and the damned thing appeared!"

"A devil?" one of the mages said, his eyes widening. "An actual lord of Hell?"

"Well, I don't know which one, obviously. We weren't about to land and ask the cursed orcs for an introduction, now, were we?"

"Which hell or which devil?" asked the other mage as he rubbed his chin.

"Either!" expostulated Terfielon. He jabbed a finger toward the glow beyond the walls. "Look, either we banish that devil and send it back to whatever inferno from which it crawled, or we need to fly at once to the Collegium for help!"

"I should think we would require the Magistras Daimonae, or at least one of his senior colleagues, for a proper banishing." The first mage looked genuinely frightened. "I don't think any of us here have the necessary influence in the nether realms."

The Prince-General frowned. "I don't suppose we can simply kill it?"

"With what? It's a manifestation from the lower realms! There's nothing to kill!"

Terfiellon's voice was full of fear. His second colleague, marginally calmer, attempted to explain the situation to the Prince-General.

"A major summoning like this will have material substance, but it's more akin to that of a rock than an elf, or even a living thing like a tree. If the substance being utilized is destroyed, the spirit can still manifest in other substances while retaining a quantity of its puissance."

"And that assumes one can destroy the substance in the first place!" Terfielon all but wailed.

The Prince-General nodded coolly. "I see," he said. His eyes were locked onto the blazing enemy bonfire.

"You see what?" demanded Lord Malchderas.

"We must retreat. At once. Save the mages first. Every sky rider must carry as many elves as he can bear, in his claws if need be. We cannot assume the walls will stand against such a being. The orcs know this, or they would not have summoned it."

"We don't have nearly enough hawks to carry off the entire garrison!" the cavalry commander objected. "And we certainly can't leave this fortress entirely unguarded."

"We can and we will!" He pointed to the mages. "Summon your colleagues. Tell them to abandon their personal effects and come here immediately. Malchderas, find the regimental commanders and order them to march the *catrodau* back to Bryn Hardd at double time. You will ride before them with your entire complement."

As the mages hastened to comply, Lord Malchderas bowed to the Prince-General. "As you command, my Prince. But Hoelion, what do you intend to do? Surely you will not stay here!"

"I would, but Fflyd-Adenyth can carry two more elfs to safety than any other hawk here. I will return to Elebrion once the fortress is evacuated and leave Valrond here with a skeleton guard to observe what happens. If the walls hold, well and good. If they are broken, at least we will retain our ability to delay the invaders and give the Collegium time to prepare a magical defense against the horde."

"I will stay behind," Lassarian declared, much to Bereth's surprise. But the Prince-General had other plans for him, as well as for her.

"No, you will depart immediately for Elebrion. Take Bereth with you, now! We'll need every eyewitness we've got to convince the king you're not imagining things. I'll send the mage with Lord Kelethan as soon as he gets here. When you arrive, you will go straight to the king and give him a message from me. You will tell him Tir Diffaith is on the verge of falling, and the only certain answer is Bessarias!"

SEVERA

S EVERA stared down at her exposed belly, in equal parts fascinated and suspicious. She found it hard to believe that there could actually be something alive inside her. But both of the sisters-in-law in whom she'd confided were certain that she was pregnant. The signs were all there; she was late, she was ravenous, and certain smells were bothering her that had never bothered her before. Even Sextus, who for all his many wonderful attributes could not be described as the most attentive of husbands, had noticed that her breasts were a little larger and considerably more sensitive.

While her belly was not yet protruding, some of her skirts felt a little tight, as if her waist had mysteriously thickened in recent weeks. Which, she supposed, it had.

"You need to eat more," Caerilla reprimanded her, while placing a plate of fruit in front of her. "This is not the time to think of your figure. Think of your baby!"

Severa hastily pulled her dress down and blushed. She hadn't realized that her sister-in-law was in the room.

"Don't be shy! This is a new experience for you, little sister. When I was first pregnant, I used to stare at my tummy for hours!" Caerilla looked off into the distance, seemingly drawn back into her memories. But then she blinked and smiled. "All the same, don't do it around the men. They don't understand and it makes them nervous."

"Or the slaves."

"No, it makes them even more uncomfortable."

Severa smiled back and dutifully began to peel an orange. She didn't have any strange cravings as yet, but she was feeling restless for no apparent reason.

"Caerilla, how do you feel about a walk along the river?"

"I shouldn't mind, but I told Pompilia I'd help her with the cena. Drusus took a delivery of oxtails this morning and she wants to make *cauda bovis* for Tertius. It's his favorite, you know. Why don't you ask Carvilia?"

"I didn't know that." Severa wondered if she knew what Sextus's favorite dish was, and was a little displeased to realize that she didn't. She reminded herself to ask him later what it was; she felt it was the sort of thing that a good wife and mother really should know about her husband. Or maybe it would be better to ask his brothers, surely one of them would have an idea about his preferences. Then a thought struck her and she wrinkled her nose. Marcipor, the slave Sextus had somehow inherited from his cousin Marcus, would almost certainly know.

Fortunately, the handsome and unbearably insouciant slave hadn't been around much since the Valerian brothers had fallen into public disgrace, though she wasn't sure if that was on orders from Sextus or simply the result of the self-centered young man pursuing his own interests. She didn't really care what kept him away from the domus so long as he stayed away.

She pushed herself up from the couch, grabbed the remaining pieces of the orange, smiled at Pompilia, and went in search of her other sister-in-law. It didn't take her long to find Potitus's wife, as she was shouting out the window at her two sons.

"Titus, get down from there! Get down from there now!"

Severa smiled. Carvilia's two young boys were both the blessing and the bane of her life. No doubt the elder of the two was climbing in the olive tree again. Her beautiful sister-in-law muttered an oath under her breath, turned around, and startled at the sight of Severa standing in the doorway, eating an orange slice.

"Severa! I didn't hear you come in!"

"Titus Valerius in the tree again?"

"I swear, you'd think he was part-monkey!" Carvilia blew a long strand of auburn hair out of her eyes. "I told Gallio to keep an eye on the two of them, but he's no doubt got his hands full with Publius."

Severa offered the taller woman an orange piece. "I want to go somewhere. I was thinking we might walk down to the river, since Caerilla and Pompilia are apparently occupied with oxtails."

"That would be perfect!" her sister-in-law exclaimed, somewhat to her surprise. "I promised Saint Leonardus I'd light fifty candles for him if he'd see that Potitus came to no harm in prison, and the chapel he shares with Saint Romaldus isn't far from the Pontus Nicolatia."

That wasn't the direction Severa had had in mind, but since she really just wanted to get out of the domus, she figured it would do as well as any other destination. And perhaps she should light at least one candle in gratitude to the saint for her own husband's reprieve, even if he hadn't been imprisoned himself. She nodded, and finished off the remaining orange slices as her sister-in-law, as was her wont, took charge of their little expedition and found Galerus to arrange for a pair of trusted slaves to accompany them. It wasn't long before they were able to depart, strolling arm-in-arm down the cobblestoned street, trailed by their armed bodyguard.

The city streets were less crowded than usual this time of year, partly because of the thousands of city men being trained for the legions, but also due to the absence of all the foreigners, elves, and other races who had formerly been resident in Amorr. It was an unexpected pleasure to stroll through the city and see nothing but Amorran faces, and hear nothing but Amorran being spoken on every side. Only now that they were gone did she realize how many foreigners and foreign tongues had made their homes in Amorr.

The wind was coming from the west, across the great river that bisected the city, and it was refreshingly cool to their bodies warmed to the point of overheating from the quick pace that Carvilia, with her long legs, had set them. As they walked under the canopy of the trees planted on the riverbank, they passed the seven-arched front of the headquarters of the Falconian Bank, the domed cupola of the cathedral of Sanctus Ioannes Baptista, and a series of orderly apartment buildings that housed merchants and other well-off plebians. They turned left onto the wide bridge that was decorated with a statue of a long-dead centurion, presumably the Nicolatus after whom it was named, and caught the full force of the wind as they lost the protection of the trees that had shielded them.

"We should have put our hair back," Severa complained as she pushed her hair out of her face for the second time.

"Here, hold still a moment," Carvilia said, and grabbing two fists of Severa's thick hair, quickly twisted it into a braid that she tied off with a ribbon. "If you have a daughter, you'll need to learn to carry a ribbon or two with you."

"Thanks, sister," Severa said unthinkingly. Carvilia, pleased, beamed at her and placed her hand over her heart.

The little church they sought was just across the bridge, less than a block to the south. It was a small church but the interior decoration was magnificent. Only the two of them entered, as their two escorts remained outside. It was laid out in a simple rectangular, with a tiny apse, and was connected to what appeared to be a small residence on one side, though whether it was for priests, monks, or nuns, Severa couldn't tell. Despite its size, it featured an octagonal dome over the presbyterium with a drum and a tiled saucer of six pitches. A central lantern was suspended from the ceiling, and the main altar was decorated with an ornate altarpiece that showed the Holy Mother with both of the church's titular saints.

A paltry seven or eight candles of varying heights burned before the altar, and a single petitioner prayed silently on his knees in front of them.

Carvilia dropped a few coins in the collection box and withdrew a pair of slender white candles from the wicker basket beside it. She offered one to Severa, who took it and stared quizzically at the lone candle in her sister-in-law's hand.

"I thought you promised him fifty?"

"Saint Leonardus? I have?"

"Then why did you only buy one?"

Carvilia laughed. It echoed off the pale-veined white marble covering the floor and the walls. "Fifty candles, fifty days, little sister. I can't just give them all at once."

"Ah, I see." Severa smiled and shook her head, and the older woman rose higher in her estimation. "So this is where you disappear every day!"

"For the last two weeks and another thirty-five days." Carvilia held up the candle. "Do you know, I believe more in the power of prayer now, when I have to fight the temptation not to keep my end of the bargain, than I did when it was first answered. Isn't that strange?"

But Carvilia didn't wait for an answer, instead, she turned and walked down between the six rows of wooden pews and kneeled down to light her candle from a flame that was guttering and about to give up its smoky ghost. Severa, feeling a little self-conscious despite the fact that the only two other people in the building were paying her no attention, took a deep breath, and followed her sister-in-law's lead.

Her knees felt as if they were burning from their direct contact with the hard floor. She accepted the pain as a penance and ignored it as she touched the candle's wick to one dancing flame, then sat back on her heels and closed her eyes. "*Gratias ago tibi, Sanctus Leonardus.* I want to thank you, Saint Leonardus, for your intercession. Thank you for my husband's freedom, and for the freedom of his brothers and cousins. Please convey my gratitude to our Heavenly Father. *In nomine sanctissimi et immaculati salvatoris nostri, amen.*"

She rose uncomfortably to her feet, wiped at her eyes, bowed to the tranquil figure on the tree and made the sign on her breast, then walked quietly out of the little church. The sunlight outside was blindingly bright, and she had to shield her eyes against the light until they adjusted. She had just gotten used to the light outside when she was joined by Carvilia, who went through the same routine of squinting her eyes and shielding them.

"Goodness," she said, shaking her head. Then her eyes narrowed again, and she frowned. "Oh, I don't like the look of them."

Severa turned her head to see what Carvilia was staring at, and was alarmed to see a group of six or seven plebian thugs walking aggressively toward them. Fortunately, the two Valerian slaves had been paying attention, and they quickly walked across the street to interpose themselves between the two Valerian women and the approaching men.

"Hey, aren't they two o' them Valerian bitches," one young man with close-cropped hair pointed the club he was carrying at them.

"Their House is treason!"

"Let's teach 'em a lesson!"

"Get back, dogs," growled one of their two guards, waggling his weighted staff in warning. But the ruffians were undeterred.

"Severa, go back to the bridge," her sister-in-law ordered. "Walk quickly, but don't run. Go to the cathedral, the priests will send help."

"What about you?"

"I'm taller than most of them and they don't know I'm armed." Carvilia revealed the jagged-edge blade in her hand. "Now hurry!"

Severa nodded, and without looking back, began walking swiftly north along the river. Behind her, she heard the noise of violence erupting, the thud of wood on flesh followed quickly by angry shouts. Just as she reached the bridge, she saw two strapping young men standing beside an ox cart, seemingly unoccupied or waiting for someone. One was leaning against the cart, the other was stroking the ears of the white-nosed ox that drew the cart.

"Oh, sirs, will you not come to our aid! Those criminals are attacking my sister!"

"Lady Valerius," the young man leaning against the cart smiled at her. His use of her name took her by surprise, but not as much as when his companion leaped behind her and pulled her arms behind her back. She opened her mouth to scream, and the first man deftly inserted a foul-tasting rag into her mouth, stifling her cries. As she writhed helplessly in the grip of the man holding her, a heavy sack was pulled down over her head, then someone grabbed her feet and she was lifted bodily onto the cart. As one of the men encouraged the ox into motion, the other expertly bound her wrists and feet with rope, then pulled a canvas tarp over her to conceal her body from view.

She was too shocked to struggle against her bonds. Behind her, the sounds of combat in front of the church faded away as the heavy clod-clod of the ox hooves on the cobblestones drowned them out.

It was hard to say how long her kidnappers drove the cart, but she felt several turns, and at least twice the path underneath changed from cobblestones to dirt, then back again. The man riding next to her checked on her periodically, to make sure she was still breathing, but otherwise showed no concern for her. It was almost as if the whole attack had been staged so they could get her alone to grab her, but how could they have known where she would be? And why would they have any interest in her instead of her sister-in-law who had been burning candles there everyday for the past two weeks?

Then a thought struck her and her blood froze. What if she had been taken in reprisal by a group of foreigners, angry at their enforced exile and eager to strike back against the officer who had been forcing it on them? No, that made no sense, both the thugs and her kidnappers had been Amorrans by accent and by appearance. A political motivation seemed unlikely; all the Senate factions were more or less of one mind these days and focused on their war with the two leagues.

Finally, the cart stopped. The canvas was drawn away, and once more, she was lifted up, but this time she wasn't put back down. Instead, the young man carried her easily on his shoulder, as if she were nothing more than a sack of flour. They entered a building, but this time, he laid her down more gently.

"Hold still, Lady Valerius," he said, and she heard the unmistakable sound of a knife being drawn. She tensed, afraid that he was going to stab her or slit her throat, but instead, she felt him cutting away at the ropes with which he'd tied her. As the ropes fell free, the pain of the blood rushing back into her hands and feet made her gasp. But what she saw when the man freeing her lifted her into a seated position and pulled the sack from her head truly took her breath away.

"You," she breathed in astonishment.

Before her was seated someone she never thought she'd see again, the aged crone from the little village in Salventum. The witch of Seijiss. The priestess of the false saint, Saint Malachus.

"I see you remember me, my Lady. And I remember you. Oh, I do remember you!" The witch's smile was eager and too hungry for Severa's liking. "I told you those curves were made to be ridden, and ridden they have been, I see!"

"You have a filthy tongue, witch!" Her eyes narrowed. She couldn't recall the woman's name, but if she was behind this, or even just involved with it, then the attack by the street thugs couldn't have been an accident. "What happened to my sister and our men?"

The old woman brushed her twisted white-streaked locks out of her wrinkled face and looked up past Severa at the kidnapper behind her. "I know nothing about them. They are of no interest to the Goddess. If you know anything, tell her."

"One of the slaves has a broken arm. The other was untouched. The highborn lady will have a nice bruise on her face and well she earned it. She stabbed Rusticus in the guts and he may not last the night."

Severa felt relief wash over her whole body. Carvilia was unharmed, that was the most important thing. And she was glad that their two loyal guards had not been too badly injured.

"They were just a distraction, weren't they. So you could take me."

The witch shrugged. "You owe the Goddess a life, Severa Valerius. And that is a debt that can only be paid in kind."

"What life do I owe her?"

"Why, yours, of course, my dear girl. Who do you think made sure your letters to your infatuation went straight to your father? Who do you think alerted your father on the night you slipped out of the house to meet your ill-fated gladiator? Do you not realize that to take such a low-born creature as your lover would have meant your death?"

"My father would never have harmed me!"

"Think again, Lady Valerius. The late Princeps Senatus didn't spare your gladiator, did he? No more would he have spared a rebellious daughter who not only brought shame to one of the most noble Houses in Amorr, but to the Senate itself! Why, your own father-in-law is now waging war against the city because his own brother executed his son! The annals of Amorr are fairly strewn with all the sons, daughters, nieces, and nephews killed to spare the blushes of their families."

"Well, even so, that makes no sense! I didn't meet you until after Father sent me to Salventum!"

"The goddess and her servants have had their eye on you for much longer than you think, Valerius Severa. And I am not her only servant."

"You're an awful, evil, terrible old woman!" Severa spat, her anger inflamed by fear. Had there been spies in her father's house? There must have been, if the witch was telling her the truth.

"I am a servant of the Goddess, Lady Valerius. And whether you like it or not, so are you!" The old woman leered at her. "A life she has demanded and a life she shall have!"

Severa bared her teeth. "She'll have a lot more than just one life. My husband and his family will hunt you down. They will kill you and they will kill everyone who had anything to do with hurting me. The Valerians are warriors, witch, true warriors, and they will go through your thugs and hired men like a scythe cutting grass."

"Oh, my dear, we have no intention of harming you!" The witch's expression was tender, but there was a hint of gleeful malice in her eyes. She reached out and placed her wrinkled hand on Severa's belly. "The goddess doesn't want your life. She merely demands an offering, a sacrifice from your body!"

"My baby!" Severa knocked the witch's hand away and placed her own protectively over the faint swelling. "She wants to take my baby!"

The witch sneered. "What she wants, she will have, mother-to-be. But what she wants is not for me to say. My task here is done."

"Your task?"

"To confirm that you are the woman sought by the goddess." She waved to the young man who had been standing silently behind Severa. "It's her. You can take her now. You need not bind her unless she is difficult."

"No!" Severa protested, but despite her best efforts to fight it off, the heavy sack came down over her head again. This time, knowing the futility of struggling, she sat there mutely and meekly on the floor, until her kidnapper, not unkindly, lifted her to her feet.

THEUDERIC

THE SOLDIER grimaced as Theuderic tightened the bandage on his wounded arm. The goblin arrow hadn't passed all the way through, but fortunately, the crudely carved wooden shafts weren't barbed, so it had been easy to extricate it, clean the wound with wine, and wrap the arm with the clean cloth that the marquis had thoughtfully taken care to provide for them.

"I can still fight," the young man assured him.

Theuderic smiled. "Yes, you certainly can. But your lord's orders were clear. If it's more than a scratch, you're to leave with the cart."

"But it's just my shield arm! I don't need to go back with the others."

"You do understand that I am a royal battlemage, do you not?"

"Yes," the soldier replied uncertainly.

Theuderic smiled again, but this time he showed his teeth. "So, would you like me to see that you actually need to leave on the cart? I can assure you, I know a wide catalog of spells from which you might choose."

The young soldier blinked, wide-eyed. "Nossir! I mean, no, monseigneur mage! I'll just collect my things and go!"

"Good!" Theuderic patted him on his bare shoulder. "Be sure to get that cleaned and changed again before nightfall. You won't be any good to the marquis if it gets infected and the doctor needs to take your arm off."

"Is that the last of them?" He heard de Ponchaux's behind him as the wounded young man hurried off towards the bridge, presumably where he'd removed his armor.

"You're lucky. Only twelve wounded, and just two of them serious."

"Will they survive?"

"I should think so. I know you told me not to waste any magery on them, but honestly, Ansoult, we didn't exert ourselves in the slightest."

The marquis snorted. He was a tall man, nearly as tall as Theuderic, and carried himself confidently, as befitted a commander of men. "I didn't see it, but the men are all still talking about how one of you made a sorcerer's head explode."

"Yes, it's a rather nasty little counterspell, really."

"I suspected you might have been behind that one. It seemed a little cruel for any of your lads. They're far too wet behind the ears to be that evil-minded."

"I don't know, was I at that age?"

"You were born evil-minded, my friend." The marquis laughed. "It's good to see you haven't changed, Theuderic. I'd heard about you here and there, although I could scarcely credit that any of it could be true. First they said you'd disappeared, then they said you were eaten by a dragon, and finally I'd heard you'd run off to Elebrion or some such nonsense."

"Amorr, actually. Although there was an elf involved. Elfille, to be precise."

"Oh, was there now?"

"The less said, the better," Theuderic's tone shut down any invitation to inquiry. "How are your men holding up?"

"Splendidly. Between having you lot here and turning back the goblins at so little cost, they're ready to take on the whole damned orc army."

Theuderic stretched out his shoulders and looked in the direction of the river. "It was good of you to arrange for the carts for the wounded. How many more are there?"

"Only four, I'm afraid. But it should be sufficient, so long as we don't break and lose the bridge before you can destroy it. I expect Comte Favre-Rapin's man is going to be rather cross with me upon my return. He only agreed to loan the one, but I borrowed the others when I went to retrieve it."

"How did you manage that?"

"I arrived early and told the guard I had the comte's permission. He wasn't about to wake him up to ask him."

Theuderic laughed. "So long as you return them and wash off the blood, I expect he'll forgive you. If the next wave goes half so well, I shouldn't be surprised if he claims half the credit."

"Bah. He's welcome to it if his wagons permit me to bring my wounded back to camp safely."

Theuderic recognized that de Poncheaux wasn't merely posturing. The marquis truly didn't care about court politics, which was why he would likely never rise in the ranks of the aristocracy. It was always thus. The true warriors fought and bled and died, while the prancing courtiers did their best to pretend that any victory won by their betters was somehow all their doing.

The true warrior lay buried in the ground, while the princeling sat in his tent in the midst of his army, pretending to be a general. Bitterness filled him for a moment, until the marquis interrupted his thoughts.

"What's the matter?"

"Oh, I was merely thinking that Charles-Phillippe would be here, if he were alive." Not sitting safely back at camp, hoping that others would win his battles for him.

De Poncheaux nodded. "I was sorry to hear of his death. Is it true? Was he really murdered by a monster across the White Sea?"

"More or less." Theuderic didn't want to talk about it. "What do you think of his younger brother?"

"Chênevin? He's not his brother, but you know that. I think he's learned from his previous mistakes."

"Do you?"

"Well, I hope so, at any rate."

Theuderic snorted. "Don't we all."

"What do you think the chances are that he can beat the orc?"

"About the same as you holding this bridge against them." Theuderic met de Poncheaux's eyes, which were uncharacteristically dark with something akin to despair. He smiled and shook his head at his old friend. "You've done your part, Ansoult. You've done more than your part. If you were to return to your lands instead of to the camp when we leave here, there is hardly a man there who would think to blame you."

"The prince would."

"Well, yes," Theuderic admitted. And in light of the fact that the Duc de Chênevin was the heir to the throne, it might be wise for a petty border lord to avoid making an enemy of him. On the other hand, it might be better to be alive and out of favor with the king one day than to not survive to see him crowned. "I understand he has a rare talent for holding grudges."

De Poncheaux shrugged. "The orc will come for us all sooner or later. The more we kill today, the more we kill tomorrow, the more time we give His Majesty to assemble a proper army that can send these creatures back to Hell. No, Theuderic, the rats may scurry for fear of the ship sinking, but I will not be one of them."

"I didn't think there was much chance of talking any sense into you."

"Monseigneur magie!" One of the poacher's men was calling down from the rooftop. "They're coming!"

At almost the same time, there was a commotion from the direction of the bridge, followed by a horn blowing the agreed-upon signal. De Poncheaux looked at Theuderic and sighed. "And so it begins. Whatever happens, don't let them cross the river."

"I won't." Theuderic stood up and extended his hand to the marquis. "Look at the sky, Ansoult. See how blue it is! It's far too lovely a day to die."

"I pray you're right."

Theuderic watched as the marquis collected his helmet and his shield, slung the latter over his back, and strode off towards the bridge. He smiled, silently wishing good fortune to his old friend, and shook his head, then made his own way towards the rooftop

The approaching army made for an impressive sight. The assault force was already assembled into a broad column of perhaps six hundred armored orc foot, presumably as a result of the previous failure of the goblin cavalry to shake off their ranged defenses. A pair of wider columns, made up of smaller figures, flanked the main column. Those would be goblin archers, Theuderic guessed, meant to provide cover for the orc infantry as they attempted to smash through the outnumbered men on the bridge. It was also possible, though, that the orc intended for them to try to swim the fast-moving waters of the river; he had yet to encounter an orc general who spared a thought for the lives of his light infantry.

Behind the three columns was the enormous mass of the main army. He could barely distinguish between the hulking shapes of the boar-riders, in the center, and the smaller wolfriders on the enemy left. The right was comprised of infantry, mostly orcs, he presumed, although he could not say. It was an intimidating sight, and in his considered opinion, did not bode well for when the Red Prince would meet them in the field in a few days. For a moment, he was tempted to call the men from the bridge and cast the incendiary spell to demolish it, so great were the enemy numbers. But he restrained himself. Every orc, goblin, and more importantly, shaman, killed today was one less to face tomorrow.

As the three columns came closer, it became clear that the orc's plan was to cast caution to the winds and simply overwhelm the defenders' archers and mages. He was wrong; neither of the two flanking columns were comprised of archers, the goblins were neither carrying bows nor were they armored. Instead, they were carrying thick wooden poles that were too thick to be lances, but just might be buoyant enough to keep a goblin head above water. He smiled grimly. The orc might spare his mages this way, but he would pay a heavy price in green blood, and for nothing.

He turned to Talbot. "It looks as if you'll find old Gaston's spell useful today. But don't be alarmed when I augment it."

The younger mage nodded, his eyes narrowed as he peered out at the approaching enemy. "How close do you want to let them approach before we hit them?"

"We're going to ignore the main body. We'll have to trust the marquis and his men to hold back their initial charge without our help. Our job is to ensure the goblins can't flank them and take them from behind by crossing the river."

"So you think they're going to swim for it?"

"I'm certain they are. Look what they're carrying. Those aren't lances they're holding; those poles aren't even tapered to a point. But put one under a goblin's chest and he should be able to kick his way across the river even if he can't swim very well."

"The lightning spell, then?"

Theuderic nodded. "Hit them with it as soon as the first three ranks are in the water. It will be much more effective there than on the bank. Then hit them again as long as you can find the energy, or until they give up. I expect the third or fourth should be enough."

"I can manage four," Talbot said, although he looked uncertain. "The left column?"

"Leave the right column to me. I hope that Ambroys has the wherewithal to deal with them, but if not, I have an idea or two."

"What about us," asked Regnaut. "You don't sound too bothered about the enemy archers."

"Keep an eye out. Just because they haven't moved any forward yet doesn't mean they won't. But until they do, target the orcs in the middle column and help relieve the pressure on the Marquis. Look for chieftains and those carrying banners in particular."

The old poacher nodded and withdrew to pass on the instructions to his men. Theuderic grimaced. He wasn't exactly surprised that the enemy was resorting to such crude and expensive tactics, the problem was that the orcs had the raw numbers to make them work. While he was confident that de Ponchaux's men would hold off the initial rush, he was worried about the goblins. Damn the clever greenskin who had come up with the idea of floating them across on poles! Even if they killed scores of them with lightning in the water, he and the young mages would exhaust themselves long before the orc ran out of goblin bodies to throw against them.

Then he smiled. He was no elf, to summon a naiad or river god and thereby raise the waters to an uncrossable barrier. But he could speed up the flow of the water, particularly on the surface, by summoning a strong breeze blowing in the same direction as the river.

It took a moment to recall the words of *Montalban's Encan Flottant* to his mind, but once he had them firmly fixed in order, he raised his staff and pointed to the north, from which direction the river flowed. He called out the words of the spell clearly, without hurry, even as the goblins were beginning to approach the river banks on either side of the bridge. When he finished, he lowered the staff and looked over at Talbot, whose face was a mask of incomprehension and disappointment.

"It didn't work?" the younger mage said, sounding dismayed.

"Not all spells are so immediately gratifying as that lightning spell that you should probably be readying about now." Theuderic indicated the river bank below, where, with fearful cries echoed by curses from the orcs driving them forward, the first goblins were descending the bank and trying to summon up the courage to enter the water. "Everything is as it should be; concentrate on your own responsibilities and leave mine to me."

A roar echoed off the buildings as the orcs in the center began to close the gap that separated them from the soldiers on the bridge with a full-speed charge. A horn answered the bestial howling, and Theuderic saw the first two ranks of men bend their knees and crouch behind their shields as they prepared to withstand the initial onslaught. On either side of the bridge, goblins were entering the river, some leaping in boldly, others wading in more gingerly, while still others were shoved forward by those behind them to fall clumsily into the rushing waters with awkward splashes.

He saw one goblin stumble into the river, lose its grip on the pole it was carrying and disappear beneath the rippling surface without making a sound or even appearing to struggle. Others spun aimlessly about, unable to control their direction as they were swept harmlessly back to the near bank towards the south of the town. But many, too many, managed to keep their poles under their chests and kick their legs to propel themselves forward, even as the current pushed them southward.

As he turned to see what was delaying Talbot, a brilliant flash seared his eyes and was followed almost instantly by a huge, deafening crash.

He blinked, half-stunned and half-blinded by the lightning strike, then shielded his eyes as a second strike, just a little further away, hammered down from the sky nearby.

"Merde!" he expostulated. "You might have warned me!"

"Shall I hit them again?"

Theuderic looked down at the river below, his vision still somewhat disturbed by the lightning bolts. The river was littered with floating bodies, some of them burned, others seemingly unmarred, but dead all the same. More were dead on the slope of the far bank; others further back had only been knocked unconscious and were beginning to moan and stir. As those killed by the first strike were pulled downstream by the current, the victims of the second one, presumably Ambroys's doing, began to arrive from under the bridge. A quick scan of the near bank showed that not a single goblin had managed to cross the river.

Despite that, the goblins were far from demoralized. With a great deal of shouting and more than a few blows, the goblin chieftains gradually managed to get the front ranks back on their feet with their poles in their arms again. But they did not do so uninterrupted. Theuderic watched one goblin with a helmet pick up a pole and shove it into the shaking hands of an unwilling fellow, but no sooner had he done so than an arrow took him through the throat. The second goblin stared, amazed, at the death throes of his officer, then cast down the pole and ran back into the mass of goblins behind him.

"Looks like they're up for a second attempt," he said to Talbot. "Are you?"

The younger mage grinned. "Certainly, monseigneur. Would you like a little warning this time?"

Theuderic only snorted. The young bastard had cheek; much better than cowardice. He took advantage of the brief respite the two blasts had given them to close his eyes and listen to the atmosphere as the boreal forces he had summoned continued to gather. It wouldn't be long now.

He looked down at the bridge, where the tightly constricted battle between the orcs and the marquis's men was raging. The force of the initial charge had driven the soldiers back nearly one third of the way across the bridge, but the orcs' momentum had faded and the narrow space prevented them from bringing their greater numbers to bear. And while the powerful, green-skinned arms hammered down heavy blow after heavy blow on the shields of the men, the soldiers, with their discipline and well-made steel armor, were able to withstand the poorly forged iron of the orcs. Theuderic saw one orc smash a spiked mace down upon one soldier's upraised shield; it snapped off at the haft, leaving him staring at it in befuddlement. But not for long, as a soldier from the second rank thrust forward a spear that took the big orc right under the chin. Caught in the press of bodies and unable to collapse, the dying orc thrashed and convulsed, spraying dark green blood left and right, to the obvious dismay of his fellows.

The archers were also helping relieve the pressure on the bridge's defenders, picking off those in the second and third ranks. At such close range, the skilled poachers could hardly miss, and there was nothing the orcs could do but roar in futile anger and hope that the next shaft would find someone else. Dead and wounded orcs soon impeded the attacking column, and prevented the orcs from using their greater collective weight to simply push back the lighter men.

An idea occurred to Theuderic. It was too soon to try it, but if it worked, it might well buy the men on the bridge the time and space they would need to disengage from the orcs before he destroyed the stone structure. He wished he had time to tell de Poncheaux of his intentions, but he would have to hope the marquis, or one of his men, had the wits to recognize the opportunity Theuderic was giving them.

"Cover your eyes," Talbot warned.

Theuderic and the archers made haste to comply, and there was another searing bolt from the cloudless blue heavens. Again, scores of goblins were slain in the river, and on the river bank, but this time, the survivors were not so quick to recover. Goblin shrieked at goblin as the ranks closest to the river tried to retreat, only to be pushed back by the ranks behind them. Larger shapes could be seen rushing forward from the mass of the main army behind the column; orcs, and by the movement of their arms, Theuderic could see they were bearing whips, lashing those goblins that had already run away from the column.

"They'll be coming in again soon and this time they're not going to stop," he told Talbot. He could see the younger mage was now showing some signs of strain. Two such spells, cast in quick succession, would tire out any mage. "How many more are you good for?"

"Three, maybe four."

"One after the other?"

"All right, two, then."

Theuderic nodded. That would suffice, as the boreal forces he had summoned were still gathering strength. Perhaps too much, as it happened, but there was nothing to be done about it now.

A fiery flare to the north caught his eye. He looked to the right and swore, belatedly realizing that he had not heard the expected thunderclap following Talbot's second spell. Six or seven of the goblins had been set alight by what he deduced was a spell cast by Maussart, who must have moved to assist Ambroys for some reason. But why hadn't Ambroys hit the goblins with a second lightning strike? Had he been wounded, or perhaps worse?

I am not cut out for this, he thought bitterly. Étienne-Henri would rightly have some harsh words for him if he managed to lose a second mageling under his command. He closed his eyes and swiftly prayed to the God in whom he did not believe that the bright young man would survive; sadly, prayer was all he had to offer Ambroys now. There was no time for anything else, as a score of paddling goblins had very nearly reached the near bank.

"Hit them there, now!" he shouted at Talbot, pointing past the bridge to the north. "Now, damn you!"

"Where?" Talbot queried, puzzled, as the goblins on their side of the bridge had not even begun to descend the riverbank again. Then his eyes widened as he looked north and saw how close the enemy was to crossing the river."

Theuderic shielded his eyes with his arm, and as the bright flash faded, grabbed the old poacher by the arm and pointed towards Ambroys's position. "Take your men up to the wall behind the bridge. I think one of my men is down. Bring him back to the square here. And be careful! They must have more archers on their left flank."

Regnaut nodded. "What about you two, monseigneur?"

"We'll be fine. They will not cross here."

The old poacher raised a white eyebrow in the direction of Talbot, who was sweating and breathing heavily.

"Never mind him, go!" He snarled at Talbot. "What are you waiting for? Hit them again!"

The young mage nodded, took a deep breath, and closed his eyes. Theuderic did the same, and again there was a bright flash, followed by a crashing boom as the sky was violently torn asunder. Talbot nodded to him, then his eyes rolled back in his head and he slumped to the rooftop before Theuderic could catch him.

The poacher shrugged and gestured for the other archers to follow him before descending the ladder to the square. Theuderic looked past the bridge and noted with satisfaction that Maussart and the archers with him

had swiftly followed up Talbot's two sorcerous strikes with a veritable storm
of hellfire and arrows, combining to kill the few goblins that the barrage of
lightning had somehow spared. He wasn't worried about Talbot; a little
magical overexertion seldom hurt anyone and it was a useful lesson in
learning one's limits. He was, however, deeply concerned about Ambroys
and desperately hoped the lad wasn't too badly harmed.

The air suddenly grew cool on his face, alerting him to the fact that
the spirits of the air had answered his imperious summons. The wind
had picked up and blew his hair across his face. He looked down where
the goblins were again beginning to enter the water and smiled in savage
satisfaction. They would not cross, not with the increasingly strong breeze
already rippling the surface of the waters.

The men and orcs battling on the bridge were impervious to it, of course.
It appeared the marquis's men had managed to extricate several of their
wounded from the vicious struggle, as there were four or five men being
bandaged behind the shelter of the heavy stone bridgehead. The men had
forced the orcs very nearly back to the edge of the bridge, but they had no
sooner done so than a mighty brute with horns thrust through his shoulder
armor and one broken tusk pushed his way to the fore, seized a man in the
front rank, and hurled him over the south side of the bridge.

Armored as he was, the man sank like a stone, of course, dismaying the
men and encouraging the big orc to a second feat of strength. This time, he
managed to get his hands on a struggling soldier and somehow threw him
over the heads of his fellows and the north side of the bridge. His fellow
orcs roared with triumph, and redoubled their efforts, forcing the men to
grudgingly give up several steps that they had fought so hard to regain.

But by the time the muscular monster tried to pick up a third soldier to
send to a watery doom, his quick-witted victim threw himself backwards
as the beast grabbed at his breastplate. His action caused the orc to lean
forward and stretch out his arms, thereby exposing both his unarmored
throat and armpits. The soldier's companions were alert to the opportunity
presented, and immediately pierced the orc's hide with a pair of swords
and a spear. The big orc fell back into the arms of his green-skinned
fellows, dying, as his would-be victim was pulled back to his feet and
promptly slew the next orc to move forward with a sword-thrust to the
eye.

As the battle on the bridge continued to rage, everyone else on either side
of the river was beginning to notice the increasingly powerful wind. Goblins
were glancing to the north even as they were driven towards the river by

whip-wielding orcs and archers frowned in frustration as they attempted to compensate for the driving winds as they took aim.

"What happened?" an unsteady Talbot asked him, leaning against a chimney for support.

"You drained yourself with that last spell. But you did well. They didn't cross."

The younger mage staggered forward and looked down at the river in front of them. "They're coming again. But I don't know if I can cast another one so soon."

"Never you mind. Just brace yourself and watch." He could feel the spirits of the air growing ever more palpable as their anger swelled, rebelling against the summoning. But they were no test for his will; this was far from the first time he had cast the spell and he knew what to expect. Already, the lighter goblins were beginning to find it hard to stand against the wind on land, and in the water, first one, then a second was overturned by the frothing waters and disappeared beneath the surface.

"Better get down," he told Talbot, not wanting to see the young mage hurled from the rooftop, and he kneeled down himself, taking shelter behind another chimney that partially protected him from the buffeting of the wind. The sky was howling louder than the enemy now, and dark grey clouds were rushing rapidly toward them from the north. The goblins who were not overturned or did not lose their grasp on the poles that supported them were washed down the river, disappearing from view as they were swept away by the now-rapid current. Even if they wound up on the west bank, they would be too far downriver to flank the defenders before it was time to withdraw.

Which, Theuderic decided, would have to be soon. They had not killed as many orcs as he would have liked, and if they had lost Ambroys, the price had been much too dear. Although he had been able to withdraw his wounded, the constant pressure from the orcs had prevented the marquis from rotating his front rank, and the exhausted soldiers were being slowly pushed back. Despite their courageous efforts, the orcs were now nearing the mid-point of the bridge. It was time to act.

First, the agreed-upon signal. Without releasing his hold upon the boreal forces, he jabbed his staff at the sky. A green fireball emerged from the tip and arced high above the enemy on the other side of the river before exploding harmlessly well over their heads. Even occupied as they were, none of the marquis's men could have missed it. Only then did he relinquish the winds, but before they had even begun to die down, he aimed his staff at the section of the bridge on which the orcs were standing and recited the trigger for *Charcot's Tempête Hivernale*. He could almost feel the energy leaving his body as the invisible, but bone-chilling cold engulfed the eastern half of the bridge, immediately transforming the water that the winds had sprayed over the bridge into ice.

A horn sounded once, and the front ranks of the men, having been warned of Theuderic's plan, immediately took advantage of the startled orcs' confusion and crashed forward into the orcs, using their shields and armored shoulders as battering rams. With their footing suddenly rendered treacherous and their feet encased with ice, the front two ranks of orcs simply slid backwards and fell over, causing many of their fellows behind them to stumble and fall as well. But no sooner had the men shoved forward than they retreated quickly backwards, holding their shields up high as they abandoned the bridge they had so determinedly defended. A few desultory arrows smacked into their shields and snapped in two as they fell back from the bridge, but the enemy seemed too shocked by the unexpected sorcery to make a more serious effort.

"Fall back! Fall back!" Theuderic heard the marquis shouting, and his order was echoed by his sergeants. A horn sounded, three times this time, signaling that the men were to retreat to the square and the wagons prepared for the wounded there.

The orcs, seeing that the defenders had finally given way, were heartened and roared triumphantly. Those whose clawed feet were unimpeded rushed for the bridge, slowed a little by the ice that coated the stones of the bridgehead, only to be met by an intense wall of flame and a mini-hail of arrows. Theuderic smiled. Maussart was certainly proving himself to be worthy of his blue cloak.

"Monseigneur le magie!" he heard someone call behind him. It was Regnaut.

"The boy, he will live. An arrow to the shoulder."

Theuderic nodded, pleased at the news. "Can he ride?"

"If he is led, I think he can."

Theuderic pushed Talbot towards the old poacher. "Take all three of them and ride for the camp now! Don't wait for the others."

"But what about you, monseigneur?"

"Never mind me. I will return with the marquis and his men."

Regnaut bowed and touched his bald forehead with his knuckle, with a good deal more respect than he had shown this morning. Theuderic stifled a smile, nodded to Talbot, who was trying to apologize unnecessarily for his spell-weakened state, and turned back to the scene below, waiting for the right moment to strike.

The bridge was a stone hell of ice, fire, and charred bodies. Undeterred, fresh orc warriors kicked and shoved their way past their dead and dying fellows, then made their way carefully over the slippery ice until they reached the middle of the bridge.

Theuderic smiled grimly. The orcs roared as their feet found firmer purchase on the still-wet stones, and raised their weapons as they began to charge the rest of the way across the undefended bridge. He spoke a single word, awakening the incendiary sigils he'd prepared earlier, then threw himself flat on the rooftop and curled into a fetal position with his arms over his head.

A massive blast nearly deafened him, and was followed immediately by the clatter and thudding of shattered pieces of stones landing on the rooftop and smashing against the side of the building below. He felt a few bits of gravel harmlessly pepper him, waited a moment, then opened his eyes to see dozens of broken chunks of bridge matter scattered all across the rooftop. He couldn't help laughing when he saw, mixed amongst the stones and the other debris, a large green hand, torn off at the wrist and oozing thick, dark green blood.

He pushed himself to his feet, brushed off some of the dust that was covering him, and made his way back towards the edge to see the extent of the devastation. The bridge, he was relieved to confirm, was entirely destroyed. Only a crumbled, blackened remnant of either bridgehead survived, the rest of the stone structure was simply gone, either vanished into the depths of the river or scattered across both the east and west banks. The far bank was littered with bodies, some crushed beneath stone-and-mortar, others torn apart, and the shrieking and wailing of the wounded sounded like the travails of the damned.

Dozens of orcs had been killed, and scores more wounded by the blast alone. Taking into account those slain by the marquis's men, his own little group, and their archers, he estimated that the enemy had lost around five hundred foot, divided almost equally between orcs and goblins. And while he didn't know their own butcher's bill, he would be surprised if they'd lost more than ten or twelve in return.

But when he looked out over the mass of the enemy army across the river, he knew that their efforts had amounted to nothing more than a mere token of defiance. The orc could afford to lose ten times that many and he would still march into the heart of the realm without fear or hesitation, so great were his numbers. It was a sight that might well have driven a man to despair. But Theuderic only shrugged.

He heard someone climbing up the ladder behind him, and was surprised to see it was Maussart, followed by the Marquis de Poncheaux. The latter was smiling, and holding up a wineskin triumphantly in his right hand.

"What are you doing here? You were supposed to go back to the camp with Regnaut!"

"I had no such orders. I stayed to make sure none of them made it across before you ignited the sigils."

"You're lucky you didn't get brained!" Theuderic gestured at the debris strewn around their feet.

"Don't be so hard on the lad, Theudo!" The marquis put a fatherly arm around the young mage and thumped his shoulder. "He damn well roasted those buggers who thought they'd steal a march on us! *Mon dieu*, my friend, but if I'd known you held the key to the gates of Hell in your hand, I'd never have stolen that innkeeper's fat daughter out from under your nose!"

Theuderic chuckled and accepted the proffered skin. He took a long and much-needed draught. The wine was warm and it was bitter, but to his parched throat, it was as fine as any that had ever been served at the royal table. He handed it to Maussart, with a nod of absolution.

"The wine of victory, kingsmage."

Maussart lifted it in a salute, then drank from it before handing it to the marquis. De Poncheaux stepped forward to the edge of the roof and held it up as he looked down over the battlefield, though whether it was to acknowledge the fallen or mock the frustrated enemy, Theuderic did not know. The victorious nobleman drank deeply from it, then turned to face them.

"The orc will cross the river, monseigneurs," he declared. "But he will not cross here and he will not cross today!"

BERETH

LTHOUGH the night flight to Elebrion was fast-paced and cold, Bereth missed most of it, having fallen asleep in the saddle not long after they'd fled Tir Diffaith. She awoke with a start as the warhawk was climbing the sky above the mountain to the white city. It was still obscured by the clouds above them, but once they broke through the wet, suffocating darkness, the lights of the city reflected off the white marble were so bright she nearly needed to shield her eyes.

"I see you're still with us," Lassarian called as he leaned back into her. "Good thing I tightened those straps."

Bereth didn't bother with a response, she just wiped the saliva from the corner of her mouth away with the sleeve of her sky jacket and twisted back and forth in a mostly futile attempt to relieve the tightness of the muscles in her lower back. She could feel Mellt straining as he beat his wings, laboring to lift them higher, and her skyrider's instincts made her worried for the bird.

"Why are you pushing him so hard?"

Lassarian pointed at the large figure moving, nearly invisible in the dark sky, in front and above them. It appeared to be headless. That unlikely observation, combined with the repeated flashes of light-colored feathers under its wings, told her it was Ilriathas's black-headed hawk, Ebon. She whistled, amazed that her would-be lover's bird had managed to make up the lead they'd had so easily.

"Lord Kelethan caught up to us half an hour ago. He ordered me to keep up with him. I think the Prince-General is worried that if we don't manage to convince the king it's necessary, he won't go to the Collegium."

"Do you know anything about that mage he mentioned? I've heard the name, but I don't know why."

"Yeah, he's been around forever. Used to be one of the magisters, but I don't remember which. They say he's the one who created the Glass Desert, so I presume he's got the spells to deal with a summoning of that magnitude."

"*Anhygoel!*" Bereth was amazed. "I wonder if we'll get to meet him."

"Probably." Lassarian yawned. "I could use a nap myself."

"You'll get one soon enough. We're almost there."

Above them, Ebon was beginning to level off as the high walls of the White City came into view. Soon Mellt was able to relax his exhausted wings and extend them as the two hawks soared over the walls and past the bronze-helmed sentries who saluted them as they flew past. Ilriathas led them past the infantry barracks, over a bridge that spanned the unlikely waters of the Huduchul River, created more than three thousand years ago through the collective efforts of the Collegium, and past the great library. They were going straight to the royal palace, it seemed, although before they reached it, they were intercepted by a pair of skyriders wearing the white tunics of the *Gard Gwyn*. They sat astride falcons that were smaller than the warhawks of the High Guard, but faster and more agile.

Bereth saw Ilriathas pump his right arm three times, make a half-circle gesture with his left arm, and then tap his chest and his forehead in rapid succession. *Emergency. Message. King.* The lead guardsman nodded and held up a thumb to indicate he understood, then pointed to the second-tallest tower before extending his arm and sweeping it forward.

"He wants us to go to the king's private landing," Lassarian observed as the first falcon swung around and led the way. The second one waited for them to follow the lead bird before swinging in behind them. "That's a good sign, I think."

As the two warhawks rose above the crenellated tower, then turned to make their descent onto the roof, the first falcon banked its wings and moved out of their path as its rider indicated that they should descend. Ilriathas threw the guardsman a casual salute by way of thanks, then guided Ebon to an enviously smooth landing. As the big warhawk extended its legs and beat its wings to slow itself, Bereth saw guards wearing white tunics over their silver mail rushing out to attach Ilriathas's hawk to a ring and offer assistance to its riders. While Ilriathas spurned their proffered hands and swung down from his saddle with practiced ease, his passenger, the mage, seemed glad enough of the help.

Then they were rushing toward the rough, dark stone of the tower top and Bereth grunted as Mellt touched down rather more roughly than his fellow warhawk and pressed her up hard against Lassarian's back. She pushed herself away from the skyrider and began unfastening the straps that secured her to the warhawk's back. When she saw Ilriathas standing below her with his hands up, she was tempted to snap at him, but restrained herself when she recalled that this was not the time for personal affairs to interfere with their mission. She leaped down into his arms; he caught her without effort and swung her lightly to her feet.

Her legs were a little wobbly at first, as always, but before she could even take a breath, the elf lord had taken her arm and was rushing her toward the light of an open door that led to a spiral staircase.

"I sent one of the guards down to let the king know we are coming." Ilriathas looked back and beckoned irritably toward Lassarian. "Leave your pack and follow me. We have no time for that. The guards will bring our packs down later!"

"Do you know where you're going?" Bereth had been in the palace before, but she'd never entered it from above.

"Of course." He released her before they passed through the doorway in order to take the lead as they dashed down the stairs. His earlier assistance aside, the tall elf lord seemed to have no concern for her or interest in talking to her at all, which, for some reason, she found as intriguing as it was disquieting. And for all that he was irritatingly attentive of her, she couldn't help but notice how commanding he was when he was taking charge of things.

And he clearly knew his way around the palace, as after racing down the stairs, taking two at a time, he led them through a landing that led to a broad red-carpeted corridor. A left, a right, and another right brought them to within sight of a large set of carved sylvanwood doors, outside of which two ceremonially-armored White Guards were standing on either side. As Iliriathas stalked toward them, they saluted and turned to open the doors before his approach.

"Find the Magister Bessarias," he snapped at the one on the right. "Tell him to come at once, that it is urgent."

"The Lady Caitlys has already gone to fetch him."

"Excellent." He turned to Bereth. "This will be an informal audience, but try not to forget that he is the High King."

"I know that!" She couldn't believe he thought she needed to be told to mind her manners, as if she was a rustic tree-elf. He really could be loathsome sometimes.

"I mean, watch your tongue. I know better than anyone how sharp it can be. And you don't tolerate fools well."

Before she could respond, he was already walking into the royal chamber, which was less imposing and more comfortable than she'd expected. But beyond the fire crackling in the large fireplace on the left side of the room and the absence of any seat that looked like a throne, she barely noticed anything. Was he really calling the king a fool? Or was he simply warning her to keep her temper in case they weren't believed? She wasn't about to forgive him for speaking to her so rudely, but she decided it was something to be dealt with later.

"Greetings, Lord Kelethan. I see you have come straight from the battlefield, which I surmise does not bode happy tidings."

"Your Majesty!" Ilriathas bowed deeply. "I fear not, but at least let me put your mind at ease about our forces at Tir Diffaith. They remain entirely intact and the walls were, at the time of our departure, unbreached."

The king was visibly relieved. It was clear that he had been steeling himself for even worse news than that which they bore. To Bereth's surprise, Ilriathas did not proceed to provide the king with any more details, but instead presented her, Lassarian, and the mage, Terfielon, to him instead. She had met the king before, of course, on several formal occasions, but she was nevertheless pleased that he remembered her. It wasn't until she saw Ilriathas glancing impatiently toward the door that she realized he was waiting for the legendary Bessarias so that they need not give their accounts twice.

When the ancient magister finally arrived, Bereth understood why it had taken him so long to navigate the stairs. Accompanied by a short, but beautiful elf she recognized as a minor royal, the great Collegian more closely resembled a desiccated corpse risen from its crypt than a living elf. His legs were bowed, his back was bent, and his hair was thin and yellowed with extreme age. As he slowly drew closer with the assistance of the elfenwy, Bereth was shocked to see that his face was deeply lined, as if it was made out of clay and someone had carved canals into it. And she was dismayed. How could this poor, decrepit creature she could hardly think to call an elf possibly save them from a mighty being of the sort they'd seen summoned by the devil magic of the orcs. He didn't have the strength to walk without support, let alone stand before a lord of the nether hells and defeat him.

Ilriathas, however, showed no sign of any similar consternation. He bowed even more deeply than he had to the king.

"Thank you for coming, Magistras. I am Ilriathas, a captain of the High Guard recently come from Tir Diffaith."

"Tir Diffaith?" Even his voice was weak and querulous. "Then I expect you've given Mael a good reason for dragging me out of my bed. Ilriathas, is it? I knew your great-grandfather. If you're half the elf he was, you'll do well enough."

The king shook his head. "Never mind him, Lord Kelethan. But now that he's here, perhaps you can enlighten me as to why four elves are required to bring me what I presume is a message from the Prince-General."

"I can indeed, your Majesty," Ilriathas assured the king. "I am here to vouch for the reliability of the other three. They are here to tell you what they have seen earlier tonight outside the gates of Tir Diffaith."

At Ilriathas's gesture, Terfelion went first. He described the ceremony first, including an estimate of the number of lives sacrificed, before mentioning the terrible being that had been successfully summoned. Having learned only rudimentary spellcraft, Bereth found it hard to follow some of the more technical details he described, but she gathered that the mage didn't believe the summoning was an elemental or a demon, but rather, a genuine devil. She wasn't quite sure what the differences between the different magical creatures were, but neither the old magister nor the king seemed inclined to argue with his conclusions.

After asking the mage several questions, Lassarian was asked for his account, but he had nothing useful to add. When Bereth mentioned that she had been riding with Lassarian, and could offer nothing more than confirmation of what the other two had said, the king nodded and turned to the elderly elf.

"What do you think, Magistras?" The king's expression was serious, but if he was worried, he did not show it. "Is such *cythraul* capable of breaking the walls of Tir Diffaith?"

"We can simply wait a few days and find out," Bessarias answered with a smile, but when the elfenwy glared at him, he sighed and shrugged his thin, sloping shoulders. "We must assume it will suffice, or the orcs would not have gone to such trouble. I have some small knowledge of their race, and they are more than merely beasts that talk. For all their crudities and their wicked ways, I believe they are ensouled, even as we are, and therefore there is no reason to assume their knowledge of the Nether and Higher Realms is inferior to our own."

"Do spare us your religious obsessions, Bessarias! This is hardly the time for that!"

"Better you don't speak in ignorance, Mael." Bereth wasn't the only one who was astonished by the way the old magistras spoke to the High King, or by the way the king neither took offense nor seemed surprised. "The true hell-dwellers harbor a particular interest in souls, sentient souls, though I've never been able to determine if it is primarily as currency or power, to the extent we can even say there is a difference."

"I don't understand the significance," the king said, and Bereth felt he was speaking for all of them, judging by the confusion on the others' faces.

"If the orcs are beings with souls, and their most powerful sorcerors traffic with the devils that trade in them, then we can safely conclude that they know considerably more about the capabilities of those beings than we do. Even our Magistras Daimonae knows little more of them beyond what he has heard second-hand from his demonic familiars and summonings, and you know what a collection of shameless liars those foul spirits are. What little knowledge we have is unreliable."

"Do you possess the knowledge to destroy it, or banish it?"

"The hell-dweller they described? I couldn't say. But I could certainly destroy those who summoned it, and I doubt it would be inclined to remain on this plane once those who drew it here are gone."

"Then we should fly you there at once," Ilriathas declared. "Our hawks are exhausted, Your Majesty, but surely you can send him there tonight with one of the skyriders of the White Guard!"

The king glanced sourly at the magister and snorted, a little bitterly. "I could. But there is no reason to do so."

"Why not?" If the situation hadn't been so serious, Bereth would have laughed at the incredulous expression on Ilri's face.

"He won't do it." The king sighed. "Unfortunately, the most powerful sorcerer in all the Elven realms refuses to work magic, even in a situation as dire as this."

"Not even at the High King's express command," Bessarias added, unnecessarily.

The sun was already high in the clear blue sky when Bereth awoke. She wriggled contentedly in the soft bed with its silken sheets and copious down pillows, enjoying the warmth of the morning light and luxuriating in the creature comforts that were distinctly absent from the besieged fortress from whence she'd come. She was vaguely under the impression that she was back at her parents house again, until she recalled their hasty flight back to Elebrion and the late night audience with High King Mael himself. She must be in the royal palace, she suddenly realized, and when she leaped from the bed, naked as a swamp goblin, she was able to confirm from the view outside her window that she had indeed been an overnight guest of His Majesty.

She panicked, wondering why no one had woken her earlier, and cast about the room looking for her clothes. They were piled in a corner, and although her nose wrinkled at the smell of her well-used flight leathers, she put them on as quickly as she could. They were cold and they were filthy, but she didn't see any other option, as she wasn't about to fly wearing nothing more than her own white skin. After dressing, she ran her hands through her tangled hair, and finally made do with a loose braid that would at least keep her hair out of her eyes. She opened the door out onto a corridor that was only vaguely familiar, and made her way uncertainly down the hall in search of a staircase or something that might lead her to someone who knew what was happening. But as she wandered, an elfenwy dressed in the palace livery called out after her.

"Are you Bereth mer Eulenarias?"

When Bereth, taken aback, demanded to know how the elfess knew who she was, the elfess handed her a scroll sealed with green wax imprinted with the High King's sigil, then observed that the palace corridors were seldom traversed by elfonwys wearing High Guard leathers. Bereth, belatedly realizing how awful her behavior would be regarded by the palace staff, apologized profusely. Fortunately, the elfonwy did not appear to have taken any offense, as she gave Bereth directions to a dining hall where she could break her fast, as well as to the baths reserved for female elves, and, very much to Bereth's surprise, told her that she shouldn't expect to leave the palace until the morrow at the soonest.

"Why do you say that?" Bereth was confident that the place staff didn't know anything about the travails of Tir Diffaith yet, and she was puzzled by the elfonwy's confidence that she wouldn't be going anywhere.

"There is going to be a great event tonight," she was informed excitedly. "Dozens of scrolls like yours have been sent out to all the highest families. It's said that they aren't invitations, but royal summons! Perhaps there's going to be a ball!"

"Perhaps," Bereth said. But she doubted it. She doubted it very much indeed.

After thanking the elfenwy and apologizing to her once more, Bereth took her leave and made her way to the nearest window to open the scroll. After cracking the seal, she unrolled it and saw that it was, indeed, a summons. It was written in a beautiful hand and in the form of an invitation addressed specifically to her, but it told her little more than when she should present herself at the royal reception hall. A postscript at the bottom informed her that she should wear the dress that would be provided to her, which was a great relief as she didn't think that the king would look quite as favorably on her current attire as he had at the previous night's considerably less formal audience.

She dined, bathed, and somehow made her way back to the room in which she'd awoken with only two false turns. The bed she'd left in disarray was neatly made, and a white silk dress was laid out upon it, as well as a simple silver coronet. There were no shoes, but the simplicity of the dress suggested that she, and presumably the other female attendees, would be expected to go barefoot. Was it some sort of ritual, she wondered? Did it have something to do with the summoning of the terrible *preswylydd uffern* by the orcs? She instinctively felt that the two events must be connected, but she couldn't imagine what the connection might be.

Well, it wasn't her problem. The comfort of the neatly-made bed called out to her, and with a sigh of relief, she took the dress off the bed, stripped off her clothes, and slipped beneath the covers for a much-needed nap. As she floated blissfully down into the welcoming darkness, her last conscious thoughts were of soaring high above the clouds on Merlian's back.

> Into the endless blue I rise,
> Above red nature's tooth and claw.
> A perfect jewel, these sapphire skies,
> And I alone their only flaw.

She had just finished braiding her hair, as there didn't seem to be much else she could do with it, given how she lacked a proper brush, and was slipping on the white dress when there was a knock on her door. Assuming it was Ilriathas, she flung the door open and was already starting to harangue him about how she'd been left to her own devices all day when she realized it was not, in fact, the High Guard captain standing before her, but the noble elfonwy who had accompanied the ancient magister.

"My Lady, I am sorry!" she exclaimed.

"Bereth, is it?" The elfess, who was wearing an identical white dress as well as a golden coronet holding back her long, alabaster hair, eyed her up and down with a critical eye. She was also carrying a leather satchel. "Caitlys. You'll remember me from last night, I'm sure. I was sent to bring you to the king's fete, but you really shouldn't wear your hair braided tonight. The Queen says we're all to wear it down."

"Who is we're?"

"As near as I can tell, every maiden elf between the ages of thirty and one hundred twenty."

"Do you know why?"

"I have my suspicions," Caitlys said darkly. "But whatever Mael has in mind, I know it has something to do with that dried-up lunatic of a mage!"

"The magistras?" Bereth raised her hand to her mouth as she recalled the horrific scene from the night before. "You don't think he's going to sacrifice all of us?"

"Bessarias?" Caitlys snorted derisively. "I do wish he'd try! Then at least we'd know he's willing to use his damned arts to defend the realms!"

Bereth relaxed. For just a moment, she'd imagined dozens of white-robed elf maidens in the place of all those poor goblins who'd been massacred by the orcs in order to accomplish their dreadful summoning. Did not the king wish for the ancient sorceror to fight fire with literal hellfire? But it seemed the Lady Caitlys was unconcerned, and Bereth found it difficult to imagine that such a well-placed member of the royal family would be left completely in the dark about a murderous plan of such magnitude, even if she was one of the intended victims.

"Now, let's do something about that hair of yours," said the other elfess, brandishing an ivory brush she'd produced

At Caitlys's command, she turned around and felt the other's hands deftly undoing her hastily-wound braids. Then she was wincing as Caitlys forced the brush through her sky-tangled hair.

"Always a bear, sky-riding. I sometimes wish I could simply shave my head. It must be worse for you in the High Guard, especially these days."

Bereth was silent for a moment, swaying as the other elfess's repetitive movements pulled at her head. "I lost my bird," she finally said, softly.

"Oh no!" The brushing stopped, then resumed. "I'm so sorry. And that means you're the one that Kelethan follows around like a lost puppy."

"What do you mean!" Her sorrow vanished in a flash of embarrassment and anger. "What do you know about Ilri?"

"Ilri, is it?" Caitlys's lips twitched with amusement. "Pretty much everything. He's my mother's cousin. And that egg you're waiting for, he bought from my uncle."

"Does everyone know about it?" Bereth was horrified.

"Only everyone in the White City. Besides the orc invasion and the Queen's sister's affair with one of her guards, it's the most interesting thing that's happened in months. There are all sorts of rumors. Were you really having it off with a cavalry officer?"

"No!"

"All right. Now, hold still and I'll put that circlet on." Caitlys eyed her handiwork, reached out to adjust the silver hairpiece, and then stepped back, satisfied. "That should give them all something to talk about," she said.

"I don't want them to talk about me!"

"Well, they will anyhow, so you might as well not make it easy for them. Anyhow, my dear High Guard, you're quite clearly mad to spurn poor Kelethan. He's brave, handsome, and rich. If he wasn't family, I'd marry him myself."

"It's not like that!"

"I'm sure it isn't." Caitlys kissed her on the cheek. "Now, you look lovely, so come down to the fete with me. We'll walk in together and give them all something to gossip about!"

Feeling rather overwhelmed, Bereth nodded. Then a thought struck her, and she went to the pile of her clothes and extricated her dagger, still in its sheath, from her flight leathers.

"Where exactly do you think you're going to put that?" Caitlys laughed as Bereth stared down at the delicate white shift that barely sufficed to cover her body. "There won't be any orcs to kill downstairs."

Shaking her head and still confused as to what was happening, Bereth tossed the dagger onto her clothes and followed Caitlys out the door.

LODI

I T WAS more like a turn-and-a-half than the promised half-turn before Thorald, Myf, and Lodi were summoned to be brought before the king. Fortunately, Lodi had noted the passage of time and substituted fresh mushroom juice for the sweetwater Myf had been drinking before any lasting damage had been done. He himself had switched to ale, and sighed with delight at the first delectable taste of Zlaty Smady Dark he'd had in two years.

Although Myf was still nervous about meeting the king, she had relaxed considerably, and was listening with great interest as Thorald and Lodi reminded each other of some of the lighter aspects of their adventures in the mountains and forests of the east.

"I vow, lad, I thought that cursed wyrm had plucked you off the mountain when I saw it flying overhead!"

Thorvald chortled. "Ah, Myf, you should have seen his face when he finally climbed over the ledge and saw me waiting for him inside the cave. I think he thought I was a ghost!"

Thorald opened his eyes wide and dropped his jaw. It was a most amusing sight, and inspired both Myf and Lodi to laughter. But Myf quickly sobered up when she realized what Lodi had said.

"I thought you said the dragon wasn't there, Lodi, that you sneaked in when it was gone! But you actually saw it flying?"

"Well, I did. You see, I thought the beast was going to be gone rather longer than he was; he came home sooner than I would have liked."

"Plenty o' good hunting in those parts," Thorald explained. "The orcs were gathering for their war nearby, so the dragon didn't have to do much more than pop outside his door for a snack. But we didn't know that at the time. So when Lodi saw him returning with an orc in his claws, he thought the wretched monster had me!"

"And damned sorry I was to lose ye too, lad," Lodi said consolingly.

Myf was shaking her head. "So, dragons and now orcs?"

"Loads o' them! We counted, what was it, lad, forty thousand?"

"Nay, at least fifty." Thorald took a pull at his ale. "The Great Orc had his drums going day and night, bringing in orcs from every corner of the mountains, goblins from the forests, and even a few trolls! That dragon must have thought he died and went to dragon-heaven; probably got too fat to fly before they marched on south toward the elves."

"Dragons, orcs, goblins, and trolls," Myf repeated. "I didn't really believe such creatures existed above the Mountain."

"Don't forget the riverfolk!" Lodi reminded Thorald. "They were nasty pieces of work, they were!"

"All those teeth!" Thorald brought his hands to his mouth and wriggled them as they were jaws chomping on something. "Ar-rar-ar-rar-ar-rar-rar! Horrible, ugly creatures."

"But useful in their way." Lodi raised his stone mug in salute to the mer. "And they kept their word better than some I've known."

"Dare I even ask?" Myf said to Thorald.

"The riverfolk are fishdwarfs, of a sort. Imagine a beardless dwarf with a fish body, no, make that a very ugly beardless dwarf with very sharp teeth."

"Ugh! They sound atrocious! Surely they are creatures of Nahoru Otek!"

"Ugly as they are, they smell even worse," Lodi commented. "Fermenting mushrooms wouldn't mask the stench. But we struck a bargain, threw a few orcs to them in exchange for safe passage over the river. They didn't eat us, so here we are."

The sound of rapidly-approaching footsteps interrupted whatever Myf was going to say, and Thorald leaped to his feet as three dwarves marched into the chamber, two of them armored in pure silver, the third wearing a sumptuous red robe with the king's sigil stitched on the breast in silver thread.

"Drinking on duty, Vodnekh?"

"Nossir! I'm off my official duties today, I only came to welcome home an old friend."

The dapper dwarf's eyes narrowed as he glanced pointedly at the mugs of ale sitting on the counter behind them. "Very well then. I hope you remain in a fit state to appear before His Majesty. You are the Kingsguard Lodi, son of Dunmorin, are you not?"

"I am," answered Lodi. "And who be ye?"

"All that you need to know is that I am the royal herald for today's court session and I will be the one announcing the three of you, so you will forgive me if I trouble to get your names right." He nodded at Myf. "And you, tesnik, how are you called?"

"Her name is Myf, second daughter of Horin of the Third Southeastern Deep, called the Horinhold," Lodi answered for her.

"Very well." The dwarf scribbled something on his shale tablet, presumably Myf's name. "Then you will come with me, and you will wait outside the door with the guards until you hear your names called. Then you will enter, and Vodnekh, I hope you will show a bit more decorum in the King's chamber than you have demonstrated here."

"Absolutely, sir!" Thorald confirmed.

The herald led them out of the sparkling chamber, accompanied by the guards. They followed a corridor leading into the interior of the palace, then came to a stop at a door that Lodi recognized as the entrance to the elevator from puffs of steam being emitted regularly from the iron grills at floor and ceiling.

"What's this," Myf asked, confused.

"It's a lifter. It's like the train, only it goes up and down. It's nothing to worry about."

Myf nodded uncertainly and moved closer to him. Lodi put out an arm to steady her, and was surprised, though not at all disappointed, when she curled herself inside it and clung to his forearm.

"I don't like this," she explained unnecessarily.

"You'll be fine, lass," he assured her as the lifter rose with a jerk. She squeaked with alarm and tightened her grasp on his arm while he closed his eyes and enjoyed the intoxicating scent of her hair.

All too soon, the ride was over and the doors were opening before them. The hallway onto which they opened was nearly four times broader than the one below, and the floor was a dark grey marble shot through with veins of scarlet and sparkling pyrite crystals. The doors at the end of the corridor were massive, nearly six paslid high, and gleamed as if they were pure gold, although Lodi knew there was carbonized iron beneath the gilded surface.

What looked like carved decorations was actually a series of protective runes. One never knew when the doors would need to hold against a determined enemy, after all. They were further protected by the squad of silver-armored Palace Guard who, despite their showy armor, looked like a tough collection of hard bastards. As he walked toward them, Lodi met their eyes without flinching and was pleased to see that two of them nodded, ever so faintly, to him.

He returned the nods. Respect for respect, that was the way of it. They might be hard jobs, but then, so was he.

"Wait here," the herald ordered as the doors opened just enough for four dwarves to stride aside, and entered the room. The doors closed again behind him with a dull booming sound that resonated through his chest, and he smiled at the expression on Myf's face.

"You the Kingsguard," one of the guards nearest to him murmured.

"Aye," he answered, raising an eyebrow.

"Thought so," the guard said. "My old dad was Kingsguard. Died in the siege."

"Yurrah," Lodi said, with a subtle flick of his thumb on his left shoulder. "Zatra zlotakha."

The younger dwarf caught the gesture and smiled, satisfied, as the doors began to open again.

"Good luck, Kingsguard."

The throne room was a familiar sight to Lodi and Thorald, but Myf gasped with wonder at the massive chamber. The floor was the same grey marble as the hallway, but a path of pure white marble led directly to the ornate throne, which was made of gold and platinum, and encrusted with diamonds. Stalactites hung from the high ceiling, gilded to prevent them from dripping on the floor below, and the soft white light that filled the chamber was provided by elven magelights so cunningly placed that not a single shadow could be seen.

But what truly caught the eye was the massive skull that was mounted on a pair of crossed oversized spears above and behind the throne, with two giant garnets set in the empty eyesockets. Lodi smiled grimly at the sight, for he had slain its former owner, Guldur Goblinsbane the troll king, and thus brought an end to the terrible siege of Iron Mountain.

"The Kingsguard Lodi, son of Dunmorin of the Sixty-Third Northern Vein, the Vodnekh Thorald Thoraldsson of the Royal Household Guard, and Tesnik Myf, daughter of Holin of the Twenty-Fourth Deep Shaft!"

Lodi led his two companions down the white marble pathway toward the white-bearded dwarf sitting on the throne. It wasn't as uncomfortable as it looked, for he knew that King Borgo had ordered gold-threaded pillows attached about a week after he'd inherited the crown. Borgo, who was technically the twenty-fourth of his name, had been king for almost fifty years, but Lodi had known him since he was only the Crown Prince. He had, in fact, served under him and they had fought side by side on at least six occasions.

And yet, he was an imposing sight, seated on that magnificent throne. He was wearing the Iron Crown, which was constructed from the humble metal which gave it its name, but the seven great rubies set within it were anything but humble.

As they approached, the king pushed himself up from the throne before they could begin their formal obeisances and stepped forward to take Lodi in a crushing embrace.

"Son of Dunmorin, it is good to see you take time from your busy schedule of being stabbed, whipped, beaten, and otherwise abused to visit with your king."

"I've got a nice scar from a wolf bite I could show you if you like, but I'd have to drop my trousers."

"Perhaps we'll save that for later." He eyed Lodi's abbreviated beard with approval. "I see your beard is finally beginning to recover. Now you might almost be confused with a dwarf of forty!"

"And you might be confused with one of two hundred. When did your beard get so white?"

The king leaned forward and whispered in his ear. "Essence of salamander liver. Gives it a regal sheen, don't you think?"

"It does indeed." He indicated Myf and Thorvald with his hand. "Your Majesty, you know Thorald, son of Thorald. This, here, is Myf Holinsdaughter, who kindly helped nurse me back to health when I was injured, and whom I am charged with accompanying to her family's mine."

"Your Majesty," said Thorald, bowing deeply. Myf bowed gracefully enough, but Lodi could see that she was overawed by the magnificence of King Borgo as well as by his own familiarity with the king.

"You needn't hold your tongue, lass. He's your sovereign too."

"It's a very great honor, your Majesty," she said softly. She glanced sideways at the king and blushed.

"So, the Deep, is it?" The king smiled paternally at the pretty young divci, then turned his attention to Lodi. "Your destination suits my purposes even better than I'd expected. How would you feel about having an armed guard accompany you to the Twenty-Fourth Shaft?"

"She's really not that much trouble, my liege." Lodi grinned at the way Myf's green eyes widened with embarrassment. "I haven't required any assistance thus far."

"The guard isn't so much for either of you as it is for the zematurges I'm sending to the Deep. I imagine her family's steading shouldn't be far out of your way."

"Zematurges?" While Lodi was familiar with the dwarven arcanists who were responsible for everything from the omnipresent witchlights and mushroom fields to the more esoteric aspects of the sacred arts of the forge, he didn't see why the king should be ordering any of them into the roots of the mountain. "Why are you sending them below?"

The king nodded at Thorvald. The younger dwarf reached into a leather pouch and pulled out a metallic object that reflected the lights of the throne room. It was a scale, Lodi saw, and it was of precisely the sort that he'd seen covering the skin of the strange creatures he'd fought at Hotstone Station with the lads from the train. His eyes narrowed, and he looked at Thorvald, who smiled grimly.

"You've seen them, then." It wasn't a question.

"Ay, the cursed creatures attacked a station where we stopped along the way. Vicious bastards. Killed twenty, twenty-five good dwarves before we drove them off. What are they?"

"We don't know. Even the archivists can't find any sign of them in their records. That's why I'm sending a pair of zematurges below with an escort of twenty Household Guards." The king's eyes were grave with foreboding. "There is something amiss down there, Lodi, and there is no one I trust more to find trouble than you, my old friend."

Lodi groaned and ran his hand through his hair. "I'd be happier if you'd give me forty. And I'd prefer proper Kingsguards, if you please, Your Majesty."

"Thirty. But you'll be the only Kingsguard. We are at war, after all, and I can't commit half a company of my best warriors to what is nothing more than a reconnaissance mission. No one is expecting you to resolve the situation, Lodi, or wipe out the zlotakha. I just need you to help the zematurges discover what the situation actually is!"

Lodi growled low in his throat, but he nodded in acquiescence. The king had the right of it. And besides, what did he care, so long as he got Myf to her family without incident? Thirty armed guards of any kind were thirty more than he'd been expecting to have. And it wasn't as if the Household couldn't fight, they just lacked age and experience, for the most part.

"At least this time we won't be bearding a wyrm in his lair, eh, Lodi?" Thorvald slapped him on the back.

"You're going too?" Both Myf and Lodi looked at the royal courtier in surprise.

Thorvald bowed. "In addition to my other royal duties, I have the honor of being a Captain of the Household Guard."

"He begged for the command as soon as we heard you were headed this way," the king said. "And if half the things he told me about your travels through the Elvenwood are true, he might even prove to be useful."

"Honored, Your Majesty," Thorvald bowed again, a little theatrically, before turning to Myf. "Now, if you'd care to let me escort you from the royal presence, Tesnik, I'm told we have some spiced slugs that you absolutely must try before embarking on the next stage of your journey!"

"A safe journey to you, Tesnik Myf," the king said, with an enigmatic smile.

Lodi nodded as Myf looked to him, though whether it was for permission or reassurance he could not tell. It was clear that the king wanted to talk to him without anyone else around. And although he preferred not to leave her alone with young Thorvald, who was bound to make an ass of himself as well as telling the lass things about Lodi she shouldn't hear, a royal dismissal wasn't something even a Kingsguard could deny.

"Don't listen to a word he tells you," he warned her as she bowed once more to the king.

She merely sniffed and took Thorvald's arm by way of response. He watched the two of them march back up the white marble aisle, and turned back to see the king smiling broadly at him.

"And how the mighty are fallen!"

"Don't talk rot," he growled, but his heart wasn't in it. "Is it that obvious?"

"Probably not to those who don't know you as well as I do," the king admitted.

"Well, there's a relief, anyhow."

The king patted his arm and beckoned to him, indicating that Lodi should follow as he began to make his way toward a well-concealed door in the rear of the tremendous hall. The dwarf king, who moved easily despite his snow-white beard, opened the door and nodded to the four guards who were positioned inside a wide corridor of black basalt that was lined with witchlights on either side. Lodi couldn't help noticing that two of the dwarves were armed with axes, the other two with crossbows, and surmised that there were probably others in position overlooking the throne. When he commented on this, King Borgo chuckled.

"The last attempt on a King of Iron Mountain was in my great-great grandfather's era. His brother didn't see why he should be denied the throne by a mere accident of birth, and some of the wealthier families backed him, seeing an opportunity to make use of the young fool. But their attempts to suborn the Household Guard were ill-considered, and one of the two groups of assassins were butchered in these very halls!"

"I never heard about that."

"It's not something either my family or the families responsible were particularly keen to get out, so it's never been taught in the schools. My father tried to cut down on the number of dwarves stationed around the chamber—he was something of a miser, you may recall—but the Guards would have none of it. I suppose they see it as a bit of an honor. Foolish idea, if you think about it."

"Why's that?"

"My philosophy is that if one is going to surround one's royal self with dwarves armed with crossbows, one is well-advised not to quibble with them."

Lodi nodded. He'd always felt that Iron Mountain would be in very good hands under the rule of a dwarf as pragmatic as Borgo.

"Here we are," said the king, stopping before a wooden door and producing a silver key from somewhere underneath his sumptuous robes. After opening it, he snapped his fingers to illuminate the witchlights. "Behold the royal storeroom, or rather, my contribution to the royal collection."

The metal in the small chamber gleamed under the pallid glow of the arcane dwarflights. There was gold enough to make a dragon drool with desire, including a beautiful, though useless in battle, full suit of plate armor emblazoned with the iron crown over the mountain that served as the royal crest. There were small chests of silver coins of ancient minting, necklaces encrusted with so many precious jewels that only a strong and stiff-necked pasla could hope to wear one, and a platined orc skull with sapphires embedded in the empty eye sockets. There were silvered axes, gilded swords, and even a dagger with a blade carved from a single rectangular ruby.

"I like to come in here to relax when things get difficult," the king confessed. "It's astonishing how restorative it is for a dwarf to bask in the pleasures of a place like this."

Lodi was feeling neither relaxed nor restored. To the contrary, he could feel his fingers itching with the urge to claim a treasure or two for his own.

"Isn't that the shield from the wyrm's cave?" He pointed to a device hung in a place of pride on the far wall.

"It is indeed!" The king beamed. "And in fact, the reason I brought you here was to express my gratitude for your doughty efforts in reclaiming it for me."

"That's not necessary, Borgo."

"True, but it is my privilege." The king was rooting around in a small wooden chest that, aside from the contents, was otherwise unremarkable. "Ah, here it is!"

The King of Iron Mountain held up a dainty filigree gold chain, which was so delicate that it rather resembled spider's silk. And yet, it was somehow strong enough to support an alluring three-carat emerald surrounded by round brilliant cut diamonds. Even to a dwarf who'd spent far more time in battle than at the forge, it was obvious there was magic involved in its creation.

"Elven work," he explained unnecessarily, as he offered it to Lodi. "Give it to the lass after you ask her father for her hand. I thought of it right away; it will suit her eyes."

"It's spectacular, Borgo. But I can't take this."

"Don't talk nonsense." His friend's eyes twinkled. "I'm your king, after all. As the King of Iron Mountain, I have the right to expect obedience from the Kingsguard, and I damn well order you to accept it!"

"Very well," Lodi grumbled, knowing he was beaten. He took the necklace and marveled at how small it appeared in his thick, well-callused hand. "Thank you, Your Majesty. It will look beautiful on her."

"She is a pretty one, isn't she? A little young for you, but perhaps that's for the best." The king put his arm around Lodi. "And now that we have the important business out of the way, let's discuss those zematurges."

Five days later and three miles deeper, Lodi stared in disbelief as Hulor, one of the arcanists with whom he'd been saddled by the king, ordered Thorvald to halt their march through the dark tunnel through which they'd been making their way. No sooner had the guards captain done so than the rotund dwarf produced a dried lizard and a flask from a hidden pocket in his voluminous robes and settled down happily for a snack. Lodi fumed. Every day, they got started later and later, and each breakfast seemed to take longer and longer. The delay was particularly aggravating today because they were less than an hour away from the Grundledum steading, according to Myf, and because they'd barely been on the move for an hour since breakfast.

"Tell him to stop stuffing his belly and start walking or we'll leave him behind to wander the depths until he starves!" Lodi hissed at Thorvald.

"I can't do that, Lodi. My orders are to guard him, not you. And don't forget, he outranks me!"

"Really?" In nearly seven years away from Iron Mountain, Lodi had forgotten some of the intricacies of the palace hierarchy, or perhaps he had simply never paid enough attention.

"As arcanists, both he and Dugnor hold rank equivalent to a captaincy, but they're both senior to me. Also, this their mission, I'm just in charge of their bodyguard."

"I see." Lodi thought about it and realized that neither he nor Myf were under any constraints to stay with the zematurges at the moment. He walked over to where Myf was impatiently glaring at the seated zematurge and gently took her hand in the darkness.

"What is he doing? It's not as if he's about to starve!"

"No, lass, not if he skipped his meals for a month. Listen, I know you're impatient to see your ma and your da, so why don't you and me push on, and let these slowbeards catch up with us. It's not far, is it?"

"Oh yes, Lodi!" Her pretty face lit up and she took his other hand. "Let's do that!"

However, Thorvald was less enthusiastic about the idea of splitting up the party. He pointed out that although there were no zlotakha previously known to inhabit these parts, the scaled creatures Lodi had encountered at Hotstone could be anywhere under the mountain, perhaps even somewhere in the vicinity. But a few withering comments questioning the courage and dwarfhood of the Household Guard, especially in comparison with the Kingsguards with whom Lodi had served, combined with Myf fluttering her green eyes at the younger dwarf, managed to convince Thorvald to let them proceed, albeit in the company of eight of his dwarves.

Once free of the slow-moving zematurges, they made very good time despite their heavy packs. In addition to his axe, Lodi was weighed down with an astonishing array of spices, herbs, and medicines that could not easily be obtained this far below the city. Myf, too, carried her fair share of the load, although her pack was perhaps half the size of his own. Fortunately, they didn't need to carry much in the way of foodstuffs or water, as Lodi had been assured he could replenish his supplies at the steading. But the tunnel was a very good one, with a perfectly flat stone floor with nary a stray rock or pebble to trip wayfarers, and it was wide enough to permit five dwarves to walk side-by-side.

It wasn't very well-lit, however, as more than half of the glowmoss emplaced along the walls seemed to have dried out and died, so Lodi had lit a torch and instructed one of the guards to do so as well. It struck him as a little strange that Myf's clan should have let the moss expire without replacing it, but there were a myriad of good reasons why a steading would have other priorities than tunnel-maintenance, especially when the tunnel was otherwise in good order.

"They've let it get a little run down," Myf said, echoing his own thoughts. "Da probably put Meldo in charge of it. He's shamefully lazy."

"I'm sure you'll have him put it to rights soon enough," Lodi said, feeling a twinge in his chest at the thought that their journey together would soon be at an end.

"I hope you'll stay for supper tonight. Ma and Da will be proud to host a real Kingsguard at the table. Da fought in the siege, alongside his brothers, but they were only militia."

"Wouldn't miss it," Lodi said gruffly. He was wondering whether the proper time to talk to her father would be before leaving with the zematurges or upon his return.

They turned a corner and saw a metal plaque embedded in the wall. The runes said HOLINHOLD. Myf's eyes lit up at the sight, and she took Lodi's free hand, pulling him along as she rushed ahead in her enthusiasm.

But Lodi didn't share it. A vague feeling of foreboding nagged at him, although he couldn't quite tell why. As they grew closer, the glowmoss was in better shape, and the tunnel grew brighter, until eventually Lodi was able to put out his torch. And that was when the first indication that something might be amiss struck him, as, once freed of the burning scent of the torch, his nose detected a faint, but familiar smell. At first, he couldn't quite put his finger on what it was, and then he came to a stop when he realized what it was. It was something he had smelled all too many times before, in the arena, on the battlefield, and in the burned-out ruins of villages and smallholdings he'd encountered in the wilds.

It was the stench of death.

Myf was the next to notice it, although she had no idea what it was.

"Now that's an odd smell," she said, sniffing loudly at the air. "Lodi, do you notice that? I wonder what it is?"

"Mm," Lodi grunted. He exchanged a glance with one of the guards, an older dwarf with a braided beard shot with gray. Judging by the grim expression on the dwarf's face, he knew what it was too. Whatever lay ahead of them, it almost certainly wasn't good. And it definitely wasn't something that Myf should be allowed to see. He came to a quick decision.

"Lass, it might not be safe ahead. You and me, we'll wait here." He pointed to the graybeard. "You take three dwarves ahead with you. You two, hurry back to Thorvald and tell him to get those zematurges here on the double even if he has to personally drag their fat backsides behind him."

"Kingsguard!" the dwarves chorused, and the older dwarf threw in a salute. Both the group of four going ahead and the pair going back shucked their packs, then moved out without delay, leaving Lodi and Myf together in the company of the two remaining guards.

"You can take your packs off too, lads," Lodi said, as he slipped the straps of his own overstuffed pack from his shoulders and laid it on the ground. "We may be here a while."

"What aren't you telling me, Lodi?" Myf brushed his hands away, suspicious, when he reached out to help her remove her own pack. "I can tell you think something is wrong."

"Just being cautious, lass. Can't be too careful down here."

"Don't lie to me!" she shouted. "Don't you dare lie to me, Lodi Dunmorinson!"

She wrestled off her pack and fairly hurled it to the stone floor. She pushed past Lodi and stood staring down the tunnel in the direction of her family home, her hands on her hips, as if she could penetrate the darkness and the stone by the sheer force of her will. She was breathing hard, as if she had just run a long distance, but her cheeks were still dry when she turned back to face him.

"So what is it," she demanded. "What has you jumping like a toad touched by fire?"

Lodi nodded slowly. He knew it was fear, not anger, that sharpened her voice so.

"That smell you noticed. I know what it is. There's something dead ahead."

"Dead!" She raised a hand to her mouth.

"Something is dead. We don't know what it is. It could be something like we saw at Hotstone. It could be something worse. Or it could be something else entirely." He took her by the shoulders and forced her to look at him. "It's my duty to protect you and that's what I'm doing. You don't have to like it, and right now I expect you don't. But I will protect you, no matter what, whether you like it or not!"

She stared at him and her lower lip began to quiver. "I'm scared, Lodi!"

"I know, lass. I know."

He took her in his arms and he held her there in the darkness, tightly, without saying a word. He could feel her shaking against him, but whether she was crying or not, he could not tell. He closed his eyes, breathing in the scent of her, of her hair, and prayed silently to Provni Otcovi that her family would be found safe and sound.

He heard the two remaining guards rising to their feet and readying their axes, then heard the heavy footsteps approaching that had sparked their response. When he opened his eyes, he saw it was the graybeard, followed by the three other guards. The older dwarf's face was grim. Lodi raised an inquisitive eyebrow and the graybeard shook his head, followed by a two-handed gesture. Lodi swallowed hard, took a deep breath and shook his head.

This was not going to be easy.

MARCUS

THE FAMILIAR SIGHT of the castra was a welcome one after the morning's hard riding. Marcus was grateful that today, at least, he would not have to spend from dawn until dusk in the saddle. He wondered how the message riders managed to survive as he shifted his weight gingerly in the saddle. While he had ridden all his life, even an experienced rider's thighs could only endure so much abuse before they began to chafe and grow tender. He could see that the legion had finished their fortification of the walls, giving him hope that by now someone would have taken the time to build some sort of bath, even if it was little more than a rudimentary wooden sweat lodge.

The riders patrolling the perimeter recognized his banner as they approached, and the decurion leading them saluted smartly before falling in with the rest of his escort. He had left the prince and Trebonius behind him in Lutece, having departed the city within a bell of hearing of the arrival of the second army of orcs. But the Savondese had insisted on providing him with a squadron of twenty knights, led by an elderly count whose garrulousness might have irritated Marcus were it not for how desperately he sought any useful information about the ground, about the enemy, and about his allies.

It was entirely possible, Marcus thought, that no Amorran legate had ever faced the prospect of battle in a more complete state of ignorance than he was right now. He didn't know how large the enemy forces were, he didn't know the terrain, he had no idea how accurate the maps they'd been provided were, and he had little more than a rough estimate of how many men the prince would have at his disposal. While the Savondese system of vassalage appeared to have its merits, timeliness and precision were not two of them. Each nobleman might owe a certain number of footmen or mounted men-at-arms to the king, but he only owed them for a limited period of time, and in any event, most of them made a regular habit of showing up with fewer men than they were supposed to have. Not only that, but their equipment was entirely irregular, so one knight might show up with ten pikeman, while another was accompanied by twenty men carrying swords and round wooden shields. His allies, such as they were, nearly made the damned orcs look organized!

"We're fortunate the orc is making his move now," the comte explained. "A month ago, we're in the spring planting season and the petty lords are reluctant to give up their manpower, as you can surely understand. Of course, it's even worse in the fall when the harvest comes in. One counts his blessings if even half one's vassals show up in their allotted numbers."

"Don't the malingerers suffer some sort of penalty for their disobedience?" Marcus was incredulous.

"Well, there was a time when the Red Prince, not the current one, his elder brother, may le bon Dieu rest his soul, took offense to one of his lords failing to appear when summoned. Sieur Bernard of Le Cluhey, if I recall correctly. Legitimized bastard of the baron, actually, got a bit carried away with himself once his father recognized him, if you ask me. It often happens, you know, when a bastard finally wins his place. He'd only held Le Cluhey four years when he thumbed his nose at the prince, and the prince turned about as red as his name when his man came back with the news."

"What happened?"

"You can probably imagine. After he took care of the affair in the south— I don't rightly remember what it was, those southern lords are always fractious about land disputes or other petty matters—he brought his army to Le Cluhey and put it to siege. After his pet battlemage knocked the crown off the keep with a lightning strike or two, Sieur Bernard agreed to come out and submit to the prince's justice." The baron laughed, a dry, hoarse chuckle. "The prince told him, 'a bastard you were born and a bastard you will die!' The poor fool begged for a beheading, but in vain; the prince wouldn't even grant him that. Put a rope around his neck and had him thrown off his own ruddy battlements!"

Marcus nodded appreciatively as the old man chuckled again. It seemed the Savondese didn't entirely lack discipline, which was some relief. But one thing puzzled him.

"Why did he wish to be beheaded? I should think most men would prefer to be hanged."

The baron stared at him and tugged at a white mustache in surprise. "Hanged? Like a common criminal? I don't know what it's like down there in your Empire, but any man of noble blood would prefer a clean death by the blade."

Marcus nodded. Being a Valerius, vanity even in the face of death was something he could appreciate. How it must have grated the rebel's soul, to have his hard-earned legitimacy denied even in death! The late Red Prince had apparently been a ruthless man. Was his brother the same? There were suggestions, to be sure. There were hints of steel beneath the silk. But the younger de Mirid was clearly neither the warrior nor the general that his brother had been. That was to be regretted, as Marcus had concluded he would not be able to rely upon Étienne-Henri once battle was joined. He still remembered, very clearly, how confused and afraid and completely unable to think he had felt during his first battle, and that had been a minor one in which he had been the most junior officer in the legion, not a complicated affair in which he was the senior commander.

He could not imagine what it would be like to try to command one's first proper battle when one was as badly outnumbered as they were almost certain to be, and he was forced to reach the unsettling conclusion that Étienne-Henri was almost certain to run once the dire reality of war, and its deadly risks, abruptly penetrated his supercilious self-regard. Moreover, in the event that anyone survived the ensuing battle, the heir to the throne would be eager, if not desperate, to ensure that word of his cowardice never got back to the capital. Nor, in light of the Chancelier's warning, could Marcus overlook the possibility that Étienne-Henri was deliberately planning to sacrifice the legion, and in doing so, kill two birds with a single treacherous stone.

His thoughts returned to the enemy they would be facing. They're only orcs, he tried to tell himself, but the ravaged bodies he'd seen in the forest were mute witness to the strength and savagery of the green-skinned monsters. And the warriors of their main army would be better armed, better armored, and better disciplined than the scavengers and skirmishers Cassabus and his five centuries had butchered in the night. What would Magnus do, he wondered? Aim for a double-envelopment? Produce an unexpected stratagem that would somehow catch them off-guard? He shook his head. Brilliance and maneuver simply would not suffice to make up for the tremendous gap in numbers. Even a decisive strike, executed flawlessly, would bounce off the quantities they anticipated like a child's wooden sword off an iron breastplate.

He closed his eyes and contemplated the geometries of which Saturnius had spoken so many times. He could almost hear the fat little legate's voice in his head now, and remembered him talking about a campaign in the north, when Saturnius led two centuries against an newly declared king who'd raised half a legion's worth of men against Amorr. "We had to make them bleed," he'd said with satisfaction. "We atritted them like a butcher slicing meat, and slowed them down until your father arrived with his cohort and three decuria of auxiliaries."

"We'll make them bleed," he said, startling the old comte, who had been marveling at the earthworks dug out by the legionaries. "But who will come to help us?"

"That's one hell of a ditch your men are digging. What good will it do? And who are you bleeding, the orcs?"

"Even between the border lords and the prince's levies, we won't have enough men to beat them." Marcus looked over the castra, which looked imposing with its wooden walls rising high above the earthen mound. But it was a fortress that could be expected to hold off fifteen or twenty thousand attackers, not three times that number. "I had them build it thinking it would buy the king sufficient time to gather his forces. But if he won't come to our assistance, what is the point of buying more time?"

"Maybe they'll get bored and go home." The baron grinned at his startled expression. "It's been known to happen."

"They wouldn't be here in these numbers now if that was likely, not after the way we already bloodied their ugly faces."

"That's true enough, I should say."

The numbers were bad enough. But what nagged at him now was the unknown factor that was the magical aspect of the battle. He'd shied away from even thinking about it, and he had avoided any serious discussion of it with the blue-robed men he'd seen in Lutece, but it was a nettle that would have to be grasped, and soon. He could only hope that the cursed kingsmage, Theuderic, had been successful in the mission with which he'd been charged. While it would be nice to imagine that Cassabus and his machines would suffice to deal with any unholy threat, as they had been against the goblins, it would be foolish to assume so, especially since they would desperately need to bring the full force of their artillery to bear against the enemy infantry in order to relieve the expected pressure on his outnumbered men.

"Ave, Valerius!" he heard someone shout at him, and saw that it was Senarius Arvandus riding towards him. The senior decurion was mounted on a big grey, and was bare-headed and unarmored, although he still wore his curved cavalry sword strapped to his belt. Marcus nodded his thanks to the comte and indicated the side of the castra toward which he should ride to have his men's horses stabled, then greeted Arvandus.

"I have to say, General, I was expecting you to arrive with more than a half-squadron of horse and a fat old senator!" They clasped forearms, and the decurion smiled, but his eyes were dark with concern. "That can't be all the reinforcements we'll be receiving."

"No, I left at once and rode ahead of the prince. I expect he'll arrive with his army around noon the day after tomorrow. Trebonius is with him; he's bringing back the silver with Vitalis and the others. Where are the orcs? Are they close?"

"They're a solid two-days' march away. They wasted a day and half the night sacking a village full of fools who were stupid enough not to flee, then lazed about the next day raping and torturing the survivors."

Marcus nodded grimly. It was hard on the villagers, to be sure, but their inadvertent sacrifice had probably delayed the invading army more effectively than five thousand Savondese men-at-arms could have managed. He regretted their fate, and yet he couldn't help welcoming the additional day's respite it provided. "Do they know where we are?"

"It appears not. The marcher lords have been maintaining patrols in force and hunting down any scouts they encounter. Our own patrols haven't seen any sign of them within a half-day's ride."

"Any skirmishes?"

"None worth speaking of. A pair of scouts from the Second was ambushed by wolfriders three days ago, but they managed to fight their way clear without losing anyone. Another pair of my men surprised a group of scavenging goblins, took two captives, and killed the rest. We couldn't find anyone who speaks gobbo, though, so Proculus executed them."

"Pity," Marcus remarked. Then again, he doubted the wretched creatures would have been able to tell them anything useful. From what he understood of the enemy hierarchy, orcs were not inclined to include goblins in their councils. "Do we have an accurate count?"

"Of the orcs?"

"I thought it might be of interest, yes," Marcus said patiently.

"The praefectus has worked out what he thinks is a pretty close calculation of their formations. As I recall, the overall count is between forty-five and fifty-five thousand. He estimates six thousand are heavy cavalry."

Marcus sighed. He'd been hoping the frightened Savondese were exaggerating the numbers they'd reported, but it seemed that was not the case after all. Titus Cassabus was nothing if not precise. Although his cavalry was now fully mounted, he still had only four hundred horse to throw against a legion's worth of boar riders. He would have to hope that between the marcher lords and the prince's forces, there would be enough knights to ride out against them. Despite more than a week of preparations, he was not sanguine about their chances for success, and he had little faith that any infantry other than the legion would stand against what he had learned were the most powerful, most intimidating cavalry on Selenoth. If he was honest with himself, he wasn't entirely sure of his legionaries either.

After all, it was one thing to read about an evil-minded creature three times the mass of a horse, and another one entirely to hold your ground as the bloody-minded beast did its best to trample you beneath its horny hooves.

He looked out towards the east, past the castra and the laboring legionaries to the peaceful green fields beyond. Somewhere out there was a ravenous horde of monsters, a mighty force bigger than any army Corvus, or Saturnius, or even Magnus himself had ever faced. In three days, four or five at most, his men would find themselves in battle again, this time against an enemy more pitiless than any human foe. In three days, the fate of an entire kingdom would be in his inexperienced, incapable hands.

I am alone and I am afraid and you have abandoned me. If only you will stand by me now! Be with me, Father, he silently prayed, although he could not have said with any certainty if it was his Heavenly Father or his fallen earthly father to whom his desperate plea was directed. Then he looked up, startled, at the sound of a loud caw coming from the sky over his head.

It was a single crow, flying east, towards the distant forest and the invaders. It cawed a second time, and then a third. Despite himself, despite his fears, Marcus found himself smiling.

"You're flying the wrong way, little friend," he called after it. "Come back soon and we will feed you well."

"What's that?" Arvandus asked.

"A sign," Marcus replied, watching as the small black shape disappeared. "I dearly hope it is a sign."

Étienne-Henri arrived in the castra not long after sundown, in the company of various nobles and regimental commanders. The royal army was setting up its camp to the south; its banners could just barely be made out from the castra's elevated ramparts. With some difficulty, Marcus managed to convince the prince that it would be best to limit their conference to the two of them and their senior commanders;

As the Savondese commanders argued amongst themselves, far too rapidly for Marcus to follow with his less-than-perfect understanding of their tongue, he returned his attention to the parchment Cassabus had hastily written up for him upon the arrival of the royal reinforcements. While the situation was marginally less desperate than he'd feared, it was considerably worse than he'd hoped. As the Chancelier had warned him, the king refused to risk exposing his rear to the rebellious nobles in the south and had given his son less than half the knights and mounted men-at-arms requested. Even worse, he had substituted a levy of three thousand refugee northmen for the trained pikemen from the royal militia that Étienne-Henri previously assured Marcus would be forthcoming. The northmen might be strong and tall of stature, but they were pirates, not soldiers, and Marcus very much doubted that they would prove much more reliable than the peasant auxiliaries that were the despair of his centurions.

Just getting the militia to stand in a line and point their pikes the right way was proving to be a challenge very nearly beyond their capabilities. One could hardly expect their regiments to stand firm under even the most gentle of battlefield pressures. He looked back at the parchment, hoping against hope that the numbers would somehow magically have changed.

Legio
Cavalry 402, Two wings, seven squadrons in the first, six in the second.
Infantry 4,558, 62 centuries.
Artillery 258, 30 ballistae, 13 scorpios.
Infirmary 37
Additional 7, 3 Michaelines (former), 4 other priests

Baron Albin de Courtaman
Cavalry 1,200, 45 knights, 1,155 men-at-arms

Infantry 1,600 militia (half-trained, some armor)
Infantry 2,000 peasants (pikes)
Artillery none

Prince EH
Cavalry: 500, 150 knights, 350 men-at-arms
Infantry 2,000 heavy foot (armor)
Infantry 4,000 militia (pikes, light armor)
Infantry 3,000 Northmen (axes and shields)
Artillery none
Additional 21

That meant about 2,100 horse, 17,000 foot, and 43 war machines, against which would come 15,000 wolf- and boar-riders, 10,000 goblins, and 20,000 orcs. If the whole 17,000 foot had been legionaries, Marcus would have gone into battle cheerfully and with a considerable amount of confidence, but seeing as he had only one legion instead of three, and that the two legions-worth of allied troops were of poor quality and led by a commander with even less experience than himself, the situation made him feel as if he had a bad case of the stomach cramps. Even if the king wasn't intending to sacrifice the legion for some nefarious political purpose, the fact that at least one, and quite possibly both of its flanks were considerably weaker than they should be meant that it risked being fearfully mauled by the foe.

Marcus decided that, no matter what, the safety of the legion would have to come first, even if that meant allowing the invading army to ravage freely over the countryside. So long as the legion survived intact, he might hope to engage the orcs in more favorable circumstances, perhaps even taking them in their rear as the king brought up the forces he'd thus far refused to commit to this battlefield. And the only way to ensure the legion's safety meant convincing the prince to accept battle within a reasonable retreat to the castra.

"My suggestion, my lords, is that we bring the enemy to battle close enough to the castra here to enable a retreat in the event the enemy numbers prove too great." He pointed to the map, indicating the place near where the River Valloye made an L-shaped curve. "If our skirmishers contest their crossing here at the ford, we can draw them onto higher ground near these three hills. Unfortunately, the hills are not steep enough to dissuade their cavalry from attacking, but they will allow us to disguise our disposition somewhat, which will be to our advantage."

"I assume you Amorrans will take the central hill, Général Valerius?"

"I think it would be wiser to place the legion on the left," Marcus responded quickly, having anticipated the Savondese. "Since the Prince is in command, he will need to be in between the legion and his various regiments for the purposes of effective communications. It would be a mistake, I think, to attempt to pass his orders through us. There is too much chance of miscommunication in the confusion of battle. However, I am willing to place ten of the legion's ballistae on the central hill, each of them manned, of course, by a team of our architects."

Marcus was relieved to see Étienne-Henri nod in response to the offer as he rubbed thoughtfully at his chin. The Red Prince didn't appear to be overwhelmed by the level of detail being discussed, in fact, he was remarkably calm for a young commander facing his first proper battle. "Orcs usually put their best infantry on the right; those big shields the Amorrans carry would serve them well there on the left. So, I concur with your proposal, Général Valerius. Can I persuade you to accept any of my battlemages in return?"

"I will accept two, to bolster the Michaelines protecting the artillery from magical assault. But they will be used for defensive purposes only, by which I mean defeating any enemy spells being directed at the machines or the men. And it would be best if one of them is Theuderic."

The Red Prince raised his eyebrows, showing an active interest for the first time since the conference began. "Really? My impression was that you did not harbor any liking for the man."

"I don't. But he knows us, and I can trust that he will obey the orders of my officers." Also, Marcus had a dark thought, if he had to order a disobedient sorcerer beheaded for resorting to witchcraft, he would just as soon have that head be Theuderic's. "And my men know him as well."

"As you wish. I shall inform him." The prince turned to his senior adviser, Comte Yvenches, a wiry little man with an old white scar lining one cheek. "How do you recommend we dispose our infantry, Milord Comte? I assume we'll keep the cavalry in reserve until we see what the orc intends with his boars."

"He'll save them for last." The comte spoke with assurance, confident in his years and his orc-fighting experience. "They'll throw the goblins and lesser clans at us first, try to wear us down while they see where our weak spots are. Once their warleader figures out where we're most likely to crack, that's where he'll throw his big boys at us. They don't use their cavalry for pursuit because the pigs don't have the endurance of a horse. They use the wolves for that. So, we have to assume they'll direct their charge on our right, assuming the Baron's men don't break and run from the first two or three waves."

A tall blond man, presumably the commander of the northmen, whispered something to the prince. Étienne-Henri nodded and pointed to the map. "Sieur Brynjolf suggests that we establish his axemen with the baron. He believes that between them and the border cavalry, they will be able to hold the right flank against their infantry."

"That will weaken the center," Marcus pointed out. He didn't like what the Savondese was implicitly suggesting, but he had to admit that the legion was much better equipped to withstand the orc's heavy cavalry than either the undisciplined royal regiments or the lightly armored militia, even if the latter was bolstered by the northmen's three thousand axes. On the battlefield, quality mattered far more than quantity, but when two armies as foreign to each other as these two met, numbers would be all the enemy general had to go by. And that meant that so long as the right and center held, it should be possible to tempt the orc to hurl his cavalry at the legion. "However, I think we can convince the orc to commit his cavalry to our left."

"Marcus–" Trebonius started to protest, but Marcus silenced him with a glance.

"The hill on the left is steep enough to hide two cohorts behind it. As long as we keep his skirmishers and light cavalry from getting a good look behind the hill, we can bait him into thinking that our left is our most vulnerable point. Both cohorts will be fresh and armed with the pig-stickers we've made; they'll take a beating, to be sure, but if Monseigneur the Prince's knights can ride around behind us to the north, they can take the enemy cavalry in the flank once it's fully engaged with the legion."

The other commanders fell silent as he traced the route the Savondese knights would have to take. First down the central hill, then back around the left hill in a curving path that would allow them to hit the enemy's right flank. All that would be necessary was for the Amorran cavalry to drive off whatever forces, most likely skirmishers or wolfriders, were accompanying the primary assault, from behind the hills. And, of course, for the two specially-armed cohorts to hold long enough to give them time to cover the ground required for the ride.

Gaius Trebonius pointed to the gaps between the two hills. The southern gap was nearly twice as large as the northern one. "What if they ride through one of these? Their light cavalry could cut off any of our three armies from the others, then envelop them from both sides."

"We should pray that the orc will be foolish enough to try it." Count Yvenches dismissed the concern. "I doubt he will prove to be such a fool. With small pickets of one hundred or so men between the left and center, and perhaps two hundred between center and right, the gaps would be nothing more than a death trap for the goblins. Even if they did manage to force the pickets before being taken in one flank or the other, the reserves your general is holding for the boars could seal the northern gap, and the Prince's cavalry the southern one."

Trebonius nodded to indicate he had withdrawn his objection and stepped back.

"Do you wish to discuss our esoteric resources?" The prince addressed Marcus directly with a faintly contemptuous expression on his face. "Or do you prefer to operate in ignorance of their actions?"

Marcus smiled faintly. It was not his wishes that mattered, but rather, what his duty as legate demanded of him. "I would prefer to know your intentions, of course, as well as to better understand what my men are likely to face."

The prince gestured, and the comte briefly exited the tent. When he returned, he was accompanied by Theuderic and an older royal mage, both of whom were wearing the rich blue cloaks that indicated their status. Theuderic maintained a straight face as he nodded respectfully to the Amorrans, although his eyes sparkled with irony as he met Marcus's disapproving gaze without flinching.

"I understand you have conferred with the men who have encountered their scouts and forward units. Tell us what you have concluded of their magical capabilities, monseigneurs." The prince did not see fit to introduce the magicians, Marcus noticed. To him, the battlemages were weapons, no more worthy of his personal interest than a horse or a catapult.

The older mage appeared to be startled at the prince's brusqueness, but Theuderic smoothly stepped forward and addressed the waiting commanders. "I am Theuderic, one of the senior royal mages present, monseigneur generals. My experience of orc shamanics is, admittedly, less than extensive, but I encountered several shamans during my year serving with the border patrol. Their spells are neither refined nor disciplined, but they do possess an amount of raw power that is derived from the blood magic they favor.

My understanding is that their shamen will perform various sacrifices, both the night before and on the morning of battle, intended to enhance the potency of their spells. They may also augment their capabilities by slashing themselves to draw their own blood."

"Is there any way we can interrupt these sacrifices?"

Theuderic dismissively eyed the border lord who'd spoken. "Not unless you think you can penetrate their lines, monseigneur."

"I meant magically. Isn't there anything you mages can do to disrupt them at that point? It sounds like it might be a weak link, of sorts."

"I can understand why you might think so, but it doesn't work like that. We can no more prevent them from slashing a goblin's throat at a distance with magic than you can with your spears and arrows."

"I see." The lord shrugged and nodded.

Theuderic glanced at Marcus. "The three primary forms of magic your men are likely to witness and encounter are *vauderie, sanguerie*, and *diablerie*. The first is the form practiced by our royal mages. In the battlefield context, it primarily involves some of the pyrotechnics I know you've previously seen utilized by goblin sorcerers, as well as various enchantments and illusions. As our abilities in this discipline are considerably superior to theirs, you need not concern yourselves overmuch. I expect your engineers will be able to answer any vauderic threats without too much trouble, and in any case, orcs are little given to the use of illusions."

"Especially when they already have the benefit of greater numbers," the older mage added. "They won't be trying to scare us off with any illusionary beasties, they'll be hoping we try to stand and fight them!"

Marcus and Trebonius exchanged a skeptical glance.

"So, what's the purpose of having mages among our men when they're not needed to stop the illusions and they can't stop the other sorceries either."

Theuderic interceded before the older mage could respond. "With all due respect, General Valerius, you are not familiar with the multitude of possibilities that are potentially in play. While we cannot prevent the sacrifices that fuel their blood magic, we can disrupt their spells once they cast them. And although we can't stop their summonings, we will try to banish any demons or other creatures of evil they raise against the legion."

"Try," Trebonius said sourly.

"There are various forms of mitigation and dispelling capabilities," said the older mage. "Some will be applicable on the morrow, others, perhaps not. That is why we have offered to stand with your men, monseigneur. If we did not believe we could assist your men, we would not have made the offer to stand with you."

Marcus sighed. "Very well. Give me examples of what our priests can do, and what they cannot do, that I can use to deal with the inevitable objections among my staff tonight."

Theuderic nodded, thought for a moment, then explained. "Orcs often have their shamans cast spells inspiring mindless rage on their infantry, to send them berserk and prevent them from running. This is the sort of thing your priests can hope to prevent by suppressing the magic in the vicinity. But if a fire spell were to ignite a catapult, there is nothing they could do to extinguish the flames that any other man could not."

"But you mages could put out the fire?" Trebonius asked.

Theuderic simply smiled and held up a finger. A single word, and a flame erupted from his finger. With another word, it was gone, leaving only a faint wisp of smoke trailing up toward the ceiling of the tent.

"Without a doubt," he said.

The prince, who had remained silent throughout the mage's elucidation, raised an expectant eyebrow. Marcus grimaced and nodded in acquiescence. It was impossible to deny the potential utility of the battlemages, and it would be a dereliction of his duty to his men to deny them the protection from enemy magic the two men could provide.

And if it was a sin he was committing by doing his duty, well, that was but one more black mark against his soul for which he would simply have to pay the price.

"Very well," Étienne-Henri said, a little impatiently. "Now that we've settled that and the dispositions, is there anything else that requires discussion?"

"Signals," Trebonius said. "And, of course, a fallback plan in case we're forced to retreat."

"Retreat?" The prince practically spat the word as if it were an obscenity. "There will be no retreat tomorrow, Amorran! Therefore, there is no need for us to make any plan to do so."

Marcus closed his eyes. This was exactly the sort of idiocy he'd feared from the arrogant, inexperienced prince. The substitution of posturing for planning, the reliance upon bold statements instead of proven stratagems, could be very nearly as dangerous to the legion as the enemy itself. He hadn't forgotten how his own inexperience had cost the legion dearly at Montmila, and while the orc chieftain was no Valerius Magnus, the creature was almost certainly a battle-hardened veteran of dozens, if not hundreds, of vicious battles.

"Your Highness, with all due respect, it is neither demoralizing nor defeatist for the men to go into battle knowing what they are to do should events not proceed in accordance with our expectations. Even our greatest generals, from Severus Attalus to Publius Claudius, have been forced to withdraw from the battlefield in defeat, and in doing so they preserved their forces to win future battles."

"Indeed, to this day, some of them are known more for the brilliance of their withdrawals than for the methods of their victories," Gaius Trebonius added. "It is a necessary aspect of our preparations."

"Enough!" snarled the prince. "This is my realm, and you, monseigneur le comte, are a sworn vassal to my father the king. Retreats, withdrawals, and arrangements to fall back may be a necessary aspect of your preparations, but as I have already told you, they are not required in this place or at this time!"

He glared first at Trebonius, then at Marcus. Somewhat to Marcus's surprise, his dark eyes did not glint with madness nor did they show even the least sign of trepidation or uncertainty. To the contrary, they were cool and filled with a calm confidence that, were it not for the obvious absurdity of Étienne-Henri's ignorance of military matters, would have been reassuring.

"Any further objections, monseigneurs?" When none were forthcoming, he nodded curtly and dismissed them. "You need not further trouble yourselves about any possibility of defeat. We will be victorious tomorrow. If you simply do what I know you are capable of doing, all will be well. You have my word as the Crown Prince of the Realm on this."

Knowing any more protests would be worse than useless, Marcus thumped his chest and bowed with a precision so correct it bordered on insubordination. Gaius Trebonius did likewise, and the two Amorrans marched from the tent, followed shortly afterward by Theuderic.

As they walked past the royal guards and toward the pegs where their horses were tethered, Trebonius laughed shortly.

"At least he permitted us to take the hill nearest the castra."

"Why not, since the thought of retreating to it most certainly won't be crossing my mind."

"What are you going to tell the centurions?"

"We'll make our own plans. The legion is my responsibility. Its survival is my first priority. The fate of the prince's men is not my problem."

"Wait!" Theuderic called from behind them. "I'll ride back with you."

"Well, then I suppose I'd better consult chapter twelve before we go over the dispositions with the centurions," Trebonius said grimly as they halted, waiting for the tall battlemage.

"Twelve? I don't recall any adverse omens."

"No, book two."

"Ah, yes, of course. Yes, that might well be in order. Go back now, I'll wait for him to get his mount."

Trebonius waved his hand in what might have been a half-hearted salute and mounted his horse, then urged it away in the direction of the Amorran castra.

"Thanks for waiting," Theuderic told him. "I couldn't help but overhear you talking with the tribune. What is book two?"

"*What to do for the Defence of the Camp, in the Event a Commander lacks Confidence in his Present Forces.* Unfortunately, it appears to be all too relevant to our present situation."

"Ah, a snippet of your vaunted military lore. I can hardly fault you, Marcus. I will admit to lacking a certain amount of confidence in our present forces myself, and by present forces, I will confess that I mean Étienne-Henri!"

"Is he mad? He doesn't look mad, and yet I would swear that he's not even remotely frightened about tomorrow. And he should be! I barely slept the night before my first battle as a commander, or my second, come to think of it. I doubt I'll sleep at all tonight either!"

"He's not mad. And he's not stupid either. Just ignorant, pig-headed, lazy, and entirely lacking in good sense."

Theuderic whistled to draw the attention of a nearby man-at-arms. He pointed to himself, then to Marcus's horse, and the man nodded, then broke into a run.

"I'm glad to be stationed with you. I assume the plan will be to fall back to the camp when either the center or the right-wing breaks?"

Marcus didn't see any point in dissembling. Theuderic might be a spy, but he obviously wasn't reporting to the Red Prince. "That, or if the orc makes any significant attempt to cut us off from it that looks like succeeding. Do you think the orc will take our bait and send his heavy cavalry against us?"

"It's impossible to say. Who knows what passes for thinking in a greenskin's skull?"

"Can the knights be trusted to ride out? That's the one thing that worries me. If the boars hit the left and we're pressed on our front, it could be very difficult to disengage if the royal cavalry doesn't hit that flank."

"Oh, they'll ride," Theuderic assured him. "They can always be trusted to ride out. Whether they will be patient enough to wait for the signal to do so, that's the question that should worry you."

Marcus shrugged. "Even an early arrival would suffice to extricate our foot. They'd kill considerably fewer pigs, though, and our withdrawal would leave the center's flank exposed." He didn't bother pretending that the decision would pose him any sort of dilemma. He would save his legionaries at all costs, and if that meant leaving every last Savonner on the battlefield to the tender mercies of the ravenous orcs, he would not hesitate to give the order to fall back under the cover of the knights' attack.

"As I said, General, I'm very glad to be with you on the left. And if you're interested in a little wager, I'll give you two gold royals to one that the right holds longer than the center."

"Done," Marcus said, after a moment's reflection on the undisciplined mass of oversized, fair-haired islanders that would make up the right wing tomorrow. "I hope you're wrong, though. We'll have more time to withdraw if the northerners break first."

The man-at-arms approached, leading a powerful stallion that looked fast and strong enough to bear a fully-armored knight. Theuderic took the reins with a nod of thanks to the man, and stepped expertly up into the saddle. Marcus did the same, then turned to address the mage.

"That's quite the horse you've got there."

The mage shrugged. "Savondese mage lore also has its fallback plans."

LUGBOL

FACE DOWN in the dirt, Lugbol groaned as it gradually dawned on him that the ominous thud-thudding that seemed to rise up from the cool earth to penetrate his skull was neither a hangover from the previous night's excesses nor a figment of his imagination. Rolling over onto his back, he listened to the slow, pounding rhythm of the Great Orc's war drums.

Boom. Boom. Boom. Boom-Boom. There was a pause, which lasted just long enough to fool him into thinking the drums had fallen silent, and then they began again. Boom. Boom. Boom. Boom-Boom.

He carefully cracked one eye open. He could see nothing, so he opened the other. Only after passing his hand in front of his face twice and barely being able to make out the movement did he realize that it was still pitch black outside. A summoning so early could only mean one thing. Commanders' confab. He groaned again, and began to push himself to his feet, careful not to put too much weight on his still-injured arm.

He was fumbling around his newly-acquired blankets, which still smelled like smoke from the fire his kors had set in the hut from which he'd claimed them. They were warm, though, and he rather thought that come winter, Meighar might value them more highly than some glittering Man baubles. Not that he hadn't made sure to gather a few of those as well for the beautiful kwee who had haunted his thoughts since the unforgettable three days he'd had with her.

A glow appeared in the darkness, and grew larger as it approached his tent, accompanied by the rapid drumbeat of footsteps. Before the messenger reached the entrance, Lugbol was already stepping through it, his hand on the bone handle of his sword, scowling as if he'd been waiting ages for the big, armored orc to arrive.

"Yez be de hadvezer, yah?"

"Yah," he confirmed. He was a little surprised to see that the Felsig Kral had done him the honor of sending one of his own body guards as an escort.

"Come along, den. Best stick close, Hadvezer. Dey told me yez be a small 'un, but dey don' say yez be lookin' like a gobbo wid a bad wing."

Lugbol grunted. It seemed that the bodyguard's presence was less an honor than a precaution. But either way, it was a thoughtful gesture, and one for which he was sincerely grateful. Knowing how the blood of his own kors was up on the morning of battle, he couldn't begin to imagine what the Blue Hide Boyz and the other vicious killers among the big mountain orc clans would be like.

He followed the big orc as they made their way through the still-sleeping camp. The sky was pitch black, with the stars having been snuffed out by the clouds below them, although he could see a small number of flickering lights converging toward a bonfire near the center of the encampment. Any lingering doubt that today would be the day that Kral hurled them against the waiting Man army vanished at the sight of the various infantry and cavalry commanders being summoned to assembly well before the break of dawn.

Even with his massive escort preceding him, it was intimidating to walk out of the darkness and into the torchlight in the shadows of his fellow war captains. The enormous Gor-Zug, the general of the orc infantry and captain of the notorious Blue Hide Boyz, was there, as well as the legendary Barghak Bearsquagger, warleader of the Blue Hide's great rivals, the Split-Top Mountain Kill Crew. To Lugbol's surprise, to say nothing of his relief, Gor-Zug appeared to recognize him on sight and even deigned to honor him with a brief nod. Kral Nekheru was there, of course, bandy-legged and looking squattier than usual amidst the Hagahornu giants, and he greeted Lugbol with a friendly roar.

"Lugbol! What took you so long, little Goghu? Spending too much time playing with your Man-ghash?"

"No excuses, Felsig Kral!" Lugbol started to salute, but the kral waved it off and slugged him on the back.

"I know you been out scouting, Hadvezer. Good you got some rest afore we start the killing."

"It will take a while. There's a lot of them to kill, Felsig Kral."

"Da more o' dem, da more meat for uns to eat!"

Lugbol was surprised to see there were two, no, he corrected himself, three goblins present at the conclave. One was a shaman, the other two looked as if they might be goblin krals, given the way they carried themselves proudly and did not cringe or cower despite finding themselves in the midst of the greatest and most powerful of their superiors. They certainly looked more comfortable than Lugbol felt himself.

General Gor-Zug stepped forward, hawked, and spit a massive green snot-grume into the fire. The commanders swiftly fell silent, so swiftly that Lugbol could hear the snot sizzling.

"Right! Shut yez gobs and listen up to what tha Felsig Kral wants yez to do today."

"Nekheru, Nekheru," the hadvezer'ugh chanted as the Hagahornu king swaggered past his guards and stood beside the huge orc in front of the fire. "Walsig Kor Nekheru!"

They abruptly stopped chanting when the kral glared at them, shaking his head in contempt.

"What part o' shut yez gobs didn't yez grok? Any hadvezer who can't do what he's told today will be eating his own bollocks come sundown, grozu? This ain't no time for firin' up the kors, yez gotta keep yez skulls hard and yez vanks harder! Grozu?"

"Oi, Walsig Kor!"

"Right. Now, we got the numbers, but they got some hard kors that might be harder to crack than a troll sqwaak's arse. So we gonna have to be patient. We gonna have to be persistent! We ain't gonna hit them turtleshells once or twice and think they'ze gonna run, right?" He punched his fist into his palm. "One! Two! Three! Four! Five! We got the numbers, so we gonna hit them, and hit them, and hit them again until somethin' breaks. Six! Seven! Eight! Nine! Ten! Whattever it takes! Grozu?"

"Oi, Walsig Kor!"

"Lugbol, it's yez kors done the rekky. Tell 'em the layout, Hadvezer."

Lugbol managed to compose himself in time to thump his chest and bark out a quick "Oi, Felsig Kral!" before addressing the mighty assembly. He forced himself to stare directly into the faces of the towering mountain orcs, reminding himself that with only a few exceptions, he was now the equal of any kor standing there. He was a little surprised to see no sign of contempt or disdain on any their tusked faces or in their cruel yellow eyes, only focus and attention.

"The Szavon'agh have divided their forces in three. They're setting up on three hills a short march from the kral's camp. The kral is on the left, and the turtleshells are on the right. The turtleshells have built a big fort about a half-morning's march from their hill, but judging by the works they've been putting up in front o' their hill, they ain't gonna stay in it."

"The more dey leave in dere, de better!" grunted Barghak.

"There aren't as many turtleshells as either set o' krals'agh, but we know they'ze hard. They know it too, cuz they squagged us real hard in the Korokhurmagh when we was under Zlatagh. So, I'm thinking they expect one o' the two other sets to crack first, then they'll fall back to the fortress. Felsig Kral, it's yez call, but mebbe we just keep them busy, then let them go and turtle-up when t'others start running."

Nekheru didn't answer, but he grunted thoughtfully before turning and looking at Gor-Zug.

"Can we send riders between da hills and cut dem off, or mebbe ride around and hit one o' dem hills tail-side?" the Blue Hide warleader mused. "Only thing better'n hittin' th'enemy in th'arse is proper kwee ghash!"

"Uh, uh, uh," several of the commanders grunted approvingly. Even the Felsig Kral grinned, before shaking his head.

"We can try, but they got riders covering both gaps and the left. And it ain't a good bet, cuz their horse is too big for our wolves and too fast for our boars."

"Don't matter how fast they are if they ain't got room to move," observed Barghak. "We ain't afeared to bleed."

"No need to make things tricksy," Nekheru growled, before the two commanders started arguing. "And we need to teach them turtleshells a lesson. Forget their cavalry, Gor-Zug. Once you warm them up, we'll smash their damn shells with our boars. How they divided on the left and middle, Hadvezer?"

"Looks like the kral's mandokki on the big hill in the middle, and some big yellowhairs of a sort we ain't seen afores on the left. They carry big tree-choppers, but their armor ain't no better than ourn. Probably ain't even as good, since our pigskin is tougher'n anything they got. And unless I miss my guess, they're light on archers."

"The hell you say!" Gor-Zug expostulated. "Why you say dat?"

"Cuz nobody seen 'em. See, the turtleshells have a lot of machines. Rock-throwers, spear-chuckers, and fire-throwers. We seen 'em in the forest, and they can rain hell from farther away than Alvu archers. So, my thought is they don't think they need'em."

"I ain't heard nothin' to change the plan," the king broke in. "Barghak, what do you say?"

"Smash 'em, den smash 'em again. If dat don't work, we smash 'em again until one o' dem break."

Gor-Zug was nodding slowly. "You want my boyz to crack the hard nut first, Walsig Kor?"

"After we let the Farkh'agh warm 'em up a little first. Let's see what them turtleshells got for bollocks afore we bust 'em."

"Walsig Kor!" Every orc present, Lugbol included, looked over in disbelief as one of the goblin krals spoke up. He was big for a gobbo, and his yellow skin had a greenish tint, but even so, he made Lugbol look like a mountain orc by comparison. But the Hagahornu king didn't rip his long-nosed head off or order him gutted, as Lugbol half-expected, he only grunted and granted the gobbo permission to speak with a nod.

"I know my people's place, Walsig Kor. You'll throw my goblins against the foe to soften them up, you will weaken them by drowning them in our blood. We know our duty to you, our cousins, and we will obey you as our rightful king of kings. But I would ask you one favor before the sun rises and we march off to die before it hits its peak."

Gor-Zug rumbled low in his throat, but Nekheru waved him off.

"So ask, Kral Murpwarden."

The goblin bowed deeply, as much at the orc king's knowledge of his name as the acknowledgment of his status among his people.

"I beg you, do not send us against the turtleshells on the right. Not against the black-iron infantry. Our wolfriders will harry them, our archers will blot out the sun with their shafts, but I ask you to send our first infantry waves against the Savon'agh on the left and center, Walsig Kor.

It was with a sinking feeling in the pit of his stomach that Lugbol watched the kral nod his approval of the goblin's request. And he knew, even before Gor-Zug pronounced the fatal words, upon whose green shoulders the fatal responsibility would fall.

"Well, yez got some experience o' dem afors, Hadvezer Lugbol. We'z been hearin' how good dat Black Fist Infantry is, so yez gots da first wave onna right."

"Oi, General!" And because he was pretty sure he, too, would be dead before sun-high anyway, for once he didn't bother watching his mouth in front of the monstrous mountain orcs. "We'll show yez damn Hagahornus how it's done!"

Lugbol looked on the hesitant advance of the goblin archers toward the waiting lines of the turtleshells on the hill and he sighed. The morning was nearly gone and against all expectations he was still alive, but that was about the only positive thing he could observe at the moment. The Felsig Kral's orders to him had been clear enough: send the archers forward, have them release all ten of the shafts in their quivers, then advance on the enemy lines as the wolfriders rode forward to threaten the enemy's flank and the shamans unleashed the spells they'd spent all night preparing. It should have gone smoothly, and if it had, the right wing under his command would already be fully engaged with the deadly turtleshells.

Unfortunately, one of the goblin krals somehow neglected to tell his shugaba'agh that the goblin infantry would be leading the attack on the left wing rather than the right. Then, after Lugbol finally managed to convince the goblin infantry that they were in the wrong position, Ghurash had been forced to chase down and literally murder the idiotic shugaba trying to lead the archers away from the right wing.

"Sorry, Hadvezer," his sour-faced galvebel had apologized as he held up the dead goblin's head by its hair. "I tried to tell him they was supposed to stay on the right, but he wouldn't listen."

"Was that really necessary?"

"Well, after he wouldn't listen, I told him I'd rip his head off if he didn't give the order to turn around. He didn't, so I did." The galvebel shrugged. "T'other shugaba'agh was willing to give the order then, seeing as how they was next."

"By Gor-Gor's stinking arse, how they must hate us."

"Who hates us?" Ghurash whirled the head around once, twice, and then released it. It flew an impressive distance, before landing with a wet thud in between two startled kors.

"The gobbos."

"Pfffff, who cares what the pesky little bastards think? Don't see how they manage to spawn without no bollocks. I'm just glad we don't have to deal with they'ze infantry. It's gonna be hard enough keeping the archers in line, and they don't even have to close with the enemy!"

The older kor's contempt wasn't undeserved, Lugbol now admitted to himself, as he watched the archers shuffling fearfully toward the silent enemy line, and the big wooden structures that loomed ominously behind the armored troops on the hilltop. The archers were supposed to stop and release their shafts once they came within twenty paces of the beginning of the incline, which was another thirty paces from the enemy's front line, but it was beginning to look as if they were halting early.

"Forward, forward!" he shouted uselessly. Even if they could hear him, which they couldn't, they wouldn't have any idea who was shouting at them amidst the clamor and clangor of the mass of kors behind him. His infantry was shuffling in their lines, shouting and sneering at the inept display by the yellowskins, and placing bets on everything from how many volleys of shafts would be released before the goblins ran to how many corpses they would leave behind them after they tried to flee the field.

Lugbol just hoped the twenty kors and thirty wolfriders he'd assigned to drive the archers back into the battle would be enough. They were armed with whips studded with bone, which normally would suffice to keep a goblin in line, but if the archers fled en masse, his kors would be overwhelmed. He wished he'd paid more attention to how Zlatagh and the other commanders handled cowardly troops who were reluctant to fight; the Black Fists might not be as feared or ferocious as any of the famed orc regiments, but the one thing you could say for them was that they were never afraid to get stuck in.

The shugaba leading the archers finally raised his arm and called for a halt, about twenty paces short of the mark, but close enough to ensure even the shafts launched by the rearmost archers should be able to reach the enemy lines. Lugbol held his breath as he heard the shugaba's high-pitched voice screaming out orders and saw the goblins nocking their shafts to their bowstrings. But even as the archers began to raise their bows, an answering shout came from the hillside. Almost immediately, what had been row after row of armored, but vulnerable soldiers transformed into large rectangles of impenetrable black metal. The discipline of the turtleshells, and the speed of their uniform obedience, was breathtaking!

"Loose!" he heard the shugaba scream. It was followed by a ragged series of twangs as over two thousand bowstrings were released, sending a black cloud of shafts into the air. The cloud rapidly covered the distance separating the archers from the enemy, and descended upon the black rectangles like a swarm of insects rushing to devour their prey. But with only a very few exceptions, the wooden shafts splintered and shattered harmlessly upon striking the upraised, interlocking metal shields that protected the men beneath them.

"Dammit, they'ze barely going to scratch them!" Ghurash complained.

"It's only the first volley. We'll see how long they can keep holding those heavy shields up."

He looked to the south, but it was impossible to see how the center of the army was faring, much less the left wing. He saw a green fireball ascend into the sky and explode; it was obviously a signal of some kind, but what it signified, he did not know.

"Are yez ready to cast some magicks against them machines," he asked the chief shaman, a tall, cadaverously-thin orc wearing a plumed bearskull on his head and holding a twisted staff adorned with feathers and bits of horn. "Can yez spells reach that far?"

The shaman smiled, showing jagged, yellow teeth. He patted a large bone dagger that was thrust through a cracked troll-skin leather belt.

"If'n they don't, weze'll make sure they do. We got all the blood we need."

Lugbol glanced behind the chief shaman and restrained an instinctive shudder. Kneeling behind the thirty or so shamans were three times that many naked orcs and goblins, their eyes wild with terror and their hands bound behind them with gutstring. They were the criminals, deserters, and cowards who had been condemned by their galvebels and grun-kors for trying to run away, for shirking their duties, or in some cases, for being unpopular in the ranks. But the Great Orc had found a way to make use for every orc and goblin in his army, no matter how otherwise useless they might seem to be, and Kral Nekheru followed Azzakhar's cruel example. Neither the cookpot nor the sacrificial altar required much in the way of strength, courage, or discipline.

"Is there anything yez could do about them shields? Maybe melt the iron or something?"

"Sure. Or we could just make the ground underneath 'em swallow 'em all up, yeah?"

"You can do that?"

The shaman regarded him with open contempt. "No, Hadvezer, of course I can't do that! If I could do things like that, then I'd be the faszhek Great Orc, wouldn't I?"

For a moment, the temptation to bash the chief shaman over the head nearly overwhelmed Lugbol, but he managed to resist the urge. Neither Kral Nekheru nor General Gor-Zug would look favorably upon him bashing the brains out of what might, despite their apparent limitations, be his most effective weapon against the turtleshells.

"Loose!" the shugaba cried again, and a second volley of shafts flew aloft, only to descend again in clattering futility.

"This ain't working," he heard Ghurash mutter. His galvebel was right. The attack was clearly failing to do any harm to the enemy. As far as he could tell, not a single turtleshell had fallen under the rain of arrows. The black rectangles dissolved into lines of enemy troops, still standing in perfect order, with no sign of any casualties.

And then, the enemy responded.

Lugbol heard a horn sound from the hilltop, in response to which the enemy machines launched what appeared to be at least ten giant spears into the mass of archers at the foot of the hill. The incline of the hillside protected the first five or six rows, but each of the large missiles struck home, impaling one or more screaming goblins apiece before bouncing off the ground and knocking down more helpless victims. No sooner had the spear-chuckers loosed than was the great crack of the rock-throwers snapping as they hurled large boulders into the air, arching skyward before plunging down to crush bones, smash skulls, and leave a green smear of dead goblins three or four rows deep. The screams and wails were heart-rending, and sapped the courage of the watching orcs, but the doughty shugaba didn't hesitate to order a response.

"Loose!" he shouted, and the archers, though shaken by the enemy artillery, bravely responded. But again, before the missiles could reach their mark, the enemy was able to raise their shields and, for the most part, render the attack ineffective. Three, perhaps four, shields fell, as shafts dropped into gaps created by soldiers who had been slow to respond, but the enemy troops simply moved closer together and restored their defenses before the fourth volley fell upon them. Even worse, the men stationed at the machines had been actively loading them with new missiles, and were already cranking back the massive ropes that were required to launch them.

"Better do something soon, Hadvezer," Ghurash growled. "They can't take much more o' this."

"No, they can't." Lugbol turned to the chief shaman. "Can you burn those machines?"

"We can try."

"So try." He grimaced as the horn sounded, the enemy artillery struck again, and once more smashed broad swaths of horror through the mass of archers. Again, the front rows were spared, but they gnashed their teeth and shook their fists in vain as their comrades lost limbs and lives to the merciless bombardment.

Lugbol looked up at the leather standards that surrounded him. He realized that as soon as the shamans struck back at the machines, they would almost certainly become the primary target for the hail of death from the sky. But before they made targets of themselves, he realized there was something they could probably do that might be useful.

"The berserk spell the Red Claw Slayers use, do you know that?"

The chief shaman looked up from his preparations and nodded.

"Will it work on goblins?"

"Certainly. Though I don't see what difference it will make."

Lugbol pointed to the thousands of archers who stood between them and the enemy on the hillside. "I want them frothing at the mouth, attacking the enemy with their hands, teeth, and claws. Can you do that?"

"All of them?"

"All of them."

"We're going to need more blood, but we can do it. Before we attack the machines?"

"As soon as you can. How long will the spell last?"

"A ten-sun, maybe a little less."

"Do it," he barked at the shaman before turning to Ghurash and the various galvebels and grun-kors that surrounded him. "Let's move. We need to get the cavalry onto their flanks."

He ignored the terrible screams that began to erupt from the prisoners behind him as the shamans fell upon them with their blades, uttering their dark spells. They weren't the real sacrifice. And it wouldn't be their deaths that would haunt him if somehow, against every expectation, he survived this battle. The real sacrifice would be the thousands of goblins, lightly armed and barely armored, being cast against the black iron wall that waited for them on the hillside.

The wall wouldn't break beneath the tide of maddened gobbos, but the task of murdering them in their thousands would exhaust the men inside the turtleshells, and maybe, just maybe, it would tire them enough to give Lugbol's Black Fists and the rest of his light infantry a chance to break their lines.

"What do you want with the wolves," shouted Ghurash as they pushed their way through orc after orc. "Even if they drive off the enemy cavalry and turn their flank, they can't do much attacking uphill against armored infantry!"

"We don't need them to do much. We just need them to worry at the enemy."

Lugbol knew the galvebel didn't understand. Then again, he wasn't entirely sure he understood what he was doing himself. What he knew was that his orders were to weaken the enemy enough to let Kral Nekheru and his boar riders ride over the turtleshells, and he couldn't accomplish that by standing around watching the enemy artillery drop rocks on the heads of his kors while they died helplessly in their lines.

He smelled the wolves before he saw them. Then he pushed through the last line of kors separating him from the waiting wolfriders and was hit by the overpowering scent of more than two thousand unwashed wolves. The wolves were milling about, mostly unmounted, growling, snarling, sleeping, pissing, and defecating, seemingly at random, next to their lightly-armored riders who, on the whole, didn't smell much better than their filthy beasts.

A wolf wrinkled its snout and snarled at him as he walked past it; he glared at the goblin who held the animal's reins loosely in his fist.

"If that cursed thing bites one of my kors, I'll smash your skull!"

"Ay, Hadvezer!" The goblin took a firmer grip on the reins and pulled them in short.

Lugbol contented himself with a final glare at the wolfrider, who cringed satisfyingly as Ghurash and the other kors swaggered past the vicious beast. Then his galvebel stopped and uttered a thunderous oath, as he stared down at his right foot, the bottom of which was now smeared with a stinking brown substance.

"Gwan-ghash! Those anyafaszhek beasts are faszhek filthier than the felsig kral's faszhek pigs!"

As he stifled a smile, Lugbol could see the other kors around the galvebel doing the same, and even a few of the nearby goblins dared to smirk a little. Ghurash demonstrated that he was a true galvebel's galvebel, as he hopped on one leg and dragged his other foot across the broken, trampled ground attempting to scrape off the scat, cursing profusely all the while.

"Where's your commander," he demanded of a goblin who was standing beside his sleeping wolf.

"Over there!" the wolfrider pointed toward a series of faded leather banners. "Near the front!"

Lugbol pushed his way past beast and goblin until he saw a tall goblin, mounted on the back of the biggest wolf he'd ever seen, surrounded by a group of large riders wearing wolf-skulls as helmets.

"Oi, gran-gol!" he shouted to get the goblin's attention.

The sound of an orc's voice must have alerted the wolfrider to his presence, as the goblin whipped his head around, wheeled his wolf around, and immediately dismounted.

"You in command o' these here wolves?"

"Ay, you got a message from the damn hadvezer?"

"I am the damn hadvezer!" Lugbol informed him brusquely, without taking offense.

"You?" The goblin snorted, then nearly choked as Lugbol continued to stare at him. "Ah, yer the one what spoke up for us goblins afore the kral!"

"That be me." Lugbol returned the goblin's suddenly crisp salute. "Now, I need you to send round about half your wolves to keep the enemy cavalry off them archers' arses. And I need you to do it now!"

The goblin looked at the enemy on the hill and back at Lugbol. "I can't do that, hadvezer! We ride out now, that infantry'll march right down the hill and hit us on the left flank once we engage!"

"No, it won't."

"Why not?"

"Those archers are gonna keep 'em too busy to come down at yez."

"Them archers ain't doin' nothin' but gettin' themselves kilt!"

"They ain't doin' nothin' now. Once the shaman gives 'em a little poke up the wizzy, they'll get stuck in."

The wolfrider scowled. "Yez gonna berserk 'em, ain't yez."

"Unless you got a better idea, then yeah, that's what we'll do."

As he remounted his wolf, the goblin muttered something under his breath about orcs that Lugbol was fairly certain was both an obscenity and an anatomical impossibility, but since he also saluted and acknowledged his orders, Lugbol just laughed and let it go.

"Get a move on, gran-gol!"

"Oi, hadvezer. I'll lead 'em out. Just don't leave us with our arses hanging out too long."

Lugbol and Ghurash watched as the goblin commander summoned his captains to him, soon after which a series of the high-pitched horn blasts that their smaller cousins seemed to favor were sounded in rapid succession, and the stinking gray mass of wolves gradually began to move under the impetus of their screeching, cursing riders.

"That should keep them turtleshells on they'ze toes," Ghurash remarked.

"Until they get skeered and run. They're only goblins after all."

But even as the lupine cavalry began to move toward the hill, there came a terrifying sound from that direction that Lugbol had only heard once or twice before. It began as a sort of moaning wail, and crescendoed into a bone-chilling scream that sounded as if it was erupting straight from one of the deeper Hells.

"Looks like the shamans got they'ze hooks into them gobbos." Ghurash pointed toward the archers, who were snarling and screaming as they rushed en masse toward the waiting Man lines without hesitation or discipline.

"Looks like." Lugbol agreed. "Now let's get back with our kors. If'n the turtleshells crack, the kral'll string me up by my vank if we don't follow up on it."

As Ghurash signaled to his guards to turn around, Lugbol saw the Man artillery loose again, and he winced as he watched the massive boulders arc high into the air, knowing the devastation they would soon wreak on his helpless kors below.

SKULI

I T WAS no surprise that repairing the abandoned vessel and making it
seaworthy proved to be a challenge. For one thing, his raiders lacked
the proper tools for such a large task, although they were able to find
six hammers and two saws while digging through the ruins of the ransacked
town. There was even a forge, although it was useless without any coal.
But axes and men they had in plenty, and most of them were veteran sea
reavers well-versed in the art of makeshift ship repair. The ship was a fat,
wallowing, grain transport of Southern design that had probably been full
of the oats, wheat, and other foodstuffs it had been carrying when captured,
judging by the rotting remnants of burlap that filled the interior. Even now,
there was an astonishing number of rats living in the hulk, and Skuli set
the young girls to hunting them, mostly in an effort to keep them occupied
and prevent them from distracting the men, whom they found fascinating
after spending most of their lives without ever having seen a human male.

The ship was, predictably, in very poor condition after what he estimated
was six or seven years floating in the dock battered by the wind and waves,
but it was structurally sound. The mast needed to be replaced, and tattered
vestiges were all that remained of the sail, but there was no shortage of canvas
to be found in the remains of the harbor and Skuli enlisted the women's
help to stitch a crude one together. The anchor was retrieved from the
sea floor and several coils of good, thick rope were found, which relieved
him greatly. Since the vessel would only be required to make a single, short
voyage, instead of cutting out the worm-eaten wood that was determined to
be unsound, they simply hammered freshly cut boards over it, and slathered
them with tar. One wouldn't want to attempt to spend many days at sea

in it, but Skuli was confident it would serve its final purpose before sinking into the depths.

In order to permit the vast bulk of the *draugamóðirin* to fit within the body of the vessel, it was necessary to remove most of the deck as well as the interior bulkheads. This meant, of course, that the ship would need to be sailed by a skeleton crew, so Skuli picked out six of his oldest and most experienced warriors, men who would not be terrified by several days of proximity to the ghastly, undead creature and who would not shirk from any order given. Mord Redcheek, the freed captives, and most of the rest of his men would sail on Ulvdraeber, which, he explained to the monster, would allow the longship to be rowed and tow the bigger vessel in the event the winds should fail or be contrary. Fortunately, the creature was content to oversee their progress from a distance; it was intelligent enough to understand that the men and women would not be able to work toward her objectives if they were paralyzed with fear and horror.

The men had a vague idea what they were about, necessarily, since it was obvious to even the slowest warrior among them that they were going to be transporting something very large in the abandoned hulk on which they were working. When Skuli finally called them all together and explained the situation, most of them were quietly accepting, and the few who seemed inclined to suspect that Skuli had inexplicably gone mad were quickly dissuaded by the Barkman and Gudrik the Glum giving their accounts of what they had seen with their own eyes. And Mord Redcheek stood squarely at Skuli's side, his narrow-eyed glare quickly silencing any man who raised any doubts or objections.

Skuli did find it necessary to take one man into his confidence. Kolfinn the Lame was one of the few members of *Ulfdraeber*'s crew who was older than he was, and considering how the man had managed to survive the siege at Ragnarborg despite a withered leg, he was arguably tougher too. He was the ship's carpenter, and it had been his advice that Skuli and the Redcheek relied upon to make the transport ready for the voyage. Upon being given Skuli's final instructions for the interior of the hulk, he didn't blink or ask any questions, he just smiled and nodded as if the request was a perfectly normal one that he'd been anticipating. But Skuli saw the fire that burned at the heart of the true warrior alight in Kolfinn's eyes, and he knew there was no need to tell the man to keep quiet about Skuli's plans.

He spent most of the next morning laboring alone in the bowels of the ship. Not long after the sun hit its height, he emerged from the hulk and found Skuli standing on the dock from where he customarily oversaw the men's labors.

"It's done." He met Skuli's eyes, proud and unafraid. "You'll need two more, besides you and me."

"Three more. Plus a man for the rudder. Six men, including the two of us, should be enough to sail her."

"You honor me, Skullbreaker." Kolfinn put out his hand, and Skuli took his forearm in the warrior's way.

"The honor is mine." Skuli slapped the older man's shoulder with his free hand. "Whatever you might be thinking, you keep your thoughts to yourself, my friend."

Kolfinn nodded. His grey-bearded face was grave as he turned toward the land, but as he limped up the dock, Skuli could hear him whistling. Skuli smiled. How fortunate he was, to find himself here, among such men as these. He felt as proud now as he imagined he would standing in the Halls of the Heroes beside the Strongbow.

Their labors took them three days longer than Skuli would have preferred, but at last, the new mast was erected and the patchwork sail was raised for the first time well before noon.

"She's an ugly pig, and she'll lay low in the water if that thing is anywhere nearly as heavy as you say, but she'll stay afloat so long as we don't run into any major squalls on the way."

Kolfinn the Lame looked weary, but pleased with the men's efforts. Skuli raised a hand to acknowledge the raising of the sail and an impromptu cheer went up. He heard someone step upon the dock behind him and turned to see Mord Redcheek, red-faced and sweating despite the cool morning breeze.

"*Ulvdraeber* is watered and stocked, Skullbreaker. Shall we get the women and children on board, then put her out to sea?"

Skuli nodded. They had agreed it would be best if the longship and its precious cargo were well out into deep waters before the *draugamóðirin* showed itself. The panic the creature would inevitably cause might cost lives, or worse, damage one of the vessels. Also, if Kolfinn's judgment was in error and the battered hulk could not bear the great weight of the undead thing, the monster could only wreak havoc on the six men who made up the crew.

"Take her out. At least three bows-lengths. Those wings don't look like flying, but only Hela knows what that monster's limits are. Stay in sight though. Jorund needs to see this for his saga."

"That ship of yours will need a name, Skullbreaker," the Redcheek observed. "Bad luck to sail her without one."

"Kolfinn, you've earned the right."

The grey-bearded shipwright frowned and contemplated his work. It was, quite possibly, the ugliest and most awkward vessel anyone had ever seen upon the White Sea.

"*Dypetsgris*," he said, hawking once and spitting on her stained timbers. Pig of the Deep.

Mord and Skuli, both taken by surprise, laughed. It was, somehow, appropriate. Then the Redcheek reached out and took Kollfin's forearm.

"Fare you well, Kollfin the Lame. The skalds will remember your name."

"We'll fare well enough, Redcheek. See you on the other coast." Kollfin released Mord's arm. "Shall I find the Halfhand and have him tell the *draugamóðirin* it's time?"

"Do that." They watched him make his halting way off the dock together, then Skuli slapped Mord's back.

"Best be on your way, old friend. Keep your distance, and don't hesitate to cut the rope at the first sign of trouble."

He embraced his second-in-command. Mord held him tight for a moment, then let him go and stepped back, his eyes uncharacteristically bright.

"No death song from the Skullbreaker? I know I'd sing one before I'd embark upon that wallowing sow of a ship."

"I'll let the skalds make one up for me. They will anyhow."

"They will indeed. Fare you well, Skuli Skullbreaker."

"And you, Mord Redcheek."

It was a certain tightness in his chest that Skuli watched the Redcheek walk away, gesturing, shouting, and giving orders. He looked inland, toward the southwest, knowing that an unspeakable evil would be coming his way before the morning was over. He licked his finger, felt the cool sensation against his finger, and smiled. At least the gods and the winds were with him on this day.

The sky was just beginning to redden as the first sign of sunset, though Hvit Måne was already visible very low on the horizon to the south. Skuli, standing at the hulk's prow, gripped the taut tow rope that connected them to *Ulvdraeber* as he looked at the sun behind them. They had sailed due east from the start and had been out of sight of land for most of the afternoon. These were deep waters and largely unknown to even the oldest reavers, but there were enough sons and grandsons of fishermen among them to tell him where he could find what he wanted.

The loading of the *draugamóðirin* had been every bit as terrifying as he'd anticipated, and for one frightening moment, when the undead monster waded into the water surrounding the docks, then spread its tattered wings and used them to somehow rise out of the water, he'd feared that it might be able to fly far enough to reach *Ulvdraeber*, but the exhausted tone of the voice in his mind quickly disabused him of his concerns, and so it was with a light heart that he'd stepped onto the remnants of the deck that surrounded the creature and given the signal for the longship to spread its sails. At first, they'd barely moved away from the docks, but once the longship's rowers began to add their muscle to the wind, and Kolfinn raised the hulk's own square sail, they began to make better speed than he'd ever imagined possible.

Even at the stern of the hulk, with the wind blowing toward the monster, the stench of it was overpowering. Here, at the fore, it was downright eye-watering, and only the fact that he hadn't breakfasted prevented Skuli from emptying his stomach on the calm and easy seas. Each of the other five men he'd hand-picked for the voyage had vomited, and most of them more than once. He looked down at the huge white wyrmskull, and saw that the mystical fires in its empty eye sockets were little more than sparks now. The voice in his head was silent too, and he wondered if it was possible for an undead thing to be seasick. Or perhaps it was only sleeping until the misery of its uncomfortable sea passage was over.

The grotesque cargo aside, the evening sea was a beautiful sight. A sailor's delight, as it was said. The gentle waves were dappled red and gold with the sparkling light of the setting sun, and the familiar rippling sound of the sail made him feel finally at peace with himself and with a world that had gone mad. He thought of Dagna, her beautiful face, the white skin of her body, and he smiled in rueful amusement at the way his weary, wounded body still stirred, however faintly, at the mere recollection of her. By Mardöll, what a woman she was! How fortunate he had been, how blessed by the gods, to take her to wife!

His thoughts turned naturally to his children. Brynjolf would never be a true jarl, nor did he have the proper makings of a warrior. But he was kind, his heart was true, and he was loyal by nature. With the assistance of his sister and the guidance of his mother, he would lead the Dalarn tribes in a way that would help them find a place within the kingdom of Savondir. Fjotra was the stronger, and, like her mother, she would have influence over both her brother and her husband, the future king of the southrons. And through her, and through the marriages of her children and grandchildren, Dalarn blood would infuse the throne of Savondir with strength and beauty, until at last the ruling line was more Northern than Southern.

And then, his children's grandchildren would be strong enough to reclaim the Isles lost by his generation.

It was nothing more than a beautiful dream, but he had laid the foundations for it to one day become reality. And now, he must lay the last and most important stone, lest all of his other preparations come undone. He closed his eyes and looked up at the sky, indulging himself in one last moment of feeling the fading sun's rays upon his face. Then he opened them. It was time to bring the Skullbreaker's Saga to its glorious end.

He drew his sword and raised it high, turning the blade slightly to reflect the light toward *Ulvdraeber*. As he expected, the Redcheek was ready and waiting for him, as a return flash from either a well-honed sword or burnished copper shield came instantly. He leaned forward, and struck down at the tow rope with all his strength, severing it in a single blow.

There is strength in my sword yet, he thought with savage satisfaction. Before him, shed of the burden of the wallowing hulk, *Ulvdraeber* seemed to leap ahead, swiftly increasing the distance between the vessels as the Redcheek ordered the rowers back into action. Then came a thumping sound from deep within the hull, and Skuli staggered as the overloaded ship lurched, almost as if it had become entangled with something under the surface of the sea. It was followed by another, fainter sound, and the vessel slowed, almost to a complete halt, although the east wind remained strong.

What happened? Is aught amiss?

"It's nothing, just a minor problem," he answered the voice in his head out loud and calmly. "The tow rope snapped. I've signaled the other ship. We'll drop anchor so they can come around and tie the rope on again."

He resisted the urge to taunt the ancient evil. Its fate was not yet sealed, not yet.

"Kolfinn, Vog, drop the anchor!"

There was a big splash on the left side of the stern, and the rope played out until the hulk came to a halt with a jerk that made Skuli stumble, even though he was prepared for it. He held his breath for a moment, then looked over the side and was pleased to confirm that the ship was indeed settling deeper into the waves. He raised his sword again, angling it to flash a second message to the longship that was rapidly pulling even further away from the anchored hulk. But not too rapidly to put the great patchwork sail beyond bowshot, as the response to his second signal was the gift of the Barkman, a shaft wrapped in an oiled rag and set alight, which arched high from the deck of the longship before it buried itself in the thick canvas and set the sail on fire. A second arrow arrived, then a third, before the longship was out of the Barkman's range.

Skuli raised his sword and waved it to salute the Barkman's heroic efforts. Hrolf, Ornolf, and Trud Crook-Nose, all soaking wet from their previous task, had clambered up from the depths of the hulk and were breaking open the small casks that looked as if they were used for storing water. In truth, however, each cask was full of pitch recovered from the abandoned docks, and the three old warriors methodically went about spreading it over the timbers of the deck and sides. Just as Kolfinn and Vog joined them on the deck, which was already beginning to catch fire, the *draugamóðirin* addressed Skuli again.

Why is there fire in the sail? Why do I feel water under my belly?

Skuli laughed with the victorious glee of a mortally wounded warrior who stands over the body of his last and greatest foe.

"Because, you cursed evil Jotunspawn, you are going to die! You are going to die by fire, water, and the sword of the Skullbreaker!"

I cannot die, you fool!

"Then dwell forever in the depths of the sea and be damned!"

The great square sail was now fully aflame, the leaping fires fanned by the east wind, and burning sections of canvas were beginning to fall on the forward section of the hulk. Soon the timbers were starting to burn, and the vessel sank even lower into the sea as cold salt water poured in through the four holes in the bottom of the hull that had been cut out and corked by Kolfinn the Lame.

The voice inside Skuli's head was no longer coherent. He did not hear any words, just a wordless, anguished roaring, and he could feel the *draugamóðirin*'s terror as the death it had eluded for so long now came to claim it. No sooner had the great wings risen than the flames from the sail were licking at them, and the torn leather and dried bone proved to be every bit as flammable as the canvas sail and the pitch-covered timber. The undead beast, now thoroughly panicked, thrashed about in pain, and in doing so, broke vital timbers inside the hull. The burning hulk, already sinking, was beginning to lose its structural integrity and break apart as the first waves began to lap over the sides.

Skuli did not cower as the massive white skull rose up toward him, its jaws gaping and its empty eye sockets glowing with undead rage. No fear, just one single savage thought filled his mind. *Thus endeth the Skullbreaker's Saga!*

He shouted with triumph and leaped down off the deck to meet the rising skull, swinging his sword with both arms, throwing every last vestige of his strength and weight into his final act. There was a tremendous crack, though Skuli could not tell if the sound was his sword smashing through bone or the *draugamóðirin's* terrible teeth severing his spine.

He saw wood and metal, water and fire. The world whirled violently around in a vicious circle, spinning faster and faster as it cast him into darkness.

And then he saw, shining in the dark on either side of him, the proud shield maidens of the Halls, braided, blue-eyed, and blonde, their spears raised in salute. And beyond them stood the towering figure of the Aldaföðr himself, tall and fierce in his guise as Sigtýr, the god of war, holding out his left hand.

"*Velkommen, Váði vitnis!*" the Aldaföðr said, and he winked his one remaining eye.

AULAN

T HE CASTRA to which his sizable escort accompanied him was familiar to Aulan, as it was located only a morning's ride from the villa in which he'd spent most of the summers throughout his childhood. Castra Mendrisus was a permanent fortification, with stone-and-mortar walls surrounding enough buildings to house three legions. Aulan knew the stables well, as most of his father's horses were still housed there, although he imagined most of the highly-prized creatures would have been commandeered by the senior decurions by now. But as they rode closer, he saw that more than a few additional changes had been made over the course of the winter.

The gates, which he had never seen shut, and previously consisted of weathered, worm-ridden timbers suspended from rusty hinges, were now closed. The wood was freshly painted and the iron hinges no longer exhibited even a speckle of corrosion. More importantly, the ditch, filled in long before he had been born, had been re-dug and now surrounded the castra, making the walls look nearly twice as tall. A scorpio was mounted on either side of the watchtower that overlooked the gate, and he could see the two bolt-throwers were supported by a pair of carroballistae as well. This was no longer the exciting, empty fort he had explored so often in his youth with his brothers, it was once more a mighty temple to the red gods of war.

He wondered where they might have put all the excavated dirt. When a legion dug in for the night, the earth removed from the ditch normally served as the foundation for the wooden walls that were erected upon the piled-up dirt. But as Castra Mendrisas already had its walls in place, that meant there was a very large quantity of earth that must have gone somewhere nearby. He looked around, but saw no signs of any suspicious hills that had not previously been there. There was, however, a large and bustling village less than two hundred paces to the south of the ditch; it replaced the old, abandoned brick and wood buildings that had once run right up to the walls and must have been demolished before the ditch was dug. Unless he missed his bet, most of the now-missing materials would have gone into the new buildings, and a fair amount of silver into the pockets of Regulus and a few of his favored centurions.

"Who ordered the castra restored?" he asked Strabo, who was riding ahead of him.

"Your brother."

Aulan nodded, marveling that his older brother had actually managed to accomplish something substantive for once in his life. He was aware that Regulus had always been better on parade or in drill than in the field, or so he'd been informed on several occasions by eminently reliable sources. Not that Regulus was cowardly or prone to shirk his duties, only that he had no more idea what to do with a century than with a ballista. The thought of his brother attempting to command entire legions in battle struck Aulan as something that bordered on the ridiculous, and he reminded himself that the worst thing he could do to hinder his mission was to offend his sensitive older brother's pride. He would have to be very, very careful, not only about his words, but even his facial expressions. One ill-timed roll of his eyes might undo the good work of a thousand honeyed bon mots.

"He did well," he commented in an approving tone of voice.

"It is suitable for war," the centurion allowed. "Against whom, we've yet to learn. Maybe Magnus, yes?"

"I sincerely hope not."

"One way or another, I expect we'll see legion fighting legion before the summer's over. And maybe not only the allied legions."

"You may be right," Aulan allowed. In truth, Strabo was almost certainly right, but he sincerely hoped to avoid actual fratricide, if at all possible. Killing didn't bother him, not when it was necessary, but there were moral lines he still feared to cross.

The gates creaked slowly open upon their approach and the guards saluted, unaware that Aulan was, at least nominally, a prisoner at the moment. Strabo looked back and raised an eyebrow as Aulan returned the salute, although he made no attempt to correct the guards' misapprehension.

"I am still a tribune of the legion, Strabo."

The centurion merely snorted. That did not strike Aulan as a particularly optimistic sign, but he shrugged and continued to sit straight in his saddle, as an officer should. They rode down the Via Principalis toward the headquarters without attracting much attention. The castra was in good order, Aulan noted, which was again something of a surprise. Appius Mallicus appeared to be something of an improvement on Buteo, at least when it came to maintaining camp discipline. Then again, he imagined the prospect of having to fight another Amorran legion or three would tend to focus the legionaries and their officers in a way that suppressing the forces of a rebel province had not. Certainly Magnus hadn't hesitated to use the possibility as motivation for his men. Still, he found himself impressed.

When they reached the forum, a pair of decurions approached them. Strabo dismounted with a grunt, handed his reins to one of the cavalry officers, and indicated that Aulan should follow suit. He was gratified to receive a nod of recognition from the young man to whom he gave his horse, and searched his memory for the decurion's name. It wouldn't come to him, though, so he made do with a brisk nod and a safely general greeting.

"Good to see you again, Decurion."

"Likewise, sir."

He resisted the urge to flash a triumphant glance at Strabo. The sour-faced centurion might consider him to be in the legion's disfavor, but the decurion's response reassured him that the cavalry, at least, had not forgotten him. The legate's quarters, too, had been rebuilt, in dark red brick, and there were even olive trees planted outside the entryway, and the four legionaries standing guard had positioned themselves in such a way as to be standing in their shade. Had they been planted out of affectation or genuine concern for his men? Given what he knew of his brother, either explanation was equally likely.

His back began to itch as Strabo indicated that he should enter the building first. It was hard not to tense himself in preparation for a treacherous blow from behind from an assassin waiting inside the entrance. He didn't really think Regulus would simply murder him out of hand, but he would have felt considerably more at ease if he'd been permitted to keep his sword. And, of course, if the centurion had not told him that his arrest had been ordered. He resisted the urge to nervously finger the dagger hidden under his tunic; no doubt it would be taken away from him too if they knew it was there.

As the centurion closed the door behind him, Aulan looked about the foyer. It had a high ceiling and was tiled in white, with a large S encircled by olive branches that represented House Severus. That struck him as a good sign; it might well have been a letter R standing for Regulus. There were several large amphors of Vallyrian wine that appeared to be empty placed against the walls, each of which were painted with a mural featuring one of their illustrious forebears. Aulan recognized his father and his great-grandfather, and he suspected the one on the wall to his left was one of his earlier namesakes, also named Aulus Severus Aulan. There were three entries into the adjacent rooms, but none of them were guarded.

He peered more closely at the mural on the wall facing the entryway. It was a good likeness of Severus Patronus addressing the Senate, and suggested that the painter had been personally acquainted with their father. For a moment, he felt an unbidden flash of anger rise, and it was with some difficulty that he suppressed it. Regulus would test his temper soon enough, and going in to see his brother in a wrathful state of mind was unlikely to help him achieve his objectives. The last thing he wanted was to cause their meeting to devolve into the sort of fraternal pissing contest in which they had found themselves regularly engaged since they were boys. For some reason, just the tone of his voice or a momentary expression of skepticism could be enough to set off his older brother.

And, to be fair, there was something about Regulus's unshakable self-regard and pompous carriage that seemed to bring out the acid in his own tongue.

He looked back at Strabo, who indicated that he should take the path to the right. He nodded in acknowledgment and led the way, with the centurion's hobnails clack-clacking noisily on the tile behind him. He passed through a brief hallway with a lowered ceiling, which then opened up again into large, well-lit room that obviously served as a triclinium. Titus Severus Regulus was sprawled casually on a couch, holding a goblet of wine in one hand and a piece of cheese in another. He looked relaxed and at his ease, the very portrait of a young man certain to enter the Senate in his year. And, rather to Aulan's surprise, his brother was alone rather than surrounded by guards or his usual coterie of friends and hangers-on.

At the sight of Aulan, Regulus smiled broadly and rose adroitly to his feet, not spilling a single drop of wine despite the goblet being nearly full.

"At last, the prodigal returneth!"

"I trust I am not also the fatted calf, to be slain upon my return, then?"

"Why ever should we do that, little brother? Whatever sins you may have committed as an officer of the legion, I hereby absolve. Mark that, Strabo! Let the mutterings and murmurings be done with. My brother is safely back where he belongs and I have no doubts concerning his loyalties to House Severus or to Amorr. None whatsoever!"

Aulan smiled through gritted teeth. Regulus had always been charming, but it seemed that somewhere along the way, he had apparently learned to slip the odd barb in with his honeyed words. It was a welcome, but it was a warning too. He heard it loud and clear. *You are safe, but you are not well-loved here, and you dare not even think of challenging me.* That was the real message his brother was sending him.

"I am but a humble servant of House Severus, Legate."

And that, in return, was his message. *I serve the House. I do not serve you, big brother.*

Regulus returned his smile, but it was a broad, seemingly genuine one that showed all his straight white teeth. Anyone less familiar with his brother would be fooled, and in most cases, charmed, but Aulan knew better. Smiles came even more easily to Regulus's lips than self-serving lies.

"Begone now, Strabo. I would speak with my brother alone!"

The centurion saluted, somehow managing to convey his disapproval of both Aulan and his own dismissal by the precise correctness of his posture, and marched out of the triclinium. Regulus followed his subordinate's departure, then turned toward Aulan and raised a single eloquent eyebrow. Aulan couldn't help it; he laughed, and a moment later, Regulus joined him.

"Gods, they're so damned pompous sometimes!" his brother said.

"I'm afraid you've disappointed him. I expect he was at least hoping you'd make me sweat it out for a few days in the stockade."

"Our copious differences of opinion notwithstanding, little brother, there is no time for that sort of thing. What does Magnus want from me?"

"Your legion. Your obedience. He'll treat you well and grant you every respect so long as you do as he tells you and stay out of his way."

"And if I don't?" Regulus raised his left eyebrow again, but this time in skeptical curiosity rather than mockery.

Aulan produced his dagger from underneath his cloak and laid it on the marble-inlaid table. "In that case, I have orders to kill you and assume your command."

He was not surprised when his elder brother coolly ignored both the weapon and the implicit threat of the words. Like their father, Regulus well understood the power of public imperturbability, be it feigned or real.

"I would have thought you would be wise to conceal any such orders."

"Despite what you may think, I've never thought you were an idiot, Regulus. I'll admit, I thought there was a chance you'd have transformed this castra into some sort of heathen potentate's pleasure palace and surrounded yourself with whores and bootlickers, but as soon as I saw the defenses in good order, I realized that your more sensible side won out."

Regulus smiled, and this time the bright smile was truly genuine.

"It pains me sometimes, to see how well you know me, Aulan. You're right. The thought of crowning myself a king and aligning House Severus with the allies did cross my mind on occasion, particularly after those damned plebians murdered father. To Hell with Amorr! To Hell with the Senate and People! These are our legions, and they are loyal to our House, not to a God-cursed city of ill-blooded bastards that kills and casts out its betters!"

Aulan said nothing. He knew Regulus was merely venting the same rage that he still felt from time to time in his darker moments.

"They don't deserve us, Aulan. They didn't deserve him. But while I'm no Severus Patronus, brother, I'm not entirely ignorant of history. This is just another episode in the long, tedious story of our nation. It doesn't matter who steps out of line. It doesn't matter who rebels. It doesn't even matter which side wins, because the end of the story is always the same. The legions march and Amorr triumphs over all. No tribe, no petty kingdom, is going to survive in the shadow of Amorr, not very long, anyhow."

His brother smiled, but ruefully this time.

"And so, I manfully resist the sordid temptations the Devil whispers in my ear. I do my duty to my House and to Amorr as a true patrician and a proper general should." He drained the remains of the goblet in a single, well-practiced effort. "God, I need another drink! Will you join me?"

"Certainly." Aulan blinked, for the first time taking in his brother's flushed face and the reddened nose that he'd initially assumed was simply too much exposure to the sun. It seemed Regulus had not managed to render himself entirely immune to the demons of vice over the course of the previous winter. But he held his tongue and watched as his brother poured a generous serving of wine into a second goblet before refilling his own.

"Thanks," he accepted the wine with a half-nod and held it up in a mock salute. "To Severus Patronus! May men long remember his name, and may his sons prove worthy of him."

"Severus Patronus!" Regulus echoed him, and although his expression was characteristically sardonic, his eyes glittered with what looked suspiciously like genuine emotion. "That was… the right thing to say, Aulan. I find myself somewhat at a loss for words."

"Do you want my opinion?"

"I don't know. It seems to me I usually regret asking for it."

"Fair enough." Aulan sipped at his goblet. "Where did you get this? It's excellent!"

"Isn't it though?" Regulus stared down at him for a moment, his dark eyes narrowed. "Very well, little brother. Tell me what you think. Pronounce your unsparing verdict, if you must."

Aulan almost laughed, but managed to stop himself before he choked on his wine. Regulus never could resist hearing one talk about his favorite subject, even if it was only to denigrate him.

"Try not to let it go to your oversized head, Titus Severus, but in truth, I think you've done extremely well. You've certainly exceeded my expectations."

"Truthfully?"

"When have I ever bothered to lie to you? One of the reasons I dreaded coming here was that I was afraid you'd be drunk, decked out in silk robes, lining your eyes with kohl, surrounded by a harem of barbarian beauties, and in complete abandonment of your duties. And what do I find but a rebuilt castra, soldiers in good order, officers who respect their commander, and a legion that is ready to march to war!"

"I'm not entirely sober," Regulus confessed unnecessarily. "But the legion is ready to fight. And I swear, this is only my fourth cup today!"

"I hadn't noticed," Aulan lied. "Not to worry, Magnus will be on his sixth by now."

"Ah, so I may hope to aspire to greatness yet!" He raised his goblet. "So what inspires these kindly words, brother? You know I have not yet agreed to anything. Nor have you given me any reason to do so."

"What inspires me? Nothing more than what I see, elder brother. And any man who is sensible enough to resist the temptations you've faced over the last few months isn't going to be foolish enough to defy Magnus in the present circumstances. He can be very persuasive, Regulus. He's well-worthy of the name. I can assure you, by the time he marches on Amorr, half the allies will be calling him king. And there isn't a centurion in this legion who would be willing to stand against him."

"Yes, it seems that holds true for its tribunes as well," said Regulus, a little slyly. It took Aulan a moment to realize to whom his brother was referring, which only made Regulus laugh all the harder when he finally did. "Magnus or no Magnus, Aulan, you do realize that you are still a tribune of this legion, and I am still your commanding officer, do you not? So, do you actually think the men would have followed you, if you had… followed his orders?"

"Thanks to your good sense, we'll never find out!" Aulan raised his goblet, knowing what merely voicing the question had cost his proud, prickly brother.

"But do you think they would have?"

"Regulus, these are uncertain times. The men, the officers in particular, they knew we were on the verge of some sort of civil war even before our father was murdered. Maybe the war would not have been between the Houses, maybe it would have just been between the Senate and the Allies, but they knew war was coming. And if you ever learned anything from Master Tisias, then I'm sure you'll recall how, in difficult times, men turn to those they know are strong."

"House Severus is strong!" Regulus broke in.

"As a House Martial, yes. But we have no leader. We have no experienced generals, no ex-consuls. And without Patronas, we have no one for them to rally behind. His generation is too weak and ours is still too young, too untested. I think that's why Father instructed us to support Magnus in his rebellion. If nothing else, it breaks House Valerius in two and prevents the Valerians from running roughshod over the Senate and People."

Regulus nodded slowly. "So you're saying that if they had followed you, they would have done it because they know you've thrown in with Magnus, not because they preferred you to me."

Aulan smiled and slapped his brother's shoulder. It seemed nothing, no amount of height, beauty, privilege, or adulation, would ever fill the endless need for attention that lurked at the core of Regulus's being.

"Of course not!" he assured him. "The men have little love for me, especially after I abandoned them last autumn. Why, that damned Strabo was glowering at me from the moment he told me I was under arrest to when he marched me in here! I was half expecting him to sheathe his gladius in my back!"

"So you think they'll support me if I tell them we're throwing in with Magnus."

"I'm sure of it."

"Do you think Magnus will leave the legion to me?"

Aulan briefly considered whether a reassuring lie might be in order, but decided that shattering the fragile trust that seemed to be forming between the two of them was too high price to pay for something that was bound to come out in a matter of days. He knew perfectly well that there was no chance the highly experienced general would leave a vital fifth of his forces in the hands of an neophyte member of a rival House.

"There's no chance of that. He hasn't told me anything, of course, but I expect he'll embrace you like a son, praise you to the skies, and then give you some sort of high-profile, but harmless task like governing a province for him. He doesn't trust inexperienced commanders, probably because he's defeated so many of them."

Regulus pursed his lips and looked up at the ceiling. Aulan had the feeling he was contemplating whether or not his prospective duties were sufficiently close to his vision of himself. His next words surprised Aulan with their uncharacteristic insight.

"You know, it wouldn't be the worst thing for one of us to avoid having Amorran blood on our hands. I expect you'll be commanding a cavalry wing for him?"

"Yes, I assume so."

"Of course, that makes sense. You've already made something of a reputation in that regard. And while I need to get more battle experience, at this point, it will probably be rather more important to stay well away from the battlefield. Once this is all over, I expect there will be a need for Senators who weren't directly involved in the war, whose hands remained clean."

"And here I thought Father intended Tertius to be the family politician!" Aulan said, and nodded thoughtfully. Perhaps Titus Severus would make for a formidable Senator one day when he came of age; but for his tender years, he already looked the part.

"Have you heard from Tertio?"

"I haven't heard from anyone in the family since I left Amorr. If anyone wrote me, I haven't seen it, but then, I've been riding with Magnus all over Vallyria."

Regulus drained the last of his wine. "Yes, of course, how would he have even known where you could be found? Well, brother, I do commend your honesty. It can't have been easy for you to come here, even if it was on the orders of the Valerian. But now that you've told me what I needed to know, I don't know that I have much use for you anymore."

Aulan froze. Had his brother's unexpectedly warm welcome just been a facade? He wouldn't have thought Regulus could be so subtle.

"Now hold on, Regulus–"

His brother ignored him and waved an imperious hand.

"Centurion! Take this man to the place that has been prepared for him. And make sure his guards know that he's been stripped of his rank!"

Aulan sighed as he was roughly forced toward his unknown destination by the pair of legionaries. He wasn't sure which irritated him more, his brother's foolishness or the fact that for a moment, he'd actually believed that Regulus might do something reasonable for once.

"I knew it was too good to be true," he told his uncaring captors. "I just knew it!"

They did not respond. They marched him through the camp, past dozens of curious legionaries, merchants, and camp-followers, until they reached a small building near the southeast end of the castra with six fully-armored soldiers from the First Cohort standing outside it. He was shoved inside, and the door slammed behind him, then barred from the outside. There was nothing inside, but a cot, a flickering candle, and a desk. In the dim light from the candle, he saw there was a sealed scroll lying on the desk. He picked it up, cracked the seal, unrolled it, and immediately recognized the hand as belonging to Regulus.

To Aulus Severus,

If you are reading this, then you are my prisoner. I will not tell you not to be afraid, because I know you are a true Amorran who does not fear to die. But allow me to assure you that I do not wish you ill, nor do I intend that you should come to any harm. Instead, you shall simply remain here, under guard, until matters are resolved. If you elect to serve me, your older brother, it would please me greatly indeed, but I will understand if you prefer not to do so in light of your present circumstances and my own responsibility for them.

I hope that for your part, you will understand my actions once they have been explained to you. You see, I have decided that our late, great father, the eminent Severus Patronus, erred greatly when he instructed us to side with Magnus against the Senate and People of Amorr. I do not question his loyalty, but rather, his judgment. So, my intention is to go to him and have my men fall upon him once we are given entry into his castra.

Aulan groaned. And to think he had been worried that Regulus was merely going to crown himself a king! The fool was actually going to set himself directly against Amorr's foremost general, thinking that surprise and hatred of House Valerius would suffice to grant him victory.

Lest you think I am unprepared, I assure you, I am prepared for any eventuality. If he is suspicious and we are not permitted to join my legion with his, for whatever reason, my spies within his camp will arrange to open the gates by night and take him unawares.

Spies? His idiot brother was relying upon what he thought were traitors to the Valerian cause, no doubt imagining they were motivated by riches, or rather, empty promises of riches. Aulan would bet his horse on the likelihood that those purported spies were some of Magnus's most trusted centurions, and that the cunning Valerian had laid a trap into which Regulus would stick his neck without hesitation or a second thought.

Dear God, what if Magnus imagined he were somehow in on this charade with his brother! No, he reassured himself. First, Magnus knew he wasn't an imbecile. Second, the fact that his brother had held him captive would speak well for him, and indeed, the very letter in his hand would testify to his innocence. And third, if he was correct and the spies in his camp were reporting to him, Magnus had known of Regulus's stupid plot even before he'd ordered Aulan to demand Regulus's legion from him.

He returned to the letter.

Brother, I pray you will trust me to know what is best for our family. Now that Father is gone, it falls to me to serve as the Paterfamilias. Do not fear, I shall devote myself entirely to restoring House Severus to its rightful place at the fore of the Senate and in the hearts of the People. Maledicite domui Valerii!

Titus Severus Regulus

He sighed and put the letter back on the desk. If he did not miss his bet, his elder brother would be joining their father in the grave before the year was out.

He looked around the small room again and shrugged. As a prison, it wasn't bad. It was certainly more comfortable than most of the places he'd slept over the last year. And if Regulus was gracious enough to keep him well supplied with women and wine, they might well need a squadron of knights and all their horses to drag him out.

SEVERA

I want a bath!" Severa shouted as she banged angrily on the wooden
door that held her imprisoned. For three days, she'd been held in this
new location, which as far as she had been able to tell while being
transported, was still within the walls of Amorr. The room in which she
was being held was comfortable enough, with a rug over the wooden floor
and plenty of blankets on a big, soft bed to keep her warm. Three windows,
all small, barred, and high above her head kept the air fresh, and although
the ignominy of being forced to use a night bucket infuriated her, at least
her captors came promptly to replace it as soon as she'd made use of it and
demanded a clean one.

They fed her simply, but well. Nothing more than cheese, bread, fruit,
and a little wine, but the quality was every bit as good as that to which she
was accustomed in the Valerian household. Whether it was the height of
the chamber or the well-polished and unscratched condition of the floors,
she did not know, but she had the sense that she was being held in a manor
house or possibly a wealthy nunnery.

However, three days was far too long for any Amorran noblewoman to
go without a bath, and Severa was more fastidious than most.

"I said I want a bath," she shouted again.

She waited, expectantly, to hear footsteps outside the door. In the meantime, she could hear birds chirping, leaves rustling, and the indeterminate
sounds of people passing by and talking in the distance, which was why
she was fairly certain she was being held in an urban environment. Despite
the windows, she hadn't bothered shouting for help, as it was evident that
no one outside was near enough to be able to hear her, and she knew her
captors wouldn't hesitate to gag her if they felt it necessary.

Finally, she could hear the footsteps for which she'd been waiting. Two women, if she judged rightly. The locking bar was moved, the door creaked open, and she congratulated herself at the sight of two servant-women, both dressed in unassuming white shifts that told her nothing about whom they served. She was surprised, however, when they bowed to her, and the one on the right held up a piece of black silk.

"The goddess is pleased to grant your wish, Lady Valerius. You shall have your bath. However, we are to escort you and you must wear this until you return to this room. If you seek to remove it, we will be forced to bind your hands."

Severa laughed, a little mordantly, and shrugged her shoulders. Better the silk blindfold than the burlap sack. She turned around compliantly to make it easier for the woman to tie the silk around her head.

"Thank you, Lady Valerius."

One of the women took her arm and led her out of the chamber and down a stone-floored corridor, although Severa lost track of where she was after the third turn. She could feel the warm heat and sense the wet air of the calidarium before she even stepped upon the marble flooring of the room, and it was with great relief that she allowed her escorts to disrobe her before they helped her carefully step down into the steaming hot water. It was a small, rectangular bath with room for no more than eight people, which suggested that she was in a manor house rather than a commune of some kind. It was sheer ecstasy as she felt the filth and grime that had encrusted her wash away from her body, and it was hard to resist the urge to plunge her face into the water in order to be completely engulfed by it.

She heard a pair of dresses drop to the floor, followed by her escorts joining her in the bath. She couldn't help emitting a moan of pleasure when one of them began scrubbing her back with a sponge, and quite cheerfully submitted to their ministrations.

"If I cover my eyes with my hands, may I put my face in the water too?" she asked in as humble a voice as she could manage.

"There's nothing to see in here," one of the women said to the other. A moment later, the blindfold was removed, and Severa glanced quickly around the calidarium before she plunged her head entirely underneath the surface, reveling in the sensation of the water penetrating her curly masses to the scalp. But aside from the walls being made of the same marble as the floors and a brazier burning incense that she had already smelled, she learned nothing useful from that momentary glimpse.

One of the women began running her long fingers through Severa's hair, working out the tangles with gentle expertise, as Severa dutifully held her hands over her eyes. Only when she heard soft footsteps pattering across the wet marble and heard a soft male voice murmuring something about oils did she dare to risk moving her hands aside for a second quick peek. So startled was she by what, or rather, by whom she saw that she couldn't quite stifle a gasp. To conceal her reaction, she plunged her head back under the hot water, wondering if she could possibly have seen who she thought she'd seen.

If she wasn't seeing things, the young blond man wearing the white robe of a house slave actually belonged to her husband. If it wasn't Marcipor, it was someone whose resemblance to him was uncanny. She surfaced again, hoping she'd have the chance to take a second look at him. But it proved to be unnecessary, as he politely addressed her two escorts.

"The oils are on the labrum. Will you be requiring anything else, ladies? Perhaps some wine in the cubarium?"

Severa thought she detected a flirtatious note in the hasty denials of her escorts' voices. That gave her all the confirmation she needed; Marcipor always had that effect on women, patrician, plebian, or slave. But he was a little wordy for a mere bath slave. Perhaps he was hoping for a sign from her?

"Some mulsum would be nice," Severa said, holding her hands firmly over her eyes so as not to attract suspicion.

"I shall return with it soon," Marcipor replied easily. "Certainly before nightfall, ladies."

As her two escorts tittered, no doubt in response to Marcipor winking suggestively at one or both of them, Severa's heart leaped at the prospects of her rescue. Her kidnappers hadn't harmed her in nearly four days, surely she could survive another few hours before sunset! And hadn't the witch—Venfica was her name, she suddenly recalled, Idemeta Venfica—hadn't Venfica told her they were after her child? If that were true, then she was in no danger whatsoever!

If Marcipor was here, then Sextus had to be near! And he would not permit the goddess or anyone else to harm her!

"Shall we go to the cubarium," she asked her escorts, a little less humbly than before.

After an application of oils that felt like an eternity in paradise after being left to languish in her own filth for so long, Severa was provided with a plain white dress and her ear was repierced with a silver earring to replace the one she'd stopped wearing. Severa accepted it without protest. Maiden, but soon Mother, she reminded herself grimly, biting her lip against the brief, but biting pain. Sextus would be coming soon, of that she was certain, but she needed to make sure she was alive to greet him. And, she thought as she caressed the barely perceptible swelling of her belly, she needed to defend their child. Against the Moon, against the goddess, and if necessary, against the world.

She was still forced to wear the blindfold, but the darkness held no terrors for her now. He is coming, he is coming! Her lips moved unconsciously as she repeated the comforting thought over and over to herself. She could still see him standing on the sands of the Coliseum, holding his sword high, shouting back at the roaring crowd like a lion standing before a pack of worshipful jackals! No goddess, no Moon Sisters, could hope to stand before her tall young husband's wrath. Once she had despised the martial strutting of House Valerius as gauche, even primitive. Now, she fairly exulted in it; it was like a wall standing between her and utter despair.

Unless, she thought with sudden horror, unless Marcipor was truly one of them! The witch had once told her that the followers of Saint Malachus were everywhere; there were servants of House Severus in their number, why not the slaves of House Valerius as well? She stumbled, as for a moment, her courage abandoned her, and it was all she could do to keep herself from crying out. No! No, she told herself. Sextus's slave was too proud, too sure of himself, too open to the world, to be drawn to a cult. He was a creature of the day, of high noon, not a creeper in the night. And what did the quiet Sisters of the Moon have to offer him that he could not pluck at will in the noble houses of Amorr?

They entered a room and her escorts, one on either side, stopped. She could hear and feel them kneel beside her.

"Lune lunae vivimus
"Per cor Lunae, sanguinem
"Per lunae tenebras morimur.
"Per virginem, per matrem, per cronam, benedicta dea."

"*Benedictus et ter benedictus.* You may remove her blindfold," replied a voice that was, despite the circumstances, distressingly familiar. She felt a pair of hands gently untie the black silk and the pressure on her eyes disappeared. She opened them and saw standing before her a small, round woman in her sixties with grey-streaked hair, deeply-lined bronze skin, and dark, piercing eyes that she recalled very well.

"Quinta Jul!"

Her former slave, or at least, the woman she thought had been her former slave, smiled at her.

"My lady Severa. I am so pleased to see you!"

Severa raised her hand to her breast. She was blinking rapidly and finding it hard to breathe. "Is it... it can't be... did you do this to me!"

"Do what, precisely?" The older lady was still smiling. "Congratulations on your wedding. And, of course, on the child. He is more important than you can possibly know."

"Kidnap me! Attack my sister-in-law! And locking me up to live in my own filth for a week!"

"So dramatic, my dear Severa! Always so dramatic!" The woman reached out and took both of Severa's hands in her own. "I did order you brought here. Carvilia Valerius was unharmed, and although I know you may not realize this, being as high-born as you are, but going without a bath and wearing the same clothes for three straight days has never proven fatal to anyone. Ever."

Whether it was Quinta Jul's apparent amusement or her complete lack of repentance in the face of Severa's accusations, Severa didn't know, but she began to understand that whatever else this woman was, she simply wasn't her slave anymore. Anger and a haughty attitude, she realized, would accomplish less than nothing. So, she growled low in her throat, forced herself to smile, and did her best to speak in a more pleasant voice.

"Are you the one they call the goddess."

"I am." Quinta Jul admitted.

"And are you a goddess?"

"That's a more difficult question, my lady. In several senses, yes, I am. In others, I would not say so."

"But you're not human?"

"No, my dear, that I am not. I have lived a very, very long time. I am not only older than House Severus, I am older than Amorr itself."

Severa blinked. The woman sounded completely serious, but what she was saying was more than just impossible, it was insane. Play along, she reminded herself. Just play along. Sextus is coming! Soon he would come to rescue her and it would all be over!

She just wished she knew how long it would be before nightfall, and wondered if she dared to ask Quinta Jul. Better not, she decided. She didn't want to make her former slave suspicious.

"You know me well enough to know I don't believe you, Quinta. Or shall I call you Goddess?"

"I see no reason why we shouldn't speak to each other as we did before, my lady. And I don't expect you to believe me yet. But you will by the time I need you to do so."

"And when is that?"

Quinta Jul stretched out a hand and placed it on Severa's stomach. "I'd say in about five months, give or take a week."

Severa repressed her rage. "Wouldn't a goddess know the precise date?"

"That's one of the senses in which I'm clearly not, Severa."

"Well, it would have been nice to know. So, you're planning on holding me captive until then? I assume you know my family is looking for me. Probably both my families by now."

"They won't find you. You know Amorr is descending into a war in which tens of thousands will die, and you will not be safe here. And you need to bear your child somewhere else, if more wars, and more death, are to be prevented. I know it sounds impossible, but once I explain it to you, I believe you will not hesitate to do what I am asking you to do."

"Never!"

The goddess, or whatever she was, smiled sadly. "I have not yet explained anything to you. Will you permit me to tell you a story?"

"Why not? It seems I'm not going anywhere anytime soon."

"Then let us sit down. Let me tell you something that very, very few have ever had the privilege of knowing."

And so Severa listened as what looked like her former slave, but was actually an ancient goddess from a long-dead race, told her of a time before Elf, before Man, before Mer, before Dwarf, Orc, and Goblin. She told her of the terrible wars between the kings of that cruel people, and the cataclysms that had led, over time, to the appearance of the Younger Races, and eventually, their rise. Severa listened, rapt with fascination, as Quinta Jul told how the elves and their terrible magics had defeated those they once worshipped as gods, and how defeated, those gods chose to abandon their world.

But what began as an epic tale of ancient history unexpectedly became an intimate recounting of pain, sorrow, and never-ending tragedy. Each of those who chose to stay behind had a different reason for doing so. For her, it had been a broken heart. For another, it had been pride. For a third, it had been pure spite. And always, over the centuries, over the millennia, the door between worlds remained closed.

Until one day, it opened, and an envoy from their long-absent fellows came through it. He bore news that was welcome to some of those who had stayed behind and abhorrent to others. Their people, or at least a significant portion of them, would be coming back. But one of the strongest of those who was not pleased by the news was bold enough to take action. He slew the envoy and sealed the door inside a stone with great and powerful spells. The door between worlds could no longer be opened from the other side, and it could only be opened from this side once every three centuries if the stone and the spells in which it had been encased could be broken.

Thus began the war of the demigods. Each time the *diebus lapis* approached, the opposing factions among the *reliquiae* would attempt to take control of the doorstone using a variety of alliances and approaches, most of which involved the manipulation of the younger and more innocent races. New religions were formed, demonic new races were created, kingdoms thrown down and empires raised up in their place, always in service to the struggle between the ancient ones for access to the stone. What had begun with a simple confrontation between two godlike beings transformed over time into a ceaseless cycle of war of all against all, as first one side, then the other, would gain the advantage, only to lose it before the next opportunity presented itself.

The one thing that never changed was the doorstone. Despite the best efforts of the *reliquiae* who sought to break the spell and open it, it remained closed. Despite the best efforts of those who sought to destroy it once and for all, it survived intact.

The current cycle had begun ten years ago. Quinta Jul's faction, which was the more extreme of the two factions that wished to keep the door between world's shut, had planned to make use of Amorr's mighty legions to defend the stone from any army that might be raised to take it. With Moon Sisters and secret votives of Saint Malachus in every House Martial and most of the more important minor Houses, she'd been in a position to influence the Senate's policy in any direction desired, if necessary. What she hadn't anticipated, however, was that one of the opposing *reliquiae ex antiquis* might circumvent her decades of preparation by virtue of a direct intervention through the Church.

"The sanctiff who died in fire with Sextus's uncle was one of you?" Severa was incredulous. The tale was so extraordinary, so beyond all of her imagining, that she almost forgot she was a prisoner."

"He was."

"Was he behind my father's assassination and my father-in-law's rebellion?" A dark thought struck her. "Or was it you?"

"It was none of our doing." Quinta Jul smiled sadly. "We influence events, Severa. We don't control them. We are too few, and there are too many parties involved. You would not believe the number of times that the vagaries of Man, or Elf, or Orc, have disrupted well-laid plans that were centuries in the making."

"And what does my child have to do with any of this?"

"Your child is the key to ending this terrible cycle of bloodshed and war. To break the spell and shatter the stone requires the blood of kings, and it flows in him from his mother and his father."

"I'm having a boy?" Severa barely heard anything else. She placed a hand over her stomach, over her child, over her little boy. Sextus would be so pleased to know his firstborn would be a son! "My God, I'm having a little boy!"

"You are."

"Then you must be truly mad to think I will give him to you. Even if you are telling me nothing but the truth, what do I care about your stupid stone, or ending your endless wars? Amorr is a city built on war! House Valerius isn't just a House Martial, it is the House of War! Do you know what the Valerians love to say? 'War is the air we breathe and blood is the water in which we swim!'"

Quinta Jul shook her head and sighed. "You humans are so simple and single-minded. Your son, he will be a Valerius, and therefore, most likely a warrior."

"He will," said Severa proudly.

"And so, when he comes to manhood, he will serve in the legions and go to war with them?"

"He will walk the *Cursus Honorem* like his father and his father's father. He will serve as a tribune, and eventually, as a legate."

"And so you know there is a chance that he might fall in battle."

"There is a chance, yes."

"And if he falls in battle, what will his death have accomplished? What purpose will it have served? Who will benefit by it?"

"He will have served his House and the Senate and People of Amorr." Severa paused. She thought she'd heard something in the distance that might have been the ring of metal on metal. Was that a muffled cry of pain. "What higher purpose is there for a man."

"Don't you see, Severa? Even if your son lives to a great age, even if he proves to be an exemplary Valerian, a greater and more successful general than his grandfather Magnus, he cannot accomplish one-half, one-tenth, one-one-hundredth of what he will do for the race of Man, the race of Elf, even the races of Dwarf, Orc, Goblin and Troll, by sealing the doorstone!"

"Find another king. Make your appeal to him."

"It must be a child! The nature of the spell protecting the stone demands it!"

"Then make it to his mother." Yes, she thought. That was most definitely someone screaming. Her confidence growing, Severa shrugged indifferently. "That's your problem, Quinta Jul, or whatever your true name is. I will never, ever, give you my son."

The other woman's eyes flared inhumanly gold and for just a moment her pupils seemed to simultaneously narrow and expand into a reptilian line. "This will not be the last time I ask you, my lady. You have months to go, and I will do my best to convince you. But rest assured, if I cannot, I will do what needs to be done!"

"No, you won't."

"You sound remarkably self-assured for a woman who was crying about being forced to live in her own filth for a few days."

Severa pushed herself up to her feet and smiled scornfully at the thing that had once feigned to serve her. "Do you hear that sound, goddess? Doesn't it ring as sweetly in your ear as it does in mine? Do you not know it? Then let me tell you! It is the sound of your servants dying on the swords of my husband and his men!"

Quinta Jul blinked, taken aback by her unexpected defiance. She cocked her head, and now that they were both silent, the sounds of violent struggle and combat could clearly be heard. She leaped to her feet as easily as a cat, her agility belying her apparent age, and glared at Severa in frustration. She snarled and made as if to grab Severa with her wiry hands, but she retreated when Sextus Valerius burst through the doorway, in full legionary armor except for his helm, and with blood splashed on his face like a barbarian's warpaint. He bore no shield, but his gladius dripped red splotches on the white marble floor.

"Severa!" he cried with heartfelt relief. "You are alive!"

He put his free arm protectively around her shoulder. She pointed. "This woman took me captive. She wants to kill our son."

Severa felt, rather than saw, her husband move. He didn't even let her go, he simply shifted his stance and snapped his hip as he brought his sword up and drove it right under Quinta Jul's breasts, so fast and hard that she saw a spray of blood accompanying the blade that erupted from her back. The goddess fell back, choking, and wine-dark liquid gushed from her mouth as she dropped to one knee, her weight supported by the sword in Sextus's hand.

"A son?" Sextus said incredulously.

Severa reached up and lovingly wiped some of the blood away from her husband's wide-eyed face. None of it was his. He was so beautiful in his savagery, like a hawk striking its prey with unrestrained violence. "He will be a warrior, Sextus Valerius. Like his father and his father's father before him."

"He will need to be," spat Quinta Jul from her bloody mouth. She placed both hands on the sword hilt and used its leverage to help her regain her feet. "He will need to be a warrior if you will not give him to me."

Sextus pulled Severa behind him and kicked the witch-goddess in the stomach with all the strength in his leg as he jerked his sword out of her body. Quinta Jul stumbled backward with the force of his kick, and before she could regain her balance, he was on her again, stabbing her in the throat and in the shoulder and in the heart. He drew the gladius back with both hands, as if to try decapitating her despite its dull edges, when the mistress of the Moon Daughters finally fell in front of the massive fireplace, bleeding copiously from her terrible wounds.

"What was that?" he exclaimed, staring at the woman's bloody corpse. "Even orcs don't go down that hard! What is she, part dwarf?"

"Leave her, Sextus," Severa urged him, as she clutched at his left arm. "Just leave her, she's dead, let's go home!"

She managed to get him turned around, but when she glanced back at the corpse to reassure herself that the cult's goddess was dead, she gasped. The woman's body was gone, and something long, thin, silvery, and scaled was disappearing up the chimney of the fireplace. Only her bloodied clothes remained behind. Alarmed by her reaction, Sextus shoved her back and stood in a combative crouch, the tip of his bloody sword moving slowly side-to-side, as he warily edged toward the fireplace.

He whirled around again at the sound of approaching footsteps behind them. Two legionaries Severa recognized as his men from his recent command entered the room. Their swords were sheathed and their manner was relaxed, but the blood on their armor belied their apparent ease. The shorter of the two soldiers saluted Sextus and addressed him.

"Sir, we've searched the entire house. There were no other captives."

"Prisoners?"

"None taken, sir." The soldier almost sounded as if the question offended him. "Shall we dispose of the bodies?"

"No, leave it to the vigiles. But write up a report for their praefectus. If he gets called before the Consul Civitas about this, he won't appreciate being left in the dark."

"Yessir!" The legionary looked from Sextus's sword to the bloody clothes near the fireplace. "Anyone in here besides Lady Valerius?"

Sextus's eyes looked a little wild, so Severa spoke up before he could reply. "Just me, soldier. And please, I have a rule. Any of my husband's men who save me from our enemies must henceforth address me as Severa."

The soldier nodded and returned her smile. "Sutorius Sejanus, at your service, Lady Severa. We're glad to find you well. Sir."

Sejanus and his fellow departed without asking further questions, and Severa exhaled with relief. Her husband, however, was staring at the rumpled clothes again.

"Severa?" His voice was a little higher-pitched than usual.

"Yes, my love?"

"I seem to recall putting my gladius through a woman just a moment ago. That did happen, did it not? It wasn't some sort of illusion or anything like that?"

"No, she was no illusion. I think she was a witch," Severa sighed, put her arms around her husband's waist, and laid her face against the cool iron of his armored back. "A very evil witch who devours children. But she's gone, because you came for me, just like I knew you would. You saved me, Sextus. And you saved our son."

Some day, she thought, she would tell him the truth, or at least what she had been told. Some day, when there was at least a fragment of a chance that he might possibly believe her. A little. But today was not that day.

"Our son," he repeated, even more stunned by that than by the disappearance of the witch's corpse. "We're going to have a son!"

"That's what she told me, anyhow. I suppose we'll learn if she was telling me the truth or not next spring." She took his hand and squeezed it. "But Sextus, however did you find me? Was that really Marcipor I saw in the bath?"

"Given all the tensions in the city and the hate for our House since my father lost his mind, I thought it would be wise to have someone follow you whenever you were out and about. So I set him to it a few months ago, and fortunately, he wasn't too distracted by chasing girls in the market to follow you and Carvilia to that little church near the bridge." He led her out of the room and down a high-ceilinged corridor. She winced at the sight of two young women lying dead in the halls, but then, she had warned her captors that her husband would show them no mercy.

"No prisoners?" she said.

"No prisoners." He looked at her and she saw the depth of fear and pain in his eyes. "I didn't know in what state we'd find you. Until Marcipor showed up the next day, I was nearly out of my mind. Carvilia kept blaming herself, Potitus had to step in and stop Galerus from whipping the slaves to death—"

"He whipped them? Sextus, they defended us bravely!"

Sextus snorted as he guided her around a dead man with blood staining his grey hair. "Bravely, perhaps, but not well. Shed no tears for them, my dear, they earned their punishment. If you want to do something for them, you may ask them to escort you again once they heal. And you should know that both of them begged to come with me today."

"I'm glad Carvilia was unhurt."

"Yes, that's what gave us hope that the attack wasn't political and they wouldn't kill you out of hand." He looked away from her as someone in a white robe moved toward them.

"Ah, Marcipor! Good to see no one stabbed you by mistake."

Her husband's body slave ignored his master and took her hands in his own much larger ones. "My Lady Severa! I am so very sorry I could not come to your aid when they grabbed you at the wagon! But your husband gave me very strict orders not to intervene unless they were trying to harm you."

Severa, a little surprised, looked askance at her husband, but Sextus was unapologetic. "Not much point in scouts who get themselves killed before they can report anything, darling."

"And I'm not much of a fighter," Marcipor admitted. "So I followed them to the first place they took you, only to learn they moved you after I returned to tell Sextus where you were."

"Then how did you find me?"

"I had to make a new friend at the first house." He shrugged. "It took a little longer to get her to talk than I anticipated. Either I'm losing my touch or I'm getting too old."

Severa reached out to him and took his hand. The handsome slave smiled at her quizzically, and she returned the smile.

"Never change, my dear friend. Never change!"

Marcipor winked at her, threw a mock salute at her husband, then took his leave of them. Sextus held her tightly by the hand as they made their way out of the mansion.

"Do you know why they took you? Marcipor said he thought it was some sort of religious cult. I didn't believe him at first, but after seeing that witch, I don't know what to believe!"

"I'll tell you everything I know," Severa promised him, wincing a little at the thought of confessing her past foolishness to him, but she knew he would need to be told why the Moon Daughters had come for her. "But not right now. And I think your brothers are going to need to hear about this too. Probably the consuls as well."

"The consuls?" Sextus goggled at her. "Is it that serious?"

"I think it will explain a lot of the strange things that have happened in the last year. And some of the strange things that are still to come."

Sextus didn't say anything, he merely shook his head and whistled. Hand in hand, surrounded by Valerian soldiers, they made their way through the streets of the city to the domus she now called home.

THEUDERIC

THEUDERIC watched, his eyes narrowed, as the goblins who'd advanced near the foot of the hill on which he stood suddenly began to throw down their bows and rush en masse toward the Amorran lines above them. What had, until moments ago, been a cowering mass of archers loosing ineffective volleys at the iron-armored legionaries, was suddenly transformed into a horde of small, yellow-skinned berserkers, charging fearlessly toward the soldiers who waited for them behind rectangular shields fixed firmly into the ground. Even from a distance of several hundred *pied du roi*, he could hear the way their unintelligible shrieks had gone from fearful screams to furious howls of unchecked rage.

"Looks like those shamans cast some sort of spell on them," observed Maussart.

"Indeed," Theuderic said, resisting the urge to caustically reprove the younger mage for pointing out the obvious. "Can you identify the spell?"

"I don't know of anything that'll affect a whole damn regiment!"

"Watch your tongue! We're royal mages, not common soldiers!"

"My apologies." Maussart had the decency to look abashed. "I don't know the spell, and I've never seen anything like it."

"That's because this is your first deployment to the borderlands. It's a mass affect spell, which in this case inflames the targeted group by converting their natural emotion, which in this case is fear, into murderous anger." He pointed at the goblins rushing madly toward the Amorran lines. They did not slow their charge, not even when, at the centurions' shouted orders, the first line of Amorrans hurled their spears into them to bloody effect. At least thirty goblins fell, transfixed by the iron-tipped wooden shafts, but their demise did not slow their screaming fellows in the slightest. "See! The effects of the spell are so strong that they've lost all sense of self-preservation."

"Dear God, they're like animals!"

The two mages watched impassively as the first goblins reached the Amorrans and hurled themselves at the soldiers. Most of them were impaled or struck down at once on the Amorran short swords, while a few failed to jump high enough and bounced comically off the iron shields that served as an effective barrier against the shorter creatures. Even fewer managed to clear the shields and avoid being stabbed, and they stabbed and scrabbled at the unprotected faces of their victims with mad abandon. None survived long, but several Amorrans fell writhing to the ground, covering their bleeding faces and crying out in pain.

"Can you dispel it, Lord Theuderic?"

"I'm afraid not. If I could see the shaman who served as the locus for the spell, I might be able to disrupt it, but it's very difficult to dispel something that one can't cast oneself." He smiled at the other mage's dismay. "However, I have an idea there is someone who can. Maussart, go and fetch the priest, the dark-haired one called Emil."

"At once, monseigneur!"

As the young mage rushed off toward the catapults, Theuderic looked past the engagement below to see if there was anything interesting taking shape in the throng of waiting formations behind the engaged goblins. His eye was naturally drawn to the largest concentration of banners, a collection of crude wood-and-leather constructions in various colors that he knew represented various warbands. The Amorran artillery was steadily raining missiles at the banners, presumably under the assumption that many of the warband leaders were gathered around them. To the left of the orcs were the goblin cavalry, a shifting grey mass of wolves and their riders. To his right, he could only see a large mass of heavy orc infantry, which suggested that the orc general's boars were positioned on the orc left to attack their weakest wing. He winced at the thought of Baron Courtemin's pikemen trying to stand up to a charge of the vicious beasts, and hoped the baron was astute enough to recognize his danger and send out his heavy cavalry against the boars before it was too late.

Of course he would, Theuderic reassured himself. Courtemin was a lifelong borderlord, and he had probably forgotten more about fighting orcs than Theuderic had ever known. And if there was one thing that he'd learned while riding the border, it was that orcs never began an attack with their best.

He grinned, remembering the advice of a gruff old ranger who had commanded his first patrol. "Never lead with your rear against the orc, mageling. Always keep your best shot in reserve." The boars wouldn't ride until the baron's motley force of half-trained militia and untrained peasants had been repeatedly tested by their lessers.

A shifting movement below him to his right caught his eye, and he saw the front lines of the wolfriders beginning to move forward. At first, he thought they might merely be altering their formation, but as the rest of the giant formation began to take shape and advance, he realized that the second stage of the orcs' attack had begun. A loud horn from the top of the hill indicated that Marcus had seen it as well, and was preparing his response. Now, where was that cursed priest!

He was just about to run up toward the catapults himself when he saw Maussart rushing down the slope with the tall priest behind him. The priest, somewhat to his surprise, was wearing a chain mail hauberk, over which he wore a white tunic and a bright yellow cape. He even wore an Amorran shortsword strapped to his hip.

"Sorry, monseigneur. It took me some time to find him."

"We were at prayer," the priest explained. "What do you want of me?"

"Do you see those goblins attacking the men below us?" Theuderic pointed. The savagery of the yellowskins remained unabated, but thanks to their armor and their position on the high ground, the legionaries were holding the creatures off without difficulty and with very light losses.

"Yes, of course." The priest pointed toward the mob of wolves, which was beginning to pick up speed. "What about them?"

"Ignore them for the nonce." Theuderic was secretly impressed that the religious had noticed the goblin cavalry, but then, his had been a military order. "We need to scatter the bespelled creatures before the wolves can ride up on them while they're engaged. Can you sense the spell?"

The priest made a sign on his chest and closed his eyes. A moment later, he opened them. "I can feel it. I can sense... the foulness."

"Can you kill it, erase it the way you did to my spells?"

This time, the priest bowed his head and raised his folded hands to his forehead. "I think... I think if we move closer, perhaps, if God wills it."

"Shall we not assume He does?" Theuderic tried not to roll his eyes. "But we can't get too close. There are still arrows flying about, and we don't want a shaman to spot our blue cloaks and target us."

"I can cast a shield spell that will protect the three of us–" Maussart broke off in the face of Theuderic's withering stare. "Ah, right. He'd suppress the shield too."

"Wait," Theuderic called after the priest, who was already marching down the hill. "Let us at least get a shield!"

"No time for that," the priest called back over his shoulder as he pointed at the approaching wolves, who were swinging wide of the legionaries with the obvious intention of taking them in the flank while they were still engaged with the goblins at their front. Theuderic growled low in his throat and held his staff in both hands to prevent it from tripping him up as he ran down the hill in pursuit of the priest.

The closer they got to the fighting, the more horrific the battle sounded. There was nothing human about the bestial shrieks and screams of the goblins, and the steady accompaniment of steel striking flesh was sickening. The legionaries were holding firm, but the insane recklessness of the ensorcelled horde clearly frightened them, if the pitch and intensity of their constant cursing was any guide. Theuderic didn't think the flank attack would break them, as the centurions were already ordering revolutions that would meet the wolfriders with a front at least four lines deep, but the situation was starting to look a little dangerous for such an early stage of the battle.

"Sancte Michael Archangele, defende nos in proelio," the priest was on one knee, praying to his god. Or rather, divine representative, Theuderic corrected himself, remembering that the priest's order was of Saint Michael.

"What are you doing? There's no time for this!" he shouted at the priest, who blithely ignored him.

Maussart grabbed his shoulder. "Leave him be, Monseigneur! It's his ritual, not ours!"

"Imperet illi Deus, supplices deprecamur: tuque, Princeps militiae caelestis, in virtute Dei, in infernum detrude satanam aliosque spiritus malignos, qui ad perditionem animarum pervagantur in mundo. Amen."

"Amen," Maussart echoed.

The priest rose to his feet and shook his head as he glanced back at Theuderic.

"Don't interrupt me again, Kingsmage. In Amorr, we burned your kind."

"I will personally hunt down five witches and hand them over to you for burning if you can break that spell, priest."

The priest smiled wryly and turned back toward the engaged legionaries, pressed his hands together, and raised them to his forehead. A moment later, he turned around again.

"God is great, Kingsmage. Never forget that."

"Is that—" Theuderic nearly choked on his words as the goblin shrieking seemed to redouble in volume, only their voices no longer filled with rage, but with abject terror. He watched, amazed, as the very goblins who just a moment ago had been flinging themselves without restraint against the swords and shields of the embattled legionaries abruptly began to flee. It was if the entire mob simply melted away and began to flow back down the hill, leaving only small dead bodies behind.

He couldn't help being impressed. There had been over a thousand goblins ensorcelled by the spell, which suggested that it had been cast jointly by ten or more shamans. And yet the priest had shattered it almost instantly, and with little more than a gesture and a prayer.

Their blood up, the front lines of the legion began to pursue the retreating enemy, but the sight of the waiting orcs and the approaching wolfriders, combined with the urgent horn blasts and curses of their centurions, reined them in before they were halfway down the hill. As the centurions were restoring order and adjusting the formation to meet the wolves, the tall young tribune who'd been commanding the detachment came running up the hill toward them. Theuderic recognized him, it was Gaius Trebonius, the Amorran who'd been made a Savondese noble by grant of the king.

"Did you do that, you cursed spawn of devils?" He grasped Theuderic's shoulders with both hands. "I could kiss you, you beautiful bastard!"

"Best kiss him, then," Theuderic said, indicating the priest. "God knows how he managed it, for I had naught to do with it."

"Praise God and thank Saint Michael, sir," the priest said humbly. "I am but an instrument."

"Praise God indeed! Now, can you do anything about them?" The tribune pointed to the wolfriders, who were beginning to pick up speed as they approached the bottom of the hill. They appeared to outnumber the three cohorts under Trebonius's command by about four-to-one.

"I fear not, sir. There is no evil spell upon them."

Theuderic glanced at Maussart and winked. "I rather think there will be. Do allow me to take my turn, good father."

"You've done more than enough," the tribune told the priest. "If you will, go to the legatus and see if he can't arrange for one of the reserves to relieve the pressure on us, preferably the horse if he can spare them."

"At once, sir," the priest saluted, legionary-style, and began making his way toward the top of the hill.

"So what can you do for us, magicien?" Trebonius asked. "Tell me quick, I have to get back to my men."

"Tell the men to expect fire. We'll avoid the front lines, but we'll hit their middle and wherever they're far enough from your lines."

"Good. If you can keep them from rounding our flanks, that would be useful."

Theuderic nodded. He liked this young Amorran, who seemed to grasp the utility of battlefield magic much more readily than his general.

"Good luck, sir."

"You too." The tribune nodded at Maussart and began loping down the hill, to where his cohorts were now extended sideways in a wide line facing the approaching wolves, forming the longer part of an L with the shorter base still facing the orcs. The Amorran discipline was, as always, a wonder, but the number and speed of the wolves was such that the formation was in danger of being overridden on its left.

That, Theuderic decided, was where he and Maussart should concentrate their efforts. He eyeballed the range and decided they could afford to fall back about thirty *pied du roi*.

"We have to move," he ordered the younger mage. "But first we're going to cast *Malebranche's Flamme Illusoire*, then *Grandier's Mur du Feu* behind it. Of the two, which do you prefer?"

"*Malebranche*, Maussart answered without hesitation. "Where do you want it?"

"There!" Theuderic pointed to the ground halfway between the lead wolfrider and what had become the new Amorran front line. "Make it quick now! We don't have much time."

As the younger mage raised his staff and began uttering the words of the spell, Theuderic eyed a spot twenty paces nearer the Amorrans and began the incantation required for the genuine incendiary. He wasn't surprised Maussart had chosen the illusion, as it always took less effort to fool the senses than to genuinely alter reality.

"*Qu'ils voient ce que je veux qu'ils voient! Comme je le dis, il doit en être ainsi!*" Maussart completed his spell just before Theuderic finished his own.

"*Allumé!*"

One after the other, two seeming walls of fire erupted on the hillside, sparking immediate terror among wolves, goblins, and men alike. The legionaries fared better, as after their initial shock and instinctive retreat of a few steps, their discipline held despite the heat from the raging fire to their fore and their line was soon restored. The wolfriders on the other hand, were severely disrupted, as the first two or three lines abruptly attempted to sheer off to the left and right, and more than a few of the leading goblins were thrown from their furry mounts as the animals reacted in fear to the illusionary flames. Some wolves lost their footing and rolled as they attempt to turn too sharply, others reared up like horses and fell over backwards to be trampled by the onrushing wolves behind them.

"Follow me," he shouted at Maussart, who was gawking at the confusion in the screaming mass of wolfriders. He knew they had to get farther away from the goblins before they cast their next spells and drew their attention. He could only hope that the orc shamans below were too far away, and too distracted by the Amorran artillery that continued to pound their assumed position, to notice a single pair of magiciens in the chaos. Using their staves as support, they quickly moved further up the hill and far enough away from the goblin flank to let them cast another wall of flame if a detachment should break off and head their way.

The middle ranks of the goblin cavalry continued to drive forward into the confusion at the front, until inevitably, a squadron of wolfriders found themselves pushed into the false fire. For a moment they stood there in shock, wreathed in flames that twisted and leaped about them. And then, upon realizing they were unharmed, they began to shout to the others and gambol about inside the illusory flames, encouraging their fellows to ride through them.

"Drop it," Theuderic told Maussart. "Quickly, break the spell!"

In a trice, the first wall of fire vanished. Maussart lifted his staff, ready to hurl a fireball down the hill, but Theuderic bade him wait. He did not want to risk drawing the enemy's attention until they were fully engaged with the legionaries and distracted.

"Where is the damn cavalry?" he shouted in the general direction of the commander, but he knew the young Amorran general could not hear him. He hoped the center and the right wing were less of a shambles than the battle on this side appeared to be shaping up to be. Then he heard high-pitched screams and panicked howls coming from down the hill.

"Look!" Maussart pointed and laughed.

Theuderic turned back and couldn't help but grin a little mordantly himself. After gathering themselves and shaking off the turmoil of Maussart's illusion, the leading goblins had forced their reluctant wolves directly into the actual fire. The panicked beasts, their fur engulfed in flames, were fleeing blindly in every direction, including into the shields and spears of the waiting legionaries. Once more, the front lines of the goblin cavalry disintegrated, but this time the Amorrans did not stand and watch. A horn blew and the front three lines marched toward the hellish fires, dispatching the wolfriders as they came staggering out of the flames.

"Now!" Theuderic commanded, and he swept his staff across the sky, launching three bright sparks that transformed into burning white fireballs as they arched through the sky. Maussart did the same, and three more fireballs followed as one of the sigils carved on the younger mage's staff momentarily glowed red. The six fireballs descended in two deadly lines in the middle of the grey mass of the goblin cavalry, and detonated as they landed, sending goblins and wolves flying and carving small gouges out of the massive formation.

"Again!" Once more deadly flowers blossomed in the midst of the enemy cavalry. Theuderic knew they wouldn't kill many wolfriders nor would they persuade the goblin captain to break off his attack, but they would disrupt them a little, and give hope to the outnumbered legionaries. Apparently one of the cavalry officers felt the same way, as Theuderic saw a skull-helmed goblin on a big wolf point his sword at them and break from the formation, followed by about thirty riders.

"Think you can manage *Grandier* this time?"

"You've not exhausted yourself already?"

"Don't be absurd. Let's see what you can do."

Maussart eyed the charging wolfriders, who were brandishing their weapons and screaming unintelligibly. "I'm not sure the Grandmagicien would regard this as the proper time for a lesson, Monseigneur."

Theuderic briefly explained, in a manner to which the master of L'Académie des Sage Arts would certainly have taken great offense, that he was not interested in the younger mage's idea about what Grandmagicien D'Arseille's opinion might, or might not, be. His explanation made Maussart laugh, and served as enough of a distraction from the shrieking goblins enough to let him cast the spell without trouble.

"*Allumé!*" Maussart finished with a shout and the wolfriders vanished behind a sheet of flame that leaped higher than the height of a mounted man.

"Well done!" Theuderic praised his young companion. He waited, and watched carefully with his staff at the ready just in case any murderously-inclined wolves might emerge suddenly from the inferno, but it appeared the goblin leading the breakaway squadron recognized that the roaring flames were no illusion. So Theuderic shifted his grip on the staff to invoke a different sigil and hurled three more fireballs above the black smoke rising from the wall of fire, knowing they would land somewhere within the mass of wolves beyond. He expected Maussart to do the same, but when the younger mage didn't follow suit, he glanced over to see him staring pensively at the point where the orc infantry was still being held in reserve, waiting for their turn to advance.

"Those shamans. They're up to something. I can feel it."

Theuderic closed his eyes to shut out the chaos of battle that surrounded them. Almost at once, he could feel it. His skin crawled with the sensation of a powerful array of forces being aimed in their direction. What it was, he did not know, but he was certain it didn't bode well.

"Can you dispel it?"

Theuderic shook his head. It was a collective effort, the swelling power was such that it had to be, but there was nothing coherent behind it that he could hope to disrupt. Perhaps if he could cast *Legendre's Lentille d'Eau* and see the summoners... he suddenly realized what the spell was just as the ground began to shake.

"They're summoning something!"

"Summoning what?"

"I don't know!" Theuderic stumbled as the earth beneath his feet began to shudder and crumble. He had to plant his staff and grip it with both hands to prevent himself from falling over. Maussart was having similar difficulties; he was standing with his legs spread wide and was shifting his weight back and forth in time with the quaking earth. Then Theuderic saw the dirt begin to fly up from the grass in a spinning circle less than twenty paces to his left. As he watched, the soil began to fountain into the air, almost as if the ground itself was vomiting, and he suddenly realized he knew what was being summoned by the orcs.

"Elemental!" he shouted. "They're calling up an earth elemental!"

"Can they do that?"

"*Évidemment!*"

The two battlemages were showered with dirt and clumps of grass as the elemental rose from the earth, waving its massive arms about, roaring, and exposing its stony teeth.

"What should we do?" The cracking of Maussart's voice betrayed his fear.

"How should I know?" Theuderic snapped. He aimed his staff and sent a vicious blast of wind at the thing, but that accomplished nothing except to remove a thin layer of dirt from its upper torso. So much for air, he thought. What about fire?

The force of the fireball igniting against the elemental's chest so close by hurled him to the ground. But when he rolled over and rose to his knees, he saw the magical fire appeared to have done no more than irritate the creature, if that was indeed the right word for such a being.

"I can't dispel it!" Maussart cried in despair.

"Of course you can't!" Theuderic shouted. "It's an elemental, not a golem! It exists in its own right!"

"So banish it?"

"To where? It's a creature of the earth, not the hells!"

"Water!" cried Maussart inexplicably.

"What?"

"Air and fire don't work. Try water!"

"I don't know any water spells!"

That wasn't strictly true, but Theuderic didn't feel he had the time to explain his opinion that sluicing the elemental with even a copious amount of water wasn't going to serve any useful purpose except perhaps to wash a little dirt off its surface. And even if he did know a spell that would produce enough water to turn that much earth and stone into mud, which he didn't, he wasn't convinced that transforming the thing into a mud elemental would render it harmless to the two of them.

The towering creature, which was half again the height of a man, tried to stomp on him, but he rolled sideways to avoid the giant earthen foot. It wasn't quick, but its power was tremendous, as the ground shook under its ponderous steps. Up close, what passed for its flesh looked more like clay than proper dirt, although here and there he could see stones embedded in it. It had no eyes, and just a wedge in the place of a nose, but somehow it was still able to sense the two of them. With Theuderic having evaded it, it turned toward Maussart and swiped at him with a massive fingerless hand that resembled the square foundation of a pillar.

The younger mage was nimble enough to duck under the blow that would have crushed him, and even had the presence of mind to invoke a sigil that sent balefire streaming from the iron-tipped end of his staff at the thing's knee. This time, the elemental appeared to feel the concentrated flames, as it roared and backed away from Maussart, as a glowing liquid leaked from its superheated joint. It was lava, Theuderic realized, as the stones that were embedded in the clay must have melted. Perhaps they could render it immobile by essentially firing the clay that was its essence as if it were in a kiln. And they didn't need to bake the whole mass, only enough of its knees to render it immobile.

He was about to invoke a similar stream of fire when another thought occurred to him. If sufficient heat could affect the constituent parts of the elemental, then presumably removing the water inside could render it equally unable to harm them. It should have much the same effect as removing all the water from a living being, and he had an excellent spell for that. The only problem was that it wasn't one that could be invoked through any of the sigils on his staff, since it was better suited for leisurely assassinations than active combat.

"Keep it occupied!" he shouted at Maussart. "I have something that might work!"

The younger mage nodded grimly and sent a fiery blast at the elemental's legs before throwing himself backward to avoid another powerful blow at the last second. Theuderic's heart was in his mouth as the huge being tried to crush the prone magicien, but Maussart adroitly rolled to one side and back up to his feet.

Now, how did *du Closneuf's Desiccation Mortelle* go again? The words seemed right on the tip of his tongue, but they would not come, until he remembered that physical contact with the target was necessary. He stared at the broad back of the thing, wondering how he was going to maintain contact long enough for the spell to take effect. Then he let his staff fall to the ground, took a deep breath, and ran at the elemental.

Fortunately, just as he rushed toward it, the inhuman monstrosity bent down to take a swipe at Maussart. Theuderic took advantage of the opportunity to leap as high as he could and half-climb, half-run up its posterior before grasping its huge earthen shoulders with a hand on either side of the blockish head. He dug his fingers as deeply as he could into the reddish-brown clay of the summoned being, and kicked his heels hard enough to embed his boots into its sides. The elemental was too broad for him to get any grip around its torso with his legs, but fortunately, and against his expectations, it didn't seem to feel him or realize he was on its back.

"*Sèches comme des os…*" he began the spell. "*Extraites de chair vos!*"

Although it was unaware of his presence, the elemental was still in pursuit of the elusive Maussart, who was holding its attention by blasting it repeatedly with the air sigil engraved in his staff. Since Maussart was staying clear of the creature's deadly appendages by moving steadily in a circle, Theuderic found it hard to maintain his hold on its back as the lumbering creature turned, and turned again. He gritted his teeth, tried to sink his fingers even deeper into the hard-packed earth of its pseudoflesh, and continued with the spell.

"*L'eau de la vie éphémère…*"

Maussart, alert as ever, realized how he was contributing to Theuderic's difficulties and promptly began retreating straight backward, up the hill and away from the still-crackling wall of flame. Theuderic chanted the words of the spell as rapidly as they came back to him, and fortunately, the recitation of each rhyming couplet served to prompt his memory with the next. Finally, he reached the end.

"*Il faut ma volonté se manifeste. Que pas une seule goutte ne reste!*"

The elemental suddenly stiffened and came to an abrupt halt. A low moan issued from its stony mouth. Under his fingers, Theuderic could feel the clay softening, as his death grip on the thing's shoulders caused them to drive even deeper into the creature's earthen substance, until they were in beyond the second knuckle. He wondered where the water was going, and looked down to see a dark circle of moisture spreading out around the elemental's wide, toeless feet. The water was draining from the summoning back into the ground from which it had come, and with it, apparently, was vanishing the *magie verte* that animated it.

Theuderic closed his eyes and sighed with relief, even as he maintained his grasp. He could feel the elemental literally crumbling in his hands, and as the last vestiges of water drained out of it into the earth, the summoning finally collapsed into nothing more than a mound of extremely dry dirt. He plucked a smooth white stone from the pile that looked as if it might have served as a tooth for good luck, then leaped carefully to the ground. There was still a battle raging below them and it wouldn't do to turn an ankle now.

"What spell was that," demanded Maussart. The younger mage was still breathing hard, but he was clearly awed by the way in which Theuderic had accomplished the complete disintegration of the monster. "You must tell me!"

"It's an old one of du Closneuf's. You'll find it in a few of the older textbooks from two, two-and-a-half centuries ago, when *l'école naturelle* was in vogue. It's usually used on living things, but fortunately, even elementals require an amount of water to sustain themselves." He thought for a moment. "Probably wouldn't work so well on a fire elemental, of course."

"How did you ever happen to learn it?"

"Oh, it's the sort of thing that comes in handy in certain circumstances when you're not in a hurry."

"What sort of circumstances?"

But Theuderic had no intention of telling the younger mage about his arrangement with the royal chancelier. "I think we've done all we can at the moment for the tribune and his men. We should go back and see if the general has any need of us to send a message to the Prince."

"What about the shamans who summoned the elemental?"

"What about them?" Theuderic pointed in their general direction. "There's nothing we can do except hope the artillery cracks a few of their skulls."

"Very well. Do you want me to dispel that?" Maussart indicated the still-burning flames that blocked their view of the battle below them, although they could still hear the clash of metal on metal, the yelps of wolves, and the deathshrieks of their riders. It sounded as if the legionaries had stopped the goblin cavalry in their tracks, despite their tremendous numbers.

"Let it burn. Wait until we get further up the hill and farther away from the fighting."

Theuderic looked over the nearby ground, searching for his staff. He hoped the elemental hadn't stepped on it in all the confusion of the melee, but between the sizable hole in the ground created by the summoning and the way in which the summoned elemental had torn up the grass, he didn't see it anywhere.

"Theuderic!" he heard Maussart shout and the terror in the young man's voice made him whip his head around.

Goblins! It was all he had time to think before hurling himself to the side, narrowly evading a crudely-sharpened lance that would have spitted him had it not been for the warning. He let himself roll down the hill toward the fire and at least ten wolfriders galloped past him, with one wolf very nearly running over him and snapping viciously at his face as it flashed by. He could feel the heat of the magical flames at his back and his staff was nowhere to be found, so he drew his sword, thinking only to kill as many as the wretched creatures as he could before he fell. There must be thirty of them, he thought, and they were only two.

Curse the luck! How was it possible that he, Savondese noble and royal battlemage, had survived a battle with an elemental only to fall to half-naked goblins armed with little more than badly-carved tree branches? A wolfrider came at him and he slipped sideways to avoid the goblin's club while thrusting hard into the wolf's side. The beast went down, spilling its rider, but Theuderic didn't have time to finish off the goblin because two more wolfriders were immediately upon him.

They must have ridden around the fire, he realized, even as he slashed with his blade and took off half a goblin's face. It screamed and dropped the studded club it had been brandishing, but something smashed into Theuderic and he fell to the ground with the fetid breath of a snarling wolf in his face. He grabbed its throat and managed to hold it off, snarling and snapping, for a moment, until the ugly yellow face of its rider suddenly loomed over him. The goblin, its inhuman green eyes sparkling with triumph, grabbed the front of his cape with one clawed hand and raised a rusty dagger with the other.

Theuderic found himself desperately wishing that the legends of the wizard's deathcurse were true. But all he could do was scream in helpless fury as he tried to keep the wolf from tearing out his throat. Then, instead of stabbing him, the goblin suddenly let him go and vanished from his sight. A moment later, the wolf threw its head back, howled in agony, and collapsed heavily onto Theuderic's chest. He lay there for a few seconds, breathing with some difficulty, until the foul stench of the lupine fur in his face and the heat from the nearby fire convinced him that he wasn't actually dead.

As he rolled out from under the body of the dead wolf, he heard the welcome sound of battle. Weapons were clashing, men were grunting with effort and shouting with the senseless rage of slaughter. But it wasn't until the noise was punctuated with some familiar Amorran curses that he understood what had just happened. The dead goblin at his feet was only one of about fifteen that had fallen swiftly to the half-century of Amorran legionaries who had come to his rescue. He located his sword, picked it up, and looked around, hoping the legionaries had arrived in time to save Maussart as well. But his young colleague was nowhere in sight.

"Looking for this, Kingsmage?"

Before him was Father Emil, holding out his missing staff to him. In the priest's other hand, he held a gladius that was dripping with green blood that covered his right arm up to the elbow. In fact, he was half covered in goblin gore; the entire right side of his face looked as if he'd painted it green.

"Holy Mother of God!" The words slipped out as he took the staff. "I thought they were exaggerating when they said you were warrior priests."

"The Order of Saint Michael is a sword in the hand of the Savior's Bride."

"You'll get no argument from me, priest. Have you seen Maussart?"

"Your young companion? He was wounded, but he'll survive. A wolf tore up his forearm a bit, so he'll need to get that cleaned out. Two legionaries already brought him to the medicus."

Theuderic exhaled deeply. That was a relief. He'd known the younger
mage was alive or his *Grandier* spell would have ended, but it was good to
know he wasn't bleeding out somewhere on the hillside.

"What happened? How did you manage to find Marcus Valerius and get
him to give you a detachment in time?"

The priest laughed and wiped ineffectually at his bloodstained face with
his free hand.

"I haven't seen the legate. I was about to come back and see if I could
help you with that magical creature that came out of the ground when I saw
the wolfriders below you looking for a way around the fire. I thought you
and the young man stood a better chance stopping the magic thing than a
cavalry squadron, so I found the nearest centurion and told him to give me
enough men to drive them off."

"You must have been persuasive. I haven't found the Amorrans to be
much inclined to ignore the orders of their superior officers."

"There is no higher authority than God, Kingsmage. Not even a legatus
outranks Him."

Theuderic laughed and mock-bowed with a hand on his chest. He
realized that he rather liked this priest who feared neither mage nor general.

"I should like you to know that I hereby wholeheartedly repent... not
so much of my many sins as for any unflattering thought, or ungenerous
sentiment, I may have harbored about you and your order."

The priest smiled beneath his half-mask of goblin blood and held up his
hand in a gesture of forgiveness. "It's a start, Kingsmage. It is a start."

LUGBOL

LUGBOL glowered at the boar rider, unintimidated despite the way the orc towered over him on the back of his massive mount. Even as he spoke, he crumpled the hastily scribbled scroll in his horny hand. The order from Kral Nekhuru was as obviously stupid as it was straightforward.

"He's wrong. Them turtleshells are not about to crack!"

The rider shrugged, indifferently. "Mebbe so, mebbe not. It ain't my problem, yez got tha word. But yez'll know the Felsig Kral'll skin yez hide and use it for 'iz next warbanner if'n yez don't throw yez kors in there quick!"

Lugbol sighed, knowing the messenger from the Hagahorn king was right. "Yeah, you ain't wrong. Tell the kral I'm on it."

The kor saluted. "Hadvezer!" He kicked the sides of his boar, and with a grunt of complaint, it was off, its massive shoulders sending two banner-kors sprawling to the ground as it went.

"Ghurash!" Lugbol bellowed. The mass of kors behind him stirred, and his galvebel appeared.

"I saw the boar. Bad news?"

"The fazhdak kral wants us to get stuck in."

"On the hill?"

"Yes, on the squagging hill!"

The galvebel pressed his finger to his nose and snotted a nostril. Then he shrugged. "We knew it was coming once them wolfriders came back yelping like pups. Now it's our turn for the grinder."

"So it is. Summon the graborghs and the gran-kors."

Ghurash was right, he thought, as his galvebel pushed his way back through the ranks. A bone grinder it was indeed. Lugbol had no idea how well the battle was progressing on the center or the left wing, but here on the right, the approach to the hill on two sides was fairly littered with the bodies of dead goblins, while the bottom half of the hill itself looked dappled due to the lighter color of the wolf corpses interspersed with those of poorly armored goblins. Five pushes they'd made, twice with the cavalry and three times with the archers, and five times his goblins had been thrown back by the well-armored Kornj'agh, who were proving to be as hard as Lugbol had feared. The hill's defenders had taken casualties too, but not anywhere nearly as many as the goblins, and they'd rotated the regiment that served as their front line three times to keep their kors fresh.

Worse, the Kornj'agh artillery had successfully disrupted the magic spells of the shamans with their relentless, methodical pounding of the positions in the rear that had previously always been safe. The worthless shamans' attempts to stop the artillery barrage through the use of magic had completely failed, and after nearly a third of them had been killed or badly wounded, the lead shaman apologetically informed Lugbol that he was retreating with the survivors outside the range of the deadly missiles. Lugbol didn't try to stop him; he'd nearly been crushed twice by a rock falling from the sky himself, and if the shaman wanted to run the risk of being boiled alive in the blood of his fellow cowards by General Gor-Zug, that was his affair.

His own kors had taken a beating too, although they hadn't been the focus of the artillery's attention, it had been bad enough that he knew some of them would be relieved to be ordered into action. There was nothing worse than standing there in formation, helpless to strike back, while enduring a bombardment that might snuff one's life out without warning. Their discipline made him proud to be their commander, and he prayed to Gor-Gor to somehow give them a way to crush the turtleshells.

"Hadvezer!"

There were four graborghs and eleven gran-kors who'd come at his command. They were mostly Hagahornu, veteran warriors whose scars and tattoos testified to their experience. There was also a kor he hadn't seen before, who wore the tattoo of a grun-kor on his bare left bicep.

"What are you doing here, Grun-kor?" he demanded.

"Dorghul, senior Grun-kor, for the Second Big Vank. Gran-kor Noghur got squished by one o' them rocks they dropped on our heads."

"I knows 'im. I can vouch for 'im," said another gran-kor whose obscene tattoos indicated that he was with the grun-kor's sister unit. "Bhughudul, Gran-kor o' the First Big Vank."

"Good enough for me. Dorghul, you're acting Gran-kor now. Your kors show out hard against those Kornj'agh, I'll see that the Felsig Kral makes it permanent."

"Hadvezer!" the delighted kor saluted crisply as the other officers nodded in approval.

Lugbol was pleased too, but he didn't let it show on his face. His rank and his brand were sufficient to ensure obedience, for now, but dropping a hint that he was in good with Kral Nekhuru should inspire them to drive their kors harder to impress him. And he intended to push them to do exactly that.

"Yez all hard kors. I can see that. This ain't yez first warbang. But the Kornj'agh are hard too, yez all seen what they done to the gobbos. The fashzek Farkh'agh did their best, the shamans even berserked them, and they barely scratched the damn shells on those turtles."

"Theyz best ain't murdu," rumbled one Gran-kor.

"Then show me yez can do better," Lugbol shot back. "Today, we'ze all leading from the front. Starting with me. So, unless any o' yez is hard enough, the Black Fist Infantry takes first crack."

"Hadvezer!" Dorghul, the newly-appointed acting gran-kor, was the first to protest. "Second Big Vank 'spectfully calls first crack!"

"No, First Big Vank is senior," barked the gran-kor who'd vouched for him.

"And Sharp Stone is senior to all o' yez," snarled the biggest and oldest graborgh. His tusks were yellowed and grooved with age, his belly was nearly bursting out from under his breastplate, and a cataract covered one eye. "Widger'spect, Hadvezer, I'm senior here, exceptin' yer own self. Sharp Stoners has earned the right to first crack!"

Lugbol nodded coolly. He wasn't at all averse to not being the first to throw himself, and his lightly-armored kors, on the lethal short swords of the Kornj'agh. For turtles, they sure had a hellish sting. But since he'd threatened to steal the honor of first crack away from the heavy infantry, the Hagahornu grabkors were just about ready to fight each other for the opportunity to be the first to land the killing blow.

"Sharp Stoners get first crack. Second Big Vank follows, while First Big Vank, you sees if you can do a better job o' getting round their side than the Farkhut'agh did. Standard horn signals; yez don't unstick yez kors unless and until yez hears the signal! Yez got it?"

"Hadvezer!" they shouted.

"Who's got it?"

"Dorghul!"

"Bhugudul!"

"Whagren! Whagren gots it!"

As each of the grabkors shouted their names, Lugbol could see how their excitement and aggression were growing. Their hands shook with savage anticipation, and their lips curled back to expose their teeth and gums. He could feel his own battle-lust rising too, but he forced himself to stay calm and resist the urge to rush forth and charge toward the enemy.

"Graborgh, once the advance sounds, get your kors moving fast." He addressed the commander of the Sharp Stoners who had claimed first crack. "The Kornj'agh will target yez with their artillery, and it don't take them long to find their range. The sooner you get stuck in, the sooner you get under their arc."

"Hadvezer!" the old graborgh saluted, his eyes fairly blazing in the deep folds of his age-lined face. Then he spun on his heel and pushed past the other grabkors to return to his unit. Dorghul and Bhugudul followed suit, leaving the rest of the grabkors waiting expectantly.

"You, third," he pointed to the senior graborgh remaining. "You, fourth. You, replace First Big Vank." He quickly ran through the rest of them, leaving two regiments plus his own Black Fists as his reserve. "Now get to your kors and get the moving when you hear the advance."

"Hadvezer!"

As the nine grabkors left in pursuit of their units, Lugbol pointed at the nearby banners, where the hornblowers were stationed.

"Get three of them and bring them with us. We're going to need to keep them with us and we need to spread those banners out before the damned turtleshells start targeting them again."

"Be nice if our stick-wigglers was worth a damn."

"Well, they scrammed, so we got nothing but Gor-Gor and our guts. Let's hope that's enough to do for the turtleshells."

He looked toward the center, but aside from a few distant screams and the occasional sound of an explosive spell detonating on one side or the other, he simply couldn't tell what was happening there or who was winning, let alone on the right. Well, he couldn't worry about any of that now. Once he threw the infantry forward, there would be nothing to protect their left flank if the enemy forced the Great Orc to retreat and leave them exposed. The battered goblin infantry was holding their ground thanks to the whip-kors he'd positioned behind them; so far they were more afraid of the brutal savagery of their own rear guard than they were of the enemy, but whips or no, they would run at the first sight of an attack from the left.

Only Gor-Gor knew where the surviving wolfriders were now. They'd retreated in disarray after the Kornj'agh cavalry rode out from behind the hill to scatter them after their second charge, and although he had some confidence in the ability of the goblin shugaba'agh to gather their dispersed gungiyars, he knew they would be useless for anything but a pursuit after the infantry finally broke and routed the turtleshells.

It would all come down to his kors. And they were no longer sqwaaks, not a single one wore the white paint of the battle virgin across his nose any longer. They were vicious hardened killers, they were well-rested and well-fed on flesh after pillaging the Man village, and they outnumbered the Kornj'agh at least five-to-one. Turtleshells or no turtleshells, his kors would crack them and eat them raw today!

He nodded to Ghurash, whose grim face was set with fierce resolve.

"It's time. Have the hornblowers sound the advance. Let's see what the Sharp Stoners have got."

The mid-day sun was at its height when it became apparent that the time to order the second retreat had come. The Sharp Stoners and their elderly graborgh had done well, certainly much better than the initial waves of goblins, but after initially buckling under the fury of the orc assault, the Kornj'agh line stiffened. It was hard to see how many of the turtleshells had actually fallen, hidden as they were behind their tall shields, but Ghurash said he'd counted at least thirty, although some of them might only have been wounded. Lugbol recalled the Sharp Stone much sooner than he might have, hoping that a second savage thrust might actually break through if it hit quickly enough, but his attempt at piling pressure upon pressure failed due to the swift rotation of the Kornj'agh lines, as the Man general replaced his exhausted front soldiers with fresh ones from the rear.

Despite the desperate exhortations of acting Gran-kor Droghul, the Second Big Vank's courage failed them when the two new lines of men at the front met the orc charge with a brutal volley of spears hurled at close range, and Lugbol suspected that without the heroics of Droghul, the entire regiment might have run. But the young korgrab, despite having lost his weapon, heroically threw himself on the black shields of the Kornj'agh, ripped off a man's head with his bare hands held it aloft, roaring with savage triumph, as he was quickly stabbed to death by at least four vengeful soldiers. Their hearts inspired by the heroic death of their commander, the Second

Big Vank attacked with renewed fervor, but the impetus had been lost, the Kornj'agh were fresh, and their discipline was as iron-hard as their shields.

It was a slaughter.

Lugbol let the butchery continue, watching calmly as one kor after another fell before the swift, biting swords that licked out from behind the giant shields, seemingly harmless, to punch through armor and leave kors staggering away, holding their bellies, with green blood leaking through their hands. Sometimes, one couldn't even see the short blades, and the only sign was when a kor suddenly fell to the ground, mortally wounded, with blood erupting from his throat or an eye. He was hoping that the First Big Vank would arrive on the enemy flank in time to help their sister regiment break through, but before they could even come close to the raging infantry battle, a tornado of sorcerous fire came out of nowhere and engulfed Bughudul, the gran-kor commanding the regiment. As he shrieked and flailed his arms in agony, finally falling to the ground and flopping around screaming like a river mer that had leaped off the barbecue, his horrified kors came to a halt. Shocked by his unexpected death and the horrific manner of his demise, they were easy prey for the Kornj'agh cavalry, which rode out on their tall horses and drove them off while seizing their warbanner. It was a feeble performance, truly embarrassing, and Lugbol decided that if neither General Gor-Zug nor King Nekhuru ordered the regiment decimated, he'd do it himself.

If he survived the day. And that was a matter that was very far from settled.

The Second Big Vank had visibly shrunk, but they were still pressing hard against the turtleshell line despite having lost perhaps a third of their number. They'd showed well, and Lugbol regretted the loss of their bold young commander, but it was no use wasting more brave kors to no avail.

"Call 'em back," he told Ghurash. As his galvebel conveyed his order, he tugged at the straps of the unfamiliar and ill-fitting breastplate he'd found in the Man town, then swung his scarred sword around a few times, loosening his muscles. He turned to face the line of kors behind him, and he was pleased to see that although they were tense and grim-faced, there was no fear in their eyes. The front two lines were comprised of his biggest, best-armored kors, each of them bearing a shield, and behind them were three rows of kors armed with a spear, but no shield. He hoped that by presenting the Kornj'agh shield wall with their own shield wall, enough of them would to survive the initial volley and let the kors behind get their longer-reaching weapons past the enemy shields.

He nodded at a few familiar faces, pointed at a few more, and did his best to show his confidence in them before drawing his cleaver and holding it high.

"Black Fist!" he shouted at them.

"Black Fist!" they shouted back.

"You're the best in the whole damn army!"

And they were, they really were, he thought proudly. Maybe they were smaller, maybe they were lighter, and maybe they didn't have all that much in the way of armor or weapons, but Lugbol would be damned if he wouldn't bet on them against the fashzek Red Claw Slayers themselves!

"Let's go squag us some turtles!"

With his fired-up kors roaring like rabid trollkillers, Lugbol spun around, and without waiting for the horns to sound, began marching forward, toward the hill, and toward the deadly black shields that awaited them all. Ghurash caught up with him just as the horns sounded the retreat, and he saw the surviving kors of the Second Big Vank immediately start falling back from the terrible Kornj'agh shield wall, leaving their dead behind.

"You might wait for the rest of us, Hadvezer!"

Lugbol didn't break stride. "I hope they're following or we're going to look pretty damned stupid, by Gor-Gor's rancid arse."

"Not for long, we won't." Ghurash's dismal tone made Lugbol laugh.

The bottom of the hill in front of them resembled a green volcano as the retreating kors streamed down it toward them. Behind them, the horns finally blew the advance, and was answered by a great shout that, to Lugbol's relief, sounded as if it came from only a few paces behind them. But he resolutely refused to look back, instead he stared intently at the tall black shields in front and above them. They looked immense, and the tall men behind them, their pale skin all but hidden behind the metal armor that covered most of their faces, looked like implacable demons. All they lacked was the wings of fire that they'd worn in the forest the night that Zlatagh Maneater had fallen.

He had survived that terrible night. And he would survive this day, he promised himself, however terrible it might be. Already, he was forced to begin being careful where he stepped, as he nearly tripped over the body of a disemboweled goblin. A large boulder sitting in a small crater, out from which poked three arms and two pairs of goblin legs, forced him to detour around it. Soon, he could see the retreating kors approaching and he waved them toward his left, urging them to stay out of the way of the Black Fist advance.

"Left! Left!" Ghurash promptly bellowed. "Get out of the fashzek way! Left!"

For the most part, they complied. And, for the most part, the defeated Big Vankers refused to meet his eyes, staring at the ground as they fled ignominiously past him toward the questionable safety of the orc lines. He ignored them in favor of keeping watch on the great catapults at the top of the hill, seeing the artillerists hard at work loading the big rocks and adjusting the range again. He knew it wouldn't be long before the lethal stone rain would be directed at them.

As the number of fallen bodies over which he had to step increased, he came upon the first severely wounded kors who were necessarily retreating more slowly. Some were shambling along, dragging wounded legs or cradling injured arms, others were crawling or even just dragging themselves over the bloody, trampled ground. He did his best to avoid them, even as he ignored their cries for help, and winced as he heard the shrieks as they were trampled by the massed kors behind him. But there was nothing that could be done for them, and indeed, when he saw the first catapult fling its stone burden into the sky, he waved his arm to encourage the kors to speed up into a jog.

"Go! Go! Go!" Ghurash shouted, and the other galvebels took up the cry. Soon he was at the foot of the hill and as he began mounting the slope, flanked now on either side by his best kors, the first thuds behind him, followed by shouts of fury and dismay, told him that their front was, as he'd hoped, already inside their range. Now, for the hard part.

They were barely a spear's throw away from the black shield wall. Seen from up close, and from downslope, the Man-kors looked even taller and more fearsome than they had from afar. He could see the raised runes on their shields, and on their armor. Their elongated white legs were only armored from ankle to knee, and only in the front, and their legs were hairy. Some of them even had hair covering what could be seen of their faces, like dwarves. But their arms were thin and their chests were hollow. They were weak and they could be killed. Of this, he was suddenly certain.

"Black Fist, Black Fist, ubruhl gwaz'ughu!" he shouted, and he began to run up the hill.

"Ubruhl! Ubruhl gwaz'aghu!"

As they rushed toward the shield wall, the eyes of the Kornj'agh narrowed and the line of their shields began to drop. Lugbol immediately stopped, braced himself, and crouched down to put as much of his body behind his round shield as he could.

"Shields up! Shield up!" the galvebels roared as they'd been ordered, and the rest of the kors came to a halt, bringing their shields up and supporting them with both of their muscular arms just as the front lines of the Kornj'agh hurled their strange black-tipped spears. They slammed violently into the mass of orcs with a series of dull thuds, but there were far fewer screams of pain this time as most of them were buried into the metal-lined wood of the shields rather than flesh.

Lugbol grunted as first one spear, then another, hammered into his shield. A third one skidded harmlessly along the blood-slicked grass at his feet. The shield, suddenly heavy, sagged with the weight of the two broken spears, but when he tugged at one shaft and tried to dislodge it, it would not come out. They were designed that way, he realized, to foul an enemy's shield, and force him to drop it. He cursed as he threw the now-useless shield to the ground, then drew his cleaver.

His kors, their shields similarly encumbered, mostly did the same, although one thick-limbed brute simply grabbed both spears and used them as handles, transforming his shield into a crude two-handed flail.

"Ubruhl gwaz'aghu!" Lugbol shouted again, and he leaped upon the waiting foe with his sword raised. But instead of trying to bash his sword against the big shield of the turtleshell in front of him, he swept it down in a feint, knowing that the stubby sword of the Man-kor would thrust out at him in a moment. When it came, he was ready and he stepped aside, then jumped up and gripped the edge of the shield with his left hand, pulling it down and allowing him to jam his own sword right into the open space he'd created.

He fell to the ground and landed on his back with the heavy turtleshield on top of him as the Man-kor dropped to his knees, clutching his chest. Lugbol pushed off the shield, somersaulted backwards to rise to his feet, and raised his dripping sword high.

"They bleed red!" he shouted. "They bleed red!"

A bestial roar from the kors behind him filled him with reckless courage despite the kors who had fallen, wounded or dead, on either side. He saw the big kor with the shield-flail bashing away one, twice, and then again at a black shield, until at the third stroke, the Man-kor behind it cried out and reeled backward with his arm broken. Another turtleshell stepped in to take his place in the line, and this time the kor threw the shield over his head and tugged on the spears, pulling the Kornja stumbling forward. The Man-kor went down to his hands and knees, and he was quickly dispatched by the spears of the Black Fists in the third line.

"Spears!" Lugbol cursed their slow wits. "Get in there and stab them with your spears!"

He rushed forward again, but this time, the Kornja didn't fall for the feint. Instead, he slammed the big iron shield right into Lugbol's face, breaking his noise with a vicious crack. Lugbol shrieked, despite himself, as pain exploded right between his eyes. He swung his sword blindly, but it struck nothing. And, in an instant, without any warning, everything went black.

He opened his eyes. Above him was nothing but blue sky. It was pretty and the sun was warm on his face. He smiled. So it had all just been a very bad dream.

Then red lightning struck him squarely in the head and he groaned as his memories came flooding back to him along with the pain.

He gingerly gripped the bridge of his nose and discovered that it moved.

"No worries, it's mostly straight, Hadvezer," said Ghurash, looming over him. "And you wasn't that pretty anyhow. It ain't like that sweet kwee the Great Orc gifted you likes you for yez face."

"What in the name of Gor-Gor happened?"

"You damned near got yez skull crushed. I saw you went down harder than a stunned goat, so me and Koltogh grabbed you by the arms and dragged you back here."

Lugbol tried to sit up, but the invisible hammer struck him between the eyes again.

"Easy there, Hadvezer. You got yez brains rattled but something good."

"The Black Fists. Are they still stuck in?"

"Nah, the graborgh for the Famine Peak took over when he saw you go down. He pulled us out and sent the Bloodscummers in. Said our kors did real good, killed more Kornj'agh than the first four waves combined." The galvebel brushed a pair of flies away from his left arm, and for the first time Lugbol noticed that Ghurash was wounded too. But when he realized Lugbol was staring at the bleeding gash in his forearm, Ghurash only snorted.

"It ain't nothing. Them stubby swords is sharper than they look, is all. Koltogh got it worse than me, he's gettin' bandaged up by the leeches, but he'll make it."

"Good." Lugbol held out his good arm. "Help me up. Be good to let the kors see me in case we got to get back in there."

"You ain't goin' nowhere," the galvebel promised. "I'll bash yez head again meself if'n you even try." But he gently helped Lugbol to his feet all the same, and steadied him with a sturdy arm when he swayed with sudden nausea. "Look, they're finally fallin' back!"

Lugbol looked, and what he saw on the hill was a welcome sight indeed. The ferocious assault of the Black Fist Infantry had indeed weakened the enemy line, and now it was beginning to retreat up the hill. There was a veritable stream of wounded Man-kors being assisted by their fellows around the back side of the hill, and while reinforcements were marching down to cover the flanks of the retreat, it was obvious that the Kornj'agh were beginning to feel overwhelmed by the weight of the sheer numbers the orcs could bring to bear.

"Hadvezer!"

Lugbol slowly, and carefully, turned around to see who was calling him. He was surprised, and a little alarmed, to see it was one of King Nekhuru's most senior graborghs striding his way. A black-armored kor was holding the reins of his ill-tempered boar, but he was otherwise unaccompanied, so Lugbol assumed he must be a messenger from the Felsig Kral. The graborgh wasn't much taller than Lugbol, but he was nearly twice as wide.

Lugbol grimaced as his head throbbed with pain, but he managed to salute the other korgrab. Technically, he was senior, but the boar rider was almost certainly speaking for the kral. "Graborgh," he managed to get out through gritted teeth.

"They told us you was dead, but the kral, he didn't believe it. Said you was too hard to kill. Good to see he's right. Who's got command now?"

"Famine Peak, they tell me." He glanced at Ghurash, who nodded. "I was out for a while. Forgot to duck."

"Good. He's a tough old squagger, but he knows his vank from his arse." The graborgh looked up at the situation on the hill with satisfaction. "You done good, Hadvezer. Kral sent me here to tell you Gor-Zug is sending over a regiment of Blue Hide Boyz to bust 'em now that they look like runnin', and the Kral is throwin' in three squadrons of boars to keep them damn riders too busy to get on they tails."

"He can spare 'em?"

"Course he can," growled Ghurash. "We bleed 'em, we crack 'em, and now that theyz fallin' back, the Blue Hides come and take all the credit! We might as well be anyafashzek gobbos!"

"Stuff it, galvebel. If the general says his boyz get the bust, they get the bust. It is what it is. You had your crack and you done good. Your hadvezer gets it, he ain't crying about it."

"Blue Hides can hit them turtleshells harder than we can anyhow."
Lugbol shrugged. "The fewer Black Fists we lose, the better. We ain't
got nothing to prove, Ghurash. Like he said, the Kral knows we got the
stuff."

"Yez can join in the chase too." The boar rider paused, and looked Lugbol
up and down. "Maybe not you, Hadvezer. You ain't–"

The graborgh didn't finish his sentence, because Lugbol rudely interrupted him by dropping to his hands and knees and vomiting on the rider's
yellow goblinskin boots. The graborgh swore as Ghurash laughed.

"Sorry 'bout that," Lugbol said, swaying a little as Ghurash helped him
rise again. "Feel better now, though."

"Ain't yez fault. My fault, I knew you took one in the noggin. It
happens."

"Yeah. So it's looking good over there?"

"Took us a few tries, but we finally rode over their right wing. The kral's
havin' the devil's own time reining 'em in, otherwise they'd be here by now.
Enemy center is holding, but we're gonna hit 'em from the left, then from
this side once the Slayers make 'em run. If their kral don't have the sense to
fall his center back soon, we'll wipe 'im out."

"That's good." Lugbol wished his wing had been the first to drive the
opposing wing from the field, but then, his wing had been the weakest of
the three by far. Simply by keeping the pressure on and refusing to run, his
kors had done what King Nekheru required of them and more. Then he
squinted, wondering if he'd actually seen what he thought he'd seen. No, he
must be seeing things, he'd taken a near-killshot to the head, after all. But
if he wasn't mistaken, a kor that had been lying on the ground, presumably
dead, was clumsily pushing itself up to its feet.

Well, the kor had probably just been knocked out, same as Lugbol had
been. There was something about its movements, though, that seemed
wrong. Downright unnatural, as a matter of fact.

"Yez seeing what I'm seeing," he asked the others, finding it hard, under
the circumstances, to put much faith in his eyes.

"I don't see nothin'" the graborgh said. Ghurash was silent as he held a
hand over his eyes to shield them from the sun. Then he shook his head.

"Somethin's wrong. Somethin' ain't right."

Now there were two kors standing awkwardly upright, shambling
unsteadily in their direction.

"Go get the head shaman," Lugbol hissed at Ghurash. The galvebel
saluted and rushed off as if Gor-Gor his own bad self was at his heels.

"Yeah, that don't quite look right." The graborgh wrinkled his lip as he stared at the battlefield.

A third figure was now rising slowly from the ground. The kor seemed to be pulled up from above, as if drawn by an invisible string, as its arms hung limply at its sides, its knees sagged, and its head lolled to one side on its breast. It seemed, at first, to have a tail, until Lugbol realized, with horror, what he was actually seeing. The graborgh saw it too.

"That kor is dragging his own guts!"

A pair of kors were approaching the first stumbling kor, ready to help him reach the leeches, where he could get help. But as they reached him, the wounded kor snapped his head forward and buried into one of his rescuer's shoulder. There was an agonized scream, and then, after a moment of shocked hesitation, the second rescuer unslung his club from his back and beat the attacking kor to the ground with three savage blows to his head. But even as he went to look after his injured companion, the first kor, which should have been unconscious at the very least, began to push itself back up again.

"Those kors are dead," Lugbol said, knowing even as he spoke how crazy he sounded. "It's got to be some Mandokki devil magic. Look, there's two goblins coming this way now!"

"What do we do?" The graborgh sounded stunned.

"Go back to Kral Nekheru and tell him what you seed. He's got better shamans, tell him he better send his best. Not even the Blue Hide Boyz are gonna help if we can't make the dead stay where they lay!"

"Hadvezer!"

Lugbol ignored the throbbing pain in his head and limped toward a group of thirty or so kors who were watching the progress of the battle on the hill. The Kornj'agh were still in good order, but their rear was getting close to the top where the artillery and command staff were positioned. Soon, they would have no choice but to start retreating down the other side, and before long the chase would be on. If the Blue Hides didn't get a move on fast, they might well lose their chance to break through the enemy lines.

"You! All of you!" He pointed to the shambling figures he assumed were dead, there were ten of them now, including three goblins. "Some dirty necro is walking those corpses. Go cut 'em to pieces, and burn the pieces."

"Hadvezer!"

The kors wasted no time in rushing the shamblers and cutting them down. They were just starting a fire to burn the remains when Ghurash returned with a wiry old shaman who wore a crown of four goat horns on his white-haired head.

"You see those kors over there? They just chopped up ten or twelve corpses that were coming this way! Can you tell if there's some sort o' devil magic that's possessing them and get rid of it?"

The shaman stroked the wispy white hairs on his chin. "I see 'em. And past them, I see three, four more kors that are walking strangely. Is that what you mean?"

When Lugbol confirmed that the shamblers were, indeed, his concern, the shaman closed his eyes and began to hum. As he began swaying back and forth, he began to mutter an incantation that chiefly consisted of sounds made low in his throat. He dropped to the ground, like an animal, and dug his fingers into the dirt as he pressed his forehead to the ground. Then he looked up, his eyes snapped open, and Lugbol saw they were half-mad with terror. The old shaman's jaw worked, silently at first, until he finally managed to gasp out the words.

"The hunger. The hunger! So much hunger!"

And then he collapsed to the ground, with his tongue lolling out of the side of his mouth.

"That cain't be good," Ghurash commented, a little unnecessarily in Lugbol's opinion. He knelt down and felt the side of the shaman's throat, then pressed a hand against the old orc's side. There wasn't even a hint of a pulse or a heartbeat to be found.

"Old bastard's stone dead!"

Ghurash's response was vulgar enough to make Gor-Gor blanch. The galvebel helped Lugbol to his feet, then pointed to where a veritable heap of corpses had been piled to get them out of the way. They were beginning to writhe and wiggle.

"When's it gonna stop? Ten or twenty, we can handle it. Chop 'em up, burn 'em, no problem. One or two hundred, we'ze okay so long as the kors don't panic. But one or two thousand…" His voice trailed off. He didn't need to spell the consequences out for Lugbol.

"So where are those cursed Blue Hides?" Lugbol could see there were more and more corpses rising. The kors he'd sent out to deal with them were cutting them down nearly as fast as they rose, and they'd managed to start a bonfire, but if the situation got much worse, they'd soon be overwhelmed.

His heart just about stopped when he felt something grab his ankle. He tried kicking himself free, but the grip was too tight. He spat and shook his head in dismay, dreading what he was pretty sure he was going to see if he looked down. Then there was a loud chunk, followed by two, three, four in quick succession, and then his foot was free. Ghurash, his face white with shock underneath fresh spatters of green blood, was holding his cleaver in both hands.

"I thought you said he was stone dead!"

"He was," Lugbol fairly screamed. "I swear to Gor-Gor, he was!"

"Well, he don't seem to know it!"

The headless, handless body of the old shaman was still rolling back and forth, trying to get up. Lugbol kicked it, more out of helpless frustration than anything, and looked out at the battlefield. The turtleshells were still retreating, but the kors of the Bloodscum warband were no longer pursuing them. In fact, the kors in the rear were now facing downhill and fighting a bizarre mix of corpses, which included wolves and men as well as orcs and goblins.

"Run and find the hornblowers. Sound the general retreat, then lead the Black Fists back to the town we sacked. I'll gather up the shamans and meet you there. Maybe they can figure out how to shut down this evil Man magic."

"What about the Kral? He might have your head for retreating!"

Lugbol snorted bitterly. "Then I'll come back and bite him in the arse like them zombies!"

"Hadvezer!" Ghurash gripped Lugbol's shoulders. "Take care o' yerself, Luggo! Don't you worry about the boyz, I'll get 'em out safe."

As his galvebel rushed off, Lugbol stared at what had been a battlefield, but was now a dark tapestry of shambling horror, as the dead stalked the living and added to their number. What sort of terrible magic could work necromancy on such a massive scale? And what sort of hellish creature was Man, that he could ruin even the brutal glories of war with his wickedness?

And then, before any more of the newly raised dead noticed him or came any closer, he broke into a run.

FJOTRA

FJOTRA sat anxiously in the chair, fretting as the young lady-in-
waiting, whose name she could never quite seem to recall, wrestled
clumsily with her long blonde hair. Word had come to the city that
her betrothed was intending to meet the orcs in battle that morning, and as
it was already well past noon, the fate of the Red Prince and his patchwork
army could arrive at any time.

"Your hair is so marvelous thick, your 'ighness" the girl prattled on as she
braided Fjotra's hair. "Usually a lady's hair so fair is much finer, but I dare
say the sailors could make a fine rope out of yours!"

"Are you suggesting I should cut my hair off and sell it for rope?"

"Oh, by 'is bones, never, your 'ighness!"

Fjotra tried not to snicker. While her own elocution still left a great deal
to be desired, if the rolled eyes and suppressed smiles of some of the nastier
ladies at court were any guide, her Savondese had improved to the point
that she could now hear the difference between some of the different accents,
and when Lady Jean—finally she recalled the lady-in-waiting's name—was
unsettled, her fine Lutècean accent tended to disappear as her voice grew
nasal and her h's dropped.

"I'm teasing you, Jean. Don't mind me, I'm just nervous about what's
happening to the east."

It wasn't just her prince for whom she was anxious. A good part of the
Dalarn men who'd made it across the sea were now battling a new type of
monster, and although she'd never seen a *gobelin* except in pictures shown
to her by Father Francois, they were said to be very nearly as terrible as the
Aalvarg from whom her people had fled. Her brother, thank Valfreyja and
the Aldaföðr, was among the jarls commanding them, since his equestrian

skills were rightly deemed insufficient to permit him to ride with the detachment of royal cavalry that had been allotted to her betrothed.

"Don't worry yourself, your highness. The Red Prince will smash them into pieces! They say he is even braver and more skilled in battle than his elder brother, may he rest in peace."

"Do they really?"

"Oh, yes, my lady! And he's ever so handsome, isn't he! Not so tall as his brother was, but much more attractive, if you don't mind my saying so."

"No, he isn't so tall," Fjotra agreed, inclining her head to the right as Jean worked on that side.

Étienne-Henri was actually a little shorter than she was, which would have bothered her more if he wasn't so intimidatingly self-assured. It almost made her laugh at times, the way her little bantam of a betrothed stalked silently into a room, and immediately all of the bigger, stronger men, some of whom could have picked him up and thrown him out the window without straining themselves, suddenly became wary and deferential.

It wasn't just that he was heir to the throne of Savondir. It was something about his eyes, she thought. Something about the way he looked at you, as if you were little more than a mouse that he might as easily step on as pet. But while his coldly superior gaze made men circumspect, and her mother downright distrustful, it sent delicious shivers up her spine, and, it appeared, not only hers. She would have given herself to him that last night before he departed, had he wanted, despite the admonitions of Father Francois and her mother alike, but he had shown no interest in taking her, and sent her away with little more than a kiss, a kind word, and a smile.

She could hardly complain, as he'd been under siege by a constant stream of generals, regimental commanders, messengers, and even the occasional blue-robed magicien throughout the afternoon and evening. But having lost one betrothed to battle before the marriage, she wasn't eager to lose a second before missing another chance to become a woman.

Let him live through this, Lady of Battles! She prayed silently for Étienne-Henri as she sat in the chair. *Let him be worthy of you, but not yet, not this day. Even if you do not grant him victory, at least let him return to me!*

The bell began to sound the hours. Fjotra didn't think anything of it, until it rang well past what she knew to be the proper hour. Seven rings, then eight, and then, for no discernible reason, other church bells began ringing. The noise was startling, and more than a little overwhelming, and she wondered if perhaps it was a signal that the enemy had been sighted. That shouldn't be possible; she'd been assured they were many leagues to the east, but perhaps the *gobelins* had stolen a march on her prince's army and somehow managed to avoid them.

"Do you hear that? Do you hear that, my lady!" Lady Jean was beaming, her bright eyes wide with joy, and she seized both of Fjotra's hands in her own. "All the churches are ringing their bells!"

"Yes, yes, I can hear that!" It was with some difficulty that she extracted her hands from the other young woman. "I don't know what it means. Are we in danger?"

"Not at all! Don't you understand? He won! Your betrothed has defeated the *gobelins!* Did I not tell you he would smash them to bits? The bells are ringing out a thanksgiving for his victory!"

"Oh, thank the gods!" Fjotra didn't notice Lady Jean blinking in surprise at her infelicitous outburst, as she had risen from her chair and had thrown her arms around the young lady-in-waiting. "He did it! He actually did it!"

Now the clangor of the bells was no longer alarming, but triumphant. The thundering of their ringing filled her with sudden exuberance. She grabbed the other girl's arms. "I have to go to the palace! Am I presentable?"

Lady Jean laughed. She, too, was caught up in the joy of victory and the ecstatic release from the fear under which they'd lived for weeks. "A little kohl for your eyes and two more ribbons for your hair and you'll be ready for court, your highness!"

Fjotra toyed with a braid. "Make them red," she decided. "The ribbons. In honor of my victorious prince!"

The walk to the palace would not be a long one, as she had been provided her own apartments in a large manor with a walled garden that belonged to her future mother-in-law, the queen. Although she was the only formal inhabitant of the residence, her life there was far from lonely, as in addition to the estate staff and her pair of Dalarn attendants, she had been assigned a small army of ladies-in-waiting of various ages, all of whom appeared to understand the significance of her position as the Red Prince's betrothed much better than she did.

But she was learning, and learning fast. Only a few months ago, she would have run to the palace alone, without troubling to make herself presentable or surround herself with an acceptable entourage. Now she knew better, as she was beginning to understand that at court, both words and appearances were weapons in an unending war of all against all. And though she was handicapped in the verbal aspect with her northern accent, primitive grammar, and limited vocabulary, her youth, her face, her fair hair, her height, and her figure combined to give her an advantage that was almost unfair, given her demi-royal rank. Even so, it would not do to be seen at the palace without a proper entourage providing her with a shield against the verbal volleys that were all but inevitable at court.

"Who is coming with me?" she demanded of Lady Jean as she examined herself one last time in the mirror in the foyer. Then, necessarily, she corrected herself. "Who is ready to come with me now?"

"Mathilde, Eshina, Emmelyn, and Avalyn," the younger girl promptly recited, counting the names off on her fingers. "And Svanhvit and Geirrid, of course. I haven't seen Flannery yet, but she will certainly want to come too, she's desperate to see if Lord Donzeau will come back with the prince or not."

Fjotra grimaced at the name of the red-haired girl, who was not so much the sorceror's lover as his servant and his spy. But she could hardly deny the girl her place, and it would be monstrous for her to do so in the great moment of their two lords' shared triumph.

"Tell them all we are leaving now! I wish to be there before the Red Prince arrives. And if Emmelyn is going to fuss about her hair not being ready, she can cut it off!"

"At once, Highness!" Lady Jean fled up the stairs, shouting the names of her attendants.

Instead of waiting in the entrance hall, Fjotra opened the door and waved her hands impatiently before the two royal guards standing attendance could begin paying their respects. "Yes, yes," she interrupted them. "Find your captain and tell him I want an escort to the palace now. I wish to leave immediately."

The taller of the two armored men nodded and swiftly disappeared into the garden in the direction of the gatehouse. Despite being near the center of the city, the manor was surrounded on four sides by greenery that obscured the high stone walls that rose nearly to the height of the first-floor windows. Her mother insisted that the palatial residence was as much prison as it was protection, but Fjotra didn't see it that way for what she felt was the perfectly good reason that no one had ever stood in the way of her leaving it. And after spending the greater portion of her life living in terror behind little more than wooden palisades erected on top of mounds of dirt, she was quite happy to sleep behind stone walls with iron-barred windows.

The captain was the first to arrive, followed by four of his men. He was a tall, middle-aged Savondese man, handsome despite the wrinkles around his eyes and the receding hairline that was hidden by his peaked silver helmet. He took his responsibilities very seriously, did not permit his men to flirt with her or her ladies, and she had never once seen him smile. But he was distant, not indifferent. She felt safe around the older man, and she would not be at all surprised to learn that he had daughters of his own.

"I understand you wish to go to the palace, your Highness."

"If you please, Captain. My ladies are a little late, but seven of them will be attending me." She heard the door creak open behind her. "And I very much hope that all seven of them are arriving now."

"Would you like for me to arrange for a pair of carriages?"

"No, it's not far. I should prefer to walk."

"As you wish, your Highness."

"Let's go, go, go, ladies!" she heard Flannery ordering the others out the door. There was much confusion, as all seven of the young women seemed to be talking excitedly at once, just as the church bells began ringing again. But the captain didn't appear to be overwhelmed at all, and Fjotra could have sworn she saw the merest ghost of a smile flicker across his narrow lips as he shared a look with one of his guardsmen.

"Jean-Charles, see to the gate!" he barked, causing the ladies to stop chattering with his deep baritone voice. "Guy and Stéphane, bring up the rear. My ladies, if you will please follow young Quennel there, we shall be on our way!"

Fjotra took Svanhvit's arm as her ladies fell in before and behind her. There seemed to be some order of precedence that still remained a mystery to her, which meant that the two oldest girls, Flannery and Mathilde, took the lead while Jean and Geirrid, brought up the rear. Thus arranged, they marched two-by-two through the garden and sallied out the wide iron gate, which closed behind them with an audible clang.

The cobblestoned streets were filled with the people of Lutèce happily celebrating their prince's unexpected victory. Urchins ran amok, screeching joyfully as they dodged men gesticulating and the occasional carriage making its way toward the center of the city. Groups of young women, the daughters of merchants and other respectable citizens by their dress, were skipping and singing cheerfully, although upon spotting Fjotra and her entourage, they stopped, pointed at her, and whispered to each other behind their open hands. Svanhvit bristled at their attention, but Fjotra quickly shut down her flaxen-haired friend's complaints by artfully pinching her side.

"How dare they—ouch!"

"Let them stare and say what they like, Svana. Étienne says presenting a spectacle is the chief duty of a princess."

"Well, not the chief one, surely!" Svanhvit giggled.

"Stop that!" Fjotra made as if to pinch her again. "We present the spectacle and they do us the honor of noticing it. Do you see that young man there?"

"The tall one? Ooh, he's blowing kisses at us."

"I know. Wink at him!"

"Do what?"

"Look at him, close one eye, then open it."

Svanhit rolled her eyes at Fjotra, but she glanced back at the young man and favored him with a wink. He gaped and pointed at her as his friends waved their hats and shouted their approval.

"The Princess! The Red Princess! *Allez!*"

Fjotra nodded with satisfaction. She was no longer the Wolf Princess, but the Red Princess. That boded well. Of course, it would take more than one victory for her betrothed to win the favor of the Savondese people, and he might never be as well-loved by them as his charismatic older brother was, but there was no reason why she shouldn't make herself a favorite with them. Something Roheis had told her once came back to her. Smile at them and they will smile at you. Show them you love them and they will love you. The beautiful southerner might be a traitor to the realm, but even now, her guidance was sound.

As the church bells and the cheers of the crowd rang in their ears, they came within sight of the royal palace, towering over the half-filled plaza that stood before its gates. It was a lively scene, with at least three bonfires and what appeared to be an impromptu market that had sprung up near the central fountain. But instead of entering the plaza, the captain led their little parade toward a narrow street on the left which took them on a short, but circuitous route to a considerably less-conspicuous side gate that appeared to be unmanned until the captain banged his armored greave against the solid black iron door. A slot slid back, revealing a pair of dark and suspicious eyes, but after a verbal exchange that Fjotra couldn't quite make out, the heavy door was cranked upon and they were permitted entry to the palace grounds.

A stone path led them across a grassy lawn to a simple wooden door that was unguarded from the outside. Upon entering, Fjotra saw they were in a section of the palace she'd never seen before, but judging by the movements of the royal staff who were passing rapidly through the corridor to which the small entry room was attached, they weren't too far from the kitchens.

"This way, your Highness," a courtier wearing the queen's livery gestured, bowing after he indicated which way she should go. The guards stayed behind as he led them through several hallways, up a small set of stairs, then through a series of small rooms, before stopping beside an ornately-carved door. "Her Majesty gave instructions that you should enter this way, in order to avoid you being mobbed by well-wishers."

"Thank you, kind sir," she did him the courtesy of acknowledging him as he opened the door, which, it turned out, led to the grand ballroom in which she had learned how to dance, and where she had attended several royal balls. The chamber was a breathtaking testament to the wealth and elegance of Savondir that she had come to love since crossing the White Sea. Adorned with soaring ceilings and walls lavishly decorated with rich tapestries depicting scenes of heroic battles and royal hunts, the vast expanse exuded a sense of regal splendor. Intricately crafted chandeliers, suspended from the heights, cast a warm, golden glow that danced upon the polished marble floor below. Tall, arched windows lined the great room, allowing the red rays of the setting sun to cast a rosy hue over the nobles and courtiers gathered within, accentuating the ethereal ambiance.

Gilded columns, intricately carved with delicate foliage motifs, adorned the chamber, adding to its stately grandeur. At the far end, a raised dais awaited the honored guests, embellished with ornate thrones draped in sumptuous velvet. From the graceful arches to the meticulously arranged floral arrangements, every detail spoke of the refinement and sophistication befitting the royal gatherings that took place within these walls.

To her surprise, the first person she recognized in the ballroom was her mother, who was decidedly underdressed for the occasion, and was apparently unattended as well.

"Mother?" she said, incredulous.

"Oh, good, you're here." Her mother stepped forward and took her hands. "I came as soon as I heard the news!"

"I can see that," Fjotra said, a little displeased by her mother's appearance. She was wearing a simple cream linen shift that was entirely inappropriate for a royal audience, although it was fortuitously adorned with a blue silk scarf which did, admittedly, set off her eyes rather nicely. "Why? What was so urgent!"

"I wanted to make sure you did not permit the prince to take any liberties with you upon his return."

"Mother!"

"Listen to me, Fjotra. I know men much, much better than you do. When they are victorious in battle, they feel they can do no wrong. They feel immortal! They feel they are masters of the whole world, and naturally they want a woman."

"I am not listening to this, mother!" She glanced over at her ladies, who were fortunately far too interested in seeing who was, and who was not already present to be paying any attention to her mother. Thank the gods she was speaking in their own tongue, so only Svanhvit and Geirrid could have understood her, not that either of them were paying any attention, thank the gods.

"Fjotra! The fate of our people rests upon your marriage! And these southerners place a very high importance on their future queen's purity, I suppose it's mostly in order to prevent succession complications and squabbles, but it doesn't really matter why they do, it only matters what they think! And that is why you cannot permit the prince any liberties, no matter how he importunes you!"

"No one is importuning anyone, Mother! He may not even be coming here tonight, or tomorrow either, for that matter!" She sniffed dismissively, then shot an arch look at her mother. "But you have to admit that he's not such a little snake now, don't you!"

"I admit nothing of the kind," her mother snapped back imperiously. "He's always been clever, so it's hardly astonishing that he should prove to be competent in the field."

"From what they said about the tremendous number of orcs involved, it required more than mere competence to defeat them."

"Perhaps. And perhaps not. I'll give him his due, young lady, but I don't trust him and you shouldn't either. An evil might be necessary, but it is still an evil!"

"Do you think Brynjolf will return with him?" Fjotra decided to change the subject.

"I don't believe so. The jarls will remain with the men after the battle. And I suggest that we should wait to see how many of our people survived the battle before we celebrate anything."

Fjotra frowned. "Hjaldrgoð grant that they are all hale and whole!"

"Especially Brynjolf," her mother concurred. Then she smiled at her daughter. "Even so, I think your father would have been well-pleased to know that his son-in-law was victorious in his first battle."

A sudden pang struck Fjotra's chest at the mention of her father. It was almost a physical blow, and she felt tears begin to fill her eyes. But she swallowed hard, smiled brightly, and somehow managed to control herself before hugging her mother just a little harder than usual.

"Come, mother, now that you've warned me not to jeopardize my wedding, let's find Étienne-Henri's mother and congratulate her on her son's victory. She must be so very proud!" She pulled her mother by the hand toward the center of the room. It didn't take them long to spot the king and queen at the center of a collection of elderly nobles, white-bearded generals, and the odd ecclesiastic or two. But before they could even start making their way toward the royal pair, a tall blue-cloaked figure pushed his way past the king's coterie, and after making a perfunctory obeisance, put his bearded lips to his liege's ear.

It was impossible to know what the royal mage said, but whatever it was, it inspired an immediate, and drastic, reaction from the king. In response to some unknown signal, what seemed like a host of hard-faced courtiers and armored guardsmen appeared from out of nowhere and began directing the mystified guests toward the exits. But before more than a few people had been escorted from the room, a great cry went up from those who were closest to the doors.

"The Prince! The Prince! The Red Prince!"

There was a clamor at the entrance that drew nearly everyone's attention, but Fjotra, glancing at the king and queen, was surprised to see that neither of them looked pleased at the news that their victorious son had arrived. The king's face was scarlet with what she supposed must be anger, given his expression, and the queen looked worried, indeed, almost fearful.

"Mother, something's wrong," she hissed in the Dalarn tongue.

"Yes, I think there is." Her mother looked around, narrow-eyed, and when she spotted the door from which Fjotra and the others had entered, urged her towards it.

"What are you doing? Don't push me!"

"I think we should leave, Fjotra. Right now."

"Now? Mother, we're perfectly safe! No one would dare raise a finger to me here. The king would never permit it!"

"The king's opinion may not matter now," her mother said ominously. Having taken a firm grip on Fjotra's sleeve, she was now pulling her toward the door. "Svanhvit! Geirrid! Find the other girls and come with us!"

But as she retreated under her mother's duress, she saw the crowd parting before a squad of crimson-cloaked soldiers. Their breastplates were dull and dented, their cloaks and pantalons were travel-stained, their boots were dusty, and what she could see of their faces behind their helms were gaunt and dirty, but their eyes were full of pride and they carried themselves with the confidence of conquerors. They were, she realized, her fiancé's bodyguard, and indeed, as they spread out to flank the king and queen, they preceded both Étienne-Henri and his constant companion, the trollmand Guilhem Donzeau.

Her prince looked extraordinarily self-satisfied, as well he might under the circumstances. But Fjotra knew her intended well enough to see that he was in a temper of some sort, even though he was keeping himself under control. Like his men, he was still wearing his armor, and both his tunic and his cape were stained and torn. He was carrying a large burlap sack which appeared to be heavy despite being only half-full, and in contrast to what Fjotra knew to be the custom in Savondir, both he and his men were still wearing their swords in their scabbards. Donzeau looked uncharacteristically tired, but though his face was pale with exhaustion, his dark eyes still flickered with inhuman arrogance.

"His Royal Highness, the Duc de Chênevin!" a courtier announced belatedly, and unnecessarily.

"Greetings, Mother dearest." The prince had to lift his face and extend his neck to kiss her on both cheeks. "I bring you a princely gift, Father!"

With a flourish, he reached into the sack and withdrew a very large crown made of a dark metal, presumably iron, in which were mounted green, red, and purple jewels of some kind. He presented it to the king with a theatrical bow, who took it in both hands and examined it with a frown on his face.

"Behold the crown of the Great Orc, the king of Necrotic Gooleegoo or some other unpronounceable orcish hellhole from which the cursed creatures spawned. I expect you will be pleased to know that he, along with tens of thousands of his unspeakable *verdards*, are presently residing in Hell, courtesy of me and my loyal men-at-arms."

A great cheer went up at his announcement, but the king only nodded and handed the crown to a courtier at his side.

"And what else is in the sack?"

"Oh, it's just his head. Since you appreciated that gift of ears earlier this summer, I thought I'd go the Amorrans one better and bring you the whole thing. But I have to say, it is rather large for a goblet."

A titter of amusement spread through the crowd, but not even a hint of a smile flashed across the king's face. "You dare to wear a sword in my presence, Étienne-Henri?" He indicated the red-cloaked guards. "You permit your men to bear their weapons before me?"

"What has His Majesty to fear from men who have wielded those weapons to defend his kingdom and crown?" Donzeau said, unlike the others, swordless, but equally as indifferent to every rule of royal protocol.

The king's eyes flashed with anger at the impertinent interruption, but the queen forestalled him by placing a hand on his arm. "Your father asked you a question, Étienne-Henri."

"I do," he answered proudly. "I dare that and I daresay a great deal more!"

"I know, and I am heartsick with the knowledge," the king said softly. "What profit it a prince to win the day at the cost of his own soul? Guards, arrest the Duc de Chênevin and his sorcerer!"

But before the royal guards, or anyone else, could react, there was a brilliant flash of light, like a bolt of lightning before the thunder rolls. Fjotra blinked, unable to see anything for a moment, and then her mother was tugging at her arm again, urging her to leave.

"Run, Fjotra! We have to leave now!"

Confused and dismayed, and more than a little frightened, this time, Fjotra obeyed her mother without hesitation. Her two Dalarn attendants followed her, as did all of her Savondese ladies as well, except one. She looked back to see if she could spot Flannery, but instead her eyes were drawn to the glowing semicircle of red light in which someone, presumably Donzeau, had enclosed both Étienne-Henri and his parents, as well as himself. Outside the circle, guards in both red cloaks and blue were drawing their swords, and at least two royal mages were shouting at each other as they desperately tried to dispel the magical construction.

It was all too much to take in. All she knew was that her mother was right and that this was not a safe place to be. Fjotra ran.

LODI

A S HE FOLLOWED the glow-bearers down the unlit tunnel, Lodi felt an empty sense of desperation he had never known before. He was holding Myf's hand as they walked through the flickering darkness together, and yet he had never felt further away from her. Not even when he was lying wounded in his bed and she would not talk to him at all had he felt so helpless, and so unable to engage with her.

He'd tried to spare her the worst of it by having the bodies of her family decently laid out and covered before he'd brought her into the steading to identify them, and while it had been the right thing to do, it hadn't lessened her grief at all in the moment. She'd howled like a goblin being eviscerated at the sight of her mother and father, but her cries grew fainter with every additional friend or family member that she saw, until she fell silent, struck dumb by the sheer magnitude of her loss. Brothers, sisters, aunts, uncles, nieces, nephews, every single member of her little community was gone now, murdered by the strange scaled creatures whose corpses were also scattered here and there around the caves.

"Skála Otek, I don't know how much more of this I can take," Thorald had muttered at the sight of a pretty young divci whose face was peaceful and unmarred, in stark contrast to her bloody and brutalized body. "Lodi, what are we going to do about Myf?"

"We're going to do right by her, lad. That's all we can do."

And so they did what they had to do. There was no other choice. They gathered the bodies, one by one, then gently laid them to rest in the steading's mushroom gardens. After one of the zematurges led the group in the ritual prayers to the First Fathers, they brought Myf with them on their royal mission, traveling ever deeper into the depths below the mountains.

Lodi had his misgivings, and he would have preferred to take her back to Iron Mountain, but they all had their orders and it would have been unthinkable to permit her to return alone. No one even suggested the idea.

Every night, she cried herself to sleep, pressing her face against Lodi's chest, her body shaking with violent, but silent sobs. In other circumstances, he might have enjoyed their growing closeness, but he was shut out from her grief. She did not speak, not to him or to anyone else, and although she still responded to his words and followed his instructions, her face was blank and her eyes were all but unseeing. He did his best to respect her silence, and for the most part, met it with his own. He knew better than to offer her meaningless platitudes and foolish reassurances. She was lost in her grief, and the most he could do was to be there for her and stand ready for the moment when she would need his help to extricate herself from it.

But he knew it was a moment that might well never come. There were wounds that did not heal, and the wound to her heart was grievous indeed.

It wasn't until the evening of the third day after they'd left the dead holding behind that she finally broke her silence. They were sitting apart from the others, next to a small fire that the zematurges had determined to be safe, when she unexpectedly spoke up.

"I don't see how I believe anymore."

"Believe what?"

"Believe in Hublok Otek and Nahoru Otek. In everything I was taught. The whole idea of good and evil. The idea that if you are a good dwarf, then good things will happen to you." She didn't look at him as she spoke, but stared fixedly into the fire. "My father was a good dwarf. He listened to the skalknahi and he always made the offerings to the Provni Otcovi. He brought us up in the old ways, the true ways of the dwarves, and what difference did it make? He had seven children, and yet his line ended with him!"

Lodi took a deep breath. He'd known it was coming, sooner or later, he'd thought a great deal about it as they'd continued their journey downward into the depths, but he had no idea what to say to her.

"My family is dead, Lodi! My family is dead and I don't know why!"

He patted her hand, knowing even as he did so how inadequate it was. "They didn't deserve it," he told her. "But if I learned one thing from my time under the sky, it's that being good ain't no guarantee that evil won't touch you, just like being bad don't necessarily mean bad things'll happen to you."

"Then what does any of it matter?"

"Maybe it matters for its own sake. I don't know, lass." He reflected for a moment. "I will say that the worse the dwarf, the worse he usually ends up. I knowed a few bad dwarves in my day, and ain't one of them that ended well. But in the war, you know, the big siege, things didn't go so well for anybody. The orc don't care if you was good or not."

"Oh, Lodi, what is going to become of me?"

Her tear-streaked face was beautiful in the dancing firelight. There were so many things he wanted to say to her, but he knew this was absolutely not the time. So he simply took her pretty, delicate little hand in one hand and brushed a stray hair out of her eyes with the other.

"I swore to Morits, son of Morits, and to the Bodel-wife that I'd stay by you, keep you safe. And I swore to the king that I'd see you safely home."

"I have no home, Lodi," she whispered. "Not anymore."

"I know. So I'll stay by you until you do. No matter how long it takes. And that, I'm swearing to you, lass, by stone and by sky if you don't believe in the First Fathers no more."

"Thank you, Lodi." She squeezed his hand. "I know I'm safe when I'm with you."

Lodi leaned back against the warm stone of the tunnel walls, as grim and taciturn as ever. But inside, his heart was singing.

It was two days later when the zematurges abruptly halted their march along the downward-sloping tunnels. After a brief conference with Thorald, a guard was sent for Lodi, who was walking at the rear of the group with Myf, asking him to come forward and join them.

"Isn't it a little soon to stop for lunch?" He poked at the fatter zematurge's belly. "Don't think you'll be starving in the next hour."

The arcanist neither smiled nor took offense, which was worrisome.

"There is a cavern ahead. A very large cavern."

"You think we found where these things live?"

"No, it's something else." The fat zematurge pulled at his beard. "It's something very big, very old, and it exudes a very powerful magic."

Lodi looked at Thorald. For once, the younger dwarf's face was as grim as his own. "Is he really saying what I think he might be getting at?"

"They think it's a dragon, Lodi."

"No, we know it's a dragon," the taller zematurge broke in. "Which is to say, we aren't actually certain that it is a dragon, there are a number of other creatures, most of them mythical or whose existence has never actually been established. But of the various possibilities that fit our observations, a dragon is by far the most likely."

Lodi first placed his hand against the tunnel wall, then his forehead. "Skála Otek, spare us your surprises!"

Thorald patted him on the back. "Here's another one for you, Kings-guard. Since you're the only one with actual experience of entering a dragon's den, we've decided that you're just the dwarf to scout the situation."

"It was a wyrm!"

"Wyrm, dragon." Thorald shrugged.

"Actually, they are customarily cataloged as members of the same phylum," the fat zematurge pronounced loftily. "Along with the wyvern—"

"Shut up!" Lodi interrupted his lecture before he could really get rolling. "How far away is this thing."

"Not far at all. Perhaps three hundred paces."

Lodi looked at the walls on either side. There was no way it was big enough for a dragon to crawl through it, so there was no need to fear its teeth and claws. But if it was a fire-breather, or worse, some sort of poison gas-belcher, they might already be too close to the monster. But they couldn't simply abandon the mission without confirming that the dragon was actually there; the king would never be content with the mere word of a pair of arcanists. And if the dragon actually was there, then they would not only have an excuse to leave off their investigations and return to Iron Mountain, they would have an absolute responsibility to do so. In fact, it was incumbent upon them to send a pair of messengers back immediately, just in case things went awry and the rest of them never made it back to the king.

For there was nothing, except perhaps volcanoes, that the dwarves feared more than dragons. And the thought of one actually living under the great city was downright appalling! Even if it was just a possibility, they had to alert the king to it, and they had to do so right away.

"I'll do it," he told Thorald. "But you need to send word back to the king, right now. Send him," he pointed to the fat zematurge, "and send Myf, along with as many guards as you think you can spare."

Thorald smiled and shook his head. "No, Lodi. I'd like to send her back too, but it would be too dangerous. This patrol is small enough as it is. We split it up, we run the risk of neither group making it back to the king safely. And I don't think Myf will go along with the idea of leaving you down here, at least, not while you're alive."

Lodi sighed. His friend was right. Splitting up the party might actually present a greater risk to everyone.

"Okay, forget I suggested it. But I need three guards to go with me."

"You need three guards to go look at the dragon?"

"No, I need them to help me kill it."

It took Lodi longer than he thought it would to convince Thorald and the zematurges of the wisdom of his plan. His idea was that Thorald would lead everyone back up the tunnels far enough to ensure their safety from any deadly dragonish emissions, while he and his three companions would sneak down, and if possible, drive an impromptu dragonlance through one of the sleeping beast's eyes. He figured they needed to make an oversized stake about six dwarf-lengths long for it to penetrate the brain and kill the mighty creature, and so he suggested himself, the greybeard, and the two strongest guards as the four with the best chance of driving the stake in deep enough.

Making the weapon was simple enough. They commandeered two axes, a spear, and over vociferous protests, the taller zematurge's staff. Removing the axe heads was simple enough, but carving out hollows in the butts of the spear and both axes to accommodate the subsequent shaft, then wrapping each joining tight with leather wraps took a little longer. The wraps were then secured with metal screws scavenged from a pair of shields. By the time they were finished, Lodi's fingers ached from forcing the screws into the hard wood, but the makeshift lance held together better than he'd expected, and certainly well enough for the task he had in mind.

Myf was as impressed as she was worried. She lifted the front of the crude weapon from the stone floor and marveled at its weight.

"You really think you can kill a dragon with this?"

"I killed a troll with a similar contraption. O' course, we rigged up what was more or less a giant crossbow, so we was nice and far away. We're going to have to get up close and personal with this, but troll, goblin, or dragon, I ain't never heard o' nothing that can survive getting stuck in the eye if'n you shove it in there far enough." He paused reflectively. "The nose'll work too, on most things, but probably not on a dragon. We'd need a longer lance and more dwarves."

"I always wondered what you were thinking about when you were sitting there next to me on the train, all strong and silent. Now I know you were just thinking about how to kill things." Her pretty smile took any sting out of her words.

"That's about all the Kingsguard are good for, lass."

She placed a hand on his shoulder, leaned in, and kissed his bearded cheek.

"Be careful, Lodi."

He watched her as she quickly walked away, bent over to retrieve her pack, and made her way along the stone corridor to where Thorald and the others were waiting. He waited until she was around the corner and out of sight before he turned around, only to see that his three remaining companions were all staring at him. He waved off their sympathy, and bent over to grasp the front of what he hoped would be the dragon-killer.

"One o' ye grab the back end. We only need two to carry it until we're ready for business, so we'll switch off once we get close and I'll go ahead to take a look-see. And when we get there, remember that we thrust right on three. That means one, two, and then stab it forward on three. Not one, two, three, and then stab on four. You all got that?"

The two younger dwarves quickly nodded, observably in awe of him. The greybeard, less impressed, just smiled.

"I hear the Kingsguard do it that way because they can't count to four."

"Just for that, you get on the tail, old dwarf," Lodi ordered. "And remember, once we stab, ye don't let go! Throw all yer body weight into it and push. We got to make sure we drive this lizard-sticker all the way in through its tiny little brain. Push like yer lives depend upon it, because they do!"

How do I get myself into these stupid situations again and again, he asked himself. For some reason, though, he wasn't scared. Setting out to impale the troll king, he'd been petrified with fear. His heart had been in his mouth the whole time he'd been in the Amorran arena. And nothing, but absolutely nothing, had been more terrifying than riding way too high above the ground on the back of an elf's giant bird.

Maybe he was just getting too old for fear. He hadn't been frightened at Hotstone, or before then, when the wolfriders had him surrounded. He'd just felt a sense of resignation. But now, he didn't feel anything. Maybe because carrying a stick into a dragon's den just seemed too ridiculous to be real.

"Even by Kingsguard standards, this is unbelievably stupid," the greybeard behind him muttered.

Lodi couldn't really find it in his heart to disagree.

"Pipe down back there," he growled. There was a faint glow ahead, as if there was a patch of golden glowmoss growing around the corner. He could feel a rush of air that ruffled his beard, then it stopped, until it picked up again. It was the dragon breathing, he realized, as he eyed the bend in the tunnel in front of him that likely led to the cavern in which it slept.

Signaling to the others to wait for him, he slipped forward as stealthily as an armored dwarf could manage. He rounded the bend and froze.

Sprawled out in a what was clearly an artificial cavern was an enormous golden dragon. It was a beautiful, magnificent creature, slumbering contentedly on a stone floor that felt warm even through Lodi's thick leather boots. How such a huge beast could have entered the cavern was a mystery, as he saw no other entrances that were any bigger than the dwarf-carved tunnel in which he was standing. There was, lamentably, no gold nor jewels anywhere that he could see, but he noticed the golden scales that covered its skin were, except for their size, very much akin to the scales that adorned the draktakha.

There must be some connection between this ancient monstrosity and the cruel, murderous lizardlings responsible for murdering Myf's family and the Hotstoners. A thought occurred to him, and he went down to one knee in order to press his palm against the floor. Zatra! He very nearly swore aloud, startled by how hot the stone was. Every dwarf knew of the Earthblood, the burning liquid stone that flowed through the bowels of the Earth, but he had not thought they were so deep as to have reached it already. Well, that was a matter for the zematurges to contemplate, in the meantime, he had an alarmingly large dragon to kill.

Fortunately, the dragon's horned skull was resting on its clawed forelegs in a position facing the tunnel exit, so he and his dwarves wouldn't have to take more than ten steps inside the cavern to reach its closed right eye.

The graybeard gestured a query. Lodi nodded, and pressed a finger to his lips. He pointed to where each dwarf should take hold of the dragon-sticker, then assumed his position behind the point of the spear and knelt down. Holding up his left hand, he counted one, two, and then lifted the spear with his right on three. It came up easily, being rather light for the four of them, and he took a firm grip with both hands before stepping forward slowly and silently. It belatedly occurred to him that it would be impossible to use a hand count when they actually stuck the beast in the eye, so they would simply have to hope that either the beast wouldn't hear a whispered count or it wouldn't react to it in time.

He didn't relish his breastplate's chances against the claws he'd seen, which were bigger than any orc's cleaver, and he imagined the creature's teeth would be even bigger. And that was assuming it didn't cough some noxious gas or spit a vicious acid in their faces. He could hear the dwarves behind him hiss with astonishment as they rounded the bend; as soft as the noise was, to Lodi it sounded louder than the royal forge in full clangor.

But they were good lads, they didn't freeze, or stop, or worse, drop the lance and run, they just kept walking as quietly as they could toward the round, gold object that was their target.

Lodi was so close to the dragon now that he held his breath, fearing that even a single exhalation might wake the beast. When the point of the spear was nearly touching the creature's eyelid and he was nearly close enough to reach out and touch the scaled ridges of its cheek, he stopped and held up a hand.

He was just about to glance backward and whisper the first number when the giant eye, larger than his head, abruptly opened. And a deep voice rumbled in his head.

I wouldn't do that if I were you, little dwarf.

It was nearly ten days later when they finally marched their weary way up the last incline and approached Iron Mountain. The king had left orders for his household guards to keep watch for them, for they were greeted warmly, with glad cries and shouts, as they rushed toward Thorald and the others. But neither Thorald nor Lodi would say anything about their weeks-long journey into the depths, while Myf walked silently by Lodi's side, holding his hand.

"Take us to His Majesty," Thorald ordered, and he waved off every offer of rest or refreshment, insisting on an immediate royal audience. But when word came that only the captain and the Kingsguard were to be permitted one right away, Lodi forestalled Myf's protests by putting two gold coins in the graybeard's hand and asking him to serve as her escort in the city until Lodi was free again. They arranged to meet at an alehouse near the palace known to both of them, and somewhat to his surprise, Myf acceded without complaint.

It was possible, Lodi thought, that she felt the fat zematurge had taken sufficient offense for both of them.

"I'm pleased to hear you're all back safe," was the king's first comment upon their arrival in the throne room. "Although there is one more of you than I was expecting. And you look exhausted, so I surmise you have unhappy news that you hurried back to tell me."

"We do," Thorald said. "Your Majesty, the reason the divci Myf returned with us is because her family's steading was wiped out by the draktakha. There were no survivors."

"I'm truly sorry to hear that. I shall make sure we find a place for her in the palace. She's presentable enough, perhaps the Queen might want her as an attendant." His eyes narrowed. "But sad as the unfortunate fate of a deep steading may be, that's not the sort of word one rushes back to tell one's king."

Thorald and Lodi looked at each other.

"I think he's more likely to believe you," the younger dwarf said.

"We'll see about that." Lodi was dubious. "First, would you send out for some ale, Your Majesty? Second, there was this dragon, you see…"

They were well into their third mug of ale by the time Lodi reached the part of his tale when the dragon opened its eyes.

"So what did you do?" the king asked, leaning forward on his throne.

"The only thing I could do in the circumstances. I apologized as sincerely as I ever done anything in my whole life, I respectfully begged his pardon, and I asked if he'd seen any draktakha about, seeing as we'd come across him while huntin' 'em."

"And he spared your lives? Even though you were caught trying to kill him?"

"Well, you see, as it turns out, dragons don't kill so easy, so he wasn't too inclined to get upset. Now, I know you'll find it hard to believe and you ain't gonna like this, but after I described the draktakha to him and told him what they was about, he apologized to us. Said he was real sorry."

"And to you, Your Majesty!" Thorald broke in. "He done apologized to you too."

"Yeah, that's right, to you as well. I forgot that, sorry. So, the reason he was apologizing was because when dragons sleep, they tend to give off a bit o' their magic. Affects their surroundings. And it seems that magic can cause things to go a bit topsy-turvy. Give 'em enough time, like centuries, and rats start talking, rocks come alive, or mortals, they change."

The king looked stricken. "So the reason those cursed creatures resemble dwarves is because once they were dwarves."

"That's exactly right. Some o' those holdings and steadings you thought got wiped out by them was actually them. Course, others, like Myf's folk and the Hotstoners, they just had the bad luck to be too close to them as got changed by the dragon's magic."

"Is there anything we can do for those poor dwarves?"

"Put 'em out of their misery, is all. The transformation did their heads all in, when it comes to brains, there's less there than with orcs or goblins. They shouldn't breed true, he says, but they might, and we don't want that. We definitely don't want that! Among other things, they don't hesitate to eat dwarf, if given the chance."

"They will," Thorald confirmed. "We saw some o' the remains."

"Porbit ho!" the king swore. "This dragon must be a son of the Sky Father, if he is not Nahotakh himself."

"Well, you ain't all that far off." Lodi pulled at his beard. "Now, you knowed me long enough to know I ain't crazy, Borgo. So try to keep that in mind, and remember that Thorald weren't there, so he can't testify as to whether what I'm telling you is true or not. But here's the thing. That dragon's been sleeping a long, long time. I mean centuries, not years. He knew what we were, and he said that he was there when we was made. The dwarves, I mean of course, not me and t'other three that was with me."

"That's impossible! Are you saying that the First Fathers were actually dragons?"

"In a manner of speaking, maybe. Look, the arcanists said they don't know how long dragons live. And this dragon said they don't die natural and they can't really be killed, which was why he wasn't inclined to take no offense to us looking to stab him in the eye. He just took us for ignorant, which was fair enough, since we was. Now, some o' the things he told me made me think that maybe they can be killed, but it needs an amount of magic to do it, because he said a long, long time ago, his people got into a big war with the elves. It was such a big war, with such terrible magics being thrown around that it created the oceans, which don't make no sense to me since there's more oceans than land, but that's what he said."

Lodi paused to pull at his beer, and continued. "Anyhow, neither side really won the war, but the dragon's people decided they had enough and so they went somewhere else. Not into the sky, but through some sort o' magic door that took them to another world somehow. The elves didn't have the magic, or the know-how, or maybe they didn't know about the other world. But regardless, the dragon's people, or most of them, anyhow, they went away, and the world shaped up to be the way we know it now."

The king readjusted the crown on his head. "This is all very interesting and the scholars are no doubt going to interrogate you to within an inch of your life once they hear about this, but what made getting word of this back to me so urgent?"

Lodi and Thorald looked at each other. Lodi cleared his throat. "That's just it, see. It seems they might be coming back."

"Who, not the dragons?"

"Yep. Or at least, some o' the dragons that was left behind want to open up the door and let 'em back in. And others want to open it so they can join t'others, and then a third group, which I think would be the one he was in, wants to leave well enough alone."

"Lodi, you have the knack for making your liege's life very difficult. How many of these dragons are there, did you think to ask?"

"O' course I did! There are thirteen o' the bastards left, which is why they like to sort out their differences by proxy. See, this door can only open every so often, like once in centuries, and they all have a pretty good idea when and where it'll be. I guess it moves or something, and has something to do with the skies, maybe with the two moons. So what they do is stir up some o' what they call the younger folk, which is to say elves and orcs and men and trolls and such, and sort out their differences that way. So what I was thinking—"

"You think this invasion of the Elfwood and the Man lands by the orcs might actually be caused by these ancients fighting amongst themselves."

"Exactly," said Lodi, wiping foam off his beard.

"But how can they possibly achieve so much influence over orcs, or men, or even us, I suppose? If a dragon tried to tell us what to do, mortal or not, we'd chop him into bits!"

Lodi and Thorald looked at each other again. This time it was Thorald who spoke up.

"My liege, you may recall that Lodi said four dwarves entered the cavern, including himself. However, when they caught up to us afterward, there wasn't four of them. There were *five* of them. And then, later that same day, there weren't. That fifth dwarf, he just vanished at some point along the way."

The king was silent for a long moment, pondering the implications of what he was being told. Then he sighed.

"So these dragons can not only change their shape, but their size as well. Which means they can become anything they want, they can appear like anyone they want. Magic like that is far beyond the dwarves, it might even exceed what the elven wizards can do."

"It does explain how the beast got into that cavern in the first place," Lodi added. "I couldn't figure out how he got in there without there being no entrances big enough for him. The good news is that at least now we don't need to worry about no giant dragon undermining the foundations o' the city while he claws his way out from below."

"There is that." The king shook his head, visibly overwhelmed by what he'd been told. "I can see you're both exhausted, so go and get some rest. I don't know who to call first, the royal scholars, the arcanists, or my generals, but you've given me a good deal to think about. And I thank you, I think some medals will be appropriate, especially for the three guards who accompanied you into the dragon's chamber, Lodi."

"Your Majesty!" They both bowed deeply, recognizing that they were being dismissed. But as Lodi started to turn away, Thorald caught his arm and winked at the king. "Your Majesty, I believe the Kingsguard would like to request a royal boon of you."

"Ask away, Kingsguard," the king commanded.

Lodi suddenly found it difficult to look anywhere but his feet. He cleared his throat. He pulled at his beard, then rubbed at his face. "Well, Borgo, you see, it's like this. It seems I be, um, well, I might have found myself in a situation."

"A situation?" For the first time in the audience, the king looked amused. "And what sort of situation would that be, Kingsguard?"

"One of the marrying sort, I guess. See, Myf don't have a father to give her away now, so I was thinking perhaps you might be willing to stand with her in the place o' her da."

At that, the king smiled broadly and clapped his hands. "And so, the mighty fall at last!" He stepped down from the throne, and embraced Lodi warmly in his powerful arms. "Congratulations, my friend. This is the best news I have had in weeks. The Queen will be delighted."

Then he released him and raised his voice, so that it could be heard throughout the chamber.

"Seeing as how we are, as King, the father of all the dwarves of Iron Mountain, we should count it as no less than our duty to stand beside our most favored daughter Myf, and see her wed to our well-beloved Kingsguard, Lodi, son of Dunmorin, whom I herewith name my Royal Councillor for Draconic Relations." When Lodi tried to protest, he raised a royal hand to forestall it and addressed his new councillor in a quieter, though no less authoritative voice. "I am well aware of your talent for finding trouble, Lodi, and I have no intention of allowing you to get yourself killed and turn that lovely young wife-to-be of yours into a widow at the earliest opportunity. I'm afraid you shall have to adapt to a less arduous way of life and learn to keep me company here at court!"

Lodi bowed, but while he appreciated the great favor which Borgo was showing him, he was troubled by the king's apparent lack of concern for the news they had just brought him. "I'd like nothing better, Your Majesty, but you heard what we told you! There's a war up there, and there's a lot we better learn about them dragons afore they open that sky-burned door o' theirs!"

"Indeed," Borgo acknowledged. "But perhaps it is time you permit others to beard the dragon, old friend. However many of them there might be."

The king glanced at Thorald, who bowed gracefully in silent acquiescence. "Now, go to your pretty lass, Lodi, and don't you dare return without giving me a date to tell the Queen!"

BERETH

THE GREAT FETE in the reception hall was far less dire than she'd feared, Bereth thought after her third goblet of sparkling golden wine. She was actually beginning to enjoy herself, as Caitlys introduced her to the daughters of some of the greatest families in the elven realms and humble seamstresses and housemaids with equal ease. Somehow, Caitlys always seemed to know every elfonwy's name, no matter what her rank, and it soon became evident that she was one of the more popular members of the royal family, as her two cousins, the royal princesses, refused to mingle, and instead stood together in splendid isolation, protected by a phalanx of their young ladies-in-waiting.

The entire crowd of elfedd, some five-hundred strong, was abuzz with rumors of why their collective presence had been demanded by the king, and their curiosity, as well as the volume of noise in the room, began to grow when the massive doors at the front of the room opened to the sound of a trumpet blast and a platoon of White Guards entered. The guards immediately began shepherding all of the elfedd to the left side of the high-ceilinged chamber; not even the princesses were permitted to remain in their corner near the right front, where the steps led up to the dais. Caitlys laughed at the expression on the face of the elder sister, who, if not for the large diamond in the center of her gold coronet, could have easily been mistaken for any of the other maidens.

"Oh, she did not like that, not at all," Caitlys chuckled at her royal cousin.

But if the noise and excitement had risen with the entrance of the guards, it rose to a crescendo when a grand parade of elves began entering in lines of five. They were all male, and like their female counterparts, they were all dressed alike, only in bright green capes worn over light grey tunics and pantalons of a slightly darker shade of grey. They were a little older, on average, which Caitlys quickly noted as she rattled off one name after another.

"There's Orithain, and there's Lord Rylle. Oh, I haven't seen Chelsoras in a while! And my goodness, will you look at how long Arden-Mergrin's hair has grown?" She dug an elbow into Bereth's side. "Now, whoever could that tall elf with the beautiful profile be?"

Bereth first wrinkled her nose and then her lip by way of reply. It was Ilriathas, of course, or 'Kelethan' as Caitlys insisted on calling him, and annoyed as she was, she had to admit that the captain of the High Guard looked rather magnificent, and that even amidst all the male splendor of his fellows, he tended to draw the eye to him. She sought to spot Lassarian as well, but he did not appear to have been included in the masculine parade, which rendered the whole dazzling display even more mysterious and inexplicable.

Line after line of elves, most of them of noble, or at least respectable, birth, marched in, aligning themselves in extended lines of twenty facing the front. When the last group entered, Bereth quickly counted and realized that there were exactly twenty-five lines arrayed before the dais. There was a trumpet blast, and as one, all five hundred elves turned to their left to face their female counterparts.

Ilriathas looked pale and unusually somber. She wondered if he was unwell, or if he simply hadn't been given the opportunity to sleep since their arrival. He was faced in her direction, but didn't seem to see her even though she was on the front edge of the elf maidens.

"Is this some sort of royal dance or something?" she whispered to Caitlys.

"I don't know," her new friend said slowly. She sounded suspicious, of but what, Bereth could not imagine. "I've never even heard of anything like this before! They say Tir Diffaith is besieged, so perhaps we're all being ordered to take up arms and do battle with the orcs."

"I'm already in the High Guard," Bereth reminded her. "So is Ilri."

"And I can count at least ten cavalry officers from here. Yes, that doesn't seem very likely now, does it."

"I shouldn't think so."

A melodious fanfare sounded.

"Well, now we'll find out. My uncle is coming."

And indeed, High King Mael was sweeping grandly up the stairs onto the dais, having entered by one of the side doors on the right side of the hall. He was wearing a gold circlet rather than his crown, but was preceded by the *Canghellor Tir Uchel* and followed by the *Arglwydd Lywodraethwr y Ddinas*, both of whom carried white staves and were dressed in the full pomp of their royal offices. The two lords stood on either side of the king, as twenty White Guards in ceremonial armor covered by green cloaks took their places behind them in an arc.

It suddenly occurred to Bereth that green was traditionally the color of an elven groom's cloak. Her eyes narrowed as she took in the fact that there were also a roughly equal number of elves and elfonwydd, and that she didn't see a single elf in all the gathering whom she knew to be married.

"Caitlys," she hissed, but before she could say more, the king raised both his hands in salutation.

"Welcome, children! We would like to say that we are pleased to see you here tonight, but tonight we must speak of hard truths, and we must do so in complete honesty. First, we must tell you that some of the rumors you have heard are true. Last night, messengers from the great fortress of Tir Diffaith arrived with word that the servants of the Great Orc worked a powerful sorcery against the magical defenses of the fortress. Today, more messengers arrived with word that although this fell sorcery failed to break the mighty walls, their defenses have been substantially weakened, to the point they will not withstand a second such assault."

The assembled gathering gasped, almost as one, at the incredible news. Even Bereth, though she knew full well of Tir Diffaith's peril, felt as if she'd been kicked in her stomach. The great fortress of the elves had defended the eastern border against the savage depredations of the orcs for dozens of centuries, and the realization that the orc horde would likely be rampaging over elven lands within a few days filled her with terror.

Nor was she the only one, judging by the protests and wails of fear that rose from the assembly. But even the most frightened elfonwy fell silent when the king held up his hand.

"The orcs are preparing for a second assault on the walls of Tir Diffaith, but it will not come tonight. The effort has exhausted their sorcerers and they will require time to restore themselves. And that is why we will take our leave of you tomorrow, in the company of the seven Magistrae of the Collegium Occludum, to ensure that not only does their second attempt fail, but to eliminate, once and entirely, Zoth Ommog's threat to our realm."

In a moment, the fear that filled the room was transformed into an ecstatic joy that bordered on mania. Bereth felt her own heart leap, and Caitlys grabbed her arm and squeezed it so tightly that she knew it had left a mark without needing to look at it. Every elf there knew there was no power on Selenoth, or anywhere else in the world, that could stand against the arcane knowledge of the Collegium. Even the dread Witchkings, before whom Dwarf, Man, Orc, and Troll alike had quailed, had fallen when the magisters finally came out of their mysterious towers to strike them down in their wicked pride. And yet, she wondered, why had the king initially turned to the ancient elf whom she had met last night instead of the wizards of the College?

"Before we depart, however, there is something we must do. And that is why we have summoned you here tonight." Unexpectedly, the king looked down at his feet. He was silent for an uncomfortably long time, to the point that the elf maidens around her begin to stir and whisper. Finally, King Mael raised his head, and his face was even more frighteningly bloodless than Ilriathas's had been earlier.

"Children, as your king, we have failed you. And you, children, you have failed yourselves. Together, we have failed the realm and we have failed the race. Once there were seven kingdoms over which my forefathers ruled as high kings. Now there are three. Once the elves were a great and mighty race who ruled over all the peoples and creatures of Selenoth. Now we hide behind our walls and our magics for fear of degenerates and savages who know nothing and care less about art, beauty, poetry, and nature!

"And the fault, children, the fault is in ourselves. But do not think we blame you! No, for you were failed by your ancestors, by your parents, and by your liege. You were not taught, we did not teach you, that by virtue of your being, by virtue of the blessings of your race, you owe a duty to those who came before you. And you owe a duty to those who will follow you, to your children and to your children's children!"

The king paused. His face was no longer pale, it was now suffused with blood, though with passion, with anger, or with shame, Bereth could not tell.

"He can't possibly be thinking... he wouldn't..." she heard one elf maiden behind her say.

"Before me stand one thousand elves. And not one single elf here has fathered a child! Not one single elfess here has birthed a child! Some of you have seen a century, a few of you have seen a century-and-a-half, and yet you tell yourselves there is no need to think beyond today, or to think beyond yourself. Are you not of the elves? Do you not have all the time in the world? Can you not let love, and marriage, and children wait for another year, another decade, another century?" He smiled coldly. "No. For we tell you tonight, my elves and elfedd, you have no more time. You will marry, and you will marry tonight!"

The female half of the assembly fairly swayed backward with astonishment and shock. But they were too stupefied by the king's unexpected declaration to speak, let alone protest. The male half was equally silent, but none of them appeared to be even remotely surprised.

They were told, Bereth thought, even as her mind reeled before the implications of the king's words. They were told what he intended, they knew what he would demand of them, and yet they are here. And yet, *he* is here. Without meaning to, she craned her neck to the right and sought out Ilrithias. He was facing forward, but she could tell by the way his head was thrown back and how his lips were tightly pressed together that he was taut with inner turmoil.

Was he thinking of her? Or after her many spurnings, her repeated rejections, did he have another in mind.

"How dare you!" she heard one elf maiden cry, and her protest was echoed by at least a score of similarly outraged elfedd.

"How dare *you* deny your High King!" roared the king, pointing a long, accusatory finger at the protesting elfess. "Hear us well, children! From this day forward, any elf or elfonwy who refuses marriage at the king's command will be deemed guilty of *mawredd anafus*, an offense against the crown, the realm, and the Elves!"

"*Cyfaddef*," chorused the two lords on either side as they raised their staffs of office.

"Let it be known that any elf here this night who is not engaged to be married by the thirteenth bell shall be deemed to have volunteered for the city militia and shall report to Lord Arthenrod before noon tomorrow. Should any volunteer fail to report for his duty by the appointed hour, he shall be deemed a deserter, he shall be stripped of all honors and property, and he shall be expelled from the Three Realms!"

None of the elves being addressed reacted to the word of the king's unthinkably harsh threats, least of all Ilriathas, further confirming Bereth's suspicions that the king had already informed them of his intentions and that this was mostly theater performed for the benefit of the gathered elf maidens. But it was effective theater, if the faint cries and urgent whispers that surrounded her could be trusted. For whom did they most fear, their brothers or their lovers, she wondered. And what would Ilriathas do, if she refused him again? Would he really give up his title, his wealth, and his captaincy? Would he ever even consider giving up Ebon, and with the great black-headed warhawk, the sky?

No, she realized, as she stared at his noble profile and his well-shaped ears. He would do his duty. And if the king was ordering him to marry, then he would marry, even if he remained secretly devoted to her.

"And let it be known, daughters, that any elfess here this night who is not engaged to be married by the thirteenth bell shall be designated the property of the crown, and she shall report to one of the Gardens of Delight before noon tomorrow. There, she shall serve as a *rhosyn hyfryd* until such time as she has birthed two children, who shall be wards of the crown. Should any elfess fail to report for her duty by the appointed hour, she shall be sold to the highest bidder for a period of time no less than ten years and no more than thirty. Any children born during the time of her service shall be wards of the owner."

It was worse than Bereth had thought. It was worse than she would have imagined possible.

"He can't possibly mean it!" she said, stunned.

"Oh, he absolutely does," Caitlys said bitterly. "I've never known him to change his mind. He must be terrified of something. Was this thing at Tir Diffaith really as bad as they said?"

"It was worse," Bereth said, shuddering at the memory of the demonic eyes looking out from the terrible inferno and seeing her, even in the darkness of the night sky. "But surely the Collegium–"

"The Collegium are a collection of aged cowards who've spent centuries staring at their own navels. I doubt he's got any faith in them. I know I don't."

The great chamber was now divided into feminine chaos on the left, as the young elfesses vented their fear and anger at the king, and silent male discipline on the right. Some of the elf maidens were excited at the prospect of an imminent marriage, many of them were, like Bereth, too astonished and bewildered to be angry, and more than a few were red-faced and shaking with fury.

"No, no, never, never!" screamed one yellow-haired elfonwy.

"What does the Queen say about this," another elfess shouted at the king.

"*Melltithio di i uffern!*" shrieked one particularly irate maiden.

But most of the elfedd, like Bereth, were wide-eyed and quiet as they tried to digest the unthinkable turn of events. *What does this mean for me? Is this truly happening? What if I'm not the one he actually wants? Who is my best option? How will I choose between him and him? They wouldn't really sell me into slavery, would they? How can this happen to me? What will my parents say?*

High King Mael did not react to any of the angry shouts directed his way from the left side of the hall, much less respond to them. Instead, he faced the elves on the right and raised his hand. *"Mae gennych eich archebion!"* he called out to them.

The thundering sound of the elves standing to attention drowned out the protests from the other side.

"We hear and we obey!" the cry echoed off the walls.

The king conferred briefly with the captain of the White Guards, then preceded the white-armored elves down the steps and out of sight in the company of the *Arglwydd*. A group of musicians replaced the guards on the dais, and as they began tuning their instruments, the *Canghellor* raised his white staff again, which was the sign for one of the musicians to ring a single bell.

"The king orders you to dance, to drink, to mingle, and to make merry. You have until the next bell to make your decision, at which time the High King of the Three Realms and his Queen will return to conduct the ceremony."

Bereth glanced over at Ilriathas and saw the Captain of the High Guard had finally turned her way. She stared at him defiantly, and for a second, she thought he might turn away. But then the tall elf took a deep breath and began walking toward her just as the musicians began to play a slow, romantic tune that was often heard at Eritide balls.

"This is madness," she told him.

"This is not how I would have had it," he replied. "Shall we dance?"

She nodded, and placed her hand in his.

She had danced with him many times before over the years, but never before had she been so conscious of him, of how he moved, how he breathed, how he held her in his arms.

"I don't care about the magic. But I don't want to give up the sky, Ilri."

"With me, you never will. We shall ride the sky together, you and I."

"It isn't the same."

"No, it won't be. It never is."

The thought of never again soaring high above the world in perfect solitude was like a dagger between her breasts. She could feel the pain in her body as well as in her soul. And yet, she took strength from his tranquility, and she found solace in the gentle swaying of their bodies together to the melody. All around them, elves were talking, dancing, arguing, crying, apologizing, accusing, wheedling, sneering, rejecting, and accepting, but she paid no heed to any of them. Her fears, her worries, began to melt away as she closed her eyes, allowed herself to stop thinking, and gave into the sensations of the moment.

"I like you, Ilri. You've always been there for me. But I don't know—"

"I do. You've always kept me at arms length because you know it is real between us, it's not something you could fly away from whenever you feel scared or bored or tied down. You and me, we are real, Bereth. Lassarian and the others, they were nothing more than illusions you could banish at will."

"You knew about Lasri?" She looked up at him, wide-eyed with surprise, and, much to her astonishment, a little shame.

"Of course. There are very few secrets in the High Guard, given all of the eyes in the skies."

"Where is Lassarian anyhow," she said quickly, hoping to change the subject. "Shouldn't he be here?"

"Once the king told me what he intended tonight, I sent him back to Tir Diffaith."

"You did what?" She stared at him, not knowing what to think. "Were you afraid that I'd choose him instead of you?"

Of all his possible responses, the one she least expected was that he would laugh at her. Which, to her surprise, was precisely what he did. "I wasn't thinking about you at all, my love. I've known Lassarian much longer than you have. He is of modest birth, he has no property to lose, and he is a valuable skyrider. As I'm sure you are aware, he has no desire to marry or confine his attentions to just one elfess, and he is just stupid and stubborn and self-centered enough to believe the king's mandate will not apply to him."

"So you sent him away rather than see him lose the sky."

"Oh, hardly that. Arthenrod would have seconded him to the High Guard before sunrise; I would have made sure of it. We cannot afford to lose any skyriders, least of all one so tireless and so willing to fly low. But he would have needlessly harmed his prospects for the future."

"And so you sent him away." She shook her head. "I am not good enough for you, Lord Kelethan.

He smiled, and for the first time, dared to lean in and kiss her. She was pleased to discover that he was rather better at it than she'd ever have imagined.

"You have always been the only one for me, Lady Kelethan-to-be."

She kissed him again, more thoroughly this time. Perhaps, she thought. Perhaps he was right. Perhaps he had been right all along.

She pulled back and stared at him, as if she was seeing him for the very first time. He was handsome, she had always known that, but how had it escaped her attention that his green eyes had flecks of gold in them, or that the intensity with which he held her gaze made her shiver down to the base of her spine. There was a firmness to him, an iron core, that had somehow eluded her even in the midst of a war. He was strong, not only in body, but in spirit and willpower as well, and it struck her that what she had always taken for stolidness and boring reliability was actually the arrogant patience of a far-seeing mind. He was like an elf from the age of the Seven Kingdoms, splendid and self-assured, and she suddenly felt grieved that she had wasted what could have already been years, even decades, together.

He said nothing. He did not look away. And finally, he smiled, as if to say 'now, at last, you see me true.' Then he held up a ring, a simple, unadorned circle of gold.

"They gave us these to give those who accepted us. You'll need to take it if you wish to avoid spending the next decade as a captive rose."

She put out her hand. "Far be it from me to fail in my duty to Elebrion and the Elves."

But with that same clever sleight of hand he had shown her once before, the plain ring vanished, and in its place was a gorgeous platinum annulus, gossamer-thin, with tiny diamonds woven around a stunning central sapphire.

"This, I think, is more suitable for the elfonwy who is to be my wife. It is precisely the color of your eyes."

He slipped it on her finger and she held up her hand to admire it properly. "Mother is going to love it. I love it. Oh, but Ilri, you know I don't care about wealth and power and all these lovely things. Just promise me that we will always have the skies!"

He took her hands in his and kissed them, first the right, then the left on which she wore his ring. "I promise you this, Bereth mer Eulenarias," he vowed. "Until the day we die, we will share the sky."

That will do, she thought. That will do. It wasn't the future that she'd thought she wanted, but it just might be a better fate than she deserved.

It belatedly occurred to her that she'd been ignoring Caitlys, and that her newly acquired friend should really see her ring.

"I need to find the elfonwy who brought me here, the Lady Caitlys!"

"She's right over there," Ilriathas pointed her out.

"You know her?"

"Of course. For ages. We're second cousins on one side, and another sort of cousin on the other."

"I should have known."   Taking his hand, she fairly dragged him through the crowd of dancing couples, kissing couples, and couples deep in conversation holding hands, past bitter elves tight-lipped with rejection, and anxious elfonwydd waiting for someone to save them from their peril. "Caitlys! It seems I'm going to marry Ilri!"

"Congratulations, High Guard," the royal elfess said offhandedly. "About time you finally talked her round, Kelethan. At least I won't have to listen to your endless mooning over her anymore."

"How about you, Shadowsong? Any likely prospects."

"Gods, no! I sent a few ambitious ear-ticklers scurrying off with what I sincerely hope will be permanent scars to their self-esteem."

"I'd expect nothing less."

Bereth was gaping at the two of them, astonished, and more than a little alarmed, at how well Ilri and Caitlys seemed to be acquainted.

"Relax, High Guard. He's the one who sent me to you in the first place." She eyed Ilriathas and raised a slender eyebrow. "Don't you have something for me, Kelethan?"

"Indeed." He produced the plain ring he'd shown Bereth before and handed it to Caitlys. The pretty elfess slipped it on her finger and shrugged at Bereth.

"If I have to marry, Lord Caerwych is my only reasonable option. He's a *marchog y dderwen wen* now, but he knows enough magic to learn how to control Vengirasse. Kelethan promised me he'd find a place for Caerwy in the High Guard once he takes to the sky."

"Oh, well, that's good, I suppose." Teaching her husband to fly her hawk would be small consolation for giving up the bond between rider and bird, Bereth knew. But she also knew that flying with another would be much, much better than remaining bound to the ground for the rest of her life.

"I'm truly sorry for both of you," Ilriathas said. "But I'm afraid that's the best I could do, in the circumstances."

"It's not your fault, Kelethan."   Bereth didn't say anything, but she squeezed his hand and leaned into his side.

Caitlys held up her hand and examined the ring Ilriathas had given her. "Kelethan, seeing as how I won't be getting married tonight, do you think you can get the three of us out of here? You'll be wanting to have a proper ceremony anyhow if we survive whatever the king and the college have in mind for us tomorrow."

"You're coming to Tir Diffaith with us?"

"I should think so! You'll have a devil of a time getting Bessarias to ride out there with anyone else." The pretty elfess made a wry face. "Besides, we should probably let Lord Caerwych know that he's acquired a royal fiancée before he does something foolish and gets himself killed. Kelethan, it might be best if you break the news to him."

"I tend to agree," her own newly-minted fiancé replied gravely, although she saw amusement dancing in his gold-flecked eyes. "I will confess, I can't wait to see his face!"

Still holding her hand tightly, the handsome skyrider led them through the mass of couples toward the exits.

FJOTRA

N O SOONER had Fjotra and her attendants followed her mother outside the palace and through the grounds toward the gate they'd entered previously, than her mother suddenly brought them all up in a halt.

"Put this over your hair," Dagna ordered as she ripped off the blue scarf she'd been wearing and forced it into her hands. "Geirrid, take off your cloak and give it to Fjotra, now!"

"Of course, madame," the girl answered, looking as confused as Fjotra felt.

"And let your hair down."

"Mother, what are you doing?"

Her mother ignored her as she arranged Geirrid's blonde hair in a manner that resembled Fjotra's own. The two young women were of a height, and with both her hair and her dress now covered, Fjotra now looked more like an attendant than a lady being attended. But what was the point of a disguise if they were all returning to the manoir from whence they'd come?

"Mother, what do you have in mind?"

Her mother looked from the one Dalarn girl to the other, then shrugged. "It should do. Fjotra, I don't know if your fiancé has gone mad or if he's being controlled by that wretched trollmand, but you are in great danger from him. You cannot allow yourself to fall into his clutches!"

"What do you mean? How am I in danger?"

"He's making a play for the throne! I don't know if he'll actually kill his father or not, but whatever his intentions are, you will be vital to his plans. Without you, he has no claim on the Isles or to command our men. So you can't go back to the manoir with your ladies now."

"But where am I to go?" Fjotra felt panic rising inside her. She had no powerful friends at court, and even if she could reach the rebels in the south, they would spurn her for her betrayal of the comtesse. And most of the Dalarn warriors were still with the Red Prince's army, leagues to the East. "What am I to do?"

"It has to be someone strong enough to resist the prince and his men, especially if the king does not survive the night. Perhaps one of the archbishops? No, if the prince does not respect his father, he will not hesitate to violate the sanctity of the Church."

"The magiciens," suggested Lady Jean shyly. "Surely one sorceror is no match for the entire Assembly!"

"Perhaps, but who can trust the trollmands? They would have the means to resist, but they have no reason to protect her, not at the price of angering the heir to the throne, or even the crown itself."

"The soldiers," Fjotra said, as she recalled an afternoon that suddenly seemed to be a very long time ago. "The soldiers from the south."

"The Amrans?" her mother said, looking thoughtful. "It's said there are ten thousand of them. And they are supposed to be formidable warriors."

"I met their commander," Fjotra said. "At the tournament." She could picture the tall young man now; with his eyes and nose that reminded her of an eagle. Although she hadn't spoken to him, she'd never forgotten the way he'd stared at her like a starving wolf. He'd wanted her, she'd known it at the time, but she'd been entirely absorbed with her engagement to Étienne-Henri and so she'd thought no more of him. But now, would his apparent interest be enough to provide her protection from an angry heir to the throne? "I do not think he liked the prince. And I do not think he would hand me over to him."

But if it came to that, what would his protection cost her, she wondered.

"Don't they have that fort they built outside the city?" Geirrid said reflectively. "Most of them marched east to fight the orcs, but I've seen their patrols and their guards outside it when I was out riding with Lord Vaullion. And no one would think to look for you there!"

"How will I get there? I don't know where it is!" Fjotra thought for a moment. "The captain should know. What is his name, Joubert?"

"Jaubert," corrected Lady Jean. "But will he still be outside the gate?"

"He'd better be," said her mother grimly. "If not, we'll find another way."

Fortunately, as the little group of women made their way out of the palace grounds and past the pair of indifferent palace guards still at their post, they were greeted by the welcome sight of the captain and his men seated at their ease on the other side of the alley, dicing to while away the time. The captain was facing the gate, and he leaped to his feet with alacrity at the sight of his previous escorts and bowed to her.

"My apologies, Your Highness! I did not expect you back so soon!" He blinked at the sight of her mother, then bowed even more deeply to her. "Captain Amédée Jaubert at your service, Madame la Duchesse."

"Captain," her mother said loftily, giving him her hand to kiss as if she had been born to the custom. "You may indeed do me a service, but I fear it may be one that could cost you dearly at court." Quickly, she explained the situation, and the captain swore a thunderous oath when she described the Red Prince's alarming actions.

"Magique, and black magique at that!" The captain shook his head. "He'll never see the throne now, not if he surrounds himself with a thousand devils summoned from Hell! There's not a noble in the kingdom who will abide such a wicked blasphemer! What do you need me to do?"

"The princess is in danger. You must take her to the Amran fort, where she will be safe from the prince's men. Can you get her out of the city?"

The captain smiled. "Without a doubt. The commander of the East Gate is an old friend. But it would be best if his men didn't know she had left the city through it, or he'll know where to start looking for her." He looked from Fjotra to one of his men. "Fortunately, Your Royal Highness is a tall young lady. Quennel, give her your helmet, and gauntlets. Sword too! And swap cloaks with her."

As Fjotra did her best to tuck all of her long hair under the helm the young guard gave her, her mother took the captain by both hands.

"Swear that you will see her safely to the fort, by your god and his dead son!"

"I'll get her there, Duchesse. I understand your concerns; I have three daughters not much younger than her. I'll let you know she's safe upon my return."

"Thank you, Captain. Our people will be in your debt." Her mother turned to Fjotra and smiled at the strange sight she made. "I'll send Erland or Ketil for you as soon as we know where Brynjolf and the other jarls are. *Den lille slange* won't dare to send his knights against three thousand of our axes! May Váði vitnis go with you and guard you, daughter!"

"And you, mother dearest."

"Quennel, Jean-Charles, get the ladies back to the manoir, then summon the next shift early. Stéphane, you will stay with Madame la Duchesse and escort her wherever she wants to go until she releases you. And God help you if any of you breathe a word of this to anyone!" Jaubert took her arm. "Come, Highness, we'll find you some pantalons at the stables before we ride out. With any luck, we'll have you safely there before nightfall!"

However, the captain's assessment proved optimistic. Although they reached the stables that belonged to the city guard without incident, and managed to find her a man's tunic, pantalons, and even a brass breastplate that accommodated her modest curves, the combination of the recent victory over the *gobelins* with rumors concerning the subsequent events at the palace had excited the population to the point that the streets were packed with children, revelers, merchants taking advantage of the impromptu festival atmosphere, and thieves taking advantage of the festival-goers. As they urged their horses past a pack of young men marching behind a papier-mâché orc's head and chanting something about victory, blood, and slaughter, Fjotra glanced down an alley, then swiftly averted her eyes in alarm at the sight of one woman of easy virtue plying her trade.

"Sit up straighter," Jaubert hissed. "Things are getting out of hand and they'll be sending the guards out as soon as a few of these idiots start setting fires. Just sit straight and keep your mouth shut!"

She nodded compliantly and did her best to imitate the stiff-backed posture of the guards she'd seen at the manoir, although she found it didn't take long before she felt a swelling pain in the center of her lower back. How did Brynjolf ever learn to ride while encased in this metal, let alone try to fight in it? If only the Skullbreaker could see her now, how he would laugh! Strangely, she felt no fear, perhaps because the whole situation was so far beyond her imaginings that it was hard to believe it was real. Was she really wearing men's armor, fleeing from her sorcerous betrothed in the hopes that complete strangers would hide her from him?

Sol was dipping very low and red in the sky, and bright Fulla had already risen, though her dark and twisted brother was yet to join her by the time they finally reached the East Gate. It was open, she was relieved to see, and there were still more people seeking to enter than leave.

"Captain Jaubert!" the oldest of the six guards at the gate saluted him. "Good to see you, sir! I assume you've heard the news?"

"A great victory! And I don't mind admitting, a load off my mind, Sergeant. I wasn't looking forward to joining you at the gate here to defend it against the stinking verdards!"

"We'd have kept the bastards out," the sergeant grinned, exposing a missing left canine. "So where are you off to this late in the day, Captain?"

Jaubert beckoned the sergeant closer, and leaned down to speak softly in his ear. "You're going to hear some funny business coming out of the palace soon, Vaquelin. So I was never here and no one was with me."

The sergeant glanced at Fjotra, then quickly looked away and swore under his breath. She didn't think he recognized her, there was no reason he should, but it was impossible to know either way.

"How bad is it?"

"Not sure. But it doesn't look good."

"I don't know nothing. And I don't want to know nothing." He looked up at Jaubert. "So I can't say nothing."

"Good man." The captain pressed a pouch into the other man's hand. "I won't insult you, Vaquelin, but it might be advisable to take the lads out for a jar or two…"

"None taken, sir!" He winked. "I'll see none o' them boys can remember their own names tonight! And you know, Captain, I think I heard tell that two o' Lord Jongny's men was riding out the South Gate around sundown."

"Indeed? Headed south to Écarlate to join the Grand Duc, no doubt."

"That's what I heard, Captain." The sergeant saluted, then turned around and immediately started bawling out a pair of his men who were dawdling over a wine merchant's cart, presumably in the hopes of obtaining a sample of the merchandise.

Jaubert didn't hurry, in fact, he didn't even urge his horse into a canter, but was content to leave the walls of Lutéce behind at a leisurely trot. It wasn't until they were well past the lines of carts and travelers waiting to pass through the gates that he glanced at her and touched his heels to the sides of his horse. Fjotra's mount was bigger and more powerful than she was accustomed to, but fortunately it was a gelding and it obediently picked up its pace into a rhythmic canter without any need of a hint from her. They rode past an outgoing cart or two, as well as several groups of people on foot, but didn't see any riders coming or going.

"We'll need to slow down when we lose the light," he shouted to her. She nodded; just trying to stay in the saddle despite the unfamiliar armor on her head and torso that made her top-heavy and upset her sense of balance. Fortunately, when darkness fell and it became difficult to distinguish the packed-dirt road from the grass on either side, the captain slowed his horse to a walk and reached out to take the reins from her. Ahead, it was just possible to make out what looked like a pair of torches in the distance, though whether it was the Amran fort or merely a guide post, she had no way of knowing.

The torches turned out to be a guard post about two hundred paces south of the main road. The soldiers, clad in their outlandish iron armor, with strange helms that covered most of their deeply-tanned faces, spoke little Savonnais, and appeared to be perplexed by their presence until Jaubert managed to get it across to them that he was a royal officer with a message for their commander.

One of the guards lit a torch, then escorted them along a well-worn path through an old forest that eventually brought them within sight of the great wooden fortress that was larger than most of the castles Fjotra had seen while traveling across Savondir. It was bigger, in fact, than any of the towns in which she'd lived in her home isles.

"They built that in a single day," Jaubert commented. "Not all of the towers and platforms, of course, or the buildings inside the walls, but the ditch and the greater part of it, that was all done well before sundown."

"That's not possible!"

"It's incredible what six thousand men can accomplish if they are well-disciplined." He snorted dismissively. "That may serve you well, if it comes to it."

Their escort was hailed by the guards at the gates, and upon his provision of what she assumed was a password, they were allowed to enter. They rode across a wide, wooden bridge that spanned the ditch, and were greeted inside the gates by a man wearing gleaming silver armor and a crest that ran from side to side rather than front to back. An officer of some kind, Fjotra assumed.

"Who are?" he said in very bad Savonnais. "Why come here?"

"I am Captain Amédée Jaubert of the Lutéce City Guard. I would like to speak with your commander. It is a matter of urgency."

"A matter of money?" The officer looked more confused than suspicious.

"I'm sorry, no. It is a matter of danger, perhaps war." Jaubert spoke slowly and clearly, then patted his sword. "Fighting, swords."

The confusion on the man's face vanished, replaced by a keen, hawk-eyed clarity. Fjotra had the impression that this was a man her father would have recognized as a proper warrior. "You wait here. I take my chief."

He turned on his heel and marched off toward one of the buildings in the center of the fort. Fjotra couldn't see much in the flickering firelight of the torches, but everything looked very orderly and organized, not unlike the soldiers themselves. She hoped they would have some sort of accommodation for women, if they agreed to let her stay.

She saw the bobbing flames approaching before she heard the tromping of the men coming toward them. There were six men besides the officer accompanying the commander; all six of them were bearing torches, so she could see him quite clearly. He was a tall young man, clean-shaven, and while he wore the same sort of helm as the others, the crest ran front to back. He also looked extremely weary, and his blue cloak was still stained with the dust of the road. His Savonnais was strongly accented, but to her relief, it was surprisingly good.

"I am the Tribune Gaius Trebonius. Because General Valerius is not here, I speak for the legion. Who are you?"

Jaubert looked at her. She nodded, and removed her helm.

"As I told your man, I am Captain Amédée Jaubert of the City Guard. And it is my honor to present Her Royal Highness, Fjotra Skulisdattir, Princess of the Wolf Isles."

"I know you!" The tribune's eyes widened. "I've seen you before! You were at the tournament. The tall blonde girl in the blue dress. You're the one who is going to marry the king's son!"

"Not anymore," she said. "Will you help me?"

AULAN

A CHALLENGE outside the door caught his attention. One of his guards appeared to be addressing someone demanding entrance.

"Sir, with all due respect, our orders are to let no one speak to the prisoner!"

"Those orders are countermanded, legionary, on my authority! Now stand aside or I'll have you flogged for insubordination!"

"Yessir!" He heard more than one guard saluting his incipient visitor. The visitor's voice sounded familiar. He wondered who it could be. It had to be an officer. One of the tribunes? No, it had to be someone of higher rank than that, judging by how quickly the guards accepted his countermanding of their orders and allowed him entrance.

The door flew open, and to his surprise, it was Falconius Buteo, the Legatus of Legio III himself.

"My apologies for the inconvenience, Aulan. But it was necessary. Good to see you again."

"Good to see you, General. At least, I hope so. It's been a while since I've seen a friendly face." Aulan took the older man's hand warily. He was confused as to why the former commander of Fulgetra was here at Castrus Mendrisus; the last he'd heard of the Falconian, he'd been in the northwestern provinces. "Why are you here?"

"To let you out, of course!"

"Secondus Falconius, I have to tell you that my lunatic brother thinks he is going to betray Magnus and thereby save Amorr from his royal aspirations."

The general laughed, a hearty chuckle that was alarming in such a large and ugly man. "Yes, I know. The centurions have already taken Titus

A SEA OF SKULLS

Severus into custody. I have him being held secure in his domus by my own men; Magnus has ordered that you will decide what to do with him." Buteo extended a hand to him, and Aulan gladly took it. "Come along now. Best we settle this thing speedily, so the men can be presented with a *fait accompli*."

Aulan stared at Buteo in astonishment. "You've been with Magnus from the start?"

"I wouldn't say from the start. But we've been in regular communication since the beginning of this whole debacle." He shrugged. "The politicians play their games in the Senate, but it inevitably falls to those of us who actually command the legions to keep civil order in the end. He may not be to everyone's liking, but with the empire, the church, and the allies all in chaos, Amorr needs someone like Magnus to take a firm grasp of things."

"Yes, my father reached a similar conclusion."

"Severus Patronus was a great man. A great loss to the Senate and People."

Aulan, feeling a little overwhelmed by the sudden turn of events, followed the older man out of the makeshift prison. He gratified to see in the flickering torchlight outside that he was greeted with friendly nods and other small gestures of encouragement by the centurions who had accompanied Buteo. They escorted him and the general back to the brick headquarters building where his brother had betrayed him.

"And my men?"

"They are well. Your brother had them imprisoned too, but either he did not dare to mistreat them or saw no reason to do so. I gave orders for their release before I went to fetch you, so I expect they are already free."

"I hope you also had them informed that I was to be freed as well."

The general laughed. "Aye, we'd not want that decurion of yours stirring up trouble. He's a hard lad, that one. He'd have made a fine centurion if he didn't know how to ride."

Aulan made a mental note to pass the comment on to Lucarus; that was high praise indeed from the old Falconian. "What does Magnus want me to do with Titus Severus?"

"He said to do as you saw fit." Buteo raised a bushy grey eyebrow. "If you know anything about Magnus, Aulan, then you have to know this is more about you than your brother. I imagine he wishes to see what you'll do when faced with a difficult choice. Many a good tribune has failed as a general; sometimes the right decision requires a cold heart."

"So you're saying I should have him executed for treason."

"Not at all." The general shook his head. "Maybe Magnus thinks you're too ruthless and hopes to see that you're able to show mercy. Or perhaps he thinks you're too soft. I'm just a simple infantry commander, I'm not a clever fox like him. Had he left it up to me, I'd have had your brother's pretty head off in a trice."

Aulan nodded. The Law of the Eagles was clear enough. Gross insubordination was the least of Regulus's offenses, but that alone was sufficient to merit an officer's execution. On the other hand, Magnus had broken with his own brother, and to some extent, with the Senate and People too, as a consequence of his fury at Valerius Corvus's lawful, and by all accounts well-merited, execution of Valerius Fortex.

As they turned the corner, he saw the torchlight reflected off the gleaming armor of the assembled legion, and realized that Buteo had ordered the entirety of *Fulgetra* to turn out and witness the fate of their erstwhile commander. He swallowed hard and did his best to resist the urge to look into the faces of the soldiers as he passed them. The rest of Fulgetra's tribunes were on the wooden stage, flanking his brother, with one notable exception.

For in front of the stage, the body of Appius Mallicus, formerly the legion's laticlavius, and briefly its nominal legatus, was lying on the ground. The unlucky officer was missing his head, which lay bare and sightless in a dark pool of blood several steps away, presumably courtesy of the powerful legionary who was standing with an axe in hand next to a large, bloodstained wooden block.

As they approached the three steps leading up to the stage, Buteo stopped and gestured that Aulan should precede him. A momentary qualm unsettled him, until the sight of his brother's bound arms reminded him that he was here to serve as the judge, not the sentenced man. He met Regulus's eyes without flinching, and was pleased to see that despite the dire situation, his brother was maintaining the dignity appropriate to a member of House Severus even in the most dire of circumstances.

"Men of the Legion, you have already witnessed the justice of the Senate and People once tonight," Buteo spoke loudly and clearly. "Your false tribune, who usurped a command that was not granted to him, has paid the price for his treachery. Now it is time for the fate of Titus Severus Regulus, who as a senior member of House Severus styled himself your Dux Domus, to be settled."

"Ave!" cried assembled men.

Buteo gestured toward Aulan. "Legio III is a House legion. As such, it is not for the Legatus Legionis to mete out justice to a son of the sponsoring House. Therefore, I present to you Aulus Severus Aulan, tribune of the legion and son of House Severus. Many of you know him. Many of you have ridden with him and served with him. He enjoys the trust of the great Valerius Magnus himself and stands here as his representative. He is also the brother of the accused, Titus Severus Regulus. Men of the Legion, will you accept his verdict in this matter?"

The legion shouted its approval, though not quite so loudly as before.

The Falconian turned to Aulan. "You heard them," he said in a low voice. "Pronounce the verdict."

Aulan nodded and stepped before his brother. He had to look up, as Regulus was taller than him. His brother's bronzed face was pale and he was blinking rapidly, but otherwise he showed no outward signs of fear.

"You gambled and you lost, Titus Severus."

"Not for the first time, little brother." Regulus actually grinned, flashing his white teeth in the smile that had charmed so many, men and women alike, over the years.

Aulan sighed. Even now, Regulus failed to recognize that for once, his charm would not allow him to escape the consequences of his foolish actions.

"No, not for the first time, elder brother. But it will be the last." Aulan spoke quietly, so that only Buteo and the tribunes on the stage could hear.

"You cannot seriously intend to sentence me to death! How will that look, Aulan? The Senate will see you as a fratricide! No matter what I have done, your enemies, and all the enemies of our House, will insist that you did it only to steal my inheritance!"

"There is that." Aulan realized just how perilous was the position in which Magnus was placing him. Was it, as Buteo suggested, a test? Or did the Valerian merely think to permanently hobble a young Severan who might one day rise to challenge the scions of House Valerius? And Regulus was not wrong; if he did not spare his brother, he would forever be seen as a kinslayer, whose actions, however justified by legionary law, were mostly motivated by greed and ambition.

"You're right, Regulus," he said. "No matter what I do, I will be damned. But what you don't understand, what you have never understood, is that I could not care less about your inheritance, the Cursus Honorum, or even the Senate. My sole concern is the good of our House!"

He saw his brother exhale with relief, and turned away from him, toward the silent gathering of soldiers awaiting his word.

"Men of *Fulgetra*! I am Aulus Severus Aulan, son of Aulus Severus Patronus, the late Princeps Senatus and Paterfamilias of House Severus. At the order of your commanding officer, Legatus Lucius Falconius Buteo, I shall now pronounce my verdict. I find the accused, Titus Severus Regulus, to be guilty of gross insubordination to a superior officer, to be guilty of conspiring against a superior officer, to be guilty of exceeding his authority as a tribune of the legion, and to be guilty of treason against this legion and against the Senate and People of Amorr!"

"*Nocens!*" The men shouted. "Guilty! He is guilty!"

"Men of Fulgetra, you know the penalty for these crimes!"

"*Mors! Mors! Poena mors est!*"

The roar was deafening as the soldiers shouted the ancient formulation: *the penalty is death!* It seemed Regulus was not quite as popular with the men as he'd imagined. But Aulan did not stand aside nor did he turn his brother over to the executioner. Instead, he held up an open palm and waited for them to settle down. It seemed to take ages, but finally, they fell silent except for a few jeers and catcalls from the legionary jesters.

"Titus Severus Regulus is guilty of the crimes of which he is accused. The Law of the Eagles states that the penalty for those crimes is death. However, Legio III is a legion sworn to the service of House Severus, and as a senior member of that House, I hereby commute his sentence on the grounds of *summa prioritas!*"

His words were met with an initial gasp of disbelief, and then, as anger swept across the crowd like a furious tide, a cacophony of bitter protest arose. There were shouts of anger and accusations of familial favoritism, but most of all, there was a repeated cry for justice to be served.

"*Nocens! Nocens! Poena mors est!*"

Buteo approached him and put a meaty hand on his shoulder. "Aulan, do you have any idea what you're doing? Don't risk your own life in trying to save his worthless hide!"

Aulan shrugged the elder man off. "Magnus told you to leave it to me. So leave it to me, Secondus Falconius."

"All right. I just hope you know what you're doing."

Aulan smiled bitterly as the general obediently stepped back. Oh, he knew exactly what he was doing. And he also knew he was going to pay for it for the rest of his life, however long or short it might be.

He faced the angry legionaries without rancor or fear. His dismissal of Buteo initially seemed to surprise them, as a number of them murmured in confusion with one another as the rest of them continued to loudly, vigorously, and obscenely object to his commutation of his brother's sentence. But soon they joined their voices to those of their fellows, and their furious words crashed over him like a waterfall to no avail, as he endured them patiently and impassively, waiting for them to tire themselves out.

After their rage had crescendoed and begun to subside, he drew his gladius and held it high over his head. Out of curiosity, if nothing else, enough of the soldiers stopped shouting so he could speak over them.

"Men of *Fulgetra*, the crimes against the Legion are not the only crimes committed by Severus Regulus! As I have already told you, I am a senior member of House Severus, and in the absence of our late paterfamilias, I have claimed the right of *summa prioritas* to judge my brother's offenses against our House and against our father." He pointed the tip of the sword at Regulus. "Titus Severus Regulus, I find you to be guilty of treason against House Severus, guilty of disobedience to your father and paterfamilias, Aulus Severus Patronus, and therefore, I denounce you as unfit to serve House Severus in any capacity!"

The soldiers roared with surprise and approval. He lowered his sword and leaned in close to Regulus. "You're also guilty of being a fool, brother! A cursed, self-centered fool!"

"Don't do this, Aulan," his brother hissed, his eyes wide with terror. "For the love of God, don't throw me to them!"

"I won't, brother," he promised, sincerely, and Regulus closed his eyes and swayed, as if he might faint with the relief of sudden reprieve.

Aulan raised the gladius high. Then he brought it around in an underhanded sweep that culminated in a deep thrust to his brother's midsection. He angled the blade up to evade the ribs and cut his brother's heart in two before withdrawing it. Regulus sank down to his knees, dying, as blood spilled from both his mouth and from the terrible wound in his belly.

"*Poena mors est!*" Aulan shouted.

As he raised the bloody sword, the legion erupted with savage joy and echoed his cry. The stage fairly rocked with their chanting combined with the stomping of their feet

"Severus! Severus! Aulus Severus!"

This time, he allowed himself to feel the legion's adulation. It was more intoxicating than wine. The Senate may not let me forget what I have done, he told himself, but I will not forget this. He closed his eyes and took a deep breath, seeing again the shock and confusion on his older brother's face when he'd realized that death was upon him. For better or for worse, it was done.

He wondered what Magnus would make of his decision.

"You didn't need to do that, Aulus Severus. Not by your own hand!"

He met Falconius Buteo's gaze and held it without saying anything. The Falconian was the first to blink and look away, but not before Aulan saw respect, and something that just might have been a small measure of wariness, in the older man's eyes.

Tell that to the Valerian, he thought, as the legion continued to chant his name.

BESSARIAS

THERE WAS a knock on his door. Bessarias looked up from the pages of his well-worn leather testament, wondering if it was Kilios and if his blind friend had managed to find any informative new documents in the royal library. He knew the entire contents of the holy scripture by memory, but now that his eyesight had sharpened, he found both solace and pleasure in reading the words again and carefully turning the thin, fragile pages, one by one.

The knock came again, a little louder and more agitated this time.

"Enter, if you please." He was surprised to look up and see the High King step through the doorway. Unlike the last time he had seen him, King Mael was beautifully attired, as if he had just come from court, although he was not wearing his crown, opting instead for a thin circlet of precious red ferleth that Bessarias couldn't recall having seen before and stood out starkly against his long white hair.

"I see you're still wasting your time with those Man fancies," he grumbled. "Well, I've done what you insisted, and now two-thirds of the noble families are in a state of near-revolt. If the orcs and their demonic summonings don't account for me, it's entirely possible that the lords and ladies of Elebrion will, courtesy of your lunacy."

"Decades from now, you'll understand that I was right to force your hand."

The king snorted dismissively and waved his hand. "Oh, there's no need to wait. I may be arrogant and mule-headed, but I'm not too proud to admit when I'm wrong. I daresay there's three times more mothers who are delighted than not, even if most of them feel the need to slander my name and lineage in public just to keep their image up. *Lese-haut majeste* is all the rage this morning."

"Ironic, that they criticize you for the first proper kingly action you've taken in centuries."

"I don't need to hear it from you too, you decrepit old relic!"

Bessarias laughed. He was pleased to hear that Mael had followed through on his promise, although he knew that now it would be time for him to do likewise.

"How many marriages?"

"Four hundred and seventeen. Another sixty maids formally affianced to elves not present in the city last night, including your friend and my niece Caitlys. Most of the unsuspecting bridegrooms are either at Tir Diffaith or with one of the regiments en route there."

"So you started from the top."

"The nobility great and small, the wealthy, and a few from families with a promising younger generation, for the most part. They were the most likely, and able, to resist, so I thought it best to begin with them. I have no doubt that the common folk will fall in line upon our return, but you'll have to take that on faith, since we must leave this morning. I'm told the walls are failing, and they will almost certainly fall to another sorcerous assault tonight."

"I will take you at your word, Mael." Bessarias smiled at the high king. He seemed uncommonly cheerful despite being under assault within and without the White City. It was the peace of a long-troubled conscience finally at rest, he had no doubt. "Any holdouts?"

"Not many. More elves than elfesses." Mael shrugged his velvet-caped shoulders. "They'll be sent to whatever regiment most requires reinforcements. The maids will be sent to a Garden house–"

"You would dishonor them?" Bessarias was incredulous, but the high king only laughed. "You wound me, Magistras. Of course not! They won't be touched. I've given strict orders to the elder sisters to put them to work scrubbing the floors on their knees and carrying out the nightpails. Between the potential shame to their families and the drudgery to which absolutely none of them is at all accustomed, I expect they'll be begging for husbands before we're back from Tir Diffaith." "Cruel, but subtle. I expect you're right."

"There might be a few to whom the lifestyle appeals, but we'll send in their mothers, and if necessary, their fathers as well, to change their minds. Any maid who still wants to stay in the Gardens after that would likely end up there sooner or later anyhow." The high king sighed. "So, I've delivered what you required. Are you prepared to do your part?"

"I am," Bessarias said. And he was ready, although his conscience remained unsettled even in the aftermath of his decision. Then again, what was one more sin added to the literally countless number for which he was already going to have to answer soon. "However, I will require the presence of Gilthalas and his three strongest adepts."

"What do you want with the Magistras Daemonae? He has never spoken well of you, and you have never spoken of him at all."

"Old differences of opinion. Water long under the bridge. It's his knowledge and strength that matter now. I will be occupied with material matters, and so we will need to be prepared for any magical assaults by the orcish sorcerors. From what the High Guard reported, the sheer amount of blood they spill more than makes up for their relative lack of talent. Their raw power is formidable."

"I'll send skyriders to the Collegium at once. Do you want them to meet us at Tir Diffaith?"

"Yes. I think it would also be well to have the Magistras Duellicus and at least one of his adepts as well. If I fail, or if I am struck down before my preparations are complete, you'll want them there to assist Gilthalas and his masters. And I might have a use for them myself."

"I'll send hawks for them as well. Anything else?"

Bessarias rose wearily from his chair, grimacing with the customary aches that afflicted his every movement now. He reached out and took Mael's left hand in both of his own, and raised it to his lips. "And now, O high king, understand, and receive instruction, you that rule the Three Realms. Serve ye the Lord with fear and rejoice unto him with trembling."

Mael smiled wryly, but he did not pull his hand away. "Advice from your dead god?"

"No, just a king of men, long dead. But he understood something you do not, my young friend, for all your arcane knowledge hard-won over the centuries. God changes times and ages, He raises up kingdoms and He takes them away. He gives wisdom to the wise, and knowledge to them that have understanding. He reveals deep and hidden things, and the light is with him."

"Thus spake the Magistras Gnossi."

Bessarias chuckled. "I hear the Collegium has a new and better one. Ah, Mael, do you not understand that as a king, you yourself are God's own tool? If I could have just one wish for you, it would be that one day, you would find the truth that I have found." He pointed to the testament he had been reading. "I am leaving that here for you. I will not need it where I am going."

The king's eyes grew dark with understanding. "You do not intend to return to Elebrion."

"My journey ends today, Mael. Whether I succeed or fail, it ends today." He patted Mael's hand. "Nine centuries is enough, as I expect you will discover in another five hundred years or so. But I go gladly to meet my fate, because you have given me hope for the future of the Elven race."

"I pray you are incorrect." The king sighed. "Will you ride with me to Tir Diffaith? If things go poorly there, our journeys may well end together."

"No, I shall ride with Caitlys. I owe it to her to let her bend my ear about her upcoming nuptials. I may even learn a few new words along the way!"

The king laughed. "I rather suspect you will. I can't imagine she's happy about giving up the sky." Then, very much to Bessarias's surprise, the High King of the Elves suddenly bowed, deeply and respectfully, to him. "Thank you for everything, old teacher, old friend. I will never forget you or the lessons you have taught me."

By way of response, Bessarias raised his hand. "*Kyrie, eleison. Propitius esto ab omni malo, ab omni peccato, ab insidiis diaboli.*" He knew Mael didn't understand a word, but the abbreviated litany seemed especially appropriate in light of the circumstances they were facing.

The king started to say something, stopped, shook his head, and left the room, closing the door softly behind him.

And there goes the last hope of the once-fair realms of Elebrion, Merithaim, Kir Donas, Glaislael, Kir Kalithel, Arathaim, and Falas, Bessarias thought, not without a modicum of satisfaction. Of the seven realms, only three remained. And now it fell to him to ensure that Mael would have the time and the opportunity to salvage the last three kingdoms, and perhaps one day restore the other four. The High King's actions of the previous night had been an important step forward, but it was nothing more than the first of many that would be necessary if the elves were to survive.

Now, where was that leather jacket Caitlys had given him? He could make do with blankets covering his spindly legs, but he had no wish to spend his last flight shivering the whole way to the ancient fortress. After searching the room, he finally found it neatly folded in the larger of the two wooden chests. A pair of thick woolen pantalons were underneath it, so he put them on under his white robe and marveled at how warm and soft they were.

Caitlys entered the room without knocking. The short, pretty elfess was rather more subdued than he expected, and she said nothing about the events of the night before, contenting herself with digging out a wool shirt that matched the pantalons and instructing him to put it on under the jacket. Mael must have told her that he would not be returning to the White City. Only after she helped him button the flight jacket and tighten the leather straps on the side to keep the wind out did she look at him directly.

"I'm honored that you chose to fly with me, Magistras. I'm sorry if I badgered you into doing this. I know that whatever it is you intend to do troubles you."

"Not anymore, child." He reached out and gently stroked her cheek. "I'm doing this for you, and for your children, and, God willing, their children's children."

She threw her arms around him and hugged him tightly. "I know. So, let's be on our way. And try not to fall off, old elf!"

The severity of the situation could be easily seen from the air as they approached Tir Diffaith. Although the tremendous army of orcs was still maintaining a safe distance from the catapults and scorpios mounted on the towers of the fortress, the scanty numbers of defenders made it clear that the fortress could not possibly hold once the spells infused in the walls failed before the relentless assault of the orc sorcery. There were still scattered flames burning from the glowing ashes of what had clearly been a considerable structure outside the encampment, and scores of orcs swarmed a second structure that was being erected nearby.

"Let's take a closer look at that," Bessarias shouted in Caitlys's ear, pointing toward the burned-out circle. She nodded and checked her hawk's descent toward the nearest tower, and urged the bird to climb a little higher, out of likely bowshot range. As they soared over the remnants of the still-glowing summoning circle, ignoring the cursing and shouting of the orcs below, Bessarias used his newly-restored sight to take in the details of the recent ritual.

Although most of the bones were charred and blackened, Bessarias could still see from their size that they had been goblins, not orcs. There were scores of them, which tended to confirm the High Guard's description of a truly massive offering to the lords of the Nether Hells. It wasn't that he hadn't believed them, but it was one thing to be told of such an unusual occurrence and another to see the actual evidence for oneself.

It was evident that whatever entity the orcs had summoned was a terrible one indeed. Looking back at the fortress, he could now see the outfacing walls were blackened and scorched by hellfire, although the ancient spells had protected them well enough that there were no visible cracks and their core integrity appeared sound. He couldn't tell how weakened they were without relaxing the tight hold he maintained on his magic, but that was a task for the Magistras Duellicus and of little concern to him. However, judging by the size of the new structure the orcs were assembling, it appeared that Gilthalas and his adepts would be facing a serious challenge indeed if his own attempt to turn the Great Orc back failed. It didn't look like they would be ready to perform the sacrifices and summoning tonight, as the sky was already showing a tinge of red, but it was safe to assume they would be testing the fortress walls again tomorrow night.

"Take me back," he told Caitlys. A moment later, the great hawk turned on its wing and began to ascend toward one of the towers. The landing was a little rough on his aged bones, and he required her help both unstrapping himself and dismounting from the bird's back, but he waved off all further offers of assistance as he walked over to the buttresses overlooking the eastern wasteland and the army occupying it as far as his eyes could see.

"Forgive me, Almighty God, for what I am about to do," he prayed with his eyes wide open. "Grant them wisdom, O Lord, grant them even a modicum of good sense, that this dreadful cup might pass from me!"

He bowed his head. "Grant me the courage to do what must be done, Heavenly Father. Your son did not wish to bear his terrible burden, and no more do I. But I shall follow his lead and lay down my life that others might live. I only ask, I only pray, that in this terrible thing I am about to do, I do Your Will. *In nomine patris et fili et spiritus sancti.*"

Stretching out his arms as if to embrace the setting sun, he lowered the barriers he'd erected and allowed the magic of the stones beneath his feet, the magic of the earth supporting the walls, the magic of the water flowing under the earth, to enter his body. The sensation was indescribable, it was agony and pleasure and delight and sorrow that first infused his soles and rapidly flowed to the tips of his fingers and the top of his head. The innumerable aches and pains of the centuries fell away in an instant, and when he opened his eyes, he realized that he could see nearly twice as far as before, although still not to the end of the orc encampment.

He turned around and smiled when Caitlys and the various guards and skyriders gasped at the sight of him.

"Magistras! You are... you are young again!"

"No, I am older than I ever was. I am merely permitting my body to draw life from the land like the rest of you." His heart leaped at the sight of her. How pretty she was! He laughed at himself as his body responded with the first desire he'd felt in more than two hundred years. This was neither the time nor the place for such things, and he was going to need every bit of his concentration if he was going to perform the deed for which he had come. "Tell the Prince-General to open the East Gate and send out a flag of truce to the Great Orc. Tell him to leave it open and tell the two Magistrae and their adepts to join me in front of it. Caitlys, if you will tell one of these guards who knows the way to lead me down to it, it has been so long since I have been here that I fear I will never get there."

"Of course, Magistras." She nodded and beckoned toward one of the white-armored elves. "May I join you as well?"

"No, I have one final charge for you. When you see me raise my hands and press them together above my head, you must immediately close your eyes and turn your back on the east. And keep them closed! You will know when it is over." He demonstrated. "You must swear that when you see me do that, you will close your eyes and turn to the west! And you must order every single elf upon these walls and towers to do the same, in the name of the High King. Will you do that for me?"

"I swear I will, by earth, by stone, and by tree, Magistras." Her face was grief-stricken, but her voice was steady. "Goodbye, Bessarias."

"Fare you well, child." He pointed an unwithered finger at her. "And heed my words!"

"I will."

"Very well." He gestured to the guard Caitlys had selected. "Then shall we descend?"

The journey down flight after flight of stone stairs was a veritable pleasure in his newly-rejuvenated body. The physical exertion that would have exhausted him within minutes now filled his body with newfound energy; by the time they reached the bottom of the stairs he was in a state of exhilaration that not even an army of orcs could quench.

The mighty East Gate, some fifty *cufydd* high and twelve *cufydd* thick, had already been opened by the time the guard led him through the tunnel that led to it. Gilthalas was standing in the middle of the opening, staring out at the vastness of the bestial army waiting for them. The Magistras Demonae turned around and raised a single white eyebrow when he saw Bessarias approaching. Then, to Bessarias's surprise, Gilthalas smiled and held out his arms to his former colleague and occasional rival.

"Welcome Magistras," he said, embracing him briefly. "It has been a very long time."

"It has indeed, Magistras." Their rivalry had not been bitter, as their interests rarely overlapped, but their very different visions for the Collegium Occludum had often led them into conflict in the days when they both had been members of the Seven. "You have grown magnanimous, Gilthalas. I no longer merit that honor."

"I disagree. I know exactly what you intend, and I honor both the intention and the elf. I hope you will believe that I would do the same, had I the knowledge."

"I believe you. You know that if I fail, it will fall to you to save the walls."

"You will not fail, Bessarias. And may I say, I am glad you asked for me. If you don't mind, before you go to face the Great Orc, I should like to know that we are reconciled."

Bessarias smiled and raised his hand. "*Ego te absolvo*, my friend."

"What does that mean?"

"It means we are reconciled."

"Then I am glad, Bessarias."

"As am I, Gilthalas."

A cloud of dust in the distance was the first sign that the Prince-General's embassy had been successful. Bidding Gilthalas goodbye, Bessarias walked toward the galloping riders as a warhawk landed nearby and disgorged a pair of passengers before flying back up to the fortress. It was the Magistras Duellicus and the adept he had chosen to accompany him.

"Greetings, Bessarias!"

"Thank you for coming, Magistras. You comprehend what is required?"

"I do indeed. Spare no worries for us. We have the strength and we will do our part."

Bessarias glanced at the adept. He was less than two hundred years old, so he was unknown to Bessarias, but he carried himself with an air of perfect confidence and a complete lack of fear.

"Very well. When I begin to raise my hands, you must cast the spell. Hold nothing back! It need not last longer than a minute or two, but it must be absolutely impermeable to a force more powerful than anything you have ever experienced, than anything you have ever even imagined!"

"It will be." The magistras chuckled. "You need have no concerns, Bessarias. We have advanced the art somewhat since you abandoned your office."

"I should hope so." Bessarias raised a hand to acknowledge the knight-captain who was riding up to them, bearing a tattered blue leather banner mounted on a crude wooden construction, flanked by five other knights. "Is this our safe passage?"

The armored young elf grimaced. "I'm afraid so, Magistras. Stinks to high heaven, it does, but the orc general that gave it to me said it's the Great Orc's own device. You're to plant it into the ground in front of their encampment, then wait for the Great Orc to come to you."

"I think it's trollskin," the adept said, rubbing the leather between his fingers. "Not very well cured, though."

"You can carry it," Bessarias told him. "Tell the Prince-General to shut the East Gate behind you," he ordered the knight-captain.

"Magistras!" the elf saluted, then rode off with considerable alacrity at the head of his squadron.

It took longer than Bessarias would have thought to reach the orcs, although the stench of their encampment greeted them long before they encountered the first foot patrol guarding the perimeter. One look at the blue banner, however, was enough to dissuade the orcs from interfering with their progress. They next came across a pair of goblins riding on the back of scrawny wolves, and one yellow-skinned rider nearly fell off his mount at the unexpected sight of them before both wolfriders fled with alacrity.

"This will do," Bessarias announced once they were nearly within a stone's throw of the crude tents and waste pits that marked the true edge of the orc camp. At his behest, the adept carrying the Great Orc's banner sank the shaft into the ground, and Bessarias sat down, cross-legged, in front of it. "Stand behind the banner," he told the Magistras. "And do not disturb me now. I must make my preparations."

He closed his eyes and gradually severed his sensory connections to the outside world. He closed his ears to the harsh babbles of the orcs in the distance, to the sawing and pounding of the great sacrificial structure being constructed, and to the soft whispers of the elves behind him. Next, and with some relief, he shut off his sense of smell, thereby removing himself from the overpowering stench of orc sweat, orc filth, and acrid smoke from their greenwood fires. Finally, he detached himself from his sense of touch, freeing himself of ground and gravity alike, leaving his consciousness floating in a dark space where nothing existed except his own body.

Now for the difficult part. He focused on the interior of his body, diving through skin, blood, muscle, and bone, until he found himself in a massive red chamber, throbbing slowly in time with the universe. But it was not enough. He forced himself to go even deeper, bringing his concentration into sharper and sharper focus, until he reached the endless dance of the *calengalads*, and found himself surrounded by the beautiful little constructions swirling around him on every side.

The rest was so trivially easy that it didn't even feel like magic. He simply reached out, took one of the delicate objects, and with the words that were engraved upon his soul, bound it to the rhythm that was engulfing him. So, so, and so. And it was done.

He opened his eyes. There was a rippling disturbance in the lines of orcs before him as the sounds of their evil drums grew ominously louder. It appeared the Great Orc was approaching. The front lines parted, revealing a black-armored bodyguard of huge orcs, most of them as tall as an elf but at least twice an elf's width, strutting toward him under a black banner that featured a clawed red hand. Twenty of them marched his way, then parted into two columns, one to his left and the other to his right. Behind them was the Great Orc himself, less physically imposing than his bodyguards or the giant blue-hued companion who stood at his right shoulder, but a phenomenal specimen in his own way. His bare arms were massive and covered with scars, from white ones inflicted by weapons to raised ones burned into his green flesh with hot metal. His yellow eyes were bright with intelligence, but the superior sneer on his tusked face suggested a tendency toward cruelty of a particularly insidious kind.

You will not have the wisdom to walk away, Bessarias concluded as he studied the orc king's visage. *And yet, it would not surprise me if you feign at being inclined toward reason.*

The orc strode toward him and came to a halt. He looked down at Bessarias, snorted in what might have been disdain or respect, then addressed him in a straightforward manner.

"So, elf, I am told you wish to talk rather than fight. Well and good! Here are my demands: Open the gate behind you before nightfall and I will give you bird-squaggers a night and a day to run away. Neither orc nor goblin, neither boar nor wolf, will enter the gate until the sun is down tomorrow night."

"What about demons and devils?" Bessarias asked.

The orc smiled thinly. "I'll call off the shamans too. No demons, no devils, nothing enters at all. But I want that gate opened immediately as a gesture of good faith. No running away and then 'oopsies, we done forgot to open it for yez.'"

"A fair offer. Will you permit me to propose a counteroffer?"

"We'ze here to talk, so talk."

"Here is my offer. If you leave now, before nightfall, I will spare your life and the lives of all your army. Return to your mountains, return to Zoth Ommog, and never cross the wastelands again. In the name of Brother Grimfang, whose memory I cherish, I assure you that I wish you no ill, and if you depart I will do you no harm."

"Do you believe this *alva ghash*?" The Great Orc snorted as he addressed his oversized companion out of the side of his mouth. Then he raised his voice. "What do yez think, boyoze, should we tuck our tails and run away like fresh sqwaaks afeared o' gettin' a good squaggin'?"

"No *fashzek* way, *Waznig Kral!*" the bodyguard roared.

The Great Orc stepped forward, looming over Bessarias. "Now who in the name of Gor-Gor's slimy, stinking butthole do you think you are, elf? Do you know why they call me the Great Orc? Because I'm the greatest *anyafashzek kor* there's ever been! I've killed trolls, I've killed giants, I've killed men, and I've killed elves. And I can kill you as easy as I take a *fashzek* piss!"

"I have no doubt. For my part, I am responsible for the most lifeless part of the wasteland you crossed," Bessarias replied calmly. "Where the poison is infused in the land itself, and to drink the water is to die."

"That waren't you! The Dead Waste has been dead as long as anyone knows!"

"And yet, it was me. I am old, orc. I am very old. In my day, those lands were known as the Glass Desert." For the first time, he saw an element of wariness enter the orc's yellow eyes and he sensed the moment of crisis had arrived. "*Waznig Kral*, you can see I am not mad. I have more power than you could possibly imagine. If you refuse me, if you strike me down, it will be your death and it will be the death of every orc, goblin, boar, and wolf that stands before me now. This is the only warning I have to offer. So please, I beg you, take your army and return to the north."

He raised his arms above his head, as if in supplication. And then he clasped his hands together.

The big brute behind the Great Orc put a massive, clawed hand on the orc king's shoulder. "Th' witch won't take kindly to you runnin' out on her plans for fear o' one single elf, no matter what you tell her 'e said. And half the tribes'll revolt if'n you show yez got a yeller belly after all. Mebbe more'n half."

The Great Orc was staring intently into Bessarias's face. The elf could see the orc struggling to make sense of the situation. Pride warred with wisdom, and fear warred with instinct. Bessarias said nothing, he merely stared calmly back into the orc king's cruel yellow eyes, hoping against hope that the vile creature would rise to the occasion and choose life over death.

"Forget the witch. Forget the tribes. What if he ain't talkin' murdu?"

"Then we better not take no chances!" The huge half-troll drew a giant cleaver from his side and leaped toward him in a single violent motion. Bessarias saw the sudden movement and the silvery gleam of the metal out of the corner of his eye, but he did not flinch nor did he look away from the orc king's troubled face.

Dyro i mi faddeuant, gollyngdod, a madd–

The cleaver struck home and bit deep, severing flesh, muscle, and bone as it clove Bessarias in two from clavicle to waist. And in doing so, it also severed the vital link that Bessarias had magically forged between the *giloi* inside his heart, unleashing the dreadful power contained within each and every *calengalad*.

Caitlys watched from the battlements, alone, as the elves still guarding the fortress were inside behind tons of magic-infused stone and King Mael had ordered all of the skyriders to fly to the west as soon as Bessarias led his pathetic little sortie out from the East Gate. Vengirasse's eyes were covered with leather blinders, and for good measure, Caitlys had tied him to a hitching ring behind a wooden structure that normally served as a shelter for off-duty guards to sleep in the shade while remaining on the tower.

She had watched with her heart in her mouth as the three elves, protected by nothing more than a tattered blue orc's banner, approached the vastness of the besieging army.

The High King did not question her desire to remain behind, but the Prince-General personally ordered her to take to the sky and fly away from the fortress with the rest of the High Guard and the king's skyriders.

"Bessarias told me to bear witness," she had lied, smiling sweetly at her cousin. And not even the Prince-General dared to contradict that. Not on this day, of all days.

She was relieved when she saw the Great Orc himself making his way through the army, behind an array of brutal bodyguards that simply shoved aside the orcs who moved too slowly to get out of their liege's path. Surely Bessarias would force the orc to see that there was no victory waiting for him here!

The orc addressed the seated magistras, his powerful body language radiating pure confidence and contempt. And then, as the orc stepped forward with a snarling expression on his face, Caitlys saw Bessarias raise his hands and put them together in precisely the manner of the signal he'd described.

Remembering her vow, she whirled around, took a seat behind the protection of the thick stones of the crenellated rampart, pulled her flight jacket over her head, and pressed her hands to her eyes. But nothing happened. She sat there feeling foolish, wondering if perhaps Bessarias's spell had failed or if the orcs had struck him down before he was able to cast it. Or was it merely a false alarm?

She started to push the leather jacket off her head, then thought better of it. *"You will know when it is over."* She decided to count to one hundred before taking a swift peek over the battlements to see what was happening. She had just reached sixteen when there was an ungodly noise that she didn't hear so much as feel it penetrate her to her core, and white lightning flashed before her closed and covered eyes. The whole tower seemed to swim underneath her, as if the ground on which the great fortress stood had magically transformed into an ocean before a wave passed under it, and she screamed in abject fear.

But once the wave had passed, the ground ceased to move. Everything was silent, far too silent, in fact. The light had vanished, and she quickly cast the jacket off her head and leaped to her feet to see what had happened. What she saw on the field below staggered her, literally staggered her, and she was forced to clutch at the stone ramparts to keep herself from falling to her knees.

Where the huge orc army had been, there was now nothing but a scorched black scar in the earth for as far as her keen elven eyes could see. A tremendous cloud of smoke was rising in the strange shape of an ancient maple tree, albeit with a massive canopy that stretched toward the heavens and darkened the sky to the point it appeared the sun had already descended below the horizon.

But there was a sharp line of demarcation immediately behind where Bessarias had been seated. Both her old friend and the blue banner were gone, completely and utterly gone. In their place was a cliff marking the lip of a new crater that was deeper than the walls of Tir Diffaith were high. At the very edge she could see two elves, their white robes still spotless, sitting on the ground and staring in awe at the devastation wrought by the former Magister Gnossi. It was the Magister Duellicus and his adept, and from the straight line of the near side of the crater, Caitlys could see it must have been their mighty magic that had protected them and Tir Diffaith from the unthinkable power of the blast, and by reflecting its fury toward the east, made the extent of the destruction all the more terrible for the orcs.

No wonder Bessarias had refused her so many times. No wonder he had been so reluctant to return to the White City. And finally, she understood why he had demanded such an outrageous price from the High King to defend the Three Realms. He had known what none of them had even suspected, he had known full well what the cost would be. Reluctant to the end, he had finally paid that price with his life and with his legacy.

She sank to her knees and began to cry. She wept with relief at the end of the invasion. She wept for the land, and for the terrible scar it would bear, and for the lifeless desert of poisoned waste it would become. She wept for the tens of thousands of vanished dead, all slain in an instant of pure horror.

But most of all, she wept for an elderly elf whom she had come to love, and who was now no more.

ÉTIENNE-HENRI

THE SUMMER SUN was warm on the prince's face as he rode his big roan stallion out through the East Gate to the muted cheers of the city's rabble who curiosity had drawn out of their homes and hovels to witness his departure. It had been three weeks since his astonishing victory over the Great Orc in the Eastmarch, but the passage of time, along with the vicious rumors circulating throughout Lutéce, had since somewhat managed to tarnish his luster. The crowd's observable lack of enthusiasm for him brought the realization home to him in a way that no courtier's warning ever could.

"You had better be right about this, Donzeau," he muttered darkly to the man riding beside him.

"Of course I'm right. When have you ever known my sources to be unreliable."

"I don't really want to know anything about whatever infernal spirit you summoned. I've got enough trouble with the Church already, thanks to you!"

The sorceror laughed, and for a moment, his sharp features lost their habitual expression of sneering contempt.

"Ah, Étienne, I fear you overrate me at times! My source is a young woman from a nearby village who washes clothes for the soldiers. She lives in the camp outside the walls, and she swears she has seen the princess with her own eyes no less than three times."

"So, a whore," the prince said sourly. "Which is to say, a woman who will tell you anything you want to hear for a few coppers."

"Au contraire, my friend. This is a fresh and unplucked flower of whom we speak, though sadly, one that is more dandelion than rose. Perhaps to describe her as an unplucked weed would do her more justice." Donzeau sighed. "The lack of beauty is a terrible curse from which none of the afflicted ever truly recover."

"Your empathy moves me to tears," said the prince drily. "But why would the Amorrans give Fjotra shelter or seek to hide her from me? Marcus has never shown even the slightest interest in the court or its politics."

"General Valerius is both a prig and a priest, and a failed priest at that. Neither occupation is an attractive failing in a man of his age and stature."

"Is being a prig an occupation?"

"I imagine it must be. What would you know of it?"

The Red Prince laughed. "More than you, Donzeau! More than you!"

"My wickedness is unsurpassed in these parts," the sorceror admitted, with no little satisfaction. "At least, not until you kill your father. Alas, that is one sin forever denied to me by the cruel vagaries of fate!"

"Be silent!" the prince hissed. "And watch your tongue!"

"First, no one can hear us over the horses. Second, these are your men, sworn to you and you alone. Third, half these men already believe the king is dead at your command. And fourth, the other half, who know that he isn't, wish you would get over your filial delicacy sooner rather than later and do what the realm requires!"

The prince looked at the men-at-arms around him, wondering if any of them had heard too much, and if so, what the consequences might be. Was Donzeau right? Were these men, clad beautifully in his red-and-white livery, beginning to lose patience with him? Was he being foolish to harbor reservations over openly claiming the crown that was as good as in his hand already? Did not fortune favor the bold?

He shook his head and once more put off answering the terrible question with which he'd been wrestling since his oh-so-loving father had sent him off to die fighting what should have been an unwinnable battle against a horde of countless orcs. Against every expectation, including at times his own, he had lived. More than that, he had won! And, he knew very well, he had only survived by thinking the unthinkable, and by deciding to do what no other royal or noble or mage in the realm would have dared.

"I should blame it on you," he told Donzeau. "A public execution, followed by a tearful repentance, a suitable penance, a lavish offering to the Church, and a vow to never dabble in *la magique noire* again would go over very well with the court and the commons alike, I think."

"It's not a bad plan, to be honest," the sorceror allowed. He showed no sign of feeling either anger or fear. "Will no one rid you of this troublesome *sorcière satanique?*"

"Don't be ridiculous. Even if you weren't the only man I can trust, I'm not that stupid. The realm was already split. The times of chaos are coming. And you've proven that you're worth more than any Grandmagicien or Immortel." He shook his head. "No, we shall rule, we shall fight, and we shall be damned together, my friend."

"How very inspiring. And you wonder why I discourage you from speaking to the knights before battle? Ah, there they are!" Donzeau pointed to the road before them, where an Amorran cavalry squad waited with a decurion at its head, along with four legionaries armed with crossbows.

"Your Royal Highness!" the decurion called in passable Savonnais before gracefully inclining his head. "The Legatus awaits you and the gates of the castra are open before you."

Étienne-Henri held up a hand to acknowledge their welcome and turned his horse onto the path that led to the Amorran fort. The Amorran riders allowed the Savondese party to pass before falling in behind them.

The prince didn't deign to look back, knowing that Donzeau would keep him informed.

"The cavalry follows. The footmen remain."

"I don't like the crossbows."

"Neither do I, but the Amorrans never change their routines. Those crossbows have nothing to do with us."

They rode in through the open gates. The prince was pleased to see a red-and-white banner with the two-headed lion of Savondir had been mounted on one of the two watchtowers that stood on either side of the gates, companion to the red banner with the letters SPA that was mounted, as always, on the other. He felt the honor being accorded him was a healthy sign that General Valerius would not prove excessively recalcitrant in the matter at hand.

They dismounted from their horses, which were adroitly taken from them and led toward the stables by their previous escorts. They did not have to wait long, though, before the Amorran commander arrived, bearing in his wake twenty or more centurions, decurions, and a pair of men Étienne-Henri assumed to be officers, or possibly surgeons, wearing yellow cloaks. The young general was irritatingly tall, and as always, carried himself with the unconscious arrogance of a man who was descended from a long and distinguished line of leaders of men. Although his demeanor was annoying, Étienne-Henri found the Amorran's tone to be pleasingly accommodating.

"How may I serve you, your Royal Highness?"

"Good morning, Marcus Valerius. I should appreciate it very much indeed if you would be so kind as to return my betrothed to me. She went missing a few weeks ago, and I understand she is now here."

"Yes, that is correct. She is here. I will send for her now."

The prince, a little taken aback at the total absence of any resistance to his demand, glanced over at Donzeau and raised his eyebrows. The sorceror shrugged, unimpressed.

"Thank you, Marcus. I hope your men are well."

"They are indeed, your Royal Highness. We lost fewer men than we'd expected. A great victory!"

"A great victory indeed," Étienne-Henri agreed warmly. "And one in which the part played by your brave footmen will never be forgotten!"

The Amorran smiled, a little, and for the first time, Étienne-Henri sensed a slight chill in the air.

"I should hope not, your Royal Highness. I should very much hope not." There was a rustling sound as the men behind the Amorran general shifted themselves out of the way of his runaway betrothed, and then Marcus himself stepped aside with an almost imperceptible bow. "Your Royal Highness, I believe you are already acquainted with the Princess of the Isles."

Étienne-Henri looked up at his bride-to-be. Had she always been so much taller than him? Her face was cold and white, a true princess of the northern ice and snow, her grey-blue eyes were wintry, and her high-cheekboned beauty, so much cleaner and finer and harder than the softer, prettier flowers of the court, seemed to stab him to the quick. She did not smile or speak, she simply extended her hand to him, palm-up.

On it rested a small golden object, one that he recognized right away.

"Your ring, your Royal Highness. Take it, if you please. I will not marry you."

He swallowed hard and somehow resisted the urge to take a step backward in shock. It was only by closing his eyes and breathing in deeply through his nose that he managed to maintain his self-control. He could feel the fury rising within him, and with it, a powerful sense of shame and humiliation, the likes of which he hadn't felt in years. How dare she! He was the heir to the throne, he was for all intents and purposes the king already, if he wished! With a single snap of his fingers, he would rule over the whole realm, with the right to the high justice and the low over every single man, woman, and child in the land!

How dare she reject him! But he mastered his ire, and did his best to smile at her.

"This is not an appropriate venue for a matter of such import, Fjotra. I won't pretend to understand why you left the manoir, or why you wish to betray your vows, but this is not the time or the place."

"Take the ring, please," she repeated. "Your Royal Highness."

He took her hand in his, and folded her fingers over her palm to close the ring inside it. His eyes met her cold blue gaze, and he smiled again, more easily this time, when she was the first to look away.

"Fjotra, come with me. We will discuss this later, in private and at our leisure. If, in the end, you truly do not wish to sit by my side and rule over Savondir as my queen, if you truly do not wish to let me help your people reclaim their islands, I will release you from our betrothal. I swear it!"

He could see her hesitation. He could feel her hand inside his shaking. She was afraid, he realized. She was going to submit, surely she had to submit to him. So much depended upon it!

It felt like a slap in the face when she abruptly pulled away from him, grunting slightly as she jerked her hand out of his grasp. Before he realized what she was doing, she tossed the ring into the air, and as the little gold object flashed in front of his face, he instinctively reached up and caught it. Dumbfounded, he stared at it for a moment before taking another deep breath and closing his hand around it.

Without meaning to do so, he stepped toward her and started to raise his fist.

"Don't," said the tall Amorran as he moved protectively in front of Fjotra. Or was it possessively? Étienne-Henri's eyes narrowed with suspicion as he looked up at the young, the very young, southern general, who he knew was much of an age with himself.

"As you said, this is not the time or the place, Étienne," Donzeau whispered urgently in his ear. "Leave it to me!"

Too angry to speak, but well aware of the fact that he and his party were hopelessly outnumbered by the legionaries, Étienne-Henri nodded mutely and stared furiously at the Amorran, whose face remained irritatingly calm. Did Marcus not realize what this foolish interference in his affairs could do to further unsettle the realm?

He had been thinking to send the Amorran and his legion south with the Marechal, to put down the Grand Duc's rebellion. But now, he realized, he might be facing a second rebellious lord, only one with nearly five thousand battle-hardened veterans less than a two-hour's march from Lutéce!

"Monseigneur le General," Donzeau stepped forward to Étienne-Henri's side and addressed the Amorran. "You are, I think, aware that your five thousand swords would avail you nothing if you were to set yourself against me."

"I know what you can do, seigneur le sorcière. I was there."

"Then I suggest you tell the princess that she cannot stay here, you will not keep her from her lawful betrothed, and you will order her to return to the palace with her rightful lord."

"No!" shouted Fjotra, her blue eyes blazing. "I gave back the ring. You can't make me marry him!"

"We can, perhaps, persuade you of the wisdom of doing so, your Highness." Donzeau's voice was calm and soft, but held ominous undertones that promised a myriad of unspeakable threats to her, or worse, her loved ones. "And if we can't, then, after a certain amount of time passes, you will be free to leave Savondir and go anywhere you please. Your person will not be harmed, as the Prince has sworn."

Étienne-Henri stifled a frown. He assumed the sorceror was lying, but he wasn't sure. He, for one, had absolutely no intention of giving up either his claim to the Wolf Isles or the three thousand axes that came as her dowry. And while he'd hate to have to use Brynjolf against her, it would be a pleasure to let Donzeau torture that bitch mother of hers until she came to her senses.

"The princess will not go anywhere. She has the protection of Amorr for as long as she wants it. So, your Royal Highness, I suggest you and your men leave and enjoy a nice ride back to the city. I understand it is a lovely day."

Étienne-Henri was just drawing breath to denounce the arrogant Amorran when Donzeau placed a hand on his shoulder. He shut his mouth and did his best to quell his rage, and allowed the sorceror to speak for him.

"Please recall that I did warn you, General Valerius."

The Amorran nodded and smiled slightly. "Yes, you did, seigneur le sorcière. But there are no dead bodies for you to work your black magick here."

"I fear your grasp of the vast range of possibilities at my disposal is limited, Monseigneur le General."

Donzeau raised his right hand. Étienne-Henri smiled and folded his arms, wondering what his esoteric friend had in mind. Would it be a warning of some kind? Or would he strike the Amorran and his men down, infested with carnivorous worms, or perhaps infected with a disease that rotted their organs within them?

But then, a look of consternation flashed across the sorceror's olive-skinned face. He shook his head, muttered something under his breath, and made another gesture, apparently to no avail.

"It's no use, magicien," said one of the soldiers wearing a yellow cloak. He was holding a white pendant in his left hand, and with the other he sketched the Tree of the Immaculate in the air. *"Artes pessimae nomine Immaculatae prohibentur."*

"That's impossible," snarled Donzeau. Again, he mumbled something unintelligible, and again, nothing happened.

"I should order you killed, sorcière," Marcus said, as if he was still musing on the possibility. "But I think the realm is troubled enough already, and it is too fine a morning to shed a man's blood, no matter how wicked he might be. So leave now, your Royal Highness, and take your magicker with you before I burn you both on a stake!"

Étienne-Henri glanced at Donzeau and saw the sorceror's eyes were wild with helpless outrage and alarm. He swiftly reviewed his options. He had no doubt that Marcus was capable of ordering his companion's death on the spot; he was well-acquainted with the Amorran's hatred for magic and magic-users alike. But he also knew the Amorran weakness for discipline and authority.

"You have no right to the high justice in this realm, Monseigneur le General. Do not forget that you are obligated to the crown, by your own signature, by your word, and by your honor!"

"Damn their honor," cursed a hard-looking officer behind the Valerian. "And damn the crown. This puppy is only going to cause us trouble if we don't put him and his pet magicker to the sword!"

"Hold your tongue, Proculus." The general's tall subordinate stepped forward and put a hand on his commanding officer's shoulder. "Marcus, the court might choose to look past your interference in a marital affair, but it will never ignore the usurpation of the king's rights over his own subjects."

Étienne-Henri nodded. "Make no mistake, my friend, if you give that order, you declare war on Savondir. You and your men will never see the southlands again."

The two young men locked eyes for a long moment that was filled with tension. Leather creaked as the gloved and gauntleted hands of their men shifted their grips on their sword hilts. Étienne-Henri smiled grimly when

the Amorran growled low in his throat and shook his head, knowing that
he had at least won one battle of wills today.

He raised a finger in warning.

"I will give you one week to return her, General Valerius. If the princess
is not back in Lutéce by sundown one week from today, I shall come back
here with considerably more than a guard of honor."

Marcus nodded calmly, then reached back and received a sealed scroll
that was placed in his hand by the tall, young officer. He offered it to
Étienne-Henri. "I understand. Now, if you will be so kind, please deliver
this to Chancelier du Moulin. It terminates the legion's contract with the
crown of Savondir."

"You wouldn't... you can't do that!"

"I doubt you are familiar with our terms of employment, your Royal
Highness, as they predate your elevation to your current position, but the
fact of the matter is that I most certainly can." The Amorran general bowed
very, very slightly. "But lest our actions disturb the sound sleep of the
king and his high council, please assure them that we will not be offering
the legion's services to the Écarlateans or anyone else. The orcs are gone,
Savondir is safe, and we have fulfilled our obligations."

Stunned and at a loss, Étienne-Henri did not know what to say. In one
fell swoop, he had somehow lost his betrothed and the legion, and now the
crown faced the prospect of suppressing the rebellion in the south without
both of its most powerful armies. He suddenly felt very, very glad that he
had not given the order to bring his father's reign to an abbreviated end.
And he started when Marcus Valerius unexpectedly leaned down toward
him to whisper in his ear.

"We are going home to Amorr, my dear prince. So do not even think of
standing in our way!"

closing time

ARTS OF DARK AND LIGHT

Summa Elvetica

A Throne of Bones

A Sea of Skulls

A Grave of Gods

Printed in the USA
CPSIA information can be obtained
at www.ICGtesting.com
JSHW081141300824
68936JS00001B/2

9 783039 440344